The Editor

ALAN SHELSTON is Honorary Senior Research Fellow in English Literature at the University of Manchester. He is Visiting Professor at the Centro Universitario di Studi Vittoriani e Edoardiani at the Università degli Studi "G. d'Annunzio," Pescara, Italy. He has written extensively on Elizabeth Gaskell and other nineteenth-century authors and, with John Chapple, is the editor of *Further Letters of Mrs. Gaskell*.

W. W. NORTON & COMPANY, INC.
Also Publishes

For a complete list of Norton Critical Editions, visit
www.wwnorton.com/college/english/nce_home.htm

A NORTON CRITICAL EDITION

Elizabeth Gaskell

NORTH AND SOUTH

AN AUTHORITATIVE TEXT

CONTEXTS

CRITICISM

Edited by

ALAN SHELSTON

UNIVERSITY OF MANCHESTER

W • W • NORTON & COMPANY • *New York* • *London*

W. W. Norton & Company has been independent since its founding in 1923, when William Warder Norton and Mary D. Herter Norton first published lectures delivered at the People's Institute, the adult education division of New York City's Cooper Union. The Nortons soon expanded their program beyond the Institute, publishing books by celebrated academics from America and abroad. By mid-century, the two major pillars of Norton's publishing program—trade books and college texts—were firmly established. In the 1950s, the Norton family transferred control of the company to its employees, and today—with a staff of four hundred and a comparable number of trade, college, and professional titles published each year—W. W. Norton & Company stands as the largest and oldest publishing house owned wholly by its employees.

Composition by Binghamton Valley Composition.
Manufacturing by the Courier Companies—Westford Division.
Production manager: Benjamin Reynolds.

Library of Congress Cataloging-in-Publication Data

Gaskell, Elizabeth Cleghorn, 1800–1865.
North and South: an authoritative text, contexts, criticism / Elizabeth Gaskell; edited by Alan Shelston.
p. cm. — (A Norton critical edition)
Includes bibliographical references.

ISBN 0–393–97908–3 (pbk.)

1. Young women—Fiction. 2. Gaskell, Elizabeth Cleghorn, 1810–1865. North and South. 3. Mothers and daughters—Fiction. 4. Children of clergy—Fiction. 5. England, Northern—Fiction. 6. Social classes—Fiction. I. Shelston, Alan. II. Title. III. Series.

PR4710.N6 2004

823'.8—dc22   2004053195

W. W. Norton & Company, Inc., 500 Fifth Avenue,
New York, N.Y. 10110–0017
www.wwnorton.com

W. W. Norton & Company Ltd., Castle House,
75/76 Wells Street, London W1T 3QT

2 3 4 5 6 7 8 9 0

Contents

Criticism 497

Preface

North and South, published as a serial in Dickens's *Household Words* between 2 September 1854 and 27 January 1855, and then in volume form, was Elizabeth Gaskell's third full-length novel. Gaskell came late to professional authorship: her first novel, *Mary Barton: A Tale of Manchester Life*, was published in 1848 when she was thirty-eight years of age. However she soon made up for lost time. The success of *Mary Barton* led Dickens to invite her to contribute to his new journal, *Household Words*: her story *Lizzie Leigh* (reprinted in this Norton Critical Edition) was the opening item in the very first number. It was followed by a variety of essays and stories from Gaskell, not least the chain of stories that make up *Cranford* (1853), the work with which she has very often been associated. The commission for *North and South* therefore was to an author who was rapidly establishing herself on the literary scene of the 1850s and who, as disputes with Dickens would show, was becoming increasingly aware of her own literary priorities and standards.[1]

Gaskell's first writings had a strongly philanthropic agenda. *Mary Barton*, as she herself claimed, was written to "give some utterance to the agony which from time to time convulses this dumb people"— i.e., the industrial workforce—an agony intensified by their sense of their own helplessness.[2] In *Ruth* (1853) she addressed the inflammatory subject of the heroine's sexual fall. *Lizzie Leigh* combines the urban setting of the Manchester streets with its own story of female experience (not only that of the woman betrayed, but that of the mother who searches for her and the woman who takes in her child), and it skillfully places these women's histories in the context of the shift from a rural to an urban society, thus anticipating *North and South*. It was Dickens who recommended the title of *North and South* for Gaskell's second "industrial" novel, with its wider frame of social reference; for Gaskell her novel was "Margaret," or "Margaret Hale," the story of its heroine. *Mary Barton* too was a title that had been wished upon Gaskell, not inappropriately since this first novel also had a heroine who comes to discover her own moral strength.

1. See the correspondence between Gaskell and Dickens reprinted in this Norton Critical Edition (pp. 399–413).
2. "Preface" to *Mary Barton* (1848).

All of these stories and novels thus have a dual focus: a conscious-ness of social change, and of the challenges that it provokes, and an awareness of the implications of such change in particular for the lives of women, especially women negotiating their own significant change from girlhood (one uses the Victorian term deliberately) to adulthood—whether working-class women like Mary, Lizzie, and Ruth, or a solidly middle-class figure like Margaret Hale. The central character of *North and South* is Gaskell's first full-scale study of a heroine from her own social background. It is to the point that Gas-kell had four daughters of her own, aged between twelve and twenty at about the time that *North and South* was completed, and her letters to them, in particular to the eldest, Marianne, show how care-ful she was in the matter of their upbringing. If Gaskell's heroines often seem more complex, especially psychologically, than those of many of her fellow novelists that is because in this particular area she is likely to have known what she was talking about.

It is useful to set Elizabeth Gaskell's work in the context of that of her fellow novelists at mid century. The year of the publication of *Mary Barton*, 1848, saw the first installments of *David Copperfield*, while one year previously Charlotte Brontë had published *Jane Eyre*. "I have tried to write truthfully," Gaskell wrote in her "Preface" to *Mary Barton*, and each of her contemporaries might have said the same. "Writing truthfully" was the key objective of the realist novel at mid-century, as was an assumed relationship with the reader that could eliminate the barriers between literature and life. "Millions have suffered a fate far worse than mine," Jane suddenly exclaims in chapter 12 of *Jane Eyre*, in a direct appeal to the reader—or is it Charlotte Brontë herself who is speaking at this point? Certainly the rhetoric assumes the reader's complicity in the fiction, and makes it more than fictional in its agenda. In the same way, in *Mary Barton*, Gaskell appeals directly to the sensibilities of her readership when revealing the injustices suffered by the Manchester poor. And when Aunt Betsey sets the moral standard for David Copperfield—" 'Never,' said my aunt, 'be mean in anything; never be false; never be cruel' " (chap. 15)—she is setting a standard not just for an indi-vidual but for a generation.

In his "Preliminary Word" to the first number of *Household Words*, Dickens expressed his aspiration to "live in the Household affections, and to be numbered amongst the Household thoughts, of our read-ers." The awareness of the readership could not be more clearly stated, and in particular of a readership conceived in family terms. *David Copperfield*, whose completion overlapped the opening of *Household Words*, fulfills his aspiration to a degree that even he might not have imagined. There is, moreover, a further dimension. If Dickens's venture had a moral agenda, the morality was not to be prescriptive. The "Preliminary Word" explicitly rejects the negative aspects of "reality": "No mere utilitarian spirit, no iron binding of the mind to grim realities, will give a harsh tone to our Household Words." Instead "we would tenderly cherish that light of Fancy. . . . To show to all, that in all familiar things . . . there is Romance enough, if we will find it out . . . [We shall] teach the hardest workers at this whirling wheel of toil, that their lot is not necessarily a moody, brutal fact." Finally, the editorial policy will be "to bring the greater and the lesser in degree, together . . . and mutually dispose them to a better acquaintance and a kinder understanding. [This] is one main object of our Household Words."[3]

With Dickens's words before us we can see why the Gaskell of *Mary Barton* had seemed such an ideal choice as his first contributor. She too had written with the declared intention of bringing together those whom the new social developments had divided, and of assuring them of their community of interest, and she also had referred to the "romance" which might be found "in the lives of some of those who elbowed me daily in the busy streets of the town in which I resided" ("Preface" to *Mary Barton*). Dickens's "there is Romance, enough if we will find it out" is almost a direct echo of Gaskell's credo, and it shows how realism—meaning here the concentration on "real" lives in recognizable situations—was to be a criterion not just for its own sake, but as part of a larger social and moral agenda, asserting the value of lives that conventional "romantic" fiction had neglected. The belief in family—or what Dickens called "Household affections"—is asserted on every page of *Mary Barton*, as it is throughout Dickens's writings of the period, and to an extent that the present-day reader will often find sentimental. Suffice it to say that both authors give evidence enough that there is another side to the picture.

It is worth investigating in some detail the situation in which Gaskell found herself when Dickens so eagerly accepted *North and South* for *Household Words* if only because Gaskell's second "industrial" novel in important ways fails to conform to the journal's proclaimed agenda. As the correspondence between them shows, Dickens became increasingly dissatisfied with Gaskell's narrative, while she in her turn was frustrated by his attempt to impose his will on her writing. Mostly the disputes are about matters of planning and length, but the correspondence between them invariably has a subtext with larger implications. Dickens was concerned about the length of Gaskell's exposition of Mr. Hale's doubts, for example— this was hardly the kind of subject matter that he had promised his readers. Gaskell for her part felt that he had not allowed her the

3. *Household Words*, vol. 1, no. 1, 30 March 1850, p. 1.

space she needed to complete her narrative, so essential for the coherence of her heroine's story. It is to the point that the staple fare of *Household Words* was shorter fiction and discursive articles: Dickens's first approach to Gaskell suggested "a *short* tale, or any number of tales." In fact *Hard Times* and *North and South* were the only preplanned novels of any distinction to be published in *Household Words* in the nine years of its existence.[4] But the real development in Gaskell's art revealed by *North and South* is to be found in the clear-mindedness of its realism—in the absence in fact of just that element of "romance" that Dickens had identified as his priority. That element is clear enough in the scenes of working-class family life in *Mary Barton*: the comparable scenes in *North and South* are much more astringent in their presentation of life in a working-class environment. Furthermore both the geographical and the psychological realities of *North and South* are more complex than anything Gaskell had attempted before, and perhaps than the *Household Words* readership might have been accustomed to. In a letter to John Forster, Gaskell wrote "I seldom see the Household Words"[5]—and this as early as 1853, when she was writing regularly for the journal. The decision to publish *North and South* in *Household Words* may well have been misjudged therefore, and by both parties. In spite of her protest when she had finished *North and South* that she would never write for *Household Words* again, Gaskell was to continue to write for the magazine until 1859, when the title was withdrawn. Nevertheless there is certainly a very real sense in which *North and South* marks a considerable step forward in her career as a novelist and it is a step which perhaps took her beyond Dickens's agenda.

Dickens's choice of title—"*North and South*"—has a fine rhetorical ring. It is taken from a comment by the working man, Nicholas Higgins, to Margaret Hale, early in the novel when she tells him of her home at Helstone: " 'That's beyond London, I reckon? And I come fro' Burnley-ways, and forty mile to th' North. And yet, yo see, North and South has both met and made kind o' friends in this big smoky place' " (p. 67). The Victorians liked the signification of these opposed polarities: Thomas Carlyle's *Past and Present* provided a precedent if one were needed; Cardinal Newman called his polemical religious novel of 1848 *Loss and Gain*. Furthermore it signified where Dickens's priorities lay; that is, in the novel's engagement with the pressing issues raised by the new industrialism. Dickens himself of course, had addressed the same topic in *Hard Times*, which immediately preceded *North and South* in his magazine. But, as can be seen from the Chronology (pp. 581–82), Gaskell had an unusually varied formative experience of her native country and, as W. A. Craik

---

4. *The Dead Servant*, by Wilkie Collins, also appeared January–June 1857.
5. *Further Letters*, p. 87.

shows in the extract from her book reprinted in this Norton Critical Edition (pp. 524–31), *North and South* has a much wider and thus more suggestive frame of geographical reference than its title implies. While it juxtaposes the new northern industrialism with the traditional rural environment of the South, it opens and effectively closes in a London populated by lawyers, members of parliament, and other professionals. "South" is not only representative of the rural way of life, therefore, it is where England has always been governed from, and by a government from which until 1832 cities like Manchester had largely been excluded. *North and South* thus engages with central issues of authority. Hale is an establishment clergyman and his wife a daughter of the English landed gentry: they are members of a class accustomed to govern, and when Hale leaves the church in which he is a beneficed clergyman and goes to live amongst dissenters the gesture is a political as well as a theological one. His son, for his part, has challenged the authority of his superior officer in the Navy. Hale is an Oxford-educated classical scholar, and in its references to Oxford *North and South* anticipates Matthew Arnold's *Culture and Anarchy* (1869), which similarly invokes not only the classics but the spirit of Oxford in a search for cultural authority at a time of political instability. (Gaskell was a friend of the Arnold family and she developed friendships with a number of Oxford acquaintances.) Furthermore, beyond England lies the naval base of Corfu—it is a fascinating accident of circumstance that having initiated her novel with a reference to the pleasures of this military posting Gaskell finished writing it in the home of Florence Nightingale just as the military at Corfu were being drawn into the Crimean War. Beyond England too lie the oceans on which Frederick Hale has pursued his naval career in the defense of British trading and imperialist interests. *North and South* was certainly recognized by contemporary commentators primarily as a contribution to the debates over industrialism, and this has remained the priority for some later critics. But clearly it is not just about the simple geographical opposition identified by its title. Rather is it, to adopt Carlyle's term, a total "condition of England" novel—a novel, that is, about the whole political culture of England at the midpoint of the nineteenth century.

But for Gaskell the novel was "Margaret," and it is clear from her own references to the novel in her correspondence that the story of . its heroine was her central focus. The opening chapters are entirely focused on Margaret Hale, and in particular on her sense of frustration—a frustration that she herself cannot fully define—in polite middle-class London society. And when she returns to London at the end of the novel, in the chapters that Gaskell expanded for the volume publication, it is again with this sense of frustration, now intensified by the fact that after the excitements of life in Milton-Northern she has a life of apparently inescapable emptiness in front of her. Charlotte Brontë, of course, made this the subject of her fiction—perhaps the only subject of her fiction—"Millions are condemned to a stiller doom than mine." Margaret Hale is closer perhaps to Caroline Helstone, in *Shirley* (1850), than to Jane Eyre among Charlotte Brontë's heroines, not least in that she seeks fulfillment in making some contribution to the wider world, but for the daughters of the middle class that fulfillment was not easily to be found. It is an interesting point that in the new industrial society working-class women were able to take paid employment, albeit of a physically demanding and often degrading kind, whereas the outlets for their middle-class equivalents were more limited.[6] Gaskell knew of highly capable young women among her daughters' friends and acquaintances who did in fact forge independent lives of their own, and she had the example of Florence Nightingale—about whom in fact she had some misgivings—immediately before her.[7] But Margaret's problem at the outset of the novel is clear enough: it is the simple one expressed by Caroline Helstone: " 'How am I to get through this day?' " (*Shirley*, chap. 7).

The problem is ultimately solved, in terms of the narrative, by the needs of John Thornton, and by the fortunate inheritance which enables Margaret to supply them. But, to use George Eliot's terms,[8] to reduce *North and South* to the diagram is to do serious injustice to the picture with which we are presented. Margaret's difficulties are defined in a way that rejects the schematic. Gaskell is especially astute on the mental processes of her heroine: for example we have not only her frustration in the London setting but, when she is alone in the garden at Helstone, her psychological vulnerability on the point of departure from the home she loves (vol. I, chap. 6). As critics have pointed out, her relationships with her potential suitors, both

---

6. See the extracts by Aina Rubenius (pp. 516–20).

7. For example, the Winkworth sisters, pupils of William Gaskell and friends of the Gaskell daughters. Catherine Winkworth in particular, who remained unmarried, became a considerable student of German and a theological scholar; she was later prominent in the field of girls' education. Of Florence Nightingale Gaskell wrote:

> "She & I had a grand quarrel one day. She is, I think, too much for institutions, sisterhoods, & associations, & she said if she had influence enough not a mother should bring up a child herself; there should be créches [*sic*] for the rich as well as the poor. If she had 20 children she would send them all out to a créche seeing of course that it was a well-managed créche. That exactly tells of what seems to me *the* want,—but then this want of love for individuals becomes a *gift*, & a very rare one, if one takes it in conjunction with her love for the *race*: her utter unselfishness in serving & ministering." (*Further Letters*, p. 116).

The passage is worth quoting at length, since it is typical of Gaskell's way of coming to a worked-out moral judgment.

8. George Eliot uses these terms at the opening of *Scenes of Clerical Life* (1858): "new-varnished efficiency . . . will yield endless diagrams, plans, elevations but alas! no picture" (*The Sad Fortunes of Amos Barton*, 1858, chap. 1).

Henry Lennox and more potently, John Thornton, are conducted
with a real sense of what is involved sexually as well as socially and
psychologically. If Gaskell is allusive rather than direct in this area
her allusions can be more readily decoded than those of many of her
contemporaries, some of whom in fact were disturbed by them.[9] In
all of this Margaret increasingly has to find her own way: morality is
not something given, in this novel, but something which has to be
discovered, as in her attempts to protect her brother from the law.
It is one of Gaskell's great qualities as a novelist that she is aware of
the complexities of moral issues and aware too that they cannot be
easily, or sometimes indeed entirely, resolved. An early chapter is
titled "Doubts and Difficulties" (vol. I, chap. 4), and these are things
that Gaskell handles well. Writing to her friend Tottie Fox about
conflicting priorities in her own life, she says: "I try to drown myself
. . . by saying it's W[illia]m who is to decide on all these things . . .
only that does not quite do."[1] For the novelist until recently invariably known as *Mrs.* Gaskell, even her husband's authority cannot
resolve the problem. In her fiction she was prepared to concede the
difficulties of resolution, even as the fictional form demands it. In
Milton-Northern Margaret has to find her own way through these
difficulties. She is brought up against not only love, but the sickness
and death of those whom she most loves and most depends upon.
Volume II, chapter 17, which follows on the death of Margaret's
father, is headed "Alone! Alone!" The quotation is from Coleridge
but it was Gaskell's fellow Victorian, Matthew Arnold, who wrote
that "We mortal millions live *alone*."[2] In a paragraph which Gaskell
inserted toward the conclusion in the second edition of the novel,
she wrote of her heroine: "On some such night as this she remembered promising to herself to live as brave and noble a life as any
heroine she ever read or heard of in romance . . . it had seemed to
her then that she had only to will, and such a life would be accomplished."[3] But as things turn out for Margaret Hale it is not as easy
as that. If, more than any other Victorian novelist except perhaps—
and only perhaps—George Eliot, Gaskell is able to register the deepest experiences of a young woman's development it is because she
oversimplifies neither the problems nor their solution.

Many of Gaskell's later titles—*My Lady Ludlow* (1858); *The Grey
Woman* (1861); *Sylvia's Lovers* (1863); *Cousin Phillis* (1863–64);
and the posthumously completed *Wives and Daughters* (1864–66)—
identify her as a novelist of women's experience. In that sense *North
and South* is pivotal, looking back to *Mary Barton*, the "Tale of Man-

9. See, e.g., the review by Margaret Oliphant (pp. 421–23).
1. *Letters*, p. 108.
2. In his poem "To Marguerite—Continued" (1852). The emphasis is Arnold's own.
3. See pp. 373–74.

chester Life" that launched her career, and forward to these later works. Like so many of the novelists of the Victorian period, her fictions record the changes that were taking place in contemporary society. Unlike so many of them however—and here again comparison with George Eliot is to the point—she always reacted positively to the prospect of change. If there is affection for the past in her work it is never transformed into conservatism: she recognizes that the world of the new brings its own challenges which must be met on their own terms. This is clear in the story both of Margaret Hale's personal life, and that of the world in which she finds herself. For that reason, if for no other, *North and South* is one of the most astutely observed novels of its time.

North and South originally appeared in *Household Words* under the editorship of Charles Dickens from 2 September 1854 to 27 January 1855.[4] As was standard practice, Gaskell was not named as the author: Dickens's attribution of her novel to "the author of *Mary Barton*," without mention of her other works, clearly identifies where its interest for him lay. It was then published in book form by Chapman and Hall in two volumes on 26 March 1855. This English first edition was preceded by a two-volume edition published by Harper and Brothers of New York on 14 February 1855, and followed in England by a "second edition" in June 1855, which included a number of significant corrections, and then by a one-volume "cheap edition" in 1859.[5] For the English first edition Gaskell inserted chapter titles and mottoes for the first time: these had not been a feature of the *Household Words* text. She also made a number of changes from the *Household Words* version; in particular she revised the ending of the novel, redrafting the final chapters. I have identified the point at which these changes become significant in my notes. This edition is based on the English first edition. I have corrected a few minor typographical errors and altered archaic spellings (for example "sate" to "sat") throughout. I have also regularized punctuation where the conventions observed by Gaskell no longer apply. I have retained the chapter numbering, with a separate sequence for each volume: readers who require a single sequence should add twenty-five to the chapter numbers of the first volume. I am grateful to the Librarian of the Portico Library, Manchester, for allowing me access to its copy of the first edition for the preparation of the text.

4. *Household Words*, vol. 10, nos. 232–53, 2 September 1854 to 27 January 1855.
5. The history of the publication of *North and South* during Gaskell's lifetime is given in Walter Smith, *Elizabeth Gaskell: A Bibliographical Guide* (Los Angeles: Heritage Book Shop, 1998). Readers interested in matters textual and contextual should also consult John Geoffrey Sharps, *Mrs. Gaskell's Observation and Invention* (Fontwell, Sussex: The Linden Press, 1970); Sharps's book is a mine of information on all aspects of Gaskell's literary career.

I have incurred debts too extensive to acknowledge individually. But I cannot allow the help I have had from Nancy Weyant, associate professor and coordinator of Reference Services, Bloomsburg University, whose generosity with her up-to-date knowledge of what has been written about Gaskell in recent years has been invaluable, to be anonymized under a general acknowledgment, nor that of my editor at W. W. Norton & Company, Carol Bemis, who answered every one of my many queries with patience and with such precision that I never had to ask twice. And especially I must thank Dr. Graham Handley for his generous gift to me of the second edition of *North and South*.

In my annotations I have tried to provide explanations that will enhance the reading of the text. Inevitably I am much indebted to the work of previous editors, and especially to Professor Angus Easson, whose "World's Classics" edition of *North and South* covers the ground comprehensively.[6] On matters of industrial history my greatest debt is to my wife, Dorothy Shelston. John Chapple read much of my material and saved me from many errors. Gaskell was an author who used literary reference and allusion instinctively and extensively, and two aspects of her practice in this respect call for comment. First, as I have indicated, for her volume edition she introduced mottoes at the head of each chapter. Where the writers involved are well known I have identified the works from which the quotations are taken. Where the writers are less familiar I have provided basic information about them, without necessarily identifying the specific works referred to. I have usually left as such material that is unidentified. Second, embedded in her writing are frequent references to the Bible, some of them casual, not all of them accurate. Here I have identified the most obvious examples, giving a reference to the King James Bible, but without correcting any accidental misquotation. Finally, Gaskell attempts to achieve authenticity in the speech of her working-class characters by her use of Lancashire dialect. (Her husband's two lectures on this topic were published in the fifth edition of *Mary Barton* [1854].) Where the sense is clear from the context I have not provided a gloss, but I have done so wherever the sense is not easily understood. Throughout I have annotated only the first instance of a particular reference or usage. In all of this I am indebted to friends and colleagues too numerous to mention. I hope though that they will accept my thanks.

---

6. Elizabeth Gaskell, *North and South*, ed. Angus Easson (Oxford and New York: Oxford UP, 1973 ["World's Classics"]); hereafter *Easson 1973*.

ABBREVIATIONS

Throughout this volume the following abbreviations have been adopted:

Letters: The Letters of Mrs. Gaskell, edited by J. A. V. Chapple and Arthur Pollard. Manchester: Manchester (1966).
Further Letters: Further Letters of Mrs. Gaskell, edited by John Chapple and Alan Shelston. Manchester: Manchester (2000).

The Text of
NORTH AND SOUTH

NORTH AND SOUTH.

BY

THE AUTHOR OF "MARY BARTON," "RUTH,"
"CRANFORD," &c.

IN TWO VOLUMES.

VOL. I.

LONDON :
CHAPMAN AND HALL, 193, PICCADILLY.
1855.

[The right of Translation is reserved.]

Facsimile title page from the first edition. Courtesy of The Portico Library and Gallery,
Manchester.

On its first appearance in "Household Words," this tale was obliged to conform to the conditions imposed by the requirements of a weekly publication, and likewise to confine itself within certain advertised limits, in order that faith might be kept with the public. Although these conditions were made as light as they well could be, the author found it impossible to develop the story in the manner originally intended, and, more especially, was compelled to hurry on events with an improbable rapidity towards the close. In some degree to remedy this obvious defect, various short passages have been inserted; and several new chapters added. With this brief explanation, the tale is commended to the kindness of the reader;

> "Beseking hym lowly, of mercy and pité,
> Of its rude makyng to have compassion."[1]

---

1. This note was placed at the head of the novel to clarify Gaskell's revision of her text after her dissatisfaction with the *Household Words* version. *Easson 1973* suggests that the couplet at the conclusion is of her own devising.

Volume I

Chapter I.

"Haste to the Wedding."

"Wooed and married and a'."[1]

"Edith!" said Margaret, gently, "Edith!"

But, as Margaret half suspected, Edith had fallen asleep. She lay curled up on the sofa in the back drawing-room in Harley Street, looking very lovely in her white muslin and blue ribbons. If Titania had ever been dressed in white muslin and blue ribbons, and had fallen asleep on a crimson damask sofa in a back drawing-room, Edith might have been taken for her. Margaret was struck afresh by her cousin's beauty. They had grown up together from childhood, and all along Edith had been remarked upon by every one, except Margaret, for her prettiness; but Margaret had never thought about it until the last few days, when the prospect of soon losing her companion seemed to give force to every sweet quality and charm which Edith possessed. They had been talking about wedding dresses, and wedding ceremonies; and Captain Lennox, and what he had told Edith about her future life at Corfu,[2] where his regiment was stationed; and the difficulty of keeping a piano in good tune (a difficulty which Edith seemed to consider as one of the most formidable that could befall her in her married life), and what gowns she should want in the visits to Scotland, which would immediately succeed her marriage; but the whispered tone had latterly become more drowsy; and Margaret, after a pause of a few minutes, found, as she fancied, that in spite of the buzz in the next room, Edith had rolled herself up into a soft ball of muslin and ribbon, and silken curls, and gone off into a peaceful little after-dinner nap.

1. In the *Household Words* version of the text, the novel was headed by a stanza from Tennyson's "Will Waterproof's Lyrical Monologue" which concluded, "But for some true result of good / All parties work together," thus emphasizing the social theme of the novel. Gaskell's chapter-motto, from a traditional song, was not included in the *Household Words* text; this suggests that Gaskell considered her heroine's story to be the main priority.
2. The largest of the Greek islands, and from 1815 until 1864 a British protectorate; as such it was an important military base. Gaskell presents the soldier's life there as a comfortable one, but this was shortly to be overtaken by events with the invasion of the Crimea by the British in September 1854 and the subsequent Crimean War.

Margaret had been on the point of telling her cousin of some of
the plans and visions which she entertained as to her future life in
the country parsonage, where her father and mother lived; and where
her bright holidays had always been passed, though for the last ten
years her aunt Shaw's house had been considered as her home. But
in default of a listener, she had to brood over the change in her life
silently as heretofore. It was a happy brooding, although tinged with
regret at being separated for an indefinite time from her gentle aunt
and dear cousin. As she thought of the delight of filling the important
post of only daughter in Helstone parsonage, pieces of the conversation out of the next room came upon her ears. Her aunt Shaw was
talking to the five or six ladies who had been dining there, and whose
husbands were still in the dining-room. They were the familiar
acquaintances of the house; neighbours whom Mrs. Shaw called
friends, because she happened to dine with them more frequently
than with any other people, and because if she or Edith wanted
anything from them, or they from her, they did not scruple to make
a call at each other's houses before luncheon. These ladies and their
husbands were invited, in their capacity of friends, to eat a farewell
dinner in honour of Edith's approaching marriage. Edith had rather
objected to this arrangement, for Captain Lennox was expected to
arrive by a late train this very evening; but, although she was a spoiled
child, she was too careless and idle to have a very strong will of her
own, and gave way when she found that her mother had absolutely
ordered those extra delicacies of the season which are always supposed to be efficacious against immoderate grief at farewell dinners.
She contented herself by leaning back in her chair, merely playing
with the food on her plate, and looking grave and absent; while all
around her were enjoying the mots[3] of Mr. Grey, the gentleman who
always took the bottom of the table at Mrs. Shaw's dinner parties,
and asked Edith to give them some music in the drawing-room. Mr.
Grey was particularly agreeable over this farewell dinner, and the
gentlemen stayed down stairs longer than usual. It was very well they
did—to judge from the fragments of conversation which Margaret
overheard.

"I suffered too much myself; not that I was not extremely happy
with the poor dear General, but still disparity of age is a drawback;
one that I was resolved Edith should not have to encounter. Of
course, without any maternal partiality, I foresaw that the dear child
was likely to marry early; indeed, I had often said that I was sure she
would be married before she was nineteen. I had quite a prophetic
feeling when Captain Lennox"—and here the voice dropped into a
whisper, but Margaret could easily supply the blank. The course of

3. Literally "words" (French), but with the implication of witticisms.

true love in Edith's case had run remarkably smooth. Mrs. Shaw had given way to the presentiment, as she expressed it; and had rather urged on the marriage, although it was below the expectations which many of Edith's acquaintances had formed for her, a young and pretty heiress. But Mrs. Shaw said that her only child should marry for love,—and sighed emphatically, as if love had not been her motive for marrying the General. Mrs. Shaw enjoyed the romance of the present engagement rather more than her daughter. Not but that Edith was very thoroughly and properly in love; still she would certainly have preferred a good house in Belgravia, to all the pictur-esqueness of the life which Captain Lennox described at Corfu. The very parts which made Margaret glow as she listened, Edith pre-tended to shiver and shudder at; partly for the pleasure she had in being coaxed out of her dislike by her fond lover, and partly because anything of a gipsy or make-shift life was really distasteful to her. Yet had any one come with a fine house, and a fine estate, and a fine title to boot, Edith would still have clung to Captain Lennox while the temptation lasted; when it was over, it is possible she might have had little qualms of ill-concealed regret that Captain Lennox could not have united in his person everything that was desirable. In this she was but her mother's child; who, after deliberately marrying Gen-eral Shaw with no warmer feeling than respect for his character and establishment, was constantly, though quietly, bemoaning her hard lot in being united to one whom she could not love.

"I have spared no expense in her trousseau," were the next words Margaret heard. "She has all the beautiful Indian shawls and scarfs the General gave to me, but which I shall never wear again."

"She is a lucky girl," replied another voice, which Margaret knew to be that of Mrs. Gibson, a lady who was taking a double interest in the conversation, from the fact of one of her daughters having been married within the last few weeks. "Helen had set her heart upon an Indian shawl, but really when I found what an extravagant price was asked, I was obliged to refuse her. She will be quite envious when she hears of Edith having Indian shawls. What kind are they? Delhi? with the lovely little borders?"

Margaret heard her aunt's voice again, but this time it was as if she had raised herself up from her half-recumbent position, and were looking into the more dimly lighted back drawing-room. "Edith! Edith!" cried she; and then she sank as if wearied by the exertion. Margaret stepped forward.

"Edith is asleep, Aunt Shaw. Is it anything I can do?"

All the ladies said "Poor child!" on receiving this distressing intel-ligence about Edith; and the minute lap-dog in Mrs. Shaw's arms began to bark, as if excited by the burst of pity.

"Hush, Tiny! you naughty little girl! you will waken your mistress.

It was only to ask Edith if she would tell Newton to bring down her shawls: perhaps you would go, Margaret dear?"

Margaret went up into the old nursery at the very top of the house, where Newton was busy getting up some laces which were required for the wedding. While Newton went (not without a muttered grumbling) to undo the shawls, which had already been exhibited four or five times that day, Margaret looked round upon the nursery; the first room in that house with which she had become familiar nine years ago, when she was brought, all untamed from the forest, to share the home, the play, and the lessons of her cousin Edith. She remembered the dark, dim look of the London nursery, presided over by an austere and ceremonious nurse, who was terribly particular about clean hands and torn frocks. She recollected the first tea up there—separate from her father and aunt, who were dining somewhere down below an infinite depth of stairs; for unless she were up in the sky (the child thought), they must be deep down in the bowels of the earth. At home—before she came to live in Harley Street— her mother's dressing-room had been her nursery; and, as they kept early hours in the country parsonage, Margaret had always had her meals with her father and mother. Oh! well did the tall stately girl of eighteen remember the tears shed with such wild passion of grief by the little girl of nine, as she hid her face under the bed-clothes, in that first night; and how she was bidden not to cry by the nurse, because it would disturb Miss Edith; and how she had cried as bitterly, but more quietly, till her newly-seen, grand, pretty aunt had come softly upstairs with Mr. Hale to show him his little sleeping daughter. Then the little Margaret had hushed her sobs, and tried to lie quiet as if asleep, for fear of making her father unhappy by her grief, which she dared not express before her aunt, and which she rather thought it was wrong to feel at all after the long hoping, and planning, and contriving they had gone through at home, before her wardrobe could be arranged so as to suit her grander circumstances, and before papa could leave his parish to come up to London, even for a few days.

Now she had got to love the old nursery, though it was but a dismantled place; and she looked all round, with a kind of cat-like regret, at the idea of leaving it for ever in three days.

"Ah Newton!" said she, "I think we shall all be sorry to leave this dear old room."

"Indeed, miss, I shan't for one. My eyes are not so good as they were, and the light here is so bad that I can't see to mend laces except just at the window, where there's always a shocking draught— enough to give one one's death of cold."

"Well, I dare say you will have both good light and plenty of warmth at Naples. You must keep as much of your darning as you can till then. Thank you, Newton, I can take them down—you're busy."

So Margaret went down laden with shawls, and snuffing up their spicy Eastern smell. Her aunt asked her to stand as a sort of lay figure on which to display them, as Edith was still asleep. No one thought about it; but Margaret's tall, finely made figure, in the black silk dress which she was wearing as mourning for some distant relative of her father's, set off the long beautiful folds of the gorgeous shawls that would have half-smothered Edith. Margaret stood right under the chandelier, quite silent and passive, while her aunt adjusted the draperies. Occasionally, as she was turned round, she caught a glimpse of herself in the mirror over the chimney-piece, and smiled at her own appearance there—the familiar features in the usual garb of a princess. She touched the shawls gently as they hung around her, and took a pleasure in their soft feel and their brilliant colours, and rather liked to be dressed in such splendour—enjoying it much as a child would do, with a quiet pleased smile on her lips. Just then the door opened, and Mr. Henry Lennox was suddenly announced. Some of the ladies started back, as if half-ashamed of their feminine interest in dress. Mrs. Shaw held out her hand to the new-comer; Margaret stood perfectly still, thinking she might be yet wanted as a sort of block for the shawls; but looking at Mr. Lennox with a bright, amused face, as if sure of his sympathy in her sense of the ludicrousness at being thus surprised.

Her aunt was so much absorbed in asking Mr. Henry Lennox—who had not been able to come to dinner—all sorts of questions about his brother the bridegroom, his sister the bridesmaid (coming with the Captain from Scotland for the occasion), and various other members of the Lennox family, that Margaret saw she was no more wanted as shawl-bearer, and devoted herself to the amusement of the other visitors, whom her aunt had for the moment forgotten. Almost immediately, Edith came in from the back drawing-room, winking and blinking her eyes at the stronger light, shaking back her slightly-ruffled curls, and altogether looking like the Sleeping Beauty just startled from her dreams. Even in her slumber she had instinctively felt that a Lennox was worth rousing herself for; and she had a multitude of questions to ask about dear Janet, the future, unseen sister-in-law, for whom she professed so much affection, that if Margaret had not been very proud she might have almost felt jealous of the mushroom rival. As Margaret sank rather more into the background on her aunt's joining the conversation, she saw Henry Lennox directing his look towards a vacant seat near her; and she knew perfectly well that as soon as Edith released him from her questioning, he would take possession of that chair. She had not been quite sure, from her aunt's rather confused account of his engagements, whether he would come that night; it was almost a surprise to see him; and now she was sure of a pleasant evening. He liked and disliked pretty nearly the same things that she did. Margaret's face was lightened up into an honest, open brightness. By-and-by he came. She received him with a smile which had not a tinge of shyness or self-consciousness in it.

"Well, I suppose you are all in the depths of business—ladies' business, I mean. Very different to my business, which is the real true law business. Playing with shawls is very different work to drawing up settlements."

"Ah, I knew how you would be amused to find us all so occupied in admiring finery. But really Indian shawls are very perfect things of their kind."

"I have no doubt they are. Their prices are very perfect, too. Nothing wanting."

The gentlemen came dropping in one by one, and the buzz and noise deepened in tone.

"This is your last dinner-party, is it not? There are no more before Thursday?"

"No. I think after this evening we shall feel at rest, which I am sure I have not done for many weeks; at least, that kind of rest when the hands have nothing more to do, and all the arrangements are complete for an event which must occupy one's head and heart. I shall be glad to have time to think, and I am sure Edith will."

"I am not so sure about her; but I can fancy that you will. Whenever I have seen you lately, you have been carried away by a whirlwind of some other person's making."

"Yes," said Margaret, rather sadly, remembering the never-ending commotion about trifles that had been going on for more than a month past: "I wonder if a marriage must always be preceded by what you call a whirlwind, or whether in some cases there might not rather be a calm and peaceful time just before it."

"Cinderella's godmother ordering the trousseau, the wedding-breakfast, writing the notes of invitation, for instance," said Mr. Lennox, laughing.

"But are all these quite necessary troubles?" asked Margaret, looking up straight at him for an answer. A sense of indescribable weariness of all the arrangements for a pretty effect, in which Edith had been busied as supreme authority for the last six weeks, oppressed her just now; and she really wanted some one to help her to a few pleasant, quiet ideas connected with a marriage.

"Oh, of course," he replied with a change to gravity in his tone. "There are forms and ceremonies to be gone through, not so much to satisfy oneself, as to stop the world's mouth, without which stoppage there would be very little satisfaction in life. But how would you have a wedding arranged?"

"Oh, I have never thought much about it; only I should like it to be a very fine summer morning; and I should like to walk to church through the shade of trees; and not to have so many bridesmaids, and to have no wedding-breakfast. I dare say I am resolving against the very things that have given me the most trouble just now."

"No, I don't think you are. The idea of stately simplicity accords well with your character."

Margaret did not quite like this speech; she winced away from it more, from remembering former occasions on which he had tried to lead her into a discussion (in which he took the complimentary part) about her own character and ways of going on. She cut his speech rather short by saying:

"It is natural for me to think of Helstone church, and the walk to it, rather than of driving up to a London church in the middle of a paved street."

"Tell me about Helstone. You have never described it to me. I should like to have some idea of the place you will be living in, when ninety-six Harley Street will be looking dingy and dirty, and dull, and shut up. Is Helstone a village, or a town, in the first place?"

"Oh, only a hamlet; I don't think I could call it a village at all. There is the church and a few houses near it on the green—cottages, rather—with roses growing all over them."

"And flowering all the year round, especially at Christmas—make your picture complete," said he.

"No," replied Margaret, somewhat annoyed, "I am not making a picture. I am trying to describe Helstone as it really is. You should not have said that."

"I am penitent," he answered. "Only it really sounded like a village in a tale rather than in real life."

"And so it is," replied Margaret, eagerly. "All the other places in England that I have seen seem so hard and prosaic-looking, after the New Forest.[4] Helstone is like a village in a poem—in one of Tennyson's poems. But I won't try and describe it any more. You would only laugh at me if I told you what I think of it—what it really is."

"Indeed, I would not. But I see you are going to be very resolved. Well, then, tell me that which I should like still better to know: what the parsonage is like."

"Oh, I can't describe my home. It is home, and I can't put its charm into words."

"I submit. You are rather severe to-night, Margaret."

4. A wooded area in Hampshire, in the south of England.

"How?" said she, turning her large soft eyes round full upon him. "I did not know I was."

"Why, because I made an unlucky remark, you will neither tell me what Helstone is like, nor will you say anything about your home, though I have told you how much I want to hear about both, the latter especially."

"But indeed I cannot tell you about my own home. I don't quite think it is a thing to be talked about, unless you knew it."

"Well, then"—pausing for a moment—"tell me what you do there. Here you read, or have lessons, or otherwise improve your mind, till the middle of the day; take a walk before lunch, go a drive with your aunt after, and have some kind of engagement in the evening. There, now fill up your day at Helstone. Shall you ride, drive, or walk?"

"Walk, decidedly. We have no horse, not even for papa. He walks to the very extremity of his parish. The walks are so beautiful, it would be a shame to drive—almost a shame to ride."

"Shall you garden much? That, I believe, is a proper employment for young ladies in the country."

"I don't know. I am afraid I shan't like such hard work."

"Archery parties—pic-nics—race-balls—hunt-balls?"

"Oh no!" said she, laughing. "Papa's living is very small; and even if we were near such things, I doubt if I should go to them."

"I see, you won't tell me anything. You will only tell me that you are not going to do this and that. Before the vacation ends, I think I shall pay you a call, and see what you really do employ yourself in."

"I hope you will. Then you will see for yourself how beautiful Helstone is. Now I must go. Edith is sitting down to play, and I just know enough of music to turn over the leaves for her; and besides, Aunt Shaw won't like us to talk."

Edith played brilliantly. In the middle of the piece the door half-opened, and Edith saw Captain Lennox hesitating whether to come in. She threw down her music, and rushed out of the room, leaving Margaret standing confused and blushing to explain to the astonished guests what vision had shown itself to cause Edith's sudden flight. Captain Lennox had come earlier than was expected; or was it really so late? They looked at their watches, were duly shocked, and took their leave.

Then Edith came back, glowing with pleasure, half-shyly, half-proudly leading in her tall handsome Captain. His brother shook hands with him, and Mrs. Shaw welcomed him in her gentle kindly way, which had always something plaintive in it, arising from the long habit of considering herself a victim to an uncongenial marriage. Now that, the General being gone, she had every good of life, with as few drawbacks as possible, she had been rather perplexed to find an anxiety, if not a sorrow. She had, however, of late settled upon her own health as a source of apprehension; she had a nervous little cough whenever she thought about it; and some complaisant doctor ordered her just what she desired,—a winter in Italy. Mrs. Shaw had as strong wishes as most people, but she never liked to do anything from the open and acknowledged motive of her own good will and pleasure; she preferred being compelled to gratify herself by some other person's command or desire. She really did persuade herself that she was submitting to some hard external necessity; and thus she was able to moan and complain in her soft manner, all the time she was in reality doing just what she liked.

It was in this way she began to speak of her own journey to Captain Lennox, who assented, as in duty bound, to all his future mother-in-law said, while his eyes sought Edith, who was busying herself in rearranging the tea-table, and ordering up all sorts of good things, in spite of his assurances that he had dined within the last two hours.

Mr. Henry Lennox stood leaning against the chimney-piece, amused with the family scene. He was close by his handsome brother; he was the plain one in a singularly good-looking family; but his face was intelligent, keen, and mobile; and now and then Margaret wondered what it was that he could be thinking about, while he kept silence, but was evidently observing, with an interest that was slightly sarcastic, all that Edith and she were doing. The sarcastic feeling was called out by Mrs. Shaw's conversation with his brother; it was separate from the interest which was excited by what he saw. He thought it a pretty sight to see the two cousins so busy in their little arrangements about the table. Edith chose to do most herself. She was in a humour to enjoy showing her lover how well she could behave as a soldier's wife. She found out that the water in the urn was cold, and ordered up the great kitchen tea-kettle; the only consequence of which was that when she met it at the door, and tried to carry it in, it was too heavy for her, and she came in pouting, with a black mark on her muslin gown, and a little round white hand indented by the handle, which she took to show to Captain Lennox, just like a hurt child, and, of course, the remedy was the same in both cases. Margaret's quickly-adjusted spirit-lamp was the most efficacious contrivance, though not so like the gypsy-encampment which Edith, in some of her moods, chose to consider the nearest resemblance to a barrack-life.

After this evening all was bustle till the wedding was over.

Chapter II.

Roses and Thorns.

"By the soft green light in the woody glade,
   On the banks of moss where thy childhood played;
By the household tree, thro' which thine eye
   First looked in love to the summer sky."

MRS. HEMANS.[1]

Margaret was once more in her morning dress, travelling quietly home with her father, who had come up to assist at the wedding. Her mother had been detained at home by a multitude of half-reasons, none of which anybody fully understood, except Mr. Hale, who was perfectly aware that all his arguments in favour of a grey satin gown, which was midway between oldness and newness, had proved unavailing; and that, as he had not the money to equip his wife afresh, from top to toe, she would not show herself at her only sister's only child's wedding. If Mrs. Shaw had guessed at the real reason why Mrs. Hale did not accompany her husband, she would have showered down gowns upon her; but it was nearly twenty years since Mrs. Shaw had been the poor, pretty Miss Beresford, and she had really forgotten all grievances except that of the unhappiness arising from disparity of age in married life, on which she could descant by the half-hour. Dearest Maria had married the man of her heart, only eight years older than herself, with the sweetest temper, and that blue-black hair one so seldom sees. Mr. Hale was one of the most delightful preachers she had ever heard, and a perfect model of a parish priest. Perhaps it was not quite a logical deduction from all these premises, but it was still Mrs. Shaw's characteristic conclusion, as she thought over her sister's lot: "Married for love, what can dearest Maria have to wish for in this world?" Mrs. Hale, if she spoke truth, might have answered with a ready-made list, "a silver-grey glacé silk, a white chip bonnet,[2] oh! dozens of things for the wedding, and hundreds of things for the house."

Margaret only knew that her mother had not found it convenient to come, and she was not sorry to think that their meeting and greeting would take place at Helstone parsonage, rather than, during the confusion of the last two or three days, in the house in Harley Street, where she herself had had to play the part of Figaro,[3] and was wanted everywhere at one and the same time. Her mind and body ached now

---

1. Felicia Dorothea Hemans (1793–1835). Her works were extremely popular in the pre-Victorian and Victorian periods.
2. "Glacé silk": a smooth and shiny form of silk, used in dressmaking. "chip bonnet": a bonnet woven of "chip"—layers of straw or wood chip—and thus for outside wear.
3. The manservant in Rossini's opera *The Barber of Seville* (1816); one of his arias refers to his need to be everywhere at once.

with the recollection of all she had done and said within the last forty-eight hours. The farewells so hurriedly taken, amongst all the other good-byes, of those she had lived with so long, oppressed her now with a sad regret for the times that were no more; it did not signify what those times had been, they were gone never to return. Margaret's heart felt more heavy than she could ever have thought it possible in going to her own dear home, the place and the life she had longed for for years—at that time of all times for yearning and longing, just before the sharp senses lose their outlines in sleep. She took her mind away with a wrench from the recollection of the past to the bright serene contemplation of the hopeful future. Her eyes began to see, not visions of what had been, but the sight actually before her; her dear father leaning back asleep in the railway carriage. His blue-black hair was grey now, and lay thinly over his brows. The bones of his face were plainly to be seen—too plainly for beauty, if his features had been less finely cut; as it was, they had a grace if not a comeliness of their own. The face was in repose; but it was rather rest after weariness, than the serene calm of the countenance of one who led a placid, contented life. Margaret was painfully struck by the worn, anxious expression; and she went back over the open and avowed circumstances of her father's life, to find the cause for the lines that spoke so plainly of habitual distress and depression.

"Poor Frederick!" thought she, sighing. "Oh! if Frederick had but been a clergyman, instead of going into the navy, and being lost to us all! I wish I knew all about it. I never understood it from Aunt Shaw; I only knew he could not come back to England because of that terrible affair. Poor dear papa! how sad he looks! I am so glad I am going home, to be at hand to comfort him and mamma."

She was ready with a bright smile, in which there was not a trace of fatigue, to greet her father when he awakened. He smiled back again, but faintly, as if it were an unusual exertion. His face returned into its lines of habitual anxiety. He had a trick of half-opening his mouth as if to speak, which constantly unsettled the form of the lips, and gave the face an undecided expression. But he had the same large, soft eyes as his daughter,—eyes which moved slowly and almost grandly round in their orbits, and were well veiled by their transparent white eyelids. Margaret was more like him than like her mother. Sometimes people wondered that parents so handsome should have a daughter who was so far from regularly beautiful; not beautiful at all, was occasionally said. Her mouth was wide; no rosebud that could only open just enough to let out a "yes" and "no," and "an't please you, sir." But the wide mouth was one soft curve of rich red lips; and the skin, if not white and fair, was of an ivory smoothness and delicacy. If the look on her face was, in general, too dignified and reserved for one so young, now, talking to her father, it was bright as the morning,—full of dimples, and glances that spoke of childish gladness, and boundless hope in the future.

It was the latter part of July when Margaret returned home. The forest trees were all one dark, full, dusky green; the fern below them caught all the slanting sunbeams; the weather was sultry and broodingly still. Margaret used to tramp along by her father's side, crushing down the fern with a cruel glee, as she felt it yield under her light foot, and send up the fragrance peculiar to it,—out on the broad commons into the warm scented light, seeing multitudes of wild, free, living creatures, revelling in the sunshine, and the herbs and flowers it called forth. This life—at least these walks—realised all Margaret's anticipations. She took a pride in her forest. Its people were her people. She made hearty friends with them; learned and delighted in using their peculiar words; took up her freedom amongst them; nursed their babies; talked or read with slow distinctness to their old people; carried dainty messes to their sick; resolved before long to teach at the school, where her father went every day as to an appointed task, but she was continually tempted off to go and see some individual friend—man, woman, or child—in some cottage in the green shade of the forest. Her out-of-doors life was perfect. Her in-doors life had its drawbacks. With the healthy shame of a child, she blamed herself for her keenness of sight, in perceiving that all was not as it should be there. Her mother—her mother always so kind and tender towards her—seemed now and then so much discontented with their situation; thought that the bishop strangely neglected his episcopal duties, in not giving Mr. Hale a better living; and almost reproached her husband because he could not bring himself to say that he wished to leave the parish, and undertake the charge of a larger. He would sigh aloud as he answered, that if he could do what he ought in little Helstone, he should be thankful; but every day he was more overpowered; the world became more bewildering. At each repeated urgency of his wife, that he would put himself in the way of seeking some preferment, Margaret saw that her father shrank more and more; and she strove at such times to reconcile her mother to Helstone. Mrs. Hale said that the near neighbourhood of so many trees affected her health; and Margaret would try to tempt her forth on to the beautiful, broad, upland, sun-streaked, cloud-shadowed common; for she was sure that her mother had accustomed herself too much to an in-doors life, seldom extending her walks beyond the church, the school, and the neighbouring cottages. This did good for a time; but when the autumn drew on, and the weather became more changeable, her mother's idea of the unhealthiness of the place increased; and she repined even more frequently that her husband, who was more learned than Mr. Hume, a better parish priest than Mr. Houldsworth, should not have met with the preferment that these two former neighbours of theirs had done.

This marring of the peace of home, by long hours of discontent, was what Margaret was unprepared for. She knew, and had rather revelled in the idea, that she should have to give up many luxuries, which had only been troubles and trammels to her freedom in Harley Street. Her keen enjoyment of every sensuous pleasure, was balanced finely, if not overbalanced, by her conscious pride in being able to do without them all, if need were. But the cloud never comes in that quarter of the horizon from which we watch for it. There had been slight complaints and passing regrets on her mother's part, over some trifle connected with Helstone, and her father's position there, when Margaret had been spending her holidays at home before; but in the general happiness of the recollection of those times, she had forgotten the small details which were not so pleasant.

In the latter half of September, the autumnal rains and storms came on, and Margaret was obliged to remain more in the house than she had hitherto done. Helstone was at some distance from any neighbours of their own standard of cultivation.

"It is undoubtedly one of the most out-of-the-way places in England," said Mrs. Hale, in one of her plaintive moods. "I can't help regretting constantly that papa has really no one to associate with here; he is so thrown away; seeing no one but farmers and labourers from week's end to week's end. If we only lived at the other side of the parish, it would be something; there we should be almost within walking distance of the Stansfields; certainly the Gormans would be within a walk."

"Gormans," said Margaret. "Are those the Gormans who made their fortunes in trade at Southampton? Oh! I'm glad we don't visit them. I don't like shoppy people. I think we are far better off, knowing only cottagers and labourers, and people without pretence."

"You must not be so fastidious, Margaret, dear!" said her mother, secretly thinking of a young and handsome Mr. Gorman whom she had once met at Mr. Hume's.

"No! I call mine a very comprehensive taste; I like all people whose occupations have to do with land; I like soldiers and sailors, and the three learned professions, as they call them. I'm sure you don't want me to admire butchers and bakers, and candlestick-makers, do you, mamma?"

"But the Gormans were neither butchers nor bakers, but very respectable coach-builders."

"Very well. Coach-building is a trade all the same, and I think a much more useless one than that of butchers or bakers. Oh! how tired I used to be of the drives every day in Aunt Shaw's carriage, and how I longed to walk!"

And walk Margaret did, in spite of the weather. She was so happy out of doors, at her father's side, that she almost danced; and with the soft violence of the west wind behind her, as she crossed some heath, she seemed to be borne onwards, as lightly and easily as the fallen leaf that was wafted along by the autumnal breeze. But the evenings were rather difficult to fill up agreeably. Immediately after tea her father withdrew into his small library, and she and her mother were left alone. Mrs. Hale had never cared much for books, and had discouraged her husband, very early in their married life, in his desire of reading aloud to her, while she worked. At one time they had tried backgammon as a resource; but as Mr. Hale grew to take an increasing interest in his school and his parishioners, he found that the interruptions which arose out of these duties were regarded as hardships by his wife, not to be accepted as the natural conditions of his profession, but to be regretted and struggled against by her as they severally arose. So he withdrew, while the children were yet young, into his library, to spend his evenings (if he were at home), in reading the speculative and metaphysical books which were his delight.

When Margaret had been here before, she had brought down with her a great box of books, recommended by masters or governess, and had found the summer's day all too short to get through the reading she had to do before her return to town. Now there were only the well-bound little-read English Classics, which were weeded out of her father's library to fill up the small book-shelves in the drawing-room. Thomson's Seasons, Hayley's Cowper, Middleton's Cicero,[4] were by far the lightest, newest, and most amusing. The book-shelves did not afford much resource. Margaret told her mother every particular of her London life, to all of which Mrs. Hale listened with interest, sometimes amused and questioning, at others a little inclined to compare her sister's circumstances of ease and comfort with the narrower means at Helstone vicarage. On such evenings Margaret was apt to stop talking rather abruptly, and listen to the drip-drip of the rain upon the leads of the little bow-window. Once or twice Margaret found herself mechanically counting the repetition of the monotonous sound, while she wondered if she might venture to put a question on a subject very near to her heart, and ask where Frederick was now; what he was doing; how long it was since they had heard from him. But a consciousness that her mother's delicate health, and positive dislike to Helstone, all dated from the time of the mutiny in which Frederick had been engaged,— the full account of which Margaret had never heard, and which now

---

4. *The Seasons*, by James Thomson (1700–1748), was a poem published 1726–30; William Hayley (1745–1820) published a biography of the poet William Cowper, and Conyers Middleton (1683–1750) published *The Life of Cicero* in 1741. The rural associations of the English references are appropriate to the Helstone context at this point.

seemed doomed to be buried in sad oblivion,—made her pause and turn away from the subject each time she approached it. When she was with her mother, her father seemed the best person to apply to for information; and when with him, she thought that she could speak more easily to her mother. Probably there was nothing much to be heard that was new. In one of the letters she had received before leaving Harley Street, her father had told her that they had heard from Frederick; he was still at Rio, and very well in health, and sent his best love to her; which was dry bones, but not the living intelligence she longed for. Frederick was always spoken of, in the rare times when his name was mentioned, as "Poor Frederick." His room was kept exactly as he had left it; and was regularly dusted, and put into order by Dixon, Mrs. Hale's maid, who touched no other part of the household work, but always remembered the day when she had been engaged by Lady Beresford as ladies' maid to Sir John's wards, the pretty Miss Beresfords, the belles of Rutlandshire. Dixon had always considered Mr. Hale as the blight which had fallen upon her young lady's prospects in life. If Miss Beresford had not been in such a hurry to marry a poor country clergyman, there was no knowing what she might not have become. But Dixon was too loyal to desert her in her affliction and downfall (alias her married life). She remained with her, and was devoted to her interests; always considering herself as the good and protecting fairy, whose duty it was to baffle the malignant giant, Mr. Hale. Master Frederick had been her favourite and pride; and it was with a little softening of her dignified look and manner, that she went in weekly to arrange the chamber as carefully as if he might be coming home that very evening.

Margaret could not help believing that there had been some late intelligence of Frederick, unknown to her mother, which was making her father anxious and uneasy. Mrs. Hale did not seem to perceive any alteration in her husband's looks or ways. His spirits were always tender and gentle, readily affected by any small piece of intelligence concerning the welfare of others. He would be depressed for many days after witnessing a death-bed, or hearing of any crime. But now Margaret noticed an absence of mind, as if his thoughts were pre-occupied by some subject, the oppression of which could not be relieved by any daily action, such as comforting the survivors, or teaching at the school in hope of lessening the evils in the generation to come. Mr. Hale did not go out among his parishioners as much as usual; he was more shut in his study; was anxious for the village postman, whose summons to the household was a rap on the back-kitchen window-shutter—a signal which at one time had often to be repeated before any one was sufficiently alive to the hour of the day to understand what it was, and attend to him. Now Mr. Hale loitered about the garden if the morning was fine, and if not, stood dreamily by the study window until the postman had called, or gone down the lane, giving a half-respectful, half-confidential shake of the head to the parson, who watched him away beyond the sweet-briar hedge, and past the great arbutus,[5] before he turned into the room to begin his day's work, with all the signs of a heavy heart and an occupied mind.

But Margaret was at an age when any apprehension, not absolutely based on a knowledge of facts, is easily banished for a time by a bright sunny day, or some happy outward circumstance. And when the brilliant fourteen fine days of October came on, her cares were all blown away as lightly as thistledown, and she thought of nothing but the glories of the forest. The fern-harvest was over; and now that the rain was gone, many a deep glade was accessible, into which Margaret had only peeped in July and August weather. She had learnt drawing with Edith; and she had sufficiently regretted, during the gloom of the bad weather, her idle revelling in the beauty of the woodlands while it had yet been fine, to make her determined to sketch what she could before winter fairly set in. Accordingly, she was busy preparing her board one morning, when Sarah, the house-maid, threw wide open the drawing-room door, and announced, "Mr. Henry Lennox."

Chapter III.

"The More Haste the Worse Speed."

"Learn to win a lady's faith
Nobly, as the thing is high;
Bravely, as for life and death—
With a loyal gravity.

Lead her from the festive boards,
Point her to the starry skies,
Guard her, by your truthful words,
Pure from courtship's flatteries."
                                MRS. BROWNING.[1]

"Mr. Henry Lennox." Margaret had been thinking of him only a moment before, and remembering his inquiry into her probable occupations at home. It was "parler du soleil et l'on en voit les rayons;"[2] and the brightness of the sun came over Margaret's face as she put down her board, and went forward to shake hands with him. "Tell mamma, Sarah," said she. "Mamma and I want to ask you so

5. An evergreen tree, often cultivated for ornamental purposes.
1. Elizabeth Barrett Browning (1806–1861). The lines are from "The Lady's Yes," a poem which begins by describing a lady's withdrawal of her acceptance of a marriage proposal.
2. "Speak of the sun and you will see its beams" (French).

many questions about Edith; I am so much obliged to you for coming."

"Did not I say that I should?" asked he, in a lower tone than that in which she had spoken.

"But I heard of you so far away in the Highlands that I never thought Hampshire could come in."

"Oh!" said he, more lightly, "our young couple were playing such foolish pranks, running all sorts of risks, climbing this mountain, sailing on that lake, that I really thought they needed a Mentor to take care of them. And indeed they did; they were quite beyond my uncle's management, and kept the old gentleman in a panic for sixteen hours out of the twenty-four. Indeed, when I once saw how unfit they were to be trusted alone, I thought it my duty not to leave them till I had seen them safely embarked at Plymouth."

"Have you been at Plymouth? Oh! Edith never named that. To be sure, she has written in such a hurry lately. Did they really sail on Tuesday?"

"Really sailed, and relieved me from many responsibilities. Edith gave me all sorts of messages for you. I believe I have a little diminutive note somewhere; yes, here it is."

"Oh! thank you," exclaimed Margaret; and then, half wishing to read it alone and unwatched, she made the excuse of going to tell her mother again (Sarah surely had made some mistake) that Mr. Lennox was there.

When she had left the room, he began in his scrutinising way to look about him. The little drawing-room was looking its best in the streaming light of the morning sun. The middle window in the bow was opened, and clustering roses and the scarlet honeysuckle came peeping round the corner; the small lawn was gorgeous with verbenas and geraniums of all bright colours. But the very brightness outside made the colours within seem poor and faded. The carpet was far from new; the chintz had been often washed; the whole apartment was smaller and shabbier than he had expected, as back-ground and frame-work for Margaret, herself so queenly. He took up one of the books lying on the table; it was the Paradiso of Dante, in the proper old Italian binding of white vellum and gold; by it lay a dictionary, and some words copied out in Margaret's hand-writing. They were a dull list of words, but somehow he liked looking at them. He put them down with a sigh.

"The living is evidently as small as she said. It seems strange, for the Beresfords belong to a good family."

Margaret meanwhile had found her mother. It was one of Mrs. Hale's fitful days, when everything was a difficulty and a hardship; and Mr. Lennox's appearance took this shape, although secretly she felt complimented by his thinking it worth while to call.

"It is most unfortunate! We are dining early to-day, and having nothing but cold meat, in order that the servants may get on with their ironing; and yet, of course, we must ask him to dinner—Edith's brother-in-law and all. And your papa is in such low spirits this morning about something—I don't know what. I went into the study just now, and he had his face on the table, covering it with his hands. I told him I was sure Helstone air did not agree with him any more than with me, and he suddenly lifted up his head, and begged me not to speak a word more against Helstone, he could not bear it; if there was one place he loved on earth it was Helstone. But I am sure, for all that, it is the damp and relaxing air."

Margaret felt as if a thin cold cloud had come between her and the sun. She had listened patiently, in hopes that it might be some relief to her mother to unburden herself; but now it was time to draw her back to Mr. Lennox.

"Papa likes Mr. Lennox; they got on together famously at the wedding breakfast. I dare say his coming will do papa good. And never mind the dinner, dear mamma. Cold meat will do capitally for a lunch, which is the light in which Mr. Lennox will most likely look upon a two o'clock dinner."

"But what are we to do with him till then? It is only half-past ten now."

"I'll ask him to go out sketching with me. I know he draws, and that will take him out of your way, mamma. Only do come in now; he will think it so strange if you don't."

Mrs. Hale took off her black silk apron, and smoothed her face. She looked a very pretty lady-like woman, as she greeted Mr. Lennox with the cordiality due to one who was almost a relation. He evidently expected to be asked to spend the day, and accepted the invitation with a glad readiness that made Mrs. Hale wish she could add something to the cold beef. He was pleased with everything; delighted with Margaret's idea of going out sketching together; would not have Mr. Hale disturbed for the world, with the prospect of so soon meeting him at dinner. Margaret brought out her drawing materials for him to choose from; and after the paper and brushes had been duly selected, the two set out in the merriest spirits in the world.

"Now, please, just stop here for a minute or two," said Margaret. "These are the cottages that haunted me so during the rainy fortnight, reproaching me for not having sketched them."

"Before they tumbled down and were no more seen. Truly, if they are to be sketched—and they are very picturesque—we had better not put it off till next year. But where shall we sit?"

"Oh! You might have come straight from chambers in the Temple,[3]

3. London's legal center, where barristers had offices and sometimes resided.

instead of having been two months in the Highlands! Look at this beautiful trunk of a tree, which the wood-cutters have left just in the right place for the light. I will put my plaid over it, and it will be a regular forest throne."

"With your feet in that puddle for a regal foot-stool! Stay, I will move, and then you can come nearer this way. Who lives in these cottages?"

"They were built by squatters fifty or sixty years ago. One is uninhabited; the foresters are going to take it down, as soon as the old man who lives in the other is dead, poor old fellow! Look—there he is—I must go and speak to him. He is so deaf you will hear all our secrets."

The old man stood bareheaded in the sun, leaning on his stick at the front of his cottage. His stiff features relaxed into a slow smile as Margaret went up and spoke to him. Mr. Lennox hastily introduced the two figures into his sketch, and finished up the landscape with a subordinate reference to them—as Margaret perceived, when the time came for getting up, putting away water, and scraps of paper, and exhibiting to each other their sketches. She laughed and blushed: Mr. Lennox watched her countenance.

"Now, I call that treacherous," said she. "I little thought you were making old Isaac and me into subjects, when you told me to ask him the history of these cottages."

"It was irresistible. You can't know how strong a temptation it was. I hardly dare tell you how much I shall like this sketch."

He was not quite sure whether she heard this latter sentence before she went to the brook to wash her palette. She came back rather flushed, but looking perfectly innocent and unconscious. He was glad of it, for the speech had slipped from him unawares—a rare thing in the case of a man who premeditated his actions so much as Henry Lennox.

The aspect of home was all right and bright when they reached it. The clouds on her mother's brow had cleared off under the propitious influence of a brace of carp, most opportunely presented by a neighbour. Mr. Hale had returned from his morning's round, and was awaiting his visitor just outside the wicket gate that led into the garden. He looked a complete gentleman in his rather threadbare coat and well-worn hat. Margaret was proud of her father; she had always a fresh and tender pride in seeing how favourably he impressed every stranger; still her quick eye sought over his face and found there traces of some unusual disturbance, which was only put aside, not cleared away.

Mr. Hale asked to look at their sketches.

"I think you have made the tints on the thatch too dark, have you not?" as he returned Margaret's to her, and held out his hand for Mr. Lennox's, which was withheld from him one moment, no more.

"No, papa! I don't think I have. The house-leek and stone-crop have grown so much darker in the rain. Is it not like, papa?" said she, peeping over his shoulder, as he looked at the figures in Mr. Lennox's drawing.

"Yes, very like. Your figure and way of holding yourself is capital. And it is just poor old Isaac's stiff way of stooping his long rheumatic back. What is this hanging from the branch of the tree? Not a bird's nest, surely."

"Oh no! that is my bonnet. I never can draw with my bonnet on; it makes my head so hot. I wonder if I could manage figures. There are so many people about here whom I should like to sketch."

"I should say that a likeness you very much wish to take you would always succeed in," said Mr. Lennox. "I have great faith in the power of will. I think myself I have succeeded pretty well in yours." Mr. Hale had preceded them into the house, while Margaret was lingering to pluck some roses, with which to adorn her morning gown for dinner.

"A regular London girl would understand the implied meaning of that speech," thought Mr. Lennox. "She would be up to looking through every speech that a young man made her for the arrière-pensée[4] of a compliment. But I don't believe Margaret,—Stay!" exclaimed he, "Let me help you;" and he gathered for her some velvety cramoisy[5] roses that were above her reach, and then dividing the spoil he placed two in his button-hole, and sent her in, pleased and happy, to arrange her flowers.

The conversation at dinner flowed on quietly and agreeably. There were plenty of questions to be asked on both sides—the latest intelligence which each could give of Mrs. Shaw's movements in Italy to be exchanged; and in the interest of what was said, the unpretending simplicity of the parsonage-ways—above all, in the neighbourhood of Margaret, Mr. Lennox forgot the little feeling of disappointment with which he had at first perceived that she had spoken but the simple truth when she had described her father's living as very small.

"Margaret, my child, you might have gathered us some pears for our dessert," said Mr. Hale, as the hospitable luxury of a freshly-decanted bottle of wine was placed on the table.

Mrs. Hale was hurried. It seemed as if desserts were impromptu and unusual things at the parsonage; whereas, if Mr. Hale would only have looked behind him, he would have seen biscuits and marmalade, and what not, all arranged in formal order on the sideboard.

4. Hidden motive (French).
5. Crimson.

But the idea of pears had taken possession of Mr. Hale's mind, and was not to be got rid of.

"There are a few brown beurrés[6] against the south wall which are worth all foreign fruits and preserves. Run, Margaret, and gather us some."

"I propose that we adjourn into the garden, and eat them there," said Mr. Lennox. "Nothing is so delicious as to set one's teeth into the crisp, juicy fruit, warm and scented by the sun. The worst is, the wasps are impudent enough to dispute it with one, even at the very crisis and summit of enjoyment."

He rose, as if to follow Margaret, who had disappeared through the window: he only awaited Mrs. Hale's permission. She would rather have wound up the dinner in the proper way, and with all the ceremonies which had gone on so smoothly hitherto, especially as she and Dixon had got out the finger-glasses from the store-room on purpose to be as correct as became General Shaw's widow's sister; but as Mr. Hale got up directly, and prepared to accompany his guest, she could only submit.

"I shall arm myself with a knife," said Mr. Hale: "The days of eating fruit so primitively as you describe are over with me. I must pare it and quarter it before I can enjoy it."

Margaret made a plate for the pears out of a beetroot leaf, which threw up their brown gold colour admirably. Mr. Lennox looked more at her than at the pears; but her father, inclined to cull fastidiously the very zest and perfection of the hour he had stolen from his anxiety, chose daintily the ripest fruit, and sat down on the garden bench to enjoy it at his leisure. Margaret and Mr. Lennox strolled along the little terrace-walk under the south wall, where the bees still hummed and worked busily in their hives.

"What a perfect life you seem to live here! I have always felt rather contemptuously towards the poets before, with their wishes, 'Mine be a cot beside a hill,' and that sort of thing: but now I am afraid that the truth is, I have been nothing better than a Cockney. Just now I feel as if twenty years' hard study of law would be amply rewarded by one year of such an exquisite serene life as this—such skies!" looking up—"such crimson and amber foliage, so perfectly motionless as that!" pointing to some of the great forest trees which shut in the garden as if it were a nest.

"You must please to remember that our skies are not always as deep a blue as they are now. We have rain, and our leaves do fall, and get sodden: though I think Helstone is about as perfect a place as any in the world. Recollect how you rather scorned my description of it one evening in Harley Street: 'a village in a tale.' "

6. A mellow variety of pear.

"Scorned, Margaret! That is rather a hard word."

"Perhaps it is. Only I know I should have liked to have talked to you of what I was very full at the time, and you—what must I call it then?—spoke disrespectfully of Helstone as a mere village in a tale."

"I will never do so again," said he, warmly. They turned the corner of the walk.

"I could almost wish, Margaret——" he stopped and hesitated. It was so unusual for the fluent lawyer to hesitate that Margaret looked up at him, in a little state of questioning wonder; but in an instant—from what about him she could not tell—she wished herself back with her mother—her father—anywhere away from him, for she was sure he was going to say something to which she should not know what to reply. In another moment the strong pride that was in her came to conquer her sudden agitation, which she hoped he had not perceived. Of course she could answer, and answer the right thing; and it was poor and despicable of her to shrink from hearing any speech, as if she had not power to put an end to it with her high maidenly dignity.

"Margaret," said he, taking her by surprise, and getting sudden possession of her hand, so that she was forced to stand still and listen, despising herself for the fluttering at her heart all the time; "Margaret, I wish you did not like Helstone so much—did not seem so perfectly calm and happy here. I have been hoping for these three months past to find you regretting London—and London friends, a little—enough to make you listen more kindly" (for she was quietly, but firmly, striving to extricate her hand from his grasp) "to one who has not much to offer, it is true—nothing but prospects in the future—but who does love you, Margaret, almost in spite of himself. Margaret, have I startled you too much? Speak!" For he saw her lips quivering almost as if she were going to cry. She made a strong effort to be calm; she would not speak till she had succeeded in mastering her voice, and then she said:

"I was startled. I did not know that you cared for me in that way. I have always thought of you as a friend; and, please, I would rather go on thinking of you so. I don't like to be spoken to as you have been doing. I cannot answer you as you want me to do, and yet I should feel so sorry if I vexed you."

"Margaret," said he, looking into her eyes, which met his with their open, straight look, expressive of the utmost good faith and reluctance to give pain, "Do you"—he was going to say—"love any one else?" But it seemed as if this question would be an insult to the pure serenity of those eyes.

"Forgive me! I have been too abrupt. I am punished. Only let me hope. Give me the poor comfort of telling me you have never seen any one whom you could——" Again a pause. He could not end his sentence. Margaret reproached herself acutely as the cause of his distress.

"Ah! if you had but never got this fancy into your head! It was such a pleasure to think of you as a friend."

"But I may hope, may I not, Margaret, that some time you will think of me as a lover? Not yet, I see—there is no hurry—but some time——"

She was silent for a minute or two, trying to discover the truth as it was in her own heart, before replying; then she said:

"I have never thought of—you, but as a friend. I like to think of you so; but I am sure I could never think of you as anything else. Pray, let us both forget that all this" ("disagreeable," she was going to say, but stopped short) "conversation has taken place."

He paused before he replied. Then, in his habitual coldness of tone, he answered:

"Of course, as your feelings are so decided, and as this conversation has been so evidently unpleasant to you, it had better not be remembered. That is all very fine in theory, that plan of forgetting whatever is painful, but it will be somewhat difficult for me, at least, to carry it into execution."

"You are vexed," said she, sadly; "yet how can I help it?"

She looked so truly grieved as she said this, that he struggled for a moment with his real disappointment, and then answered more cheerfully, but still with a little hardness in his tone:

"You should make allowances for the mortification, not only of a lover, Margaret, but of a man not given to romance in general—prudent, worldly, as some people call me—who has been carried out of his usual habits by the force of a passion—well, we will say no more of that; but in the one outlet which he has formed for the deeper and better feelings of his nature, he meets with rejection and repulse. I shall have to console myself with scorning my own folly. A struggling barrister to think of matrimony!"

Margaret could not answer this. The whole tone of it annoyed her. It seemed to touch on and call out all the points of difference which had often repelled her in him; while yet he was the pleasantest man, the most sympathising friend, the person of all others who understood her best in Harley Street. She felt a tinge of contempt mingle itself with her pain at having refused him. Her beautiful lip curled in a slight disdain. It was well that, having made the round of the garden, they came suddenly upon Mr. Hale, whose whereabouts had been quite forgotten by them. He had not yet finished the pear, which he had delicately peeled in one long strip of silver-paper thinness, and which he was enjoying in a deliberate manner. It was like the story of the eastern king, who dipped his head into a basin of water, at the magician's command, and ere he instantly took it out went through the experience of a lifetime.[7] Margaret felt stunned, and unable to recover her self-possession enough to join in the trivial conversation that ensued between her father and Mr. Lennox. She was grave, and little disposed to speak; full of wonder when Mr. Lennox would go, and allow her to relax into thought on the events of the last quarter of an hour. He was almost as anxious to take his departure as she was for him to leave; but a few minutes light and careless talking, carried on at whatever effort, was a sacrifice which he owed to his mortified vanity, or his self-respect. He glanced from time to time at her sad and pensive face.

"I am not so indifferent to her as she believes," thought he to himself. "I do not give up hope."

Before a quarter of an hour was over, he had fallen into a way of conversing with quiet sarcasm; speaking of life in London and life in the country, as if he were conscious of his second mocking self, and afraid of his own satire. Mr. Hale was puzzled. His visitor was a different man to what he had seen him before at the wedding-breakfast, and at dinner to-day; a lighter, cleverer, more worldly man, and, as such, dissonant to Mr. Hale. It was a relief to all three when Mr. Lennox said that he must go directly if he meant to catch the five o'clock train. They proceeded to the house to find Mrs. Hale, and wish her good-bye. At the last moment, Henry Lennox's real self broke through the crust.

"Margaret, don't despise me; I have a heart, notwithstanding all this good-for-nothing way of talking. As a proof of it, I believe I love you more than ever—if I do not hate you—for the disdain with which you have listened to me during this last half-hour. Good-bye, Margaret—Margaret!"

Chapter IV.

Doubts and Difficulties.

> "Cast me upon some naked shore,
> Where I may tracke
> Only the print of some sad wracke,
> If thou be there, though the seas roare,
> I shall no gentler calm implore."
>
> HABINGTON.[1]

He was gone. The house was shut up for the evening. No more deep blue skies or crimson and amber tints. Margaret went up to dress for the early tea, finding Dixon in a pretty temper from the interruption

7. A popular oriental story; Dickens also refers to it in *Hard Times* (bk. 2, chap. 1).
1. William Habington (1605–1654), English metaphysical poet.

which a visitor had naturally occasioned on a busy day. She showed it by brushing away viciously at Margaret's hair, under pretence of being in a great hurry to go to Mrs. Hale. Yet, after all, Margaret had to wait a long time in the drawing-room before her mother came down. She sat by herself at the fire, with unlighted candles on the table behind her, thinking over the day, the happy walk, happy sketching, cheerful pleasant dinner, and the uncomfortable, miserable walk in the garden.

How different men were to women! Here was she disturbed and unhappy, because her instinct had made anything but a refusal impossible; while he, not many minutes after he had met with a rejection of what ought to have been the deepest, holiest proposal of his life, could speak as if briefs, success, and all its superficial consequences of a good house, clever and agreeable society, were the sole avowed objects of his desires. Oh dear! how she could have loved him if he had but been different, with a difference which she felt, on reflection, to be one that went low—deep down. Then she took it into her head that, after all, his lightness might be but assumed, to cover a bitterness of disappointment which would have been stamped on her own heart if she had loved and been rejected.

Her mother came into the room before this whirl of thoughts was adjusted into anything like order. Margaret had to shake off the recollections of what had been done and said through the day, and turn a sympathising listener to the account of how Dixon had complained that the ironing-blanket had been burnt again; and how Susan Lightfoot had been seen with artificial flowers in her bonnet, thereby giving evidence of a vain and giddy character. Mr. Hale sipped his tea in abstracted silence; Margaret had the responses all to herself. She wondered how her father and mother could be so forgetful, so regardless of their companion through the day, as never to mention his name. She forgot that he had not made them an offer.

After tea Mr. Hale got up, and stood with his elbow on the chimney-piece, leaning his head on his hand, musing over something, and from time to time sighing deeply. Mrs. Hale went out to consult with Dixon about some winter clothing for the poor. Margaret was preparing her mother's worsted work, and rather shrinking from the thought of the long evening, and wishing bed-time were come that she might go over the events of the day again.

"Margaret!" said Mr. Hale, at last, in a sort of sudden desperate way, that made her start. "Is that tapestry thing of immediate consequence? I mean, can you leave it and come into my study? I want to speak to you about something very serious to us all."

"Very serious to us all." Mr. Lennox had never had the opportunity of having any private conversation with her father after her refusal, or else that would indeed be a very serious affair. In the first place,

Margaret felt guilty and ashamed of having grown so much into a woman as to be thought of in marriage; and secondly, she did not know if her father might not be displeased that she had taken upon herself to decline Mr. Lennox's proposal. But she soon felt it was not about anything, which having only lately and suddenly occurred, could have given rise to any complicated thoughts, that her father wished to speak to her. He made her take a chair by him; he stirred the fire, snuffed the candles, and sighed once or twice before he could make up his mind to say—and it came out with a jerk after all—"Margaret! I am going to leave Helstone."

"Leave Helstone, papa! But why?"

Mr. Hale did not answer for a minute or two. He played with some papers on the table in a nervous and confused manner, opening his lips to speak several times, but closing them again without having the courage to utter a word. Margaret could not bear the sight of the suspense, which was even more distressing to her father than to herself.

"But why, dear papa? Do tell me!"

He looked up at her suddenly, and then said with a slow and enforced calmness:

"Because I must no longer be a minister in the Church of England."[2]

Margaret had imagined nothing less than that some of the preferments which her mother so much desired had befallen her father at last—something that would force him to leave beautiful, beloved Helstone, and perhaps compel him to go and live in some of the stately and silent Closes which Margaret had seen from time to time in cathedral towns. They were grand and imposing places, but if, to go there, it was necessary to leave Helstone as a home for ever, that would have been a sad, long, lingering pain. But nothing to the shock she received from Mr. Hale's last speech. What could he mean? It was all the worse for being so mysterious. The aspect of piteous distress on his face, almost as imploring a merciful and kind judgment from his child, gave her a sudden sickening. Could he have become implicated in anything Frederick had done? Frederick was an outlaw. Had her father, out of a natural love for his son, connived at any—

"Oh! what is it? do speak, papa! tell me all! Why can you no longer be a clergyman? Surely, if the bishop were told all we know about Frederick, and the hard, unjust—"

"It is nothing about Frederick; the bishop would have nothing to

2. As this and further references in this chapter indicate, Mr. Hale's doubts are not doubts about belief, but he is convinced that his conscience does not allow him to subscribe to his obligations as a clergyman of the Church of England.

do with that. It is all myself, Margaret, I will tell you about it. I will answer any questions this once, but after to-night let us never speak of it again. I can meet the consequences of my painful, miserable doubts; but it is an effort beyond me to speak of what has caused me so much suffering."

"Doubts, papa! Doubts as to religion?" asked Margaret, more shocked than ever.

"No! not doubts as to religion; not the slightest injury to that."

He paused. Margaret sighed, as if standing on the verge of some new horror. He began again, speaking rapidly, as if to get over a set task:

"You could not understand it all, if I told you—my anxiety, for years past, to know whether I had any right to hold my living—my efforts to quench my smouldering doubts by the authority of the Church. Oh! Margaret, how I love the holy Church from which I am to be shut out!" He could not go on for a moment or two. Margaret could not tell what to say; it seemed to her as terribly mysterious as if her father were about to turn Mahometan.

"I have been reading to-day of the two thousand who were ejected from their churches,"[3]—continued Mr. Hale, smiling faintly,—"trying to steal some of their bravery; but it is of no use—no use—I cannot help feeling it acutely."

"But, papa, have you well considered? Oh! it seems so terrible, so shocking," said Margaret, suddenly bursting into tears. The one staid foundation of her home, of her idea of her beloved father, seemed reeling and rocking. What could she say? What was to be done? The sight of her distress made Mr. Hale nerve himself, in order to try and comfort her. He swallowed down the dry choking sobs which had been heaving up from his heart hitherto, and going to his bookcase he took down a volume, which he had often been reading lately, and from which he thought he had derived strength to enter upon the course in which he was now embarked.

"Listen, dear Margaret," said he, putting one arm round her waist. She took his hand in hers and grasped it tight, but she could not lift up her head; nor indeed could she attend to what he read, so great was her internal agitation.

"This is the soliloquy of one who was once a clergyman in a country parish, like me; it was written by a Mr. Oldfield,[4] minister of

3. Clergymen in the seventeenth century who would not subscribe to the Act of Uniformity (1662), which required them to give their consent to everything prescribed in the Book of Common Prayer.
4. See previous note. John Oldfield (c. 1627–1682) was one such minister. His "soliloquy" was quoted in *An Abridgement of Mr Baxter's History of his Life and Times*, by Edmund Calamy. See Angus Easson, "Mr Hale's Doubts in *North and South*." *Review of English Studies*, 31 (1980): 30–40.

Carsington, in Derbyshire, a hundred and sixty years ago, or more. His trials are over. He fought the good fight." These last two sentences he spoke low, as if to himself. Then he read aloud,—

"When thou canst no longer continue in thy work without dishonour to God, discredit to religion, foregoing thy integrity, wounding conscience, spoiling thy peace, and hazarding the loss of thy salvation; in a word, when the conditions upon which thou must continue (if thou wilt continue) in thy employments are sinful, and unwarranted by the word of God, thou mayest, yea, thou must believe that God will turn thy very silence, suspension, deprivation, and laying aside, to His glory, and the advancement of the Gospel's interest. When God will not use thee in one kind, yet He will in another. A soul that desires to serve and honour Him shall never want opportunity to do it; nor must thou so limit the Holy One of Israel, as to think He hath but one way in which He can glorify Himself by thee. He can do it by thy silence as well as by thy preaching; thy laying aside as well as thy continuance in thy work. It is not pretence of doing God the greatest service, or performing the weightiest duty, that will excuse the least sin, though that sin capacitated or gave us the opportunity for doing that duty. Thou wilt have little thanks, O my soul! if, when thou art charged with corrupting God's worship, falsifying thy vows, thou pretendest a necessity for it in order to a continuance in the ministry."

As he read this, and glanced at much more which he did not read, he gained resolution for himself, and felt as if he too could be brave and firm in doing what he believed to be right; but as he ceased he heard Margaret's low convulsive sob; and his courage sank down under the keen sense of suffering.

"Margaret, dear!" said he, drawing her closer, "think of the early martyrs; think of the thousands who have suffered."

"But, father," said she, suddenly lifting up her flushed, tear-wet face, "the early martyrs suffered for the truth, while you—oh! dear, dear papa!"

"I suffer for conscience' sake, my child," said he, with a dignity that was only tremulous from the acute sensitiveness of his character; "I must do what my conscience bids. I have borne long with self-reproach that would have roused any mind less torpid and cowardly than mine." He shook his head as he went on. "Your poor mother's fond wish, gratified at last in the mocking way in which over-fond wishes are too often fulfilled—Sodom apples[5] as they are—has brought on this crisis, for which I ought to be, and I hope I am thankful. It is not a month since the bishop offered me another living; if I had accepted it, I should have had to make a fresh declaration

5. Traditionally, fruit that was attractive to the eye, but unpleasant to eat.

of conformity to the Liturgy at my institution.[6] Margaret, I tried to do it; I tried to content myself with simply refusing the additional preferment, and stopping quietly here,—strangling my conscience now, as I had strained it before. God forgive me!"

He rose and walked up and down the room, speaking low words of self-reproach and humiliation, of which Margaret was thankful to hear but few. At last he said,

"Margaret, I return to the old sad burden: we must leave Helstone."

"Yes! I see. But when?"

"I have written to the bishop—I dare say I have told you so, but I forget things just now," said Mr. Hale, collapsing into his depressed manner as soon as he came to talk of hard matter-of-fact details, "informing him of my intention to resign this vicarage. He has been most kind; he has used arguments and expostulations, all in vain—in vain. They are but what I have tried upon myself, without avail. I shall have to take my deed of resignation, and wait upon the bishop myself, to bid him farewell. That will be a trial. But worse, far worse, will be the parting from my dear people. There is a curate appointed to read prayers—a Mr. Brown. He will come to stay with us to-morrow. Next Sunday I preach my farewell sermon."

Was it to be so sudden then? thought Margaret; and yet perhaps it was as well. Lingering would only add stings to the pain; it was better to be stunned into numbness by hearing of all these arrangements, which seemed to be nearly completed before she had been told. "What does mamma say?" asked she, with a deep sigh.

To her surprise, her father began to walk about again before he answered. At length he stopped and replied:

"Margaret. I am a poor coward after all. I cannot bear to give pain. I know so well your mother's married life has not been all she hoped—all she had a right to expect—and this will be such a blow to her, that I have never had the heart, the power to tell her. She must be told though, now," said he, looking wistfully at his daughter. Margaret was almost overpowered with the idea that her mother knew nothing of it all, and yet the affair was so far advanced!

"Yes, indeed she must," said Margaret. "Perhaps, after all, she may not—Oh yes! she will, she must be shocked"—as the force of the blow returned upon herself in trying to realise how another would take it. "Where are we to go to?" said she at last, struck with a fresh wonder as to their future plans, if plans indeed her father had.

"To Milton-Northern,"[7] he answered, with a dull indifference, for

6. On being appointed to a new parish, Anglican clergymen are required to reaffirm their commitment to the prescriptions of the Book of Common Prayer.
7. Undoubtedly Manchester, as Darkshire is Lancashire. Here, as elsewhere, Gaskell deliberately fictionalizes her geographical settings. This is a departure from her practice in her first Manchester novel, *Mary Barton*.

he had perceived that, although his daughter's love had made her cling to him, and for a moment strive to soothe him with her love, yet the keenness of the pain was as fresh as ever in her mind.

"Milton-Northern! The manufacturing town in Darkshire?"

"Yes," said he, in the same despondent, indifferent way.

"Why there, papa?" asked she.

"Because there I can earn bread for my family. Because I know no one there, and no one knows Helstone, or can ever talk to me about it."

"Bread for your family! I thought you and mamma had"—and then she stopped, checking her natural interest regarding their future life, as she saw the gathering gloom on her father's brow. But he, with his quick intuitive sympathy, read in her face, as in a mirror, the reflections of his own moody depression, and turned it off with an effort.

"You shall be told all, Margaret. Only help me to tell your mother. I think I could do anything but that: the idea of her distress turns me sick with dread. If I tell you all, perhaps you could break it to her to-morrow. I am going out for the day, to bid farmer Dobson and the poor people on Bracy Common good-bye. Would you dislike breaking it to her very much, Margaret?"

Margaret did dislike it, did shrink from it more than from anything she had ever had to do in her life before. She could not speak, all at once. Her father said, "You dislike it very much, don't you, Margaret?" Then she conquered herself, and said, with a bright strong look on her face:

"It is a painful thing, but it must be done, and I will do it as well as ever I can. You must have many painful things to do."

Mr. Hale shook his head despondingly: he pressed her hand in token of gratitude. Margaret was nearly upset again into a burst of crying. To turn her thoughts, she said: "Now tell me, papa, what our plans are. You and mamma have some money, independent of the income from the living, have not you? Aunt Shaw has, I know."

"Yes. I suppose we have about a hundred and seventy pounds a year of our own. Seventy of that has always gone to Frederick, since he has been abroad. I don't know if he wants it all," he continued in a hesitating manner. "He must have some pay for serving with the Spanish army."

"Frederick must not suffer," said Margaret, decidedly; "in a foreign country; so unjustly treated by his own. A hundred is left. Could not you, and I, and mamma live on a hundred a year in some very cheap—very quiet part of England? Oh! I think we could."

"No!" said Mr. Hale. "That would not answer. I must do something. I must make myself busy, to keep off morbid thoughts. Besides, in a country parish I should be so painfully reminded of

Helstone, and my duties here. I could not bear it, Margaret. And a hundred a year would go a very little way, after the necessary wants of housekeeping are met, towards providing your mother with all the comforts she has been accustomed to, and ought to have. No: we must go to Milton. That is settled. I can always decide better by myself, and not influenced by those whom I love," said he, as a half apology for having arranged so much before he had told any one of his family of his intentions. "I cannot stand objections. They make me so undecided."

Margaret resolved to keep silence. After all, what did it signify where they went, compared to the one terrible change?

Mr. Hale continued: "A few months ago, when my misery of doubt became more than I could bear without speaking, I wrote to Mr. Bell—you remember Mr. Bell, Margaret?"

"No; I never saw him, I think. But I know who he is. Frederick's godfather—your old tutor at Oxford, don't you mean?"

"Yes. He is a Fellow of Plymouth College[8] there. He is a native of Milton-Northern, I believe. At any rate he has property there, which has very much increased in value since Milton has become such a large manufacturing town. Well; I had reason to suspect—to imagine—I had better say nothing about it, however. But I felt sure of sympathy from Mr. Bell. I dont know that he gave me much strength. He has lived an easy life in his college all his days. But he has been as kind as can be. And it is owing to him we are going to Milton."

"How?" said Margaret.

"Why he has tenants, and houses, and mills there; so, though he dislikes the place—too bustling for one of his habits—he is obliged to keep up some sort of connection; and he tells me that he hears there is a good opening for a private tutor there."

"A private tutor!" said Margaret, looking scornful; "What in the world do manufacturers want with the classics, or literature, or the accomplishments of a gentleman?"

"Oh," said her father, "some of them really seem to be fine fellows, conscious of their own deficiencies, which is more than many a man at Oxford is. Some want resolutely to learn, though they have come to man's estate. Some want their children to be better instructed than they themselves have been. At any rate, there is an opening, as I have said, for a private tutor. Mr. Bell has recommended me to a Mr. Thornton, a tenant of his, and a very intelligent man, as far as I can judge from his letters. And in Milton, Margaret, I shall find a busy life, if not a happy one, and people and scenes so different that I shall never be reminded of Helstone."

There was the secret motive, as Margaret knew from her own feel-

8. Like Milton-Northern, an invented name.

ings. It would be different. Discordant as it was—with almost a detestation for all she had ever heard of the North of England, the manufacturers, the people, the wild and bleak country—there was this one recommendation—it would be different from Helstone, and could never remind them of that beloved place.

"When do we go?" asked Margaret, after a short silence.

"I do not know exactly. I wanted to talk it over with you. You see, your mother knows nothing about it yet: but I think, in a fortnight;—after my deed of resignation is sent in, I shall have no right to remain."

Margaret was almost stunned.

"In a fortnight!"

"No—no, not exactly to a day. Nothing is fixed," said her father, with anxious hesitation, as he noticed the filmy sorrow that came over her eyes, and the sudden change in her complexion. But she recovered herself immediately.

"Yes, papa, it had better be fixed soon and decidedly, as you say. Only mamma to know nothing about it! It is that that is the great perplexity."

"Poor Maria!" replied Mr. Hale tenderly. "Poor, poor Maria! Oh, if I were not married—if I were but myself in the world, how easy it would be! As it is—Margaret, I dare not tell her!"

"No," said Margaret, sadly, "I will do it. Give me till to-morrow evening to choose my time. Oh, papa," cried she with sudden passionate entreaty, "say—tell me it is a night-mare—a horrid dream—not the real waking truth! You cannot mean that you are really going to leave the Church—to give up Helstone—to be for ever separate from me, from mamma—led away by some delusion—some temptation! You do not really mean it!"

Mr. Hale sat in rigid stillness while she spoke.

Then he looked her in the face, and said in a slow, hoarse, measured way—"I do mean it, Margaret. You must not deceive yourself into doubting the reality of my words—my fixed intention and resolve." He looked at her in the same steady, stony manner, for some moments after he had done speaking. She, too, gazed back with pleading eyes before she would believe that it was irrevocable. Then she arose and went, without another word or look, towards the door. As her fingers were on the handle he called her back. He was standing by the fireplace, shrunk and stooping; but as she came near he drew himself up to his full height, and, placing his hands on her head, he said, solemnly:

"The blessing of God be upon thee, my child!"

"And may He restore you to His Church," responded she, out of the fulness of her heart. The next moment she feared lest this answer to his blessing might be irreverent, wrong—might hurt him as coming from his daughter, and she threw her arms round his neck. He held her to him for a minute or two. She heard him murmur to himself, "The martyrs and confessors had even more pain to bear—I will not shrink."

They were startled by hearing Mrs. Hale inquiring for her daughter. They started asunder in the full consciousness of all that was before them. Mr. Hale hurriedly said—"Go, Margaret, go. I shall be out all to-morrow. Before night you will have told your mother."

"Yes," she replied, and she returned to the drawing-room in a stunned and dizzy state.

Chapter V.

Decision.

"I ask Thee for a thoughtful love,
    Through constant watching wise,
To meet the glad with joyful smiles,
    And to wipe the weeping eyes;
And a heart at leisure from itself
    To soothe and sympathise."

ANON.[1]

Margaret made a good listener to all her mother's little plans for adding some small comforts to the lot of the poorer parishioners. She could not help listening, though each new project was a stab to her heart. By the time the frost had set in, they should be far away from Helstone. Old Simon's rheumatism might be bad and his eyesight worse; there would be no one to go and read to him, and comfort him with little porringers of broth and good red flannel: or if there was, it would be a stranger, and the old man would watch in vain for her. Mary Domville's little crippled boy would crawl in vain to the door and look for her coming through the forest. These poor friends would never understand why she had forsaken them; and there were many others besides. "Papa has always spent the income he derived from his living in the parish. I am, perhaps, encroaching upon the next dues, but the winter is likely to be severe, and our poor old people must be helped."

"Oh, mamma, let us do all we can," said Margaret eagerly, not seeing the prudential side of the question, only grasping at the idea that they were rendering such help for the last time; "we may not be here long."

"Do you feel ill, my darling?" asked Mrs. Hale, anxiously, misun-

1. Anonymous in Gaskell's text, but in fact by the Victorian hymn-writer Anna Laetitia Waring (1823–1910).

derstanding Margaret's hint of the uncertainty of their stay at Helstone. "You look pale and tired. It is this soft, damp, unhealthy air."

"No—no, mamma, it is not that: it is delicious air. It smells of the freshest, purest fragrance, after the smokiness of Harley Street. But I am tired: it surely must be near bedtime."

"Not far off—it is half-past nine. You had better go to bed at once, dear. Ask Dixon for some gruel. I will come and see you as soon as you are in bed. I am afraid you have taken cold; or the bad air from some of the stagnant ponds—"

"Oh, mamma," said Margaret, faintly smiling as she kissed her mother, "I am quite well—don't alarm yourself about me; I am only tired."

Margaret went upstairs. To soothe her mother's anxiety she submitted to a basin of gruel. She was lying languidly in bed when Mrs. Hale came up to make some last inquiries and kiss her before going to her own room for the night. But the instant she heard her mother's door locked, she sprang out of bed, and throwing her dressing-gown on, she began to pace up and down the room, until the creaking of one of the boards reminded her that she must make no noise. She went and curled herself up on the window-seat in the small, deeply-recessed window. That morning when she had looked out, her heart had danced at seeing the bright clear lights on the church tower, which foretold a fine and sunny day. This evening—sixteen hours at most had passed by—she sat down, too full of sorrow to cry, but with a dull cold pain, which seemed to have pressed the youth and buoyancy out of her heart, never to return. Mr. Henry Lennox's visit—his offer—was like a dream, a thing beside her actual life. The hard reality was, that her father had so admitted tempting doubts into his mind as to become a schismatic—an outcast; all the changes consequent upon this grouped themselves around that one great blighting fact.

She looked out upon the dark-gray lines of the church tower, square and straight in the centre of the view, cutting against the deep blue transparent depths beyond, into which she gazed, and felt that she might gaze for ever, seeing at every moment some farther distance, and yet no sign of God! It seemed to her at the moment, as if the earth was more utterly desolate than if girt in by an iron dome, behind which there might be the ineffaceable peace and glory of the Almighty: those never-ending depths of space, in their still serenity, were more mocking to her than any material bounds could be—shutting in the cries of earth's sufferers, which now might ascend into that infinite splendour of vastness and be lost—lost for ever, before they reached His throne. In this mood her father came in unheard. The moonlight was strong enough to let him see his daughter in her unusual place and attitude. He came to her and touched her shoulder before she was aware that he was there.

"Margaret, I heard you were up. I could not help coming in to ask you to pray with me—to say the Lord's Prayer; that will do good to both of us."

Mr. Hale and Margaret knelt by the window-seat—he looking up, she bowed down in humble shame. God was there, close around them, hearing her father's whispered words. Her father might be a heretic; but had not she, in her despairing doubts not five minutes before, shown herself a far more utter sceptic?[2] She spoke not a word, but stole to bed after her father had left her, like a child ashamed of its fault. If the world was full of perplexing problems she would trust, and only ask to see the one step needful for the hour. Mr. Lennox—his visit, his proposal—the remembrance of which had been so rudely pushed aside by the subsequent events of the day— haunted her dreams that night. He was climbing up some tree of fabulous height to reach the branch whereon was slung her bonnet: he was falling, and she was struggling to save him, but held back by some invisible powerful hand. He was dead. And yet, with a shifting of the scene, she was once more in the Harley Street drawing-room, talking to him as of old, and still with a consciousness all the time that she had seen him killed by that terrible fall.

Miserable, unresting night! Ill preparation for the coming day! She awoke with a start, unrefreshed, and conscious of some reality worse even than her feverish dreams. It all came back upon her; not merely the sorrow, but the terrible discord in the sorrow. Where, to what distance apart, had her father wandered, led by doubts which were to her temptations of the Evil One? She longed to ask, and yet would not have heard for all the world.

The fine crisp morning made her mother feel particularly well and happy at breakfast-time. She talked on, planning village kindnesses, unheeding the silence of her husband and the monosyllabic answers of Margaret. Before the things were cleared away, Mr. Hale got up; he leaned one hand on the table, as if to support himself:

"I shall not be at home till evening. I am going to Bracy Common, and will ask Farmer Dobson to give me something for dinner. I shall be back to tea at seven."

He did not look at either of them, but Margaret knew what he meant. By seven the announcement must be made to her mother. Mr. Hale would have delayed making it till half-past-six, but Margaret was of different stuff. She could not bear the impending weight

---

2. The distinction drawn here between a "heretic" and a "sceptic" is important. Hale is a "heretic" in that he plans to leave the established church. The effect of his decision upon Margaret is that she has temporarily questioned her religious faith.

on her mind all the day long: better get the worst over; the day would be too short to comfort her mother. But while she stood by the window, thinking how to begin, and waiting for the servant to have left the room, her mother had gone up stairs to put on her things to go to the school. She came down ready equipped, in a brisker mood than usual.

"Mother, come round the garden with me this morning; just one turn," said Margaret, putting her arm round Mrs. Hale's waist.

They passed through the open window. Mrs. Hale spoke—said something—Margaret could not tell what. Her eye caught on a bee entering a deep-belled flower: when that bee flew forth with his spoil she would begin—that should be the sign. Out he came.

"Mamma! Papa is going to leave Helstone!" she blurted forth. "He's going to leave the Church, and live in Milton-Northern." There were the three hard facts hardly spoken.

"What makes you say so?" asked Mrs. Hale, in a surprised incredulous voice. "Who has been telling you such nonsense?"

"Papa himself," said Margaret, longing to say something gentle and consoling, but literally not knowing how. They were close to a garden-bench. Mrs. Hale sat down, and began to cry.

"I don't understand you," she said. "Either you have made some great mistake, or I don't quite understand you."

"No, mother, I have made no mistake. Papa has written to the bishop, saying that he has such doubts that he cannot conscientiously remain a priest of the Church of England, and that he must give up Helstone. He has also consulted Mr. Bell—Frederick's godfather, you know, mamma; and it is arranged that we go to live in Milton-Northern." Mrs. Hale looked up in Margaret's face all the time she was speaking these words: the shadow on her countenance told that she, at least, believed in the truth of what she said.

"I don't think it can be true," said Mrs. Hale, at length. "He would surely have told me before it came to this."

It came strongly upon Margaret's mind that her mother ought to have been told: that whatever her faults of discontent and repining might have been, it was an error in her father to have left her to learn his change of opinion, and his approaching change of life, from her better-informed child. Margaret sat down by her mother, and took her unresisting head on her breast, bending her own soft cheeks down caressingly to touch her face.

"Dear, darling mamma! we were so afraid of giving you pain. Papa felt so acutely—you know you are not strong, and there must have been such terrible suspense to go through."

"When did he tell you, Margaret?"

"Yesterday, only yesterday," replied Margaret, detecting the jealousy which prompted the inquiry. "Poor papa!"—trying to divert her mother's thoughts into compassionate sympathy for all her father had gone through. Mrs. Hale raised her head.

"What does he mean by having doubts?" she asked. "Surely, he does not mean that he thinks differently—that he knows better than the Church."

Margaret shook her head, and the tears came into her eyes, as her mother touched the bare nerve of her own regret.

"Can't the bishop set him right?" asked Mrs. Hale, half impatiently.

"I'm afraid not," said Margaret. "But I did not ask. I could not bear to hear what he might answer. It is all settled at any rate. He is going to leave Helstone in a fortnight. I am not sure if he did not say he had sent in his deed of resignation."

"In a fortnight!" exclaimed Mrs. Hale, "I do think this is very strange—not at all right. I call it very unfeeling," said she, beginning to take relief in tears, "He has doubts, you say, and gives up his living, and all without consulting me. I dare say, if he had told me his doubts at the first I could have nipped them in the bud."

Mistaken as Margaret felt her father's conduct to have been, she could not bear to hear it blamed by her mother. She knew that his very reserve had originated in a tenderness for her, which might be cowardly, but was not unfeeling.

"I almost hoped you might have been glad to leave Helstone, mamma," said she, after a pause. "You have never been well in this air, you know."

"You can't think the smoky air of a manufacturing town, all chimneys and dirt like Milton-Northern, would be better than this air, which is pure and sweet, if it is too soft and relaxing. Fancy living in the middle of factories, and factory people! Though, of course, if your father leaves the Church, we shall not be admitted into society anywhere. It will be such a disgrace to us! Poor dear Sir John! It is well he is not alive to see what your father has come to! Every day after dinner, when I was a girl, living with your aunt Shaw, at Beresford Court, Sir John used to give for the first toast—'Church and King, and down with the Rump.' "[3]

Margaret was glad that her mother's thoughts were turned away from the fact of her husband's silence to her on the point which must have been so near his heart. Next to the serious vital anxiety as to the nature of her father's doubts, this was the one circumstance of the case that gave Margaret the most pain.

"You know, we have very little society here, mamma. The Gor-

3. A traditional toast referring to the religious conflicts of the seventeenth century, "Church and King" emphasizes the king's position as head of the established church; "Rump" refers to those members of parliament who resisted the king's challenge to Parliament, and remained in office, forming what was known as the "Rump Parliament."

mans, who are our nearest neighbours (to call society—and we hardly ever see them), have been in trade just as much as these Milton-Northern people."

"Yes," said Mrs. Hale, almost indignantly, "but, at any rate, the Gormans made carriages for half the gentry of the county, and were brought into some kind of intercourse with them; but these factory people, who on earth wears cotton that can afford linen?"

"Well, mamma, I give up the cotton-spinners; I am not standing up for them, any more than for any other trades-people. Only we shall have little enough to do with them."

"Why on earth has your father fixed on Milton-Northern to live in?"

"Partly," said Margaret, sighing, "because it is so very different from Helstone—partly because Mr. Bell says there is an opening there for a private tutor."

"Private tutor in Milton! Why can't he go to Oxford, and be a tutor to gentlemen?"

"You forget, mamma! He is leaving the Church on account of his opinions—his doubts would do him no good at Oxford."

Mrs. Hale was silent for some time, quietly crying. At last she said:—

"And the furniture—How in the world are we to manage the removal? I never removed in my life, and only a fortnight to think about it!"

Margaret was inexpressibly relieved to find that her mother's anxiety and distress was lowered to this point, so insignificant to herself, and on which she could do so much to help. She planned and promised, and led her mother on to arrange fully as much as could be fixed before they knew somewhat more definitively what Mr. Hale intended to do. Throughout the day Margaret never left her mother; bending her whole soul to sympathise in all the various turns her feelings took; towards evening especially, as she became more and more anxious that her father should find a soothing welcome home awaiting him, after his return from his day of fatigue and distress. She dwelt upon what he must have borne in secret for long; her mother only replied coldly that he ought to have told her, and that then at any rate he would have had an adviser to give him counsel; and Margaret turned faint at heart when she heard her father's step in the hall. She dared not go to meet him, and tell him what she had done all day, for fear of her mother's jealous annoyance. She heard him linger, as if awaiting her, or some sign of her; and she dared not stir; she saw by her mother's twitching lips, and changing colour, that she too was aware that her husband had returned. Presently he opened the room-door, and stood there uncertain whether to come in. His face was gray and pale; he had a timid, fearful look in his eyes; something almost pitiful to see in a man's face; but that look of despondent uncertainty, of mental and bodily languor, touched his wife's heart. She went to him, and threw herself on his breast, crying out:—

"Oh! Richard, Richard, you should have told me sooner!"

And then, in tears, Margaret left her, as she rushed up stairs to throw herself on her bed, and hide her face in the pillows to stifle the hysteric sobs that would force their way at last, after the rigid self-control of the whole day.

How long she lay thus she could not tell. She heard no noise, though the housemaid came in to arrange the room. The affrighted girl stole out again on tip-toe, and went and told Mrs. Dixon that Miss Hale was crying as if her heart would break: she was sure she would make herself deadly ill if she went on at that rate. In consequence of this, Margaret felt herself touched, and started up into a sitting posture; she saw the accustomed room; the figure of Dixon in shadow, as the latter stood holding the candle a little behind her, for fear of the effect on Miss Hale's startled eyes, swollen and blinded as they were.

"Oh, Dixon! I did not hear you come into the room!" said Margaret, resuming her trembling self-restraint. "Is it very late?" continued she, lifting herself languidly off the bed, yet letting her feet touch the ground without fairly standing down, as she shaded her wet ruffled hair off her face, and tried to look as though nothing were the matter; as if she had only been asleep.

"I hardly can tell what time it is," replied Dixon, in an aggrieved tone of voice. "Since your mamma told me this terrible news, when I dressed her for tea, I've lost all count of time. I'm sure I don't know what is to become of us all. When Charlotte told me just now you were sobbing, Miss Hale, I thought, no wonder, poor thing! And master thinking of turning Dissenter at his time of life, when, if it is not to be said he's done well in the Church, he's not done badly after all. I had a cousin, miss, who turned Methodist preacher after he was fifty years of age, and a tailor all his life; but then he had never been able to make a pair of trousers to fit, for as long as he had been in the trade, so it was no wonder; but for master! as I said to missus, 'What would poor Sir John have said? he never liked your marrying Mr. Hale, but if he could have known it would have come to this, he would have sworn worse oaths than ever, if that was possible!' "

Dixon had been so much accustomed to comment upon Mr. Hale's proceedings to her mistress (who listened to her, or not, as she was in the humour), that she never noticed Margaret's flashing eye and dilating nostril. To hear her father talked of in this way by a servant to her face!

"Dixon," she said, in the low tone she always used when much

excited, which had a sound in it as of some distant turmoil, or threatening storm breaking far away. "Dixon! you forget to whom you are
speaking." She stood upright and firm on her feet now, confronting
the waiting-maid, and fixing her with her steady discerning eye. "I
am Mr. Hale's daughter. Go! You have made a strange mistake, and
one that I am sure your own good feeling will make you sorry for
when you think about it."

Dixon hung irresolutely about the room for a minute or two. Margaret repeated, "You may leave me, Dixon. I wish you to go." Dixon
did not know whether to resent these decided words or to cry; either
course would have done with her mistress: but, as she said to herself,
"Miss Margaret has a touch of the old gentleman about her, as well
as poor Master Frederick; I wonder where they get it from?" and she,
who would have resented such words from any one less haughty and
determined in manner, was subdued enough to say, in a half humble,
half injured tone:

"Mayn't I unfasten your gown, miss, and do your hair?"

"No! not to-night, thank you." And Margaret gravely lighted her
out of the room, and bolted the door. From henceforth Dixon obeyed
and admired Margaret. She said it was because she was so like poor
Master Frederick; but the truth was, that Dixon, as do many others,
liked to feel herself ruled by a powerful and decided nature.

Margaret needed all Dixon's help in action, and silence in words;
for, for some time, the latter thought it her duty to show her sense
of affront by saying as little as possible to her young lady; so the
energy came out in doing rather than in speaking. A fortnight was a
very short time to make arrangements for so serious a removal; as
Dixon said, "Any one but a gentleman—indeed almost any other
gentleman—" but catching a look at Margaret's straight, stern brow
just here, she coughed the remainder of the sentence away, and
meekly took the horehound drop[4] that Margaret offered her, to stop
the "little tickling at my chest, miss." But almost any one but Mr.
Hale would have had practical knowledge enough to see, that in so
short a time it would be difficult to fix on any house in Milton-
Northern, or indeed elsewhere, to which they could remove the furniture that had of necessity to be taken out of Helstone vicarage.

Mrs. Hale, overpowered by all the troubles and necessities for
immediate household decisions that seemed to come upon her at
once, became really ill, and Margaret almost felt it as a relief when
her mother fairly took to her bed, and left the management of affairs
to her. Dixon, true to her post of body-guard, attended most faithfully
to her mistress, and only emerged from Mrs. Hale's bedroom to
shake her head, and murmur to herself in a manner which Margaret

4. An herbal remedy.

did not choose to hear. For, the one thing clear and straight before her, was the necessity for leaving Helstone. Mr. Hale's successor in the living was appointed; and, at any rate, after her father's decision, there must be no lingering now, for his sake, as well as from every other consideration. For he came home every evening more and more depressed, after the necessary leave-taking which he had resolved to have with every individual parishioner. Margaret, inexperienced as she was in all the necessary matter-of-fact business to be got through, did not know to whom to apply for advice. The cook and Charlotte worked away with willing arms and stout hearts at all the moving and packing; and as far as that went, Margaret's admirable sense enabled her to see what was best, and to direct how it should be done. But where were they to go to? In a week they must be gone. Straight to Milton, or where? So many arrangements depended on this decision that Margaret resolved to ask her father one evening, in spite of his evident fatigue and low spirits. He answered:

"My dear! I have really had too much to think about to settle this. What does your mother say? What does she wish? Poor Maria!"

He met with an echo even louder than his sigh. Dixon had just come into the room for another cup of tea for Mrs. Hale, and catching Mr. Hale's last words, and protected by his presence from Margaret's upbraiding eyes, made bold to say, "My poor mistress!"

"You don't think her worse to-day," said Mr. Hale, turning hastily.

"I'm sure I can't say, sir. It's not for me to judge. The illness seems so much more on the mind than on the body."

Mr. Hale looked infinitely distressed.

"You had better take mamma her tea while it is hot, Dixon," said Margaret, in a tone of quiet authority.

"Oh! I beg your pardon, miss! My thoughts was otherwise occupied in thinking of my poor——of Mrs. Hale."

"Papa!" said Margaret, "it is this suspense that is bad for you both. Of course, mamma must feel your change of opinions: we can't help that," she continued, softly; "but now the course is clear, at least to a certain point. And I think, papa, that I could get mamma to help me in planning, if you could tell me what to plan for. She has never expressed any wish in any way, and only thinks of what can't be helped. Are we to go straight to Milton? Have you taken a house there?"

"No," he replied. "I suppose we must go into lodgings, and look about for a house."

"And pack up the furniture so that it can be left at the railway station, till we have met with one?"

"I suppose so. Do what you think best. Only remember, we shall have much less money to spend."

They had never had much superfluity, as Margaret knew. She felt

that it was a great weight suddenly thrown upon her shoulders. Four
months ago, all the decisions she needed to make were what dress
she would wear for dinner, and to help Edith to draw out the lists of
who should take down whom in the dinner parties at home. Nor was
the household in which she lived one that called for much decision.
Except in the one grand case of Captain Lennox's offer, everything
went on with the regularity of clockwork. Once a year, there was a
long discussion between her aunt and Edith as to whether they
should go to the Isle of Wight, abroad, or to Scotland; but at such
times Margaret herself was secure of drifting, without any exertion
of her own, into the quiet harbour of home. Now, since that day
when Mr. Lennox came, and startled her into a decision, every day
brought some question, momentous to her, and to those whom she
loved, to be settled.

Her father went up after tea to sit with his wife. Margaret
remained alone in the drawing-room. Suddenly she took a candle
and went into her father's study for a great atlas, and lugging it back
into the drawing-room, she began to pore over the map of England.
She was ready to look up brightly when her father came down stairs.

"I have hit upon such a beautiful plan. Look here—in Darkshire,
hardly the breadth of my finger from Milton, is Heston, which I have
often heard of from people living in the north as such a pleasant
little bathing-place. Now, don't you think we could get mamma there
with Dixon, while you and I go and look at houses, and get one all
ready for her in Milton? She would get a breath of sea air to set her
up for the winter, and be spared all the fatigue, and Dixon would
enjoy taking care of her."

"Is Dixon to go with us?" asked Mr. Hale, in a kind of helpless
dismay.

"Oh, yes!" said Margaret. "Dixon quite intends it, and I don't know
what mamma would do without her."

"But we shall have to put up with a very different way of living, I
am afraid. Everything is so much dearer in a town. I doubt if Dixon
can make herself comfortable. To tell you the truth, Margaret, I
sometimes feel as if that woman gave herself airs."

"To be sure she does, papa," replied Margaret; "and if she has to
put up with a different style of living, we shall have to put up with
her airs, which will be worse. But she really loves us all, and would
be miserable to leave us, I am sure—especially in this change; so,
for mamma's sake, and for the sake of her faithfulness, I do think
she must go."

"Very well, my dear. Go on. I am resigned. How far is Heston from
Milton? The breadth of one of your fingers does not give me a very
clear idea of distance."

"Well, then, I suppose it is thirty miles; that is not much!"

"Not in distance, but in—. Never mind! If you really think it will do your mother good, let it be fixed so."

This was a great step. Now Margaret could work, and act, and plan in good earnest. And now Mrs. Hale could rouse herself from her languor, and forget her real suffering in thinking of the pleasure and the delight of going to the sea-side. Her only regret was that Mr. Hale could not be with her all the fortnight she was to be there, as he had been for a whole fortnight once, when they were engaged, and she was staying with Sir John and Lady Beresford at Torquay.

Chapter VI.

Farewell.

"Unwatch'd the garden bough shall sway,
    The tender blossom flutter down,
    Unloved that beech will gather brown,
The maple burn itself away;

Unloved, the sun-flower, shining fair,
    Ray round with flames her disk of seed,
    And many a rose-carnation feed
With summer spice the humming air;

*   *   *   *   *   *

Till from the garden and the wild
    A fresh association blow,
    And year by year the landscape grow
Familiar to the stranger's child;

As year by year the labourer tills
    His wonted glebe, or lops the glades;
    And year by year our memory fades
From all the circle of the hills."

TENNYSON.[1]

The last day came; the house was full of packing-cases, which were being carted off at the front door, to the nearest railway station. Even the pretty lawn at the side of the house, was made unsightly and untidy by the straw that had been wafted upon it through the open door and windows. The rooms had a strange echoing sound in them,—and the light came harshly and strongly in through the uncurtained windows,—seeming already unfamiliar and strange. Mrs. Hale's dressing-room was left untouched to the last; and there she and Dixon were packing up clothes, and interrupting each other every now and then to exclaim at, and turn over with fond regard, some forgotten treasure, in the shape of some relic of the children

---

1. The lines are from *In Memoriam* (1850), lyric no. 101. The lyric that follows begins, "We leave the well-beloved place."

while they were yet little. They did not make much progress with their work. Down-stairs, Margaret stood calm and collected, ready to counsel or advise the men who had been called in to help the cook and Charlotte. These two last, crying between whiles, wondered how the young lady could keep up so this last day, and settled it between them that she was not likely to care much for Helstone, having been so long in London. There she stood, very pale and quiet, with her large grave eyes observing everything—up to every present circumstance however small. They could not understand how her heart was aching all the time, with a heavy pressure that no sighs could lift off or relieve, and how constant exertion for her perceptive faculties was the only way to keep herself from crying out with pain. Moreover, if she gave way, who was to act? Her father was examining papers, books, registers, what not, in the vestry with the clerk; and when he came in, there were his own books to pack up, which no one but himself could do to his satisfaction. Besides, was Margaret one to give way before strange men, or even household friends like the cook and Charlotte! Not she. But at last the four packers went into the kitchen to their tea; and Margaret moved stiffly and slowly away from the place in the hall where she had been standing so long, out through the bare echoing drawing-room, into the twilight of an early November evening. There was a filmy veil of soft dull mist obscuring, but not hiding, all objects, giving them a lilac hue, for the sun had not yet fully set; a robin was singing,—perhaps, Margaret thought, the very robin that her father had so often talked of as his winter pet, and for which he had made, with his own hands, a kind of robin-house by his study-window. The leaves were more gorgeous than ever; the first touch of frost would lay them all low on the ground. Already one or two kept constantly floating down, amber and golden in the low slanting sun-rays.

Margaret went along the walk under the pear-tree wall. She had never been along it since she paced it at Henry Lennox's side. Here, at this bed of thyme, he began to speak of what she must not think of now. Her eyes were on that late-blowing rose as she was trying to answer; and she had caught the idea of the vivid beauty of the feathery leaves of the carrots in the very middle of his last sentence. Only a fortnight ago! And all so changed! Where was he now? In London,—going through the old round; dining with the old Harley Street set, or with gayer young friends of his own. Even now, while she walked sadly through that damp and drear garden in the dusk, with everything falling and fading, and turning to decay around her, he might be gladly putting away his law-books after a day of satisfactory toil, and freshening himself up, as he had told her he often did, by a run in the Temple Gardens, taking in the while the grand inarticulate mighty roar of tens of thousands of busy men, nigh at hand, but not seen, and catching ever, at his quick turns, glimpses of the lights of the city coming up out of the depths of the river. He had often spoken to Margaret of these hasty walks, snatched in the intervals between study and dinner. At his best times and in his best moods had he spoken of them; and the thought of them had struck upon her fancy. Here there was no sound. The robin had gone away into the vast stillness of night. Now and then, a cottage door in the distance was opened and shut, as if to admit the tired labourer to his home; but that sounded very far away. A stealthy, creeping, cranching sound among the crisp fallen leaves of the forest, beyond the garden, seemed almost close at hand. Margaret knew it was some poacher. Sitting up in her bedroom this past autumn, with the light of her candle extinguished, and purely revelling in the solemn beauty of the heavens and the earth, she had many a time seen the light noiseless leap of the poachers over the garden-fence, their quick tramp across the dewy moonlit lawn, their disappearance in the black still shadow beyond. The wild adventurous freedom of their life had taken her fancy; she felt inclined to wish them success; she had no fear of them. But to-night she was afraid, she knew not why. She heard Charlotte shutting the windows, and fastening up for the night, unconscious that any one had gone out into the garden. A small branch—it might be of rotten wood, or it might be broken by force—came heavily down in the nearest part of the forest; Margaret ran, swift as Camilla, down to the window, and rapped at it with a hurried tremulousness which startled Charlotte within.

"Let me in! Let me in! It is only me, Charlotte!" Her heart did not still its fluttering till she was safe in the drawing-room, with the windows fastened and bolted, and the familiar walls hemming her round, and shutting her in. She had sat down upon a packing-case; cheerless, chill was the dreary and dismantled room—no fire, nor other light, but Charlotte's long unsnuffed candle. Charlotte looked at Margaret with surprise; and Margaret, feeling it rather than seeing it, rose up.

"I was afraid you were shutting me out altogether, Charlotte," said she, half-smiling. "And then you would never have heard me in the kitchen, and the doors into the lane and churchyard are locked long ago."

"Oh, miss, I should have been sure to have missed you soon. The men would have wanted you to tell them how to go on. And I have put tea in master's study, as being the most comfortable room, so to speak."

"Thank you, Charlotte. You are a kind girl. I shall be sorry to leave you. You must try and write to me, if I can ever give you any little help or good advice. I shall always be glad to get a letter from Helstone, you know. I shall be sure and send you my address when I know it."

The study was all ready for tea. There was a good blazing fire, and unlighted candles on the table. Margaret sat down on the rug, partly to warm herself, for the dampness of the evening hung about her dress, and overfatigue had made her chilly. She kept herself balanced by clasping her hands together round her knees; her head dropped a little towards her chest; the attitude was one of despondency, whatever her frame of mind might be. But when she heard her father's step on the gravel outside, she started up, and hastily shaking her heavy black hair back, and wiping a few tears away that had come on her cheeks she knew not how, she went out to open the door for him. He showed far more depression than she did. She could hardly get him to talk, although she tried to speak on subjects that would interest him, at the cost of an effort every time which she thought would be her last.

"Have you been a very long walk to-day?" asked she, on seeing his refusal to touch food of any kind.

"As far as Fordham Beeches. I went to see Widow Maltby; she is sadly grieved at not having wished you good-bye. She says little Susan has kept watch down the lane for days past.—Nay, Margaret, what is the matter, dear?" The thought of the little child watching for her, and continually disappointed—from no forgetfulness on her part, but from sheer inability to leave home—was the last drop in poor Margaret's cup, and she was sobbing away as if her heart would break. Mr. Hale was distressingly perplexed. He rose, and walked nervously up and down the room. Margaret tried to check herself, but would not speak until she could do so with firmness. She heard him talking, as if to himself.

"I cannot bear it. I cannot bear to see the sufferings of others. I think I could go through my own with patience. Oh, is there no going back?"

"No, father," said Margaret, looking straight at him, and speaking low and steadily. "It is bad to believe you in error. It would be infinitely worse to have known you a hypocrite." She dropped her voice at the last few words, as if entertaining the idea of hypocrisy for a moment in connection with her father savoured of irreverence.

"Besides," she went on, "it is only that I am tired to-night; don't think that I am suffering from what you have done, dear papa. We can't either of us talk about it to-night, I believe," said she, finding that tears and sobs would come in spite of herself. "I had better go and take mamma up this cup of tea. She had hers very early, when I was too busy to go to her, and I am sure she will be glad of another now."

Railroad time[2] inexorably wrenched them away from lovely, beloved Helstone, the next morning. They were gone; they had seen the last of the long low parsonage home, half-covered with China-roses and pyracanthus—more homelike than ever in the morning sun that glittered on its windows, each belonging to some well-loved room. Almost before they had settled themselves into the car, sent from Southampton to fetch them to the station, they were gone away to return no more. A sting at Margaret's heart made her strive to look out to catch the last glimpse of the old church tower at the turn where she knew it might be seen above a wave of the forest trees; but her father remembered this too, and she silently acknowledged his greater right to the one window from which it could be seen. She leant back and shut her eyes, and the tears welled forth, and hung glittering for an instant on the shadowing eyelashes before rolling slowly down her cheeks, and dropping, unheeded, on her dress.

They were to stop in London all night at some quiet hotel. Poor Mrs. Hale had cried in her way nearly all day long; and Dixon showed her sorrow by extreme crossness, and a continual irritable attempt to keep her petticoats from even touching the unconscious Mr. Hale, whom she regarded as the origin of all this suffering.

They went through the well-known streets, past houses which they had often visited, past shops in which she had lounged, impatient, by her aunt's side, while that lady was making some important and interminable decision—nay, absolutely past acquaintances in the streets; for though the morning had been of an incalculable length to them, and they felt as if it ought long ago to have closed in for the repose of darkness, it was the very busiest time of a London afternoon in November when they arrived there. It was long since Mrs. Hale had been in London; and she roused up, almost like a child, to look about her at the different streets, and to gaze after and exclaim at the shops and carriages.

"Oh, there's Harrison's, where I bought so many of my wedding-things. Dear! how altered! They've got immense plate-glass windows, larger than Crawford's in Southampton. Oh, and there, I declare—no, it is not—yes, it is—Margaret, we have just passed Mr. Henry Lennox. Where can he be going, among all these shops?"

Margaret started forwards, and as quickly fell back, half-smiling at herself for the sudden motion. They were a hundred yards away by this time; but he seemed like a relic of Helstone—he was associated with a bright morning, an eventful day, and she should have liked to have seen him, without his seeing her,—without the chance of their speaking.

The evening, without employment, passed in a room high up in

2. The coming of the railways synchronized time-keeping in Britain. Before the railways, time-keeping was fairly localized and informal. "Railroad time" was an accepted term.

an hotel, was long and heavy. Mr. Hale went out to his bookseller's, and to call on a friend or two. Every one they saw, either in the house or out in the streets, appeared hurrying to some appointment, expected by, or expecting somebody. They alone seemed strange and friendless, and desolate. Yet within a mile, Margaret knew of house after house, where she for her own sake, and her mother for her aunt Shaw's, would be welcomed, if they came in gladness, or even in peace of mind. If they came sorrowing, and wanting sympathy in a complicated trouble like the present, then they would be felt as a shadow in all these houses of intimate acquaintances, not friends. London life is too whirling and full to admit of even an hour of that deep silence of feeling which the friends of Job[3] showed, when "they sat with him on the ground seven days and seven nights, and none spake a word unto him; for they saw that his grief was very great."

Chapter VII.

New Scenes and Faces.

"Mist clogs the sunshine,
Smoky dwarf houses
Have we round on every side."
Matthew Arnold.[1]

The next afternoon, about twenty miles from Milton-Northern, they entered on the little branch railway that led to Heston. Heston itself was one long straggling street, running parallel to the sea-shore. It had a character of its own, as different from the little bathing-places in the south of England as they again from those of the continent. To use a Scotch word, every thing looked more "purposelike." The country carts had more iron, and less wood and leather about the horse-gear; the people in the streets, although on pleasure bent, had yet a busy mind. The colours looked grayer—more enduring, not so gay and pretty. There were no smock-frocks, even among the country folk; they retarded motion, and were apt to catch on machinery, and so the habit of wearing them had died out. In such towns in the south of England, Margaret had seen the shopmen, when not employed in their business, lounging a little at their doors, enjoying the fresh air, and the look up and down the street. Here, if they had any leisure from customers, they made themselves business in the shop—even, Margaret fancied, to the unnecessary unrolling and re-

---

3. Traditionally known as Job's comforters—i.e., the companions of Job during his hardships, as described in the Old Testament. The quotation is from Job 2:13.
1. The quotation is of the opening lines of Arnold's poem "Consolation" (1852). The third line is misquoted and should read "Hem me round everywhere."

rolling of ribbons. All these differences struck upon her mind, as she and her mother went out next morning to look for lodgings.

Their two nights at hotels had cost more than Mr. Hale had anticipated, and they were glad to take the first clean, cheerful rooms they met with that were at liberty to receive them. There, for the first time for many days, did Margaret feel at rest. There was a dreaminess in the rest, too, which made it still more perfect and luxurious to repose in. The distant sea, lapping the sandy shore with measured sound; the nearer cries of the donkey-boys;[2] the unusual scenes moving before her like pictures, which she cared not in her laziness to have fully explained before they passed away; the stroll down to the beach to breathe the sea-air, soft and warm on that sandy shore even to the end of November; the great long misty sea-line touching the tender-coloured sky; the white sail of a distant boat turning silver in some pale sunbeam:—it seemed as if she could dream her life away in such luxury of pensiveness, in which she made her present all in all, from not daring to think of the past, or wishing to contemplate the future.

But the future must be met, however stern and iron it be. One evening it was arranged that Margaret and her father should go the next day to Milton-Northern, and look out for a house. Mr. Hale had received several letters from Mr. Bell, and one or two from Mr. Thornton, and he was anxious to ascertain at once a good many particulars respecting his position and chances of success there, which he could only do by an interview with the latter gentleman. Margaret knew that they ought to be removing; but she had a repugnance to the idea of a manufacturing town, and believed that her mother was receiving benefit from Heston air, so she would willingly have deferred the expedition to Milton.

For several miles before they reached Milton, they saw a deep lead-coloured cloud hanging over the horizon in the direction in which it lay. It was all the darker from contrast with the pale gray-blue of the wintry sky; for in Heston there had been the earliest signs of frost. Nearer to the town, the air had a faint taste and smell of smoke; perhaps, after all, more a loss of the fragrance of grass and herbage than any positive taste or smell. Quick they were whirled over long, straight, hopeless streets of regularly-built houses, all small and of brick. Here and there a great oblong many-windowed factory stood up, like a hen among her chickens, puffing out black "unparliamentary" smoke,[3] and sufficiently accounting for the cloud which Margaret had taken to foretell rain. As they drove through the larger and

2. Boys who looked after donkeys for hire on the beach.
3. So described because an Act of Parliament of 1847 was supposed to have controlled the emission of smoke in these circumstances: the Act had little effect. The reference is repeated in chapter 10.

wider streets, from the station to the hotel, they had to stop constantly; great loaded lurries[4] blocked up the not over-wide thoroughfares. Margaret had now and then been into the city in her drives with her aunt. But there the heavy lumbering vehicles seemed various in their purposes and intent; here every van, every waggon and truck, bore cotton, either in the raw shape in bags, or the woven shape in bales of calico. People thronged the footpaths, most of them well-dressed as regarded the material, but with a slovenly looseness which struck Margaret as different from the shabby, threadbare smartness of a similar class in London.

"New Street," said Mr. Hale. "This, I believe, is the principal street in Milton. Bell has often spoken to me about it. It was the opening of this street from a lane into a great thoroughfare, thirty years ago, which has caused his property to rise so much in value. Mr. Thornton's mill must be somewhere not very far off, for he is Mr. Bell's tenant. But I fancy he dates from his warehouse."

"Where is our hotel, papa?"

"Close to the end of this street, I believe. Shall we have lunch before or after we have looked at the houses we marked in the Milton Times?"

"Oh, let us get our work done first."

"Very well. Then I will only see if there is any note or letter for me from Mr. Thornton, who said he would let me know anything he might hear about these houses, and then we will set off. We will keep the cab; it will be safer than losing ourselves, and being too late for the train this afternoon."

There were no letters awaiting him. They set out on their house-hunting. Thirty pounds a-year was all they could afford to give, but in Hampshire they could have met with a roomy house and pleasant garden for the money. Here, even the necessary accommodation of two sitting-rooms and four bed-rooms seemed unattainable. They went through their list, rejecting each as they visited it. Then they looked at each other in dismay.

"We must go back to the second, I think. That one,—in Crampton, don't they call the suburb? There were three sitting-rooms; don't you remember how we laughed at the number compared with the three bed-rooms? But I have planned it all. The front room down-stairs is to be your study and our dining-room (poor papa!), for, you know, we settled mamma is to have as cheerful a sitting-room as we can get; and that front room up-stairs, with the atrocious blue and pink paper and heavy cornice, had really a pretty view over the plain, with a great bend of river, or canal, or whatever it is, down below. Then I could have the little bed-room behind, in that projection at the

4. Trucks; the modern English spelling is "lorries."

head of the first flight of stairs—over the kitchen, you know—and you and mamma the room behind the drawing-room, and that closet in the roof will make you a splendid dressing-room."

"But Dixon, and the girl we are to have to help?"

"Oh, wait a minute. I am overpowered by the discovery of my own genius for management. Dixon is to have—let me see, I had it once— the back sitting-room. I think she will like that. She grumbles so much about the stairs at Heston; and the girl is to have that sloping attic over your room and mamma's. Won't that do?"

"I dare say it will. But the papers. What taste! And the overloading such a house with colour and such heavy cornices!"

"Never mind, papa! Surely, you can charm the landlord into re-papering one or two of the rooms—the drawing-room and your bed-room—for mamma will come most in contact with them; and your book-shelves will hide a great deal of that gaudy pattern in the dining-room."

"Then you think it the best? If so, I had better go at once and call on this Mr. Donkin, to whom the advertisement refers me. I will take you back to the hotel, where you can order lunch, and rest, and by the time it is ready, I shall be with you. I hope I shall be able to get new papers."

Margaret hoped so too, though she said nothing. She had never come fairly in contact with the taste that loves ornament, however bad, more than the plainness and simplicity which are of themselves the framework of elegance.

Her father took her through the entrance of the hotel, and leaving her at the foot of the staircase, went to the address of the landlord of the house they had fixed upon. Just as Margaret had her hand on the door of their sitting-room, she was followed by a quick-stepping waiter:

"I beg your pardon, ma'am. The gentleman was gone so quickly, I had no time to tell him. Mr. Thornton called almost directly after you left; and, as I understood from what the gentleman said, you would be back in an hour, I told him so, and he came again about five minutes ago, and said he would wait for Mr. Hale. He is in your room now, ma'am."

"Thank you. My father will return soon, and then you can tell him."

Margaret opened the door and went in with the straight, fearless, dignified presence habitual to her. She felt no awkwardness; she had too much the habits of society for that. Here was a person come on business to her father; and, as he was one who had shown himself obliging, she was disposed to treat him with a full measure of civility. Mr. Thornton was a good deal more surprised and discomfited than she. Instead of a quiet, middle-aged clergyman, a young lady came forward with frank dignity,—a young lady of a different type to most of those he was in the habit of seeing. Her dress was very plain: a close straw bonnet of the best material and shape, trimmed with white ribbon; a dark silk gown, without any trimming or flounce; a large Indian shawl, which hung about her in long heavy folds, and which she wore as an empress wears her drapery. He did not understand who she was, as he caught the simple, straight, unabashed look, which showed that his being there was of no concern to the beautiful countenance, and called up no flush of surprise to the pale ivory of the complexion. He had heard that Mr. Hale had a daughter, but he had imagined that she was a little girl.

"Mr. Thornton, I believe!" said Margaret, after a half-instant's pause, during which his unready words would not come. "Will you sit down. My father brought me to the door, not a minute ago, but unfortunately he was not told that you were here, and he has gone away on some business. But he will come back almost directly. I am sorry you have had the trouble of calling twice."

Mr. Thornton was in habits of authority himself, but she seemed to assume some kind of rule over him at once. He had been getting impatient at the loss of his time on a market-day, the moment before she appeared, yet now he calmly took a seat at her bidding.

"Do you know where it is that Mr. Hale has gone to? Perhaps I might be able to find him."

"He has gone to a Mr. Donkin's in Canute Street. He is the landlord of the house my father wishes to take in Crampton."

Mr. Thornton knew the house. He had seen the advertisement, and been to look at it, in compliance with a request of Mr. Bell's that he would assist Mr. Hale to the best of his power: and also instigated by his own interest in the case of a clergyman who had given up his living under circumstances such as those of Mr. Hale. Mr. Thornton had thought that the house in Crampton was really just the thing; but now that he saw Margaret, with her superb ways of moving and looking, he began to feel ashamed of having imagined that it would do very well for the Hales, in spite of a certain vulgarity in it which had struck him at the time of his looking it over.

Margaret could not help her looks; but the short curled upper lip, the round, massive up-turned chin, the manner of carrying her head, her movements, full of a soft feminine defiance, always gave strangers the impression of haughtiness. She was tired now, and would rather have remained silent, and taken the rest her father had planned for her; but, of course, she owed it to herself to be a gentlewoman, and to speak courteously from time to time to this stranger; not over-brushed, nor over-polished, it must be confessed, after his rough encounter with Milton streets and crowds. She wished that he would go, as he had once spoken of doing, instead of sitting there, answering with curt sentences all the remarks she made. She had taken off her shawl, and hung it over the back of her chair. She sat facing him and facing the light; her full beauty met his eye; her round white flexile throat rising out of the full, yet lithe figure; her lips, moving so slightly as she spoke, not breaking the cold serene look of her face with any variation from the one lovely haughty curve; her eyes, with their soft gloom, meeting his with quiet maiden freedom. He almost said to himself that he did not like her, before their conversation ended; he tried so to compensate himself for the mortified feeling, that while he looked upon her with an admiration he could not repress, she looked at him with proud indifference, taking him, he thought, for what, in his irritation, he told himself he was—a great rough fellow, with not a grace or a refinement about him. Her quiet coldness of demeanour he interpreted into contemptuousness, and resented it in his heart to the pitch of almost inclining him to get up and go away, and have nothing more to do with these Hales, and their superciliousness.

Just as Margaret had exhausted her last subject of conversation—and yet conversation that could hardly be called which consisted of so few and such short speeches—her father came in, and with his pleasant gentlemanly courteousness of apology, reinstated his name and family in Mr. Thornton's good opinion.

Mr. Hale and his visitor had a good deal to say respecting their mutual friend, Mr. Bell; and Margaret, glad that her part of entertaining the visitor was over, went to the window to try and make herself more familiar with the strange aspect of the street. She got so much absorbed in watching what was going on outside that she hardly heard her father when he spoke to her, and he had to repeat what he said:

"Margaret! the landlord will persist in admiring that hideous paper, and I am afraid we must let it remain."

"Oh dear! I am sorry!" she replied, and began to turn over in her mind the possibility of hiding part of it, at least, by some of her sketches, but gave up the idea at last, as likely only to make bad worse. Her father, meanwhile, with his kindly country hospitality, was pressing Mr. Thornton to stay to luncheon with them. It would have been very inconvenient to him to do so, yet he felt that he should have yielded, if Margaret by word or look had seconded her father's invitation; he was glad she did not, and yet he was irritated at her for not doing it. She gave him a low, grave bow when he left, and he felt more awkward and self-conscious in every limb than he had ever done in all his life before.

"Well, Margaret, now to luncheon, as fast we can. Have you ordered it?"

"No, papa; that man was here when I came home, and I have never had an opportunity."

"Then we must take anything we can get. He must have been waiting a long time, I'm afraid."

"It seemed exceedingly long to me. I was just at the last gasp when you came in. He never went on with any subject, but gave little, short, abrupt answers."

"Very much to the point though, I should think. He is a clear-headed fellow. He said (did you hear?) that Crampton is on gravelly soil, and by far the most healthy suburb in the neighbourhood of Milton."

When they returned to Heston, there was the day's account to be given to Mrs. Hale, who, was full of questions which they answered in the intervals of tea-drinking.

"And what is your correspondent, Mr. Thornton, like?"

"Ask Margaret," said her husband. "She and he had a long attempt at conversation, while I was away speaking to the landlord."

"Oh! I hardly know what he is like," said Margaret, lazily; too tired to tax her powers of description much. And then rousing herself, she said, "He is a tall, broad-shouldered man, about—how old, papa?"

"I should guess about thirty."

"About thirty—with a face that is neither exactly plain, nor yet handsome, nothing remarkable—not quite a gentleman; but that was hardly to be expected."

"Not vulgar, or common though," put in her father, rather jealous of any disparagement of the sole friend he had in Milton.

"Oh no!" said Margaret. "With such an expression of resolution and power, no face, however plain in feature, could be either vulgar or common. I should not like to have to bargain with him; he looks very inflexible. Altogether a man who seems made for his niche, mamma; sagacious, and strong, as becomes a great tradesman."

"Don't call the Milton manufacturers tradesmen, Margaret," said her father. "They are very different."

"Are they? I apply the word to all who have something tangible to sell; but if you think the term is not correct, papa, I won't use it. But, oh mamma! speaking of vulgarity and commonness, you must prepare yourself for our drawing-room paper. Pink and blue roses, with yellow leaves! And such a heavy cornice round the room!"

But when they removed to their new house in Milton, the obnoxious papers were gone. The landlord received their thanks very composedly; and let them think, if they liked, that he had relented from his expressed determination not to repaper. There was no particular need to tell them, that what he did not care to do for a Reverend Mr. Hale, unknown in Milton, he was only too glad to do at the one short sharp remonstrance of Mr. Thornton, the wealthy manufacturer.

Chapter VIII.

Home Sickness.

"And it's hame, hame, hame,
Hame fain wad I be."

It needed the pretty light papering of the rooms to reconcile them
to Milton. It needed more—more that could not be had. The thick
yellow November fogs had come on; and the view of the plain in the
valley, made by the sweeping bend of the river, was all shut out when
Mrs. Hale arrived at her new home.

Margaret and Dixon had been at work for two days, unpacking and
arranging, but everything inside the house still looked in disorder;
and outside a thick fog crept up to the very windows, and was driven
in to every open door in choking white wreaths of unwholesome mist.

"Oh, Margaret! are we to live here?" asked Mrs. Hale in blank
dismay.

Margaret's heart echoed the dreariness of the tone in which this
question was put. She could scarcely command herself enough to
say, "Oh, the fogs in London are sometimes far worse!"

"But then you knew that London itself, and friends lay behind it.
Here—well! we are desolate, Oh Dixon, what a place this is!"

"Indeed, ma'am, I'm sure it will be your death before long, and
then I know who'll—stay! Miss Hale, that's far too heavy for you to
lift."

"Not at all, thank you, Dixon," replied Margaret coldly. "The best
thing we can do for mamma is to get her room quite ready for her
to go to bed, while I go and bring her a cup of coffee."

Mr. Hale was equally out of spirits, and equally came upon Margaret for sympathy.

"Margaret, I do believe this is an unhealthy place. Only suppose
that your mother's health or yours should suffer. I wish I had gone
into some country place in Wales; this is really terrible," said he,
going up to the window.

There was no comfort to be given. They were settled in Milton,
and must endure smoke and fogs for a season; indeed, all other life
seemed shut out from them by as thick a fog of circumstance. Only
the day before, Mr. Hale had been reckoning up with dismay how
much their removal and fortnight at Heston had cost, and he found
it had absorbed nearly all his little stock of ready money. No! here
they were, and here they must remain.

At night when Margaret realised this, she felt inclined to sit down
in a stupor of despair. The heavy smoky air hung about her bed-

room, which occupied the long narrow projection at the back of the house. The window, placed at the side of the oblong, looked to the blank wall of a similar projection, not above ten feet distant. It loomed through the fog like a great barrier to hope. Inside the room everything was in confusion. All their efforts had been directed to make her mother's room comfortable. Margaret sat down on a box, the direction card upon which struck her as having been written at Helstone—beautiful, beloved Helstone! She lost herself in dismal thought: but at last she determined to take her mind away from the present; and suddenly remembered that she had a letter from Edith which she had only half read in the bustle of the morning. It was to tell of their arrival at Corfu; their voyage along the Mediterranean—their music, and dancing on board ship; the gay new life opening upon her; her house with its trellised balcony, and its views over white cliffs and deep blue sea.

Edith wrote fluently and well, if not graphically. She could not only seize the salient and characteristic points of a scene, but she could enumerate enough of indiscriminate particulars for Margaret to make it out for herself. Captain Lennox and another lately married officer shared a villa, high up on the beautiful precipitous rocks overhanging the sea. Their days, late as it was in the year, seemed spent in boating or land pic-nics; all out-of-doors, pleasure-seeking and glad, Edith's life seemed like the deep vault of blue sky above her, free—utterly free from fleck or cloud. Her husband had to attend drill, and she, the most musical officer's wife there, had to copy the new and popular tunes out of the most recent English music, for the benefit of the bandmaster; those seemed their most severe and arduous duties. She expressed an affectionate hope that, if the regiment stopped another year at Corfu, Margaret might come out and pay her a long visit. She asked Margaret if she remembered the day twelve-month on which she, Edith, wrote—how it rained all day long in Harley Street; and how she would not put on her new gown to go to a stupid dinner, and get it all wet and splashed in going to the carriage; and how at that very dinner they had first met Captain Lennox.

Yes! Margaret remembered it well. Edith and Mrs. Shaw had gone to dinner. Margaret had joined the party in the evening. The recollection of the plentiful luxury of all the arrangements, the stately handsomeness of the furniture, the size of the house, the peaceful, untroubled ease of the visitors—all came vividly before her, in strange contrast to the present time. The smooth sea of that old life closed up, without a mark left to tell where they had all been. The habitual dinners, the calls, the shopping, the dancing evenings, were all going on, going on for ever, though her Aunt Shaw and Edith were no longer there; and she, of course, was even less missed. She doubted if any one of that old set ever thought of her, except Henry Lennox. He too, she knew, would strive to forget her, because of the pain she had caused him. She had heard him often boast of his power of putting any disagreeable thought far away from him. Then she penetrated farther into what might have been. If she had cared for him as a lover, and had accepted him, and this change in her father's opinions and consequent station had taken place, she could not doubt but that it would have been impatiently received by Mr. Lennox. It was a bitter mortification to her in one sense; but she could bear it patiently, because she knew her father's purity of purpose, and that strengthened her to endure his errors, grave and serious though in her estimation they were. But the fact of the world esteeming her father degraded, in its rough wholesale judgment, would have oppressed and irritated Mr. Lennox. As she realised what might have been, she grew to be thankful for what was. They were at the lowest now; they could not be worse. Edith's astonishment and her aunt Shaw's dismay would have to be met bravely, when their letters came. So Margaret rose up and began slowly to undress herself, feeling the full luxury of acting leisurely, late as it was, after all the past hurry of the day. She fell asleep, hoping for some brightness, either internal or external. But if she had known how long it would be before the brightness came, her heart would have sunk low down. The time of the year was most unpropitious to health as well as to spirits. Her mother caught a severe cold, and Dixon herself was evidently not well, although Margaret could not insult her more than by trying to save her, or by taking any care of her. They could hear of no girl to assist her; all were at work in the factories; at least, those who applied were well scolded by Dixon, for thinking that such as they could ever be trusted to work in a gentleman's house. So they had to keep a charwoman in almost constant employ. Margaret longed to send for Charlotte; but besides the objection of her being a better servant than they could now afford to keep, the distance was too great.

Mr. Hale met with several pupils, recommended to him by Mr. Bell, or by the more immediate influence of Mr. Thornton. They were mostly of the age when many boys would be still at school, but, according to the prevalent, and apparently well-founded notions of Milton, to make a lad into a good tradesman he must be caught young, and acclimated to the life of the mill, or office, or warehouse. If he were sent to even the Scotch Universities,[1] he came back unsettled for commercial pursuits; how much more so if he went to Oxford or Cambridge, where he could not be entered till he was eighteen?

---

1. The Scottish universities admitted students at a younger age than those in England in the nineteenth century. They also admitted dissenters and had a more modern curriculum in which the study of philosophy was prominent. Gaskell's husband, William, had attended Glasgow University.

So most of the manufacturers placed their sons in sucking situations[2] at fourteen or fifteen years of age, unsparingly cutting away all off-shoots in the direction of literature or high mental cultivation, in hopes of throwing the whole strength and vigour of the plant into commerce. Still there were some wiser parents; and some young men, who had sense enough to perceive their own deficiencies, and strive to remedy them. Nay, there were a few no longer youths, but men in the prime of life, who had the stern wisdom to acknowledge their own ignorance, and to learn late what they should have learnt early. Mr. Thornton was perhaps the oldest of Mr. Hale's pupils. He was certainly the favourite. Mr. Hale got into the habit of quoting his opinions so frequently, and with such regard, that it became a little domestic joke to wonder what time, during the hour appointed for instruction, could be given to absolute learning, so much of it appeared to have been spent in conversation.

Margaret rather encouraged this light, merry way of viewing her father's acquaintance with Mr. Thornton, because she felt that her mother was inclined to look upon this new friendship of her husband's with jealous eyes. As long as his time had been solely occupied with his books and his parishioners, as at Helstone, she had appeared to care little whether she saw much of him or not; but now that he looked eagerly forward to each renewal of his intercourse with Mr. Thornton, she seemed hurt and annoyed, as if he were slighting her companionship for the first time. Mr. Hale's over-praise had the usual effect of over-praise upon his auditors; they were a little inclined to rebel against Aristides being always called the Just.[3]

After a quiet life in a country parsonage for more than twenty years, there was something dazzling to Mr. Hale in the energy which conquered immense difficulties with ease; the power of the machinery of Milton, the power of the men of Milton, impressed him with a sense of grandeur, which he yielded to without caring to inquire into the details of its exercise. But Margaret went less abroad, among machinery and men; saw less of power in its public effect, and, as it happened, she was thrown with one or two of those who, in all measures affecting masses of people, must be acute sufferers for the good of many. The question always is, has everything been done to make the sufferings of these exceptions as small as possible? Or, in the triumph of the crowded procession, have the helpless been trampled on, instead of being gently lifted aside out of the roadway of the conqueror, whom they have no power to accompany on his march?

2. Positions where, as little more than children, they could be trained into the demands of the business.
3. In Plutarch's *Lives* the story is told of Aristides, the Greek philosopher and statesman, that an Athenian voter who did not recognize him asked him to copy his name on to his tablet so that he might vote for his exile. On being asked why, the voter replied that he was vexed by Aristides always being referred to as "the just."

It fell to Margaret's share to have to look out for a servant to assist Dixon, who had at first undertaken to find just the person she wanted to do all the rough work of the house. But Dixon's ideas of helpful girls were founded on the recollection of tidy elder scholars at Helstone school, who were only too proud to be allowed to come to the parsonage on a busy day, and treated Mrs. Dixon with all the respect, and a good deal more of fright, which they paid to Mr. and Mrs. Hale. Dixon was not unconscious of this awed reverence which was given to her; nor did she dislike it; it flattered her much as Louis the Fourteenth was flattered by his courtiers shading their eyes from the dazzling light of his presence. But nothing short of her faithful love for Mrs. Hale could have made her endure the rough independent way in which all the Milton girls, who made application for the servant's place, replied to her inquiries respecting their qualifications. They even went the length of questioning her back again; having doubts and fears of their own, as to the solvency of a family who lived in a house of thirty pounds a-year, and yet gave themselves airs, and kept two servants, one of them so very high and mighty. Mr. Hale was no longer looked upon as Vicar of Helstone, but as a man who only spent at a certain rate. Margaret was weary and impatient of the accounts which Dixon perpetually brought to Mrs. Hale of the behaviour of these would-be servants. Not but what Margaret was repelled by the rough uncourteous manners of these people; not but what she shrunk with fastidious pride from their hail-fellow accost, and severely resented their unconcealed curiosity as to the means and position of any family who lived in Milton, and yet were not engaged in trade of some kind. But the more Margaret felt impertinence, the more likely she was to be silent on the subject; and, at any rate, if she took upon herself to make inquiry for a servant, she could spare her mother the recital of all her disappointments and fancied or real insults.

Margaret accordingly went up and down to butchers and grocers, seeking for a nonpareil of a girl;[4] and lowering her hopes and expectations every week, as she found the difficulty of meeting with any one in a manufacturing town who did not prefer the better wages and greater independence of working in a mill. It was something of a trial to Margaret to go out by herself in this busy bustling place. Mrs. Shaw's ideas of propriety and her own helpless dependence on others, had always made her insist that a footman should accompany Edith and Margaret, if they went beyond Harley Street or the immediate neighbourhood. The limits by which this rule of her aunt's had circumscribed Margaret's independence had been silently rebelled against at the time: and she had doubly enjoyed the free walks and

4. An exceptional girl.

rambles of her forest life, from the contrast which they presented. She went along there with a bounding fearless step, that occasionally broke out into a run, if she were in a hurry, and occasionally was stilled into perfect repose, as she stood listening to, or watching any of the wild creatures who sang in the leafy courts, or glanced out with their keen bright eyes from the low brushwood or tangled furze. It was a trial to come down from such motion or such stillness, only guided by her own sweet will, to the even and decorous pace necessary in streets. But she could have laughed at herself for minding this change, if it had not been accompanied by what was a more serious annoyance.

The side of the town on which Crampton lay was especially a thoroughfare for the factory people. In the back streets around them there were many mills, out of which poured streams of men and women two or three times a day. Until Margaret had learnt the times of their ingress and egress, she was very unfortunate in constantly falling in with them. They came rushing along, with bold, fearless faces, and loud laughs and jests, particularly aimed at all those who appeared to be above them in rank or station. The tones of their unrestrained voices, and their carelessness of all common rules of street politeness, frightened Margaret a little at first. The girls, with their rough, but not unfriendly freedom, would comment on her dress, even touch her shawl or gown to ascertain the exact material; nay, once or twice she was asked questions relative to some article which they particularly admired. There was such a simple reliance on her womanly sympathy with their love of dress, and on her kindliness, that she gladly replied to these inquiries, as soon as she understood them; and half smiled back at their remarks. She did not mind meeting any number of girls, loud spoken and boisterous though they might be. But she alternately dreaded and fired up against the workmen, who commented not on her dress, but on her looks, in the same open fearless manner. She, who had hitherto felt that even the most refined remark on her personal appearance was an impertinence, had to endure undisguised admiration from these out-spoken men. But the very out-spokenness marked their innocence of any intention to hurt her delicacy, as she would have perceived if she had been less frightened by the disorderly tumult. Out of her fright came a flash of indignation which made her face scarlet, and her dark eyes gather flame, as she heard some of their speeches. Yet there were other sayings of theirs, which, when she reached the quiet safety of home, amused her even while they irritated her.

For instance, one day, after she had passed a number of men, several of whom had paid her the not unusual compliment of wishing she was their sweetheart, one of the lingerers added, "Your bonny face, my lass, makes the day look brighter." And another day, as she was unconsciously smiling at some passing thought, she was addressed by a poorly-dressed, middle-aged workman, with "You may well smile, my lass; many a one would smile to have such a bonny face." This man looked so care-worn that Margaret could not help giving him an answering smile, glad to think that her looks, such as they were, should have had the power to call up a pleasant thought. He seemed to understand her acknowledging glance, and a silent recognition was established between them whenever the chances of the day brought them across each other's paths. They had never exchanged a word; nothing had been said but that first compliment; yet somehow Margaret looked upon this man with more interest than upon any one else in Milton. Once or twice, on Sundays, she saw him walking with a girl, evidently his daughter, and, if possible, still more unhealthy than he was himself.

One day Margaret and her father had been as far as the fields that lay around the town; it was early spring, and she had gathered some of the hedge and ditch flowers, dog-violets, lesser celandines, and the like, with an unspoken lament in her heart for the sweet profusion of the South. Her father had left her to go into Milton upon some business; and on the road home she met her humble friends. The girl looked wistfully at the flowers, and, acting on a sudden impulse, Margaret offered them to her. Her pale blue eyes lightened up as she took them, and her father spoke for her.

"Thank yo, Miss. Bessy 'll think a deal o' them flowers; that hoo will; and I shall think a deal o' yor kindness. Yo're not of this country, I reckon?"

"No!" said Margaret, half sighing. "I come from the South—from Hampshire," she continued, a little afraid of wounding his consciousness of ignorance, if she used a name which he did not understand.

"That's beyond London, I reckon? And I come fro' Burnley-ways,[5] and forty mile to th' North. And yet, yo see, North and South has both met and made kind o' friends in this big smoky place."

Margaret had slackened her pace to walk alongside of the man and his daughter, whose steps were regulated by the feebleness of the latter. She now spoke to the girl, and there was a sound of tender pity in the tone of her voice as she did so that went right to the heart of the father.

5. Burnley was a cotton town in Lancashire, at roughly the distance indicated from Manchester; here Gaskell breaks her convention of fictionalizing place names. Higgins's comment—"North and South has both met and made kind o' friends"—perhaps provided Dickens with the title of the novel that he suggested to Gaskell.

"I'm afraid you are not very strong."

"No," said the girl, "nor never will be."

"Spring is coming," said Margaret, as if to suggest pleasant, hopeful thoughts.

"Spring nor summer will do me good," said the girl quietly.

Margaret looked up at the man, almost expecting some contradiction from him, or at least some remark that would modify his daughter's utter hopelessness. But, instead, he added—

"I'm afeared hoo speaks truth. I'm afeared hoo's too far gone in a waste."

"I shall have a spring where I'm boun to, and flowers, and amaranths, and shining robes besides."[6]

"Poor lass, poor lass!" said her father in a low tone. "I'm none so sure o' that; but it's a comfort to thee, poor lass, poor lass. Poor father! it'll be soon."

Margaret was shocked by his words—shocked but not repelled; rather attracted and interested.

"Where do you live? I think we must be neighbours, we meet so often on this road."

"We put up at nine Frances Street, second turn to th' left at after yo've past th' Goulden Dragon."

"And your name? I must not forget that."

"I'm none ashamed o' my name. It's Nicholas Higgins. Hoo's called Bessy Higgins. Whatten yo' asking for?"

Margaret was surprised at this last question, for at Helstone it would have been an understood thing, after the inquiries she had made, that she intended to come and call upon any poor neighbour whose name and habitation she had asked for.

"I thought—I meant to come and see you." She suddenly felt rather shy of offering the visit, without having any reason to give for her wish to make it, beyond a kindly interest in a stranger. It seemed all at once to take the shape of an impertinence on her part; she read this meaning too in the man's eyes.

"I'm none so fond of having strange folk in my house." But then relenting, as he saw her heightened colour, he added, "Yo're a foreigner, as one may say, and maybe don't know many folk here, and yo've given my wench here flowers out of yo'r own hand;—yo may come if yo like."

Margaret was half-amused, half-nettled at this answer. She was not sure if she would go where permission was given so like a favour conferred. But when they came to the town into Frances Street, the girl stopped a minute, and said,

"Yo'll not forget yo're to come and see us."

6. Here as elsewhere in her utterance Bessy draws on traditional religious symbolism. The amaranth is symbolic of immortality in that its flowers are said never to fade.

"Aye, aye," said the father, impatiently, "hoo'll come. Hoo's a bit set up now, because hoo thinks I might ha' spoken more civilly; but hoo'll think better on it, and come. I can read her proud bonny face like a book. Come along, Bess; there's the mill bell ringing."

Margaret went home, wondering at her new friends, and smiling at the man's insight into what had been passing in her mind. From that day Milton became a brighter place to her. It was not the long, bleak sunny days of spring, nor yet was it that time was reconciling her to the town of her habitation. It was that in it she had found a human interest.

Chapter IX.

Dressing for Tea.

> "Let China's earth, enrich'd with coloured stains,
>   Pencil'd with gold, and streaked with azure veins,
>   The grateful flavour of the Indian leaf,
>   Or Mocho's sunburnt berry glad receive."
>   MRS. BARBAULD.[1]

The day after this meeting with Higgins and his daughter, Mr. Hale came upstairs into the little drawing-room at an unusual hour. He went up to different objects in the room, as if examining them, but Margaret saw that it was merely a nervous trick—a way of putting off something he wished, yet feared to say. Out it came at last—

"My dear! I've asked Mr. Thornton to come to tea to-night."

Mrs. Hale was leaning back in her easy chair, with her eyes shut, and an expression of pain on her face which had become habitual to her of late. But she roused up into querulousness at this speech of her husband's.

"Mr. Thornton!—and to-night! What in the world does the man want to come here for? And Dixon is washing my muslins and laces, and there is no soft water with these horrid east winds, which I suppose we shall have all the year round in Milton."

"The wind is veering round, my dear," said Mr. Hale, looking out at the smoke, which drifted right from the east, only he did not yet understand the points of the compass, and rather arranged them ad libitum,[2] according to circumstances.

"Don't tell me!" said Mrs. Hale, shuddering up, and wrapping her shawl about her still more closely. "But, east or west wind, I suppose this man comes."

"Oh, mamma, that shows you never saw Mr. Thornton. He looks

---

1. Anna Letitia Barbauld (1743–1825), popular English poet.
2. Indiscriminately (Latin).

like a person who would enjoy battling with every adverse thing he
could meet with—enemies, winds, or circumstances. The more it
rains and blows, the more certain we are to have him. But I'll go and
help Dixon. I'm getting to be a famous clear-starcher. And he won't
want any amusement beyond talking to papa. Papa, I am really longing to see the Pythias to your Damon.[3] You know I never saw him
but once, and then we were so puzzled to know what to say to each
other that we did not get on particularly well."

"I don't know that you would ever like him, or think him agreeable,
Margaret. He is not a lady's man."

Margaret wreathed her throat in a scornful curve.

"I don't particularly admire ladies' men, papa. But Mr. Thornton
comes here as your friend—as one who has appreciated you"—

"The only person in Milton," said Mrs. Hale.

"So we will give him a welcome, and some cocoa-nut cakes. Dixon
will be flattered if we ask her to make some; and I will undertake to
iron your caps, mamma."

Many a time that morning did Margaret wish Mr. Thornton far
enough away. She had planned other employments for herself: a
letter to Edith, a good piece of Dante, a visit to the Higginses. But,
instead, she ironed away, listening to Dixon's complaints, and only
hoping that by an excess of sympathy she might prevent her from
carrying the recital of her sorrows to Mrs. Hale. Every now and then,
Margaret had to remind herself of her father's regard for Mr. Thornton, to subdue the irritation of weariness that was stealing over her,
and bringing on one of the bad headaches to which she had lately
become liable. She could hardly speak when she sat down at last,
and told her mother that she was no longer Peggy the laundry-maid,
but Margaret Hale the lady. She meant this speech for a little joke,
and was vexed enough with her busy tongue when she found her
mother taking it seriously.

"Yes! if any one had told me, when I was Miss Beresford, and one
of the belles of the county, that a child of mine would have to stand
half a day, in a little poky kitchen, working away like any servant,
that we might prepare properly for the reception of a tradesman, and
that this tradesman should be the only"—

"Oh, mamma!" said Margaret, lifting herself up, "don't punish me
so for a careless speech. I don't mind ironing, or any kind of work,
for you and papa. I am myself a born and bred lady through it all,
even though it comes to scouring a floor, or washing dishes. I am
tired now, just for a little while; but in half an hour I shall be ready
to do the same over again. And as to Mr. Thornton's being in trade,
why he can't help that now, poor fellow. I don't suppose his educa-

3. In classical mythology, two friends who were faithful until death.

tion would fit him for much else." Margaret lifted herself slowly up, and went to her own room; for just now she could not bear much more.

In Mr. Thornton's house, at this very same time, a similar, yet different, scene was going on. A large-boned lady, long past middle age, sat at work in a grim handsomely-furnished dining-room. Her features, like her frame, were strong and massive, rather than heavy. Her face moved slowly from one decided expression to another equally decided. There was no great variety in her countenance; but those who looked at it once, generally looked at it again; even the passers-by in the street, half-turned their heads to gaze an instant longer at the firm, severe, dignified woman, who never gave way in street-courtesy, or paused in her straight-onward course to the clearly-defined end which she proposed to herself.

She was handsomely dressed in stout black silk, of which not a thread was worn or discoloured. She was mending a large, long table-cloth of the finest texture, holding it up against the light occasionally to discover thin places, which required her delicate care. There was not a book about in the room, with the exception of Matthew Henry's Bible Commentaries,[4] six volumes of which lay in the centre of the massive side-board, flanked by a tea-urn on one side, and a lamp on the other. In some remote apartment, there was exercise upon the piano going on. Some one was practising up a morceau de salon,[5] playing it very rapidly, every third note, on an average, being either indistinct, or wholly missed out, and the loud chords at the end being half of them false, but not the less satisfactory to the performer. Mrs. Thornton heard a step, like her own in its decisive character, pass the dining-room door.

"John! Is that you?"

Her son opened the door, and showed himself.

"What has brought you home so early? I thought you were going to tea with that friend of Mr. Bell's; that Mr. Hale."

"So I am, mother, I am come home to dress!"

"Dress! humph! When I was a girl, young men were satisfied with dressing once in a day. Why should you dress to go and take a cup of tea with an old parson?"

"Mr. Hale is a gentleman, and his wife and daughter are ladies."

"Wife and daughter! Do they teach too? What do they do? You have never mentioned them."

---

4. *Exposition of the Old and New Testament* by Matthew Henry (1662–1714), a noncon-
    formist divine. More generally known as "Henry's Commentaries," the work was incom-
    plete at its author's death. The reference here is either to the completed edition of six
    volumes (1811), which remained a staple of dissenting theology until well into the nine-
    teenth century, or to a later six-volume abridgement (1831–35).
5. Parlor piece (French).

"No! mother, because I have never seen Mrs. Hale; I have only seen Miss Hale for half an hour."

"Take care you don't get caught by a penniless girl, John."

"I am not easily caught, mother, as I think you know. But I must not have Miss Hale spoken of in that way, which, you know, is offensive to me. I never was aware of any young lady trying to catch me yet, nor do I believe that any one has ever given themselves that useless trouble."

Mrs. Thornton did not choose to yield the point to her son; or else she had, in general, pride enough for her sex.

"Well! I only say, take care. Perhaps our Milton girls have too much spirit and good feeling to go angling after husbands; but this Miss Hale comes out of the aristocratic counties, where, if all tales be true, rich husbands are reckoned prizes."

Mr. Thornton's brow contracted, and he came a step forward into the room.

"Mother" (with a short scornful laugh), "you will make me confess. The only time I saw Miss Hale, she treated me with a haughty civility which had a strong flavour of contempt in it. She held herself aloof from me as if she had been a queen, and I her humble, unwashed vassal. Be easy, mother."

"No! I am not easy, nor content either. What business had she, a renegade clergyman's daughter, to turn up her nose at you! I would dress for none of them—a saucy set! if I were you." As he was leaving the room he said:—

"Mr. Hale is good, and gentle, and learned. He is not saucy. As for Mrs. Hale, I will tell you what she is like to-night, if you care to hear." He shut the door, and was gone."

"Despise my son! treat him as her vassal, indeed! Humph! I should like to know where she could find such another! Boy and man, he's the noblest, stoutest heart I ever knew. I don't care if I am his mother; I can see what's what, and not be blind. I know what Fanny is; and I know what John is. Despise him! I hate her!"

Chapter X.

Wrought Iron and Gold.

"We are the trees whom shaking fastens more."
                                        GEORGE HERBERT.[1]

Mr. Thornton left the house without coming into the dining-room again. He was rather late, and walked rapidly out to Crampton. He

---

1. English poet and divine (1593–1633). The line is from his poem "Affliction (V)."

was anxious not to slight his new friend by any disrespectful unpunctuality. The church-clock struck half-past seven as he stood at the
door awaiting Dixon's slow movements; always doubly tardy when
she had to degrade herself by answering the door-bell. He was ushered into the little drawing-room, and kindly greeted by Mr. Hale,
who led him up to his wife, whose pale face, and shawl-draped figure
made a silent excuse for the cold languor of her greeting. Margaret
was lighting the lamp when he entered, for the darkness was coming
on. The lamp threw a pretty light into the centre of the dusky room,
from which, with country habits, they did not exclude the night-
skies, and the outer darkness of air. Somehow, that room contrasted
itself with the one he had lately left; handsome, ponderous, with no
sign of feminine habitation, except in the one spot where his mother
sat, and no convenience for any other employment than eating and
drinking. To be sure, it was a dining-room; his mother preferred to
sit in it; and her will was a household law. But the drawing-room was
not like this. It was twice—twenty times as fine; not one quarter as
comfortable. Here were no mirrors, not even a scrap of glass to
reflect the light, and answer the same purpose as water in a landscape; no gilding; a warm, sober breadth of colouring, well relieved
by the dear old Helstone chintz-curtains and chair covers. An open
davenport[2] stood in the window opposite the door; in the other there
was a stand, with a tall white china vase, from which drooped
wreaths of English ivy, pale-green birch, and copper-coloured beech-
leaves. Pretty baskets of work stood about in different places: and
books, not cared for on account of their binding solely, lay on one
table, as if recently put down. Behind the door was another table,
decked out for tea, with a white table-cloth, on which flourished the
cocoa-nut cakes, and a basket piled with oranges and ruddy American apples[3] heaped on leaves.

It appeared to Mr. Thornton that all these graceful cares were
habitual to the family; and especially of a piece with Margaret. She
stood by the tea-table in a light-coloured muslin gown, which had a
good deal of pink about it. She looked as if she was not attending to
the conversation, but solely busy with the tea-cups, among which
her round ivory hands moved with pretty, noiseless, daintiness. She
had a bracelet on one taper arm, which would fall down over her
round wrist. Mr. Thornton watched the re-placing of this troublesome ornament with far more attention than he listened to her
father. It seemed as if it fascinated him to see her push it up impatiently, until it tightened her soft flesh; and then to mark the loos-

2. A small writing table with a number of drawers.
3. Presumably imported. In a letter of December 13, 1861, to Edward Everett Hale, Gaskell
   records receiving a gift of apples from America and regarding them as particularly delicious
   (*Further Letters* pp. 228–29).

ening—the fall. He could almost have exclaimed—"There it goes, again!" There was so little left to be done after he arrived at the preparation for tea, that he was almost sorry the obligation of eating and drinking came so soon to prevent his watching Margaret. She handed him his cup of tea with the proud air of an unwilling slave; but her eye caught the moment when he was ready for another cup; and he almost longed to ask her to do for him what he saw her compelled to do for her father, who took her little finger and thumb in his masculine hand, and made them serve as sugar-tongs. Mr. Thornton saw her beautiful eyes lifted to her father, full of light, half-laughter and half-love, as this bit of pantomime went on between the two, unobserved, as they fancied, by any. Margaret's head still ached, as the paleness of her complexion, and her silence might have testified; but she was resolved to throw herself into the breach, if there was any long untoward pause, rather than that her father's friend, pupil, and guest should have cause to think himself in any way neglected. But the conversation went on; and Margaret drew into a corner, near her mother, with her work, after the tea-things were taken away; and felt that she might let her thoughts roam, without fear of being suddenly wanted to fill up a gap.

Mr. Thornton and Mr. Hale were both absorbed in the continuation of some subject which had been started at their last meeting. Margaret was recalled to a sense of the present by some trivial, low-spoken remark of her mother's; and on suddenly looking up from her work, her eye was caught by the difference of outward appearance between her father and Mr. Thornton, as betokening such distinctly opposite natures. Her father was of slight figure, which made him appear taller than he really was, when not contrasted, as at this time, with the tall, massive frame of another. The lines in her father's face were soft and waving, with a frequent undulating kind of trembling movement passing over them, showing every fluctuating emotion; the eyelids were large and arched, giving to the eyes a peculiar languid beauty which was almost feminine. The brows were finely arched, but were, by the very size of the dreamy lids, raised to a considerable distance from the eyes. Now, in Mr. Thornton's face the straight brows fell low over the clear, deep-set earnest eyes, which, without being unpleasantly sharp, seemed intent enough to penetrate into the very heart and core of what he was looking at. The lines in the face were few but firm, as if they were carved in marble, and lay principally about the lips, which were slightly compressed over a set of teeth so faultless and beautiful as to give the effect of sudden sunlight when the rare bright smile, coming in an instant and shining out of the eyes, changed the whole look from the severe and resolved expression of a man ready to do and dare everything, to the keen honest enjoyment of the moment, which is seldom shown so fearlessly and instantaneously except by children. Margaret liked this smile; it was the first thing she had admired in this new friend of her father's; and the opposition of character, shown in all these details of appearance she had just been noticing, seemed to explain the attraction they evidently felt towards each other.

She rearranged her mother's worsted-work, and fell back into her own thoughts—as completely forgotten by Mr. Thornton as if she had not been in the room, so thoroughly was he occupied in explaining to Mr. Hale the magnificent power, yet delicate adjustment of the might of the steam-hammer, which was recalling to Mr. Hale some of the wonderful stories of subservient genii in the Arabian Nights—one moment stretching from earth to sky and filling all the width of the horizon, at the next obediently compressed into a vase small enough to be borne in the hand of a child.[4]

"And this imagination of power, this practical realisation of a gigantic thought, came out of one man's brain in our good town. That very man has it within him to mount, step by step, on each wonder he achieves to higher marvels still. And I'll be bound to say, we have many among us who, if he were gone, could spring into the breach and carry on the war which compels, and shall compel, all material power to yield to science."

"Your boast reminds me of the old lines—

'I've a hundred captains in England,' he said,
    'As good as ever was he.' "

At her father's quotation Margaret looked suddenly up, with inquiring wonder in her eyes. How in the world had they got from cog-wheels to Chevy Chace?[5]

"It is no boast of mine," replied Mr. Thornton; "it is plain matter-of-fact. I won't deny that I am proud of belonging to a town—or perhaps I should rather say a district—the necessities of which give birth to such grandeur of conception. I would rather be a man toiling, suffering—nay, failing and successless—here, than lead a dull prosperous life in the old worn grooves of what you call more aristocratic society down in the South, with their slow days of careless ease. One may be clogged with honey and unable to rise and fly."

"You are mistaken," said Margaret, roused by the aspersion on her beloved South to a fond vehemence of defence, that brought the colour into her cheeks and the angry tears into her eyes. "You do not know anything about the South. If there is less adventure or less progress—I suppose I must not say less excitement—from the gam-

4. The steam-hammer, invented by the Manchester engineer James Nasmyth in the 1830s, was famous for the precision of its action in operation. Hence the comparison with the genie in the *Arabian Nights* who similarly stands as a symbol of great power combined with compression and precision.
5. As Gaskell indicates, the quotation is from the traditional northern ballad of Chevy Chase.

bling spirit of trade, which seems requisite to force out these wonderful inventions, there is less suffering also. I see men here going about in the streets who look ground down by some pinching sorrow or care—who are not only sufferers but haters. Now, in the South we have our poor, but there is not that terrible expression in their countenances of a sullen sense of injustice which I see here. You do not know the South, Mr. Thornton," she concluded, collapsing into a determined silence, and angry with herself for having said so much.

"And may I say you do not know the North?" asked he, with an inexpressible gentleness in his tone, as he saw that he had really hurt her. She continued resolutely silent; yearning after the lovely haunts she had left far away in Hampshire, with a passionate longing that made her feel her voice would be unsteady and trembling if she spoke.

"At any rate, Mr. Thornton," said Mrs. Hale, "you will allow that Milton is a much more smoky, dirty town than you will ever meet with in the South."

"I'm afraid I must give up its cleanliness," said Mr. Thornton, with the quick gleaming smile. "But we are bidden by parliament to burn our own smoke[6]; so I suppose, like good little children, we shall do as we are bid—some time."

"But I think you told me you had altered your chimneys so as to consume the smoke, did you not?" asked Mr. Hale.

"Mine were altered by my own will, before parliament meddled with the affair. It was an immediate outlay, but it repays me in the saving of coal. I'm not sure whether I should have done it, if I had waited until the act was passed. At any rate, I should have waited to be informed against and fined, and given all the trouble in yielding that I legally could. But all laws which depend for their enforcement upon informers and fines, become inert from the odiousness of the machinery. I doubt if there has been a chimney in Milton informed against for five years past, although some are constantly sending out one-third of their coal in what is called here unparliamentary smoke."

"I only know it is impossible to keep the muslin blinds clean here above a week together; and at Helstone we have had them up for a month or more, and they have not looked dirty at the end of that time. And as for hands—Margaret, how many times did you say you had washed your hands this morning before twelve o'clock? Three times, was it not?"

"Yes, mamma."

"You seem to have a strong objection to acts of parliament and all

6. See vol. I, chap. 7, n. 3 above (p. 55).

legislation affecting your mode of management down here at Milton," said Mr. Hale.

"Yes, I have; and many others have as well. And with justice, I think. The whole machinery—I don't mean the wood and iron machinery now—of the cotton trade is so new that it is no wonder if it does not work well in every part all at once. Seventy years ago what was it? And now what is it not? Raw, crude materials came together; men of the same level, as regarded education and station, took suddenly the different positions of masters and men, owing to the motherwit, as regarded opportunities and probabilities, which distinguished some, and made them far-seeing as to what great future lay concealed in that rude model of Sir Richard Arkwright's.[7] The rapid development of what might be called a new trade, gave those early masters enormous power of wealth and command. I don't mean merely over the workmen; I mean over purchasers—over the whole world's market. Why, I may give you, as an instance, an advertisement, inserted not fifty years ago in a Milton paper, that so-and-so (one of the half-dozen calico-printers[8] of the time) would close his warehouse at noon each day; therefore, that all purchasers must come before that hour. Fancy a man dictating in this manner the time when he would sell and when he would not sell. Now, I believe, if a good customer chose to come at mid-night, I should get up, and stand hat in hand to receive his orders."

Margaret's lip curled, but somehow she was compelled to listen; she could no longer abstract herself in her own thoughts.

"I only name such things to show what almost unlimited power the manufacturers had about the beginning of this century. The men were rendered dizzy by it. Because a man was successful in his ventures, there was no reason that in all other things his mind should be well-balanced. On the contrary, his sense of justice, and his simplicity, were often utterly smothered under the glut of wealth that came down upon him; and they tell strange tales of the wild extravagance of living indulged in on gala-days by those early cotton-lords. There can be no doubt, too, of the tyranny they exercised over their work-people. You know the proverb, Mr. Hale, 'Set a beggar on horseback, and he'll ride to the devil,'—well, some of these early manufacturers did ride to the devil in a magnificent style—crushing human bone and flesh under their horses' hoofs without remorse. But by-and-by came a reaction; there were more factories, more masters; more men were wanted. The power of masters and men became more evenly balanced; and now the battle is pretty fairly waged

---

7. Richard Arkwright (1732–1792) patented a water-powered spinning machine in 1769, which marked the beginning of the transformation of cotton-spinning to a factory industry.
8. Calico-printing was a finishing trade, by means of which the original woven cloth was given patterns and designs.

between us. We will hardly submit to the decision of an umpire, much less to the interference of a meddler with only a smattering of the knowledge of the real facts of the case, even though that meddler be called the High Court of Parliament."

"Is there necessity for calling it a battle between the two classes?" asked Mr. Hale. "I know, from your using the term, it is one which gives a true idea of the real state of things to your mind."

"It is true; and I believe it to be as much a necessity as that prudent wisdom and good conduct are always opposed to, and doing battle with ignorance and improvidence. It is one of the great beauties of our system, that a working-man may raise himself into the power and position of a master by his own exertions and behaviour; that, in fact, every one who rules himself to decency and sobriety of conduct, and attention to his duties, comes over to our ranks; it may not be always as a master, but as an overlooker, a cashier, a book-keeper, a clerk, one on the side of authority and order."

"You consider all who are unsuccessful in raising themselves in the world, from whatever cause, as your enemies, then, if I understand you rightly," said Margaret, in a clear, cold voice.

"As their own enemies, certainly," said he, quickly, not a little piqued by the haughty disapproval her form of expression and tone of speaking implied. But, in a moment, his straightforward honesty made him feel that his words were but a poor and quibbling answer to what she had said, and, be she as scornful as she liked, it was a duty he owed to himself to explain, as truly as he could, what he did mean. Yet it was very difficult to separate her interpretation, and keep it distinct from his meaning. He could best have illustrated what he wanted to say by telling them something of his own life; but was it not too personal a subject to speak about to strangers? Still, it was the simple straightforward way of explaining his meaning; so, putting aside the touch of shyness that brought a momentary flush of colour into his dark cheek, he said:

"I am not speaking without book. Sixteen years ago, my father died under very miserable circumstances. I was taken from school, and had to become a man (as well as I could) in a few days. I had such a mother as few are blest with; a woman of strong power, and firm resolve. We went into a small country town, where living was cheaper than in Milton, and where I got employment in a draper's shop (a capital place, by the way, for obtaining a knowledge of goods). Week by week, our income came to fifteen shillings, out of which three people had to be kept. My mother managed so that I put by three out of these fifteen shillings regularly. This made the beginning; this taught me self-denial. Now that I am able to afford my mother such comforts as her age, rather than her own wish, requires, I thank her silently on each occasion for the early training she gave me. Now when I feel that in my own case it is no good luck, nor merit, nor talent,—but simply the habits of life which taught me to despise indulgences not thoroughly earned,—indeed, never to think twice about them,—I believe that this suffering, which Miss Hale says is impressed on the countenances of the people of Milton, is but the natural punishment of dishonestly-enjoyed pleasure, at some former period of their lives. I do not look on self-indulgent, sensual people as worthy of my hatred; I simply look upon them with contempt for their poorness of character."

"But you have had the rudiments of a good education," remarked Mr. Hale. "The quick zest with which you are now reading Homer, shows me that you do not come to it as an unknown book; you have read it before, and are only recalling your old knowledge."

"That is true,—I had blundered along it at school; I dare say, I was even considered a pretty fair classic in those days, though my Latin and Greek have slipt away from me since. But I ask you, what preparation they were for such a life as I had to lead? None at all. Utterly none at all. On the point of education, any man who can read and write starts fair with me in the amount of really useful knowledge that I had at that time."

"Well! I don't agree with you. But there I am perhaps somewhat of a pedant. Did not the recollection of the heroic simplicity of the Homeric life nerve you up?"

"Not one bit!" exclaimed Mr. Thornton, laughing. "I was too busy to think about any dead people, with the living pressing alongside of me, neck to neck, in the struggle for bread. Now that I have my mother safe in the quiet peace that becomes her age, and duly rewards her former exertions, I can turn to all that old narration and thoroughly enjoy it."

"I dare say, my remark came from the professional feeling of there being nothing like leather," replied Mr. Hale.

When Mr. Thornton rose up to go away, after shaking hands with Mr. and Mrs. Hale, he made an advance to Margaret to wish her good-bye in a similar manner. It was the frank familiar custom of the place; but Margaret was not prepared for it. She simply bowed her farewell; although the instant she saw the hand, half put out, quickly drawn back, she was sorry she had not been aware of the intention. Mr. Thornton, however, knew nothing of her sorrow, and, drawing himself up to his full height, walked off, muttering as he left the house—

"A more proud, disagreeable girl I never saw. Even her great beauty is blotted out of one's memory by her scornful ways."

Chapter XI.

First Impressions.

"There's iron, they say, in all our blood,
    And a grain or two perhaps is good;
But his, he makes me harshly feel,
    Has got a little too much of steel."

ANON.

"Margaret!" said Mr. Hale, as he returned from showing his guest downstairs; "I could not help watching your face with some anxiety, when Mr. Thornton made his confession of having been a shop-boy. I knew it all along from Mr. Bell; so I was aware of what was coming; but I half expected to see you get up and leave the room."

"Oh, papa! you don't mean that you thought me so silly? I really liked that account of himself better than anything else he said. Everything else revolted me, from its hardness; but he spoke about himself so simply—with so little of the pretence that makes the vulgarity of shop-people, and with such tender respect for his mother, that I was less likely to leave the room then than when he was boasting about Milton, as if there was not such another place in the world; or quietly professing to despise people for careless, wasteful improvidence, without ever seeming to think it his duty to try to make them different,—to give them anything of the training which his mother gave him, and to which he evidently owes his position, whatever that may be. No! his statement of having been a shop-boy was the thing I liked best of all."

"I am surprised at you, Margaret," said her mother. "You who were always accusing people of being shoppy at Helstone! I don't think, Mr. Hale, you have done quite right in introducing such a person to us without telling us what he had been. I really was very much afraid of showing him how much shocked I was at some parts of what he said. His father 'dying in miserable circumstances.' Why it might have been in the workhouse."

"I am not sure if it was not worse than being in the workhouse," replied her husband. "I heard a good deal of his previous life from Mr. Bell before we came here; and as he has told you a part, I will fill up what he left out. His father speculated wildly, failed, and then killed himself, because he could not bear the disgrace. All his former friends shrunk from the disclosures that had to be made of his dishonest gambling—wild, hopeless struggles, made with other people's money, to regain his own moderate portion of wealth. No one came forwards to help the mother and this boy. There was another child, I believe, a girl; too young to earn money, but of course she had to be kept. At least, no friend came forwards immediately, and Mrs.

Thornton is not one, I fancy, to wait till tardy kindness comes to find her out. So they left Milton. I knew he had gone into a shop, and that his earnings, with some fragment of property secured to his mother, had been made to keep them for a long time. Mr. Bell said they absolutely lived upon water-porridge for years—how, he did not know; but long after the creditors had given up hope of any payment of old Mr. Thornton's debts (if, indeed, they ever had hoped at all about it, after his suicide,) this young man returned to Milton, and went quietly round to each creditor, paying him the first instalment of the money owing to him. No noise—no gathering together of creditors—it was done very silently and quietly, but all was paid at last; helped on materially by the circumstance of one of the creditors, a crabbed old fellow (Mr. Bell says), taking in Mr. Thornton as a kind of partner."

"That really is fine," said Margaret. "What a pity such a nature should be tainted by his position as a Milton manufacturer."

"How tainted?" asked her father.

"Oh, papa, by that testing everything by the standard of wealth. When he spoke of the mechanical powers, he evidently looked upon them only as new ways of extending trade and making money. And the poor men around him—they were poor because they were vicious—out of the pale of his sympathies because they had not his iron nature, and the capabilities that it gives him for being rich."

"Not vicious; he never said that. Improvident and self-indulgent were his words."

Margaret was collecting her mother's working materials, and preparing to go to bed. Just as she was leaving the room, she hesitated— she was inclined to make an acknowledgment which she thought would please her father, but which to be full and true must include a little annoyance. However, out it came.

"Papa, I do think Mr. Thornton a very remarkable man; but personally I don't like him at all."

"And I do!" said her father laughing. "Personally, as you call it, and all. I don't set him up for a hero, or anything of that kind. But good night, child. Your mother looks sadly tired to-night, Margaret."

Margaret had noticed her mother's jaded appearance with anxiety for some time past, and this remark of her father's sent her up to bed with a dim fear lying like a weight on her heart. The life in Milton was so different from what Mrs. Hale had been accustomed to live in Helstone, in and out perpetually into the fresh and open air; the air itself was so different, deprived of all revivifying principle as it seemed to be here; the domestic worries pressed so very closely, and in so new and sordid a form, upon all the women in the family, that there was good reason to fear that her mother's health might be becoming seriously affected. There were several other signs of something wrong about Mrs. Hale. She and Dixon held mysterious consultations in her bedroom, from which Dixon would come out crying and cross, as was her custom when any distress of her mistress called upon her sympathy. Once Margaret had gone into the chamber soon after Dixon left it, and found her mother on her knees, and as Margaret stole out she caught a few words, which were evidently a prayer for strength and patience to endure severe bodily suffering. Margaret yearned to re-unite the bond of intimate confidence which had been broken by her long residence at her aunt Shaw's, and strove by gentle caresses and softened words to creep into the warmest place in her mother's heart. But though she received caresses and fond words back again, in such profusion as would have gladdened her formerly, yet she felt that there was a secret withheld from her, and she believed it bore serious reference to her mother's health. She lay awake very long this night, planning how to lessen the evil influence of their Milton life on her mother. A servant to give Dixon permanent assistance should be got, if she gave up her whole time to the search; and then, at any rate, her mother might have all the personal attention she required, and had been accustomed to her whole life.

Visiting register offices,[1] seeing all manner of unlikely people, and very few in the least likely, absorbed Margaret's time and thoughts for several days. One afternoon she met Bessy Higgins in the street, and stopped to speak to her.

"Well, Bessy, how are you? Better, I hope, now the wind has changed."

"Better and not better, if yo' know what that means."

"Not exactly," replied Margaret, smiling.

"I'm better in not being torn to pieces by coughing o' nights, but I'm weary and tired o' Milton, and longing to get away to the land o' Beulah; and when I think I'm farther and farther off, my heart sinks, and I'm no better; I'm worse."

Margaret turned round to walk alongside of the girl in her feeble progress homeward. But for a minute or two she did not speak. At last she said in a low voice,

"Bessy, do you wish to die?" For she shrank from death herself, with all the clinging to life so natural to the young and healthy.

Bessy was silent in her turn for a minute or two. Then she replied,

"If yo'd led the life I have, and getten as weary of it as I have, and thought at times, 'maybe it'll last for fifty or sixty years—it does wi' some,'—and got dizzy and dazed, and sick, as each of them sixty years seemed to spin about me, and mock me with its length of hours and minutes, and endless bits o' time—oh, wench! I tell thee thou'd been

---

1. Offices where lists of people available for employment were kept.

glad enough when th' doctor said he feared thou'd never see another winter."

"Why, Bessy, what kind of a life has yours been?"

"Nought worse than many others', I reckon. Only I fretted again it, and they didn't."

"But what was it? You know, I'm a stranger here, so perhaps I'm not so quick at understanding what you mean as if I'd lived all my life at Milton."

"If yo'd ha' come to our house when yo' said yo' would, I could maybe ha' told you. But father says yo're just like th' rest on 'em; its out o' sight out o' mind wi' you."

"I don't know who the rest are; and I've been very busy; and, to tell the truth, I had forgotten my promise—"

"Yo' offered it; we asked none of it."

"I had forgotten what I said for the time," continued Margaret quietly. "I should have thought of it again when I was less busy. May I go with you now?"

Bessy gave a quick glance at Margaret's face, to see if the wish expressed was really felt. The sharpness in her eye turned to a wistful longing as she met Margaret's soft and friendly gaze.

"I ha' none so many to care for me; if yo' care yo' may come."

So they walked on together in silence. As they turned up into a small court, opening out of a squalid street, Bessy said,

"Yo'll not be daunted if father's at home, and speaks a bit gruffish at first. He took a mind to ye, yo' see, and he thought a deal o' your coming to see us; and just because he liked yo' he were vexed and put about."

"Don't fear, Bessy."

But Nicholas was not at home when they entered. A great slatternly girl, not so old as Bessy, but taller and stronger, was busy at the wash-tub, knocking about the furniture in a rough capable way, but altogether making so much noise that Margaret shrunk, out of sympathy with poor Bessy, who had sat down on the first chair, as if completely tired out with her walk. Margaret asked the sister for a cup of water, and while she ran to fetch it (knocking down the fire-irons, and tumbling over a chair in her way), she unloosed Bessy's bonnet strings, to relieve her catching breath.

"Do you think such life as this is worth caring for?" gasped Bessy, at last. Margaret did not speak, but held the water to her lips. Bessy took a long and feverish draught, and then fell back and shut her eyes. Margaret heard her murmur to herself: "They shall hunger no more, neither thirst any more; neither shall the sun light on them, nor any heat."

Margaret bent over and said, "Bessy, don't be impatient with your life, whatever it is—or may have been. Remember who gave it you, and made it what it is!"

She was startled by hearing Nicholas speak behind her; he had come in without her noticing him.

"Now, I'll not have my wench preached to. She's bad enough as it is, with her dreams and her methodee fancies, and her visions of cities with goulden gates and precious stones. But if it amuses her I let it abe,[2] but I'm none going to have more stuff poured into her."

"But surely," said Margaret, facing round, "you believe in what I said, that God gave her life, and ordered what kind of life it was to be?"

"I believe what I see, and no more. That's what I believe, young woman. I don't believe all I hear—no! not by a big deal. I did hear a young lass make an ado about knowing where we lived, and coming to see us. And my wench here thought a deal about it, and flushed up many a time, when hoo little knew as I was looking at her, at the sound of a strange step. But hoo's come at last,—and hoo's welcome, as long as hoo'll keep from preaching on what hoo knows nought about."

Bessy had been watching Margaret's face; she half sat up to speak now, laying her hand on Margaret's arm with a gesture of entreaty. "Don't be vexed wi' him—there's many a one thinks like him; many and many a one here. If yo' could hear them speak, yo'd not be shocked at him; he's a rare good man, is father—but oh!" said she, falling back in despair, "what he says at times makes me long to die more than ever, for I want to know so many things, and am so tossed about wi' wonder."

"Poor wench—poor old wench,—I'm loth to vex thee, I am; but a man mun speak out for the truth, and when I see the world going all wrong at this time o' day, bothering itself wi' things it knows nought about, and leaving undone all the things that lie in disorder close at its hand—why, I say, leave a' this talk about religion alone, and set to work on what yo' see and know. That's my creed. It's simple, and not far to fetch, nor hard to work."

But the girl only pleaded the more with Margaret.

"Don't think hardly on him—he's a good man, he is. I sometimes think I shall be moped wi' sorrow even in the City of God, if father is not there." The feverish colour came into her cheek, and the feverish flame into her eye. "But you will be there, father! you shall! Oh! my heart!" She put her hand to it, and became ghastly pale.

Margaret held her in her arms, and put the weary head to rest upon her bosom. She lifted the thin soft hair from off the temples, and bathed them with water. Nicholas understood all her signs for

2. I tolerate it.

different articles with the quickness of love, and even the round-eyed sister moved with laborious gentleness at Margaret's "hush!" Presently the spasm that fore-shadowed death had passed away, and Bessy roused herself and said,—

"I'll go to bed,—it's best place; but," catching at Margaret's gown, "yo'll come again,—I know yo' will—but just say it!"

"I will come to-morrow," said Margaret.

Bessy leant back against her father, who prepared to carry her upstairs; but as Margaret rose to go, he struggled to say something: "I could wish there were a God, if it were only to ask Him to bless thee."

Margaret went away very sad and thoughtful.

She was late for tea at home. At Helstone unpunctuality at meal-times was a great fault in her mother's eyes; but now this, as well as many other little irregularities, seemed to have lost their power of irritation, and Margaret almost longed for the old complainings.

"Have you met with a servant, dear?"

"No, mamma; that Anne Buckley would never have done."

"Suppose I try," said Mr. Hale. "Everybody else has had their turn at this great difficulty. Now let me try. I may be the Cinderella to put on the slipper after all."

Margaret could hardly smile at this little joke, so oppressed was she by her visit to the Higginses.

"What would you do, papa? How would you set about it?"

"Why, I would apply to some good house-mother to recommend me one known to herself or her servants."

"Very good. But we must first catch our house mother."

"You have caught her. Or rather she is coming into the snare, and you will catch her to-morrow, if you're skilful."

"What do you mean, Mr. Hale?" asked his wife, her curiosity aroused.

"Why, my paragon pupil (as Margaret calls him), has told me that his mother intends to call on Mrs. and Miss Hale to-morrow."

"Mrs. Thornton!" exclaimed Mrs. Hale.

"The mother of whom he spoke to us?" said Margaret.

"Mrs. Thornton; the only mother he has, I believe," said Mr. Hale quietly.

"I shall like to see her. She must be an uncommon person," her mother added. "Perhaps she may have a relation who might suit us, and be glad of our place. She sounded to be such a careful economical person, that I should like any one out of the same family."

"My dear," said Mr. Hale alarmed. "Pray don't go off on that idea. I fancy Mrs. Thornton is as haughty and proud in her way, as our little Margaret here is in hers, and that she completely ignores that old time of trial, and poverty, and economy, of which he speaks so openly. I am sure, at any rate, she would not like strangers to know anything about it."

"Take notice that is not my kind of haughtiness, papa, if I have any at all; which I don't agree to, though you're always accusing me of it."

"I don't know positively that it is hers either; but from little things I have gathered from him, I fancy so."

They cared too little to ask in what manner her son had spoken about her. Margaret only wanted to know if she must stay in to receive this call, as it would prevent her going to see how Bessy was, until late in the day, since the early morning was always occupied in household affairs; and then she recollected that her mother must not be left to have the whole weight of entertaining her visitor.

Chapter XII.

Morning Calls.

"Well—I suppose we must."
FRIENDS IN COUNCIL.[1]

Mr. Thornton had had some difficulty in working up his mother to the desired point of civility. She did not often make calls; and when she did, it was in heavy state that she went through her duties. Her son had given her a carriage; but she refused to let him keep horses for it; they were hired for the solemn occasions, when she paid morning or evening visits. She had had horses for three days, not a fortnight before, and had comfortably "killed off" all her acquaintances, who might now put themselves to trouble and expense in their turn. Yet Crampton was too far off for her to walk; and she had repeatedly questioned her son as to whether his wish that she should call on the Hales was strong enough to bear the expense of cab-hire. She would have been thankful if it had not; for, as she said, "she saw no use in making up friendships and intimacies with all the teachers and masters in Milton; why, he would be wanting her to call on Fanny's dancing-master's wife, the next thing!"

"And so I would, mother, if Mr. Mason and his wife were friendless in a strange place, like the Hales."

"Oh! you need not speak so hastily. I am going to-morrow. I only wanted you exactly to understand about it."

"If you are going to-morrow, I shall order horses."

1. A collection of occasional writings by Sir Arthur Helps (1813–1875), author of *The Claims of Labour* (1844). See p. 462, note, below.

"Nonsense, John. One would think you were made of money."

"Not quite, yet. But about the horses I'm determined. The last time you were out in a cab, you came home with a headache from the jolting."

"I never complained of it, I'm sure."

"No! My mother is not given to complaints," said he, a little proudly. "But so much the more I have to watch over you. Now, as for Fanny there, a little hardship would do her good."

"She is not made of the same stuff as you are, John. She could not bear it."

Mrs. Thornton was silent after this; for her last words bore relation to a subject which mortified her. She had an unconscious contempt for a weak character; and Fanny was weak in the very points in which her mother and brother were strong. Mrs. Thornton was not a woman much given to reasoning; her quick judgment and firm resolution served her in good stead of any long arguments and discussions with herself; she felt instinctively that nothing could strengthen Fanny to endure hardships patiently, or face difficulties bravely; and though she winced as she made this acknowledgment to herself about her daughter, it only gave her a kind of pitying tenderness of manner towards her; much of the same description of demeanour with which mothers are wont to treat their weak and sickly children. A stranger, a careless observer might have considered that Mrs. Thornton's manner to her children betokened far more love to Fanny than to John. But such a one would have been deeply mistaken. The very daringness with which mother and son spoke out unpalatable truths, the one to the other, showed a reliance on the firm centre of each other's souls; which the uneasy tenderness of Mrs. Thornton's manner to her daughter, the shame with which she thought to hide the poverty of her child in all the grand qualities which she herself possessed unconsciously, and which she set so high a value upon in others—this shame, I say, betrayed the want of a secure resting-place for her affection. She never called her son by any name but John; "love," and "dear," and such like terms, were reserved for Fanny. But her heart gave thanks for him day and night; and she walked proudly among women for his sake.

"Fanny dear! I shall have horses to the carriage to-day, to go and call on these Hales. Should not you go and see nurse? It's in the same direction, and she's always so glad to see you. You could go on there while I am at Mrs. Hale's."

"Oh! mamma, it's such a long way, and I am so tired."

"With what?" asked Mrs. Thornton, her brow slightly contracting.

"I don't know—the weather, I think. It is so relaxing. Couldn't you bring nurse here, mamma? The carriage could fetch her, and she could spend the rest of the day here, which I know she would like."

Mrs. Thornton did not speak; but she laid her work on the table, and seemed to think.

"It will be a long way for her to walk back at night!" she remarked, at last.

"Oh but I will send her home in a cab. I never thought of her walking."

At this point, Mr. Thornton came in, just before going to the mill.

"Mother! I need hardly say, that if there is any little thing that could serve Mrs. Hale as an invalid, you will offer it, I'm sure."

"If I can find it out, I will. But I have never been ill myself, so I am not much up to invalids' fancies."

"Well! here is Fanny then, who is seldom without an ailment. She will be able to suggest something, perhaps—won't you, Fan?"

"I have not always an ailment," said Fanny, pettishly; "and I am not going with mamma. I have a headache to-day, and I shan't go out."

Mr. Thornton looked annoyed. His mother's eyes were bent on her work, at which she was now stitching away busily.

"Fanny! I wish you to go," said he, authoritatively. "It will do you good, instead of harm. You will oblige me by going, without my saying anything more about it."

He went abruptly out of the room after saying this.

If he had staid a minute longer, Fanny would have cried at his tone of command, even when he used the words, "You will oblige me." As it was, she grumbled.

"John always speaks as if I fancied I was ill, and I am sure I never do fancy any such thing. Who are these Hales that he makes such a fuss about?"

"Fanny, don't speak so of your brother. He has good reasons of some kind or other, or he would not wish us to go. Make haste and put your things on."

But the little altercation between her son and her daughter did not incline Mrs. Thornton more favourably towards "these Hales." Her jealous heart repeated her daughter's question, "Who are they, that he is so anxious we should pay them all this attention?" It came up like a burden to a song, long after Fanny had forgotten all about it in the pleasant excitement of seeing the effect of a new bonnet in the looking-glass.

Mrs. Thornton was shy. It was only of late years that she had had leisure enough in her life to go into society; and as society she did not enjoy it. As dinner-giving, and as criticising other people's dinners, she took satisfaction in it. But this going to make acquaintance with strangers was a very different thing. She was ill at ease, and looked more than usually stern and forbidding as she entered the Hales' little drawing-room.

Margaret was busy embroidering a small piece of cambric for some little article of dress for Edith's expected baby—"Flimsy, useless work," as Mrs. Thornton observed to herself. She liked Mrs. Hale's double knitting far better; that was sensible of its kind. The room altogether was full of knick-knacks, which must take a long time to dust; and time to people of limited income was money.

She made all these reflections as she was talking in her stately way to Mrs. Hale, and uttering all the stereotyped commonplaces that most people can find to say with their senses blindfolded. Mrs. Hale was making rather more exertion in her answers, captivated by some real old lace which Mrs. Thornton wore; "lace," as she afterwards observed to Dixon, "of that old English point which has not been made for this seventy years, and which cannot be bought. It must have been an heir-loom, and shows that she had ancestors." So the owner of the ancestral lace became worthy of something more than the languid exertion to be agreeable to a visitor, by which Mrs. Hale's efforts at conversation would have been otherwise bounded. And presently, Margaret, racking her brain to talk to Fanny, heard her mother and Mrs. Thornton plunge into the interminable subject of servants.

"I suppose you are not musical," said Fanny, "as I see no piano."

"I am fond of hearing good music; I cannot play well myself; and papa and mamma don't care much about it; so we sold our old piano when we came here."

"I wonder how you can exist without one. It almost seems to me a necessary of life."

"Fifteen shillings a week, and three saved out of them!" thought Margaret to herself. "But she must have been very young. She probably has forgotten her own personal experience. But she must know of those days." Margaret's manner had an extra tinge of coldness in it when she next spoke.

"You have good concerts here, I believe."

"Oh, yes! Delicious! Too crowded, that is the worst. The directors admit so indiscriminately. But one is sure to hear the newest music there. I always have a large order to give to Johnson's, the day after a concert."

"Do you like new music simply for its newness, then?"

"Oh; one knows it is the fashion in London, or else the singers would not bring it down here. You have been in London, of course."

"Yes," said Margaret, "I have lived there for several years."

"Oh! London and the Alhambra are the two places I long to see!"

"London and the Alhambra!"

"Yes! ever since I read the Tales of the Alhambra.[2] Don't you know them?"

"I don't think I do. But surely, it is a very easy journey to London."

"Yes; but somehow," said Fanny, lowering her voice, "mamma has never been to London herself, and can't understand my longing. She is very proud of Milton; dirty, smoky place, as I feel it to be. I believe she admires it the more for those very qualities."

"If it has been Mrs. Thornton's home for some years, I can well understand her loving it," said Margaret, in her clear bell-like voice.

"What are you saying about me, Miss Hale? May I inquire?"

Margaret had not the words ready for an answer to this question, which took her a little by surprise, so Miss Thornton replied:

"Oh, mamma! we are only trying to account for your being so fond of Milton."

"Thank you," said Mrs. Thornton. "I do not feel that my very natural liking for the place where I was born and brought up,—and which has since been my residence for some years, requires any accounting for."

Margaret was vexed. As Fanny had put it, it did seem as if they had been impertinently discussing Mrs. Thornton's feelings; but she also rose up against that lady's manner of showing that she was offended.

Mrs. Thornton went on after a moment's pause:

"Do you know anything of Milton, Miss Hale? Have you seen any of our factories? our magnificent warehouses?"

"No!" said Margaret. "I have not seen anything of that description as yet."

Then she felt that, by concealing her utter indifference to all such places, she was hardly speaking with truth; so she went on:

"I dare say, papa would have taken me before now if I had cared. But I really do not find much pleasure in going over manufactories."

"They are very curious places," said Mrs. Hale, "but there is so much noise and dirt always. I remember once going in a lilac silk to see candles made, and my gown was utterly ruined."

"Very probably," said Mrs. Thornton, in a short displeased manner. "I merely thought, that as strangers newly come to reside in a town which has risen to eminence in the country, from the character and progress of its peculiar business, you might have cared to visit some of the places where it is carried on; places unique in the kingdom, I am informed. If Miss Hale changes her mind and condescends to be curious as to the manufactures of Milton, I can only say I shall be glad to procure her admission to print-works, or reed-making, or the

2. The reference is presumably to Washington Irving's *Legends of the Alhambra*, first published in England in 1832. The Alhambra is a Moorish fortress in southern Spain.

more simple operations of spinning carried on in my son's mill.[3] Every improvement of machinery is, I believe, to be seen there, in its highest perfection."

"I am so glad you don't like mills and manufactories, and all those kind of things," said Fanny, in a half-whisper, as she rose to accompany her mother, who was taking leave of Mrs. Hale with rustling dignity.

"I think I should like to know all about them, if I were you," replied Margaret quietly.

"Fanny!" said her mother, as they drove away, "we will be civil to these Hales: but don't form one of your hasty friendships with the daughter. She will do you no good, I see. The mother looks very ill, and seems a nice, quiet kind of person."

"I don't want to form any friendship with Miss Hale, mamma," said Fanny, pouting. "I thought I was doing my duty by talking to her, and trying to amuse her."

"Well! at any rate John must be satisfied now."

Chapter XIII.

A Soft Breeze in a Sultry Place.

"That doubt and trouble, fear and pain,
And anguish, all, are shadows vain,
That death itself shall not remain;

That weary deserts we may tread,
A dreary labyrinth may thread,
Thro' dark ways underground be led;

Yet, if we will one Guide obey,
The dreariest path, the darkest way
Shall issue out in heavenly day;

And we, on divers shores now cast,
Shall meet, our perilous voyage past,
All in our Father's house at last!"
R. C. TRENCH.[1]

Margaret flew up stairs as soon as their visitors were gone, and put on her bonnet and shawl, to run and inquire how Bessy Higgins was, and sit with her as long as she could before dinner. As she went

---

3. In weaving, reeds were metal wires used to separate the threads of the warp. Mrs. Thornton's comment suggests that Thornton's mill was a spinning mill producing yarn, rather than a weaving mill where cotton cloth was made, although some mills combined both functions. Developments in printing machines, notably the cylinder printer, led to the specialization of the printing process, and thus to the establishment of print-works where the cloth could be finished.

1. Richard Chenevix Trench (1807–1886), theologian and poet.

along the crowded narrow streets, she felt how much of interest they
had gained by the simple fact of her having learnt to care for a dweller
in them.

Mary Higgins, the slatternly younger sister, had endeavoured as
well as she could to tidy up the house for the expected visit. There
had been rough-stoning[2] done in the middle of the floor, while the
flags under the chairs and table and round the walls retained their
dark unwashed appearance. Although the day was hot, there burnt
a large fire in the grate, making the whole place feel like an oven;
Margaret did not understand that the lavishness of coals was a sign
of hospitable welcome to her on Mary's part, and thought that perhaps the oppressive heat was necessary for Bessy. Bessy herself lay
on a squab, or short sofa, placed under the window. She was very
much more feeble than on the previous day, and tired with raising
herself at every step to look out and see if it was Margaret coming.
And now that Margaret was there, and had taken a chair by her,
Bessy lay back silent, and content to look at Margaret's face, and
touch her articles of dress, with a childish admiration of their fine-
ness of texture.

"I never knew why folk in the Bible cared for soft raiment afore.
But it must be nice to go dressed as yo' do. It's different fro' common.
Most fine folk tire my eyes out wi' their colours; but some how yours
rest me. Where did ye get this frock?"

"In London," said Margaret, much amused.

"London! Have yo' been in London?"

"Yes! I lived there for some years. But my home was in a forest; in
the country."

"Tell me about it," said Bessy. "I like to hear speak of the country,
and trees, and such like things." She leant back, and shut her eyes,
and crossed her hands over her breast, lying at perfect rest, as if to
receive all the ideas Margaret could suggest.

Margaret had never spoken of Helstone since she left it, except
just naming the place incidentally. She saw it in dreams more vivid
than life, and as she fell away to slumber at nights her memory wandered in all its pleasant places. But her heart was opened to this girl:
"Oh, Bessy, I loved the home we have left so dearly! I wish you could
see it. I cannot tell you half its beauty. There are great trees standing
all about it, with their branches stretching long and level, and making
a deep shade of rest even at noonday. And yet, though every leaf may
seem still, there is a continual rushing sound of movement all
around—not close at hand. Then sometimes the turf is as soft and
fine as velvet; and sometimes quite lush with the perpetual moisture
of a little, hidden, tinkling brook near at hand. And then in other

2. A method of cleaning the stone slabs of the floor.

parts there are billowy ferns—whole stretches of fern; some in the green shadow; some with long streaks of golden sunlight lying on them—just like the sea."

"I have never seen the sea," murmured Bessy. "But go on."

"Then, here and there, there are wide commons, high up as if above the very tops of the trees—"

"I'm glad of that. I felt smothered like down below. When I have gone for an out, I've always wanted to get high up and see far away, and take a deep breath o' fulness in that air. I get smothered enough in Milton, and I think the sound yo' speak of among the trees, going on for ever and ever, would send me dazed; it's that made my head ache so in the mill. Now on these commons I reckon there is but little noise?"

"No," said Margaret; "nothing but here and there a lark high in the air. Sometimes I used to hear a farmer speaking sharp and loud to his servants; but it was so far away that it only reminded me pleasantly that other people were hard at work in some distant place, while I just sat on the heather and did nothing."

"I used to think once that if I could have a day of doing nothing, to rest me—a day in some quiet place like that yo' speak on—it would maybe set me up. But now I've had many days o' idleness, and I'm just as weary o' them as I was o' my work. Sometimes I'm so tired out I think I cannot enjoy heaven without a piece of rest first. I'm rather afeard o' going straight there without getting a good sleep in the grave to set me up."

"Don't be afraid, Bessy," said Margaret, laying her hand on the girl's; "God can give you more perfect rest than even idleness on earth, or the dead sleep of the grave can do."

Bessy moved uneasily; then she said:

"I wish father would not speak as he does. He means well, as I telled yo' yesterday, and tell yo' again and again. But yo' see, though I don't believe him a bit by day, yet by night—when I'm in a fever, half-asleep and half-awake—it comes back upon me—oh! so bad! And I think, if this should be th' end of all, and if all I've been born for is just to work my heart and my life away, and to sicken i' this dree[3] place, wi' them mill-noises in my ears for ever, until I could scream out for them to stop, and let me have a little piece o' quiet— and wi' the fluff filling my lungs, until I thirst to death for one long deep breath o' the clear air yo' speak on—and my mother gone, and I never able to tell her again how I loved her, and o' all my troubles— I think if this life is th' end, and that there's no God to wipe away all tears from all eyes—yo' wench, yo'!" said she, sitting up, and clutching violently, almost fiercely, at Margaret's hand, "I could go

3. Sad.

mad, and kill yo', I could." She fell back completely worn out with her passion. Margaret knelt down by her.

"Bessy—we have a Father in Heaven."

"I know it! I know it," moaned she, turning her head uneasily from side to side. "I'm very wicked. I've spoken very wickedly. Oh! don't be frightened by me and never come again. I would not harm a hair of your head. And," opening her eyes, and looking earnestly at Margaret, "I believe, perhaps, more than yo' do o' what's to come. I read the book o' Revelations until I know it off by heart, and I never doubt when I'm waking, and in my senses, of all the glory I'm to come to."

"Don't let us talk of what fancies come into your head when you are feverish. I would rather hear something about what you used to do when you were well."

"I think I was well when mother died, but I have never been rightly strong sin' somewhere about that time. I began to work in a carding-room[4] soon after, and the fluff got into my lungs, and poisoned me."

"Fluff?" said Margaret, inquiringly.

"Fluff," repeated Bessy. "Little bits, as fly off fro' the cotton, when they're carding it, and fill the air till it looks all fine white dust. They say it winds round the lungs, and tightens them up. Anyhow, there's many a one as works in a carding-room, that falls into a waste, coughing and spitting blood, because they're just poisoned by the fluff."

"But can't it be helped?" asked Margaret.

"I dunno. Some folk have a great wheel at one end o' their carding-rooms to make a draught, and carry off th' dust; but that wheel costs a deal o' money—five or six hundred pound, maybe, and brings in no profit; so it's but a few of th' masters as will put 'em up; and I've heard tell o' men who did'nt like working in places where there was a wheel, because they said as how it made 'em hungry, at after they'd been long used to swallowing fluff, to go without it, and that their wage ought to be raised if they were to work in such places. So between masters and men th' wheels fall through. I know I wish there'd been a wheel in our place, though."

"Did not your father know about it?" asked Margaret.

"Yes! And he were sorry. But our factory were a good one on the whole; and a steady likely set o' people; and father was afeard of letting me go to a strange place, for though yo' would na think it now, many a one then used to call me a gradely[5] lass enough. And I did na like to be reckoned nesh[6] and soft, and Mary's schooling were

---

4. Carding was the process by which the raw cotton, which came in the form of bundles of fluff, was made into primitive thread, before spinning could begin. By this point in time it had become mechanized, but of all the processes involved in the cotton industry it remained the most injurious to health.
5. Attractive.
6. Weak.

to be kept up, mother said, and father he were always liking to buy books, and go to lectures o' one kind or another—all which took money—so I just worked on till I shall ne'er get the whirr out o' my ears, or the fluff out o' my throat i' this world. That's all."

"How old are you?" asked Margaret.

"Nineteen, come July."

"And I too am nineteen." She thought, more sorrowfully than Bessy did, of the contrast between them. She could not speak for a moment or two for the emotion she was trying to keep down.

"About Mary," said Bessy. "I wanted to ask yo' to be a friend to her. She's seventeen, but she's th' last on us. And I don't want her to go to th' mill, and yet I dunno what she's fit for."

"She could not do"—Margaret glanced unconsciously at the uncleaned corners of the room—"She could hardly undertake a servant's place, could she? We have an old faithful servant, almost a friend, who wants help, but who is very particular; and it would not be right to plague her with giving her any assistance that would really be an annoyance and an irritation."

"No, I see. I reckon yo're right. Our Mary's a good wench; but who has she had to teach her what to do about a house? No mother, and me at the mill till I were good for nothing but scolding her for doing badly what I did'nt know how to do a bit. But I wish she could ha' lived wi' yo', for all that."

"But even though she may not be exactly fitted to come and live with us as a servant—and I don't know about that—I will always try and be a friend to her for your sake, Bessy. And now I must go. I will come again as soon as I can; but if it should not be to-morrow, or the next day, or even a week or a fortnight hence, don't think I've forgotten you. I may be busy."

"I'll know yo' won't forget me again. I'll not mistrust yo' no more. But remember, in a week or a fortnight I may be dead and buried!"

"I'll come as soon as I can, Bessy," said Margaret, squeezing her hand tight. "But you'll let me know if you are worse."

"Ay, that will I," said Bessy, returning the pressure.

From that day forwards Mrs. Hale became more and more of a suffering invalid. It was now drawing near to the anniversary of Edith's marriage, and looking back upon the year's accumulated heap of troubles, Margaret wondered how they had been borne. If she could have anticipated them, how she would have shrunk away and hid herself from the coming time! And yet day by day had, of itself, and by itself, been very endurable—small, keen, bright little spots of positive enjoyment having come sparkling into the very middle of sorrows. A year ago, or when she first went to Helstone, and first became silently conscious of the querulousness in her mother's temper, she would have groaned bitterly over the idea of a long illness to be borne in a strange, desolate, noisy, busy place, with diminished comforts on every side of the home life. But with the increase of serious and just ground of complaint, a new kind of patience had sprung up in her mother's mind. She was gentle and quiet in intense bodily suffering, almost in proportion as she had been restless and depressed when there had been no real cause for grief. Mr. Hale was in exactly that stage of apprehension which, in men of his stamp, takes the shape of wilful blindness. He was more irritated than Margaret had ever known him at his daughter's expressed anxiety.

"Indeed, Margaret, you are growing fanciful! God knows I should be the first to take the alarm if your mother were really ill; we always saw when she had her headaches at Helstone, even without her telling us. She looks quite pale and white when she is ill; and now she has a bright healthy colour in her cheeks, just as she used to have when I first knew her."

"But, papa," said Margaret, with hesitation, "do you know, I think that is the flush of pain."

"Nonsense, Margaret. I tell you, you are too fanciful. You are the person not well, I think. Send for the doctor to-morrow for yourself; and then, if it will make your mind easier, he can see your mother."

"Thank you, dear papa. It will make me happier, indeed." And she went up to him to kiss him. But he pushed her away—gently enough, but still as if she had suggested unpleasant ideas, which he should be glad to get rid of as readily as he could of her presence. He walked uneasily up and down the room.

"Poor Maria!" said he, half soliloquising, "I wish one could do right without sacrificing others. I shall hate this town, and myself too, if she——Pray, Margaret, does your mother often talk to you of the old places: of Helstone, I mean?"

"No, papa," said Margaret, sadly.

"Then, you see, she can't be fretting after them, eh? It has always been a comfort to me to think that your mother was so simple and open that I knew every little grievance she had. She never would conceal anything seriously affecting her health from me: would she, eh, Margaret? I am quite sure she would not. So don't let me hear of these foolish morbid ideas. Come, give me a kiss, and run off to bed."

But she heard him pacing about (racooning,[7] as she and Edith used to call it) long after her slow and languid undressing was finished—long after she began to listen as she lay in bed.

---

7. The reference is to the raccoon's nocturnal habits. But it is a strange one, in that raccoons are not to be found in England.

Chapter XIV.

The Meeting.[1]

> "I was used
> To sleep at nights as sweetly as a child,—
> Now if the wind blew rough, it made me start,
> And think of my poor boy tossing about
> Upon the roaring seas. And then I seemed
> To feel that it was hard to take him from me
> For such a little fault."
>
> SOUTHEY.[2]

It was a comfort to Margaret about this time, to find that her mother drew more tenderly and intimately towards her than she had ever done since the days of her childhood. She took her to her heart as a confidential friend—the post Margaret had always longed to fill, and had envied Dixon for being preferred to. Margaret took pains to respond to every call made upon her for sympathy—and they were many—even when they bore relation to trifles, which she would no more have noticed or regarded herself than the elephant would perceive the little pin at his feet, which yet he lifts carefully up at the bidding of his keeper. All unconsciously Margaret drew near to a reward.

One evening, Mr. Hale being absent, her mother began to talk to her about her brother Frederick, the very subject on which Margaret had longed to ask questions, and almost the only one on which her timidity overcame her natural openness. The more she wanted to hear about him, the less likely she was to speak.

"Oh, Margaret, it was so windy last night! It came howling down the chimney in our room! I could not sleep. I never can when there is such a terrible wind. I got into a wakeful habit when poor Frederick was at sea; and now, even if I don't waken all at once, I dream of him in some stormy sea, with great, clear, glass-green walls of waves on either side his ship, but far higher than her very masts, curling over her with that cruel, terrible white foam, like some gigantic crested serpent. It is an old dream, but it always comes back on windy nights, till I am thankful to waken, sitting straight and stiff up in bed with my terror. Poor Frederick! He is on land now, so wind can do him no harm. Though I did think it might shake down some of those tall chimneys."

---

1. Editions of *North and South* since the "Knutsford" edition (1906) have adopted "The Mutiny" as the heading for this chapter, and Easson argues convincingly that the original chapter title, "The Meeting," is the result of a printer's error (*Easson 1973*, p. 440). Such a revision would be appropriate to the subject matter of the chapter, which has no reference to a meeting of any kind. However, for the sake of consistency with the first edition, I have retained the original reading.
2. From "English Eclogues" by Robert Southey (1774–1843).

"Where is Frederick now, mamma? Our letters are directed to the care of Messrs. Barbour, at Cadiz, I know; but where is he himself?"

"I can't remember the name of the place, but he is not called Hale; you must remember that, Margaret. Notice the F. D. in every corner of the letters. He has taken the name of Dickenson. I wanted him to have been called Beresford, to which he had a kind of right, but your father thought he had better not. He might be recognised, you know, if he were called by my name."

"Mamma," said Margaret, "I was at Aunt Shaw's when it all happened; and I suppose I was not old enough to be told plainly about it. But I should like to know now, if I may—if it does not give you too much pain to speak about it."

"Pain! No," replied Mrs. Hale, her cheek flushing. "Yet it is pain to think that perhaps I may never see my darling boy again. Or else he did right, Margaret. They may say what they like, but I have his own letters to show, and I'll believe him, though he is my son, sooner than any court-martial on earth. Go to my little japan cabinet, dear, and in the second left-hand drawer you will find a packet of letters."

Margaret went. There were the yellow, sea-stained letters, with the peculiar fragrance which ocean letters have. Margaret carried them back to her mother, who untied the silken string with trembling fingers, and, examining their dates, she gave them to Margaret to read, making her hurried, anxious remarks on their contents, almost before her daughter could have understood what they were.

"You see, Margaret, how from the very first he disliked Captain Reid. He was second lieutenant in the ship—the Orion—in which Frederick sailed the very first time. Poor little fellow, how well he looked in his midshipman's dress, with his dirk in his hand, cutting open all the newspapers with it as if it were a paper-knife! But this Mr. Reid, as he was then, seemed to take a dislike to Frederick from the very beginning. And then—stay! these are the letters he wrote on board the Russell. When he was appointed to her, and found his old enemy Captain Reid in command, he did mean to bear all his tyranny patiently. Look! this is the letter. Just read it, Margaret. Where is it he says—Stop—'my father may rely upon me, that I will bear with all proper patience everything that one officer and gentleman can take from another. But from my former knowledge of my present captain, I confess I look forward with apprehension to a long course of tyranny on board the Russell.' You see, he promises to bear patiently, and I am sure he did, for he was the sweetest-tempered boy, when he was not vexed, that could possibly be. Is that the letter in which he speaks of Captain Reid's impatience with the men, for not going through the ship's manœuvres as quickly as the Avenger? You see, he says that they had many new hands on board the Russell, while the Avenger had been nearly three years on the station, with nothing to do but to keep slavers off, and work her men, till they ran up and down the rigging like rats or monkeys."

Margaret slowly read the letter, half illegible through the fading of the ink. It might be—it probably was—a statement of Captain Reid's imperiousness in trifles, very much exaggerated by the narrator, who had written it while fresh and warm from the scene of altercation. Some sailors being aloft in the main-topsail rigging, the captain had ordered them to race down, threatening the hind-most with the cat-of-nine-tails. He who was the farthest on the spar, feeling the impossibility of passing his companions, and yet passionately dreading the disgrace of the flogging, threw himself desperately down to catch a rope considerably lower, failed, and fell senseless on deck. He only survived for a few hours afterwards, and the indignation of the ship's crew was at boiling point when young Hale wrote.

"But we did not receive this letter till long, long after we heard of the mutiny. Poor Fred! I dare say it was a comfort to him to write it, even though he could not have known how to send it, poor fellow! And then we saw a report in the papers—that's to say, long before Fred's letter reached us—of an atrocious mutiny having broken out on board the Russell, and that the mutineers had remained in possession of the ship, which had gone off, it was supposed, to be a pirate; and that Captain Reid was sent adrift in a boat with some men—officers or something—whose names were all given, for they were picked up by a West-Indian steamer. Oh, Margaret! how your father and I turned sick over that list, when there was no name of Frederick Hale. We thought it must be some mistake; for poor Fred was such a fine fellow, only perhaps rather too passionate; and we hoped that the name of Carr, which was in the list, was a misprint for that of Hale—newspapers are so careless. And towards post-time the next day, papa set off to walk to Southampton to get the papers; and I could not stop at home, so I went to meet him. He was very late—much later than I thought he would have been; and I sat down under the hedge to wait for him. He came at last, his arms hanging loose down, his head sunk, and walking heavily along, as if every step was a labour and a trouble. Margaret, I see him now."

"Don't go on, mamma. I can understand it all," said Margaret, leaning up caressingly against her mother's side, and kissing her hand.

"No, you can't, Margaret. No one can who did not see him then. I could hardly lift myself up to go and meet him—everything seemed so to reel around me all at once. And when I got to him, he did not speak, or seem surprised to see me there, more than three miles from home, beside the Oldham beech-tree; but he put my arm in his, and kept stroking my hand, as if he wanted to soothe me to be very quiet under some great heavy blow; and when I trembled so all over that I could not speak, he took me in his arms, and stooped down his head on mine, and began to shake and to cry in a strange muffled, groaning voice, till I, for very fright, stood quite still, and only begged him to tell me what he had heard. And then, with his hand jerking, as if some one else moved it against his will, he gave me a wicked newspaper to read, calling our Frederick a 'traitor of the blackest dye,' 'a base, ungrateful disgrace to his profession.' Oh! I cannot tell what bad words they did not use. I took the paper in my hands as soon as I had read it—tore it up to little bits—I tore it—oh! I believe Margaret, I tore it with my teeth. I did not cry. I could not. My cheeks were as hot as fire, and my very eyes burnt in my head. I saw your father looking grave at me. I said it was a lie, and so it was. Months after, this letter came, and you see what provocation Frederick had. It was not for himself, or his own injuries, he rebelled; but he would speak his mind to Captain Reid, and so it went on from bad to worse; and you see, most of the sailors stuck by Frederick.

"I think, Margaret," she continued, after a pause, in a weak, trembling, exhausted voice, "I am glad of it—I am prouder of Frederick standing up against injustice, than if he had been simply a good officer."

"I am sure I am," said Margaret, in a firm, decided tone. "Loyalty and obedience to wisdom and justice are fine; but it is still finer to defy arbitrary power, unjustly and cruelly used—not on behalf of ourselves, but on behalf of others more helpless."

"For all that, I wish I could see Frederick once more—just once. He was my first baby, Margaret." Mrs. Hale spoke wistfully, and almost as if apologising for the yearning, craving wish, as though it were a depreciation of her remaining child. But such an idea never crossed Margaret's mind. She was thinking how her mother's desire could be fulfilled.

"It is six or seven years ago—would they still prosecute him, mother? If he came and stood his trial, what would be the punishment? Surely, he might bring evidence of his great provocation."

"It would do no good," replied Mrs. Hale. "Some of the sailors who accompanied Frederick were taken, and there was a court-martial held on them on board the Amicia; I believed all they said in their defence, poor fellows, because it just agreed with Frederick's story—but it was of no use,—" and for the first time during the conversation Mrs. Hale began to cry; yet something possessed Margaret to force the information she foresaw, yet dreaded, from her mother.

"What happened to them, mamma?" asked she.

"They were hung at the yard-arm," said Mrs. Hale, solemnly. "And the worst was that the court, in condemning them to death, said they had suffered themselves to be led astray from their duty by their superior officers."

They were silent for a long time.

"And Frederick was in South America for several years, was he not?"

"Yes. And now he is in Spain. At Cadiz, or somewhere near it. If he comes to England he will be hung. I shall never see his face again—for if he comes to England he will be hung."

There was no comfort to be given. Mrs. Hale turned her face to the wall, and lay perfectly still in her mother's despair. Nothing could be said to console her. She took her hand out of Margaret's with a little impatient movement, as if she would fain be left alone with the recollection of her son. When Mr. Hale came in, Margaret went out, oppressed with gloom, and seeing no promise of brightness on any side of the horizon.

Chapter XV.

Masters and Men.

"Thought fights with thought; out springs a spark of truth
From the collision of the sword and shield."

W. S. LANDOR.[1]

"Margaret," said her father, the next day, "we must return Mrs. Thornton's call. Your mother is not very well, and thinks she cannot walk so far; but you and I will go this afternoon."

As they went, Mr. Hale began about his wife's health, with a kind of veiled anxiety, which Margaret was glad to see awakened at last.

"Did you consult the doctor, Margaret? Did you send for him?"

"No, papa, you spoke of his coming to see me. Now I was well. But if I only knew of some good doctor, I would go this afternoon, and ask him to come, for I am sure mamma is seriously indisposed."

She put the truth thus plainly and strongly because her father had so completely shut his mind against the idea, when she had last named her fears. But now the case was changed. He answered in a despondent tone:

"Do you think she has any hidden complaint? Do you think she is

1. Walter Savage Landor (1774–1864), English poet. His writings included poetry in English and Latin and essays and other prose writings on a wide variety of subjects. The lines quoted here are from *The Last Fruit off an Old Tree*, a compendium of material published in 1853, and thus contemporary with the writing of *North and South*. Correspondence between Gaskell and Landor on the subject of traditional customs survives (*Letters*, pp. 291–93).

really very ill? Has Dixon said anything? Oh, Margaret! I am haunted
by the fear that our coming to Milton has killed her. My poor Maria!"

"Oh, papa! don't imagine such things," said Margaret, shocked.
"She is not well, that is all. Many a one is not well for a time; and
with good advice gets better and stronger than ever."

"But has Dixon said anything about her?"

"No! You know Dixon enjoys making a mystery out of trifles; and
she has been a little mysterious about mamma's health, which has
alarmed me rather, that is all. Without any reason, I dare say. You
know, papa, you said the other day I was getting fanciful."

"I hope and trust you are. But don't think of what I said then. I
like you to be fanciful about your mother's health. Don't be afraid
of telling me your fancies. I like to hear them, though, I dare say, I
spoke as if I was annoyed. But we will ask Mrs. Thornton if she can
tell us of a good doctor. We won't throw away our money on any but
some one first-rate. Stay, we turn up this street."

The street did not look as if it could contain any house large
enough for Mrs. Thornton's habitation. Her son's presence never
gave any impression as to the kind of house he lived in; but, unconsciously, Margaret had imagined that tall, massive, handsomely
dressed Mrs. Thornton must live in a house of the same character
as herself. Now Marlborough Street consisted of long rows of small
houses, with a blank wall here and there; at least that was all they
could see from the point at which they entered it.

"He told me he lived in Marlborough Street, I'm sure," said Mr.
Hale, with a much perplexed air.

"Perhaps it is one of the economies he still practises, to live in a
very small house. But here are plenty of people about; let me ask."

She accordingly inquired of a passer-by, and was informed that
Mr. Thornton lived close to the mill, and had the factory lodge-door
pointed out to her, at the end of the long dead wall they had noticed.

The lodge-door was like a common garden-door; on one side of it
were great closed gates for the ingress and egress of lurries and wag-
ons. The lodge-keeper admitted them into a great oblong yard, on
one side of which were offices for the transaction of business; on
the opposite, an immense many-windowed mill, whence proceeded
the continual clank of machinery and the long groaning roar of the
steam-engine, enough to deafen those who lived within the enclosure. Opposite to the wall, along which the street ran, on one of the
narrow sides of the oblong, was a handsome stone-coped house,—
blackened, to be sure, by the smoke, but with paint, windows, and
steps kept scrupulously clean. It was evidently a house which had
been built some fifty or sixty years. The stone facings—the long,
narrow windows, and the number of them—the flights of steps up
to the front door, ascending from either side, and guarded by rail-

ing—all witnessed to its age. Margaret only wondered why people who could afford to live in so good a house, and keep it in such perfect order, did not prefer a much smaller dwelling in the country, or even some suburb;[2] not in the continual whirl and din of the factory. Her unaccustomed ears could hardly catch her father's voice, as they stood on the steps awaiting the opening of the door. The yard, too, with the great doors in the dead wall as a boundary, was but a dismal look-out for the sitting-rooms of the house—as Margaret found when they had mounted the old-fashioned stairs, and been ushered into the drawing-room, the three windows of which went over the front door and the room on the right-hand side of the entrance. There was no one in the drawing-room. It seemed as though no one had been in it since the day when the furniture was bagged up with as much care as if the house was to be overwhelmed with lava, and discovered a thousand years hence. The walls were pink and gold; the pattern on the carpet represented bunches of flowers on a light ground, but it was carefully covered up in the centre by a linen drugget, glazed and colourless. The window-curtains were lace; each chair and sofa had its own particular veil of netting, or knitting. Great alabaster groups occupied every flat surface, safe from dust under their glass shades. In the middle of the room, right under the bagged-up chandelier, was a large circular table, with smartly-bound books arranged at regular intervals round the circumference of its polished surface, like gaily-coloured spokes of a wheel. Everything reflected light, nothing absorbed it. The whole room had a painfully spotted, spangled, speckled look about it, which impressed Margaret so unpleasantly that she was hardly conscious of the peculiar cleanliness required to keep everything so white and pure in such an atmosphere, or of the trouble that must be willingly expended to secure that effect of icy, snowy discomfort. Wherever she looked there was evidence of care and labour, but not care and labour to procure ease, to help on habits of tranquil home employment; solely to ornament, and then to preserve ornament from dirt or destruction.

They had leisure to observe, and to speak to each other in low voices, before Mrs. Thornton appeared. They were talking of what all the world might hear; but it is a common effect of such a room as this to make people speak low, as if unwilling to awaken the unused echoes.

At last Mrs. Thornton came in, rustling in handsome black silk, as was her wont; her muslins and laces rivalling, not excelling, the

---

2. In the 1850s, with the expansion of the railway system, Manchester businessmen were increasingly moving out to the suburbs for their domestic residences: Thornton's decision to live at the same site as his workplace is thus an indication of his identification with his business.

pure whiteness of the muslins and netting of the room. Margaret explained how it was that her mother could not accompany them to return Mrs. Thornton's call; but in her anxiety not to bring back her father's fears too vividly, she gave but a bungling account, and left the impression on Mrs. Thornton's mind that Mrs. Hale's was some temporary or fanciful fine-ladyish indisposition, which might have been put aside had there been a strong enough motive; or that if it was too severe to allow her to come out that day, the call might have been deferred. Remembering, too, the horses to her carriage, hired for her own visit to the Hales, and how Fanny had been ordered to go by Mr. Thornton, in order to pay every respect to them, Mrs. Thornton drew up slightly offended, and gave Margaret no sympathy—indeed, hardly any credit for the statement of her mother's indisposition.

"How is Mr. Thornton?" asked Mr. Hale. "I was afraid he was not well, from his hurried note yesterday."

"My son is rarely ill; and when he is, he never speaks about it, or makes it an excuse for not doing anything. He told me he could not get leisure to read with you last night, sir. He regretted it, I am sure; he values the hours spent with you."

"I am sure they are equally agreeable to me." said Mr. Hale. "It makes me feel young again to see his enjoyment and appreciation of all that is fine in classical literature."

"I have no doubt the classics are very desirable for people who have leisure. But, I confess, it was against my judgment that my son renewed his study of them. The time and place in which he lives, seem to me to require all his energy and attention. Classics may do very well for men who loiter away their lives in the country or in colleges; but Milton men ought to have their thoughts and powers absorbed in the work of to-day. At least, that is my opinion." This last clause she gave out with "the pride that apes humility."[3]

"But, surely, if the mind is too long directed to one object only, it will get stiff and rigid, and unable to take in many interests," said Margaret.

"I do not quite understand what you mean by a mind getting stiff and rigid. Nor do I admire those whirligig characters that are full of this thing to-day, to be utterly forgetful of it in their new interest to-morrow. Having many interests does not suit the life of a Milton manufacturer. It is, or ought to be, enough for him to have one great desire, and to bring all the purposes of his life to bear on the fulfilment of that."

"And that is—?" asked Mr. Hale.

Her sallow cheek flushed, and her eye lightened, as she answered: "To hold and maintain a high, honourable place among the mer-

<hr/>

3. "And the devil did grin, for his darling sin / Is the pride which apes humility." From "The Devil's Thoughts" (1799) by S. T. Coleridge and Robert Southey.

chants of his country—the men of his town. Such a place my son has earned for himself. Go where you will—I don't say in England only, but in Europe—the name of John Thornton of Milton is known and respected amongst all men of business. Of course, it is unknown in the fashionable circles," she continued, scornfully. "Idle gentlemen and ladies are not likely to know much of a Milton manufacturer, unless he gets into parliament, or marries a lord's daughter."

Both Mr. Hale and Margaret had an uneasy, ludicrous consciousness that they had never heard of this great name, until Mr. Bell had written them word that Mr. Thornton would be a good friend to have in Milton. The proud mother's world was not their world of Harley Street gentilities on the one hand, or country clergymen and Hampshire squires on the other. Margaret's face, in spite of all her endeavours to keep it simply listening in its expression, told the sensitive Mrs. Thornton this feeling of hers.

"You think you never heard of this wonderful son of mine, Miss Hale. You think I'm an old woman whose ideas are bounded by Milton, and whose own crow is the whitest ever seen."

"No," said Margaret, with some spirit. "It may be true, that I was thinking I had hardly heard Mr. Thornton's name before I came to Milton. But since I have come here, I have heard enough to make me respect and admire him, and to feel how much justice, and truth there is in what you have said of him."

"Who spoke to you of him?" asked Mrs. Thornton, a little mollified, yet jealous lest any one else's words should not have done him full justice.

Margaret hesitated before she replied. She did not like this authoritative questioning. Mr. Hale came in, as he thought, to the rescue.

"It was what Mr. Thornton said himself, that made us know the kind of man he was. Was it not, Margaret?"

Mrs. Thornton drew herself up, and said—

"My son is not the one to tell of his own doings. May I again ask you, Miss Hale, from whose account you formed your favourable opinion of him? A mother is curious and greedy of commendation of her children, you know."

Margaret replied, "It was as much from what Mr. Thornton withheld of that which we had been told of his previous life by Mr. Bell—it was more that than what he said, that made us all feel what reason you have to be proud of him."

"Mr. Bell! What can he know of John? He, living a lazy life in a drowsy college. But I'm obliged to you, Miss Hale. Many a missy[4] young lady would have shrunk from giving an old woman the pleasure of hearing that her son was well spoken of."

4. Affected.

"Why?" asked Margaret, looking straight at Mrs. Thornton, in bewilderment.

"Why! because I suppose they might have consciences that told them how surely they were making the old mother into an advocate for them, in case they had any plans on the son's heart."

She smiled a grim smile, for she had been pleased by Margaret's frankness; and perhaps she felt that she had been asking questions too much as if she had a right to catechise. Margaret laughed outright at the notion presented to her; laughed so merrily that it grated on Mrs. Thornton's ear, as if the words that called forth that laugh, must have been utterly and entirely ludicrous.

Margaret stopped her merriment as soon as she saw Mrs. Thornton's annoyed look.

"I beg your pardon, madam. But I really am very much obliged to you for exonerating me from making any plans on Mr. Thornton's heart."

"Young ladies have, before now," said Mrs. Thornton, stiffly.

"I hope Miss Thornton is well," put in Mr. Hale, desirous of changing the current of the conversation.

"She is as well as she ever is. She is not strong," replied Mrs. Thornton, shortly.

"And Mr. Thornton? I suppose I may hope to see him on Thursday?"

"I cannot answer for my son's engagements. There is some uncomfortable work going on in the town; a threatening of a strike. If so, his experience and judgment will make him much consulted by his friends. But I should think he could come on Thursday. At any rate, I am sure he will let you know if he cannot."

"A strike!" asked Margaret. "What for? What are they going to strike for?"

"For the mastership and ownership of other people's property," said Mrs. Thornton, with a fierce snort. "That is what they always strike for. If my son's work-people strike, I will only say they are a pack of ungrateful hounds. But I have no doubt they will."

"They are wanting higher wages, I suppose?" asked Mr. Hale.

"That is the face of the thing. But the truth is, they want to be masters, and make the masters into slaves on their own ground. They are always trying at it; they always have it in their minds; and every five or six years, there comes a struggle between masters and men. They'll find themselves mistaken this time, I fancy—a little out of their reckoning. If they turn out, they mayn't find it so easy to go in again. I believe, the masters have a thing or two in their heads which will teach the men not to strike again in a hurry, if they try it this time."

"Does it not make the town very rough?" asked Margaret.

"Of course it does. But surely you are not coward, are you? Milton is not the place for cowards. I have known the time when I have had to thread my way through a crowd of white, angry men, all swearing they would have Makinson's blood as soon as he ventured to show his nose out of his factory; and he, knowing nothing of it, some one had to go and tell him, or he was a dead man; and it needed to be a woman—so I went. And when I had got in, I could not get out. It was as much as my life was worth. So I went up to the roof, where there were stones piled ready to drop on the heads of the crowd, if they tried to force the factory doors. And I would have lifted those heavy stones, and dropped them with as good an aim as the best man there, but that I fainted with the heat I had gone through. If you live in Milton, you must learn to have a brave heart, Miss Hale."

"I would do my best," said Margaret rather pale. "I do not know whether I am brave or not till I am tried; but I am afraid I should be a coward."

"South country people are often frightened by what our Darkshire men and women only call living and struggling. But when you've been ten years among a people who are always owing their betters a grudge, and only waiting for an opportunity to pay it off, you'll know whether you are a coward or not, take my word for it."

Mr. Thornton came that evening to Mr. Hale's. He was shown up into the drawing-room, where Mr. Hale was reading aloud to his wife and daughter.

"I am come partly to bring you a note from my mother, and partly to apologise for not keeping to my time yesterday. The note contains the address you asked for; Dr. Donaldson."

"Thank you!" said Margaret, hastily, holding out her hand to take the note, for she did not wish her mother to hear that they had been making any inquiry about a doctor. She was pleased that Mr. Thornton seemed immediately to understand her feeling; he gave her the note without another word of explanation.

Mr. Hale began to talk about the strike. Mr. Thornton's face assumed a likeness to his mother's worst expression, which immediately repelled the watching Margaret.

"Yes; the fools will have a strike. Let them. It suits us well enough. But we gave them a chance. They think trade is flourishing as it was last year. We see the storm on the horizon and draw in our sails. But because we don't explain our reasons, they won't believe we're acting reasonably. We must give them line and letter for the way we choose to spend or save our money. Henderson tried a dodge with his men, out at Ashley, and failed. He rather wanted a strike; it would have suited his book well enough. So when the men came to ask for the five per cent. they are claiming, he told 'em he'd think about it, and give them his answer on the pay day; knowing all the while what his answer would be, of course, but thinking he'd strengthen their conceit of their own way. However, they were too deep for him, and heard something about the bad prospects of trade. So in they came on the Friday, and drew back their claim, and now he's obliged to go on working. But we Milton masters have to-day sent in our decision. We won't advance a penny. We tell them we may have to lower wages; but can't afford to raise. So here we stand, waiting for their next attack."

"And what will that be?" asked Mr. Hale.

"I conjecture, a simultaneous strike. You will see Milton without smoke in a few days, I imagine, Miss Hale."

"But why," asked she, "could you not explain what good reason you have for expecting a bad trade? I don't know whether I use the right words, but you will understand what I mean."

"Do you give your servants reasons for your expenditure, or your economy in the use of your own money? We, the owners of capital, have a right to choose what we will do with it."

"A human right," said Margaret, very low.

"I beg your pardon, I did not hear what you said."

"I would rather not repeat it," said she; "it related to a feeling which I do not think you would share."

"Won't you try me?" pleaded he; his thoughts suddenly bent upon learning what she had said. She was displeased with his pertinacity, but did not choose to affix too much importance to her words.

"I said you had a human right. I meant that there seemed no reason but religious ones, why you should not do what you like with your own."

"I know we differ in our religious opinions; but don't you give me credit for having some, though not the same as yours?"

He was speaking in a subdued voice, as if to her alone. She did not wish to be so exclusively addressed. She replied out in her usual tone:

"I do not think that I have any occasion to consider your special religious opinions in the affair. All I meant to say is, that there is no human law to prevent the employers from utterly wasting or throwing away all their money, if they choose; but that there are passages in the Bible which would rather imply—to me at least—that they neglected their duty as stewards if they did so.[5] However, I know so little about strikes, and rate of wages, and capital, and labour, that I had better not talk to a political economist like you."

"Nay, the more reason," said he eagerly. "I shall only be too glad to explain to you all that may seem anomalous or mysterious to a

---

5. The reference is presumably to the parable of the talents (Matthew 25:14–30).

stranger; especially at a time like this, when our doings are sure to be canvassed by every scribbler who can hold a pen."

"Thank you," she answered, coldly. "Of course, I shall apply to my father in the first instance for any information he can give me, if I get puzzled with living here amongst this strange society."

"You think it strange. Why?"

"I don't know—I suppose because, on the very face of it, I see two classes dependent on each other in every possible way, yet each evidently regarding the interests of the other as opposed to their own; I never lived in a place before where there were two sets of people always running each other down."

"Who have you heard running the masters down? I don't ask who you have heard abusing the men; for I see you persist in misunderstanding what I said the other day. But who have you heard abusing the masters?"

Margaret reddened; then smiled as she said,

"I am not fond of being catechised. I refuse to answer your question. Besides, it has nothing to do with the fact. You must take my word for it, that I have heard some people, or, it may be, only some one of the workpeople speak as though it were the interest of the employers to keep them from acquiring money—that it would make them too independent if they had a sum in the savings' bank."

"I dare say it was that man Higgins who told you all this," said Mrs. Hale. Mr. Thornton did not appear to hear what Margaret evidently did not wish him to know. But he caught it, nevertheless.

"I heard, moreover, that it was considered to the advantage of the masters to have ignorant workmen—not hedge-lawyers,[6] as Captain Lennox used to call those men in his company who questioned and would know the reason for every order."

This latter part of her sentence she addressed rather to her father than to Mr. Thornton. Who is Captain Lennox? asked Mr. Thornton of himself, with a strange kind of displeasure, that prevented him for the moment from replying to her! Her father took up the conversation.

"You never were fond of schools, Margaret, or you would have seen and known before this, how much is being done for education in Milton."

"No!" said she, with sudden meekness. "I know I do not care enough about schools. But the knowledge and the ignorance of which I was speaking, did not relate to reading and writing,—the teaching or information one can give to a child. I am sure, that what was meant was ignorance of the wisdom that shall guide men and

6. Workmen who argue on points of detail as if in a court of law. The modern term is "barrack-room lawyers."

women. I hardly know what that is. But he—that is my informant—spoke as if the masters would like their hands to be merely tall, large children—living in the present moment—with a blind unreasoning kind of obedience."

"In short, Miss Hale, it is very evident that your informant found a pretty ready listener to all the slander he chose to utter against the masters," said Mr. Thornton, in an offended tone.

Margaret did not reply. She was displeased at the personal character Mr. Thornton affixed to what she had said.

Mr. Hale spoke next:

"I must confess that, although I have not become so intimately acquainted with any workmen as Margaret has, I am very much struck by the antagonism between the employer and the employed, on the very surface of things. I even gather this impression from what you yourself have from time to time said."

Mr. Thornton paused awhile before he spoke. Margaret had just left the room, and he was vexed at the state of feeling between himself and her. However, the little annoyance, by making him cooler and more thoughtful, gave a greater dignity to what he said:

"My theory is, that my interests are identical with those of my workpeople, and vice-versâ. Miss Hale, I know, does not like to hear men called 'hands,' so I won't use that word, though it comes most readily to my lips as the technical term, whose origin, whatever it was, dates before my time. On some future day—in some millenium—in Utopia, this unity may be brought into practice—just as I can fancy a republic the most perfect form of government."

"We will read Plato's Republic as soon as we have finished Homer."

"Well, in the Platonic year,[7] it may fall out that we are all—men,women, and children—fit for a republic: but give me a constitutional monarchy in our present state of morals and intelligence. In our infancy we require a wise despotism to govern us. Indeed, long past infancy, children and young people are the happiest under the unfailing laws of a discreet, firm authority. I agree with Miss Hale so far as to consider our people in the condition of children, while I deny that we, the masters, have anything to do with the making or keeping them so. I maintain that despotism is the best kind of government for them; so that in the hours in which I come in contact with them I must necessarily be an autocrat. I will use my best discretion—from no humbug or philanthropic feeling, of which we have had rather too much in the North—to make wise laws and come to just decisions in the conduct of my business—laws and decisions

---

7. Forms of government are a subject of Plato's *Republic*; the Platonic year is an ideal time in the distant future when all of the heavenly bodies will return harmoniously to their original position.

which work for my own good in the first instance—for theirs in the second; but I will neither be forced to give my reasons, nor flinch from what I have once declared to be my resolution. Let them turn out! I shall suffer as well as they: but at the end they will find I have not bated nor altered one jot."

Margaret had re-entered the room and was sitting at her work; but she did not speak. Mr. Hale answered—

"I dare say I am talking in great ignorance; but from the little I know, I should say that the masses were already passing rapidly into the troublesome stage which intervenes between childhood and manhood, in the life of the multitude as well as that of the individual. Now, the error which many parents commit in the treatment of the individual at this time is, insisting on the same unreasoning obedience as when all he had to do in the way of duty was, to obey the simple laws of 'Come when you're called,' and 'Do as you're bid!' But a wise parent humours the desire for independent action, so as to become the friend and adviser when his absolute rule shall cease. If I get wrong in my reasoning, recollect, it is you who adopted the analogy."

"Very lately," said Margaret, "I heard a story of what happened in Nuremberg only three or four years ago. A rich man there lived alone in one of the immense mansions which were formerly both dwellings and warehouses. It was reported that he had a child, but no one knew of it for certain. For forty years this rumour kept rising and falling— never utterly dying away. After his death it was found to be true. He had a son—an overgrown man, with the unexercised intellect of a child, whom he had kept up in that strange way, in order to save him from temptation and error. But, of course, when this great old child was turned loose into the world, every bad counsellor had power over him. He did not know good from evil. His father had made the blunder of bringing him up in ignorance and taking it for innocence; and after fourteen months of riotous living, the city authorities had to take charge of him, in order to save him from starvation. He could not even use words effectively enough to be a successful beggar."

"I used the comparison (suggested by Miss Hale) of the position of the master to that of a parent; so I ought not to complain of your turning the simile into a weapon against me. But, Mr. Hale, when you were setting up a wise parent as a model for us, you said he humoured his children in their desire for independent action. Now certainly, the time is not come for the hands to have any independent action during business hours; I hardly know what you would mean by it then. And I say, that the masters would be trenching on the independence of their hands, in a way that I, for one, should not feel justified in doing, if we interfered too much with the life they lead out of the mills. Because they labour ten hours a-day for us, I do not see that we have any right to impose leading-strings upon them for the rest of their time. I value my own independence so highly that I can fancy no degradation greater than that of having another man perpetually directing and advising and lecturing me, or even planning too closely in any way about my actions. He might be the wisest of men or the most powerful—I should equally rebel and resent his interference. I imagine this is a stronger feeling in the North of England than in the South."

"I beg your pardon, but is not that because there has been none of the equality of friendship between the adviser and advised classes? Because every man has had to stand in an unchristian and isolated position, apart from and jealous of his brother-man: constantly afraid of his rights being trenched upon?"

"I only state the fact. I am sorry to say, I have an appointment at eight o'clock, and I must just take facts as I find them to-night, without trying to account for them; which, indeed, would make no difference in determining how to act as things stand—the facts must be granted."

"But," said Margaret in a low voice, "it seems to me that it makes all the difference in the world—." Her father made a sign to her to be silent, and allow Mr. Thornton to finish what he had to say. He was already standing up and preparing to go.

"You must grant me this one point. Given a strong feeling of independence in every Darkshire man, have I any right to obtrude my views, of the manner in which he shall act, upon another (hating it as I should do most vehemently myself), merely because he has labour to sell and I capital to buy?"

"Not in the least," said Margaret, determined just to say this one thing; "not in the least because of your labour and capital positions, whatever they are, but because you are a man, dealing with a set of men over whom you have, whether you reject the use of it or not, immense power, just because your lives and your welfare are so constantly and intimately interwoven. God has made us so that we must be mutually dependent. We may ignore our own dependence, or refuse to acknowledge that others depend upon us in more respects than the payment of weekly wages; but the thing must be, nevertheless. Neither you nor any other master can help yourselves. The most proudly independent man depends on those around him for their insensible influence on his character—his life. And the most isolated of all your Darkshire Egos has dependants clinging to him on all sides; he cannot shake them off, any more than the great rock he resembles can shake off—"

"Pray don't go into similes, Margaret; you have led us off once already," said her father, smiling, yet uneasy at the thought that they were detaining Mr. Thornton against his will, which was a mistake;

for he rather liked it, as long as Margaret would talk, although what she said only irritated him.

"Just tell me, Miss Hale, are you yourself ever influenced—no, that is not a fair way of putting it;—but if you are ever conscious of being influenced by others, and not by circumstances, have those others been working directly or indirectly? Have they been labouring to exhort, to enjoin, to act rightly for the sake of example, or have they been simple, true men, taking up their duty, and doing it unflinchingly, without a thought of how their actions were to make this man industrious, that man saving? Why, if I were a workman, I should be twenty times more impressed by the knowledge that my master was honest, punctual, quick, resolute in all his doings (and hands are keener spies even than valets),[8] than by any amount of interference, however kindly meant, with my ways of going on out of work-hours. I do not choose to think too closely on what I am myself; but, I believe, I rely on the straightforward honesty of my hands, and the open nature of their opposition, in contra-distinction to the way in which the turn-out will be managed in some mills, just because they know I scorn to take a single dishonourable advantage, or do an underhand thing myself. It goes farther than a whole course of lectures on 'Honesty is the Best Policy'—life diluted into words. No, no! What the master is, that will the men be, without over-much taking thought on his part."

"That is a great admission," said Margaret, laughing. "When I see men violent and obstinate in pursuit of their rights, I may safely infer that the master is the same; that he is a little ignorant of that spirit which suffereth long, and is kind, and seeketh not her own."

"You are just like all strangers who don't understand the working of our system, Miss Hale," said he, hastily. "You suppose that our men are puppets of dough, ready to be moulded into any amiable form we please. You forget we have only to do with them for less than a third of their lives; and you seem not to perceive that the duties of a manufacturer are far larger and wider than those merely of an employer of labour: we have a wide commercial character to maintain, which makes us into the great pioneers of civilisation."

"It strikes me," said Mr. Hale, smiling, "that you might pioneer a little at home. They are a rough, heathenish set of fellows, these Milton men of yours."

"They are that," replied Mr. Thornton. "Rosewater surgery won't do for them. Cromwell would have made a capital mill-owner, Miss Hale.[9] I wish we had him to put down this strike for us."

8. Valets were traditionally thought to be ideally placed to act as spies.
9. Oliver Cromwell (1599–1658), who during the period of the Commonwealth (1649–60) was ruthless in his suppression of rebellion in Ireland. In the nineteenth century, his name was synonymous with rigorous authority.

"Cromwell is no hero of mine," said she, coldly. "But I am trying to reconcile your admiration of despotism with your respect for other men's independence of character."

He reddened at her tone. "I choose to be the unquestioned and irresponsible master of my hands, during the hours that they labour for me. But those hours past, our relation ceases; and then comes in the same respect for their independence that I myself exact."

He did not speak again for a minute, he was too much vexed. But he shook it off, and bade Mr. and Mrs. Hale good night. Then, drawing near to Margaret, he said in a lower voice—

"I spoke hastily to you once this evening, and I am afraid, rather rudely. But you know I am but an uncouth Milton manufacturer; will you forgive me?"

"Certainly," said she, smiling up in his face, the expression of which was somewhat anxious and oppressed, and hardly cleared away as he met her sweet sunny countenance, out of which all the north-wind effect of their discussion had entirely vanished. But she did not put out her hand to him, and again he felt the omission, and set it down to pride.

Chapter XVI.

The Shadow of Death.

"Trust in that veilëd hand, which leads
None by the path that he would go;
And always be for change prepared,
For the world's law is ebb and flow."
                                        FROM THE ARABIC.

The next afternoon Dr. Donaldson came to pay his first visit to Mrs. Hale. The mystery that Margaret hoped their late habits of intimacy had broken through, was resumed. She was excluded from the room, while Dixon was admitted. Margaret was not a ready lover, but where she loved she loved passionately, and with no small degree of jealousy.

She went into her mother's bed-room, just behind the drawing-room, and paced it up and down, while awaiting the doctor's coming out. Every now and then she stopped to listen; she fancied she heard a moan. She clenched her hands tight, and held her breath. She was sure she heard a moan. Then all was still for a few minutes more; and then there was the moving of chairs, the raised voices, all the little disturbances of leave-taking.

When she heard the door open, she went quickly out of the bed-room.

"My father is from home, Dr. Donaldson; he has to attend a pupil at this hour. May I trouble you to come into his room down stairs?"

She saw, and triumphed over all the obstacles which Dixon threw in her way; assuming her rightful position as daughter of the house in something of the spirit of the Elder Brother,[1] which quelled the old servant's officiousness very effectually. Margaret's conscious assumption of this unusual dignity of demeanour towards Dixon, gave her an instant's amusement in the midst of her anxiety. She knew, from the surprised expression on Dixon's face, how ridiculously grand she herself must be looking; and the idea carried her down stairs into the room; it gave her that length of oblivion from the keen sharpness of the recollection of the actual business in hand. Now, that came back, and seemed to take away her breath. It was a moment or two before she could utter a word.

But she spoke with an air of command, as she asked:—

"What is the matter with mamma? You will oblige me by telling the simple truth." Then, seeing a slight hesitation on the doctor's part, she added—

"I am the only child she has—here, I mean. My father is not sufficiently alarmed, I fear; and, therefore, if there is any serious apprehension, it must be broken to him gently. I can do this. I can nurse my mother. Pray, speak, sir; to see your face, and not be able to read it, gives me a worse dread than I trust any words of yours will justify."

"My dear young lady, your mother seems to have a most attentive and efficient servant, who is more like her friend—"

"I am her daughter, sir."

"But when I tell you she expressly desired that you might not be told—"

"I am not good or patient enough to submit to the prohibition. Besides, I am sure, you are too wise—too experienced to have promised to keep the secret."

"Well," said he, half-smiling, though sadly enough, "there you are right. I did not promise. In fact, I fear, the secret will be known soon enough without my revealing it."

He paused. Margaret went very white, and compressed her lips a little more. Otherwise not a feature moved. With the quick insight into character, without which no medical man can rise to the eminence of Dr. Donaldson, he saw that she would exact the full truth; that she would know if one iota was withheld; and that the with-

---

1. Presumably the reference is to the parable of the prodigal son (Luke 15), although the connection is not easy to make. Perhaps it refers to the elder brother's sense of offended dignity.

holding would be torture more acute than the knowledge of it. He spoke two short sentences in a low voice, watching her all the time; for the pupils of her eyes dilated into a black horror, and the whiteness of her complexion became livid. He ceased speaking. He waited for that look to go off,—for her gasping breath to come. Then she said:—

"I thank you most truly, sir, for your confidence. That dread has haunted me for many weeks. It is a true, real agony. My poor, poor mother!" her lips began to quiver, and he let her have the relief of tears, sure of her power of self-control to check them.

A few tears—those were all she shed, before she recollected the many questions she longed to ask.

"Will there be much suffering?"

He shook his head. "That we cannot tell. It depends on constitution; on a thousand things. But the late discoveries of medical science have given us large power of alleviation."

"My father!" said Margaret, trembling all over.

"I do not know Mr. Hale. I mean, it is difficult to give advice. But I should say, bear on, with the knowledge you have forced me to give you so abruptly, till the fact which I could not withhold has become in some degree familiar to you, so that you may, without too great an effort, be able to give what comfort you can to your father. Before then,—my visits, which, of course, I shall repeat from time to time, although I fear I can do nothing but alleviate,—a thousand little circumstances will have occurred to awaken his alarm, to deepen it— so that he will be all the better prepared.—Nay, my dear young lady—nay, my dear—I saw Mr. Thornton, and I honour your father for the sacrifice he has made, however mistaken I may believe him to be.—Well, this once, if it will please you, my dear. Only remember, when I come again, I come as a friend. And you must learn to look upon me as such, because seeing each other—getting to know each other at such times as these, is worth years of morning calls."

Margaret could not speak for crying; but she wrung his hand at parting.

"That's what I call a fine girl!" thought Dr. Donaldson, when he was seated in his carriage, and had time to examine his ringed hand, which had slightly suffered from her pressure. "Who would have thought that little hand could have given such a squeeze? But the bones were well put together, and that gives immense power. What a queen she is! With her head thrown back at first, to force me into speaking the truth; and then bent so eagerly forward to listen. Poor thing! I must see she does not overstrain herself. Though it's astonishing how much those thorough-bred creatures can do and suffer. That girl's game to the back-bone. Another, who had gone that deadly colour, could never have come round without either fainting or hysterics. But she wouldn't do either—not she! And the very force of her will brought her round. Such a girl as that would win my heart, if I were thirty years younger. It's too late now. Ah! here we are at the Archers." So out he jumped, with thought, wisdom, experience, sympathy, and ready to attend to the calls made upon them by this family, just as if there were none other in the world.

Meanwhile, Margaret had returned into her father's study for a moment, to recover strength before going upstairs into her mother's presence.

"Oh, my God, my God! but this is terrible. How shall I bear it? Such a deadly disease! no hope! Oh, mamma, mamma, I wish I had never gone to aunt Shaw's, and been all those precious years away from you! Poor mamma! how much she must have borne! Oh, I pray thee, my God, that her sufferings may not be too acute, too dreadful. How shall I bear to see them? How can I bear papa's agony? He must not be told yet; not all at once. It would kill him. But I won't lose another moment of my own dear, precious mother."

She ran upstairs. Dixon was not in the room. Mrs. Hale lay back in an easy chair, with a soft white shawl wrapped around her, and a becoming cap put on, in expectation of the doctor's visit. Her face had a little faint colour in it, and the very exhaustion after the examination gave it a peaceful look. Margaret was surprised to see her look so calm.

"Why, Margaret, how strange you look! What is the matter?" And then, as the idea stole into her mind of what was indeed the real state of the case, she added, as if a little displeased: "you have not been seeing Dr. Donaldson, and asking him any questions—have you child?" Margaret did not reply—only looked wistfully towards her. Mrs. Hale became more displeased. "He would not, surely, break his word to me, and"—

"Oh yes, mamma, he did. I made him. It was I—blame me." She knelt down by her mother's side, and caught her hand—she would not let it go, though Mrs. Hale tried to pull it away. She kept kissing it, and the hot tears she shed bathed it.

"Margaret, it was very wrong of you. You knew I did not wish you to know." But, as if tired with the contest, she left her hand in Margaret's clasp, and by-and-by she returned the pressure faintly. That encouraged Margaret to speak.

"Oh, mamma! let me be your nurse. I will learn anything Dixon can teach me. But you know I am your child, and I do think I have a right to do everything for you."

"You don't know what you are asking," said Mrs. Hale, with a shudder.

"Yes, I do. I know a great deal more than you are aware of. Let me be your nurse. Let me try, at any rate. No one has ever, shall ever try so hard as I will do. It will be such a comfort, mamma."

"My poor child! Well, you shall try. Do you know, Margaret, Dixon and I thought you would quite shrink from me if you knew—"

"Dixon thought!" said Margaret, her lip curling. "Dixon could not give me credit for enough true love—for as much as herself! She thought, I suppose, that I was one of those poor sickly women who like to lie on rose leaves, and be fanned all day. Don't let Dixon's fancies come any more between you and me, mamma. Don't, please!" implored she.

"Don't be angry with Dixon," said Mrs. Hale, anxiously. Margaret recovered herself.

"No! I won't. I will try and be humble, and learn her ways, if you will only let me do all I can for you. Let me be in the first place, mother—I am greedy of that. I used to fancy you would forget me while I was away at aunt Shaw's, and cry myself to sleep at nights with that notion in my head."

"And I used to think, how will Margaret bear our makeshift poverty after the thorough comfort and luxury in Harley Street, till I have many a time been more ashamed of your seeing our contrivances at Helstone than of any stranger finding them out."

"Oh, mamma! and I did so enjoy them. They were so much more amusing than all the jog-trot Harley Street ways. The wardrobe shelf with handles, that served as a supper-tray on grand occasions! And the old tea-chests stuffed and covered for ottomans! I think what you call the makeshift contrivances at dear Helstone were a charming part of the life there."

"I shall never see Helstone again, Margaret," said Mrs. Hale, the tears welling up into her eyes. Margaret could not reply. Mrs. Hale went on. "While I was there, I was for ever wanting to leave it. Every place seemed pleasanter. And now I shall die far away from it. I am rightly punished."

"You must not talk so," said Margaret impatiently. "He said you might live for years. Oh, mother! we will have you back at Helstone yet."

"No, never! That I must take as a just penance. But, Margaret—Frederick!"

At the mention of that one word, she suddenly cried out loud, as in some sharp agony. It seemed as if the thought of him upset all her composure, destroyed the calm, overcame the exhaustion. Wild passionate cry succeeded to cry—"Frederick! Frederick! Come to me. I am dying. Little first-born child, come to me once again!"

She was in violent hysterics. Margaret went and called Dixon in terror. Dixon came in a huff, and accused Margaret of having over-excited her mother. Margaret bore all meekly, only trusting that her father might not return. In spite of her alarm, which was even greater than the occasion warranted, she obeyed all Dixon's directions promptly and well, without a word of self-justification. By so doing she mollified her accuser. They put her mother to bed, and Margaret sat by her till she fell asleep, and afterwards till Dixon beckoned her out of the room, and, with a sour face, as if doing something against the grain, she bade her drink a cup of coffee which she had prepared for her in the drawing-room, and stood over her in a commanding attitude as she did so.

"You shouldn't have been so curious, Miss, and then you wouldn't have needed to fret before your time. It would have come soon enough. And now, I suppose, you'll tell master, and a pretty household I shall have of you!"

"No, Dixon," said Margaret, sorrowfully, "I will not tell papa. He could not bear it as I can." And by way of proving how well she bore it, she burst into tears.

"Ay! I knew how it would be. Now you'll waken your mamma, just after she's gone to sleep so quietly. Miss Margaret my dear, I've had to keep it down this many a week; and though I don't pretend I can love her as you do, yet I loved her better than any other man, woman, or child—no one but Master Frederick ever came near her in my mind. Ever since Lady Beresford's maid first took me in to see her dressed out in white crape, and corn-ears,[2] and scarlet poppies, and I ran a needle down into my finger, and broke it in, and she tore up her worked pocket-handkerchief, after they'd cut it out, and came in to wet the bandages again with lotion when she returned from the ball—where she'd been the prettiest young lady of all—I've never loved any one like her. I little thought then that I should live to see her brought so low. I don't mean no reproach to nobody. Many a one calls you pretty and handsome, and what not. Even in this smoky place, enough to blind one's eyes, the owls can see that. But you'll never be like your mother for beauty—never; not if you live to be a hundred."

"Mamma is very pretty still. Poor mamma!"

"Now don't ye set off again, or I shall give way at last" (whimpering). "You'll never stand master's coming home, and questioning, at this rate. Go out and take a walk, and come in something like. Many's the time I've longed to walk it off—the thought of what was the matter with her, and how it must all end."

"Oh, Dixon!" said Margaret, "how often I've been cross with you, not knowing what a terrible secret you had to bear!"

"Bless you, child! I like to see you showing a bit of a spirit. It's the

2. Like the poppies, decorations to a bonnet for a festive occasion.

good old Beresford blood. Why, the last Sir John but two shot his
steward down, there where he stood, for just telling him that he'd
racked the tenants, and he'd racked the tenants till he could get no
more money off them than he could get skin off a flint."

"Well, Dixon, I won't shoot you, and I'll try not to be cross again."

"You never have. If I've said it at times, it has always been to
myself, just in private, by way of making a little agreeable conversation, for there's no one here fit to talk to. And when you fire up,
you're the very image of Master Frederick. I could find in my heart
to put you in a passion any day, just to see his stormy look coming
like a great cloud over your face. But now you go out, Miss. I'll watch
over missus; and as for master, his books are company enough for
him, if he should come in."

"I will go," said Margaret. She hung about Dixon for a minute or
so, as if afraid and irresolute; then suddenly kissing her, she went
quickly out of the room.

"Bless her!" said Dixon. "She's as sweet as a nut. There are three
people I love: it's missus, Master Frederick, and her. Just them three.
That's all. The rest be hanged, for I don't know what they're in the
world for. Master was born, I suppose, for to marry missus. If I
thought he loved her properly, I might get to love him in time. But
he should ha' made a deal more on her, and not been always reading,
reading, thinking, thinking. See what it has brought him to! Many a
one who never reads nor thinks either, gets to be Rector, and Dean,
and what not; and I dare say master might, if he'd just minded missus, and let the weary reading and thinking alone.—There she goes"
(looking out of the window as she heard the front door shut). "Poor
young lady! her clothes look shabby to what they did when she came
to Helstone a year ago. Then she hadn't so much as a darned stocking
or a cleaned pair of gloves in all her wardrobe. And now—!"

Chapter XVII.

What is a Strike?

> "There are briars besetting every path,
>   Which call for patient care;
> There is a cross in every lot,
>   And an earnest need for prayer."
>   ANON.[1]

Margaret went out heavily and unwillingly enough. But the length
of a street—yes, the air of a Milton Street—cheered her young blood

---

1. Although identified as anonymous, the stanza is again by Anna Waring. See vol. I, chap.
   5, n.1.

before she reached her first turning. Her step grew lighter, her lip redder. She began to take notice, instead of having her thoughts turned so exclusively inward. She saw unusual loiterers in the streets: men with their hands in their pockets sauntering along; loud-laughing and loud-spoken girls clustered together, apparently excited to high spirits, and a boisterous independence of temper and behaviour. The more ill-looking of the men—the discreditable minority—hung about on the steps of the beer-houses and gin-shops, smoking, and commenting pretty freely on every passer-by. Margaret disliked the prospect of the long walk through these streets, before she came to the fields which she had planned to reach. Instead, she would go and see Bessy Higgins. It would not be so refreshing as a quiet country walk, but still it would perhaps be doing the kinder thing.

Nicholas Higgins was sitting by the fire smoking, as she went in. Bessy was rocking herself on the other side.

Nicholas took the pipe out of his mouth, and standing up, pushed his chair towards Margaret; he leant against the chimney-piece in a lounging attitude, while she asked Bessy how she was.

"Hoo's rather down i' th' mouth in regard to spirits, but hoo's better in health. Hoo doesn't like this strike. Hoo's a deal too much set on peace and quietness at any price."

"This is th' third strike I've seen," said she, sighing, as if that was answer and explanation enough.

"Well, third time pays for all. See if we don't dang[2] th' masters this time. See if they don't come, and beg us to come, back at our own price. That's all. We've missed it afore time, I grant yo'; but this time we'n laid our plans desperate deep."

"Why do you strike?" asked Margaret. "Striking is leaving off work till you get your own rate of wages, is it not? You must not wonder at my ignorance; where I come from I never heard of a strike."

"I wish I were there," said Bessy, wearily. "But it's not for me to get sick and tired o' strikes. This is the last I'll see. Before it's ended I shall be in the Great City—the Holy Jerusalem."

"Hoo's so full of th' life to come, hoo cannot think of th' present. Now I, yo see, am bound to do the best I can here. I think a bird i' th' hand is worth two i' th' bush. So them's the different views we take on th' strike question."

"But," said Margaret, "if the people struck, as you call it, where I come from, as they are mostly all field labourers, the seed would not be sown, the hay got in, the corn reaped."

"Well?" said he. He had resumed his pipe, and put his "well" in the form of an interrogation.

"Why," she went on, "what would become of the farmers?"

2. Defeat, implicitly comprehensively and with violence.

He puffed away. "I reckon, they'd have either to give up their farms, or to give fair rate of wage."

"Suppose they could not, or would not do the last; they could not give up their farms all in a minute, however much they might wish to do so; but they would have no hay, nor corn to sell that year; and where would the money come from to pay the labourers' wages the next?"

Still puffing away. At last he said:

"I know nought of your ways down South. I have heerd they're a pack of spiritless, down-trodden men; welly clemmed to death[3]; too much dazed wi' clemming to know when they're put upon. Now, it's not so here. We known when we're put upon; and we'en too much blood in us to stand it. We just take our hands fro' our looms, and say, 'Yo may clem us, but yo'll not put upon us, my masters!' And be danged to 'em, they shan't this time!"

"I wish I lived down South," said Bessy.

"There's a deal to bear there," said Margaret. "There are sorrows to bear everywhere. There is very hard bodily labour to be gone through, with very little food to give strength."

"But it's out of doors," said Bessy. "And away from the endless, endless noise, and sickening heat."

"It's sometimes in heavy rain, and sometimes in bitter cold. A young person can stand it; but an old man gets racked with rheumatism, and bent and withered before his time; yet he must just work on the same, or else go to the workhouse."

"I thought yo were so taken wi' the ways of the South country."

"So I am," said Margaret, smiling a little, as she found herself thus caught. "I only mean, Bessy, there's good and bad in everything in this world; and as you felt the bad up here, I thought it was but fair you should know the bad down there."

"And yo say they never strike down there?" asked Nicholas abruptly.

"No!" said Margaret; "I think they have too much sense."

"An' I think," replied he, dashing the ashes out of his pipe with so much vehemence that it broke, "it's not that they've too much sense, but that they've too little spirit."

"O, father!" said Bessy, "what have ye gained by striking? Think of that first strike when mother died—how we all had to clem—you the worst of all; and yet many a one went in every week at the same wage, till all were gone in that there was work for; and some went beggars all their lives at after."

"Ay," said he. "That there strike was badly managed. Folk got into

3. Starved to death.

th' management of it, as were either fools or not true men. Yo'll see, it'll be different this time."

"But all this time you've not told me what you're striking for," said Margaret, again.

"Why, yo see, there's five or six masters who have set themselves again paying the wages they've been paying these two years past, and flourishing upon, and getting richer upon. And now they come to us, and say we're to take less. And we won't. We'll just clem them to death first; and see who'll work for 'em then. They'll have killed the goose that laid 'em the golden eggs, I reckon."

"And so you plan dying, in order to be revenged upon them!"

"No," said he, "I dunnot. I just look forward to the chance of dying at my post sooner than yield. That's what folk call fine and honour-able in a soldier, and why not in a poor weaver-chap?"

"But," said Margaret, "a soldier dies in the cause of the Nation—in the cause of others."

He laughed grimly. "My lass," said he, "yo're but a young wench, but don't yo think I can keep three people—that's Bessy, and Mary, and me—on sixteen shilling a week? Dun yo think it's for mysel' I'm striking work at this time? It's just as much in the cause of others as yon soldier—only m'appen,[4] the cause he dies for is just that of some-body he never clapt eyes on, nor heerd on all his born days, while I take up John Boucher's cause, as lives next door but one, wi' a sickly wife, and eight childer, none on 'em factory age;[5] and I don't take up his cause only, though he's a poor good-for-nought, as can only manage two looms at a time, but I take up th' cause o' justice. Why are we to have less wage now, I ask, than two year ago?"

"Don't ask me," said Margaret; "I am very ignorant. Ask some of your masters. Surely they will give you a reason for it. It is not merely an arbitrary decision of theirs, come to without reason."

"Yo're just a foreigner, and nothing more," said he, contemptu-ously. "Much yo know about it. Ask th' masters! They'd tell us to mind our own business, and they'd mind theirs. Our business being, yo' understand, to take the bated[6] wage, and be thankful; and their business to bate us down to clemming point, to swell their profits. That's what it is."

"But," said Margaret, determined not to give way, although she saw she was irritating him, "the state of trade may be such as not to enable them to give you the same remuneration."

"State o' trade! That's just a piece o' masters' humbug. It's rate o'

4. Contraction of "may happen," thus "perhaps."
5. Old enough to work in a factory. Under the terms of factory legislation at the time, children under the age of nine could not be employed in factories.
6. Reduced.

wages I was talking of. Th' masters keep th' state o' trade in their own hands; and just walk it forward like a black bug-a-boo, to frighten naughty children with into being good. I'll tell yo it's their part,—their cue, as some folks call it,—to beat us down, to swell their fortunes; and it's ours to stand up and fight hard,—not for ourselves alone, but for them round about us—for justice and fair play. We help to make their profits, and we ought to help spend 'em. It's not that we want their brass so much this time, as we've done many a time afore. We 'n getten money laid by; and we're resolved to stand and fall together; not a man on us will go in for less wage than th' Union says is our due. So I say, 'hooray for the strike,' and let Thornton, and Slickson, and Hamper, and their set look to it!"

"Thornton!" said Margaret. "Mr. Thornton of Marlborough Street?"

"Aye! Thornton o' Marlborough Mill, as we call him."

"He is one of the masters you are striving with, is he not? What sort of a master is he?"

"Did yo' ever see a bulldog? Set a bulldog on hind legs, and dress him up in coat and breeches, and yo'n just getten John Thornton."

"Nay," said Margaret, laughing, "I deny that. Mr. Thornton is plain enough, but he's not like a bulldog, with its short broad nose, and snarling upper lip."

"No! not in look, I grant yo'. But let John Thornton get hold on a notion, and he'll stick to it like a bulldog; yo' might pull him away wi' a pitch-fork ere he'd leave go. He's worth fighting wi', is John Thornton. As for Slickson, I take it, some o' these days he'll wheedle his men back wi' fair promises; that they'll just get cheated out of as soon as they're in his power again. He'll work his fines well out on 'em, I'll warrant. He's as slippery as an eel, he is. He's like a cat,—as sleek, and cunning, and fierce. It'll never be an honest up and down fight wi' him, as it will be wi' Thornton. Thornton's as dour as a door-nail; an obstinate chap, every inch on him,—th' oud bulldog!"

"Poor Bessy!" said Margaret, turning round to her. "You sigh over it all. You don't like struggling and fighting as your father does, do you?"

"No!" said she, heavily. "I'm sick on it. I could have wished to have had other talk about me in my latter days, than just the clashing and clanging and clattering that has wearied a' my life long, about work and wages, and masters, and hands, and knobsticks."[7]

"Poor wench! latter days be farred![8] Thou'rt looking a sight better already for a little stir and change. Beside, I shall be a deal here to make it more lively for thee."

"Tobacco-smoke chokes me!" said she, querulously.

7. Strikebreakers.
8. A term of dismissal—e.g., "be blowed," "nonsense."

"Then I'll never smoke no more i' th' house!" he replied, tenderly. "But why didst thou not tell me afore, thou foolish wench?"

She did not speak for a while, and then so low that only Margaret heard her:

"I reckon, he'll want a' the comfort he can get out o' either pipe or drink afore he's done."

Her father went out of doors, evidently to finish his pipe.

Bessy said passionately,

"Now am not I a fool,—am I not, Miss?—there, I knew I ought for to keep father at home, and away fro' the folk that are always ready for to tempt a man, in time o' strike, to go drink,—and there my tongue must needs quarrel with this pipe o' his'n,—and he'll go off, I know he will,—as often as he wants to smoke—and nobody knows where it'll end. I wish I'd letten myself be choked first."

"But does your father drink?" asked Margaret.

"No—not to say drink," replied she, still in the same wild excited tone. "But what win ye have? There are days wi' you, as wi' other folk, I suppose, when yo' get up and go through th' hours, just longing for a bit of a change—a bit of a fillip,[9] as it were. I know I ha' gone and bought a four-pounder out o' another baker's shop to common on[1] such days, just because I sickened at the thought of going on for ever wi' the same sight in my eyes, and the same sound in my ears, and the same taste i' my mouth, and the same thought (or no thought, for that matter) in my head, day after day, for ever. I've longed for to be a man to go spreeing,[2] even if it were only a tramp to some new place in search o' work. And father—all men—have it stronger in 'em than me to get tired o' sameness and work for ever. And what is 'em to do? It's little blame to them if they do go into th' gin-shop for to make their blood flow quicker, and more lively, and see things they never see at no other time—pictures, and looking-glass, and such like. But father never was a drunkard, though maybe, he's got worse for drink, now and then. Only yo' see," and now her voice took a mournful, pleading tone, "at times o' strike there's much to knock a man down, for all they start so hopefully; and where's the comfort to come fro'? He'll get angry and mad—they all do—and then they get tired out wi' being angry and mad, and maybe ha' done things in their passion they'd be glad to forget. Bless yo'r sweet pitiful face! but yo' dunnot know what a strike is yet."

"Come, Bessy," said Margaret, "I won't say you're exaggerating, because I don't know enough about it: but, perhaps, as you're not well, you're only looking on one side, and there is another and a brighter to be looked to."

9. A stimulus.
1. A four-pound loaf from another baker's shop for us to eat.
2. I have wanted to be a man with the freedom to roam.

"It's all well enough for yo' to say so, who have lived in pleasant green places all your life long, and never known want or care, or wickedness either, for that matter."

"Take care," said Margaret, her cheek flushing, and her eye lightening, "how you judge, Bessy. I shall go home to my mother, who is so ill—so ill, Bessy, that there's no outlet but death for her out of the prison of her great suffering; and yet I must speak cheerfully to my father, who has no notion of her real state, and to whom the knowledge must come gradually. The only person—the only one who could sympathise with me and help me—whose presence could comfort my mother more than any other earthly thing—is falsely accused—would run the risk of death if he came to see his dying mother. This I tell you—only you, Bessy. You must not mention it. No other person in Milton—hardly any other person in England knows. Have I not care? Do I not know anxiety, though I go about well-dressed, and have food enough? Oh, Bessy, God is just, and our lots are well portioned out by Him, although none but He knows the bitterness of our souls."

"I ask your pardon," replied Bessy, humbly. "Sometimes, when I've thought o' my life, and the little pleasure I've had in it, I've believed that, maybe, I was one of those doomed to die by the falling of a star from heaven; 'And the name of the star is called Wormwood; and the third part of the waters became wormwood; and men died of the waters, because they were made bitter.'[3] One can bear pain and sorrow better if one thinks it has been prophesied long before for one: somehow, then it seems as if my pain was needed for the fulfilment; otherways it seems all sent for nothing."

"Nay, Bessy—think!" said Margaret. "God does not willingly afflict. Don't dwell so much on the prophecies, but read the clearer parts of the Bible."

"I dare say it would be wiser; but where would I hear such grand words of promise—hear tell o' anything so far different fro' this dreary world, and this town above a', as in Revelations? Many's the time I've repeated the verses in the seventh chapter to myself, just for the sound.[4] It's as good as an organ, and as different from every day, too. No, I cannot give up Revelations. It gives me more comfort than any other book i' the Bible."

"Let me come and read you some of my favourite chapters."

"Ay," said she greedily, "come. Father will maybe hear yo'. He's deaved[5] wi' my talking; he says it's all nought to do with the things o' to-day, and that's his business."

3. Revelation 8:11.
4. Revelation 7 describes the "great multitude" clad in white robes who stand before the throne of God: "These are they which came out of great tribulation, and, have washed their robes, and made them white in the blood of the Lamb" (7:14).
5. Deafened.

"Where is your sister?"

"Gone fustian-cutting.[6] I were loth to let her go; but somehow we must live; and th' Union can't afford us much."

"Now I must go. You have done me good, Bessy."

"I done you good!"

"Yes. I came here very sad, and rather too apt to think my own cause for grief was the only one in the world. And now I hear how you have had to bear for years, and that makes me stronger."

"Bless yo'! I thought a' the good-doing was on the side of gentle-folk. I shall get proud if I think I can do good to yo'."

"You won't do it if you think about it. But you'll only puzzle yourself if you do, that's one comfort."

"Yo're not like no one I ever seed. I dunno what to make of yo'."

"Nor I of myself. Good-bye!"

Bessy stilled her rocking to gaze after her.

"I wonder if there are many folk like her down South. She's like a breath of country air, somehow. She freshens me up above a bit. Who'd ha' thought that face—as bright and as strong as the angel I dream of—could have known the sorrow she speaks on? I wonder how she'll sin. All on us must sin. I think a deal on her, for sure. But father does the like, I see. And Mary even. It's not often hoo's stirred up to notice much."

Chapter XVIII.

Likes and Dislikes.

"My heart revolts within me, and two voices
Make themselves audible within my bosom."
                                    WALLENSTEIN.[1]

On Margaret's return home she found two letters on the table: one was a note for her mother,—the other, which had come by the post, was evidently from her Aunt Shaw—covered with foreign post-marks—thin, silvery, and rustling. She took up the other, and was examining it, when her father came in suddenly:

"So your mother is tired, and gone to bed early! I'm afraid, such a thundery day was not the best in the world for the doctor to see her. What did he say? Dixon tells me he spoke to you about her."

Margaret hesitated. Her father's looks became more grave and anxious:

---

6. Fustian was the coarsest form of cotton cloth; this work would thus be extremely unpleasant.
1. A drama by the German writer Johann Christian Schiller (1759–1805). It was translated by Coleridge, from the second part of whose version, *The Death of Wallenstein* (1800), the quotation is taken (scene 9, lines 10–11).

"He does not think her seriously ill?"

"Not at present; she needs care, he says; he was very kind, and said he would call again, and see how his medicines worked."

"Only care—he did not recommend change of air?—he did not say this smoky town was doing her any harm, did he, Margaret?"

"No! not a word," she replied, gravely. "He was anxious, I think."

"Doctors have that anxious manner; it's professional," said he.

Margaret saw, in her father's nervous ways, that the first impression of possible danger was made upon his mind, in spite of all his making light of what she told him. He could not forget the subject,—could not pass from it to other things; he kept recurring to it through the evening, with an unwillingness to receive even the slightest unfavourable idea, which made Margaret inexpressibly sad.

"This letter is from Aunt Shaw, papa. She has got to Naples, and finds it too hot, so she has taken apartments at Sorrento. But I don't think she likes Italy."

"He did not say anything about diet, did he?"

"It was to be nourishing, and digestible. Mamma's appetite is pretty good, I think."

"Yes! and that makes it all the more strange he should have thought of speaking about diet."

"I asked him, papa." Another pause. Then Margaret went on: "Aunt Shaw says, she has sent me some coral ornaments, papa; but," added Margaret, half smiling, "she's afraid the Milton Dissenters won't appreciate them. She has got all her ideas of Dissenters from the Quakers, has not she?"[2]

"If ever you hear or notice that your mother wishes for anything, be sure you let me know. I am so afraid she does not tell me always what she would like. Pray, see after that girl Mrs. Thornton named. If we had a good, efficient house-servant, Dixon could be constantly with her, and I'd answer for it we'd soon set her up amongst us, if care will do it. She's been very much tired of late, with the hot weather, and the difficulty of getting a servant. A little rest will put her quite to rights—eh, Margaret?"

"I hope so," said Margaret,—but so sadly, that her father took notice of it. He pinched her cheek.

"Come; if you look so pale as this, I must rouge you up a little. Take care of yourself, child, or you'll be wanting the doctor next."

But he could not settle to anything that evening. He was continually going backwards and forwards, on laborious tiptoe, to see if his wife was still asleep. Margaret's heart ached at his restlessness—his trying to stifle and strangle the hideous fear that was looming out of the dark places of his heart.

2. Dissenters here is a generic term for nonconformists, who were strongly represented in the new industrial culture. Quakers were famous for their austerity of dress.

He came back at last, somewhat comforted.

"She's awake now, Margaret. She quite smiled as she saw me standing by her. Just her old smile. And she says she feels refreshed, and ready for tea. Where's the note for her? She wants to see it. I'll read it to her while you make tea."

The note proved to be a formal invitation from Mrs. Thornton, to Mr. and Mrs., and Miss Hale to dinner, on the twenty-first instant. Margaret was surprised to find an acceptance contemplated, after all she had learnt of sad probabilities during the day. But so it was. The idea of her husband's and daughter's going to this dinner had quite captivated Mrs. Hale's fancy, even before Margaret had heard the contents of the note. It was an event to diversify the monotony of the invalid's life; and she clung to the idea of their going, with even fretful pertinacity when Margaret objected.

"Nay, Margaret? if she wishes it, I'm sure we'll both go willingly. She never would wish it unless she felt herself really stronger—really better than we thought she was, eh, Margaret?" said Mr. Hale, anxiously, as she prepared to write the note of acceptance, the next day.

"Eh! Margaret?" questioned he, with a nervous motion of his hands. It seemed cruel to refuse him the comfort he craved for. And besides, his passionate refusal to admit the existence of fear, almost inspired Margaret herself with hope.

"I do think she is better since last night," said she. "Her eyes look brighter, and her complexion clearer."

"God bless you," said her father, earnestly. "But is it true? Yesterday was so sultry every one felt ill. It was a most unlucky day for Mr. Donaldson to see her on."

So he went away to his day's duties, now increased by the preparation of some lectures he had promised to deliver to the working people at a neighbouring Lyceum.[3] He had chosen Ecclesiastical Architecture as his subject, rather more in accordance with his own taste and knowledge than as falling in with the character of the place or the desire for particular kinds of information among those to whom he was to lecture. And the institution itself, being in debt, was only too glad to get a gratis course from an educated and accomplished man like Mr. Hale, let the subject be what it might.

"Well, mother," asked Mr. Thornton that night, "who have accepted your invitations for the twenty-first?"

"Fanny, where are the notes? The Slicksons accept, Collingbrooks accept, Stephenses accept, Browns decline. Hales—father and daughter come,—mother too great an invalid—Macphersons come,

---

3. An educational institution primarily for the better class of working people. Lectures were often given there by clergymen and other educated speakers as acts of philanthropy; Gaskell's husband, the Reverend William Gaskell, sometimes did so. The classical term is typical of the cultural institutions that were establishing themselves in the industrial cities.

and Mr. Horsfall, and Mr. Young. I was thinking of asking the Porters, as the Browns can't come."

"Very good. Do you know, I'm really afraid Mrs. Hale is very far from well, from what Dr. Donaldson says."

"It's strange of them to accept a dinner-invitation if she's very ill," said Fanny.

"I didn't say very ill," said her brother, rather sharply. "I only said very far from well. They may not know it either." And then he suddenly remembered that, from what Dr. Donaldson had told him, Margaret, at any rate, must be aware of the exact state of the case.

"Very probably they are quite aware of what you said yesterday, John—of the great advantage it would be to them—to Mr. Hale, I mean, to be introduced to such people as the Stephenses and the Collingbrooks."

"I'm sure that motive would not influence them. No! I think I understand how it is."

"John!" said Fanny, laughing in her little, weak, nervous way. "How you profess to understand these Hales, and how you never will allow that we can know anything about them. Are they really so very different to most people one meets with?"

She did not mean to vex him; but if she had intended it, she could not have done it more thoroughly. He chafed in silence, however, not deigning to reply to her question.

"They do not seem to me out of the common way," said Mrs. Thornton. "He appears a worthy kind of man enough; rather too simple for trade—so it's perhaps as well he should have been a clergyman first, and now a teacher. She's a bit of a fine lady, with her invalidism; and as for the girl—she's the only one who puzzles me when I think about her,—which I don't often do. She seems to have a great notion of giving herself airs; and I can't make out why. I could almost fancy she thinks herself too good for her company at times. And yet they're not rich; from all I can hear they never have been."

"And she's not accomplished, mamma. She can't play."

"Go on, Fanny. What else does she want to bring her up to your standard?"

"Nay! John," said his mother, "that speech of Fanny's did no harm. I myself heard Miss Hale say she could not play. If you would let us alone, we could perhaps like her, and see her merits."

"I'm sure I never could!" murmured Fanny, protected by her mother. Mr. Thornton heard, but did not care to reply. He was walking up and down the dining-room, wishing that his mother would order candles, and allow him to set to work at either reading or writing, and so put a stop to the conversation. But he never thought of interfering in any of the small domestic regulations that Mrs. Thornton observed, in habitual remembrance of her old economies.

"Mother," said he, stopping, and bravely speaking out the truth, "I wish you would like Miss Hale."

"Why?" asked she, startled by his earnest, yet tender manner. "You're never thinking of marrying her?—a girl without a penny."

"She would never have me," said he, with a short laugh.

"No, I don't think she would," answered his mother. "She laughed in my face, when I praised her for speaking out something Mr. Bell had said in your favour. I liked the girl for doing it so frankly, for it made me sure she had no thought of you; and the next minute she vexed me so by seeming to think——Well, never mind! Only you're right in saying she's too good an opinion of herself to think of you. The saucy jade! I should like to know where she'd find a better!"

If these words hurt her son, the dusky light prevented him from betraying any emotion. In a minute he came up quite cheerfully to his mother, and putting one hand lightly on her shoulder, said

"Well, as I'm just as much convinced of the truth of what you have been saying as you can be; and as I have no thought or expectation of ever asking her to be my wife, you'll believe me for the future that I'm quite disinterested in speaking about her. I foresee trouble for that girl—perhaps, want of motherly care—and I only wish you to be ready to be a friend to her, in case she needs one. Now, Fanny," said he, "I trust you have delicacy enough to understand, that it is as great an injury to Miss Hale as to me—in fact, she would think it a greater—to suppose that I have any reason, more than I now give, for begging you and my mother to show her every kindly attention."

"I cannot forgive her her pride," said his mother; "I will befriend her, if there is need, for your asking, John. I would befriend Jezebel herself if you asked me. But this girl, who turns up her nose at us all—who turns up her nose at you——"

"Nay, mother; I have never yet put myself, and I mean never to put myself, within reach of her contempt."

"Contempt, indeed!"—(One of Mrs. Thornton's expressive snorts.)—"Don't go on speaking of Miss Hale, John, if I've to be kind to her. When I'm with her, I don't know if I like or dislike her most; but when I think of her, and hear you talk of her, I hate her. I can see she's given herself airs to you as well as if you'd told me out."

"And if she has," said he—and then he paused for a moment—then went on: "I'm not a lad, to be cowed by a proud look from a woman, or to care for her misunderstanding me and my position. I can laugh at it!"

"To be sure! and at her too, with her fine notions, and haughty tosses!"

"I only wonder why you talk so much about her, then," said Fanny. "I'm sure, I'm tired enough of the subject."

"Well!" said her brother, with a shade of bitterness. "Suppose we find some more agreeable subject. What do you say to a strike, by way of something pleasant to talk about?"

"Have the hands actually turned out?" asked Mrs. Thornton, with vivid interest.

"Hamper's men are actually out. Mine are working out their week, through fear of being prosecuted for breach of contract. I'd have had every one of them up and punished for it, that left his work before his time was out."

"The law expenses would have been more than the hands themselves were worth—a set of ungrateful naughts!" said his mother.

"To be sure. But I'd have shown them how I keep my word, and how I mean them to keep theirs. They know me by this time. Slickson's men are off—pretty certain he won't spend money in getting them punished. We're in for a turn-out, mother."

"I hope there are not many orders in hand?"

"Of course there are. They know that well enough. But they don't quite understand all, though they think they do."

"What do you mean, John?"

Candles had been brought, and Fanny had taken up her interminable piece of worsted-work, over which she was yawning; throwing herself back in her chair, from time to time, to gaze at vacancy, and think of nothing at her ease.

"Why," said he, "the Americans are getting their yarns so into the general market, that our only chance is producing them at a lower rate. If we can't, we may shut up shop at once, and hands and masters go alike on tramp. Yet these fools go back to the prices paid three years ago—nay, some of their leaders quote Dickinson's prices now—though they know as well as we do that, what with fines pressed out of their wages as no honourable man would extort them, and other ways which I for one would scorn to use, the real rate of wage paid at Dickinson's is less than at ours. Upon my word, mother, I wish the old combination-laws[4] were in force. It is too bad to find out that fools—ignorant, wayward men like these—just by uniting their weak silly heads, are to rule over the fortunes of those who bring all the wisdom that knowledge and experience, and often painful thought and anxiety, can give. The next thing will be—indeed, we're all but come to it now—that we shall have to go and ask— stand hat in hand—and humbly ask the secretary of the Spinner' Union to be so kind as to furnish us with labour at their own price. That's what they want—they, who haven't the sense to see that, if we don't get a fair share of the profits to compensate us for our wear and tear here in England, we can move off to some other country;

4. Laws passed in 1799 and 1800 that forbade workers from uniting in their own interests. They were repealed in 1824, thus paving the way for legalized trade unions.

and that, what with home and foreign competition, we are none of us likely to make above a fair share, and may be thankful enough if we can get that, in an average number of years."

"Can't you get hands from Ireland? I wouldn't keep these fellows a day. I'd teach them that I was master, and could employ what servants I liked."

"Yes! to be sure, I can; and I will, too, if they go on long. It will be trouble and expense, and I fear there will be some danger; but I will do it, rather than give in."

"If there is to be all this extra expense, I'm sorry we're giving a dinner just now."

"So am I,—not because of the expense, but because I shall have much to think about, and many unexpected calls on my time. But we must have had Mr. Horsfall, and he does not stay in Milton long. And as for the others, we owe them dinners, and it's all one trouble."

He kept on with his restless walk—not speaking any more, but drawing a deep breath from time to time, as if endeavouring to throw off some annoying thought. Fanny asked her mother numerous small questions, all having nothing to do with the subject, which a wiser person would have perceived was occupying her attention. Consequently, she received many short answers. She was not sorry when, at ten o'clock, the servants filed in to prayers. These her mother always read,—first reading a chapter. They were now working steadily through the Old Testament. When prayers were ended, and his mother had wished him good-night, with that long steady look of hers which conveyed no expression of the tenderness that was in her heart, but yet had the intensity of a blessing, Mr. Thornton continued his walk. All his business plans had received a check, a sudden pull-up, from this approaching turn-out. The forethought of many anxious hours was thrown away, utterly wasted by their insane folly, which would injure themselves even more than him, though no one could set any limit to the mischief they were doing. And these were the men who thought themselves fitted to direct the masters in the disposal of their capital! Hamper had said, only this very day, that if he were ruined by the strike, he would start life again, comforted by the conviction that those who brought it on were in a worse predicament than he himself,—for he had head as well as hands, while they had only hands; and if they drove away their market, they could not follow it, nor turn to anything else. But this thought was no consolation to Mr. Thornton. It might be that revenge gave him no pleasure; it might be that he valued the position he had earned with the sweat of his brow, so much that he keenly felt its being endangered by the ignorance or folly of others,—so keenly that he had no thoughts to spare for what would be the consequences of their conduct to themselves. He paced up and down, setting his teeth a little now and then. At last it struck two. The candles were flickering in their sockets. He lighted his own, muttering to himself:

"Once for all, they shall know whom they have got to deal with. I can give them a fortnight,—no more. If they don't see their madness before the end of that time, I must have hands from Ireland. I believe it's Slickson's doing,—confound him and his dodges! He thought he was overstocked; so he seemed to yield at first, when the deputation came to him,—and of course, he only confirmed them in their folly, as he meant to do. That's where it spread from."

Chapter XIX.

Angel Visits.

> "As angels in some brighter dreams
>   Call to the soul when man doth sleep,
>   So some strange thoughts transcend our wonted themes,
>   And into glory peep."
>
> HENRY VAUGHAN.[1]

Mrs. Hale was curiously amused and interested by the idea of the Thornton dinner party. She kept wondering about the details, with something of the simplicity of a little child, who wants to have all its anticipated pleasures described beforehand. But the monotonous life led by invalids often makes them like children, inasmuch as they have neither of them any sense of proportion in events, and seem each to believe that the walls and curtains which shut in their world, and shut out everything else, must of necessity be larger than anything hidden beyond. Besides, Mrs. Hale had had her vanities as a girl; had perhaps unduly felt their mortification when she became a poor clergyman's wife;—they had been smothered and kept down; but they were not extinct; and she liked to think of seeing Margaret dressed for a party, and discussed what she should wear, with an unsettled anxiety that amused Margaret, who had been more accustomed to society in her one year in Harley Street than her mother in five and twenty years of Helstone.

"Then you think you shall wear your white silk. Are you sure it will fit? It's nearly a year since Edith was married!"

"Oh yes, mamma! Mrs. Murray made it, and it's sure to be right; it may be a straw's breadth shorter or longer-waisted, according to

---

1. Welsh metaphysical poet (1622–1695). The lines quoted are from "They are all gone into a world of light," published in the second part of Vaughan's volume *Silex Scintillans* (1655).

my having grown fat or thin. But I don't think I've altered in the least."

"Hadn't you better let Dixon see it? It may have gone yellow with lying by."

"If you like, mamma. But if the worst comes to the worst, I've a very nice pink gauze which aunt Shaw gave me, only two or three months before Edith was married. That can't have gone yellow."

"No! but it may have faded."

"Well! then I've a green silk. I feel more as if it was the embarrassment of riches."

"I wish I knew what you ought to wear," said Mrs. Hale, nervously.

Margaret's manner changed instantly. "Shall I go and put them on one after another, mamma, and then you could see which you liked best?"

"But—yes! perhaps that will be best."

So off Margaret went. She was very much inclined to play some pranks when she was dressed up at such an unusual hour; to make her rich white silk balloon out into a cheese,[2] to retreat backwards from her mother as if she were the queen; but when she found that these freaks of hers were regarded as interruptions to the serious business, and as such annoyed her mother, she became grave and sedate. What had possessed the world (her world) to fidget so about her dress, she could not understand; but that very afternoon, on naming her engagement to Bessy Higgins (apropos of the servant that Mrs. Thornton had promised to inquire about), Bessy quite roused up at the intelligence.

"Dear! and are you going to dine at Thornton's at Marlborough Mills?"

"Yes, Bessy. Why are you so surprised?"

"Oh, I dunno. But they visit wi' a' th' first folk in Milton."

"And you don't think we're quite the first folk in Milton, eh, Bessy?"

Bessy's cheeks flushed a little at her thought being thus easily read.

"Well," said she, "yo' see, they thinken a deal o' money here; and I reckon yo've not getten much."

"No," said Margaret, "that's very true. But we are educated people, and have lived amongst educated people. Is there anything so wonderful, in our being asked out to dinner by a man who owns himself inferior to my father by coming to him to be instructed? I don't mean to blame Mr. Thornton. Few drapers' assistants, as he was once, could have made themselves what he is."

"But can yo' give dinners back, in yo're small house? Thornton's house is three times as big."

2. The full skirt of the dress can be made to assume a rounded shape like a cheese, either by curtseying or by twirling.

"Well, I think we could manage to give Mr. Thornton a dinner back, as you call it. Perhaps not in such a large room, nor with so many people. But I don't think we've thought about it at all in that way."

"I never thought yo'd be dining with Thorntons," repeated Bessy. "Why, the mayor hissel' dines there; and the members of Parliament and all."

"I think I could support the honour of meeting the mayor of Milton."

"But them ladies dress so grand!" said Bessy, with an anxious look at Margaret's print gown, which her Milton eyes appraised at sevenpence a yard.

Margaret's face dimpled up into a merry laugh. "Thank you, Bessy, for thinking so kindly about my looking nice among all the smart people. But I've plenty of grand gowns,—a week ago, I should have said they were far too grand for anything I should ever want again. But as I'm to dine at Mr. Thornton's, and perhaps to meet the mayor, I shall put on my very best gown, you may be sure."

"What win yo' wear?" asked Bessy, somewhat relieved.

"White silk," said Margaret. "A gown I had for a cousin's wedding, a year ago."

"That'll do!" said Bessy, falling back in her chair. "I should be loth to have yo' looked down upon."

"Oh! I'll be fine enough, if that will save me from being looked down upon in Milton."

"I wish I could see you dressed up," said Bessy. "I reckon, yo're not what folk would ca' pretty; yo've not red and white enough for that. But dun yo' know, I ha' dreamt of yo', long afore ever I seed yo'."

"Nonsense, Bessy!"

"Ay, but I did. Yo'r very face,—looking wi' yo'r clear steadfast eyes out o' th' darkness, wi' yo'r hair blown off from yo'r brow, and going out like rays round yo'r forehead, which was just as smooth and as straight as it is now,—and yo' always came to give me strength, which I seemed to gather out o' yo'r deep comforting eyes,—and yo' were drest in shining raiment—just as yo'r going to be drest. So, yo' see, it was yo'!"

"Nay, Bessy," said Margaret, gently, "it was but a dream."

"And why might na I dream a dream in my affliction as well as others? Did not many a one i' the Bible? Ay, and see visions too! Why, even my father thinks a deal o' dreams! I tell yo' again, I saw yo' as plainly, coming swiftly towards me, wi' yo'r hair blown back wi' the very swiftness o' the motion, just like the way it grows, a little standing off like; and the white shining dress on yo've getten to wear.

Let me come and see yo' in it. I want to see yo' and touch yo' as in very deed yo' were in my dream."

"My dear Bessy, it is quite a fancy of yours."

"Fancy or no fancy,—yo've come, as I knew yo' would, when I saw yo'r movement in my dream,—and when yo're here about me, I reckon I feel easier in my mind, and comforted, just as a fire comforts one on a dree day. Yo' said it were on th' twenty-first; please God, I'll come and see yo'."

"Oh Bessy! you may come and welcome; but don't talk so—it really makes me sorry. It does indeed."

"Then I'll keep it to mysel', if I bite my tongue out. Not but what it's true for all that."

Margaret was silent. At last she said,

"Let us talk about it sometimes, if you think it true. But not now. Tell me, has your father turned out?"[3]

"Ay!" said Bessy, heavily—in a manner very different from that she had spoken in but a minute or two before. "He and many another,—all Hamper's men,—and many a one besides. Th' women are as bad as th' men, in their savageness, this time. Food is high,—and they mun have food for their childer, I reckon. Suppose Thorntons sent 'em their dinner out,—th' same money, spent on potatoes and meal, would keep many a crying babby quiet, and hush up its mother's heart for a bit!"

"Don't speak so!" said Margaret. "You'll make me feel wicked and guilty in going to this dinner."

"No!" said Bessy. "Some's pre-elected to sumptuous feasts, and purple and fine linen,—may be yo're one on 'em. Others toil and moil all their lives long—and the very dogs are not pitiful in our days, as they were in the days of Lazarus. But if yo' ask me to cool yo'r tongue wi' th' tip of my finger, I'll come across the great gulf to yo' just for th' thought o' what yo've been to me here."[4]

"Bessy! you're very feverish! I can tell it in the touch of your hand, as well as in what you're saying. It won't be division enough, in that awful day, that some of us have been beggars here, and some of us have been rich,—we shall not be judged by that poor accident, but by our faithful following of Christ."

Margaret got up, and found some water: and soaking her pocket-handkerchief in it, she laid the cool wetness on Bessy's forehead,

---

3. Gone on strike.
4. The reference, here and in the following paragraph, is to the story of Dives and Lazarus (Luke 16:19–31). In Luke's account the dogs licked the sores of Lazarus, the beggar who sat at the gate of Dives, the rich man. After his death, Dives, in the fires of hell, pleads that Lazarus, now in Heaven ("Abraham's bosom"), might dip his finger in water and cool Dives's tongue. He is told however that the "great gulf" that now divides them cannot be crossed.

and began to chafe the stone-cold feet. Bessy shut her eyes, and allowed herself to be soothed. At last she said,

"Yo'd ha' been deaved out o' yo'r five wits, as well as me, if yo'd had one body after another coming in to ask for father, and staying to tell me each one their tale. Some spoke o' deadly hatred, and made my blood run cold wi' the terrible things they said o' th' masters,— but more, being women, kept plaining, plaining (wi' the tears running down their cheeks, and never wiped away, nor heeded), of the price o' meat, and how their childer could na sleep at nights for th' hunger."

"And do they think the strike will mend this?" asked Margaret.

"They say so," replied Bessy. "They do say trade has been good for long, and the masters has made no end o' money; how much father doesn't know, but, in course, th' Union does; and, as is natural, they wanten their share o' th' profits, now that food is getting dear; and th' Union says they'll not be doing their duty if they don't make the masters give 'em their share. But masters has getten th' upper hand somehow; and I'm feared they'll keep it now and evermore. It's like th' great battle o' Armageddon,[5] the way they keep on, grinning and fighting at each other, till even while they fight, they are picked off into the pit."

Just then, Nicholas Higgins came in. He caught his daughter's last words.

"Ay! and I'll fight on too; and I'll get it this time. It 'll not take long for to make 'em give in, for they've getten a pretty lot of orders, all under contract; and they'll soon find out they'd better give us our five per cent than lose the profit they'll gain; let alone the fine for not fulfilling the contract. Aha my masters! I know who'll win."

Margaret fancied from his manner that he must have been drinking, not so much from what he said, as from the excited way in which he spoke; and she was rather confirmed in this idea by the evident anxiety Bessy showed to hasten her departure. Bessy said to her,—

"The twenty-first—that's Thursday week. I may come and see yo' dressed for Thornton's, I reckon. What time is yo'r dinner?"

Before Margaret could answer, Higgins broke out,

"Thornton's! Ar' t' going to dine at Thornton's? Ask him to give yo' a bumper to the success of his orders. By th' twenty-first, I reckon, he'll be pottered in his brains how to get 'em done in time. Tell him, there's seven hundred'll come marching into Marlborough Mills, the morning after he gives the five per cent, and will help him through his contract in no time. You'll have 'em all there. My master, Hamper. He's one o' th' oud-fashioned sort. Ne'er meets a man bout an oath or a curse; I should think he were going to die if he spoke me

5. Described in Revelation 16.

civil; but arter all, his bark's waur than his bite, and yo' may tell him one o' his turn-outs said so, if yo' like. Eh! but yo'll have a lot of prize millowners at Thornton's! I should like to get speech o' them, when they're a bit inclined to sit still after dinner, and could na run for the life on 'em. I'd tell 'em my mind. I'd speak up again th' hard way they're driving on us!"

"Good-bye!" said Margaret, hastily. "Good-bye, Bessy! I shall look to see you on the twenty-first, if you're well enough."

The medicines and treatment which Dr. Donaldson had ordered for Mrs. Hale, did her so much good at first that not only she herself, but Margaret, began to hope that he might have been mistaken, and that she could recover permanently. As for Mr. Hale, although he had never had an idea of the serious nature of their apprehensions, he triumphed over their fears with an evident relief, which proved how much his glimpse into the nature of them had affected him. Only Dixon croaked for ever into Margaret's ear. However, Margaret defied the raven,[6] and would hope.

They needed this gleam of brightness in-doors, for out-of-doors, even to their uninstructed eyes, there was a gloomy brooding appearance of discontent. Mr. Hale had his own acquaintances among the working men, and was depressed with their earnestly-told tales of suffering and long-endurance. They would have scorned to speak of what they had to bear to any one who might, from his position, have understood it without their words. But here was this man, from a distant county, who was perplexed by the workings of the system into the midst of which he was thrown, and each was eager to make him a judge, and to bring witness of his own causes for irritation. Then Mr. Hale brought all his budget of grievances, and laid it before Mr. Thornton, for him, with his experience as a master, to arrange them, and explain their origin; which he always did, on sound economical principles; showing that, as trade was conducted, there must always be a waxing and waning of commercial prosperity; and that in the waning a certain number of masters, as well as of men, must go down into ruin, and be no more seen among the ranks of the happy and prosperous. He spoke as if this consequence were so entirely logical, that neither employers nor employed had any right to complain if it became their fate: the employer to turn aside from the race he could no longer run, with a bitter sense of incompetency and failure— wounded in the struggle—trampled down by his fellows in their haste to get rich—slighted where he once was honoured—humbly asking for, instead of bestowing, employment with a lordly hand. Of course, speaking so of the fate that, as a master, might be his own in the fluctuations of commerce, he was not likely to have more

6. Echoing Edgar Allan Poe's poem, "The Raven" ("croaking 'Nevermore,' " Line 72). The poem was first published in 1845 and by this time had achieved considerable popularity.

sympathy with that of the workmen, who were passed by in the swift
merciless improvement or alteration; who would fain lie down and
quietly die out of the world that needed them not, but felt as if they
could never rest in their graves for the clinging cries of the beloved
and helpless they would leave behind; who envied the power of the
wild bird, that can feed her young with her very heart's blood. Margaret's whole soul rose up against him while he reasoned in this
way—as if commerce were everything and humanity nothing. She
could hardly thank him for the individual kindness, which brought
him that very evening to offer her—for the delicacy which made him
understand that he must offer her privately—every convenience for
illness that his own wealth or his mother's foresight had caused them
to accumulate in their household, and which, as he learnt from Dr.
Donaldson, Mrs. Hale might possibly require. His presence, after
the way he had spoken—his bringing before her the doom, which
she was vainly trying to persuade herself might yet be averted from
her mother—all conspired to set Margaret's teeth on edge, as she
looked at him, and listened to him. What business had he to be the
only person, except Dr. Donaldson and Dixon, admitted to the awful
secret, which she held shut up in the most dark and sacred recess
of her heart—not daring to look at it, unless she invoked heavenly
strength to bear the sight—that, some day soon, she should cry aloud
for her mother, and no answer would come out of the blank, dumb
darkness? Yet he knew all. She saw it in his pitying eyes. She heard
it in his grave and tremulous voice. How reconcile those eyes, that
voice, with the hard, reasoning, dry, merciless way in which he laid
down axioms of trade, and serenely followed them out to their full
consequences? The discord jarred upon her inexpressibly. The more
because of the gathering woe of which she heard from Bessy. To be
sure, Nicholas Higgins, the father, spoke differently. He had been
appointed a committee-man, and said that he knew secrets of which
the exoteric[7] knew nothing. He said this more expressly and particularly, on the very day before Mrs. Thornton's dinner-party, when
Margaret, going in to speak to Bessy, found him arguing the point
with Boucher, the neighbour of whom she had frequently heard
mention, as by turns exciting Higgins's compassion, as an unskilful
workman with a large family depending upon him for support, and
at other times enraging his more energetic and sanguine neighbour
by his want of what the latter called spirit. It was very evident that
Higgins was in a passion when Margaret entered. Boucher stood,
with both hands on the rather high mantelpiece, swaying himself a
little on the support which his arms, thus placed, gave him, and
looking wildly into the fire, with a kind of despair that irritated Hig-

7. Outsiders.

gins, even while it went to his heart. Bessy was rocking herself violently backwards and forwards, as was her wont (Margaret knew by this time) when she was agitated. Her sister Mary was tying on her bonnet (in great clumsy bows, as suited her great clumsy fingers), to go to her fustian-cutting, blubbering out loud the while, and evidently longing to be away from a scene that distressed her.

Margaret came in upon this scene. She stood for a moment at the door—then, her finger on her lips, she stole to a seat on the squab[8] near Bessy. Nicholas saw her come in, and greeted her with a gruff, but not unfriendly nod. Mary hurried out of the house, catching gladly at the open door, and crying aloud when she got away from her father's presence. It was only John Boucher that took no notice whatever who came in and who went out.

"It's no use, Higgins. Hoo cannot live long a this'n. Hoo's just sinking away—not for want o' meat hersel'—but because hoo cannot stand th' sight o' the little ones clemming. Ay, clemming! Five shilling a week may do well enough for thee, wi' but two mouths to fill, and one on 'em a wench who can welly earn her own meat. But its clemming to us. An' I tell thee plain—if hoo dies, as I'm 'feard hoo will afore we've getten th' five per cent, I'll fling th' money back i' th' master's face, and say, 'Be domned to yo'; be domned to th' whole cruel world o' yo'; that could na leave me th' best wife that ever bore childer to a man!' An' look thee, lad, I'll hate thee, and th' whole pack o' th' Union. Ay, an' chase yo' through heaven wi' my hatred,—I will, lad! I will,—if yo're leading me astray i' this matter. Thou saidst, Nicholas, on Wednesday sennight—and it's now Tuesday i' th' second week—that afore a fortnight we'd ha' the masters coming a-begging to us to take back our work, at our own wage—and time's nearly up,—and there's our lile Jack lying a-bed, too weak to cry, but just every now and then sobbing up his heart for want o' food,—our lile Jack, I tell thee, lad! Hoo's never looked up sin' he were born, and hoo loves him as if he were her very life,—as he is,—for I reckon he'll ha' cost me that precious price,—our lile Jack, who wakened me each morn wi' putting his sweet little lips to my great rough fou' face, a-seeking a smooth place to kiss,—an' he lies clemming." Here the deep sobs choked the poor man, and Nicholas looked up, with eyes brimful of tears, to Margaret, before he could gain courage to speak.

"Hou'd up, man. Thy lile Jack shall na' clem. I ha' getten brass, and we'll go buy the chap a sup o' milk an' a good four-pounder this very minute. What's mine's thine, sure enough, i' thou'st i' want. Only, dunnot lose heart, man!" continued he, as he fumbled in a tea-pot for what money he had. "I lay yo' my heart and soul we'll win for a' this: it's but bearing on one more week, and yo' just see th' way

8. A low seat or couch.

th' masters 'll come round, praying on us to come back to our mills.
An' th' Union,—that's to say, I—will take care yo've enough for th'
childer and th' missus. So dunnot turn faint-heart, and go to th'
tyrants a-seeking work."

The man turned round at these words,—turned round a face so
white, and gaunt, and tear-furrowed, and hopeless, that its very calm
forced Margaret to weep.

"Yo' know well, that a worser tyrant than e'er th' masters were says,
'Clem to death, and see 'em a' clem to death, ere yo' dare go again
th' Union.' Yo' know it well, Nicholas, for a' yo're one on 'em. Yo'
may be kind hearts, each separate; but once banded together, yo've
no more pity for a man than a wild hunger-maddened wolf."

Nicholas had his hand on the lock of the door—he stopped and
turned round on Boucher, close following:

"So help me God! man alive—if I think not I'm doing best for thee,
and for all on us. If I'm going wrong when I think I'm going right,
it's their sin, who ha' left me where I am, in my ignorance. I ha'
thought till my brains ached,—Beli' me, John, I have. An' I say again,
there's no help for us but having faith i' th' Union. They'll win the
day, see if they dunnot!"

Not one word had Margaret or Bessy spoken. They had hardly
uttered the sighing, that the eyes of each called to the other to bring
up from the depths of her heart. At last Bessy said,

"I never thought to hear father call on God again. But yo' heard
him say, 'So help me God!' "

"Yes!" said Margaret. "Let me bring you what money I can spare,—
let me bring you a little food for that poor man's children. Don't let
them know it comes from any one but your father. It will be but
little."

Bessy lay back without taking any notice of what Margaret said.
She did not cry—she only quivered up her breath,

"My heart's drained dry o' tears," she said. "Boucher's been in
these days past, a telling me of his fears and his troubles. He's but
a weak kind o' chap, I know, but he's a man for a' that; and tho' I've
been angry, many a time afore now, wi' him an' his wife, as knew no
more nor him how to manage, yet, yo' see, all folks isn't wise, yet
God lets 'em live—ay, an' gives 'em some one to love, and be loved
by, just as good as Solomon. An', if sorrow comes to them they love,
it hurts 'em as sore as e'er it did Solomon.[9] I can't make it out.
Perhaps it's as well such a one as Boucher has th' Union to see after
him. But I'd just like for to see th' men as make th' Union, and put
'em one by one face to face wi' Boucher. I reckon, if they heard him,

---

9. The reference conflates two ideas associated with Solomon: his wisdom and the fact that
   he was uniquely loved. The implication is that those who are not wise are nevertheless
   equally entitled to love, and therefore suffer its emotional consequences.

they'd tell him (if I cotched 'em one by one),[1] he might go back and get what he could for his work, even if it weren't so much as they ordered."

Margaret sat utterly silent. How was she ever to go away into comfort and forget that man's voice, with the tone of unutterable agony, telling more by far than his words of what he had to suffer? She took out her purse; she had not much in it of what she could call her own, but what she had she put into Bessy's hand without speaking.

"Thank yo'. There's many on 'em gets no more, and is not so bad off,—leastways does not show it as he does. But father won't let 'em want, now he knows. Yo' see, Boucher's been pulled down wi' his childer,—and her being so cranky, and a' they could pawn has gone this last twelvemonth. Yo're not to think we'd ha' letten 'em clem, for all we're a bit pressed oursel'; if neighbours doesn't see after neighbours, I dunno who will." Bessy seemed almost afraid lest Margaret should think they had not the will, and, to a certain degree, the power of helping one whom she evidently regarded as having a claim upon them. "Besides," she went on, "father is sure and positive the masters must give in within these next few days,—that they canna hould on much longer. But I thank yo' all the same,—I thank yo' for mysel', as much as for Boucher, for it just makes my heart warm to yo' more and more."

Bessy seemed much quieter to-day, but fearfully languid and exhausted. As she finished speaking, she looked so faint and weary that Margaret became alarmed.

"It's nout," said Bessy. "It's not death yet. I had a fearfu' night wi' dreams—or somewhat like dreams, for I were wide awake—and I'm all in a swounding daze to-day,—only yon poor chap made me alive again. No! it's not death yet, but death is not far off. Ay. Cover me up, and I'll may be sleep, if th' cough will let me. Good night—good afternoon, m'appen I should say—but th' light is dim an' misty to-day."

Chapter XX.

Men and Gentlemen.

> "Old and young, boy, let 'em all eat, I have it;
> Let 'em have ten tire of teeth a-piece, I care not."
> ROLLO, DUKE OF NORMANDY.[1]

Margaret went home so painfully occupied with what she had heard and seen that she hardly knew how to rouse herself up to the duties

---

1. If I spoke to them individually.
1. A play (published 1639) by the seventeenth-century dramatist John Fletcher.

which awaited her; the necessity for keeping up a constant flow of
cheerful conversation for her mother, who, now that she was unable
to go out, always looked to Margaret's return from the shortest walk
as bringing in some news.

"And can your factory friend come on Thursday to see you
dressed?"

"She was so ill I never thought of asking her," said Margaret, dole-
fully.

"Dear! Everybody is ill now, I think," said Mrs. Hale, with a little
of the jealousy which one invalid is apt to feel of another. "But it
must be very sad to be ill in one of those little back streets." (Her
kindly nature prevailing, and the old Helstone habits of thought
returning.) "It's bad enough here. What could you do for her, Margaret? Mr. Thornton has sent me some of his old port wine since
you went out. Would a bottle of that do her good, think you?"

"No, mamma! I don't believe they are very poor,—at least, they
don't speak as if they were; and, at any rate, Bessy's illness is consumption—she won't want wine. Perhaps, I might take her a little
preserve, made of our dear Helstone fruit. No! there's another family
to whom I should like to give—Oh mamma, mamma! how am I to
dress up in my finery, and go off and away to smart parties, after the
sorrow I have seen to-day?" exclaimed Margaret, bursting the bounds
she had preordained for herself before she came in, and telling her
mother of what she had seen and heard at Higgins's cottage.

It distressed Mrs. Hale excessively. It made her restlessly irritated
till she could do something. She directed Margaret to pack up a
basket in the very drawing-room, to be sent there and then to the
family; and was almost angry with her for saying, that it would not
signify if it did not go till morning, as she knew Higgins had provided
for their immediate wants, and she herself had left money with
Bessy. Mrs. Hale called her unfeeling for saying this; and never gave
herself breathing-time till the basket was sent out of the house. Then
she said:

"After all, we may have been doing wrong. It was only the last time
Mr. Thornton was here that he said, those were no true friends who
helped to prolong the struggle by assisting the turn-outs.[2] And this
Boucher-man was a turn-out, was he not?"

The question was referred to Mr. Hale by his wife, when he came
up-stairs, fresh from giving a lesson to Mr. Thornton, which had
ended in conversation, as was their wont. Margaret did not care if
their gifts had prolonged the strike; she did not think far enough for
that, in her present excited state.

2. Strikers.

Mr. Hale listened, and tried to be as calm as a judge; he recalled all that had seemed so clear not half-an-hour before, as it came out of Mr. Thornton's lips; and then he made an unsatisfactory compromise. His wife and daughter had not only done quite right in this instance, but he did not see for a moment how they could have done otherwise. Nevertheless, as a general rule, it was very true what Mr. Thornton said, that as the strike, if prolonged, must end in the masters' bringing hands from a distance (if, indeed, the final result were not, as it had often been before, the invention of some machine which would diminish the need of hands at all), why, it was clear enough that the kindest thing was to refuse all help which might bolster them up in their folly. But, as to this Boucher, he would go and see him the first thing in the morning, and try and find out what could be done for him.

Mr. Hale went the next morning, as he proposed. He did not find Boucher at home, but he had a long talk with his wife; promised to ask for an Infirmary order[3] for her; and, seeing the plenty provided by Mrs. Hale, and somewhat lavishly used by the children, who were masters down-stairs in their father's absence, he came back with a more consoling and cheerful account than Margaret had dared to hope for; indeed, what she had said the night before had prepared her father for so much worse a state of things that, by a re-action of his imagination, he described all as better than it really was.

"But I will go again, and see the man himself," said Mr. Hale. "I hardly know as yet how to compare one of these houses with our Helstone cottages. I see furniture here which our labourers would never have thought of buying, and food commonly used which they would consider luxuries; yet for these very families there seems no other resource now that their weekly wages are stopped, but the pawn-shop. One had need to learn a different language, and measure by a different standard, up here in Milton."

Bessy, too, was rather better this day. Still she was so weak that she seemed to have entirely forgotten her wish to see Margaret dressed—if, indeed, that had not been the feverish desire of a half-delirious state.

Margaret could not help comparing this strange dressing of hers, to go where she did not care to be—her heart heavy with various anxieties—with the old, merry, girlish toilettes that she and Edith had performed scarcely more than a year ago. Her only pleasure now in decking herself out was in thinking that her mother would take delight in seeing her dressed. She blushed when Dixon, throwing the drawing-room door open, made an appeal for admiration.

3. A note allowing patients to present themselves for charitable hospital treatment.

"Miss Hale looks well, ma'am,—doesn't she? Mrs. Shaw's coral couldn't have come in better. It just gives the right touch of colour, ma'am. Otherwise, Miss Margaret, you would have been too pale."

Margaret's black hair was too thick to be plaited; it needed rather to be twisted round and round, and have its fine silkiness compressed into massive coils, that encircled her head like a crown, and then were gathered into a large spiral knot behind. She kept its weight together by two large coral pins, like small arrows for length. Her white silk sleeves were looped up with strings of the same material, and on her neck, just below the base of her curved and milk-white throat, there lay heavy coral beads.

"Oh, Margaret! how I should like to be going with you to one of the old Barrington assemblies,—taking you as Lady Beresford used to take me."

Margaret kissed her mother for this little burst of maternal vanity; but she could hardly smile at it, she felt so much out of spirits.

"I would rather stay at home with you,—much rather, mamma."

"Nonsense, darling! Be sure you notice the dinner well. I shall like to hear how they manage these things in Milton. Particularly the second course, dear. Look what they have instead of game."

Mrs. Hale would have been more than interested,—she would have been astonished, if she had seen the sumptuousness of the dinner-table and its appointments. Margaret, with her London cultivated taste, felt the number of delicacies to be oppressive; one half of the quantity would have been enough, and the effect lighter and more elegant. But it was one of Mrs. Thornton's rigorous laws of hospitality, that of each separate dainty enough should be provided for all the guests to partake, if they felt inclined. Careless to abstemiousness in her daily habits, it was part of her pride to set a feast before such of her guests as cared for it. Her son shared this feeling. He had never known—though he might have imagined, and had the capability to relish—any kind of society but that which depended on an exchange of superb meals: and even now, though he was denying himself the personal expenditure of an unnecessary sixpence, and had more than once regretted that the invitations for this dinner had been sent out, still, as it was to be, he was glad to see the old magnificence of preparation.

Margaret and her father were the first to arrive. Mr. Hale was anxiously punctual to the time specified. There was no one upstairs in the drawing-room but Mrs. Thornton and Fanny. Every cover was taken off, and the apartment blazed forth in yellow silk damask and a brilliantly-flowered carpet. Every corner seemed filled up with ornament, until it became a weariness to the eye, and presented a strange contrast to the bald ugliness of the look-out into the great mill-yard, where wide folding gates were thrown open for the admission of carriages. The mill loomed high on the left-hand side of the windows, casting a shadow down from its many stories, which darkened the summer evening before its time.

"My son was engaged up to the last moment on business. He will be here directly, Mr. Hale. May I beg you to take a seat?"

Mr. Hale was standing at one of the windows as Mrs. Thornton spoke. He turned away, saying,

"Don't you find such close neighbourhood to the mill rather unpleasant at times?"

She drew herself up:

"Never. I am not become so fine as to desire to forget the source of my son's wealth and power. Besides, there is not such another factory in Milton. One room alone is two hundred and twenty square yards."

"I meant that the smoke and the noise—the constant going out and coming in of the work-people, might be annoying!"

"I agree with you, Mr. Hale!" said Fanny. "There is a continual smell of steam, and oily machinery—and the noise is perfectly deafening."

"I have heard noise that was called music far more deafening. The engine-room is at the street-end of the factory; we hardly hear it, except in summer weather, when all the windows are open; and as for the continual murmur of the work-people, it disturbs me no more than the humming of a hive of bees. If I think of it at all, I connect it with my son, and feel how all belongs to him, and that his is the head that directs it. Just now, there are no sounds to come from the mill; the hands have been ungrateful enough to turn out, as perhaps you have heard. But the very business (of which I spoke, when you entered), had reference to the steps he is going to take to make them learn their place." The expression on her face, always stern, deepened into dark anger, as she said this. Nor did it clear away when Mr. Thornton entered the room; for she saw, in an instant, the weight of care and anxiety which he could not shake off, although his guests received from him a greeting that appeared both cheerful and cordial. He shook hands with Margaret. He knew it was the first time their hands had met, though she was perfectly unconscious of the fact. He inquired after Mrs. Hale, and heard Mr. Hale's sanguine, hopeful account; and glancing at Margaret, to understand how far she agreed with her father, he saw that no dissenting shadow crossed her face. And as he looked with this intention, he was struck anew with her great beauty. He had never seen her in such dress before; and yet now it appeared as if such elegance of attire was so

befitting her noble figure and lofty serenity of countenance, that she
ought to go always thus apparelled. She was talking to Fanny; about
what, he could not hear; but he saw his sister's restless way of continually arranging some part of her gown, her wandering eyes, now
glancing here, now there, but without any purpose in her observation; and he contrasted them uneasily with the large soft eyes that
looked forth steadily at one object, as if from out their light beamed
some gentle influence of repose: the curving lines of the red lips,
just parted in the interest of listening to what her companion said—
the head a little bent forwards, so as to make a long sweeping line
from the summit, where the light caught on the glossy raven hair, to
the smooth ivory tip of the shoulder; the round white arms, and taper
hands, laid lightly across each other, but perfectly motionless in their
pretty attitude. Mr. Thornton sighed as he took in all this with one
of his sudden comprehensive glances. And then he turned his back
to the young ladies, and threw himself, with an effort, but with all
his heart and soul, into a conversation with Mr. Hale.

More people came—more and more. Fanny left Margaret's side,
and helped her mother to receive her guests. Mr. Thornton felt
that in this influx no one was speaking to Margaret, and was restless under this apparent neglect. But he never went near her himself; he did not look at her. Only, he knew what she was doing—or
not doing—better than he knew the movements of any one else in
the room. Margaret was so unconscious of herself, and so much
amused by watching other people, that she never thought whether
she was left unnoticed or not. Somebody took her down to dinner;
she did not catch the name; nor did he seem much inclined to talk
to her. There was a very animated conversation going on among
the gentlemen; the ladies, for the most part, were silent, employing
themselves in taking notes of the dinner and criticising each
other's dresses. Margaret caught the clue to the general conversation, grew interested and listened attentively. Mr. Horsfall, the
stranger, whose visit to the town was the original germ of the
party, was asking questions relative to the trade and manufactures
of the place; and the rest of the gentlemen—all Milton men,—
were giving him answers and explanations. Some dispute arose,
which was warmly contested; it was referred to Mr. Thornton, who
had hardly spoken before; but who now gave an opinion, the
grounds of which were so clearly stated that even the opponents
yielded. Margaret's attention was thus called to her host; his whole
manner, as master of the house, and entertainer of his friends, was
so straightforward, yet simple and modest, as to be thoroughly dignified. Margaret thought she had never seen him to so much
advantage. When he had come to their house, there had been
always something, either of over-eagerness or of that kind of vexed

annoyance which seemed ready to pre-suppose that he was unjustly judged, and yet felt too proud to try and make himself better understood. But now, among his fellows, there was no uncertainty as to his position. He was regarded by them as a man of great force of character; of power in many ways. There was no need to struggle for their respect. He had it, and he knew it; and the security of this gave a fine grand quietness to his voice and ways, which Margaret had missed before.

He was not in the habit of talking to ladies; and what he did say was a little formal. To Margaret herself he hardly spoke at all. She was surprised to think how much she enjoyed this dinner. She knew enough now to understand many local interests—nay, even some of the technical words employed by the eager millowners. She silently took a very decided part in the question they were discussing. At any rate, they talked in desperate earnest,—not in the used-up style that wearied her so in the old London parties. She wondered that, with all this dwelling on the manufactures and trade of the place, no allusion was made to the strike then pending. She did not yet know how coolly such things were taken by the masters, as having only one possible end. To be sure, the men were cutting their own throats, as they had done many a time before; but if they would be fools, and put themselves into the hands of a rascally set of paid delegates, they must take the consequence. One or two thought Thornton looked out of spirits; and, of course, he must lose by this turn-out. But it was an accident that might happen to themselves any day; and Thornton was as good to manage a strike as any one; for he was as iron a chap as any in Milton. The hands had mistaken their man in trying that dodge on him. And they chuckled inwardly at the idea of the workmen's discomfiture and defeat, in their attempt to alter one iota of what Thornton had decreed.

It was rather dull for Margaret after dinner. She was glad when the gentlemen came, not merely because she caught her father's eye to brighten her sleepiness up; but because she could listen to something larger and grander than the petty interests which the ladies had been talking about. She liked the exultation in the sense of power which these Milton men had. It might be rather rampant in its display, and savour of boasting; but still they seemed to defy the old limits of possibility, in a kind of fine intoxication, caused by the recollection of what had been achieved, and what yet should be. If in her cooler moments she might not approve of their spirit in all things, still there was much to admire in their forgetfulness of themselves and the present, in their anticipated triumphs over all inanimate matter at some future time which none of them should live to see. She was rather startled when Mr. Thornton spoke to her, close at her elbow:

"I could see you were on our side in our discussion at dinner,—were you not, Miss Hale?"

"Certainly. But then I know so little about it. I was surprised, however, to find from what Mr. Horsfall said, that there were others who thought in so diametrically opposite a manner, as the Mr. Morison he spoke about. He cannot be a gentleman—is he?"

"I am not quite the person to decide on another's gentlemanliness, Miss Hale. I mean, I don't quite understand your application of the word. But I should say that this Morison is no true man. I don't know who he is; I merely judge him from Mr. Horsfall's account."

"I suspect my 'gentleman' includes your 'true man.' "

"And a great deal more, you would imply. I differ from you. A man is to me a higher and a completer being than a gentleman."

"What do you mean?" asked Margaret. "We must understand the words differently."

"I take it that 'gentleman' is a term that only describes a person in his relation to others; but when we speak of him as 'a man,' we consider him not merely with regard to his fellow-men, but in relation to himself,—to life—to time—to eternity. A cast-away lonely as Robinson Crusoe—a prisoner immured in a dungeon for life—nay, even a saint in Patmos,[4] has his endurance, his strength, his faith, best described by being spoken of as 'a man.' I am rather weary of this word 'gentlemanly,' which seems to me to be often inappropriately used, and often, too, with such exaggerated distortion of meaning, while the full simplicity of the noun 'man,' and the adjective 'manly' are unacknowledged—that I am induced to class it with the cant of the day."

Margaret thought a moment,—but before she could speak her slow conviction, he was called away by some of the eager manufacturers, whose speeches she could not hear, though she could guess at their import by the short clear answers Mr. Thornton gave, which came steady and firm as the boom of a distant minute gun. They were evidently talking of the turn-out, and suggesting what course had best be pursued. She heard Mr. Thornton say:

"That has been done." Then came a hurried murmur, in which two or three joined.

"All those arrangements have been made."

Some doubts were implied, some difficulties named by Mr. Slickson, who took hold of Mr. Thornton's arm, the better to impress his words. Mr. Thornton moved slightly away, lifted his eyebrows a very little, and then replied:

"I take the risk. You need not join in it unless you choose." Still some more fears were urged.

4. Specifically, Saint John the Divine, who isolated himself on the Greek island of Patmos. Here, simply a hermit.

"I'm not afraid of anything so dastardly as incendiarism. We are open enemies; and I can protect myself from any violence that I apprehend. And I will assuredly protect all others who come to me for work. They know my determination by this time, as well and as fully as you do."

Mr. Horsfall took him a little on one side, as Margaret conjectured, to ask him some other question about the strike; but, in truth, it was to inquire who she herself was—so quiet, so stately, and so beautiful.

"A Milton lady?" asked he, as the name was given.

"No! from the south of England—Hampshire, I believe," was the cold, indifferent answer.

Mrs. Slickson was catechising Fanny on the same subject.

"Who is that fine distinguished-looking girl? a sister of Mr. Horsfall's?"

"Oh dear, no! That is Mr. Hale, her, father, talking now to Mr. Stephens. He gives lessons; that is to say, he reads with young men. My brother John goes to him twice a week, and so he begged mamma to ask them here, in hopes of getting him known. I believe, we have some of their prospectuses, if you would like to have one."

"Mr. Thornton! Does he really find time to read with a tutor, in the midst of all his business,—and this abominable strike in hand as well?"

Fanny was not sure, from Mrs. Slickson's manner, whether she ought to be proud or ashamed of her brother's conduct; and, like all people who try and take other people's "ought" for the rule of their feelings, she was inclined to blush for any singularity of action. Her shame was interrupted by the dispersion of the guests.

Chapter XXI.

The Dark Night.

> "On earth is known to none
> The smile that is not sister to a tear."
>   ELLIOTT.[1]

Margaret and her father walked home. The night was fine, the streets clean, and with her pretty white silk, like Leezie Lindsay's gown o' green satin, in the ballad, "kilted up to her knee,"[2] she was off with her father—ready to dance along with the excitement of the cool, fresh night air.

1. Ebenezer Elliott (1781–1849), the "Corn-Law rhymer." A working man, his poetry was taken up by social reformers and middle-class readers generally.
2. From a traditional ballad; Gaskell quotes from an eighteenth-century musical version.

"I rather think Thornton is not quite easy in his mind about this strike. He seemed very anxious to-night."

"I should wonder if he were not. But he spoke with his usual coolness to the others, when they suggested different things, just before we came away."

"So he did after dinner as well. It would take a good deal to stir him from his cool manner of speaking; but his face strikes me as anxious."

"I should be, if I were he. He must know of the growing anger and hardly smothered hatred of his workpeople, who all look upon him as what the Bible calls a 'hard man,'[3]—not so much unjust as unfeeling; clear in judgment, standing upon his 'rights' as no human being ought to stand, considering what we and all our petty rights are in the sight of the Almighty. I am glad you think he looks anxious. When I remember Boucher's half mad words and ways, I cannot bear to think how coolly Mr. Thornton spoke."

"In the first place, I am not so convinced as you are about that man Boucher's utter distress; for the moment, he was badly off, I don't doubt. But there is always a mysterious supply of money from these Unions; and, from what you said, it was evident the man was of a passionate, demonstrative nature, and gave strong expression to all he felt."

"Oh, papa!"

"Well! I only want you to do justice to Mr. Thornton, who is, I suspect, of an exactly opposite nature,—a man who is far too proud to show his feelings. Just the character I should have thought beforehand, you would have admired, Margaret."

"So I do,—so I should; but I don't feel quite so sure as you do of the existence of those feelings. He is a man of great strength of character,—of unusual intellect, considering the few advantages he has had."

"Not so few. He has led a practical life from a very early age; has been called upon to exercise judgment and self-control. All that develops one part of the intellect. To be sure, he needs some of the knowledge of the past, which gives the truest basis for conjecture as to the future; but he knows this need,—he perceives it, and that is something. You are quite prejudiced against Mr. Thornton, Margaret."

"He is the first specimen of a manufacturer—of a person engaged in trade—that I had ever the opportunity of studying, papa. He is my first olive: let me make a face while I swallow it. I know he is good of his kind, and by and by I shall like the kind. I rather think I am already beginning to do so. I was very much interested by what

3. From the parable of the talents: "Lord, I knew thee that thou art an hard man, reaping where thou hast not sown and gathering where thou hast not strawed." (Matthew 25:24)

the gentlemen were talking about, although I did not understand half of it. I was quite sorry when Miss Thornton came to take me to the other end of the room, saying she was sure I should be uncomfortable at being the only lady among so many gentlemen. I had never thought about it, I was so busy listening; and the ladies were so dull, papa—oh, so dull! Yet I think it was clever too. It reminded me of our old game of having each so many nouns to introduce into a sentence."

"What do you mean, child?" asked Mr. Hale.

"Why, they took nouns that were signs of things which gave evidence of wealth,—housekeepers, under-gardeners, extent of glass, valuable lace, diamonds, and all such things; and each one formed her speech so as to bring them all in, in the prettiest accidental manner possible."

"You will be as proud of your one servant when you get her, if all is true about her that Mrs. Thornton says."

"To be sure, I shall. I felt like a great hypocrite to-night, sitting there in my white silk gown, with my idle hands before me, when I remembered all the good, thorough, house-work they had done to-day. They took me for a fine lady, I'm sure."

"Even I was mistaken enough to think you looked like a lady, my dear," said Mr. Hale, quietly smiling.

But smiles were changed to white and trembling looks, when they saw Dixon's face, as she opened the door.

"Oh, master!—Oh, Miss Margaret! Thank God you are come! Dr. Donaldson is here. The servant next door went for him, for the charwoman[4] is gone home. She's better now; but, oh sir! I thought she'd have died an hour ago."

Mr. Hale caught Margaret's arm to steady himself from falling. He looked at her face, and saw an expression upon it of surprise and extremest sorrow, but not the agony of terror that contracted his own unprepared heart. She knew more than he did, and yet she listened with that hopeless expression of awed apprehension.

"Oh! I should not have left her—wicked daughter that I am!" moaned forth Margaret, as she supported her trembling father's hasty steps upstairs. Dr. Donaldson met them on the landing.

"She is better now," he whispered. "The opiate has taken effect. The spasms were very bad: no wonder they frightened your maid; but she'll rally this time."

"This time! Let me go to her!" Half an hour ago, Mr. Hale was a middle-aged man; now his sight was dim, his senses wavering, his walk tottering, as if he were seventy years of age.

Dr. Donaldson took his arm, and led him into the bedroom.

---

4. A woman servant hired by the day to perform domestic tasks. I have modernized Gaskell's original spelling of "charewoman."

Margaret followed close. There lay her mother, with an unmistake-able look on her face. She might be better now; she was sleeping, but Death had signed her for his own, and it was clear that ere long he would return to take possession. Mr. Hale looked at her for some time without a word. Then he began to shake all over, and, turning away from Dr. Donaldson's anxious care, he groped to find the door; he could not see it, although several candles, brought in the sudden affright, were burning and flaring there. He staggered into the drawing-room, and felt about for a chair. Dr. Donaldson wheeled one to him, and placed him in it. He felt his pulse.

"Speak to him, Miss Hale. We must rouse him."

"Papa!" said Margaret, with a crying voice that was wild with pain. "Papa! Speak to me!" The speculation came again into his eyes, and he made a great effort.

"Margaret, did you know of this? Oh, it was cruel of you!"

"No, sir, it was not cruel!" replied Dr. Donaldson, with quick deci-sion. "Miss Hale acted under my directions. There may have been a mistake, but it was not cruel. Your wife will be a different creature to-morrow, I trust. She has had spasms, as I anticipated, though I did not tell Miss Hale of my apprehensions. She has taken the opiate I brought with me; she will have a good long sleep; and to-morrow, that look which has alarmed you so much will have passed away."

"But not the disease?"

Dr. Donaldson glanced at Margaret. Her bent head, her face raised with no appeal for a temporary reprieve, showed that quick observer of human nature that she thought it better that the whole truth should be told.

"Not the disease. We cannot touch the disease, with all our poor vaunted skill. We can only delay its progress—alleviate the pain it causes. Be a man, sir—a Christian. Have faith in the immortality of the soul, which no pain, no mortal disease, can assail or touch!"

But all the reply he got, was in the choked words, "You have never been married, Dr. Donaldson; you do not know what it is," and in the deep, manly sobs, which went through the stillness of the night like heavy pulses of agony.

Margaret knelt by him, caressing him with tearful caresses. No one, not even Dr. Donaldson, knew how the time went by. Mr. Hale was the first to dare to speak of the necessities of the present moment.

"What must we do?" asked he. "Tell us both. Margaret is my staff—my right hand."

Dr. Donaldson gave his clear, sensible directions. No fear for to-night—nay, even peace for to-morrow, and for many days yet. But no enduring hope of recovery. He advised Mr. Hale to go to bed, and leave only one to watch the slumber, which he hoped would be undisturbed. He promised to come again early in the morning. And, with a warm and kindly shake of the hand, he left them.

They spoke but few words; they were too much exhausted by their terror to do more than decide upon the immediate course of action. Mr. Hale was resolved to sit up through the night, and all that Margaret could do was to prevail upon him to rest on the drawing-room sofa. Dixon stoutly and bluntly refused to go to bed; and, as for Margaret, it was simply impossible that she should leave her mother, let all the doctors in the world speak of "husbanding resources," and "one watcher only being required." So, Dixon sat, and stared, and winked, and drooped, and picked herself up again with a jerk, and finally gave up the battle, and fairly snored. Margaret had taken off her gown and tossed it aside with a sort of impatient disgust, and put on her dressing-gown. She felt as if she never could sleep again; as if her whole senses were acutely vital, and all endued with double keenness, for the purposes of watching. Every sight and sound—nay, even every thought, touched some nerve to the very quick. For more than two hours, she heard her father's restless movements in the next room. He came perpetually to the door of her mother's chamber, pausing there to listen, till she, not hearing his close unseen presence, went and opened it to tell him how all went on, in reply to the questions his baked lips could hardly form. At last he, too, fell asleep, and all the house was still. Margaret sat behind the curtain thinking. Far away in time, far away in space, seemed all the interests of past days. Not more than thirty-six hours ago, she cared for Bessy Higgins and her father, and her heart was wrung for Boucher; now, that was all like a dreaming memory of some former life;—everything that had passed out of doors seemed dissevered from her mother, and therefore unreal. Even Harley Street appeared more distinct; there she remembered, as if it were yesterday, how she had pleased herself with tracing out her mother's features in her Aunt Shaw's face,— and how letters had come, making her dwell on the thoughts of home with all the longing of love. Helstone, itself, was in the dim past. The dull gray days of the preceding winter and spring, so uneventless and monotonous, seemed more associated with what she cared for now above all price. She would fain have caught at the skirts of that departing time, and prayed it to return, and give her back what she had too little valued while it was yet in her possession. What a vain show Life seemed! How unsubstantial, and flickering, and flitting! It was as if from some aërial belfry, high up above the stir and jar of the earth, there was a bell continually tolling, "All are shadows!—all are passing!—all is past!" And when the morning dawned, cool and gray, like many a happier morning before—when Margaret looked one by one at the sleepers, it seemed as if the terrible night were unreal as a dream; it, too, was a shadow. It, too, was past.

Mrs. Hale herself was not aware when she awoke, how ill she had been the night before. She was rather surprised at Dr. Donaldson's early visit, and perplexed by the anxious faces of husband and child. She consented to remain in bed that day, saying she certainly was tired; but, the next, she insisted on getting up; and Dr. Donaldson gave his consent to her returning into the drawing-room. She was restless and uncomfortable in every position, and before night she became very feverish. Mr. Hale was utterly listless, and incapable of deciding on anything.

"What can we do to spare mamma such another night?" asked Margaret on the third day.

"It is, to a certain degree, the reaction after the powerful opiates I have been obliged to use. It is more painful for you to see than for her to bear, I believe. But, I think, if we could get a water-bed it might be a good thing. Not but what she will be better to-morrow; pretty much like herself as she was before this attack. Still, I should like her to have a water-bed. Mrs. Thornton has one, I know. I'll try and call there this afternoon. Stay," said he, his eye catching on Margaret's face, blanched with watching in a sick room, "I'm not sure whether I can go; I've a long round to take. It would do you no harm to have a brisk walk to Marlborough Street, and ask Mrs. Thornton if she can spare it."

"Certainly," said Margaret. "I could go while mamma is asleep this afternoon. I'm sure Mrs. Thornton would lend it to us."

Dr. Donaldson's experience told them rightly. Mrs. Hale seemed to shake off the consequences of her attack, and looked brighter and better this afternoon than Margaret had ever hoped to see her again. Her daughter left her after dinner, sitting in her easy chair, with her hand lying in her husband's, who looked more worn and suffering than she by far. Still, he could smile now—rather slowly, rather faintly, it is true; but a day or two before, Margaret never thought to see him smile again.

It was about two miles from their house in Crampton Crescent to Marlborough Street. It was too hot to walk very quickly. An August sun beat straight down into the street at three o'clock in the afternoon. Margaret went along, without noticing anything very different from usual in the first mile and a half of her journey; she was absorbed in her own thoughts, and had learnt by this time to thread her way through the irregular stream of human beings that flowed through Milton streets. But, by and by, she was struck with an unusual heaving among the mass of people in the crowded road on which she was entering. They did not appear to be moving on, so much as talking, and listening, and buzzing with excitement, without much stirring from the spot where they might happen to be. Still, as they made way for her, and, wrapt up in the purpose of her errand, and the necessities that suggested it, she was less quick of observation than she might have been, if her mind had been at ease, she had got into Marlborough Street before the full conviction forced itself upon her, that there was a restless, oppressive sense of irritation abroad among the people; a thunderous atmosphere, morally as well as physically, around her. From every narrow lane opening out on Marlborough Street came up a low distant roar, as of myriads of fierce indignant voices. The inhabitants of each poor squalid dwelling were gathered round the doors and windows, if indeed they were not actually standing in the middle of the narrow ways—all with looks intent towards one point. Marlborough Street itself was the focus of all those human eyes, that betrayed intensest interest of various kinds; some fierce with anger, some lowering with relentless threats, some dilated with fear, or imploring entreaty; and, as Margaret reached the small side-entrance by the folding doors, in the great dead wall of Marlborough mill-yard, and waited the porter's answer to the bell, she looked round and heard the first long far-off roll of the tempest;—saw the first slow-surging wave of the dark crowd come, with its threatening crest, tumble over, and retreat, at the far end of the street, which a moment ago, seemed so full of repressed noise, but which now was ominously still; all these circumstances forced themselves on Margaret's notice, but did not sink down into her pre-occupied heart. She did not know what they meant—what was their deep significance; while she did know, did feel the keen sharp pressure of the knife that was soon to stab her through and through by leaving her motherless. She was trying to realise that, in order that, when it came, she might be ready to comfort her father.

The porter opened the door cautiously, not nearly wide enough to admit her.

"It's you, is it, ma'am?" said he, drawing a long breath, and widening the entrance, but still not opening it fully. Margaret went in. He hastily bolted it behind her.

"Th' folk are all coming up here I reckon?" asked he.

"I don't know. Something unusual seemed going on; but this street is quite empty, I think."

She went across the yard and up the steps to the house door. There was no near sound,—no steam-engine at work with beat and pant,—no click of machinery, or mingling and clashing of many sharp voices; but far away, the ominous gathering roar, deep-clamouring.

Chapter XXII.

A Blow and Its Consequences.

"But work grew scarce, while bread grew dear,
    And wages lessened, too;
For Irish hordes were bidders here,
    Our half-paid work to do."

CORN LAW RHYMES.[1]

Margaret was shown into the drawing-room. It had returned into its normal state of bag and covering. The windows were half open because of the heat, and the Venetian blinds covered the glass,—so that a gray grim light, reflected from the pavement below, threw all the shadows wrong, and combined with the green-tinged upper light to make even Margaret's own face, as she caught it in the mirrors, look ghastly and wan. She sat and waited; no one came. Every now and then, the wind seemed to bear the distant multitudinous sound nearer; and yet there was no wind! It died away into profound stillness between whiles.

Fanny came in at last.

"Mamma will come directly, Miss Hale. She desired me to apologise to you as it is. Perhaps you know my brother has imported hands from Ireland, and it has irritated the Milton people excessively—as if he hadn't a right to get labour where he could; and the stupid wretches here wouldn't work for him; and now they've frightened these poor Irish starvelings so with their threats, that we daren't let them out. You may see them huddled in that top room in the mill,—and they're to sleep there, to keep them safe from those brutes, who will neither work nor let them work. And mamma is seeing about their food, and John is speaking to them, for some of the women are crying to go back. Ah! here's mamma!"

Mrs. Thornton came in with a look of black sternness on her face, which made Margaret feel she had arrived at a bad time to trouble her with her request. However, it was only in compliance with Mrs. Thornton's expressed desire, that she would ask for whatever they might want in the progress of her mother's illness. Mrs. Thornton's brow contracted, and her mouth grew set, while Margaret spoke with gentle modesty of her mother's restlessness, and Dr. Donaldson's wish that she should have the relief of a water-bed. She ceased. Mrs. Thornton did not reply immediately. Then she started up and exclaimed—

"They're at the gates! Call John, Fanny,—call him in from the mill! They're at the gates! They'll batter them in! Call John, I say!"

---

1. By Ebenezer Elliott: see chap. 21 n.1 above.

And simultaneously, the gathering tramp—to which she had been listening, instead of heeding Margaret's words—was heard just right outside the wall, and an increasing din of angry voices raged behind the wooden barrier, which shook as if the unseen maddened crowd made battering-rams of their bodies, and retreated a short space only to come with more united steady impetus against it, till their great beats made the strong gates quiver, like reeds before the wind.

The women gathered round the windows, fascinated to look on the scene which terrified them. Mrs. Thornton, the women-servants, Margaret,—all were there. Fanny had returned, screaming upstairs as if pursued at every step, and had thrown herself in hysterical sobbing on the sofa. Mrs. Thornton watched for her son, who was still in the mill. He came out, looked up at them—the pale cluster of faces—and smiled good courage to them, before he locked the factory-door. Then he called to one of the women to come down and undo his own door, which Fanny had fastened behind her in her mad flight. Mrs. Thornton herself went. And the sound of his well-known and commanding voice, seemed to have been like the taste of blood to the infuriated multitude outside. Hitherto they had been voiceless, wordless, needing all their breath for their hard-labouring efforts to breakdown the gates. But now, hearing him speak inside, they set up such a fierce unearthly groan, that even Mrs. Thornton was white with fear as she preceded him into the room. He came in a little flushed, but his eyes gleaming, as in answer to the trumpet-call of danger, and with a proud look of defiance on his face, that made him a noble, if not a handsome man. Margaret had always dreaded lest her courage should fail her in any emergency, and she should be proved to be, what she dreaded lest she was—coward. But now, in this real great time of reasonable fear and nearness of terror, she forgot herself, and felt only an intense sympathy—intense to painfulness—in the interests of the moment.

Mr. Thornton came frankly forwards:

"I'm sorry, Miss Hale, you have visited us at this unfortunate moment, when, I fear, you may be involved in whatever risk we have to bear. Mother! had'nt you better go into the back rooms? I'm not sure whether they may not have made their way from Pinner's Lane into the stable-yard; but if not, you will be safer there than here. Go Jane!" continued he, addressing the upper servant. And she went, followed by the others.

"I stop here!" said his mother. "Where you are, there I stay." And indeed, retreat into the back rooms was of no avail; the crowd had surrounded the outbuildings at the rear, and were sending forth their awful threatening roar behind. The servants retreated into the garrets, with many a cry and shriek. Mr. Thornton smiled scornfully as he heard them. He glanced at Margaret, standing all by herself at the window nearest the factory. Her eyes glittered, her colour was deepened on cheek and lip. As if she felt his look, she turned to him and asked a question that had been for some time in her mind:

"Where are the poor imported work-people? In the factory there?"

"Yes! I left them cowered up in a small room, at the head of a back flight of stairs; bidding them run all risks, and escape down there, if they heard any attack made on the mill-doors. But it is not them—it is me they want."

"When can the soldiers be here?" asked his mother, in a low but not unsteady voice.

He took out his watch with the same measured composure with which he did everything. He made some little calculation:

"Supposing Williams got straight off when I told him, and hadn't to dodge about amongst them—it must be twenty minutes yet."

"Twenty minutes!" said his mother, for the first time showing her terror in the tones of her voice.

"Shut down the windows instantly, mother," exclaimed he: "the gates won't bear such another shock. Shut down that window, Miss Hale."

Margaret shut down her window, and then went to assist Mrs. Thornton's trembling fingers.

From some cause or other, there was a pause of several minutes in the unseen street. Mrs. Thornton looked with wild anxiety at her son's countenance, as if to gain the interpretation of the sudden stillness from him. His face was set into rigid lines of contemptuous defiance; neither hope nor fear could be read there.

Fanny raised herself up:

"Are they gone?" asked she, in a whisper.

"Gone!" replied he. "Listen!"

She did listen; they all could hear the one great straining breath; the creak of wood slowly yielding; the wrench of iron; the mighty fall of the ponderous gates. Fanny stood up tottering—made a step or two towards her mother, and fell forwards into her arms in a fainting fit. Mrs. Thornton lifted her up with a strength that was as much that of the will as of the body, and carried her away.

"Thank God!" said Mr. Thornton, as he watched her out. "Had you not better go upstairs, Miss Hale?"

Margaret's lips formed a "No!"—but he could not hear her speak, for the tramp of innumerable steps right under the very wall of the house, and the fierce growl of low deep angry voices that had a ferocious murmur of satisfaction in them, more dreadful than their baffled cries not many minutes before.

"Never mind!" said he, thinking to encourage her. "I am very sorry you should have been entrapped into all this alarm; but it cannot last long now; a few minutes more, and the soldiers will be here."

"Oh, God!" cried Margaret, suddenly; "there is Boucher. I know his face, though he is livid with rage,—he is fighting to get to the front—look! look!"

"Who is Boucher?" asked Mr. Thornton coolly, and coming close to the window to discover the man in whom Margaret took such an interest. As soon as they saw Mr. Thornton, they set up a yell,—to call it not human is nothing,—it was as the demoniac desire of some terrible wild beast for the food that is withheld from his ravening. Even he drew back for a moment, dismayed at the intensity of hatred he had provoked.

"Let them yell!" said he. "In five minutes more—. I only hope my poor Irishmen are not terrified out of their wits by such a fiendlike noise. Keep up your courage for five minutes, Miss Hale."

"Don't be afraid for me," she said hastily. "But what in five minutes? Can you do nothing to soothe these poor creatures? It is awful to see them."

"The soldiers will be here directly, and that will bring them to reason."

"To reason!" said Margaret, quickly. "What kind of reason?"

"The only reason that does with men that make themselves into wild beasts. By heaven! they've turned to the mill-door!"

"Mr. Thornton," said Margaret, shaking all over with her passion, "go down this instant, if you are not a coward. Go down and face them like a man. Save these poor strangers, whom you have decoyed here. Speak to your workmen as if they were human beings. Speak to them kindly. Don't let the soldiers come in and cut down poor creatures who are driven mad. I see one there who is. If you have any courage or noble quality in you, go out and speak to them, man to man."

He turned and looked at her while she spoke. A dark cloud came over his face while he listened. He set his teeth as he heard her words.

"I will go. Perhaps I may ask you to accompany me downstairs, and bar the door behind me; my mother and sister will need that protection."

"Oh! Mr. Thornton! I do not know—I may be wrong—only—"

But he was gone; he was downstairs in the hall; he had unbarred the front door; all she could do, was to follow him quickly, and fasten it behind him, and clamber up the stairs again with a sick heart and a dizzy head. Again she took her place by the farthest window. He was on the steps below; she saw that by the direction of a thousand angry eyes; but she could neither see nor hear anything save the savage satisfaction of the rolling angry murmur. She threw the window wide open. Many in the crowd were mere boys; cruel and thoughtless,—cruel because they were thoughtless; some were men, gaunt as wolves,

and mad for prey. She knew how it was; they were like Boucher,—
with starving children at home—relying on ultimate success in their
efforts to get higher wages, and enraged beyond measure at discovering that Irishmen were to be brought in to rob their little ones of
bread. Margaret knew it all; she read it in Boucher's face, forlornly
desperate and livid with rage. If Mr. Thornton would but say something to them—let them hear his voice only—it seemed as if it would
be better than this wild beating and raging against the stony silence
that vouchsafed them no word, even of anger or reproach. But perhaps he was speaking now; there was a momentary hush of their
noise, inarticulate as that of a troop of animals. She tore her bonnet
off; and bent forwards to hear. She could only see; for if Mr. Thornton had indeed made the attempt to speak, the momentary instinct to
listen to him was past and gone, and the people were raging worse
than ever. He stood with his arms folded; still as a statue; his face
pale with repressed excitement. They were trying to intimidate him—
to make him flinch; each was urging the other on to some immediate
act of personal violence. Margaret felt intuitively, that in an instant
all would be uproar; the first touch would cause an explosion, in
which, among such hundreds of infuriated men and reckless boys,
even Mr. Thornton's life would be unsafe,—that in another instant
the stormy passions would have passed their bounds, and swept away
all barriers of reason, or apprehension of consequence. Even while
she looked, she saw lads in the background stooping to take off their
heavy wooden clogs—the readiest missile they could find; she saw it
was the spark to the gunpowder, and, with a cry, which no one heard,
she rushed out of the room, down stairs,—she had lifted the great iron
bar of the door with an imperious force—had thrown the door open
wide—and was there, in face of that angry sea of men, her eyes smit-
ing them with flaming arrows of reproach. The clogs were arrested in
the hands that held them—the countenances, so fell not a moment
before, now looked irresolute, and as if asking what this meant. For
she stood between them and their enemy. She could not speak, but
held out her arms towards them till she could recover breath.

   "Oh, do not use violence! He is one man, and you are many;" but
her words died away, for there was no tone in her voice; it was but
a hoarse whisper. Mr. Thornton stood a little on one side; he had
moved away from behind her, as if jealous of anything that should
come between him and danger.

   "Go!" said she, once more (and now her voice was like a cry). "The
soldiers are sent for—are coming. Go peaceably. Go away. You shall
have relief from your complaints, whatever they are."

   "Shall them Irish blackguards be packed back again?" asked one
from out the crowd, with fierce threatening in his voice.

   "Never, for your bidding!" exclaimed Mr. Thornton. And instantly the storm broke. The hootings rose and filled the air,—but Margaret did not hear them. Her eye was on the group of lads who had armed themselves with their clogs some time before. She saw their gesture—she knew its meaning,—she read their aim. Another moment, and Mr. Thornton might be smitten down,—he whom she had urged and goaded to come to this perilous place. She only thought how she could save him. She threw her arms around him; she made her body into a shield from the fierce people beyond. Still, with his arms folded, he shook her off.

[margin note: Thornton sees her as making things worse]

"Go away," said he, in his deep voice. "This is no place for you."

"It is!" said she. "You did not see what I saw." If she thought her sex would be a protection—if, with shrinking eyes she had turned away from the terrible anger of these men, in any hope that ere she looked again they would have paused and reflected, and slunk away, and vanished,—she was wrong. Their reckless passion had carried them too far to stop—at least had carried some of them too far; for it is always the savage lads, with their love of cruel excitement, who head the riot—reckless to what bloodshed it may lead. A clog whizzed through the air. Margaret's fascinated eyes watched its progress; it missed its aim, and she turned sick with affright, but changed not her position, only hid her face on Mr. Thornton's arm. Then she turned and spoke again:

"For God's sake! do not damage your cause by this violence. You do not know what you are doing." She strove to make her words distinct.

A sharp pebble flew by her, grazing forehead and cheek, and drawing a blinding sheet of light before her eyes. She lay like one dead on Mr. Thornton's shoulder. Then he unfolded his arms, and held her encircled in one for an instant:

"You do well!" said he. "You come to oust the innocent stranger. You fall—you hundreds—on one man; and when a woman comes before you, to ask you for your own sakes to be reasonable creatures, your cowardly wrath falls upon her! You do well!" They were silent while he spoke. They were watching, open-eyed and open-mouthed, the thread of dark-red blood which wakened them up from their trance of passion. Those nearest the gate stole out ashamed; there was a movement through all the crowd—a retreating movement. Only one voice cried out:

[margin note: # You are bad and I knew it. He is stirring the pot.]

"Th' stone were meant for thee; but thou wert sheltered behind a woman!"

Mr. Thornton quivered with rage. The blood-flowing had made Margaret conscious—dimly, vaguely conscious. He placed her gently on the door-step, her head leaning against the frame.

"Can you rest there?" he asked. But without waiting for her answer, he went slowly down the steps right into the middle of the

[handwritten note at bottom: Margaret is the one trying to keep peace, but she ends up getting hurt]

crowd. "Now kill me, if it is your brutal will. There is no woman to shield me here. You may beat me to death—you will never move me from what I have determined upon—not you!" He stood amongst them, with his arms folded, in precisely the same attitude as he had been in on the steps.

But the retrograde movement towards the gate had begun—as unreasoningly, perhaps as blindly, as the simultaneous anger. Or, perhaps, the idea of the approach of the soldiers, and the sight of that pale, upturned face, with closed eyes, still and sad as marble, though the tears welled out of the long entanglement of eyelashes, and dropped down; and, heavier, slower plash than even tears, came the drip of blood from her wound. Even the most desperate—Boucher himself—drew back, faltered away, scowled, and finally went off, muttering curses on the master, who stood in his unchanging attitude, looking after their retreat with defiant eyes. The moment that retreat had changed into a flight (as it was sure from its very character to do), he darted up the steps to Margaret.

She tried to rise without his help.

"It is nothing," she said, with a sickly smile. "The skin is grazed, and I was stunned at the moment. Oh, I am so thankful they are gone!" And she cried without restraint.

He could not sympathise with her. His anger had not abated; it was rather rising the more as his sense of immediate danger was passing away. The distant clank of the soldiers was heard; just five minutes too late to make this vanished mob feel the power of authority and order. He hoped they would see the troops, and be quelled by the thought of their narrow escape. While these thoughts crossed his mind, Margaret clung to the doorpost to steady herself: but a film came over her eyes—he was only just in time to catch her. "Mother—mother!" cried he; "Come down—they are gone, and Miss Hale is hurt!" He bore her into the dining-room, and laid her on the sofa there; laid her down softly, and looking on her pure white face, the sense of what she was to him came upon him so keenly that he spoke it out in his pain:

"Oh, my Margaret—my Margaret! no one can tell what you are to me! Dead—cold as you lie there, you are the only woman I ever loved! Oh, Margaret—Margaret!"

Inarticulately as he spoke, kneeling by her, and rather moaning than saying the words, he started up, ashamed of himself, as his mother came in. She saw nothing, but her son a little paler, a little sterner than usual.

"Miss Hale is hurt, mother. A stone has grazed her temple. She has lost a good deal of blood, I'm afraid."

"She looks very seriously hurt,—I could almost fancy her dead," said Mrs. Thornton, a good deal alarmed.

"It is only a fainting-fit. She has spoken to me since." But all the blood in his body seemed to rush inwards to his heart as he spoke, and he absolutely trembled.

"Go and call Jane,—she can find me the things I want; and do you go to your Irish people, who are crying and shouting as if they were mad with fright."

He went. He went away as if weights were tied to every limb that bore him from her. He called Jane; he called his sister. She should have all womanly care, all gentle tendance. But every pulse beat in him as he remembered how she had come down and placed herself in foremost danger,—could it be to save him? At the time, he had pushed her aside, and spoken gruffly; he had seen nothing but the unnecessary danger she had placed herself in. He went to his Irish people, with every nerve in his body thrilling at the thought of her, and found it difficult to understand enough of what they were saying to soothe and comfort away their fears. There, they declared, they would not stop; they claimed to be sent back.

And so he had to think, and talk, and reason.

Mrs. Thornton bathed Margaret's temples with eau de Cologne. As the spirit touched the wound, which till then neither Mrs. Thornton nor Jane had perceived, Margaret opened her eyes; but it was evident she did not know where she was, nor who they were. The dark circles deepened, the lips quivered and contracted, and she became insensible once more.

"She has had a terrible blow," said Mrs. Thornton. "Is there any one who will go for a doctor?"

"Not me, ma'am, if you please," said Jane, shrinking back. "Them rabble may be all about; I don't think the cut is so deep, ma'am, as it looks."

"I will not run the chance. She was hurt in our house. If you are a coward, Jane, I am not. I will go."

"Pray, ma'am, let me send one of the police. There's ever so many come up, and soldiers too."

"And yet you're afraid to go! I will not have their time taken up with our errands. They'll have enough to do to catch some of the mob. You will not be afraid to stop in this house," she asked contemptuously, "and go on bathing Miss Hale's forehead, shall you? I shall not be ten minutes away."

"Couldn't Hannah go, ma'am?"

"Why Hannah? Why any but you? No, Jane, if you don't go, I do."

Mrs. Thornton went first to the room in which she had left Fanny stretched on the bed. She started up as her mother entered.

"Oh, mamma, how you terrified me! I thought you were a man that had got into the house."

"Nonsense! The men are all gone away. There are soldiers all round the place, seeking for their work now it is too late. Miss Hale is lying on the dining-room sofa badly hurt. I am going for the doctor."

"Oh! don't, mamma! they'll murder you." She clung to her mother's gown. Mrs. Thornton wrenched it away with no gentle hand.

"Find me some one else to go; but that girl must not bleed to death."

"Bleed! oh, how horrid! How has she got hurt?"

"I don't know,—I have no time to ask. Go down to her, Fanny, and do try to make yourself of use. Jane is with her; and I trust it looks worse than it is. Jane has refused to leave the house, cowardly woman! And I won't put myself in the way of any more refusals from my servants, so I am going myself."

"Oh, dear, dear!" said Fanny, crying, and preparing to go down rather than be left alone, with the thought of wounds and bloodshed in the very house.

"Oh, Jane!" said she, creeping into the dining-room, "what is the matter? How white she looks! How did she get hurt? Did they throw stones into the drawing-room?"

Margaret did indeed look white and wan, although her senses were beginning to return to her. But the sickly daze of the swoon made her still miserably faint. She was conscious of movement around her, and of refreshment from the eau de Cologne, and a craving for the bathing to go on without intermission; but when they stopped to talk, she could no more have opened her eyes, or spoken to ask for more bathing, than the people who lie in death-like trance can move, or utter sound, to arrest the awful preparations for their burial, while they are yet fully aware, not merely of the actions of those around them, but of the idea that is the motive for such actions.

Jane paused in her bathing, to reply to Miss Thornton's question.

"She'd have been safe enough, miss, if she'd stayed in the drawing-room, or come up to us; we were in the front garret, and could see it all, out of harm's way."

"Where was she then?" said Fanny, drawing nearer by slow degrees, as she became accustomed to the sight of Margaret's pale face.

"Just before the front door—with master!" said Jane, significantly.

"With John! with my brother! How did she get there?"

"Nay, miss, that's not for me to say," answered Jane, with a slight toss of her head. "Sarah did"——

"Sarah what?" said Fanny, with impatient curiosity.

Jane resumed her bathing, as if what Sarah did or said was not exactly the thing she liked to repeat.

"Sarah what?" asked Fanny, sharply. "Don't speak in these half sentences, or I can't understand you."

"Well, miss, since you will have it—Sarah, you see, was in the best place for seeing, being at the right-hand window; and she says, and said at the very time too, that she saw Miss Hale with her arms about master's neck, hugging him before all the people."

"I don't believe it," said Fanny. "I know she cares for my brother; any one can see that; and I dare say, she'd give her eyes if he'd marry her,—which he never will, I can tell her. But I don't believe she'd be so bold and forward as to put her arms round his neck."

"Poor young lady! she's paid for it dearly if she did. It's my belief, that the blow has given her such an ascendency of blood to the head as she'll never get the better from. She looks like a corpse now."

"Oh, I wish mamma would come!" said Fanny, wringing her hands. "I never was in the room with a dead person before."

"Stay, miss! She's not dead: her eye-lids are quivering, and here's wet tears a-coming down her cheeks. Speak to her, Miss Fanny!"

"Are you better now?" asked Fanny, in a quavering voice.

No answer; no sign of recognition; but a faint pink colour returned to her lips, although the rest of her face was ashen pale.

Mrs. Thornton came hurriedly in, with the nearest surgeon she could find.

"How is she? Are you better, my dear?" as Margaret opened her filmy eyes, and gazed dreamily at her. "Here is Mr. Lowe come to see you."

Mrs. Thornton spoke loudly and distinctly, as to a deaf person. Margaret tried to rise, and drew her ruffled, luxuriant hair instinctly over the cut.

"I am better now," said she, in a very low, faint voice. "I was a little sick."

She let him take her hand and feel her pulse. The bright colour came for a moment into her face, when he asked to examine the wound in her forehead; and she glanced up at Jane, as if shrinking from her inspection more than from the doctor's.

"It is not much, I think. I am better now. I must go home."

"Not until I have applied some strips of plaster, and you have rested a little."

She sat down hastily, without another word, and allowed it to be bound up.

"Now, if you please," said she, "I must go. Mamma will not see it, I think. It is under the hair, is it not?"

"Quite; no one could tell."

"But you must not go," said Mrs. Thornton, impatiently. "You are not fit to go."

"I must," said Margaret, decidedly. "Think of mamma. If they should hear——Besides, I must go," said she, vehemently. "I cannot stay here. May I ask for a cab?"

"You are quite flushed and feverish," observed Mr. Lowe.

"It is only with being here, when I do so want to go. The air—getting away, would do me more good than anything," pleaded she.

"I really believe it is as she says," Mr. Lowe replied. "If her mother is so ill as you told me on the way here, it may be very serious if she hears of this riot, and does not see her daughter back at the time she expects. The injury is not deep. I will fetch a cab, if your servants are still afraid to go out."

"Oh, thank you!" said Margaret. "It will do me more good than anything. It is the air of this room that makes me feel so miserable."

She leant back on the sofa, and closed her eyes. Fanny beckoned her mother out of the room, and told her something that made her equally anxious with Margaret for the departure of the latter. Not that she fully believed Fanny's statement; but she credited enough to make her manner to Margaret appear very much constrained, at wishing her good-bye.

Mr. Lowe returned in the cab.

"If you will allow me, I will see you home, Miss Hale. The streets are not very quiet yet."

Margaret's thoughts were quite alive enough to the present to make her desirous of getting rid of both Mr. Lowe and the cab before she reached Crampton Crescent, for fear of alarming her father and mother. Beyond that one aim she would not look. That ugly dream of insolent words spoken about herself, could never be forgotten—but could be put aside till she was stronger—for, oh! she was very weak; and her mind sought for some present fact to steady itself upon, and keep it from utterly losing consciousness in another hideous, sickly swoon.

Chapter XXIII.

Mistakes.

> "Which when his mother saw, she in her mind
> Was troubled sore, ne wist well what to ween."
> SPENSER.[1]

Margaret had not been gone five minutes when Mr. Thornton came in, his face all a-glow.

"I could not come sooner: the superintendent would——Where

---

1. *The Faerie Queene*, Book IV, 12, 21.

is she?" He looked round the dining-room, and then almost fiercely at his mother, who was quietly re-arranging the disturbed furniture, and did not instantly reply. "Where is Miss Hale?" asked he again.

"Gone home," said she, rather shortly.

"Gone home!"

"Yes. She was a great deal better. Indeed, I don't believe it was so very much of a hurt; only some people faint at the least thing."

"I am sorry she is gone home," said he, walking uneasily about. "She could not have been fit for it."

"She said she was; and Mr. Lowe said she was. I went for him myself."

"Thank you, mother." He stopped, and partly held out his hand to give her a grateful shake. But she did not notice the movement.

"What have you done with your Irish people?"

"Sent to the Dragon for a good meal for them, poor wretches. And then, luckily, I caught Father Grady, and I've asked him in to speak to them, and dissuade them from going off in a body. How did Miss Hale go home? I'm sure she could not walk."

"She had a cab. Everything was done properly, even to the paying. Let us talk of something else. She has caused disturbance enough."

"I don't know where I should have been but for her."

"Are you become so helpless as to have to be defended by a girl?" asked Mrs. Thornton, scornfully.

He reddened. "Not many girls would have taken the blows on herself which were meant for me;—meant with right down goodwill, too."

"A girl in love will do a good deal," replied Mrs. Thornton, shortly.

"Mother!" He made a step forwards; stood still; heaved with passion.

She was a little startled at the evident force he used to keep himself calm. She was not sure of the nature of the emotions she had provoked. It was only their violence that was clear. Was it anger? His eyes glowed, his figure was dilated, his breath came thick and fast. It was a mixture of joy, of anger, of pride, of glad surprise, of panting doubt; but she could not read it. Still it made her uneasy,—as the presence of all strong feeling, of which the cause is not fully understood or sympathised in, always has this effect. She went to the sideboard, opened a drawer, and took out a duster, which she kept there for any occasional purpose. She had seen a drop of eau de Cologne on the polished arm of the sofa, and instinctively sought to wipe it off. But she kept her back turned to her son much longer than was necessary; and when she spoke, her voice seemed unusual and constrained.

"You have taken some steps about the rioters, I suppose? You don't apprehend any more violence, do you? Where were the police? Never at hand when they're wanted!"

"On the contrary, I saw three or four of them when the gates gave way, struggling and beating about in fine fashion; and more came running up just when the yard was clearing. I might have given some of the fellows in charge then, if I had had my wits about me. But there will be no difficulty, plenty of people can identify them."

"But won't they come back to night?"

"I'm going to see about a sufficient guard for the premises. I have appointed to meet Captain Hanbury in half an hour at the station."

"You must have some tea first."

"Tea! Yes, I suppose I must. It's half-past six, and I may be out for some time. Don't sit up for me, mother."

"You expect me to go to bed before I have seen you safe, do you?"

"Well, perhaps not." He hesitated for a moment. "But if I've time, I shall go round by Crampton after I've arranged with the police and seen Hamper and Clarkson." Their eyes met; they looked at each other intently for a minute. Then she asked:

"Why are you going round by Crampton?"

"To ask after Miss Hale."

"I will send. Williams must take the water-bed she came to ask for. He shall inquire how she is."

"I must go myself."

"Not merely to ask how Miss Hale is?"

"No, not merely for that. I want to thank her for the way in which she stood between me and the mob."

"What made you go down at all? It was putting your head into the lion's mouth!"

He glanced sharply at her; saw that she did not know what had passed between him and Margaret in the drawing-room; and replied by another question:

"Shall you be afraid to be left without me, until I can get some of the police; or had we better send Williams for them now, and they could be here by the time we have done tea? There's no time to be lost. I must be off in a quarter of an hour."

Mrs. Thornton left the room. Her servants wondered at her directions, usually so sharply-cut and decided, now confused and uncertain. Mr. Thornton remained in the dining-room, trying to think of the business he had to do at the police-office, and in reality thinking of Margaret. Everything seemed dim and vague beyond—behind— besides the touch of her arms round his neck—the soft clinging which made the dark colour come and go in his cheek as he thought of it.

The tea would have been very silent, but for Fanny's perpetual description of her own feelings; how she had been alarmed—and then thought they were gone—and then felt sick and faint and trembling in every limb.

"There, that's enough," said her brother, rising from the table. "The reality was enough for me." He was going to leave the room, when his mother stopped him with her hand upon his arm.

"You will come back here before you go to the Hales'," said she, in a low, anxious voice.

"I know what I know," said Fanny to herself.

"Why? Will it be too late to disturb them?"

"John, come back to me for this one evening. It will be late for Mrs. Hale. But that is not it. Tomorrow, you will——Come back to night, John!" She had seldom pleaded with her son at all—she was too proud for that: but she had never pleaded in vain.

"I will return straight here after I have done my business. You will be sure to inquire after them?—after her?"

Mrs. Thornton was by no means a talkative companion to Fanny, nor yet a good listener while her son was absent. But on his return, her eyes and ears were keen to see and to listen to all the details which he could give, as to the steps he had taken to secure himself, and those whom he chose to employ, from any repetition of the day's outrages. He clearly saw his object. Punishment and suffering, were the natural consequences to those who had taken part in the riot. All that was necessary, in order that property should be protected, and that the will of the proprietor might cut to his end, clean and sharp as a sword.

"Mother! You know what I have got to say to Miss Hale, tomorrow?"

The question came upon her suddenly, during a pause in which she, at least, had forgotten Margaret.

She looked up at him.

"Yes! I do. You can hardly do otherwise."

"Do otherwise! I don't understand you."

"I mean that, after allowing her feelings so to overcome her, I consider you bound in honour—"

"Bound in honour," said he scornfully. "I'm afraid honour has nothing to do with it. 'Her feelings overcome her!' What feelings do you mean?"

"Nay, John, there is no need to be angry. Did she not rush down, and cling to you to save you from danger?"

"She did!" said he. "But, mother," continued he, stopping short in his walk right in front of her, "I dare not hope. I never was faint-hearted before; but I cannot believe such a creature cares for me."

"Don't be foolish, John. Such a creature! Why, she might be a duke's daughter, to hear you speak. And what proof more would you have, I wonder, of her caring for you? I can believe she has had a struggle with her aristocratic way of viewing things; but I like her the better for seeing clearly at last. It is a good deal for me to say," said Mrs. Thornton, smiling slowly, while the tears stood in her eyes; "for after to-night, I stand second. It was to have you to myself, all to myself, a few hours longer, that I begged you not to go till to-morrow!"

"Dearest mother!" (Still love is selfish, and in an instant he reverted to his own hopes and fears in a way that drew the cold creeping shadow over Mrs. Thornton's heart.) "But I know she does not care for me. I shall put myself at her feet—I must. If it were but one chance in a thousand—or a million—I should do it."

"Don't fear!" said his mother, crushing down her own personal mortification at the little notice he had taken of the rare ebullition of her maternal feelings—of the pang of jealousy that betrayed the intensity of her disregarded love. "Don't be afraid," she said, coldly. "As far as love may go she may be worthy of you. It must have taken a good deal to overcome her pride. Don't be afraid, John," said she, kissing him, as she wished him good-night. And she went slowly and majestically out of the room. But when she got into her own, she locked the door, and sat down to cry unwonted tears.

Margaret entered the room (where her father and mother still sat, holding low conversation together), looking very pale and white. She came close up to them before she could trust herself to speak.

"Mrs. Thornton will send the water-bed, mamma."

"Dear, how tired you look! Is it very hot, Margaret?"

"Very hot, and the streets are rather rough with the strike."

Margaret's colour came back vivid and bright as ever; but it faded away instantly.

"Here has been a message from Bessy Higgins, asking you to go to her," said Mrs. Hale. "But I'm sure you look too tired."

"Yes!" said Margaret. "I am tired, I cannot go."

She was very silent and trembling while she made tea. She was thankful to see her father so much occupied with her mother as not to notice her looks. Even after her mother went to bed, he was not content to be absent from her, but undertook to read her to sleep. Margaret was alone.

"Now I will think of it—now I will remember it all. I could not before—I dared not." She sat still in her chair, her hands clasped on her knees, her lips compressed, her eyes fixed as one who sees a vision. She drew a deep breath.

"I, who hate scenes—I, who have despised people for showing

emotion—who have thought them wanting in self-control—I went down and must needs throw myself into the mêlée, like a romantic fool! Did I do any good? They would have gone away without me, I dare say." But this was over-leaping the rational conclusion,—as in an instant her well-poised judgment felt. "No, perhaps they would not. I did some good. But what possessed me to defend that man as if he were a helpless child! Ah!" said she, clenching her hands together, "it is no wonder those people thought I was in love with him, after disgracing myself in that way. I in love—and with him too!" Her pale cheeks suddenly became one flame of fire; and she covered her face with her hands. When she took them away, her palms were wet with scalding tears.

"Oh how low I am fallen that they should say that of me! I could not have been so brave for any one else, just because he was so utterly indifferent to me—if, indeed, I do not positively dislike him. It made me the more anxious that there should be fair play on each side; and I could see what fair play was. It was not fair," said she vehemently, "that he should stand there—sheltered, awaiting the soldiers, who might catch those poor maddened creatures as in a trap—without an effort on his part, to bring them to reason. And it was worse than unfair for them to set on him as they threatened. I would do it again, let who will say what they like of me. If I saved one blow, one cruel, angry action that might otherwise have been committed, I did a woman's work. Let them insult my maiden pride as they will—I walk pure before God!"

She looked up, and a noble peace seemed to descend and calm her face, till it was "stiller than chiselled marble."[2]

Dixon came in:

"If you please, Miss Margaret, here's the water-bed from Mrs. Thornton's. It's too late for to-night, I'm afraid, for missus is nearly asleep: but it will do nicely for to-morrow."

"Very," said Margaret. "You must send our best thanks."

Dixon left the room for a moment.

"If you please, Miss Margaret, he says he's to ask particular how you are. I think he must mean missus; but he says his last words were, to ask how Miss Hale was."

"Me!" said Margaret, drawing herself up. "I am quite well. Tell him I am perfectly well." But her complexion was as deadly white as her handkerchief; and her head ached intensely.

Mr. Hale now came in. He had left his sleeping wife; and wanted,

2. The quotation is from Tennyson's poem "A Dream of Fair Women" (1833): "At length I saw a lady within call, / Stiller than chisell'd marble, standing there; / A daughter of the gods, divinely tall, / And most divinely fair."

as Margaret saw, to be amused and interested by something that she was to tell him. With sweet patience did she bear her pain, without a word of complaint; and rummaged up numberless small subjects for conversation—all except the riot, and that she never named once. It turned her sick to think of it.

"Good-night, Margaret. I have every chance of a good night myself, and you are looking very pale with your watching. I shall call Dixon if your mother needs anything. Do you go to bed and sleep like a top; for I'm sure you need it, poor child!"

"Good-night, papa."

She let her colour go—the forced smile fade away—the eyes grow dull with heavy pain. She released her strong will from its laborious task. Till morning she might feel ill and weary.

She lay down and never stirred. To move hand or foot, or even so much as one finger, would have been an exertion beyond the powers of either volition or motion. She was so tired, so stunned, that she thought she never slept at all; her feverish thoughts passed and repassed the boundary between sleeping and waking, and kept their own miserable identity. She could not be alone, prostrate, powerless as she was,—a cloud of faces looked up at her, giving her no idea of fierce vivid anger, or of personal danger, but a deep sense of shame that she should thus be the object of universal regard—a sense of shame so acute that it seemed as if she would fain have burrowed into the earth to hide herself, and yet she could not escape out of that unwinking glare of many eyes.

Chapter XXIV.

Mistakes Cleared Up.

> "Your beauty was the first that won the place,
> And scal'd the walls of my undaunted heart,
>   Which, captive now, pines in a captive case,
> Unkindly met with rigour for desert:—
>   Yet not the less your servant shall abide,
>   In spite of rude repulse or silent pride."
>   WILLIAM FOWLER.[1]

The next morning, Margaret dragged herself up, thankful that the night was over,—unrefreshed, yet rested. All had gone well through the house; her mother had only wakened once. A little breeze was stirring in the hot air, and though there were no trees to show the

---

1. Scottish poet and courtier (c. 1560–1612). His poetry was unpublished in his lifetime. The lines are from his sonnet sequence *The Tarantula of Love*.

playful tossing movement caused by the wind among the leaves, Margaret knew how, somewhere or another, by wayside, in copses, or in thick green woods, there was a pleasant, murmuring dancing sound,—a rushing and falling noise, the very thought of which was an echo of distant gladness in her heart.

She sat at her work in Mrs. Hale's room. As soon as that forenoon slumber was over, she would help her mother to dress; after dinner, she would go and see Bessy Higgins. She would banish all recollection of the Thornton family,—no need to think of them till they absolutely stood before her in flesh and blood. But, of course, the effort not to think of them brought them only the more strongly before her; and from time to time, the hot flush came over her pale face sweeping it into colour, as a sunbeam from between watery clouds comes swiftly moving over the sea.

Dixon opened the door very softly, and stole on tiptoe up to Margaret, sitting by the shaded window.

"Mr. Thornton, Miss Margaret. He is in the drawing-room."

Margaret dropped her sewing.

"Did he ask for me? Isn't papa come in?"

"He asked for you, miss; and master is out."

"Very well, I will come," said Margaret, quietly. But she lingered strangely.

Mr. Thornton stood by one of the windows, with his back to the door, apparently absorbed in watching something in the street. But, in truth, he was afraid of himself. His heart beat thick at the thought of her coming. He could not forget the touch of her arms around his neck, impatiently felt as it had been at the time; but now the recollection of her clinging defence of him, seemed to thrill him through and through,—to melt away every resolution, all power of self-control, as if it were wax before a fire. He dreaded lest he should go forwards to meet her, with his arms held out in mute entreaty that she would come and nestle there, as she had done, all unheeded, the day before, but never unheeded again. His heart throbbed loud and quick. Strong man as he was, he trembled at the anticipation of what he had to say, and how it might be received. She might droop, and flush, and flutter to his arms, as to her natural home and resting-place. One moment, he glowed with impatience at the thought that she might do this,—the next, he feared a passionate rejection, the very idea of which withered up his future with so deadly a blight that he refused to think of it. He was startled by the sense of the presence of some one else in the room. He turned round. She had come in so gently, that he had never heard her; the street noises had been more distinct to his inattentive ear than her slow movements, in her soft muslin gown.

She stood by the table, not offering to sit down. Her eyelids were dropped half over her eyes; her teeth were shut, not compressed; her lips were just parted over them, allowing the white line to be seen between their curve. Her slow deep breathings dilated her thin and beautiful nostrils; it was the only motion visible on her countenance. The fine-grained skin, the oval cheek, the rich outline of her mouth, its corners deep set in dimples,—were all wan and pale to-day; the loss of their usual natural healthy colour being made more evident by the heavy shadow of the dark hair, brought down upon the temples, to hide all sign of the blow she had received. Her head, for all its drooping eyes, was thrown a little back, in the old proud attitude. Her long arms hung motionless by her sides. Altogether she looked like some prisoner, falsely accused of a crime that she loathed and despised, and from which she was too indignant to justify herself.

Mr. Thornton made a hasty step or two forwards; recovered himself, and went with quiet firmness to the door (which she had left open), and shut it. Then he came back, and stood opposite to her for a moment, receiving the general impression of her beautiful presence, before he dared to disturb it, perhaps to repel it, by what he had to say.

"Miss Hale, I was very ungrateful yesterday—"

"You had nothing to be grateful for," said she, raising her eyes, and looking full and straight at him. "You mean, I suppose, that you believe you ought to thank me for what I did." In spite of herself—in defiance of her anger—the thick blushes came all over her face, and burnt into her very eyes; which fell not nevertheless from their grave and steady look. "It was only a natural instinct; any woman would have done just the same. We all feel the sanctity of our sex as a high privilege when we see danger. I ought rather," said she, hastily, "to apologise to you, for having said thoughtless words which sent you down into the danger."

"It was not your words; it was the truth they conveyed, pungently as it was expressed. But you shall not drive me off upon that, and so escape the expression of my deep gratitude, my—" he was on the verge now; he would not speak in the haste of his hot passion; he would weigh each word. He would; and his will was triumphant. He stopped in mid career.

"I do not try to escape from anything," said she. "I simply say, that you owe me no gratitude; and I may add, that any expression of it will be painful to me, because I do not feel that I deserve it. Still, if it will relieve you from even a fancied obligation, speak on."

"I do not want to be relieved from any obligation," said he, goaded by her calm manner. "Fancied, or not fancied—I question not myself to know which—I choose to believe that I owe my very life to you—

ay—smile, and think it an exaggeration if you will. I believe it, because it adds a value to that life to think—oh, Miss Hale!" continued he, lowering his voice to such a tender intensity of passion that she shivered and trembled before him, "to think circumstance so wrought, that whenever I exult in existence henceforward, I may say to myself, 'All this gladness in life, all honest pride in doing my work in the world, all this keen sense of being, I owe to her!' And it doubles the gladness, it makes the pride glow, it sharpens the sense of existence till I hardly know if it is pain or pleasure, to think that I owe it to one—nay, you must, you shall hear"—said he, stepping forwards with stern determination—"to one whom I love, as I do not believe man ever loved woman before." He held her hand tight in his. He panted as he listened for what should come. He threw the hand away with indignation, as he heard her icy tone; for icy it was, though the words came faltering out, as if she knew not where to find them.

"Your way of speaking shocks me. It is blasphemous. I cannot help it, if that is my first feeling. It might not be so, I dare say, if I understood the kind of feeling you describe. I do not want to vex you; and besides, we must speak gently, for mamma is asleep; but your whole manner offends me—"

"How!" exclaimed he. "Offends you! I am indeed most unfortunate."

"Yes!" said she, with recovered dignity. "I do feel offended; and, I think, justly. You seem to fancy that my conduct of yesterday"—again the deep carnation blush, but this time with eyes kindling with indignation rather than shame—"was a personal act between you and me; and that you may come and thank me for it, instead of perceiving, as a gentleman would—yes! a gentleman," she repeated, in allusion to their former conversation about that word, "that any woman, worthy of the name of woman, would come forward to shield, with her reverenced helplessness, a man in danger from the violence of numbers."

"And the gentleman thus rescued is forbidden the relief of thanks!" he broke in contemptuously. "I am a man. I claim the right of expressing my feelings."

"And I yielded to the right; simply saying that you gave me pain by insisting upon it," she replied proudly. "But you seem to have imagined, that I was not merely guided by womanly instinct, but"—and here the passionate tears (kept down for long—struggled with vehemently) came up into her eyes, and choked her voice—"but that I was prompted by some particular feeling for you—you! Why, there was not a man—not a poor desperate man in all that crowd—for whom I had not more sympathy—for whom I should not have done what little I could more heartily."

"You may speak on, Miss Hale. I am aware of all these misplaced sympathies of yours. I now believe that it was only your innate sense of oppression—(yes; I, though a master, may be oppressed)—that made you act so nobly as you did. I know you despise me; allow me to say, it is because you do not understand me."

"I do not care to understand," she replied, taking hold of the table to steady herself; for she thought him cruel—as, indeed, he was—and she was weak with her indignation.

"No, I see you do not. You are unfair and unjust."

Margaret compressed her lips. She would not speak in answer to such accusations. But, for all that—for all his savage words, he could have thrown himself at her feet, and kissed the hem of her garment. She did not speak; she did not move. The tears of wounded pride fell hot and fast. He waited awhile, longing for her to say something, even a taunt, to which he might reply. But she was silent. He took up his hat.

"One word more. You look as if you thought it tainted you to be loved by me. You cannot avoid it. Nay, I, if I would, cannot cleanse you from it. But I would not, if I could. I have never loved any woman before: my life has been too busy, my thoughts too much absorbed with other things. Now I love, and will love. But do not be afraid of too much expression on my part."

"I am not afraid," she replied, lifting herself straight up. "No one yet has ever dared to be impertinent to me, and no one ever shall. But, Mr. Thornton, you have been very kind to my father," said she, changing her whole tone and bearing to a most womanly softness. "Don't let us go on making each other angry. Pray don't!" He took no notice of her words: he occupied himself in smoothing the nap of his hat with his coat-sleeve, for half a minute or so; and then, rejecting her offered hand, and making as if he did not see her grave look of regret, he turned abruptly away, and left the room. Margaret caught one glance at his face before he went.

When he was gone, she thought she had seen the gleam of washed tears in his eyes; and that turned her proud dislike into something different and kinder, if nearly as painful—self-reproach for having caused such mortification to any one.

"But how could I help it?" asked she of herself. "I never liked him. I was civil; but I took no trouble to conceal my indifference. Indeed, I never thought about myself or him, so my manners must have shown the truth. All that yesterday, he might mistake. But that is his fault, not mine. I would do it again, if need were, though it does lead me into all this shame and trouble."

Chapter XXV.

Frederick.

"Revenge may have her own;
Roused discipline aloud proclaims their cause,
And injured navies urge their broken laws."
BYRON.[1]

Margaret began to wonder whether all offers were as unexpected beforehand,—as distressing at the time of their occurrence, as the two she had had. An involuntary comparison between Mr. Lennox and Mr. Thornton arose in her mind. She had been sorry, that an expression of any other feeling than friendship had been lured out by circumstances from Henry Lennox. That regret was the predominant feeling, on the first occasion of her receiving a proposal. She had not felt so stunned—so impressed as she did now, when echoes of Mr. Thornton's voice yet lingered about the room. In Lennox's case, he seemed for a moment to have slid over the boundary between friendship and love; and, the instant afterwards, to regret it nearly as much as she did, although for different reasons. In Mr. Thornton's case, as far as Margaret knew, there was no intervening stage of friendship. Their intercourse had been one continued series of opposition. Their opinions clashed; and indeed, she had never perceived that he had cared for her opinions, as belonging to her, the individual. As far as they defied his rock-like power of character, his passion-strength, he seemed to throw them off from him with contempt, until she felt the weariness of the exertion of making useless protests; and now, he had come, in this strange wild passionate way, to make known his love! For, although at first it had struck her, that his offer was forced and goaded out of him by sharp compassion for the exposure she had made of herself,—which he, like others, might misunderstand—yet, even before he left the room,—and certainly, not five minutes after, the clear conviction dawned upon her, shined bright upon her, that he did love her; that he had loved her; that he would love her. And she shrank and shuddered as under the fascination of some great power, repugnant to her whole previous life. She crept away, and hid from his idea. But it was of no use. To parody a line out of Fairfax's Tasso—

"His strong idea wandered through her thought."[2]

---

1. From Lord Byron's poem "The Island" (1823), which takes as its subject the mutiny on the *Bounty*. The lines thus relate to the situation of Frederick Hale, discussed in this chapter.
2. From Edward Fairfax's translation (1600) of Tasso's *Gerusalemme Liberata*. The original reads: "Her sweet idea wander'd through his thought." Gaskell has thus reversed the roles: Margaret is now thinking of Thornton.

She disliked him the more for having mastered her inner will. How dared he say that he would love her still, even though she shook him off with contempt? She wished she had spoken more—stronger. Sharp, decisive speeches came thronging into her mind, now that it was too late to utter them. The deep impression made by the interview, was like that of a horror in a dream; that will not leave the room although we waken up, and rub our eyes, and force a stiff rigid smile upon our lips. It is there—there, cowering and gibbering, with fixed ghastly eyes, in some corner of the chamber, listening to hear whether we dare to breathe of its presence to any one. And we dare not; poor cowards that we are!

And so she shuddered away from the threat of his enduring love. What did he mean? Had she not the power to daunt him? She would see. It was more daring than became a man to threaten her so. Did he ground it upon the miserable yesterday? If need were, she would do the same to-morrow,—by a crippled beggar, willingly and gladly,—but by him, she would do it, just as bravely, in spite of his deductions, and the cold slime of women's impertinence. She did it because it was right, and simple, and true to save where she could save; even to try to save. "Fais ce que dois, advienne que pourra."[3]

Hitherto she had not stirred from where he had left her; no outward circumstances had roused her out of the trance of thought in which she had been plunged by his last words, and by the look of his deep intent passionate eyes, as their flames had made her own fall before them. She went to the window, and threw it open, to dispel the oppression which hung around her. Then she went and opened the door, with a sort of impetuous wish to shake off the recollection of the past hour, in the company of others, or in active exertion. But all was profoundly hushed in the noonday stillness of a house, where an invalid catches the unrefreshing sleep that is denied to the night-hours. Margaret would not be alone. What should she do? "Go and see Bessy Higgins, of course," thought she, as the recollection of the message sent the night before flashed into her mind. And away she went.

When she got there, she found Bessy lying on the settle, moved close to the fire, though the day was sultry and oppressive. She was laid down quite flat, as if resting languidly after some paroxysm of pain. Margaret felt sure she ought to have the greater freedom of breathing which a more sitting posture would procure; and, without a word, she raised her up, and so arranged the pillows, that Bessy was more at ease, though very languid.

"I thought I should na' ha' seen yo' again," said she, at last, looking wistfully in Margaret's face.

3. Literally, "do what you should do, come what may" (French).

"I'm afraid you're much worse. But I could not have come yester-day, my mother was so ill—for many reasons," said Margaret, col-ouring.

"Yo'd m'appen think I went beyond my place in sending Mary for yo'. But the wranglin' and the loud voices had just torn me to pieces, and I thought when father left, oh! if I could just hear her voice, reading me some words o' peace and promise, I could die away into the silence and rest o' God, just as a babby is hushed up to sleep by its mother's lullaby."

"Shall I read you a chapter, now?"

"Ay, do! M'appen I shan't listen to th' sense, at first; it will seem far away—but when yo' come to words I like—to th' comforting texts—it'll seem close in my ear, and going through me as it were."

Margaret began. Bessy tossed to and fro. If, by an effort, she attended for one moment, it seemed as though she were convulsed into double restlessness the next. At last, she burst out: "Don't go on reading. It's no use. I'm blaspheming all the time in my mind, wi' thinking angrily on what canna be helped—Yo'd hear of th' riot, m'appen, yesterday at Marlborough Mills? Thornton's factory, yo' know."

"Your father was not there, was he?" said Margaret, colouring deep.

"Not he. He'd ha' given his right hand if it had never come to pass. It's that that's fretting me. He's fairly knocked down in his mind by it. It's no use telling him, fools will always break out o' bounds. Yo' never saw a man so down-hearted as he is."

"But why?" asked Margaret. "I don't understand."

"Why, yo' see, he's a committee-man on this special strike. Th' Union appointed him because, though I say it as shouldn't say it, he's reckoned a deep chap, and true to th' back-bone. And he and t'other committee-men laid their plans. They were to hou'd together through thick and thin; what the major part thought, t'others were to think, whether they would or no. And above all there was to be no going again the law of the land. Folk would go with them if they saw them striving and starving wi' dumb patience; but if there was once any noise o' fighting and struggling—even wi' knobsticks—all was up, as they knew by th' experience of many; and many a time before. They would try and get speech o' th' knobsticks, and coax 'em, and reason wi' 'em, and m'appen warn 'em off; but whatever came, the Committee charged all members o' th' Union to lie down and die, if need were, without striking a blow; and then they reck-oned they were sure o' carrying th' public with them. And beside all that, Committee knew they were right in their demand, and they didn't want to have right all mixed up wi' wrong, till folk can't sep-arate it, no more nor I can th' physic-powder from th' jelly yo' gave me to mix it in; jelly is much the biggest, but powder tastes it all through. Well, I've told yo' at length about this'n, but I'm tired out. Yo' just think for yo'rsel, what it mun be for father to have a' his work undone, and by such a fool as Boucher, who must needs go right again the orders of Committee, and ruin th' strike, just as bad as if he meant to be a Judas. Eh! but father giv'd it him last night! He went so far as to say, he'd go and tell police where they might find th' ringleader o' th' riot; he'd give him up to th' mill-owners to do what they would wi' him. He'd show the world that th' real leaders o' the strike were not such as Boucher, but steady thoughtful men; good hands, and good citizens, who were friendly to law and judgment, and would uphold order; who only wanted their right wage, and wouldn't work, even though they starved, till they got 'em; but who would ne'er injure property or life. For," dropping her voice, "they do say, that Boucher threw a stone at Thornton's sister, that welly killed her."

"That's not true," said Margaret. "It was not Boucher that threw the stone"—she went first red, then white.

"Yo'd be there then, were yo'?" asked Bessy languidly: for indeed, she had spoken with many pauses, as if speech was unusually difficult to her.

"Yes. Never mind. Go on. Only it was not Boucher that threw the stone. But what did he answer to your father?"

"He did na' speak words. He were all in such a tremble wi' spent passion, I could na' bear to look at him. I heard his breath coming quick, and at one time I thought he were sobbing. But when father said he'd give him up to police, he gave a great cry, and struck father on th' face wi' his closed fist, and he off like lightning. Father were stunned wi' the blow at first, for all Boucher were weak wi' passion and wi' clemming. He sat down a bit, and put his hand afore his eyes; and then made for th' door. I dunno' where I got strength, but I threw mysel' off th' settle and clung to him. 'Father, father!' said I. 'Thou'll never go peach[4] on that poor clemmed man. I'll never leave go on thee, till thou sayst thou wunnot.' 'Dunnot be a fool,' says he, 'words come readier than deeds to most men. I never thought o' telling th' police on him; though by G—, he deserves it, and I should na' ha' minded if some one else had done the dirty work, and got him clapped up. But now he has strucken me, I could do it less nor ever, for it would be getting other men to take up my quarrel. But if ever he gets well o'er this clemming, and is in good condition, he and I'll have an up and down fight, purring[5] an' a', and I'll see what I can do for him.' And so father shook me off,—for indeed, I was low and faint

4. Inform.
5. Kicking. The term was used to define clog-fights, which were known in Lancashire working-class life.

enough, and his face was all clay white, where it weren't bloody, and turned me sick to look at. And I know not if I slept or waked; or were in a dead swoon, till Mary come in; and I told her to fetch yo' to me. And now dunnot talk to me, but just read out th' chapter. I'm easier in my mind for having spit it out; but I want some thoughts of the world that's far away to take the weary taste of it out o' my mouth. Read me—not a sermon chapter, but a story chapter; they've pictures in them, which I see when my eyes are shut. Read about the New Heavens, and the New Earth,[6] and m'appen I'll forget this."

Margaret read in her soft low voice. Though Bessy's eyes were shut, she was listening for some time, for the moisture of tears gathered heavy on her eyelashes. At last she slept; with many starts, and muttered pleadings. Margaret covered her up, and left her, for she had an uneasy consciousness that she might be wanted at home, and yet, until now, it seemed cruel to leave the dying girl.

Mrs. Hale was in the drawing-room on her daughter's return. It was one of her better days, and she was full of praises of the water-bed. It had been more like the beds at Sir John Beresford's than anything she had slept on since. She did not know how it was, but people seemed to have lost the art of making the same kind of beds as they used to do in her youth. One would think it was easy enough; there was the same kind of feathers to be had, and yet somehow, till this last night she did not know when she had had a good sound resting sleep.

Mr. Hale suggested, that something of the merits of the feather-beds of former days might be attributed to the activity of youth, which gave a relish to rest; but this idea was not kindly received by his wife.

"No, indeed, Mr. Hale, it was those beds at Sir John's. Now, Margaret, you're young enough, and go about in the day; are the beds comfortable? I appeal to you. Do they give you a feeling of perfect repose when you lie down upon them; or rather, don't you toss about, and try in vain to find an easy position, and waken in the morning as tired as when you went to bed?"

Margaret laughed. "To tell the truth, mamma, I've never thought about my bed at all, what kind it is. I'm so sleepy at night, that if I only lie down anywhere, I nap off directly. So I don't think I'm a competent witness. But then, you know, I never had the opportunity of trying Sir John Beresford's beds. I never was at Oxenham."

"Were not you? Oh, no! to be sure. It was poor darling Fred I took with me, I remember. I only went to Oxenham once after I was married—to your Aunt Shaw's wedding; and poor little Fred was the baby then. And I know Dixon did not like changing from lady's maid

6. Revelation 21:1.

to nurse, and I was afraid that if I took her near her old home, and amongst her own people, she might want to leave me. But poor baby was taken ill at Oxenham, with his teething; and, what with my being a great deal with Anna just before her marriage, and not being very strong myself, Dixon had more of the charge of him than she ever had before; and it made her so fond of him, and she was so proud when he would turn away from every one and cling to her, that I don't believe she ever thought of leaving me again; though it was very different from what she'd been accustomed to. Poor Fred! Every body loved him. He was born with the gift of winning hearts. It makes me think very badly of Captain Reid when I know that he disliked my own dear boy. I think it a certain proof he had a bad heart. Ah! Your poor father, Margaret. He has left the room. He can't bear to hear Fred spoken of."

"I love to hear about him, mamma. Tell me all you like; you never can tell me too much. Tell me what he was like as a baby."

"Why, Margaret, you must not be hurt, but he was much prettier than you were. I remember, when I first saw you in Dixon's arms, I said, 'Dear, what an ugly little thing!' And she said, 'It's not every child that's like Master Fred, bless him!' Dear! how well I remember it. Then I could have had Fred in my arms every minute of the day, and his cot was close by my bed; and now, now—Margaret—I don't know where my boy is, and sometimes I think I shall never see him again."

Margaret sat down by her mother's sofa on a little stool, and softly took hold of her hand, caressing it and kissing it, as if to comfort. Mrs. Hale cried without restraint. At last, she sat straight, stiff up on the sofa, and turning round to her daughter, she said with tearful, almost solemn earnestness, "Margaret, if I can get better,—if God lets me have a chance of recovery, it must be through seeing my son Frederick once more. It will waken up all the poor springs of health left in me."

She paused, and seemed to try and gather strength for something more yet to be said. Her voice was choked as she went on—was quavering as with the contemplation of some strange, yet closely-present idea.

"And, Margaret, if I am to die—if I am one of those appointed to die before many weeks are over—I must see my child first. I cannot think how it must be managed; but I charge you, Margaret, as you yourself hope for comfort in your last illness, bring him to me that I may bless him. Only for five minutes, Margaret. There could be no danger in five minutes. Oh, Margaret, let me see him before I die!"

Margaret did not think of anything that might be utterly unreasonable in this speech: we do not look for reason or logic in the passionate entreaties of those who are sick unto death; we are stung with the recollection of a thousand slighted opportunities of fulfilling the wishes of those who will soon pass away from among us: and do they ask us for the future happiness of our lives, we lay it at their feet, and will it away from us. But this wish of Mrs. Hale's was so natural, so just, so right to both parties, that Margaret felt as if, on Frederick's account as well as on her mother's, she ought to overlook all intermediate chances of danger, and pledge herself to do everything in her power for its realisation. The large, pleading, dilated eyes were fixed upon her wistfully, steady in their gaze, though the poor white lips quivered like those of a child. Margaret gently rose up and stood opposite to her frail mother; so that she might gather the secure fulfilment of her wish from the calm steadiness of her daughter's face.

"Mamma, I will write to-night, and tell Frederick what you say. I am as sure that he will come directly to us, as I am sure of my life. Be easy, mamma, you shall see him as far as anything earthly can be promised."

"You will write to-night? Oh, Margaret! the post goes out at five—you will write by it, won't you? I have so few hours left—I feel, dear, as if I should not recover, though sometimes your father over-persuades me into hoping; you will write directly, wont you? Don't lose a single post; for just by that very post I may miss him."

"But, mamma, papa is out."

"Papa is out! and what then? Do you mean that he would deny me this last wish, Margaret? Why, I should not be ill—be dying—if he had not taken me away from Helstone, to this unhealthy, smoky, sunless place."

"Oh, mamma!" said Margaret.

"Yes; it is so, indeed. He knows it himself; he has said so many a time. He would do anything for me; you don't mean he would refuse me this last wish—prayer, if you will. And, indeed, Margaret, the longing to see Frederick stands between me and God. I cannot pray till I have this one thing; indeed, I cannot. Don't lose time, dear, dear Margaret. Write by this very next post. Then he may be here—here in twenty-two days! For he is sure to come. No cords or chains can keep him. In twenty-two days I shall see my boy." She fell back, and for a short time she took no notice of the fact that Margaret sat motionless, her hand shading her eyes.

"You are not writing!" said her mother at last. "Bring me some pens and paper; I will try and write myself." She sat up, trembling all over with feverish eagerness. Margaret took her hand down and looked at her mother sadly.

"Only wait till papa comes in. Let us ask him how best to do it."

"You promised, Margaret, not a quarter of an hour ago;—you said he should come."

"And so he shall, mamma; don't cry, my own dear mother. I'll write here, now,—you shall see me write,—and it shall go by this very post; and if papa thinks fit, he can write again when he comes in,—it is only a day's delay. Oh, mamma, don't cry so pitifully,—it cuts me to the heart."

Mrs. Hale could not stop her tears; they came hysterically; and, in truth, she made no effort to control them, but rather called up all the pictures of the happy past, and the probable future—painting the scene when she should lie a corpse, with the son she had longed to see in life weeping over her, and she unconscious of his presence—till she was melted by self-pity into a state of sobbing and exhaustion that made Margaret's heart ache. But at last she was calm, and greedily watched her daughter, as she began her letter; wrote it with swift urgent entreaty; sealed it up hurriedly, for fear her mother should ask to see it: and then, to make security most sure, at Mrs. Hale's own bidding, took it herself to the post-office. She was coming home when her father overtook her.

"And where have you been, my pretty maid?" asked he.

"To the post-office,—with a letter; a letter to Frederick. Oh, papa, perhaps I have done wrong: but mamma was seized with such a passionate yearning to see him—she said it would make her well again,—and then she said that she must see him before she died,—I cannot tell you how urgent she was! Did I do wrong?"

Mr. Hale did not reply at first. Then he said:

"You should have waited till I came in, Margaret."

"I tried to persuade her,—" and then she was silent.

"I don't know," said Mr. Hale, after a pause. "She ought to see him if she wishes it so much; for I believe it would do her much more good than all the doctor's medicine,—and, perhaps, set her up altogether; but the danger to him, I'm afraid, is very great."

"All these years since the mutiny, papa?"

"Yes; it is necessary, of course, for government to take very stringent measures for the repression of offences against authority, more particularly in the navy, where a commanding officer needs to be surrounded in his men's eyes with a vivid consciousness of all the power there is at home to back him, and take up his cause, and avenge any injuries offered to him, if need be. Ah! it's no matter to them how far their authorities have tyrannised,—galled hasty tempers to madness—or, if that can be any excuse afterwards, it is never allowed for in the first instance; they spare no expense, they send out ships,—they scour the seas to lay hold of the offenders,—the lapse of years does not wash out the memory of the offence,—it is a fresh and vivid crime on the Admiralty books till it is blotted out by blood."

"Oh, papa, what have I done! And yet it seemed so right at the time. I'm sure Frederick himself, would run the risk."

"So he would; so he should! Nay, Margaret, I'm glad it is done, though I durst not have done it myself. I'm thankful it is as it is; I should have hesitated till, perhaps, it might have been too late to do any good. Dear Margaret, you have done what is right about it; and the end is beyond our control."

It was all very well; but her father's account of the relentless manner in which mutinies were punished made Margaret shiver and creep. If she had decoyed her brother home to blot out the memory of his error by his blood! She saw her father's anxiety lay deeper than the source of his latter cheering words. She took his arm and walked home pensively and wearily by his side.

END OF VOL. I

NORTH AND SOUTH.

BY

THE AUTHOR OF "MARY BARTON," "RUTH,"
"CRANFORD," &c.

IN TWO VOLUMES.

VOL. II.

LONDON:
CHAPMAN & HALL, 193, PICCADILLY.
1855.

[*The right of Translation is reserved.*]

Facsimile title page from the first edition. Courtesy of The Portico Library and Gallery, Manchester.

Volume II

Chapter I.

Mother and Son.

"I have found that holy place of rest
Still changeless."

MRS. HEMANS.[1]

When Mr. Thornton had left the house that morning he was almost
blinded by his baffled passion. He was as dizzy as if Margaret, instead
of looking, and speaking, and moving like a tender graceful woman,
had been a sturdy fish-wife, and given him a sound blow with her
fists. He had positive bodily pain,—a violent headache, and a throb-
bing intermittent pulse. He could not bear the noise, the garish light,
the continued rumble and movement of the street. He called himself
a fool for suffering so; and yet he could not, at the moment, recollect
the cause of his suffering, and whether it was adequate to the consequences it had produced. It would have been a relief to him, if he
could have sat down and cried on a door-step by a little child, who
was raging and storming, through his passionate tears, at some injury
he had received. He said to himself, that he hated Margaret, but a
wild, sharp sensation of love cleft his dull, thunderous feeling like
lightning, even as he shaped the words expressive of hatred. His
greatest comfort was in hugging his torment; and in feeling, as he
had indeed said to her, that though she might despise him, contemn
him, treat him with her proud sovereign indifference, he did not
change one whit. She could not make him change. He loved her,
and would love her; and defy her, and this miserable bodily pain.

He stood still for a moment, to make this resolution firm and clear.
There was an omnibus passing—going into the country; the con-
ductor thought he was wishing for a place, and stopped near the
pavement. It was too much trouble to apologise and explain; so he
mounted upon it, and was borne away,—past long rows of houses—
then past detached villas with trim gardens, till they came to real

---

1. For Mrs. Hemans see vol. I, chap. 2, n. 1. The lines are from her poem "The Bride of the
   Greek Isle."

country hedge-rows, and, by-and-by, to a small country town. Then everybody got down; and so did Mr. Thornton, and because they walked away he did so too. He went into the fields, walking briskly, because the sharp motion relieved his mind. He could remember all about it now; the pitiful figure he must have cut; the absurd way in which he had gone and done the very thing he had so often agreed with himself in thinking would be the most foolish thing in the world; and had met with exactly the consequences which, in these wise moods, he had always foretold were certain to follow, if he ever did make such a fool of himself. Was he bewitched by those beautiful eyes, that soft, half-open, sighing mouth which lay so close upon his shoulder only yesterday? He could not even shake off the recollection that she had been there; that her arms had been round him, once—if never again. He only caught glimpses of her; he did not understand her altogether. At one time she was so brave, and at another so timid; now so tender, and then so haughty and regal-proud. And then he thought over every time he had ever seen her once again, by way of finally forgetting her. He saw her in every dress, in every mood, and did not know which became her best. Even this morning, how magnificent she had looked,—her eyes flashing out upon him at the idea that, because she had shared his danger yesterday, she had cared for him the least!

If Mr. Thornton was a fool in the morning, as he assured himself at least twenty times he was, he did not grow much wiser in the afternoon. All that he gained in return for his sixpenny omnibus ride, was a more vivid conviction that there never was, never could be, any one like Margaret; that she did not love him and never would; but that she—no! nor the whole world—should never hinder him from loving her. And so he returned to the little market-place, and remounted the omnibus to return to Milton.

It was late in the afternoon when he was set down, near his warehouse. The accustomed places brought back the accustomed habits and trains of thought. He knew how much he had to do—more than his usual work, owing to the commotion of the day before. He had to see his brother magistrates; he had to complete the arrangements, only half made in the morning, for the comfort and safety of his newly imported Irish hands; he had to secure them from all chance of communication with the discontented workpeople of Milton. Last of all, he had to go home and encounter his mother.

Mrs. Thornton had sat in the dining-room all day, every moment expecting the news of her son's acceptance by Miss Hale. She had braced herself up many and many a time, at some sudden noise in the house; had caught up the half-dropped work, and begun to ply her needle diligently, though through dimmed spectacles, and with an unsteady hand! and many times had the door opened, and some indifferent person entered on some insignificant errand. Then her rigid face unstiffened from its gray frost-bound expression, and the features dropped into the relaxed look of despondency, so unusual to their sternness. She wrenched herself away from the contemplation of all the dreary changes that would be brought about to herself by her son's marriage; she forced her thoughts into the accustomed household grooves. The newly-married couple-to-be would need fresh household stocks of linen; and Mrs. Thornton had clothes-basket upon clothes-basket, full of table-cloths and napkins, brought in, and began to reckon up the store. There was some confusion between what was hers, and consequently marked G. H. T. (for George and Hannah Thornton), and what was her son's—bought with his money, marked with his initials. Some of those marked G. H. T. were Dutch damask of the old kind, exquisitely fine; none were like them now. Mrs. Thornton stood looking at them long,— they had been her pride when she was first married. Then she knit her brows, and pinched and compressed her lips tight, and carefully unpicked the G. H. She went so far as to search for the Turkey-red[2] marking-thread to put in the new initials; but it was all used,—and she had no heart to send for any more just yet. So she looked fixedly at vacancy; a series of visions passing before her, in all of which her son was the principal, the sole object,—her son, her pride, her property. Still he did not come. Doubtless he was with Miss Hale. The new love was displacing her already from her place as first in his heart. A terrible pain—a pang of vain jealousy—shot through her: she hardly knew whether it was more physical or mental; but it forced her to sit down. In a moment, she was up again as straight as ever,—a grim smile upon her face for the first time that day, ready for the door opening, and the rejoicing triumphant one, who should never know the sore regret his mother felt at his marriage. In all this, there was little thought enough of the future daughter-in-law as an individual. She was to be John's wife. To take Mrs. Thornton's place as mistress of the house, was only one of the rich consequences which decked out the supreme glory; all household plenty and comfort, all purple and fine linen, honour, love, obedience, troops of friends, would all come as naturally as jewels on a king's robe, and be as little thought of for their separate value. To be chosen by John, would separate a kitchen-wench from the rest of the world. And Miss Hale was not so bad. If she had been a Milton lass, Mrs. Thornton would have positively liked her. She was pungent, and had taste, and spirit, and flavour in her. True, she was sadly prejudiced, and very ignorant; but that was to be expected from her southern breeding. A strange

2. "A brilliant and permanent red colour produced on cotton goods" (*Oxford English Dictionary*). Turkey red embroidery floss was used to produce redwork, decorative red designs on white fabric, such as pillowcases and dish towels.

sort of mortified comparison of Fanny with her, went on in Mrs. Thornton's mind; and for once she spoke harshly to her daughter; abused her roundly; and then, as if by way of penance, she took up Henry's Commentaries, and tried to fix her attention on it, instead of pursuing the employment she took pride and pleasure in, and continuing her inspection of the table-linen.

His step at last! She heard him, even while she thought she was finishing a sentence; while her eye did pass over it, and her memory could mechanically have repeated it word for word, she heard him come in at the hall-door. Her quickened sense could interpret every sound of motion: now he was at the hat-stand—now at the very room-door. Why did he pause? Let her know the worst.

Yet her head was down over the book; she did not look up. He came close to the table, and stood still there, waiting till she should have finished the paragraph which apparently absorbed her. By an effort she looked up. "Well, John?"

He knew what that little speech meant. But he had steeled himself. He longed to reply with a jest; the bitterness of his heart could have uttered one, but his mother deserved better of him. He came round behind her, so that she could not see his looks, and, bending back her gray, stony face, he kissed it, murmuring:

"No one loves me,—no one cares for me, but you, mother."

He turned away and stood leaning his head against the mantel-piece, tears forcing themselves into his manly eyes. She stood up,—she tottered. For the first time in her life, the strong woman tottered. She put her hands on his shoulders; she was a tall woman. She looked into his face; she made him look at her.

"Mother's love is given by God, John. It holds fast for ever and ever. A girl's love is like a puff of smoke,—it changes with every wind. And she would not have you, my own lad, would not she?" She set her teeth; she showed them like a dog for the whole length of her mouth. He shook his head.

"I am not fit for her, mother; I knew I was not."

She ground out words between her closed teeth. He could not hear what she said; but the look in her eyes interpreted it to be a curse,—if not as coarsely worded, as fell in intent as ever was uttered. And yet her heart leapt up light, to know he was her own again.

"Mother!" said he, hurriedly, "I cannot hear a word against her. Spare me,—spare me! I am very weak in my sore heart;—I love her yet; I love her more than ever."

"And I hate her," said Mrs. Thornton, in a low fierce voice. "I tried not to hate her when she stood between you and me, because,—I said to myself,—she will make him happy; and I would give my heart's blood to do that. But now, I hate her for your misery's sake. Yes, John, it's no use hiding up your aching heart from me. I am the

mother that bore you, and your sorrow is my agony; and if you don't
hate her, I do."

"Then, mother, you make me love her more. She is unjustly treated
by you, and I must make the balance even. But why do we talk of
love or hatred? She does not care for me, and that is enough,—too
much. Let us never name the subject again. It is the only thing you
can do for me in the matter. Let us never name her."

"With all my heart. I only wish that she, and all belonging to her,
were swept back to the place they came from."

He stood still, gazing into the fire for a minute or two longer. Her
dry dim eyes filled with unwonted tears as she looked at him; but
she seemed just as grim and quiet as usual when he next spoke.

"Warrants are out against three men for conspiracy, mother. The
riot yesterday helped to knock up the strike."

And Margaret's name was no more mentioned between Mrs.
Thornton and her son. They fell back into their usual mode of talk—
about facts, not opinions, far less feelings. Their voices and tones
were calm and cold; a stranger might have gone away and thought
that he had never seen such frigid indifference of demeanour
between such near relations.

Chapter II.

Fruit-Piece.

"For never any thing can be amiss
When simpleness and duty tender it."
MIDSUMMER NIGHT'S DREAM.[1]

Mr. Thornton went straight and clear into all the interests of the
following day. There was a slight demand for finished goods; and as
it affected his branch of the trade, he took advantage of it, and drove
hard bargains. He was sharp to the hour at the meeting of his brother
magistrates,—giving them the best assistance of his strong sense,
and his power of seeing consequences at a glance, and so coming to
a rapid decision. Older men, men of long standing in the town, men
of far greater wealth—realised and turned into land, while his was
all floating capital, engaged in his trade—looked to him for prompt,
ready wisdom. He was the one deputed to see and arrange with the
police—to lead in all the requisite steps. And he cared for their
unconscious deference no more than for the soft west wind, that
scarcely made the smoke from the great tall chimneys swerve in its
straight upward course. He was not aware of the silent respect paid

1. From William Shakespeare, *A Midsummer Night's Dream* V.1.82–83.

to him. If it had been otherwise, he would have felt it as an obstacle
in his progress to the object he had in view. As it was, he looked to
the speedy accomplishment of that alone. It was his mother's greedy
ears that sucked in, from the womenkind of these magistrates
and wealthy men, how highly Mr. This or Mr. That thought of Mr.
Thornton; that if he had not been there, things would have gone on
very differently,—very badly, indeed. He swept off his business right
and left that day. It seemed as though his deep mortification of yesterday, and the stunned purposeless course of the hours afterwards,
had cleared away all the mists from his intellect. He felt his power
and revelled in it. He could almost defy his heart. If he had known
it, he could have sang the song of the miller who lived by the river
Dee:—

> "I care for nobody—
> Nobody cares for me."[2]

The evidence against Boucher, and other ring-leaders of the riot,
was taken before him; that against the three others, for conspiracy,
failed. But he sternly charged the police to be on the watch; for the
swift right arm of the law should be in readiness to strike, as soon
as they could prove a fault. And then he left the hot reeking room
in the borough court, and went out into the fresher, but still sultry
street. It seemed as though he gave way all at once; he was so languid
that he could not control his thoughts; they would wander to her;
they would bring back the scene,—not of his repulse and rejection
the day before, but the looks, the actions of the day before that. He
went along the crowded streets mechanically, winding in and out
among the people, but never seeing them,—almost sick with longing
for that one half-hour—that one brief space of time when she clung
to him, and her heart beat against his—to come once again.

"Why, Mr. Thornton! you're cutting me very coolly, I must say.
And how is Mrs. Thornton? Brave weather this! We doctors don't
like it, I can tell you!"

"I beg your pardon, Dr. Donaldson. I really didn't see you. My
mother's quite well, thank you. It is a fine day, and good for the
harvest, I hope. If the wheat is well got in, we shall have a brisk trade
next year, whatever you doctors have."

"Ay, Ay. Each man for himself. Your bad weather, and your bad
times, are my good ones. When trade is bad, there's more under-
mining of health, and preparation for death, going on among you
Milton men than you're aware of."

2. The final lines of the popular song "The Miller of Dee": "And this the burden of his
song / Forever used to be / I care for nobody, no! not I / And nobody cares for me." Collected in Charles Mackay's *Songs for Music* (1856).

"Not with me, Doctor. I'm made of iron. The news of the worst bad debt I ever had, never made my pulse vary. This strike, which affects me more than any one else in Milton—more than Hamper,— never comes near my appetite. You must go elsewhere for a patient, Doctor."

"By the way, you've recommended me a good patient, poor lady! Not to go on talking in this heartless way, I seriously believe that Mrs. Hale—that lady in Crampton, you know—hasn't many weeks to live. I never had any hope of cure, as I think I told you; but I've been seeing her to-day, and I think very badly of her."

Mr. Thornton was silent. The vaunted steadiness of pulse failed him for an instant.

"Can I do anything, Doctor?" he asked, in an altered voice. "You know—you would see, that money is not very plentiful; are there any comforts or dainties she ought to have?"

"No," replied the Doctor, shaking his head. "She craves for fruit,— she has a constant fever on her; but jargonelle pears[3] will do as well as anything, and there are quantities of them in the market."

"You will tell me, if there is anything I can do, I'm sure," replied Mr. Thornton. "I rely upon you."

"Oh! never fear! I'll not spare your purse,—I know it's deep enough. I wish you'd give me carte-blanche for all my patients, and all their wants."

But Mr. Thornton had no general benevolence,—no universal philanthropy; few even would have given him credit for strong affections. But he went straight to the first fruit-shop in Milton, and chose out the bunch of purple grapes with the most delicate bloom upon them,—the richest-coloured peaches,—the freshest vine-leaves. They were packed into a basket, and the shopman awaited the answer to his inquiry, "Where shall we send them to, sir?"

There was no reply. "To Marlborough Mills, I suppose, sir?"

"No!" Mr. Thornton said. "Give the basket to me,—I'll take it."

It took up both his hands to carry it; and he had to pass through the busiest part of the town for feminine shopping. Many a young lady of his acquaintance turned to look after him, and thought it strange to see him occupied just like a porter or an errand-boy.

He was thinking, "I will not be daunted from doing as I choose by the thought of her. I like to take this fruit to the poor mother, and it is simply right that I should. She shall never scorn me out of doing what I please. A pretty joke, indeed, if for fear of a haughty girl, I failed in doing a kindness to a man I liked! I do it for Mr. Hale; I do it in defiance of her."

3. An early-fruiting variety of pear.

He went at an unusual pace, and was soon at Crampton. He went upstairs two steps at a time, and entered the drawing-room before Dixon could announce him,—his face flushed, his eyes shining with kindly earnestness. Mrs. Hale lay on the sofa, heated with fever. Mr. Hale was reading aloud. Margaret was working on a low stool by her mother's side. Her heart fluttered, if his did not, at this interview. But he took no notice of her,—hardly of Mr. Hale himself; he went up straight with his basket to Mrs. Hale, and said, in that subdued and gentle tone, which is so touching when used by a robust man in full health, speaking to a feeble invalid,—

"I met Dr. Donaldson, ma'am, and as he said fruit would be good for you, I have taken the liberty—the great liberty—of bringing you some that seemed to me fine." Mrs. Hale was excessively surprised; excessively pleased; quite in a tremble of eagerness. Mr. Hale with fewer words expressed a deeper gratitude.

"Fetch a plate, Margaret—a basket—anything." Margaret stood up by the table, half afraid of moving or making any noise to arouse Mr. Thornton into a consciousness of her being in the room. She thought it would be awkward for both to be brought into conscious collision; and fancied that, from her being on a low seat at first, and now standing behind her father, he had overlooked her in his haste. As if he did not feel the consciousness of her presence all over, though his eyes had never rested on her!

"I must go," said he, "I cannot stay. If you will forgive this liberty,—my rough ways,—too abrupt, I fear—but I will be more gentle next time. You will allow me the pleasure of bringing you some fruit again, if I should see any that is tempting. Good afternoon, Mr. Hale. Good-bye, ma'am."

He was gone. Not one word: not one look to Margaret. She believed that he had not seen her. She went for a plate in silence, and lifted the fruit out tenderly, with the points of her delicate taper fingers. It was good of him to bring it; and after yesterday too!

"Oh! it is so delicious!" said Mrs. Hale, in a feeble voice. "How kind of him to think of me! Margaret love, only taste these grapes! Was it not good of him?"

"Yes!" said Margaret, quietly.

"Margaret!" said Mrs. Hale, rather querulously, "you won't like anything Mr. Thornton does. I never saw anybody so prejudiced."

Mr. Hale had been peeling a peach for his wife; and, cutting off a small piece for himself, he said:

"If I had any prejudices, the gift of such delicious fruit as this would melt them all away. I have not tasted such fruit—no! not even in Hampshire—since I was a boy; and to boys, I fancy, all fruit is good. I remember eating sloes and crabs[4] with a relish. Do you remember the matted-up currant bushes, Margaret, at the corner of the west-wall at the garden at home?"

Did she not? Did she not remember every weather-stain on the old stone wall; the gray and yellow lichens that marked it like a map; the little crane's-bill that grew in the crevices? She had been shaken by the events of the last two days; her whole life just now was a strain upon her fortitude; and, somehow, these careless words of her father's, touching on the remembrance of the sunny times of old, made her start up, and, dropping her sewing on the ground, she went hastily out of the room into her own little chamber. She had hardly given way to the first choking sob, when she became aware of Dixon standing at her drawers, and evidently searching for something.

"Bless me, miss! How you startled me! Missus is not worse, is she? Is anything the matter?"

"No, nothing. Only I'm silly, Dixon, and want a glass of water. What are you looking for? I keep my muslins in that drawer."

Dixon did not speak, but went on rummaging. The scent of lavender came out and perfumed the room.

At last Dixon found what she wanted; what it was Margaret could not see. Dixon faced round, and spoke to her:

"Now I don't like telling you what I wanted, because you've fretting enough to go through, and I know you'll fret about this. I meant to have kept it from you till night, may be, or such times as that."

"What is the matter? Pray, tell me, Dixon, at once."

"That young woman you go to see—Higgins I mean."

"Well?"

"Well! she died this morning, and her sister is here—come to beg a strange thing. It seems, the young woman who died had a fancy for being buried in something of yours, and so the sister's come to ask for it,—and I was looking for a night-cap that was'nt too good to give away."

"Oh! let me find one," said Margaret, in the midst of her tears. "Poor Bessy! I never thought I should not see her again."

"Why, that's another thing. This girl downstairs wanted me to ask you, if you would like to see her."

"But she's dead!" said Margaret, turning a little pale. "I never saw a dead person. No! I would rather not."

"I should never have asked you, if you hadn't come in. I told her you wouldn't."

"I will go down and speak to her," said Margaret, afraid lest Dixon's

---

4. Both sloes (the fruit of the blackthorn bush) and crabapples, a species of miniature apple, have a sharp taste.

harshness of manner might wound the poor girl. So, taking the cap in her hand, she went to the kitchen. Mary's face was all swollen with crying, and she burst out afresh when she saw Margaret.

"Oh, ma'am, she loved yo', she loved yo', she did indeed!" And for a long time, Margaret could not get her to say anything more than this. At last, her sympathy, and Dixon's scolding, forced out a few facts. Nicholas Higgins had gone out in the morning, leaving Bessy as well as on the day before. But in an hour she was taken worse; some neighbour ran to the room where Mary was working; they did not know where to find her father; Mary had only come in a few minutes before she died.

"It were a day or two ago she axed to be buried in somewhat o' yourn. She were never tired o' talking o' yo'. She used to say yo' were the prettiest thing she'd ever clapped eyes on. She loved yo' dearly. Her last words were, 'Give her my affectionate respects; and keep father fro' drink.' Yo'll come and see her, ma'am. She would ha' thought it a great compliment, I know."

Margaret shrank a little from answering.

"Yes, perhaps I may. Yes, I will. I'll come before tea. But where's your father, Mary?"

Mary shook her head, and stood up to be going.

"Miss Hale," said Dixon, in a low voice, "where's the use o' your going to see the poor thing laid out? I'd never say a word against it, if it could do the girl any good; and I wouldn't mind a bit going myself, if that would satisfy her. They've just a notion, these common folks, of its being a respect to the departed. Here," said she, turning sharply round, "I'll come and see your sister. Miss Hale is busy, and she can't come, or else she would."

The girl looked wistfully at Margaret. Dixon's coming might be a compliment, but it was not the same thing to the poor sister, who had had her little pangs of jealousy, during Bessy's lifetime, at the intimacy between her and the young lady.

"No, Dixon!" said Margaret with decision. "I will go. Mary, you shall see me this afternoon." And for fear of her own cowardice, she went away, in order to take from herself any chance of changing her determination.

Chapter III.

Comfort in Sorrow.

"Through cross to crown!—And though thy spirit's life
   Trials untold assail with giant strength,
Good cheer! good cheer! Soon ends the bitter strife,
   And thou shalt reign in peace with Christ at length."
KOSEGARTEN.[1]

"Ay sooth, we feel too strong in weal, to need Thee on that road;
But woe being come, the soul is dumb, that crieth not on 'God.' "
MRS. BROWNING.[2]

That afternoon she walked swiftly to the Higgins's house. Mary was looking out for her, with a half-distrustful face. Margaret smiled into her eyes to re-assure her. They passed quickly through the house-place, upstairs, and into the quiet presence of the dead. Then Margaret was glad that she had come. The face, often so weary with pain, so restless with troublous thoughts, had now the faint soft smile of eternal rest upon it. The slow tears gathered into Margaret's eyes, but a deep calm entered into her soul. And that was death! It looked more peaceful than life. All beautiful scriptures came into her mind. "They rest from their labours." "The weary are at rest." "He giveth His beloved sleep."[3]

Slowly, slowly Margaret turned away from the bed. Mary was humbly sobbing in the back-ground. They went down stairs without a word.

Resting his hand upon the house-table, Nicholas Higgins stood in the midst of the floor; his great eyes startled open by the news he had heard, as he came along the court, from many busy tongues. His eyes were dry and fierce; studying the reality of her death; bringing himself to understand that her place should know her no more. For she had been sickly, dying so long, that he had persuaded himself she would not die; that she would "pull through."

Margaret felt as if she had no business to be there, familiarly acquainting herself with the surroundings of death which he, the father, had only just learnt. There had been a pause of an instant on the steep crooked stair, when she first saw him; but now she tried to steal past his abstracted gaze, and to leave him in the solemn circle of his house-hold misery.

1. Ludwig Gottland Kosegarten (1758–1818), a German theologian, teacher, and poet admired by William Gaskell.
2. The lines are from Elizabeth Barrett Browning's verse-drama *The Lay of the Brown Rosary*, first printed as *The Legend of the Brown Rosary* in *Finden's Tableaux*, an annual miscellany of verse and prose, 1840. Apart from the fact that it deals with a female death, the content of the drama has no connection with the situation in this chapter.
3. Revelation 14:13 (adapted); Isaiah 28:12 (adapted); Psalms 127:2, consecutively.

Mary sat down on the first chair she came to, and throwing her apron over her head, began to cry.

The noise appeared to rouse him. He took sudden hold of Margaret's arm, and held her till he could gather words to speak. His throat seemed dry; they came up thick, and choked, and hoarse:

"Were yo' with her? Did yo' see her die?"

"No!" replied Margaret, standing still with the utmost patience, now she found herself perceived. It was some time before he spoke again, but he kept his hold on her arm.

"All men must die," said he at last, with a strange sort of gravity, which first suggested to Margaret the idea that he had been drinking—not enough to intoxicate himself, but enough to make his thoughts bewildered. "But she were younger than me." Still he pondered over the event, not looking at Margaret, though he grasped her tight. Suddenly, he looked up at her with a wild searching inquiry in his glance. "Yo're sure and certain she's dead—not in a dwam,[4] a faint?—she's been so before, often."

"She is dead," replied Margaret. She felt no fear in speaking to him, though he hurt her arm with his grip, and wild gleams came across the stupidity of his eyes.

"She is dead!" she said.

He looked at her still with that searching look, which seemed to fade out of his eyes as he gazed. Then he suddenly let go his hold of Margaret, and, throwing his body half across the table, he shook it and every piece of furniture in the room, with his violent sobs. Mary came trembling towards him.

"Get thee gone!—get thee gone!" he cried, striking wildly and blindly at her. "What do I care for thee?" Margaret took her hand, and held it softly in hers. He tore his hair, he beat his head against the hard wood, then he lay exhausted and stupid. Still his daughter and Margaret did not move. Mary trembled from head to foot.

At last—it might have been a quarter of an hour, it might have been an hour—he lifted himself up. His eyes were swollen and bloodshot, and he seemed to have forgotten that any one was by; he scowled at the watchers when he saw them. He shook himself heavily, gave them one more sullen look, spoke never a word, but made for the door.

"Oh, father, father!" said Mary, throwing herself upon his arm,—"not to-night! Any night but to-night. Oh, help me! he's going out to drink again! Father, I'll not leave yo'. Yo' may strike, but I'll not leave yo'. She told me last of all to keep yo' fro' drink!"

But Margaret stood in the doorway, silent yet commanding. He looked up at her defyingly.

4. Dream.

"It's my own house. Stand out o' the way, wench, or I'll make yo'!"
He had shaken off Mary with violence; he looked ready to strike
Margaret. But she never moved a feature—never took her deep, serious eyes off him. He stared back on her with gloomy fierceness. If
she had stirred hand or foot, he would have thrust her aside with
even more violence than he had used to his own daughter, whose
face was bleeding from her fall against a chair.

"What are yo' looking at me in that way for?" asked he at last,
daunted and awed by her severe calm. "If yo' think for to keep me
from going what gait I choose, because she loved yo—and in my own
house, too, where I never asked yo to come, yo're mista'en. It's very
hard upon a man that he can't go to the only comfort left."

Margaret felt that he acknowledged her power. What could she
do next? He had seated himself on a chair, close to the door; half-
conquered, half-resenting; intending to go out as soon as she left her
position, but unwilling to use the violence he had threatened not five
minutes before. Margaret laid her hand on his arm.

"Come with me," she said. "Come and see her!"

The voice in which she spoke was very low and solemn; but there
was no fear or doubt expressed in it, either of him or of his compliance. He sullenly rose up. He stood uncertain, with dogged irreso-
lution upon his face. She waited him there; quietly and patiently
waited for his time to move. He had a strange pleasure in making
her wait; but at last he moved towards the stairs.

She and he stood by the corpse.

"Her last words to Mary were, 'Keep my father fro' drink.' "

"It canna hurt her now," muttered he. "Nought can hurt her now."
Then, raising his voice to a wailing cry, he went on: "We may quarrel
and fall out—we may make peace and be friends—we may clem to
skin and bone—and nought o' all our griefs will ever touch her more.
Hoo's had her portion on 'em. What wi' hard work first, and sickness
at last, hoo's led the life of a dog. And to die without knowing one
good piece o' rejoicing in all her days! Nay, wench, whatever hoo
said, hoo can know nought about it now, and I mun ha' a sup o' drink
just to steady me again sorrow."

"No," said Margaret, softening with his softened manner. "You
shall not. If her life has been what you say, at any rate she did not
fear death as some do. Oh, you should have heard her speak of the
life to come—the life hidden with God, that she is now gone to."

He shook his head, glancing sideways up at Margaret as he did so.
His pale, haggard face struck her painfully.

"You are sorely tired. Where have you been all day—not at work?"

"Not at work, sure enough," said he, with a short, grim laugh. "Not
at what you call work. I were at the Committee, till I were sickened
out wi' trying to make fools hear reason. I were fetched to Boucher's

wife afore seven this morning. She's bed-fast, but she were raving
and raging to know where her dunder-headed brute of a chap was,
as if I'd to keep him—as if he were fit to be ruled by me. The d—d
fool, who has put his foot in all our plans! And I've walked my feet
sore wi' going about for to see men who wouldn't be seen, now the
law is raised again us. And I were sore-hearted, too, which is worse
than sore-footed; and if I did see a friend who ossed[5] to treat me, I
never knew hoo lay a-dying here. Bess, lass, thou'd believe me, thou
wouldst—wouldstn't thou?" turning to the poor dumb form with wild
appeal.

"I am sure," said Margaret, "I am sure you did not know: it was
quite sudden. But now, you see, it would be different; you do know;
you do see her lying there; you hear what she said with her last
breath. You will not go?"

No answer. In fact, where was he to look for comfort?

"Come home with me," said she at last, with a bold venture, half
trembling at her own proposal as she made it. "At least you shall have
some comfortable food, which I'm sure you need."

"Yo'r father's a parson?" asked he, with a sudden turn in his ideas.

"He was," said Margaret, shortly.

"I'll go and take a dish o' tea with him, since yo've asked me. I've
many a thing I often wished to say to a parson, and I'm not particular
as to whether he's preaching now, or not."

Margaret was perplexed; his drinking tea with her father, who
would be totally unprepared for his visitor—her mother so ill—
seemed utterly out of the question; and yet if she drew back now, it
would be worse than ever—sure to drive him to the gin-shop. She
thought that if she could only get him to their own house, it was so
great a step gained that she would trust to the chapter of accidents
for the next.

"Goodbye, ou'd wench! We've parted company at last, we have!
But thou'st been a blessin' to thy father ever sin' thou wert born.
Bless thy white lips, lass,—they've a smile on 'em now! and I'm
glad to see it once again, though I'm lone and forlorn for evermore."

He stooped down and fondly kissed his daughter; covered up her
face, and turned to follow Margaret. She had hastily gone down stairs
to tell Mary of the arrangement; to say it was the only way she could
think of to keep him from the gin-palace; to urge Mary to come too,
for her heart smote her at the idea of leaving the poor affectionate girl alone. But Mary had friends among the neighbours, she
said, who would come in and sit a bit with her; it was all right; but
father—

5. Tried.

He was there by them as she would have spoken more. He had shaken off his emotion, as if he was ashamed of having ever given way to it; and had even o'erleaped himself so much that he assumed a sort of bitter mirth, like the crackling of thorns under a pot.

"I'm going to take my tea wi' her father, I am!"

But he slouched his cap low down over his brow as he went out into the street, and looked neither to the right nor to the left, while he tramped along by Margaret's side; he feared being upset by the words, still more the looks, of sympathising neighbours. So he and Margaret walked in silence.

As he got near the street in which he knew she lived, he looked down at his clothes, his hands, and shoes.

"I should m'appen ha' cleaned mysel', first?"

It certainly would have been desirable, but Margaret assured him he should be allowed to go into the yard, and have soap and towel provided; she could not let him slip out of her hands just then.

While he followed the house-servant along the passage, and through the kitchen, stepping cautiously on every dark mark in the pattern of the oil-cloth, in order to conceal his dirty foot-prints, Margaret ran upstairs. She met Dixon on the landing.

"How is mamma?—where is papa?"

Missus was tired, and gone into her own room. She had wanted to go to bed, but Dixon had persuaded her to lie down on the sofa, and have her tea brought to her there; it would be better than getting restless by being too long in bed.

So far, so good. But where was Mr. Hale? In the drawing-room. Margaret went in half breathless with the hurried story she had to tell. Of course, she told it incompletely; and her father was rather "taken aback" by the idea of the drunken weaver awaiting him in his quiet study, with whom he was expected to drink tea, and on whose behalf Margaret was anxiously pleading. The meek, kind-hearted Mr. Hale would have readily tried to console him in his grief, but, unluckily, the point Margaret dwelt upon most forcibly was the fact of his having been drinking, and her having brought him home with her as a last expedient to keep him from the gin-shop. One little event had come out of another so naturally that Margaret was hardly conscious of what she had done, till she saw the slight look of repugnance on her father's face.

"Oh, papa! he really is a man you will not dislike—if you won't be shocked to begin with."

"But, Margaret, to bring a drunken man home—and your mother so ill!"

Margaret's countenance fell. "I am sorry, papa. He is very quiet—he is not tipsy at all. He was only rather strange at first, but that might be the shock of poor Bessy's death." Margaret's eyes filled with tears. Mr. Hale took hold of her sweet pleading face in both his hands, and kissed her forehead.

"It is all right, dear. I'll go and make him as comfortable as I can, and do you attend to your mother. Only, if you can come in and make a third in the study, I shall be glad."

"Oh, yes—thank you." But as Mr. Hale was leaving the room, she ran after him:

"Papa—you must not wonder at what he says: he's an——I mean he does not believe in much of what we do."

"Oh dear! a drunken infidel weaver!" said Mr. Hale to himself, in dismay. But to Margaret he only said, "If your mother goes to sleep, be sure you come directly."

Margaret went into her mother's room. Mrs. Hale lifted herself up from a doze.

"When did you write to Frederick, Margaret? Yesterday, or the day before?"

"Yesterday, mamma."

"Yesterday. And the letter went?"

"Yes. I took it myself."

"Oh, Margaret, I'm so afraid of his coming! If he should be recognised! If he should be taken! If he should be executed, after all these years that he has kept away and lived in safety! I keep falling asleep and dreaming that he is caught and being tried."

"Oh, mamma, don't be afraid. There will be some risk no doubt; but we will lessen it as much as ever we can. And it is so little! Now, if we were at Helstone, there would be twenty—a hundred times as much. There, everybody would remember him; and if there was a stranger known to be in the house, they would be sure to guess it was Frederick; while here, nobody knows or cares for us enough to notice what we do. Dixon will keep the door like a dragon—won't you, Dixon—while he is here?"

"They'll be clever if they come in past me!" said Dixon, showing her teeth at the bare idea.

"And he need not go out, except in the dusk, poor fellow!"

"Poor fellow!" echoed Mrs. Hale. "But I almost wish you had not written. Would it be too late to stop him if you wrote again, Margaret?"

"I'm afraid it would, mamma," said Margaret, remembering the urgency with which she had entreated him to come directly, if he wished to see his mother alive.

"I always dislike that doing things in such a hurry," said Mrs. Hale.

Margaret was silent.

"Come now, ma'am," said Dixon, with a kind of cheerful authority, "you know seeing Master Frederick is just the very thing of all others you're longing for. And I'm glad Miss Margaret wrote off straight, without shilly-shallying. I've had a great mind to do it myself. And we'll keep him snug, depend upon it. There's only Martha in the house that would not do a good deal to save him on a pinch; and I've been thinking she might go and see her mother just at that very time.[6] She's been saying once or twice she should like to go, for her mother has had a stroke since she came here; only she didn't like to ask. But I'll see about her being safe off, as soon as we know when he comes, God bless him! So take your tea, ma'am, in comfort, and trust to me."

Mrs. Hale did trust in Dixon more than in Margaret. Dixon's words quieted her for the time. Margaret poured out the tea in silence, trying to think of something agreeable to say; but her thoughts made answer something like Daniel O'Rourke, when the man-in-the-moon asked him to get off his reaping-hook. "The more you ax us, the more we won't stir."[7] The more she tried to think of something—anything besides the danger to which Frederick would be exposed—the more closely her imagination clung to the unfortunate idea presented to her. Her mother prattled with Dixon, and seemed to have utterly forgotten the possibility of Frederick being tried and executed—utterly forgotten that at her wish, if by Margaret's deed, he was summoned into this danger. Her mother was one of those who throw out terrible possibilities, miserable probabilities, unfortunate chances of all kinds, as a rocket throws out sparks; but if the sparks light on some combustible matter, they smoulder first, and burst out into a frightful flame at last. Margaret was glad when, her filial duties gently and carefully performed, she could go down into the study. She wondered how her father and Higgins had got on.

In the first place, the decorous, kind-hearted, simple, old-fashioned gentleman, had unconsciously called out, by his own refinement and courteousness of manner, all the latent courtesy in the other.

Mr. Hale treated all his fellow-creatures alike: it never entered into his head to make any difference because of their rank. He placed a chair for Nicholas; stood up till he, at Mr. Hale's request, took a seat; and called him, invariably, "Mr. Higgins," instead of the curt "Nicholas" or "Higgins," to which the "drunken infidel weaver" had been accustomed. But Nicholas was neither an habitual drunkard nor a thorough infidel. He drank to drown care, as he would have himself expressed it: and he was infidel so far as he had never yet found any form of faith to which he could attach himself, heart and soul. Margaret was a little surprised, and very much pleased, when she

6. We are later told (p. 314) that Martha's mother had died before she was taken in by Mrs. Thornton. The two accounts are inconsistent.
7. Daniel O'Rourke was "a drunken folk-hero found in the chap-books." (*Easson 1973*) The name is Irish: the quotation identifies the kind of contradiction thought to be typically Irish according to Victorian stereotyping.

found her father and Higgins in earnest conversation—each speaking with gentle politeness to the other, however their opinions might clash. Nicholas—clean, tidied (if only at the pump-trough), and quiet spoken—was a new creature to her, who had only seen him in the rough independence of his own hearthstone. He had "slicked" his hair down with the fresh water; he had adjusted his neckhandkerchief, and borrowed an odd candle-end to polish his clogs with; and there he sat, enforcing some opinion on her father, with a strong Darkshire accent, it is true, but with a lowered voice, and a good, earnest composure on his face. Her father, too, was interested in what his companion was saying. He looked round as she came in, smiled, and quietly gave her his chair, and then sat down afresh as quickly as possible, and with a little bow of apology to his guest for the interruption. Higgins nodded to her as a sign of greeting; and she softly adjusted her working materials on the table, and prepared to listen.

"As I was a-sayin, sir, I reckon yo'd not ha' much belief in yo' if yo' lived here,—if yo'd been bred here. I ax your pardon if I use wrong words; but what I mean by belief just now, is a-thinking on sayings and maxims and promises made by folk yo' never saw, about the things and the life yo' never saw, nor no one else. Now, yo' say these are true things, and true sayings, and a true life. I just say, where's the proof? There's many and many a one wiser, and scores better learned than I am around me,—folk who've had time to think on these things—while my time has had to be gi'en up to getting my bread. Well, I sees these people. Their lives is pretty much open to me. They're a real folk. They don't believe i' the Bible,—not they. They may say they do, for form's sake; but Lord, sir, d'ye think their first cry i' th' morning is, 'What shall I do to get hold on eternal life?'[8] or 'What shall I do to fill my purse this blessed day? Where shall I go? What bargains shall I strike?' The purse and the gold and the notes is real things; things as can be felt and touched; them's realities; and eternal life is all a talk, very fit for—I ax your pardon, sir; yo'r a parson out o'work, I believe. Well! I'll never speak disrespectful of a man in the same fix as I'm in mysel'. But I'll just ax yo' another question, sir, and I dunnot want yo' to answer it, only to put in yo'r pipe, and smoke it, afore yo' go for to set down us, who only believe in what we see, as fools and noddies. If salvation, and life to come, and what not, was true—not in men's words, but in men's hearts' core—dun yo' not think they'd din us wi' it as they do wi' political 'conomy? They're mighty anxious to come round us wi' that piece o' wisdom; but t'other would be a greater convarsion, if it were true."

8. The quotation appears variously in the Gospels; it also appears in a slightly different form ('What shall I do to be saved?') in the opening of John Bunyan's *Pilgrim's Progress* (1678), which would have made it familiar to nineteenth-century readers.

"But the masters have nothing to do with your religion. All that they are connected with you in is trade,—so they think,—and all that it concerns them, therefore, to rectify your opinions in is the science of trade."

"I'm glad, sir," said Higgins, with a curious wink of his eye, "that yo' put in, 'so they think.' I'd ha' thought yo' a hyprocrite, I'm afeard, if yo' hadn't, for all yo'r a parson, or rayther because yo'r a parson. Yo' see, if yo'd spoken o' religion as a thing that, if it was true, it didn't concern all men to press on all men's attention, above every-thing else in this 'varsal[9] earth, I should ha' thought yo' a knave for to be a parson; and I'd rather think yo' a fool than a knave. No offence, I hope, sir."

"None at all. You consider me mistaken, and I consider you far more fatally mistaken. I don't expect to convince you in a day,—not in one conversation; but let us know each other, and speak freely to each other about these things, and the truth will prevail. I should not believe in God if I did not believe that. Mr. Higgins, I trust, whatever else you have given up, you believe"—(Mr. Hale's voice dropped low in reverence)—"you believe in Him."

Nicholas Higgins suddenly stood straight, stiff up. Margaret started to her feet,—for she thought, by the working of his face, he was going into convulsions. Mr. Hale looked at her dismayed. At last Higgins found words:

"Man! I could fell yo' to the ground for tempting me. Whatten business have yo' to try me wi' your doubts? Think o' her lying theere, after the life hoo's led; and think then how yo'd deny me the one sole comfort left—that there is a God, and that He set her her life. I dunnot believe she'll ever live again," said he, sitting down, and drearily going on, as if to the unsympathising fire. "I dunnot believe in any other life than this, in which she dreed[1] such trouble, and had such never-ending care; and I cannot bear to think it were all a set o' chances, that might ha' been altered wi'a breath o' wind. There's many a time when I've thought I didna believe in God, but I've never put it fair out before me in words, as many men do. I may ha' laughed at those who did, to brave it out like—but I have looked round at after, to see if He heard me, if so be there was a He; but to-day, when I'm left desolate, I wunnot listen to yo' wi' yo'r questions, and yo'r doubts. There's but one thing steady and quiet i' all this reeling[2] world, and, reason or no reason, I'll cling to that. It's a' very well for happy folk"——

Margaret touched his arm very softly. She had not spoken before, nor had he heard her rise.

9. Universal.
1. Endured.
2. Whirling, hence confusing.

"Nicholas, we do not want to reason; you misunderstand my father. We do not reason—we believe; and so do you. It is the one sole comfort in such times."

He turned round and caught her hand. "Ay! it is, it is"—(brushing away the tears with the back of his hand).—"But yo' know, she's lying dead at home; and I'm welly dazed wi' sorrow, and at times I hardly know what I'm saying. It's as if speeches folk ha' made—clever and smart things as I've thought at the time—come up now my heart's welly brossen.[3] Th' strike's failed as well; dun yo' know that, miss? I were coming whoam to ask her, like a beggar as I am, for a bit o' comfort i' that trouble; and I were knocked down by one who told me she were dead—just dead. That were all; but that were enough for me."

Mr. Hale blew his nose, and got up to snuff the candles in order to conceal his emotion. "He's not an infidel, Margaret; how could you say so?" muttered he reproachfully. "I've a good mind to read him the fourteenth chapter of Job."[4]

"Not yet, papa, I think. Perhaps not at all. Let us ask him about the strike, and give him all the sympathy he needs, and hoped to have from poor Bessy."

So they questioned and listened. The workmen's calculations were based (like too many of the masters') on false premises. They reckoned on their fellow-men as if they possessed the calculable powers of machines, no more, no less; no allowance for human passions getting the better of reason, as in the case of Boucher and the rioters; and believing that the representations of their injuries would have the same effect on strangers far away, as the injuries (fancied or real) had upon themselves. They were consequently surprised and indignant at the poor Irish, who had allowed themselves to be imported and brought over to take their places. This indignation was tempered, in some degree, by contempt for "them Irishers," and by pleasure at the idea of the bungling way in which they would set to work, and perplex their new masters with their ignorance and stupidity, strange exaggerated stories of which were already spreading through the town. But the most cruel cut of all was that of the Milton workmen, who had defied and disobeyed the commands of the Union to keep the peace, whatever came; who had originated discord in the camp, and spread the panic of the law being arrayed against them.

"And so the strike is at an end," said Margaret.

"Ay, miss. It's save as save can. Th' factory doors will need open wide to-morrow to let in all who'll be axing for work; if it's only just

3. Broken.
4. On the subject of the brevity of human life, its sufferings, and the inevitability of God's appointment.

to show they'd nought to do wi' a measure, which if we'd been made o' th' right stuff would ha' brought wages up to a point they'n not been at this ten year."

"You'll get work, shan't you?" asked Margaret. "You're a famous workman, are not you?"

"Hamper 'll let me work at his mill, when he cuts off his right hand—not before, and not after," said Nicholas, quietly. Margaret was silenced and sad.

"About the wages," said Mr. Hale. "You'll not be offended, but I think you make some sad mistakes. I should like to read you some remarks in a book I have." He got up and went to his book-shelves.

"Yo' needn't trouble yoursel', sir," said Nicholas. "Their book-stuff goes in at one ear and out at t'other. I can make nought on't. Afore Hamper and me had this split, th' overlooker told him I were stirring up th' men to ask for higher wages; and Hamper met me one day in th' yard. He'd a thin book i' his hand, and says he, 'Higgins, I'm told you're one of those damned fools that think you can get higher wages for asking for 'em; ay, and keep 'em up too, when you've forced 'em up. Now, I'll give yo' a chance and try if yo've any sense in yo'. Here's a book written by a friend o' mine, and if yo'll read it yo'll see how wages find their own level, without either masters or men having aught to do with them; except the men cut their own throats wi' striking, like the confounded noodles they are.' Well, now, sir, I put it to yo', being a parson, and having been in th' preaching line, and having had to try and bring folk o'er to what yo' thought was a right way o'thinking—did yo' begin by calling 'em fools and such like, or didn't yo' rayther give 'em some kind words at first, to make 'em ready for to listen and be convinced, if they could; and in yo'r preaching, did yo' stop every now and then, and say, half to them and half to yo'rsel', 'But yo're such a pack o' fools, that I've a strong notion it's no use my trying to put sense into yo'?' I were not i' th' best state, I'll own, for taking in what Hamper's friend had to say—I were so vexed at the way it were put to me;—but I thought, 'Come, I'll see what these chaps has got to say, and try if it's them or me as is th' noodle.' So I took th' book and tugged at it; but, Lord bless yo', it went on about capital and labour, and labour and capital, till it fair sent me off to sleep. I ne'er could rightly fix i' my mind which was which; and it spoke on 'em as if they was vartues or vices; and what I wanted for to know were the rights o' men, whether they were rich or poor—so be they only were men."

"But for all that," said Mr. Hale, "and granting to the full the offensiveness, the folly, the unchristianness of Mr. Hamper's way of speaking to you in recommending his friend's book, yet if it told you what he said it did, that wages find their own level, and that the most successful strike can only force them up for a moment, to sink in far greater proportion afterwards, in consequence of that very strike, the book would have told you the truth."

"Well, sir," said Higgins, rather doggedly; "it might, or it might not. There's two opinions go to settling that point. But suppose it was truth double strong, it were no truth to me if I couldna take it in. I daresay there's truth in yon Latin book on your shelves; but it's gibberish and not truth to me, unless I know the meaning o' the words. If yo', sir, or any other knowledgable, patient man come to me, and says he'll larn me what the words mean, and not blow me up if I'm a bit stupid, or forget how one thing hangs on another— why, in time I may get to see the truth of it; or I may not. I'll not be bound to say I shall end in thinking the same as any man. And I'm not one who think truth can be shaped out in words, all neat and clean, as th' men at th' foundry cut out sheet-iron. Same bones won't go down wi' every one. It'll stick here i' this man's throat, and there i' t'other's. Let alone that, when down, it may be too strong for this one, too weak for that. Folk who sets up to doctor th' world wi' their truth, mun suit different for different minds; and be a bit tender in th' way of giving it too, or th' poor sick fools may spit it out i' their faces. Now Hamper first gi'es me a box on my ear, and then he throws his big bolus[5] at me, and says he reckons it'll do me no good, I'm such a fool, but there it is."

"I wish some of the kindest and wisest of the masters would meet some of you men, and have a good talk on these things; it would, surely, be the best way of getting over your difficulties, which, I do believe, arise from your ignorance—excuse me, Mr. Higgins—on subjects which it is for the mutual interest of both masters and men should be well understood by both. I wonder"—(half to his daughter), "if Mr. Thornton might not be induced to do such a thing?"

"Remember, papa," said she in a very low voice, "what he said one day—about governments, you know." She was unwilling to make any clearer allusion to the conversation they had held on the mode of governing work-people—by giving men intelligence enough to rule themselves, or by a wise despotism on the part of the master—for she saw that Higgins had caught Mr. Thornton's name, if not the whole of the speech: indeed, he began to speak of him.

"Thornton! He's the chap as wrote off at once for these Irishers; and led to th' riot that ruined th' strike. Even Hamper wi' all his bullying, would ha' waited a while—but it's a word and a blow wi' Thornton. And, now, when th' Union would ha' thanked him for following up th' chase after Boucher, and them chaps as went right again our commands, it's Thornton who steps forrard and coolly says

5. A large pill.

that, as th' strike's at an end, he, as party injured, doesn't want to press the charge again the rioters. I thought he'd had more pluck. I thought he'd ha' carried his point, and had his revenge in an open way; but says he (one in court told me his very words) 'they are well known; they will find the natural punishment of their conduct, in the difficulty they will meet wi' in getting employment. That will be severe enough.' I only wish they'd cotched Boucher, and had him up before Hamper. I see th' oud tiger setting on him! would he ha' let him off? Not he!"

"Mr. Thornton was right," said Margaret. "You are angry against Boucher, Nicholas; or else you would be the first to see, that where the natural punishment would be severe enough for the offence, any farther punishment would be something like revenge."

"My daughter is no great friend of Mr. Thornton's," said Mr. Hale smiling at Margaret; while she, as red as any carnation, began to work with double diligence, "but I believe what she says is the truth. I like him for it."

"Well, sir, this strike has been a weary piece o' business to me; and yo'll not wonder if I'm a bit put out wi' seeing it fail, just for a few men who would na suffer in silence, and hou'd out, brave and firm."

"You forget!" said Margaret. "I don't know much of Boucher; but the only time I saw him it was not his own sufferings he spoke of, but those of his sick wife—his little children."

"True! but he were not made of iron himsel'. He'd ha' cried out for his own sorrows, next. He were not one to bear."

"How came he into the Union?" asked Margaret innocently. "You don't seem to have much respect for him; nor gained much good from having him in."

Higgins's brow clouded. He was silent for a minute or two. Then he said, shortly enough:

"It's not for me to speak o' th' Union. What they does, they does. Them that is of a trade mun hang together; and if they're not willing to take their chance along wi' th' rest, th' Union has ways and means."

Mr. Hale saw that Higgins was vexed at the turn the conversation had taken, and was silent. Not so Margaret, though she saw Higgins's feeling as clearly as he did. By instinct she felt, that if he could but be brought to express himself in plain words, something clear would be gained on which to argue for the right and the just.

"And what are the Union's ways and means?"

He looked up at her, as if on the point of dogged resistance to her wish for information. But her calm face, fixed on his, patient and trustful, compelled him to answer.

"Well! If a man doesn't belong to th' Union, them as works next looms has orders not to speak to him—if he's sorry or ill it's a' the same; he's out o' bounds; he's none o' us; he comes among us, he works among us, but he's none o' us. I' some places them's fined who speaks to him. Yo' try that, miss; try living a year or two among them as looks away if yo' look at 'em; try working within two yards o' crowds o' men, who, yo' know, have a grinding grudge at yo' in their hearts— to whom if yo' say yo'r glad, not an eye brightens, nor a lip moves—to whom if your heart's heavy, yo' can never say nought, because they'll ne'er take notice on your sighs or sad looks (and a man's no man who'll groan out loud 'bout folk asking him what's the matter?)—just yo' try that, miss—ten hours for three hundred days, and yo'll know a bit what th' Union is."

"Why!" said Margaret, "what tyranny this is! Nay, Higgins, I don't care one straw for your anger. I know you can't be angry with me if you would, and I must tell you the truth: that I never read, in all the history I have read, of a more slow, lingering torture than this. And you belong to the Union! And you talk of the tyranny of the masters!"

"Nay," said Higgins, "yo' may say what yo' like! The dead stand between yo' and every angry word o' mine. D' ye think I forget who's lying *there*, and how hoo loved yo'? And it's th' masters as has made us sin, if th' Union is a sin. Not this generation maybe, but their fathers. Their fathers ground our fathers to the very dust; ground us to powder! Parson! I reckon, I've heerd my mother read out a text, 'The fathers have eaten sour grapes and th' children's teeth are set on edge.'[6] It's so wi' them. In those days of sore oppression th' Unions began; it were a necessity. It's a necessity now, according to me. It's a withstanding of injustice, past, present, or to come. It may be like war; along wi' it come crimes; but I think it were a greater crime to let it alone. Our only chance is binding men together in one common interest; and if some are cowards and some are fools, they mun come along and join the great march, whose only strength is in numbers."

"Oh!" said Mr. Hale, sighing, "your Union in itself would be beautiful, glorious,—it would be Christianity itself—if it were but for an end which affected the good of all, instead of that of merely one class as opposed to another."

"I reckon it's time for me to be going, sir," said Higgins, as the clock struck ten.

"Home?" said Margaret very softly. He understood her, and took her offered hand. "Home, miss. Yo' may trust me, tho' I am one o' th' Union."

"I do trust you most thoroughly, Nicholas."

"Stay!" said Mr. Hale, hurrying to the bookshelves. "Mr. Higgins! I'm sure you'll join us in family prayer?"

6. Ezekiel 18:2.

Higgins looked at Margaret, doubtfully. Her grave sweet eyes met his; there was no compulsion, only deep interest in them. He did not speak, but he kept his place.

Margaret the Churchwoman,[7] her father the Dissenter, Higgins the Infidel, knelt down together. It did them no harm.

All 3 of them can find common ground and peace together

Chapter IV.

A Ray of Sunshine.

"Some wishes crossed my mind and dimly cheered it,
And one or two poor melancholy pleasures,
Each in the pale unwarming light of hope,
Silvering its flimsy wing, flew silent by—
Moths in the moonbeam!"

COLERIDGE.[1]

The next morning brought Margaret a letter from Edith. It was affectionate and inconsequent like the writer. But the affection was charming to Margaret's own affectionate nature; and she had grown up with the inconsequence, so she did not perceive it. It was as follows:—

"Oh, Margaret, it is worth a journey from England to see my boy! He is a superb little fellow, especially in his caps, and most especially in the one you sent him, you good, dainty-fingered, persevering little lady! Having made all the mothers here envious, I want to show him to somebody new, and hear a fresh set of admiring expressions; perhaps, that's all the reason; perhaps it is not,—nay, possibly, there is just a little cousinly love mixed with it; but I do want you so much to come here, Margaret! I'm sure it would be the very best thing for Aunt Hale's health; everybody here is young and well, and our skies are always blue, and our sun always shines, and the band plays deliciously from morning till night; and, to come back to the burden of my ditty, my baby always smiles. I am constantly wanting you to draw him for me, Margaret. It does not signify what he is doing; that very thing is prettiest, gracefulest, best. I think I love him a great deal better than my husband, who is getting stout, and grumpy,—what he calls 'busy.' No! he is not. He has just come in with news of such a charming pic-nic, given by the officers of the Hazard, at anchor in the bay below. Because he has brought in such a pleasant piece of news, I retract all I said just now. Did not somebody burn his hand

7. A member of the Church of England. Despite her father's defection Margaret has remained within the established church.
1. The lines quoted are a fragment from Samuel Taylor Coleridge's *Literary Remains* (1836). Gaskell slightly misquotes.

for having said or done something he was sorry for?[2] Well, I can't
burn mine, because it would hurt me, and the scar would be ugly;
but I'll retract all I said as fast as I can. Cosmo[3] is quite as great a
darling as baby, and not a bit stout, and as ungrumpy as ever husband
was; only, sometimes he is very, very busy. I may say that without
love—wifely duty—where was I?—I had something very particular
to say, I know, once. Oh, it is this—Dearest Margaret!—you must
come and see me; it would do Aunt Hale good, as I said before. Get
the doctor to order it for her. Tell him that it's the smoke of Milton
that does her harm. I have no doubt it is that, really. Three months
(you must not come for less) of this delicious climate—all sunshine,
and grapes as common as blackberries, would quite cure her. I don't
ask my uncle"—(Here the letter became more constrained, and better written; Mr. Hale was in the corner, like a naughty child, for
having given up his living.)—"because, I dare say, he disapproves of
war, and soldiers, and bands of music; at least, I know that many
Dissenters are members of the Peace Society,[4] and I am afraid he
would not like to come; but, if he would, dear, pray say that Cosmo
and I will do our best to make him happy; and I'll hide up Cosmo's
red coat and sword, and make the band play all sorts of grave, solemn
things; or, if they do play pomps and vanities, it shall be in double
slow time. Dear Margaret, if he would like to accompany you and
Aunt Hale, we will try and make it pleasant, though I'm rather afraid
of any one who has done something for conscience' sake. You never
did, I hope. Tell Aunt Hale not to bring many warm clothes, though
I'm afraid it will be late in the year before you can come. But you
have no idea of the heat here! I tried to wear my great beauty Indian
shawl at a picnic. I kept myself up with proverbs as long as I could;
'Pride must abide,'—and such wholesome pieces of pith; but it was
of no use. I was like mamma's little dog Tiny with an elephant's
trappings on; smothered, hidden, killed with my finery; so I made it
into a capital carpet for us all to sit down upon. Here's this boy of
mine, Margaret,—if you don't pack up your things as soon as you
get this letter, and come straight off to see him, I shall think you're
descended from King Herod!"

Margaret did long for a day of Edith's life—her freedom from care,
her cheerful home, her sunny skies. If a wish could have transported
her, she would have gone off; just for one day. She yearned for the

2. Thomas Cranmer (1489–1556), about to be burned at the stake for treason in the reign
   of Mary I, thrust his right hand into the flames, uttering the words, "This hand hath
   offended," since it had signed his recantation of Protestant doctrines.
3. Gaskell here gives Captain Lennox's first name as "Cosmo"; later (vol. II, chap. 23) it is
   given as "Sholto," the name also given to his son. I have retained the anomaly.
4. Founded in 1816, and still functioning at the time of Gaskell's writing of North and South,
   the Peace Society argued against the use of force in international disputes. The issue was
   topical at the time of writing, with the unrest leading up to the Crimean War. There were
   a number of such societies in Britain and America in the nineteenth century.

strength which such a change would give,—even for a few hours to be in the midst of that bright life, and to feel young again. Not yet twenty! and she had had to bear up against such hard pressure that she felt quite old. That was her first feeling after reading Edith's letter. Then she read it again, and, forgetting herself, was amused at its likeness to Edith's self, and was laughing merrily over it when Mrs. Hale came into the drawing-room, leaning on Dixon's arm. Margaret flew to adjust the pillows. Her mother seemed more than usually feeble.

"What were you laughing at, Margaret?" asked she, as soon as she had recovered from the exertion of settling herself on the sofa.

"A letter I have had this morning from Edith. Shall I read it you, mamma?"

She read it aloud, and for a time it seemed to interest her mother, who kept wondering what name Edith had given to her boy, and suggesting all probable names, and all possible reasons why each and all of these names should be given. Into the very midst of these wonders Mr. Thornton came, bringing another offering of fruit for Mrs. Hale. He could not—say rather, he would not—deny himself the chance of the pleasure of seeing Margaret. He had no end in this but the present gratification. It was the sturdy wilfulness of a man usually most reasonable and self-controlled. He entered the room, taking in at a glance the fact of Margaret's presence; but after the first cold distant bow, he never seemed to let his eyes fall on her again. He only stayed to present his peaches—to speak some gentle kindly words—and then his cold offended eyes met Margaret's with a grave farewell, as he left the room. She sat down silent and pale.

"Do you know, Margaret, I really begin quite to like Mr. Thornton."

No answer at first. Then Margaret forced out an icy. "Do you?"

"Yes! I think he is really getting quite polished in his manners."

Margaret's voice was more in order now. She replied,

"He is very kind and attentive,—there is no doubt of that."

"I wonder Mrs. Thornton never calls. She must know I am ill, because of the water-bed."

"I dare say, she hears how you are from her son."

"Still, I should like to see her. You have so few friends here, Margaret."

Margaret felt what was in her mother's thoughts,—a tender craving to bespeak the kindness of some woman towards the daughter that might be so soon left motherless. But she could not speak.

"Do you think," said Mrs. Hale, after a pause, "that you could go and ask Mrs. Thornton to come and see me? Only once,—I don't want to be troublesome."

"I will do anything, if you wish it, mamma,—but if—but when Frederick comes"——

"Ah, to be sure! we must keep our doors shut,—we must let no one in. I hardly know whether I dare wish him to come or not. Sometimes I think I would rather not. Sometimes I have such frightful dreams about him."

"Oh, mamma! we'll take good care. I will put my arm in the bolt sooner than he should come to the slightest harm. Trust the care of him to me, mamma. I will watch over him like a lioness over her young."

"When can we hear from him?"

"Not for a week yet, certainly,—perhaps more."

"We must send Martha away in good time. It would never do to have her here when he comes, and then send her off in a hurry."

"Dixon is sure to remind us of that. I was thinking that, if we wanted any help in the house while he is here, we could perhaps get Mary Higgins. She is very slack of work, and is a good girl, and would take pains to do her best, I am sure, and would sleep at home, and need never come upstairs, so as to know who is in the house."

"As you please. As Dixon pleases. But, Margaret, don't get to use these horrid Milton words. 'Slack of work:' it is a provincialism. What will your aunt Shaw say, if she hears you use it on her return?"

"Oh, mamma! don't try and make a bugbear of aunt Shaw," said Margaret, laughing. "Edith picked up all sorts of military slang from Captain Lennox, and aunt Shaw never took any notice of it."

"But yours is factory slang."

"And if I live in a factory town, I must speak factory language when I want it. Why, mamma, I could astonish you with a great many words you never heard in your life. I don't believe you know what a knobstick is."

"Not I, child. I only know it has a very vulgar sound; and I don't want to hear you using it."

"Very well, dearest mother, I won't. Only I shall have to use a whole explanatory sentence instead."

"I don't like this Milton," said Mrs. Hale. "Edith is right enough in saying it's the smoke that has made me so ill."

Margaret started up as her mother said this. Her father had just entered the room, and she was most anxious that the faint impression she had seen on his mind that the Milton air had injured her mother's health, should not be deepened,—should not receive any confirmation. She could not tell whether he had heard what Mrs. Hale had said or not; but she began speaking hurriedly of other things, unaware that Mr. Thornton was following him.

"Mamma is accusing me of having picked up a great deal of vulgarity since we came to Milton."

The "vulgarity" Margaret spoke of, referred purely to the use of local words, and the expression arose out of the conversation they had just been holding. But Mr. Thornton's brow darkened; and Margaret suddenly felt how her speech might be misunderstood by him; so, in the natural sweet desire to avoid giving unnecessary pain, she forced herself to go forwards with a little greeting, and continue what she was saying, addressing herself to him expressly.

"Now, Mr. Thornton, though 'knobstick' has not a very pretty sound, is it not expressive? Could I do without it, in speaking of the thing it represents? If using local words is vulgar, I was very vulgar in the Forest,—was I not, mamma?"

It was unusual with Margaret to obtrude her own subject of conversation on others; but, in this case, she was so anxious to prevent Mr. Thornton from feeling annoyance at the words he had accidentally overheard, that it was not until she had done speaking that she coloured all over with consciousness, more especially as Mr. Thornton seemed hardly to understand the exact gist or bearing of what she was saying, but passed her by, with a cold reserve of ceremonious movement, to speak to Mrs. Hale.

The sight of him reminded her of the wish to see his mother, and commend Margaret to her care. Margaret, sitting in burning silence, vexed and ashamed of her difficulty in keeping her right place, and her calm unconsciousness of heart, when Mr. Thornton was by, heard her mother's slow entreaty that Mrs. Thornton would come and see her; see her soon; to-morrow, if it were possible. Mr. Thornton promised that she should—conversed a little, and then took his leave; and Margaret's movements and voice seemed at once released from some invisible chains. He never looked at her; and yet, the careful avoidance of his eyes betokened that in some way he knew exactly where, if they fell by chance, they would rest on her. If she spoke, he gave no sign of attention, and yet his next speech to any one else was modified by what she had said; sometimes there was an express answer to what she had remarked, but given to another person as though unsuggested by her. It was not the bad manners of ignorance: it was the wilful bad manners arising from deep offence. It was wilful at the time; repented of afterwards. But no deep plan, no careful cunning could have stood him in such good stead. Margaret thought about him more than she had ever done before; not with any tinge of what is called love, but with regret that she had wounded him so deeply,—and with a gentle, patient striving to return to their former position of antagonistic friendship; for a friend's position was what she found that he had held in her regard, as well as in that of the rest of the family. There was a pretty humility in her behaviour to him, as if mutely apologising for the over-strong words which were the reaction from the deeds of the day of the riot.

But he resented those words bitterly. They rung in his ears; and he was proud of the sense of justice which made him go on in every kindness he could offer to her parents. He exulted in the power he showed in compelling himself to face her, whenever he could think of any action which might give her father or mother pleasure. He thought that he disliked seeing one who had mortified him so keenly; but he was mistaken. It was a stinging pleasure to be in the room with her, and feel her presence. But he was no great analyser of his own motives, and was mistaken, as I have said.

Chapter V.

Home at Last.

"The saddest birds a season find to sing."
SOUTHWELL.[1]

"Never to fold the robe o'er secret pain,
Never, weighed down by memory's clouds again,
To bow thy head! Thou art gone home!"
MRS. HEMANS.[2]

Mrs. Thornton came to see Mrs. Hale the next morning. She was much worse. One of those sudden changes—those great visible strides towards death, had been taken in the night, and her own family were startled by the gray sunken look her features had assumed in that one twelve hours of suffering. Mrs. Thornton—who had not seen her for weeks—was softened all at once. She had come because her son asked it from her as a personal favour, but with all the proud bitter feelings of her nature in arms against that family of which Margaret formed one. She doubted the reality of Mrs. Hale's illness; she doubted any want beyond a momentary fancy on that lady's part, which should take her out of her previously settled course of employment for the day. She told her son that she wished they had never come near the place; that he had never got acquainted with them; that there had been no such useless languages as Latin and Greek ever invented. He bore all this pretty silently; but when she had ended her invective against the dead languages, he quietly returned to the short, curt, decided expression of his wish that she should go and see Mrs. Hale at the time appointed, as most likely to be convenient to the invalid. Mrs. Thornton submitted with as bad a grace as she could to her son's desire, all the time liking him the

---

1. Robert Southwell (c. 1561–1595), poet and Jesuit priest. He was tortured and executed as a traitor in the reign of Elizabeth I.
2. From the poem "The Two Voices."

better for having it; and exaggerating in her own mind the same notion that he had of extraordinary goodness on his part in so perseveringly keeping up with the Hales.

His goodness verging on weakness (as all the softer virtues did in her mind), and her own contempt for Mr. and Mrs. Hale, and positive dislike to Margaret, were the ideas which occupied Mrs. Thornton, till she was struck into nothingness before the dark shadow of the wings of the angel of death. There lay Mrs. Hale—a mother like herself—a much younger woman than she was,—on the bed from which there was no sign of hope that she might ever rise again. No more variety of light and shade for her in that darkened room; no power of action, scarcely change of movement; faint alternations of whispered sound and studious silence; and yet that monotonous life seemed almost too much! When Mrs. Thornton, strong and prosperous with life, came in, Mrs. Hale lay still, although from the look on her face she was evidently conscious of who it was. But she did not even open her eyes for a minute or two. The heavy moisture of tears stood on the eyelashes before she looked up; then, with her hand groping feebly over the bed-clothes, for the touch of Mrs. Thornton's large firm fingers, she said, scarcely above her breath— Mrs. Thornton had to stoop from her erectness to listen,—

"Margaret—you have a daughter—my sister is in Italy. My child will be without a mother;—in a strange place,—if I die——will you"——[3]

And her filmy wandering eyes fixed themselves with an intensity of wistfulness on Mrs. Thornton's face. For a minute, there was no change in its rigidness; it was stern and unmoved;—nay, but that the eyes of the sick woman were growing dim with the slow-gathering tears, she might have seen a dark cloud cross the cold features. And it was no thought of her son, or of her living daughter Fanny, that stirred her heart at last; but a sudden remembrance, suggested by something in the arrangement of the room,—of a little daughter— dead in infancy—long years ago—that, like a sudden sunbeam, melted the icy crust, behind which there was a real tender woman.

"You wish me to be a friend to Miss Hale," said Mrs. Thornton, in her measured voice, that would not soften with her heart, but came out distinct and clear.

Mrs. Hale, her eyes still fixed on Mrs. Thornton's face, pressed the hand that lay below hers on the coverlet. She could not speak. Mrs. Thornton sighed, "I will be a true friend, if circumstances require it. Not a tender friend. That I cannot be,"—("to her," she was on the point of adding, but she relented at the sight of that poor,

3. In conveying Mrs. Hale's confused state of mind Gaskell perhaps confuses the reader. "Margaret" refers to her daughter; "you have a daughter" to Mrs. Thornton; "my sister is in Italy" explains why she consigns Margaret to Mrs. Thornton's protection.

anxious face.)—"It is not my nature to show affection even where I feel it, nor do I volunteer advice in general. Still, at your request,—if it will be any comfort to you, I will promise you." Then came a pause. Mrs. Thornton was too conscientious to promise what she did not mean to perform; and to perform anything in the way of kindness on behalf of Margaret, more disliked at this moment than ever, was difficult; almost impossible.

"I promise," said she, with grave severity; which, after all, inspired the dying woman with faith as in something more stable than life itself,—flickering, flitting, wavering life! "I promise that in any difficulty in which Miss Hale"——

"Call her Margaret!" gasped Mrs. Hale.

"In which she comes to me for help, I will help her with every power I have, as if she were my own daughter. I also promise that if ever I see her doing what I think is wrong"——

"But Margaret never does wrong—not wilfully wrong," pleaded Mrs. Hale. Mrs. Thornton went on as before; as if she had not heard:

"If ever I see her doing what I believe to be wrong—such wrong not touching me or mine, in which case I might be supposed to have an interested motive—I will tell her of it, faithfully and plainly, as I should wish my own daughter to be told."

There was a long pause. Mrs. Hale felt that this promise did not include all; and yet it was much. It had reservations in it which she did not understand; but then she was weak, dizzy, and tired. Mrs. Thornton was reviewing all the probable cases in which she had pledged herself to act. She had a fierce pleasure in the idea of telling Margaret unwelcome truths, in the shape of performance of duty. Mrs. Hale began to speak:

"I thank you. I pray God to bless you. I shall never see you again in this world. But my last words are, I thank you for your promise of kindness to my child."

"Not kindness!" testified Mrs. Thornton, ungraciously truthful to the last. But having eased her conscience by saying these words, she was not sorry that they were not heard. She pressed Mrs. Hale's soft languid hand; and rose up and went her way out of the house without seeing a creature.

During the time that Mrs. Thornton was having this interview with Mrs. Hale, Margaret and Dixon were laying their heads together and consulting how they should keep Frederick's coming a profound secret to all out of the house. A letter from him might now be expected any day; and he would assuredly follow quickly on its heels. Martha must be sent away on her holiday; Dixon must keep stern guard on the front door, only admitting the few visitors that ever came to the house into Mr. Hale's room down stairs—Mrs. Hale's extreme illness giving her a good excuse for this. If Mary Higgins was required as a help to Dixon in the kitchen, she was to hear and see as little of Frederick as possible; and he was, if necessary, to be spoken of to her under the name of Mr. Dickinson. But her sluggish and incurious nature was the greatest safeguard of all.

They resolved that Martha should leave them that very afternoon for this visit to her mother.[4] Margaret wished that she had been sent away on the previous day, as she fancied it might be thought strange to give a servant a holiday when her mistress's state required so much attendance.

Poor Margaret! All that afternoon she had to act the part of a Roman daughter, and give strength out of her own scanty stock to her father. Mr. Hale would hope, would not despair, between the attacks of his wife's malady; he buoyed himself up in every respite from her pain, and believed that it was the beginning of ultimate recovery. And so, when the paroxysms came on, each more severe than the last, they were fresh agonies, and greater disappointments to him. This afternoon, he sat in the drawing-room, unable to bear the solitude of his study, or to employ himself in any way. He buried his head in his arms, which lay folded on the table. Margaret's heart ached to see him; yet, as he did not speak, she did not like to volunteer any attempt at comfort. Martha was gone. Dixon sat with Mrs. Hale while she slept. The house was very still and quiet, and darkness came on, without any movement to procure candles. Margaret sat at the window, looking out at the lamps and the street, but seeing nothing,—only alive to her father's heavy sighs. She did not like to go down for lights, lest the tacit restraint of her presence being withdrawn, he might give way to more violent emotion, without her being at hand to comfort him. Yet she was just thinking that she ought to go and see after the well-doing of the kitchen fire, which there was nobody but herself to attend to, when she heard the muffled door-bell ring with so violent a pull, that the wires jingled all through the house, though the positive sound was not great. She started up, passed her father, who had never moved at the veiled, dull sound,— returned, and kissed him tenderly. And still he never moved, nor took any notice of her fond embrace. Then she went down softly, through the dark, to the door. Dixon would have put the chain on before she opened it, but Margaret had not a thought of fear in her pre-occupied mind. A man's tall figure stood between her and the luminous street. He was looking away; but at the sound of the latch he turned quickly round.

"Is this Mr. Hale's?" said he, in a clear, full, delicate voice.

Margaret trembled all over; at first she did not answer. In a moment she sighed out,

4. See p. 207, n. 6, above.

"Frederick!" and stretched out both her hands to catch his, and draw him in.

"Oh, Margaret!" said he, holding her off by her shoulders, after they had kissed each other, as if even in that darkness he could see her face, and read in its expression a quicker answer to his question than words could give,—

"My mother! is she alive?"

"Yes, she is alive, dear, dear brother! She—as ill as she can be she is; but alive! She is alive!"

"Thank God!" said he.

"Papa is utterly prostrate with this great grief."

"You expect me, don't you?"

"No, we have had no letter."

"Then I have come before it. But my mother knows I am coming?"

"Oh! we all knew you would come. But wait a little! Step in here. Give me your hand. What is this? Oh! your carpet-bag. Dixon has shut the shutters; but this is papa's study, and I can take you to a chair to rest yourself for a few minutes; while I go and tell him."

She groped her way to the taper and the lucifer matches.[5] She suddenly felt shy, when the little feeble light made them visible. All she could see was, that her brother's face was unusually dark in complexion, and she caught the stealthy look of a pair of remarkably long-cut blue eyes, that suddenly twinkled up with a droll conscious-ness of their mutual purpose of inspecting each other. But though the brother and sister had an instant of sympathy in their reciprocal glances, they did not exchange a word; only, Margaret felt sure that she should like her brother as a companion as much as she already loved him as a near relation. Her heart was wonderfully lighter as she went up stairs; the sorrow was no less in reality, but it became less oppressive from having some one in precisely the same relation to it as that in which she stood. Not her father's desponding attitude had power to damp her now. He lay across the table, helpless as ever; but she had the spell by which to rouse him. She used it perhaps too violently in her own great relief.

"Papa," said she, throwing her arms fondly round his neck; pulling his weary head up in fact with her gentle violence, till it rested in her arms, and she could look into his eyes, and let them gain strength and assurance from hers.

"Papa! guess who is here!"

He looked at her; she saw the idea of the truth glimmer into their filmy sadness, and be dismissed thence as a wild imagination.

He threw himself forward, and hid his face once more in his stretched-out arms, resting upon the table as heretofore. She heard

5. Slips of wood tipped with a substance that ignited on friction. The origin of present-day matches, they tended to ignite unpredictably.

him whisper; she bent tenderly down to listen. "I don't know. Don't tell me it is Frederick—not Frederick. I cannot bear it,—I am too weak. And his mother is dying!"

He began to cry and wail like a child. It was so different to all which Margaret had hoped and expected, that she turned sick with disappointment, and was silent for an instant. Then she spoke again—very differently—not so exultingly, far more tenderly and carefully.

"Papa, it is Frederick! Think of mamma, how glad she will be! And oh, for her sake, how glad we ought to be! For his sake, too,—our poor, poor boy!"

Her father did not change his attitude, but he seemed to be trying to understand the fact.

"Where is he?" asked he at last, his face still hidden in his prostrate arms.

"In your study, quite alone. I lighted the taper, and ran up to tell you. He is quite alone, and will be wondering why—"

"I will go to him," broke in her father; and he lifted himself up and leant on her arm as on that of a guide.

Margaret led him to the study door, but her spirits were so agitated that she felt she could not bear to see the meeting. She turned away, and ran up stairs, and cried most heartily. It was the first time she had dared to allow herself this relief for days. The strain had been terrible, as she now felt. But Frederick was come! He, the one precious brother, was there, safe, amongst them again! She could hardly believe it. She stopped her crying, and opened her bedroom door. She heard no sound of voices, and almost feared she might have dreamt. She went down stairs, and listened at the study door. She heard the buzz of voices; and that was enough. She went into the kitchen, and stirred up the fire, and lighted the house, and prepared for the wanderer's refreshment. How fortunate it was that her mother slept! She knew that she did, from the candle-lighter thrust through the keyhole of her bedroom door. The traveller could be refreshed and bright, and the first excitement of the meeting with his father all be over, before her mother became aware of anything unusual.

When all was ready, Margaret opened the study door, and went in like a serving-maiden, with a heavy tray held in her extended arms. She was proud of serving Frederick. But he, when he saw her, sprang up in a minute, and relieved her of her burden. It was a type, a sign, of all the coming relief which his presence would bring. The brother and sister arranged the table together, saying little, but their hands touching, and their eyes speaking the natural language of expression, so intelligible to those of the same blood. The fire had gone out; and Margaret applied herself to light it, for the evenings had begun to be chilly; and yet it was desirable to make all noises as distant as possible from Mrs. Hale's room.

"Dixon says it is a gift to light a fire; not an art to be acquired."

"Poeta nascitur, non fit,"[6] murmured Mr. Hale; and Margaret was glad to hear a quotation once more, however languidly given.

"Dear old Dixon! How we shall kiss each other!" said Frederick. "She used to kiss me, and then look in my face to be sure I was the right person, and then set to again! But, Margaret, what a bungler you are! I never saw such a little awkward, good-for-nothing pair of hands. Run away, and wash them, ready to cut bread-and-butter for me, and leave the fire. I'll manage it. Lighting fires is one of my natural accomplishments."

So Margaret went away; and returned; and passed in and out of the room, in a glad restlessness that could not be satisfied with sitting still. The more wants Frederick had, the better she was pleased; and he understood all this by instinct. It was a joy snatched in the house of mourning, and the zest of it was all the more pungent, because they knew in the depths of their hearts what irremediable sorrow awaited them.

In the middle, they heard Dixon's foot on the stairs. Mr. Hale started from his languid posture in his great arm-chair, from which he had been watching his children in a dreamy way, as if they were acting some drama of happiness, which it was pretty to look at, but which was distinct from reality, and in which he had no part. He stood up, and faced the door, showing such a strange, sudden anxiety to conceal Frederick from the sight of any person entering, even though it were the faithful Dixon, that a shiver came over Margaret's heart: it reminded her of the new fear in their lives. She caught at Frederick's arm, and clutched it tight, while a stern thought compressed her brows, and caused her to set her teeth. And yet they knew it was only Dixon's measured tread. They heard her walk the length of the passage,—into the kitchen. Margaret rose up.

"I will go to her, and tell her. And I shall hear how mamma is." Mrs. Hale was awake. She rambled at first; but after they had given her some tea she was refreshed, though not disposed to talk. It was better that the night should pass over before she was told of her son's arrival. Dr. Donaldson's appointed visit would bring nervous excitement enough for the evening; and he might tell them how to prepare her for seeing Frederick. He was there, in the house; could be summoned at any moment.

Margaret could not sit still. It was a relief to her to aid Dixon in all her preparations for "Master Frederick." It seemed as though she never could be tired again. Each glimpse into the room where he sat

6. A poet is born, not made (Latin).

by his father, conversing with him, about, she knew not what, nor cared to know,—was increase of strength to her. Her own time for talking and hearing would come at last, and she was too certain of this to feel in a hurry to grasp it now. She took in his appearance and liked it. He had delicate features, redeemed from effeminacy by the swarthiness of his complexion, and his quick intensity of expression. His eyes were generally merry-looking, but at times they and his mouth so suddenly changed, and gave her such an idea of latent passion, that it almost made her afraid. But this look was only for an instant; and had in it no doggedness, no vindictiveness; it was rather the instantaneous ferocity of expression that comes over the countenances of all natives of wild or southern countries—a ferocity which enhances the charm of the childlike softness into which such a look may melt away. Margaret might fear the violence of the impulsive nature thus occasionally betrayed, but there was nothing in it to make her distrust, or recoil in the least, from the new-found brother. On the contrary, all their intercourse was peculiarly charming to her from the very first. She knew then how much responsibility she had had to bear, from the exquisite sensation of relief which she felt in Frederick's presence. He understood his father and mother— their characters and their weaknesses, and went along with a careless freedom, which was yet most delicately careful not to hurt or wound any of their feelings. He seemed to know instinctively when a little of the natural brilliancy of his manner and conversation would not jar on the deep depression of his father, or might relieve his mother's pain. Whenever it would have been out of tune, and out of time, his patient devotion and watchfulness came into play, and made him an admirable nurse. Then Margaret was almost touched into tears by the allusions which he often made to their childish days in the New Forest; he had never forgotten her—or Helstone either—all the time he had been roaming among distant countries and foreign people. She might talk to him of the old spot, and never fear tiring him. She had been afraid of him before he came, even while she had longed for his coming; seven or eight years had, she felt, produced such great changes in herself that, forgetting how much of the original Margaret was left, she had reasoned that if her tastes and feelings had so materially altered, even in her stay-at-home life, his wild career, with which she was but imperfectly acquainted, must have almost substituted another Frederick for the tall stripling in his middy's uniform,[7] whom she remembered looking up to with such admiring awe. But in their absence they had grown nearer to each other in age, as well as in many other things. And so it was that the weight, this sorrowful time, was lightened to Margaret. Other light

7. That is, the uniform of a midshipman (the rank of trainee officers in the British navy).

than that of Frederick's presence she had none. For a few hours, the mother rallied on seeing her son. She sat with his hand in hers; she would not part with it even while she slept; and Margaret had to feed him like a baby, rather than that he should disturb her mother by removing a finger. Mrs. Hale wakened while they were thus engaged; she slowly moved her head round on the pillow, and smiled at her children, as she understood what they were doing, and why it was done.

"I am very selfish," said she; "but it will not be for long." Frederick bent down and kissed the feeble hand that imprisoned his.

This state of tranquillity could not endure for many days, nor perhaps for many hours; so Dr. Donaldson assured Margaret. After the kind doctor had gone away, she stole down to Frederick, who, during the visit, had been adjured to remain quietly concealed in the back parlour, usually Dixon's bedroom, but now given up to him.

Margaret told him what Dr. Donaldson said.

"I don't believe it," he exclaimed. "She is very ill; she may be dangerously ill, and in immediate danger, too; but I can't imagine that she could be as she is, if she were on the point of death. Margaret! she should have some other advice—some London doctor. Have you never thought of that?"

"Yes," said Margaret, "more than once. But I don't believe it would do any good. And, you know, we have not the money to bring any great London surgeon down, and I am sure Dr. Donaldson is only second in skill to the very best,—if, indeed, he is to them."

Frederick began to walk up and down the room impatiently.

"I have credit in Cadiz," said he, "but none here, owing to this wretched change of name. Why did my father leave Helstone? That was the blunder."

"It was no blunder," said Margaret gloomily. "And above all possible chances, avoid letting papa hear anything like what you have just been saying. I can see that he is tormenting himself already with the idea that mamma would never have been ill if we had stayed at Helstone, and you don't know papa's agonizing power of self-reproach!"

Frederick walked away as if he were on the quarter-deck. At last he stopped right opposite to Margaret, and looked at her drooping and desponding attitude for an instant.

"My little Margaret!" said he, caressing her. "Let us hope as long as we can. Poor little woman! what! is this face all wet with tears? I will hope. I will, in spite of a thousand doctors. Bear up, Margaret, and be brave enough to hope!"

Margaret choked in trying to speak, and when she did it was very low.

"I must try to be meek enough to trust. Oh, Frederick! mamma was getting to love me so! And I was getting to understand her. And now comes death to snap us asunder!"

"Come, come, come! Let us go up-stairs, and do something, rather than waste time that may be so precious. Thinking has, many a time, made me sad, darling; but doing never did in all my life. My theory is a sort of parody on the maxim of 'Get money, my son, honestly if you can; but get money.' My precept is, 'Do something, my sister, do good if you can; but, at any rate, do something.' "

"Not excluding mischief," said Margaret, smiling faintly through her tears.

"By no means. What I do exclude is the remorse afterwards. Blot your misdeeds out (if you are particularly conscientious), by a good deed, as soon as you can; just as we did a correct sum at school on the slate, where an incorrect one was only half rubbed out. It was better than wetting our sponge with our tears; both less loss of time where tears had to be waited for, and a better effect at last."

If Margaret thought Frederick's theory rather a rough one at first, she saw how he worked it out into continual production of kindness in fact. After a bad night with his mother (for he insisted on taking his turn as a sitter-up) he was busy next morning before breakfast, contriving a leg-rest for Dixon, who was beginning to feel the fatigues of watching. At breakfast-time, he interested Mr. Hale with vivid, graphic, rattling accounts of the wild life he had led in Mexico, South America, and elsewhere. Margaret would have given up the effort in despair to rouse Mr. Hale out of his dejection; it would even have affected herself and rendered her incapable of talking at all. But Fred, true to his theory, did something perpetually; and talking was the only thing to be done, besides eating, at breakfast.

Before the night of that day, Dr. Donaldson's opinion was proved to be too well founded. Convulsions came on; and when they ceased, Mrs. Hale was unconscious. Her husband might lie by her shaking the bed with his sobs; her son's strong arms might lift her tenderly up into a comfortable position; her daughter's hands might bathe her face; but she knew them not. She would never recognise them again, till they met in Heaven.

Before the morning came all was over.

Then Margaret rose from her trembling and despondency, and became as a strong angel of comfort to her father and brother. For Frederick had broken down now, and all his theories were of no use to him. He cried so violently when shut up alone in his little room at night, that Margaret and Dixon came down in affright to warn him to be quiet: for the house partitions were but thin, and the next-door neighbours might easily hear his youthful passionate sobs, so

different from the slower trembling agony of after-life, when we
become inured to grief, and dare not be rebellious against the inex-
orable doom, knowing who it is that decrees.

Margaret sat with her father in the room with the dead. If he had
cried, she would have been thankful. But he sat by the bed quite
quietly; only, from time to time, he uncovered the face, and stroked
it gently, making a kind of soft inarticulate noise, like that of some
mother-animal caressing her young. He took no notice of Margaret's
presence. Once or twice she came up to kiss him; and he submitted
to it, giving her a little push away when she had done, as if her
affection disturbed him from his absorption in the dead. He started
when he heard Frederick's cries, and shook his head:—"Poor boy!
poor boy!" he said, and took no more notice. Margaret's heart ached
within her. She could not think of her own loss in thinking of her
father's case. The night was wearing away, and the day was at hand,
when, without a word of preparation, Margaret's voice broke upon
the stillness of the room, with a clearness of sound that startled even
herself: "Let not your heart be troubled,[8]" it said; and she went steadily on through all that chapter of unspeakable consolation.

Chapter VI.

"Should Auld Acquaintance Be Forgot?"

"Show not that manner, and these features all,
The serpent's cunning, and the sinner's fall?"
CRABBE.[1]

The chill, shivery October morning came; not the October morning
of the country, with soft, silvery mists, clearing off before the sunbeams that bring out all the gorgeous beauty of colouring, but the
October morning of Milton, whose silver mists were heavy fogs, and
where the sun could only show long dusky streets when he did break
through and shine. Margaret went languidly about, assisting Dixon
in her task of arranging the house. Her eyes were continually blinded
by tears, but she had no time to give way to regular crying. The father
and brother depended upon her; while they were giving way to grief,
she must be working, planning, considering. Even the necessary
arrangements for the funeral seemed to devolve upon her.

When the fire was bright and crackling—when everything was
ready for breakfast, and the tea-kettle was singing away, Margaret
gave a last look round the room before going to summon Mr. Hale

8. John 14:1.
1. George Crabbe (1754–1832). From *The Borough*, letter 14, lines 7–8.

and Frederick. She wanted everything to look as cheerful as possible; and yet, when it did so, the contrast between it and her own thoughts forced her into sudden weeping. She was kneeling by the sofa, hiding her face in the cushions that no one might hear her cry, when she was touched on the shoulder by Dixon.

"Come, Miss Hale—come, my dear! You must not give way, or where shall we all be? There is not another person in the house fit to give a direction of any kind, and there is so much to be done. There's who's to manage the funeral; and who's to come to it; and where it's to be; and all to be settled; and Master Frederick's like one crazed with crying, and master never was a good one for settling; and, poor gentleman, he goes about now as if he was lost. It's bad enough, my dear, I know; but death comes to us all; and you're well off never to have lost any friend till now."

Perhaps so. But this seemed a loss by itself; not to bear comparison with any other event in the world. Margaret did not take any comfort from what Dixon said, but the unusual tenderness of the prim old servant's manner touched her to the heart; and, more from a desire to show her gratitude for this than for any other reason, she roused herself up, and smiled in answer to Dixon's anxious look at her; and went to tell her father and brother that breakfast was ready.

Mr. Hale came—as if in a dream, or rather with the unconscious motion of a sleep-walker, whose eyes and mind perceive other things than what are present. Frederick came briskly in, with a forced cheerfulness, grasped her hand, looked into her eyes, and burst into tears. She had to try and think of little nothings to say all breakfast-time, in order to prevent the recurrence of her companions' thoughts too strongly to the last meal they had taken together, when there had been a continual strained listening for some sound or signal from the sick-room.

After breakfast, she resolved to speak to her father, about the funeral. He shook his head, and assented to all she proposed, though many of her propositions absolutely contradicted one another. Margaret gained no real decision from him; and was leaving the room languidly, to have a consultation with Dixon, when Mr. Hale motioned her back to his side.

"Ask Mr. Bell," said he in a hollow voice.

"Mr. Bell!" said she, a little surprised. "Mr. Bell of Oxford?"

"Mr. Bell," he repeated. "Yes. He was my groom's-man."[2]

Margaret understood the association.

"I will write to-day," said she. He sank again into listlessness. All morning she toiled on, longing for rest, but in a continual whirl of melancholy business.

2. Best man, at his wedding.

Towards evening, Dixon said to her:

"I've done it, miss. I was really afraid for master, that he'd have a stroke with grief. He's been all this day with poor missus; and when I've listened at the door, I've heard him talking to her, and talking to her, as if she was alive. When I went in he would be quite quiet, but all in a maze like. So I thought to myself, he ought to be roused; and if it gives him a shock at first, it will, maybe, be the better afterwards. So I've been and told him, that I don't think it's safe for Master Frederick to be here. And I don't. It was only on Tuesday, when I was out, that I met a Southampton man—the first I've seen since I came to Milton; they don't make their way much up here, I think. Well, it was young Leonards, old Leonards the draper's son, as great a scamp as ever lived—who plagued his father almost to death, and then ran off to sea. I never could abide him. He was in the Orion at the same time as Master Frederick, I know; though I don't recollect if he was there at the mutiny."

"Did he know you?" said Margaret, eagerly.

"Why, that's the worst of it. I don't believe he would have known me but for my being such a fool as to call out his name. He were a Southampton man, in a strange place, or else I should never have been so ready to call cousins with him, a nasty, good-for-nothing fellow. Says he, 'Miss Dixon! who would ha' thought of seeing you here? But perhaps I mistake, and you're Miss Dixon no longer?' So I told him he might still address me as an unmarried lady, though if I hadn't been so particular, I'd had good chances of matrimony. He was polite enough: 'He couldn't look at me and doubt me.' But I were not to be caught with such chaff from such a fellow as him, and so I told him; and, by, way of being even, I asked him after his father (who I knew had turned him out of doors), as if they was the best friends as ever was. So then, to spite me—for you see we were getting savage, for all we were so civil to each other—he began to inquire after Master Frederick, and said, what a scrape he'd got into (as if Master Frederick's scrapes would ever wash George Leonards' white, or make 'em look otherwise than nasty, dirty black), and how he'd be hung for mutiny if ever he were caught, and how a hundred pound reward had been offered for catching him, and what a disgrace he had been to his family—all to spite me, you see, my dear, because before now I've helped old Mr. Leonards to give George a good rating,[3] down in Southampton. So I said, there were other families as I knew, who had far more cause to blush for their sons, and to be thankful if they could think they were earning an honest living far away from home. To which he made answer, like the impudent

3. A good dressing-down.

chap he is, that he were in a confidential situation, and if I knew of any young man who had been so unfortunate as to lead vicious courses, and wanted to turn steady, he'd have no objection to lend him his patronage. He, indeed! Why, he'd corrupt a saint. I've not felt so bad myself for years as when I were standing talking to him the other day. I could have cried to think I couldn't spite him better, for he kept smiling in my face, as if he took all my compliments for earnest; and I couldn't see that he minded what I said in the least, while I was mad with all his speeches."

"But you did not tell him anything about us—about Frederick?"

"Not I," said Dixon. "He had never the grace to ask where I was staying; and I shouldn't have told him if he had asked. Nor did I ask him what his precious situation was. He was waiting for a bus, and just then it drove up, and he hailed it. But, to plague me to the last, he turned back before he got in, and said, 'If you can help me to trap Lieutenant Hale, Miss Dixon, we'll go partners in the reward. I know you'd like to be my partner, now wouldn't you? Don't be shy, but say yes.' And he jumped on the bus, and I saw his ugly face leering at me with a wicked smile to think how he'd had the last word of plaguing."

Margaret was made very uncomfortable by this account of Dixon's.

"Have you told Frederick?" asked she.

"No," said Dixon. "I were uneasy in my mind at knowing that bad Leonards was in town; but there was so much else to think about that I did not dwell on it at all. But when I saw master sitting so stiff, and with his eyes so glazed and sad, I thought it might rouse him to have to think of Master Frederick's safety a bit. So I told him all, though I blushed to say how a young man had been speaking to me. And it has done master good. And if we're to keep Master Frederick in hiding, he would have to go, poor fellow, before Mr. Bell came."

"Oh, I'm not afraid of Mr. Bell; but I am afraid of this Leonards. I must tell Frederick. What did Leonards look like?"

"A bad-looking fellow, I can assure you, miss. Whiskers such as I should be ashamed to wear—they are so red. And for all he said he'd got a confidential situation, he was dressed in fustian just like a working-man."

It was evident that Frederick must go. Go, too, when he had so completely vaulted into his place in the family, and promised to be such a stay and staff to his father and sister. Go, when his cares for the living mother, and sorrow for the dead, seemed to make him one of those peculiar people who are bound to us by a fellow-love for them that are taken away. Just as Margaret was thinking all this, sitting over the drawing-room fire—her father restless and uneasy under the pressure of this newly-aroused fear, of which he had not as yet spoken—Frederick came in, his brightness dimmed, but the extreme violence of his grief passed away. He came up to Margaret, and kissed her forehead.

"How wan you look, Margaret!" said he in a low voice. "You have been thinking of everybody, and no one has thought of you. Lie on this sofa—there is nothing for you to do."

"That is the worst," said Margaret, in a sad whisper. But she went and lay down, and her brother covered her feet with a shawl, and then sat on the ground by her side; and the two began to talk in a subdued tone.

Margaret told him all that Dixon had related of her interview with young Leonards. Frederick's lips closed with a long whew of dismay.

"I should just like to have it out with that young fellow. A worse sailor was never on board ship—nor a much worse man either. I declare, Margaret—you know the circumstances of the whole affair?"

"Yes, mamma told me."

"Well, when all the sailors who were good for anything were indignant with our captain, this fellow, to curry favour—pah! And to think of his being here! Oh, if he'd a notion I was within twenty miles of him, he'd ferret me out to pay off old grudges. I'd rather anybody had the hundred pounds they think I am worth than that rascal. What a pity poor old Dixon could not be persuaded to give me up, and make a provision for her old age!"

"Oh, Frederick, hush! Don't talk so."

Mr. Hale came towards them, eager and trembling. He had over-heard what they were saying. He took Frederick's hand in both of his:

"My boy, you must go. It is very bad—but I see you must. You have done all you could—you have been a comfort to her."

"Oh, papa, must he go?" said Margaret, pleading against her own conviction of necessity.

"I declare, I've a good mind to face it out, and stand my trial. If I could only pick up my evidence! I cannot endure the thought of being in the power of such a blackguard as Leonards. I could almost have enjoyed—in other circumstances—this stolen visit: it has had all the charm which the Frenchwoman[4] attributed to forbidden pleasures."

"One of the earliest things I can remember," said Margaret, "was your being in some great disgrace, Fred, for stealing apples. We had plenty of our own—trees loaded with them; but some one had told

---

4. Untraced, but possibly a reference to Mme. de Sévigné (1626–1696), whose *Letters* give detailed information about French aristocratic life and manners in the seventeenth century, and of whom Gaskell contemplated writing a biography.

you that stolen fruit tasted sweetest, which you took au pied de la lettre,[5] and off you went a-robbing. You have not changed your feelings much since then."

"Yes—you must go," repeated Mr. Hale, answering Margaret's question, which she had asked some time ago. His thoughts were fixed on one subject, and it was an effort to him to follow the zigzag remarks of his children—an effort which he did not make.

Margaret and Frederick looked at each other. That quick momentary sympathy would be theirs no longer if he went away. So much was understood through eyes that could not be put into words. Both coursed the same thought till it was lost in sadness. Frederick shook it off first:

"Do you know, Margaret, I was very nearly giving both Dixon and myself a good fright this afternoon. I was in my bedroom; I had heard a ring at the front door, but I thought the ringer must have done his business and gone away long ago; so I was on the point of making my appearance in the passage, when, as I opened my room door, I saw Dixon coming downstairs; and she frowned and kicked me into hiding again. I kept the door open, and heard a message given to some man that was in my father's study, and that then went away. Who could it have been? Some of the shopmen?"

"Very likely," said Margaret, indifferently. "There was a little quiet man who came up for orders about two o'clock."

"But this was not a little man—a great powerful fellow; and it was past four when he was here."

"It was Mr. Thornton," said Mr. Hale. They were glad to have drawn him into the conversation.

"Mr. Thornton!" said Margaret, a little surprised. "I thought——"

"Well, little one, what did you think?" asked Frederick, as she did not finish her sentence.

"Oh, only," said she, reddening and looking straight at him, "I fancied you meant some one of a different class, not a gentleman; somebody come on an errand."

"He looked like some one of that kind," said Frederick, carelessly. "I took him for a shopman, and he turns out a manufacturer."

Margaret was silent. She remembered how at first, before she knew his character, she had spoken and thought of him just as Frederick was doing. It was but a natural impression that was made upon him, and yet she was a little annoyed by it. She was unwilling to speak; she wanted to make Frederick understand what kind of person Mr. Thornton was—but she was tongue-tied.

Mr. Hale went on. "He came to offer any assistance in his power,

5. At its word (French). The literal meaning is "at the foot of the letter."

I believe. But I could not see him. I told Dixon to ask him if he would like to see you—I think I asked her to find you, and you would go to him. I don't know what I said."

"He has been a very agreeable acquaintance, has he not?" asked Frederick, throwing the question like a ball for any one to catch who chose.

"A very kind friend," said Margaret, when her father did not answer.

Frederick was silent for a time. At last he spoke:

"Margaret, it is painful to think I can never thank those who have shown you kindness. Your acquaintances and mine must be separate. Unless, indeed, I run the chances of a court-martial, or unless you and father would come to Spain." He threw out this last suggestion as a kind of feeler; and then suddenly made the plunge. "You don't know how I wish you would. I have a good position—the chance of a better," continued he, reddening like a girl. "That Dolores Barbour that I was telling you of, Margaret—I only wish you knew her; I am sure you would like—no, love is the right word, like is so poor—you would love her, father, if you knew her. She is not eighteen; but if she is in the same mind another year, she is to be my wife. Mr. Barbour won't let us call it an engagement. But if you would come, you would find friends everywhere, besides Dolores. Think of it, father. Margaret, be on my side."

"No—no more removals for me," said Mr. Hale. "One removal has cost me my wife. No more removals in this life. She will be here; and here will I stay out my appointed time."

"Oh, Frederick," said Margaret, "tell us more about her. I never thought of this; but I am so glad. You will have some one to love and care for you out there. Tell us all about it."

"In the first place, she is a Roman Catholic. That's the only objection I anticipated. But my father's change of opinion—nay, Margaret, don't sigh."

Margaret had reason to sigh a little more before the conversation ended. Frederick himself was Roman Catholic in fact, though not in profession as yet. This was, then, the reason why his sympathy in her extreme distress at her father's leaving the Church had been so faintly expressed in his letters. She had thought it was the carelessness of a sailor; but the truth was, that even then he was himself inclined to give up the form of religion into which he had been baptised, only that his opinions were tending in exactly the opposite direction to those of his father. How much love had to do with this change not even Frederick himself could have told. Margaret gave up talking about this branch of the subject at last; and, returning to the fact of the engagement, she began to consider it in some fresh light:

"But for her sake, Fred, you surely will try and clear yourself of the exaggerated charges brought against you, even if the charge of mutiny itself be true. If there were to be a court-martial, and you could find your witnesses, you might, at any rate, show how your disobedience to authority was because that authority was unworthily exercised."

Mr. Hale roused himself up to listen to his son's answer.

"In the first place, Margaret, who is to hunt up my witnesses? All of them are sailors, drafted off to other ships, except those whose evidence would go for very little, as they took part, or sympathised in the affair. In the next place, allow me to tell you, you don't know what a court-martial is, and consider it as an assembly where justice is administered, instead of what it really is—a court where authority weighs nine-tenths in the balance, and evidence forms only the other tenth. In such cases, evidence itself can hardly escape being influenced by the prestige of authority."

"But is it not worth trying, to see how much evidence might be discovered and arrayed on your behalf? At present, all those who knew you formerly, believe you guilty without any shadow of excuse. You have never tried to justify yourself, and we have never known where to seek for proofs of your justification. Now, for Miss Barbour's sake, make your conduct as clear as you can in the eye of the world. She may not care for it; she has, I am sure, that trust in you that we all have; but you ought not to let her ally herself to one under such a serious charge, without showing the world exactly how it is you stand. You disobeyed authority—that was bad; but to have stood by, without word or act, while the authority was brutally used, would have been infinitely worse. People know what you did; but not the motives that elevate it out of a crime into an heroic protection of the weak. For Dolores' sake, they ought to know."

"But how must I make them know? I am not sufficiently sure of the purity and justice of those who would be my judges, to give myself up to a court-martial, even if I could bring a whole array of truth-speaking witnesses. I can't send a bellman about, to cry aloud and proclaim in the streets what you are pleased to call my heroism. No one would read a pamphlet of self-justification so long after the deed, even if I put one out."

"Will you consult a lawyer as to your chances of exculpation?" asked Margaret, looking up, and turning very red.

"I must first catch my lawyer, and have a look at him, and see how I like him, before I make him into my confidant. Many a briefless barrister might twist his conscience into thinking, that he could earn a hundred pounds very easily by doing a good action—in giving me, a criminal, up to justice."

"Nonsense, Frederick!—because I know a lawyer on whose honour I can rely; of whose cleverness in his profession people speak very highly; and who would, I think, take a good deal of trouble for any of—of Aunt Shaw's relations. Mr. Henry Lennox, papa."

"I think it is a good idea," said Mr. Hale. "But don't propose anything which will detain Frederick in England. Don't, for your mother's sake."

"You could go to London to-morrow evening by a night-train," continued Margaret, warming up into her plan. "He must go to-morrow, I'm afraid, papa," said she, tenderly; "we fixed that, because of Mr. Bell, and Dixon's disagreeable acquaintance."

"Yes; I must go to-morrow," said Frederick decidedly.

Mr. Hale groaned. "I can't bear to part with you, and yet I am miserable with anxiety as long as you stop here."

"Well then," said Margaret, "listen to my plan. He gets to London on Friday morning. I will—you might—no! it would be better for me to give him a note to Mr. Lennox. You will find him at his chambers in the Temple."

"I will write down a list of all the names I can remember on board the Orion. I could leave it with him to ferret them out. He is Edith's husband's brother, isn't he? I remember your naming him in your letters. I have money in Barbour's hands. I can pay a pretty long bill, if there is any chance of success. Money, dear father, that I had meant for a different purpose; so I shall only consider it as borrowed from you and Margaret."

"Don't do that," said Margaret. "You won't risk it if you do. And it will be a risk; only it is worth trying. You can sail from London as well as from Liverpool?"

"To be sure, little goose. Wherever I feel water heaving under a plank, there I feel at home. I'll pick up some craft or other to take me off, never fear. I won't stay twenty-four hours in London, away from you on the one hand, and from somebody else on the other."

It was rather a comfort to Margaret that Frederick took it into his head to look over her shoulder as she wrote to Mr. Lennox. If she had not been thus compelled to write steadily and concisely on, she might have hesitated over many a word, and been puzzled to choose between many an expression, in the awkwardness of being the first to resume the intercourse of which the concluding event had been so unpleasant to both sides. However, the note was taken from her before she had even had time to look it over, and treasured up in a pocket-book, out of which fell a long lock of black hair, the sight of which caused Frederick's eyes to glow with pleasure.

"Now you would like to see that, wouldn't you?" said he. "No! you must wait till you see her herself. She is too perfect to be known by fragments. No mean brick shall be a specimen of the building of my palace."

Chapter VII.

Mischances.

"What! remain to be
Denounced—dragged, it may be, in chains."
WERNER.[1]

All the next day they sat together—they three. Mr. Hale hardly ever spoke but when his children asked him questions, and forced him, as it were, into the present. Frederick's grief was no more to be seen or heard; the first paroxysm had passed over, and now he was ashamed of having been so battered down by emotion; and though his sorrow for the loss of his mother was a deep real feeling, and would last out his life, it was never to be spoken of again. Margaret, not so passionate at first, was more suffering now. At times she cried a good deal; and her manner, even when speaking on indifferent things, had a mournful tenderness about it, which was deepened whenever her looks fell on Frederick, and she thought of his rapidly approaching departure. She was glad he was going, on her father's account, however much she might grieve over it on her own. The anxious terror in which Mr. Hale lived lest his son should be detected and captured, far out-weighed the pleasure he derived from his presence. The nervousness had increased since Mrs. Hale's death, probably because he dwelt upon it more exclusively. He started at every unusual sound; and was never comfortable unless Frederick sat out of the immediate view of any one entering the room. Towards evening he said:

"You will go with Frederick to the station, Margaret? I shall want to know he is safely off. You will bring me word that he is clear of Milton, at any rate?"

"Certainly," said Margaret. "I shall like it, if you won't be lonely without me, papa."

"No, no! I should always be fancying some one had known him, and that he had been stopped, unless you could tell me you had seen him off. And go to the Outwood station. It is quite as near, and not so many people about. Take a cab there. There is less risk of his being seen. What time is your train, Fred?"

"Ten minutes past six; very nearly dark. So what will you do, Margaret?"

"Oh, I can manage. I am getting very brave and very hard. It is a well-lighted road all the way home, if it should be dark. But I was out last week much later."

Margaret was thankful when the parting was over—the parting

1. A poetic drama (1823) by Byron, "neither adapted, nor in any shape intended, for the stage" (Preface).

from the dead mother and the living father. She hurried Frederick into the cab, in order to shorten a scene which she saw was so bitterly painful to her father, who would accompany his son as he took his last look at his mother. Partly in consequence of this, and partly owing to one of the very common mistakes in the "Railway Guide" as to the times when trains arrive at the smaller stations, they found, on reaching Outwood, that they had nearly twenty minutes to spare. The booking-office was not open, so they could not even take the ticket. They accordingly went down the flight of steps that led to the level of the ground below the railway. There was a broad cinder-path diagonally crossing a field which lay along-side of the carriage-road, and they went there to walk backwards and forwards for the few minutes they had to spare.

Margaret's hand lay in Frederick's arm. He took hold of it affectionately.

"Margaret! I am going to consult Mr. Lennox as to the chance of exculpating myself, so that I may return to England whenever I choose, more for your sake than for the sake of any one else. I can't bear to think of your lonely position if anything should happen to my father. He looks sadly changed—terribly shaken. I wish you could get him to think of the Cadiz plan, for many reasons. What could you do if he were taken away? You have no friend near. We are curiously bare of relations."

Margaret could hardly keep from crying at the tender anxiety with which Frederick was bringing before her an event which she herself felt was not very improbable, so severely had the cares of the last few months told upon Mr. Hale. But she tried to rally as she said:

"There have been such strange unexpected changes in my life during these last two years, that I feel more than ever that it is not worth while to calculate too closely what I should do if any future event took place. I try to think only upon the present." She paused; they were standing still for a moment, close on the field side of the stile leading into the road; the setting sun fell on their faces. Frederick held her hand in his, and looked with wistful anxiety into her face, reading there more care and trouble than she would betray by words. She went on:

"We shall write often to one another, and I will promise—for I see it will set your mind at ease—to tell you every worry I have. Papa is"—she started a little, a hardly visible start—but Frederick felt the sudden motion of the hand he held, and turned his full face to the road, along which a horseman was slowly riding, just passing the very stile where they stood. Margaret bowed; her bow was stiffly returned.

"Who is that?" said Frederick, almost before he was out of hearing.

Margaret was a little drooping, a little flushed, as she replied: "Mr. Thornton; you saw him before, you know."

"Only his back. He is an unprepossessing-looking fellow. What a scowl he has!"

"Something has happened to vex him," said Margaret, apologetically. "You would not have thought him unprepossessing if you had seen him with mamma."

"I fancy it must be time to go and take my ticket. If I had known how dark it would be, we wouldn't have sent back the cab, Margaret."

"Oh, don't fidget about that. I can take a cab here, if I like; or go back by the rail-road, when I should have shops and people and lamps all the way from the Milton station-house. Don't think of me; take care of yourself. I am sick with the thought that Leonards may be in the same train with you. Look well into the carriage before you get in."

They went back to the station. Margaret insisted upon going into the full light of the flaring gas inside to take the ticket. Some idle-looking young men were lounging about with the station-master. Margaret thought she had seen the face of one of them before, and returned him a proud look of offended dignity for his somewhat impertinent stare of undisguised admiration. She went hastily to her brother, who was standing outside, and took hold of his arm. "Have you got your bag? Let us walk about here on the platform," said she, a little flurried at the idea of so soon being left alone, and her bravery oozing out rather faster than she liked to acknowledge even to herself. She heard a step following them along the flags; it stopped when they stopped, looking out along the line and hearing the whizz of the coming train. They did not speak; their hearts were too full. Another moment, and the train would be here; a minute more, and he would be gone. Margaret almost repented the urgency with which she had entreated him to go to London; it was throwing more chances of detection in his way. If he had sailed for Spain by Liverpool, he might have been off in two or three hours.

Frederick turned round, right facing the lamp, where the gas darted up in vivid anticipation of the train. A man in the dress of a railway porter started forward; a bad-looking man, who seemed to have drunk himself into a state of brutality, although his senses were in perfect order.

"By your leave, miss!" said he, pushing Margaret rudely on one side, and seizing Frederick by the collar.

"Your name is Hale, I believe?"

In an instant—how, Margaret did not see, for everything danced before her eyes—but by some sleight of wrestling, Frederick had tripped him up, and he fell from the height of three or four feet, which the platform was elevated above the space of soft ground, by the side of the railroad. There he lay.

"Run, run!" gasped Margaret. "The train is here. It was Leonards, was it? oh, run! I will carry your bag." And she took him by the arm to push him along with all her feeble force. A door was opened in a carriage—he jumped in; and as he leant out to say, "God bless you, Margaret!" the train rushed past her; and she was left standing alone. She was so terribly sick and faint that she was thankful to be able to turn into the ladies' waiting-room, and sit down for an instant. At first she could do nothing but gasp for breath. It was such a hurry; such a sickening alarm; such a near chance. If the train had not been there at the moment, the man would have jumped up again and called for assistance to arrest him. She wondered if the man had got up: she tried to remember if she had seen him move; she wondered if he could have been seriously hurt. She ventured out; the platform was all alight, but still quite deserted; she went to the end, and looked over, somewhat fearfully. No one was there; and then she was glad she had made herself go, and inspect, for otherwise terrible thoughts would have haunted her dreams. And even as it was, she was so trembling and affrighted that she felt she could not walk home along the road, which did indeed seem lonely and dark, as she gazed down upon it from the blaze of the station. She would wait till the down train passed and take her seat in it. But what if Leonards recognised her as Frederick's companion! She peered about, before venturing into the booking-office to take her ticket. There were only some railway officials standing about; and talking loud to one another.

"So Leonards has been drinking again!" said one, seemingly in authority. "He'll need all his boasted influence to keep his place this time."

"Where is he?" asked another, while Margaret, her back towards them, was counting her change with trembling fingers, not daring to turn round until she heard the answer to this question.

"I don't know. He came in not five minutes ago, with some long story or other about a fall he'd had, swearing awfully; and wanted to borrow some money from me to go to London by the next up-train. He made all sorts of tipsy promises, but I'd something else to do than listen to him; I told him to go about his business; and he went off at the front door."

"He's at the nearest vaults,[2] I'll be bound," said the first speaker. "Your money would have gone there too, if you'd been such a fool as to lend it."

"Catch me! I knew better what his London meant. Why, he has never paid me off that five shillings"—and so they went on.

And now all Margaret's anxiety was for the train to come. She hid herself once more in the ladies' waiting-room, and fancied every noise was Leonards' step—every loud and boisterous voice was his.

2. I.e., beer-shop, public house.

But no one came near her until the train drew up; when she was civilly helped into a carriage by a porter, into whose face she durst not look till they were in motion, and then she saw that it was not Leonards'.

Chapter VIII.

Peace.

"Sleep on, my love, in thy cold bed,
    Never to be disquieted!
My last Good Night—thou wilt not wake
    Till I thy fate shall overtake."
                                                            Dr. King[1]

Home seemed unnaturally quiet after all this terror and noisy commotion. Her father had seen all due preparation made for her refreshment on her return; and then sat down again in his accustomed chair, to fall into one of his sad waking dreams. Dixon had got Mary Higgins to scold and direct in the kitchen; and her scolding was not the less energetic because it was delivered in an angry whisper; for, speaking above her breath she would have thought irreverent, as long as there was any one dead lying in the house. Margaret had resolved not to mention the crowning and closing affright to her father. There was no use in speaking about it; it had ended well; the only thing to be feared was lest Leonards should in some way borrow money enough to effect his purpose of following Frederick to London, and hunting him out there. But there were immense chances against the success of any such plan; and Margaret determined not to torment herself by thinking of what she could do nothing to prevent. Frederick would be as much on his guard as she could put him; and in a day or two at most he would be safely out of England.

"I suppose we shall hear from Mr. Bell to-morrow," said Margaret.

"Yes," replied her father. "I suppose so."

"If he can come, he will be here to-morrow evening, I should think."

"If he cannot come, I shall ask Mr. Thornton to go with me to the funeral. I cannot go alone. I should break down utterly."

"Don't ask Mr. Thornton, papa. Let me go with you," said Margaret, impetuously.

---

1. Henry King, English poet (1592–1669). The lines are from "An Exequy," a funeral poem written in memory of King's wife, and are thus directly appropriate to the subject matter of this chapter.

"You! My dear, women do not generally go."[2]

"No: because they can't control themselves. Women of our class don't go, because they have no power over their emotions, and yet are ashamed of showing them. Poor women go, and don't care if they are seen overwhelmed with grief. But I promise you, papa, that if you will let me go, I will be no trouble. Don't have a stranger, and leave me out. Dear papa! if Mr. Bell cannot come, I shall go. I won't urge my wish against your will, if he does."

Mr. Bell could not come. He had the gout. It was a most affectionate letter, and expressed great and true regret for his inability to attend. He hoped to come and pay them a visit soon, if they would have him; his Milton property required some looking after, and his agent had written to him to say that his presence was absolutely necessary; or else he had avoided coming near Milton as long as he could, and now the only thing that would reconcile him to this necessary visit was the idea that he should see, and might possibly be able to comfort his old friend.

Margaret had all the difficulty in the world to persuade her father not to invite Mr. Thornton. She had an indescribable repugnance to this step being taken. The night before the funeral, came a stately note from Mrs. Thornton to Miss Hale, saying that, at her son's desire, their carriage should attend the funeral, if it would not be disagreeable to the family. Margaret tossed the note to her father.

"Oh, don't let us have these forms," said she. "Let us go alone— you and me, papa. They don't care for us, or else he would have offered to go himself, and not have proposed this sending an empty carriage."

"I thought you were so extremely averse to his going, Margaret," said Mr. Hale in some surprise.

"And so I am. I don't want him to come at all; and I should especially dislike the idea of our asking him. But this seems such a mockery of mourning that I did not expect it from him." She startled her father by bursting into tears. She had been so subdued in her grief, so thoughtful for others, so gentle and patient in all things, that he could not understand her impatient ways to-night; she seemed agitated and restless; and at all the tenderness which her father in his turn now lavished upon her, she only cried the more.

She passed so bad a night that she was ill prepared for the additional anxiety caused by a letter received from Frederick. Mr. Lennox was out of town; his clerk said that he would return by the following Tuesday at the latest; that he might possibly be at home on Monday. Consequently, after some consideration, Frederick had determined

---

2. The convention of middle-class women's not attending funerals lived on in some areas of Britain well into the twentieth century. Margaret's resistance to it is a further sign of her independence and her acceptance of responsibility.

upon remaining in London a day or two longer. He had thought of coming down to Milton again; the temptation had been very strong; but the idea of Mr. Bell domesticated in his father's house, and the alarm he had received at the last moment at the railway station, had made him resolve to stay in London. Margaret might be assured he would take every precaution against being tracked by Leonards. Margaret was thankful that she received this letter while her father was absent in her mother's room. If he had been present, he would have expected her to read it aloud to him, and it would have raised in him a state of nervous alarm which she would have found it impossible to soothe away. There was not merely the fact, which disturbed her excessively, of Frederick's detention in London, but there were allusions to the recognition at the last moment at Milton, and the possibility of a pursuit, which made her blood run cold; and how then would it have affected her father? Many a time did Margaret repent of having suggested and urged on the plan of consulting Mr. Lennox. At the moment, it had seemed as if it would occasion so little delay—add so little to the apparently small chances of detection; and yet everything that had since occurred had tended to make it so undesirable. Margaret battled hard against this regret of hers for what could not now be helped; this self-reproach for having said what had at the time appeared to be wise, but which after events were proving to have been so foolish. But her father was in too depressed a state of mind and body to struggle healthily; he would succumb to all these causes for morbid regret over what could not be recalled. Margaret summoned up all her forces to her aid. Her father seemed to have forgotten that they had any reason to expect a letter from Frederick that morning. He was absorbed in one idea—that the last visible token of the presence of his wife was to be carried away from him, and hidden from his sight. He trembled pitifully as the undertaker's man was arranging his crape draperies around him. He looked wistfully at Margaret; and, when released, he tottered towards her, murmuring, "Pray for me, Margaret. I have no strength left in me. I cannot pray. I give her up because I must. I try to bear it: indeed I do. I know it is God's will. But I cannot see why she died. Pray for me, Margaret, that I may have faith to pray. It is a great strait, my child."

Margaret sat by him in the coach, almost supporting him in her arms; and repeating all the noble verses of holy comfort, or texts expressive of faithful resignation, that she could remember. Her voice never faltered; and she herself gained strength by doing this. Her father's lips moved after her, repeating the well-known texts as her words suggested them; it was terrible to see the patient struggling effort to obtain the resignation which he had not strength to take into his heart as a part of himself.

Margaret's fortitude nearly gave way as Dixon, with a slight motion of her hand, directed her notice to Nicholas Higgins and his daughter, standing a little aloof, but deeply attentive to the ceremonial. Nicholas wore his usual fustian clothes, but had a bit of black stuff sown round his hat—a mark of mourning which he had never shown to his daughter Bessy's memory. But Mr. Hale saw nothing. He went on repeating to himself, mechanically as it were, all the funeral service as it was read by the officiating clergyman; he sighed twice or thrice when all was ended; and then, putting his hand on Margaret's arm, he mutely entreated to be led away, as if he were blind, and she his faithful guide.

Dixon sobbed aloud; she covered her face with her handkerchief, and was so absorbed in her own grief, that she did not perceive that the crowd, attracted on such occasions, was dispersing, till she was spoken to by some one close at hand. It was Mr. Thornton. He had been present all the time, standing, with bent head, behind a group of people, so that, in fact, no one had recognised him.

"I beg your pardon,—but, can you tell me how Mr. Hale is? And Miss Hale, too? I should like to know how they both are."

"Of course, sir. They are much as is to be expected. Master is terribly broke down. Miss Hale bears up better than likely."

Mr. Thornton would rather have heard that she was suffering the natural sorrow. In the first place, there was selfishness enough in him to have taken pleasure in the idea that his great love might come in to comfort and console her; much the same kind of strange passionate pleasure which comes stinging through a mother's heart, when her drooping infant nestles close to her, and is dependent upon her for everything. But this delicious vision of what might have been—in which, in spite of all Margaret's repulse, he would have indulged only a few days ago—was miserably disturbed by the recollection of what he had seen near the Outwood station. "Miserably disturbed!" that is not strong enough. He was haunted by the remembrance of the handsome young man, with whom she stood in an attitude of such familiar confidence; and the remembrance shot through him like an agony, till it made him clench his hands tight in order to subdue the pain. At that late hour, so far from home! It took a great moral effort to galvanise his trust—erewhile so perfect— in Margaret's pure and exquisite maidenliness, into life; as soon as the effort ceased, his trust dropped down dead and powerless: and all sorts of wild fancies chased each other like dreams through his mind. Here was a little piece of miserable, gnawing confirmation. "She bore up better than likely" under this grief. She had then some hope to look to, so bright that even in her affectionate nature it could come in to lighten the dark hours of a daughter newly made motherless. Yes! he knew how she would love. He had not loved her with-

out gaining that instinctive knowledge of what capabilities were in
her. Her soul would walk in glorious sunlight if any man was worthy,
by his power of loving, to win back her love. Even in her mourning
she would rest with a peaceful faith upon his sympathy. His sympathy! Whose? That other man's. And that it was another was enough
to make Mr. Thornton's pale grave face grow doubly wan and stern
at Dixon's answer.

"I suppose I may call," said he coldly. "On Mr. Hale, I mean. He
will perhaps admit me after to-morrow or so."

He spoke as if the answer were a matter of indifference to him.
But it was not so. For all his pain, he longed to see the author of it.
Although he hated Margaret at times, when he thought of that gentle
familiar attitude and all the attendant circumstances, he had a restless desire to renew her picture in his mind—a longing for the very
atmosphere she breathed. He was in the Charybdis[3] of passion, and
must perforce circle and circle ever nearer round the fatal centre.

"I dare say, sir, master will see you. He was very sorry to have to
deny you the other day; but circumstances was not agreeable just
then."

For some reason or other, Dixon never named this interview that
she had had with Mr. Thornton to Margaret. It might have been
mere chance, but so it was that Margaret never heard that he had
attended her poor mother's funeral.

Chapter IX.

False and True.

"Truth will fail thee never, never!
Though thy bark be tempest-driven,
Though each plank be rent and riven,
Truth will bear thee on for ever!"

ANON.

The "bearing up better than likely" was a terrible strain upon Margaret. Sometimes she thought she must give way, and cry out with
pain, as the sudden sharp thought came across her, even during her
apparently cheerful conversations with her father, that she had no
longer a mother. About Frederick, too, there was great uneasiness.
The Sunday post intervened, and interfered with their London letters;[1] and on Tuesday Margaret was surprised and disheartened to

3. In classical mythology, a whirlpool off the coast of Sicily, into which ships could be
   dragged. It was partner to a similar pool, Scylla: hence the expression between Scylla and
   Charybdis.
1. The Post Office was famous for the promptness and frequency of its deliveries in the
   Victorian period, but it came under pressure from religious groups to suspend its activities

find that there was still no letter. She was quite in the dark as to his plans, and her father was miserable at all this uncertainty. It broke in upon his lately acquired habit of sitting still in one easy chair for half a day together. He kept pacing up and down the room; then out of it; and she heard him upon the landing opening and shutting the bed-room doors, without any apparent object. She tried to tranquillise him by reading aloud; but it was evident he could not listen for long together. How thankful she was then, that she had kept to herself the additional cause for anxiety produced by their encounter with Leonards. She was thankful to hear Mr. Thornton announced. His visit would force her father's thoughts into another channel.

He came up straight to her father, whose hands he took and wrung without a word—holding them in his for a minute or two, during which time his face, his eyes, his look, told of more sympathy than could be put into words. Then he turned to Margaret. Not "better than likely" did she look. Her stately beauty was dimmed with much watching and with many tears. The expression on her countenance was of gentle patient sadness—nay of positive present suffering. He had not meant to greet her otherwise than with his late studied coldness of demeanour; but he could not help going up to her, as she stood a little aside, rendered timid by the uncertainty of his manner of late, and saying the few necessary common-place words in so tender a voice, that her eyes filled with tears, and she turned away to hide her emotion. She took her work and sat down very quiet and silent. Mr. Thornton's heart beat quick and strong, and for the time he utterly forgot the Outwood lane. He tried to talk to Mr. Hale: and—his presence always a certain kind of pleasure to Mr. Hale, as his power and decision made him, and his opinions, a safe, sure port—was unusually agreeable to her father, as Margaret saw.

Presently Dixon came to the door and said, "Miss Hale, you are wanted."

Dixon's manner was so flurried that Margaret turned sick at heart. Something had happened to Fred. She had no doubt of that. It was well that her father and Mr. Thornton were so much occupied by their conversation.

"What is it, Dixon?" asked Margaret, the moment she had shut the drawing-room door.

"Come this way, miss," said Dixon, opening the door of what had been Mrs. Hale's bed-chamber, now Margaret's, for her father refused to sleep there again after his wife's death. "It's nothing,

---

on Sundays. Nevertheless, there were deliveries on Sundays, although the reference here suggests that they were limited in some way. R. H. Super suggests that there were attempts to prevent the handling of mail on trains on Sundays; this may be why the letters from London have been interrupted. (R. H. Super, *Trollope in the Post Office*, Ann Arbor: U of Michigan P, 1981, p. 31)

miss," said Dixon, choking a little. "Only a police-inspector. He wants to see you, miss. But I dare say, it's about nothing at all."

"Did he name—" asked Margaret, almost inaudibly.

"No, miss; he named nothing. He only asked if you lived here, and if he could speak to you. Martha went to the door, and let him in; she has shown him into master's study. I went to him myself, to try if that would do; but no—it's you, miss, he wants."

Margaret did not speak again till her hand was on the lock of the study door. Here she turned round and said, "Take care papa does not come down. Mr. Thornton is with him now."

The inspector was almost daunted by the haughtiness of her manner as she entered. There was something of indignation expressed in her countenance, but so kept down and controlled, that it gave her a superb air of disdain. There was no surprise, no curiosity. She stood awaiting the opening of his business there. Not a question did she ask.

"I beg your pardon, ma'am, but my duty obliges me to ask you a few plain questions. A man has died at the Infirmary, in consequence of a fall, received at Outwood station, between the hours of five and six on Thursday evening, the twenty-sixth instant. At the time, this fall did not seem of much consequence; but it was rendered fatal, the doctors say, by the presence of some internal complaint, and the man's own habit of drinking."

The large dark eyes, gazing straight into the inspector's face, dilated a little. Otherwise there was no motion perceptible to his experienced observation. Her lips swelled out into a richer curve than ordinary, owing to the enforced tension of the muscles, but he did not know what was their usual appearance, so as to recognise the unwonted sullen defiance of the firm sweeping lines. She never blenched or trembled. She fixed him with her eye. Now—as he paused before going on, she said, almost as if she would encourage him in telling his tale—"Well—go on!"

"It is supposed that an inquest will have to be held; there is some slight evidence to prove that the blow, or push, or scuffle that caused the fall, was provoked by this poor fellow's half-tipsy impertinence to a young lady, walking with the man who pushed the deceased over the edge of the platform. This much was observed by some one on the platform, who, however, thought no more about the matter, as the blow seemed of slight consequence. There is also some reason to identify the lady with yourself; in which case—"

"I was not there," said Margaret, still keeping her expressionless eyes fixed on his face, with the unconscious look of a sleep-walker.

The inspector bowed but did not speak. The lady standing before him showed no emotion, no fluttering fear, no anxiety, no desire to end the interview. The information he had received was very vague; one of the porters, rushing out to be in readiness for the train, had

seen a scuffle, at the other end of the platform, between Leonards
and a gentleman accompanied by a lady, but heard no noise; and
before the train had got to its full speed after starting, he had been
almost knocked down by the headlong run of the enraged half intoxicated Leonards, swearing and cursing awfully. He had not thought
any more about it, till his evidence was routed out by the inspector,
who, on making some farther inquiry at the railroad station, had
heard from the station-master that a young lady and gentleman had
been there about that hour—the lady remarkably handsome—and
said, by some grocer's assistant present at the time, to be a Miss
Hale, living at Crampton, whose family dealt at his shop. There was
no certainty that the one lady and gentleman were identical with the
other pair, but there was great probabilty. Leonards himself had
gone, half-mad with rage and pain, to the nearest gin-palace for comfort; and his tipsy words had not been attended to by the busy waiters
there; they, however, remembered his starting up and cursing himself for not having sooner thought of the electric telegraph, for some
purpose unknown; and they believed that he left with the idea of
going there. On his way, overcome by pain or drink, he had lain down
in the road, where the police had found him and taken him to the
Infirmary: there he had never recovered sufficient consciousness to
give any distinct account of his fall, although once or twice he had
had glimmerings of sense sufficient to make the authorities send for
the nearest magistrate, in hopes that he might be able to take down
the dying man's deposition of the cause of his death. But when the
magistrate had come, he was rambling about being at sea, and mixing
up names of captains and lieutenants in an indistinct manner with
those of his fellow porters at the railway; and his last words were a
curse on the "Cornish trick"[2] which had, he said, made him a hundred pounds poorer than he ought to have been. The inspector ran
all this over in his mind—the vagueness of the evidence to prove that
Margaret had been at the station—the unflinching, calm denial
which she gave to such a supposition. She stood awaiting his next
word with a composure that appeared supreme.

"Then, madam, I have your denial that you were the lady accompanying the gentleman who struck the blow, or gave the push, which
caused the death of this poor man?"

A quick, sharp pain went through Margaret's brain. "Oh God! that
I knew Frederick were safe!" A deep observer of human countenances might have seen the momentary agony shoot out of her great
gloomy eyes, like the torture of some creature brought to bay. But
the inspector though a very keen, was not a very deep observer. He
was a little struck, notwithstanding, by the form of the answer, which

2. The reference is to wrestling, a sport associated with Cornwall, Frederick having thrown
Leonards on the station platform.

sounded like a mechanical repetition of her first reply—not changed and modified in shape so as to meet his last question.

"I was not there," said she, slowly and heavily. And all this time she never closed her eyes, or ceased from that glassy, dream-like stare. His quick suspicious were aroused by this dull echo of her former denial. It was as if she had forced herself to one untruth, and had been stunned out of all power of varying it.

He put up his book of notes in a very deliberate manner. Then he looked up; she had not moved any more than if she had been some great Egyptian statue.

"I hope you will not think me impertinent when I say, that I may have to call on you again. I may have to summon you to appear on the inquest, and prove an alibi, if my witnesses" (it was but one who had recognised her) "persist in deposing to your presence at the unfortunate event." He looked at her sharply. She was still perfectly quiet—no change of colour, or darker shadow of guilt, on her proud face. He thought to have seen her wince: he did not know Margaret Hale. He was a little abashed by her regal composure. It must have been a mistake of identity. He went on:

"It is very unlikely, ma'am, that I shall have to do anything of the kind. I hope you will excuse me for doing what is only my duty, although it may appear impertinent."

Margaret bowed her head as he went towards the door. Her lips were stiff and dry. She could not speak even the common words of farewell. But suddenly she walked forwards, and opened the study door, and preceded him to the door of the house, which she threw wide open for his exit. She kept her eyes upon him in the same dull, fixed manner, until he was fairly out of the house. She shut the door, and went half-way into the study; then turned back, as if moved by some passionate impulse, and locked the door inside.

Then she went into the study, paused—tottered forward—paused again—swayed for an instant where she stood, and fell prone on the floor in a dead swoon.

Chapter X.

Explanation.

"There's nought so finely spun
But it cometh to the sun."

Mr. Thornton sat on and on. He felt that his company gave pleasure to Mr. Hale; and was touched by the half-spoken wishful entreaty that he would remain a little longer—the plaintive "Don't go yet,"

which his poor friend put forth from time to time. He wondered
Margaret did not return; but it was with no view of seeing her that
he lingered. For the hour—and in the presence of one who was so
thoroughly feeling the nothingness of earth—he was reasonable and
self-controlled. He was deeply interested in all her father said.

> "Of death, and of the heavy lull,
> And of the brain that has grown dull."

It was curious how the presence of Mr. Thornton had power over
Mr. Hale to make him unlock the secret thoughts which he kept
shut up even from Margaret. Whether it was that her sympathy
would be so keen, and show itself in so lively a manner, that he was
afraid of the reaction upon himself, or whether it was that to his
speculative mind all kinds of doubts presented themselves at such a
time, pleading and crying aloud to be resolved into certainties, and
that he knew she would have shrunk from the expression of any such
doubts—nay, from him himself as capable of conceiving them—
whatever was the reason, he could unburden himself better to Mr.
Thornton than to her of all the thoughts and fancies and fears that
had been frost-bound in his brain till now. Mr. Thornton said very
little; but every sentence he uttered added to Mr. Hale's reliance and
regard for him. Was it that he paused in the expression of some
remembered agony, Mr. Thornton's two or three words would complete the sentence, and show how deeply its meaning was entered
into. Was it a doubt—a fear—a wandering uncertainty seeking rest,
but finding none—so tear-blinded were its eyes—Mr. Thornton,
instead of being shocked, seemed to have passed through that very
stage of thought himself, and could suggest where the exact ray of
light was to be found, which should make the dark places plain. Man
of action as he was, busy in the world's great battle, there was a
deeper religion binding him to God in his heart, in spite of his strong
wilfulness, through all his mistakes, than Mr. Hale had ever
dreamed. They never spoke of such things again, as it happened; but
this one conversation made them peculiar people to each other; knit
them together, in a way which no loose indiscriminate talking about
sacred things can ever accomplish. When all are admitted, how can
there be a Holy of Holies?

And all this while, Margaret lay as still and white as death on the
study floor! She had sunk under her burden. It had been heavy in
weight and long carried; and she had been very meek and patient,
till all at once her faith had given way, and she had groped in vain
for help! There was a pitiful contraction of suffering upon her beautiful brows, although there was no other sign of consciousness
remaining. The mouth—a little while ago, so sullenly projected in
defiance—was relaxed and livid.

"E par che de la sua labbia si mova
Uno spirito soave e pien d'amore,
Chi va dicendo a l'anima: sospira!"[1]

The first symptom of returning life was a quivering about the lips—a little mute soundless attempt at speech; but the eyes were still closed; and the quivering sank into stillness. Then, feebly leaning on her arms for an instant to steady herself, Margaret gathered herself up, and rose. Her comb had fallen out of her hair; and with an intuitive desire to efface the traces of weakness, and bring herself into order again, she sought for it, although from time to time, in the course of the search, she had to sit down and recover strength. Her head drooped forwards—her hands meekly laid one upon the other—she tried to recall the force of her temptation, by endeavouring to remember the details which had thrown her into such deadly fright; but she could not. She only understood two facts—that Frederick had been in danger of being pursued and detected in London, as not only guilty of manslaughter, but as the more unpardonable leader of the mutiny, and that she had lied to save him. There was one comfort; her lie had saved him, if only by gaining some additional time. If the inspector came again to-morrow, after she had received the letter she longed for to assure her of her brother's safety, she would brave shame, and stand in her bitter penance—she, the lofty Margaret—acknowledging before a crowded justice-room, if need were, that she had been as "a dog, and done this thing."[2] But if he came before she heard from Frederick; if he returned, as he had half threatened, in a few hours, why! she would tell that lie again; though how the words would come out, after all this terrible pause for reflection and self-reproach, without betraying her falsehood, she did not know, she could not tell. But her repetition of it would gain time—time for Frederick.

She was roused by Dixon's entrance into the room; she had just been letting out Mr. Thornton.

He had hardly gone ten steps in the street, before a passing omnibus stopped close by him, and a man got down, and came up to him, touching his hat as he did so. It was the police-inspector.

Mr. Thornton had obtained for him his first situation in the police, and had heard from time to time of the progress of his protégé, but they had not often met, and at first Mr. Thornton did not remember him.

"My name is Watson—George Watson, sir, that you got——"

"Ah, yes! I recollect. Why you are getting on famously, I hear."

"Yes, sir. I ought to thank you, sir. But it is on a little matter of

---

1. "A soothing spirit that is full of love, / Saying forever to the soul, 'Oh Sigh!' " Dante, *La Vita Nuova* (trans. D. G. Rossetti).
2. A misquotation of 2 Kings 8:13.

business I made so bold as to speak to you now. I believe you were the magistrate who attended to take down the deposition of a poor man who died in the Infirmary last night."

"Yes," replied Mr. Thornton. "I went and heard some kind of a rambling statement, which the clerk said was of no great use. I'm afraid he was but a drunken fellow, though there is no doubt he came to his death by violence at last. One of my mother's servants was engaged to him, I believe, and she is in great distress to-day. What about him?"

"Why, sir, his death is oddly mixed up with somebody in the house I saw you coming out of just now; it was a Mr. Hale's, I believe."

"Yes!" said Mr. Thornton, turning sharp round and looking into the inspector's face with sudden interest. "What about it?"

"Why, sir, it seems to me that I have got a pretty distinct chain of evidence, inculpating a gentleman who was walking with Miss Hale that night at the Outwood station, as the man who struck or pushed Leonards off the platform and so caused his death. But the young lady denies that she was there at the time."

"Miss Hale denies she was there!" repeated Mr. Thornton, in an altered voice. "Tell me, what evening was it? What time?"

"About six o'clock, on the evening of Thursday, the twenty-sixth."

They walked on, side by side, in silence for a minute or two. The inspector was the first to speak.

"You see, sir, there is like to be a coroner's inquest; and I've got a young man who is pretty positive,—at least he was at first;—since he has heard of the young lady's denial, he says he should not like to swear; but still he's pretty positive that he saw Miss Hale at the station, walking about with a gentleman, not five minutes before the time, when one of the porters saw a scuffle, which he set down to some of Leonards' impudence—but which led to the fall which caused his death. And seeing you come out of the very house, sir, I thought I might make bold to ask if—you see, it's always awkward having to do with cases of disputed identity, and one doesn't like to doubt the word of a respectable young woman unless one has strong proof to the contrary."

"And she denied having been at the station that evening!" repeated Mr. Thornton, in a low, brooding tone.

"Yes, sir, twice over, as distinct as could be. I told her I should call again, but seeing you just as I was on my way back from questioning the young man who said it was her, I thought I would ask your advice, both as the magistrate who saw Leonards on his death-bed, and as the gentleman who got me my berth in the force."

"You were quite right," said Mr. Thornton. "Don't take any steps till you have seen me again."

"The young lady will expect me to call, from what I said."

"I only want to delay you an hour. It's now three. Come to my warehouse at four."

"Very well, sir!"

And they parted company. Mr. Thornton hurried to his warehouse, and, sternly forbidding his clerks to allow any one to interrupt him, he went his way to his own private room, and locked the door. Then he indulged himself in the torture of thinking it all over, and realising every detail. How could he have lulled himself into the unsuspicious calm in which her tearful image had mirrored itself not two hours before, till he had weakly pitied her and yearned towards her, and forgotten the savage, distrustful jealousy with which the sight of her—and that unknown to him—at such an hour—in such a place—had inspired him! How could one so pure have stooped from her decorous and noble manner of bearing! But was it decorous—was it? He hated himself for the idea that forced itself upon him, just for an instant—no more—and yet, while it was present, thrilled him with its old potency of attraction towards her image. And then this falsehood—how terrible must be some dread of shame to be revealed—for, after all, the provocation given by such a man as Leonards was, when excited by drinking, might, in all probability, be more than enough to justify any one who came forward to state the circumstances openly and without reserve! How creeping and deadly that fear which could bow down the truthful Margaret to falsehood! He could almost pity her. What would be the end of it? She could not have considered all she was entering upon; if there was an inquest and the young man came forward. Suddenly he started up. There should be no inquest. He would save Margaret. He would take the responsibility of preventing the inquest, the issue of which, from the uncertainty of the medical testimony (which he had vaguely heard the night before, from the surgeon in attendance), could be but doubtful; the doctors had discovered an internal disease far advanced, and sure to prove fatal; they had stated that death might have been accelerated by the fall, or by the subsequent drinking and exposure to cold. If he had but known how Margaret would have become involved in the affair—if he had but foreseen that she would have stained her whiteness by a falsehood, he could have saved her by a word; for the question, of inquest or no inquest, had hung trembling in the balance only the night before. Miss Hale might love another—was indifferent and contemptuous to him—but he would yet do her faithful acts of service of which she should never know. He might despise her, but the woman whom he had once loved should be kept from shame; and shame it would be to pledge herself to a lie in a public court, or otherwise to stand and acknowledge her reason for desiring darkness rather than light.

Very gray and stern did Mr. Thornton look, as he passed out

through his wondering clerks. He was away about half an hour; and scarcely less stern did he look when he returned, although his errand had been successful.

He wrote two lines on a slip of paper, put it in an envelope, and sealed it up. This he gave to one of the clerks, saying:—

"I appointed Watson—he who was a packer in the warehouse, and who went into the police—to call on me at four o'clock. I have just met with a gentleman from Liverpool who wishes to see me before he leaves town. Take care to give this note to Watson when he calls."

The note contained these words:

"There will be no inquest. Medical evidence not sufficient to justify it. Take no further steps. I have not seen the coroner; but I will take the responsibility."

"Well," thought Watson, "it relieves me from an awkward job. None of my witnesses seemed certain of anything except the young woman. She was clear and distinct enough; the porter at the railroad had seen a scuffle; or when he found it was likely to bring him in as a witness, then it might not have been a scuffle, only a little larking, and Leonards might have jumped off the platform himself;—he would not stick firm to anything. And Jennings, the grocer's shopman,—well, he was not quite so bad, but I doubt if I could have got him up to an oath after he heard that Miss Hale flatly denied it. It would have been a troublesome job and no satisfaction. And now I must go and tell them they won't be wanted."

He accordingly presented himself again at Mr. Hale's that evening. Her father and Dixon would fain have persuaded Margaret to go to bed; but they, neither of them, knew the reason for her low continued refusals to do so. Dixon had learnt part of the truth—but only part. Margaret would not tell any human being of what she had said, and she did not reveal the fatal termination to Leonards' fall from the platform. So Dixon's curiosity combined with her allegiance to urge Margaret to go to rest, which her appearance, as she lay on the sofa, showed but too clearly that she required. She did not speak except when spoken to; she tried to smile back in reply to her father's anxious looks and words of tender enquiry; but, instead of a smile, the wan lips resolved themselves into a sigh. He was so miserably uneasy that, at last, she consented to go into her own room, and prepare for going to bed. She was indeed inclined to give up the idea that the inspector would call again that night, as it was already past nine o'clock.

She stood by her father, holding on to the back of his chair.

"You will go to bed soon, papa, won't you? Don't sit up alone!"

What his answer was she did not hear; the words were lost in the far smaller point of sound that magnified itself to her fears, and filled her brain. There was a low ring at the door-bell.

She kissed her father and glided down stairs, with a rapidity of motion of which no one would have thought her capable, who had seen her the minute before. She put aside Dixon.

"Don't come; I will open the door. I know it is him—I can—I must manage it all myself."

"As you please, miss!" said Dixon testily; but in a moment afterwards, she added, "But you're not fit for it. You are more dead than alive."

"Am I?" said Margaret, turning round and showing her eyes all aglow with strange fire, her cheeks flushed, though her lips were baked and livid still.

She opened the door to the Inspector, and preceded him into the study. She placed the candle on the table, and snuffed it carefully, before she turned round and faced him.

"You are late!" said she. "Well?" She held her breath for the answer.

"I'm sorry to have given any unnecessary trouble, ma'am; for, after all, they've given up all thoughts of holding an inquest. I have had other work to do and other people to see, or I should have been here before now."

"Then it is ended," said Margaret. "There is to be no further enquiry."

"I believe I've got Mr. Thornton's note about me," said the Inspector, fumbling in his pocket-book.

"Mr. Thornton's!" said Margaret.

"Yes! he's a magistrate—ah! here it is." She could not see to read it—no, not although she was close to the candle. The words swam before her. But she held it in her hand, and looked at it as if she were intently studying it.

"I'm sure, ma'am, it's a great weight off my mind; for the evidence was so uncertain, you see, that the man had received any blow at all,—and if any question of identity came in, it so complicated the case, as I told Mr. Thornton—"

"Mr. Thornton!" said Margaret, again.

"I met him this morning, just as he was coming out of this house, and, as he's an old friend of mine, besides being the magistrate who saw Leonards last night, I made bold to tell him of my difficulty."

Margaret sighed deeply. She did not want to hear any more; she was afraid alike of what she had heard, and of what she might hear. She wished that the man would go. She forced herself to speak.

"Thank you for calling. It is very late. I dare say it is past ten o'clock. Oh! here is the note!" she continued, suddenly interpreting the meaning of the hand held out to receive it. He was putting it up, when she said, "I think it is a cramped, dazzling sort of writing. I could not read it; will you just read it to me?"

He read it aloud to her.

"Thank you. You told Mr. Thornton that I was not there?"

"Oh, of course, ma'am. I'm sorry now that I acted upon information, which seems to have been so erroneous. At first the young man was so positive; and now he says that he doubted all along, and hopes that his mistake won't have occasioned you such annoyance as to lose their shop your custom. Good night, ma'am."

"Good night." She rang the bell for Dixon to show him out. As Dixon returned up the passage Margaret passed her swiftly.

"It is all right!" said she, without looking at Dixon; and before the woman could follow her with further questions she had sped upstairs, and entered her bed-chamber, and bolted her door.

She threw herself, dressed as she was, upon her bed. She was too much exhausted to think. Half-an hour or more elapsed before the cramped nature of her position, and the chilliness, supervening upon great fatigue, had the power to rouse her numbed faculties. Then she began to recall, to combine, to wonder. The first idea that presented itself to her was, that all this sickening alarm on Frederick's behalf was over; that the strain was past. The next was a wish to remember every word of the Inspector's which related to Mr. Thornton. When had he seen him? What had he said? What had Mr. Thornton done? What were the exact words of his note? And until she could recollect, even to the placing or omitting an article, the very expressions which he had used in the note, her mind refused to go on with its progress. But the next conviction she came to was clear enough;—Mr. Thornton had seen her close to Outwood station on the fatal Thursday night, and had been told of her denial that she was there. She stood as a liar in his eyes. She was a liar. But she had no thought of penitence before God; nothing but chaos and night surrounded the one lurid fact that, in Mr. Thornton's eyes, she was degraded. She cared not to think, even to herself, of how much of excuse she might plead. That had nothing to do with Mr. Thornton; she never dreamed that he, or any one else, could find cause for suspicion in what was so natural as her accompanying her brother; but what was really false and wrong was known to him, and he had a right to judge her. "Oh, Frederick! Frederick!" she cried, "what have I not sacrificed for you!" Even when she fell asleep her thoughts were compelled to travel the same circle, only with exaggerated and monstrous circumstances of pain.

When she awoke a new idea flashed upon her with all the brightness of the morning. Mr. Thornton had learnt her falsehood before he went to the coroner; that suggested the thought, that he had possibly been influenced so to do with a view of sparing her the repetition of her denial. But she pushed this notion on one side with the sick wilfulness of a child. If it were so, she felt no gratitude to him, as it only showed her how keenly he must have seen that she was disgraced already, before he took such unwonted pains to spare her any further trial of truthfulness, which had already failed so signally. She would have gone through the whole—she would have perjured herself to save Frederick, rather—far rather—than Mr. Thornton should have had the knowledge that prompted him to interfere to save her. What ill-fate brought him in contact with the Inspector? What made him be the very magistrate sent for to receive Leonards' deposition? What had Leonards said? How much of it was intelligible to Mr. Thornton, who might already, for aught she knew, be aware of the old accusation against Frederick, through their mutual friend, Mr. Bell? If so, he had striven to save the son, who came in defiance of the law to attend his mother's death-bed. And under this idea she could feel grateful—not yet, if ever she should, if his interference had been prompted by contempt. Oh! had any one such just cause to feel contempt for her? Mr. Thornton, above all people, on whom she had looked down from her imaginary heights till now! She suddenly found herself at his feet, and was strangely distressed at her fall. She shrank from following out the premises to their conclusion, and so acknowledging to herself how much she valued his respect and good opinion. Whenever this idea presented itself to her at the end of a long avenue of thoughts, she turned away from following that path—she would not believe in it.

It was later than she fancied, for in the agitation of the previous night, she had forgotten to wind up her watch; and Mr. Hale had given especial orders that she was not to be disturbed by the usual awakening. By and by the door opened cautiously, and Dixon put her head in. Perceiving that Margaret was awake, she came forwards with a letter.

"Here's something to do you good, miss. A letter from Master Frederick."

"Thank you, Dixon. How late it is!"

She spoke very languidly, and suffered Dixon to lay it on the counterpane before her, without putting out a hand to take it.

"You want your breakfast, I'm sure. I will bring it you in a minute. Master has got the tray all ready, I know."

Margaret did not reply; she let her go; she felt that she must be alone before she could open that letter. She opened it at last. The first thing that caught her eye was the date two days earlier than she received it. He had then written when he had promised, and their alarm might have been spared. But she would read the letter and see. It was hasty enough, but perfectly satisfactory. He had seen Henry Lennox, who knew enough of the case to shake his head over it, in the first instance, and tell him he had done a very daring thing in returning to England, with such an accusation, backed by such powerful influence, hanging over him. But when they had come to talk it over, Mr. Lennox had acknowledged that there might be some chance of his acquittal, if he could but prove his statements by cred- ible witnesses—that in such case it might be worth while to stand his trial, otherwise it would be a great risk. He would examine—he would take every pains. "It struck me," said Frederick, "that your introduction, little sister of mine, went a long way. Is it so? He made many inquiries, I can assure you. He seemed a sharp, intelligent fellow, and in good practice too, to judge from the signs of business and the number of clerks about him. But these may be only lawyer's dodges. I have just caught a packet on the point of sailing—I am off in five minutes. I may have to come back to England again on this business, so keep my visit secret. I shall send my father some rare old sherry, such as you cannot buy in England,—(such stuff as I've got in the bottle before me)! He needs something of the kind—my dear love to him—God bless him. I'm sure—here's my cab. P.S.— What an escape that was! Take care you don't breathe of my having been—not even to the Shaws."

Margaret turned to the envelope; it was marked "Too late."[3] The letter had probably been trusted to some careless waiter, who had forgotten to post it. Oh! what slight cobwebs of chances stand between us and Temptation! Frederick had been safe, and out of England twenty, nay, thirty hours ago; and it was only about seven- teen hours since she had told a falsehood to baffle pursuit, which even then would have been vain. How faithless she had been! Where now was her proud motto, "Fais ce que dois, advienne que pourra?"[4] If she had but dared to bravely tell the truth as regarded herself, defying them to find out what she refused to tell concerning another, how light of heart she would now have felt! Not humbled before God, as having failed in trust towards Him; not degraded and abased in Mr. Thornton's sight. She caught herself up at this with a mis- erable tremor; here was she classing his low opinion of her alongside with the displeasure of God. How was it that he haunted her imag- ination so persistently? What could it be? Why did she care for what he thought, in spite of all her pride; in spite of herself? She believed that she could have borne the sense of Almighty displeasure, because He knew all, and could read her penitence, and hear her cries for help in time to come. But Mr. Thornton—why did she tremble, and hide her face in the pillow? What strong feeling had overtaken her at last?

She sprang out of bed and prayed long and earnestly. It soothed

---

3. I.e., too late for a specific postal collection. The letter is dated two days before Margaret receives it; this slight delay has involved her in deception that would otherwise have been unnecessary. The timing is an indication of the promptness of postal deliveries at the time.
4. As before (vol. I, chap. 25), "do what you should do, come what may."

and comforted her so to open her heart. But as soon as she reviewed her position she found the sting was still there; that she was not good enough, nor pure enough to be indifferent to the lowered opinion of a fellow creature; that the thought of how he must be looking upon her with contempt, stood between her and her sense of wrong-doing. She took her letter in to her father as soon as she was drest. There was so slight an allusion to their alarm at the railroad station, that Mr. Hale passed over it without paying any attention to it. Indeed, beyond the mere fact of Frederick having sailed undiscovered and unsuspected, he did not gather much from the letter at the time, he was so uneasy about Margaret's pallid looks. She seemed continually on the point of weeping.

"You are sadly overdone, Margaret. It is no wonder. But you must let me nurse you now."

He made her lie down on the sofa, and went for a shawl to cover her with. His tenderness released her tears; and she cried bitterly.

"Poor child!—poor child!" said he, looking fondly at her, as she lay with her face to the wall, shaking with her sobs. After a while they ceased, and she began to wonder whether she durst give herself the relief of telling her father of all her trouble. But there were more reasons against it than for it. The only one for it was the relief to herself; and against it was the thought that it would add materially to her father's nervousness, if it were indeed necessary for Frederick to come to England again; that he would dwell on the circumstance of his son's having caused the death of a man, however unwittingly and unwillingly; that this knowledge would perpetually recur to trouble him, in various shapes of exaggeration and distortion from the simple truth. And about her own great fault—he would be distressed beyond measure at her want of courage and faith, yet perpetually troubled to make excuses for her. Formerly Margaret would have come to him as priest as well as father, to tell him of her temptation and her sin; but latterly they had not spoken much on such subjects; and she knew not how, in his change of opinions, he would reply if the depth of her soul called unto his. No; she would keep her secret, and bear the burden alone. Alone she would go before God, and cry for His absolution. Alone she would endure her disgraced position in the opinion of Mr. Thornton. She was unspeakably touched by the tender efforts of her father to think of cheerful subjects on which to talk, and so to take her thoughts away from dwelling on all that had happened of late. It was some months since he had been so talkative as he was this day. He would not let her sit up, and offended Dixon desperately by insisting on waiting upon her himself.

At last she smiled; a poor, weak little smile; but it gave him the truest pleasure.

"It seems strange to think, that what gives us most hope for the future should be called Dolores,"[5] said Margaret. The remark was more in character with her father than with her usual self; but to-day they seemed to have changed natures.

"Her mother was a Spaniard, I believe: that accounts for her religion. Her father was a stiff Presbyterian when I knew him. But it is a very soft and pretty name."

"How young she is!—younger by fourteen months than I am. Just the age that Edith was when she was engaged to Captain Lennox. Papa, we will go and see them in Spain."

He shook his head. But he said, "If you wish it, Margaret. Only let us come back here. It would seem unfair—unkind to your mother, who always, I'm afraid, disliked Milton so much, if we left it now she is lying here, and cannot go with us. No, dear; you shall go and see them, and bring me back a report of my Spanish daughter."

"No, papa, I won't go without you. Who is to take care of you when I am gone?"

"I should like to know which of us is taking care of the other. But if you went, I should persuade Mr. Thornton to let me give him double lessons. We would work up the classics famously. That would be a perpetual interest. You might go on, and see Edith at Corfu, if you liked."

Margaret did not speak all at once. Then she said rather gravely: "Thank you, papa. But I don't want to go. We will hope that Mr. Lennox will manage so well, that Frederick may bring Dolores to see us when they are married. And as for Edith, the regiment won't remain much longer in Corfu. Perhaps we shall see both of them here before another year is out."

Mr. Hale's cheerful subjects had come to an end. Some painful recollection had stolen across his mind, and driven him into silence. By and by Margaret said:

"Papa—did you see Nicholas Higgins at the funeral? He was there, and Mary too. Poor fellow! it was his way of showing sympathy. He has a good warm heart under his bluff abrupt ways."

"I am sure of it," replied Mr. Hale. "I saw it all along, even while you tried to persuade me that he was all sorts of bad things. We will go and see them to-morrow, if you are strong enough to walk so far."

"Oh yes. I want to see them. We did not pay Mary—or rather she refused to take it, Dixon says. We will go so as to catch him just after his dinner, and before he goes to his work."

Towards evening Mr. Hale said:

"I half expected Mr. Thornton would have called. He spoke of a book yesterday which he had, and which I wanted to see. He said he would try and bring it to-day."

---

5. Punning on the name's suggestion of sadness.

Margaret sighed. She knew he would not come. He would be too delicate to run the chance of meeting her, while her shame must be so fresh in his memory. The very mention of his name renewed her trouble, and produced a relapse into the feeling of depressed, pre-occupied exhaustion. She gave way to listless languor. Suddenly it struck her that this was a strange manner to show her patience, or to reward her father for his watchful care of her all through the day. She sat up, and offered to read aloud. His eyes were failing, and he gladly accepted her proposal. She read well: she gave the due emphasis; but had any one asked her, when she had ended, the meaning of what she had been reading, she could not have told. She was smitten with a feeling of ingratitude to Mr. Thornton, inasmuch as, in the morning, she had refused to accept the kindness he had shown her in making further inquiry from the medical men, so as to obviate any inquest being held. Oh! she was grateful! She had been cowardly and false, and had shown her cowardliness and falsehood in action that could not be recalled; but she was not ungrateful. It sent a glow to her heart, to know how she could feel towards one who had reason to despise her. His cause for contempt was so just, that she should have respected him less if she had thought he did not feel contempt. It was a pleasure to feel how thoroughly she respected him. He could not prevent her doing that; it was the one comfort in all this misery.

Late in the evening, the expected book arrived, "with Mr. Thornton's kind regards, and wishes to know how Mr. Hale is."

"Say that I am much better, Dixon, but that Miss Hale—"

"No, papa," said Margaret, eagerly—"don't say anything about me. He does not ask."

"My dear child, how you are shivering!" said her father, a few minutes afterwards. "You must go to bed directly. You have turned quite pale!"

Margaret did not refuse to go, though she was loth to leave her father alone. She needed the relief of solitude after a day of busy thinking, and busier repenting.

But she seemed much as usual the next day; the lingering gravity and sadness, and the occasional absence of mind, were not unnatural symptoms in the early days of grief. And almost in proportion to her re-establishment in health, was her father's relapse into his abstracted musing upon the wife he had lost, and the past era in his life that was closed to him for ever.

Chapter XI.

Union Not Always Strength.[1]

"The steps of the bearers, heavy and slow,
The sobs of the mourners, deep and low"
SHELLEY.[2]

At the time arranged the previous day, they set out on their walk to see Nicholas Higgins and his daughter. They both were reminded of their recent loss, by a strange kind of shyness in their new habiliments,[3] and in the fact that it was the first time, for many weeks, that they had deliberately gone out together. They drew very close to each other in unspoken sympathy.

Nicholas was sitting by the fire-side in his accustomed corner: but he had not his accustomed pipe. He was leaning his head upon his hand, his arm resting on his knee. He did not get up when he saw them, though Margaret could read the welcome in his eye.

"Sit ye down, sit ye down. Fire's welly[4] out," said he, giving it a vigorous poke, as if to turn attention away from himself. He was rather disorderly, to be sure, with a black unshaven beard of several days' growth, making his pale face look yet paler, and a jacket which would have been all the better for patching.

"We thought we should have a good chance of finding you, just after dinner-time," said Margaret.

"We have had our sorrow too, since we saw you," said Mr. Hale.

"Ay, ay. Sorrows is more plentiful than dinners just now; I reckon, my dinner hour stretches all o'er the day; yo're pretty sure of finding me."

"Are you out of work?" asked Margaret.

"Ay," he replied shortly. Then, after a moment's silence, he added, looking up for the first time: "I'm not wanting brass. Dunno yo' think it. Bess, poor lass, had a little stock under her pillow, ready to slip into my hand, last moment, and Mary is fustian-cutting. But I'm out o' work a' the same."

"We owe Mary some money," said Mr. Hale, before Margaret's sharp pressure on his arm could arrest the words.

"If hoo takes it, I'll turn her out o' doors. I'll bide inside these four walls, and she'll bide out. That's a'."

---

1. Contemporary trade union mottoes and slogans frequently proclaimed the relationship between unity, or "union," and strength. The chapter title echoes this idea.
2. The lines quoted (slightly inaccurately) are from Percy Bysshe Shelley's poem "The Sensitive Plant," published with *Prometheus Unbound* in 1820.
3. Margaret and her father are wearing mourning dress for Mrs. Hale.
4. Nearly.

"But we owe her many thanks for her kind service," began Mr. Hale again.

"I ne'er thanked yo'r daughter theer for her deeds o' love to my poor wench. I ne'er could find th' words. I'se have to begin and try now, if yo' start making an ado about what little Mary could sarve yo'."

"Is it because of the strike you're out of work?" asked Margaret gently.

"Strike's ended. It's o'er for this time. I'm out o' work because I ne'er asked for it. And I ne'er asked for it, because good words is scarce, and bad words is plentiful."

He was in a mood to take a surly pleasure in giving answers that were like riddles. But Margaret saw that he would like to be asked for the explanation.

"And good words are—?"

"Asking for work. I reckon them's almost the best words that men can say. 'Gi' me work' means 'and I'll do it like a man.' Them's good words."

"And bad words are refusing you work when you ask for it."

"Ay. Bad words is saying 'Aha, my fine chap! Yo've been true to yo'r order, and I'll be true to mine. Yo' did the best yo' could for them as wanted help; that's yo're way of being true to yo'r kind; and I'll be true to mine. Yo've been a poor fool, as knowed no better nor be a true faithful fool. So go and be d—d to yo'. There's no work for yo' here.' Them's bad words. I'm not a fool; and if I was, folk ought to ha' taught me how to be wise after their fashion. I could mappen[5] ha' learnt, if any one had tried to teach me."

"Would it not be worth while," said Mr. Hale, "to ask your old master if he would take you back again? It might be a poor chance, but it would be a chance."

He looked up again, with a sharp glance at the questioner; and then tittered a low and bitter laugh.

"Measter! if it's no offence, I'll ask yo' a question or two in my turn."

"You're quite welcome," said Mr. Hale.

"I reckon yo'n some way of earning your bread. Folk seldom lives i' Milton just for pleasure, if they can live anywhere else."

"You are quite right. I have some independent property, but my intention in settling in Milton was to become a private tutor."

"To teach folk. Well! I reckon they pay yo' for teaching them, dunnot they?"

"Yes," replied Mr. Hale, smiling. "I teach in order to get paid."

5. Contraction of "may happen," thus "perhaps."

"And them that pays yo', dun they tell yo' whatten to do, or whatten not to do wi' the money they gives you in just payment for your pains—in fair exchange like?"

"No; to be sure not!"

"They dunnot say, 'Yo' may have a brother, or a friend as dear as a brother, who wants this here brass for a purpose both yo' and he think right; but yo' mun promise not give it to him. Yo' may see a good use, as yo' think, to put yo'r money to; but we don't think it good, and so if yo' spend it a-that-ens[6] we'll just leave off dealing with yo'.' They dunnot say that, dun they?"

"No: to be sure not!"

"Would yo' stand it if they did?"

"It would be some very hard pressure that would make me even think of submitting to such dictation."

"There's not the pressure on all the broad earth that would make me," said Nicholas Higgins. "Now yo've got it. Yo've hit the bull's eye. Hampers—that's where I worked—makes their men pledge 'emselves they'll not give a penny to help th' Union or keep turn-outs fro' clemming. They may pledge and make pledge," continued he, scornfully; "they nobbut make liars and hypocrites. And that's a less sin, to my mind, to making men's hearts so hard that they'll not do a kindness to them as needs it, or help on the right and just cause, though it goes again the strong hand. But I'll ne'er forswear mysel' for a' the work the king could gi'e me. I'm a member o' the Union; and I think it's the only thing to do the workman any good. And I've been a turn-out, and known what it were to clem; so if I get a shilling, sixpence shall go to them if they axe it from me. Consequence is, I dunnot see where I'm to get a shilling."

"Is that rule about not contributing to the Union in force at all the mills?" asked Margaret.

"I cannot say. It's a new regulation at ourn; and I reckon they'll find that they cannot stick to it. But it's in force now. By-and-by they'll find out, tyrants makes liars."

There was a little pause. Margaret was hesitating whether she should say what was in her mind; she was unwilling to irritate one who was already gloomy and despondent enough. At last out it came. But in her soft tones, and with her reluctant manner, showing that she was unwilling to say anything unpleasant, it did not seem to annoy Higgins, only to perplex him.

"Do you remember poor Boucher saying that the Union was a tyrant? I think he said it was the worst tyrant of all. And I remember, at the time I agreed with him."

It was a long while before he spoke. He was resting his head on

6. In that way.

his two hands, and looking down into the fire, so she could not read the expression on his face.

"I'll not deny but what th' Union finds it necessary to force a man into his own good. I'll speak truth. A man leads a dree life who's not i' th' Union. But once i' th' Union, his interests are taken care on better nor he could do it for himsel', or by himsel', for that matter. It's the only way working men can get their rights, by all joining together. More the members, more chance for each one separate man having justice done him. Government takes care o' fools and madmen; and if any man is inclined to do himsel' or his neighbour a hurt, it puts a bit of a check on him, whether he likes it or no. That's all we do i' th' Union. We can't clap folk into prison; but we can make a man's life so heavy to be borne, that he's obliged to come in, and be wise and helpful in spite of himself. Boucher were a fool all along, and ne'er a worse fool than at th' last."

"He did you harm?" asked Margaret.

"Aye, that did he. We had public opinion on our side, till he and his sort began rioting and breaking laws. It were all o'er wi' the strike then."

"Then would it not have been far better to have left him alone, and not forced him to join the Union? He did you no good; and you drove him mad."

"Margaret," said her father, in a low and warning tone, for he saw the cloud gathering on Higgins's face.

"I like her," said Higgins, suddenly. "Hoo speaks plain out what's in her mind. Hoo doesn't comprehend th' Union for all that. It's a great power: it's our only power. I ha' read a bit o' poetry about a plough going o'er a daisy,[7] as made tears come into my eyes, afore I'd other cause for crying. But the chap ne'er stopped driving the plough, I'se warrant, for all he were pitiful about the daisy. He'd too much mother-wit for that. Th' Union's the plough, making ready the land for harvest-time. Such as Boucher—'twould be settin' him up too much to liken him to a daisy; he's liker a weed lounging over the ground—mun just make up their mind to be put out o' the way. I'm sore vexed wi' him just now. So, mappen, I dunnot speak him fair. I could go o'er him wi' a plough mysel', wi' a' the pleasure in life."

"Why? What has he been doing? Anything fresh?"

"Ay, to be sure. He's ne'er out o' mischief, that man. First of a' he must go raging like a mad fool, and kick up yon riot. Then he'd to go into hiding, where he'd a been yet, if Thornton had followed him out as I'd hoped he would ha' done. But Thornton, having got his

---

7. The reference is to Robert Burns's poem "To a Mountain Daisy: on turning one down with the plough, in April, 1786," which opens with a ploughman's lament for crushing a daisy while ploughing. The fate of the daisy is then taken as emblematic for the fate of all obscure humanity.

own purpose, didn't care to go on wi' the prosecution for the riot. So Boucher slunk back again to his house. He ne'er showed himsel' abroad for a day or two. He had that grace. And then, where think ye that he went? Why, to Hampers'. Damn him! He went wi' his mealy-mouthed face, that turns me sick to look at, a-asking for work, though he knowed well enough the new rule, o' pledging themselves to give nought to th' Unions; nought to help the starving turn-out! Why he'd a clemmed to death, if th' Union had na helped him in his pinch. There he went, ossing to promise aught, and pledge himsel' to aught[8]—to tell a' he know'd on our proceedings, the good-for-no-thing Judas! But I'll say this for Hamper, and thank him for it at my dying day, he drove Boucher away, and would na listen to him—ne'er a word—though folk standing by, says the traitor cried like a babby!"

"Oh! how shocking! how pitiful!" exclaimed Margaret. "Higgins, I don't know you to-day. Don't you see how you've made Boucher what he is, by driving him into the Union against his will—without his heart going with it. You have made him what he is!"

Made him what he is! What was he?

Gathering, gathering along the narrow street, came a hollow, mea-sured sound; now forcing itself on their attention. Many voices were hushed and low: many steps were heard, not moving onwards, at least not with any rapidity or steadiness of motion, but as if circling round one spot. Yes, there was one distinct, slow tramp of feet, which made itself a clear path through the air, and reached their ears; the measured laboured walk of men carrying a heavy burden. They were all drawn towards the house-door by some irresistible impulse; impelled thither—not by a poor curiosity, but as if by some solemn blast.

Six men walked in the middle of the road, three of them being policemen. They carried a door, taken off its hinges, upon their shoulders, on which lay some dead human creature; and from each side of the door there were constant droppings. All the street turned out to see, and, seeing, to accompany the procession, each one ques-tioning the bearers, who answered almost reluctantly at last, so often had they told the tale.

"We found him i' th' brook in the field beyond there."

"Th' brook!—why there's not water enough to drown him!"

"He was a determined chap. He lay with his face downwards. He was sick enough o' living, choose what cause he had for it."

8. The dialect here is difficult to penetrate. "Ossing" can be glossed as "trying" or "attempting," with the implication of difficulty. "Aught" can mean equally "everything," "anything," or "nothing," according to context. The general sense of Higgins's comment is that Boucher is desperate to promise anything, or commit himself to anything, to obtain work.

Higgins crept up to Margaret's side, and said in a weak piping kind of voice: "It's not John Boucher? He had na spunk enough. Sure! It's not John Boucher! Why, they are a' looking this way! Listen! I've a singing in my head, and I cannot hear."

They put the door down carefully upon the stones, and all might see the poor drowned wretch—his glassy eyes, one half-open, staring right upwards to the sky. Owing to the position in which he had been found lying, his face was swollen and discoloured; besides, his skin was stained by the water in the brook, which had been used for dying purposes. The fore part of his head was bald; but the hair grew thin and long behind, and every separate lock was a conduit for water. Through all these disfigurements, Margaret recognised John Boucher. It seemed to her so sacrilegious to be peering into that poor distorted, agonised face, that, by a flash of instinct, she went forwards and softly covered the dead man's countenance with her handkerchief. The eyes that saw her do this followed her, as she turned away from her pious office, and were thus led to the place where Nicholas Higgins stood, like one rooted to the spot. The men spoke together, and then one of them came up to Higgins, who would have fain shrunk back into his house.

"Higgins, thou knowed him! Thou mun go tell the wife. Do it gently, man, but do it quick, for we canna leave him here long."

"I canna go," said Higgins. "Dunnot ask me. I canna face her."

"Thou knows her best," said the man. "We'n done a deal in bringing him here—thou take thy share."

"I canna do it," said Higgins. "I'm welly felled wi' seeing him. We wasn't friends; and now he's dead."

"Well, if thou wunnot thou wunnot. Some one mun though. It's a dree task; but it's a chance, every minute, as she doesn't hear on it in some rougher way nor a person going to make her let on by degrees, as it were."

"Papa, do you go," said Margaret, in a low voice.

"If I could—if I had time to think of what I had better say; but all at once——" Margaret saw that her father was indeed unable. He was trembling from head to foot.

"I will go," said she.

"Bless yo', miss, it will be a kind act; for she's been but a sickly sort of body, I hear, and few hereabouts know much on her."

Margaret knocked at the closed door; but there was such a noise, as of many little ill-ordered children, that she could hear no reply; indeed, she doubted if she was heard, and as every moment of delay made her recoil from her task more and more, she opened the door and went in, shutting it after her, and even, unseen to the woman, fastening the bolt.

Mrs. Boucher was sitting in a rocking-chair, on the other side of the ill-redd-up[9] fireplace; it looked as if the house had been untouched for days by any effort at cleanliness.

Margaret said something, she hardly knew what, her throat and mouth were so dry, and the children's noise completely prevented her from being heard. She tried again.

"How are you, Mrs. Boucher? But very poorly, I'm afraid."

"I've no chance o' being well," said she querulously. "I'm left alone to manage these childer, and nought for to give 'em for to keep 'em quiet. John should na ha' left me, and me so poorly."

"How long is it since he went away?"

"Four days sin'. No one would give him work here, and he'd to go on tramp toward Greenfield. But he might ha' been back afore this, or sent me some word if he'd getten work. He might——"

"Oh, don't blame him," said Margaret. "He felt it deeply, I'm sure——"

"Willto' hold thy din, and let me hear the lady speak!" addressing herself, in no very gentle voice, to a little urchin of about a year old. She apologetically continued to Margaret, "He's always mithering me for 'daddy' and 'butty;'[1] and I ha'no butties to give him, and daddy's away, and forgotten us a', I think. He's his father's darling, he is," said she, with a sudden turn of mood, and, dragging the child up to her knee, she began kissing it fondly.

Margaret laid her hand on the woman's arm to arrest her attention. Their eyes met.

"Poor little fellow!" said Margaret, slowly; "he *was* his father's darling."

"He *is* his father's darling," said the woman, rising hastily, and standing face to face with Margaret. Neither of them spoke for a moment or two. Then Mrs. Boucher began in a low growling tone, gathering in wildness as she went on: "He *is* his father's darling, I say. Poor folk can love their childer as well as rich. Why dunno yo' speak? Why dun yo' stare at me wi' your great pitiful eyes? Where's John?" Weak as she was, she shook Margaret to force out an answer. "Oh, my God!" said she, understanding the meaning of that tearful look. She sank back into the chair. Margaret took up the child and put him into her arms.

"He loved him," said she.

"Ay," said the woman, shaking her head, "he loved us a'. We had some one to love us once. It's a long time ago; but when he were in

9. Unmade, unattended. An unmade fireplace would have contained the dead ashes of a previous fire; it was a clear visual indication of neglect.
1. Now in general use, a sandwich, but then dialect, probably for any form of bread with nourishment.

life and with us he did love us, he did. He loved this babby mappen the best on us; but he loved me and I loved him, though I was calling him five minutes agone. Are yo' sure he's dead?" said she, trying to get up. "If it's only that he's ill and like to die, they may bring him round yet. I'm but an ailing creature mysel'—I've been ailing this long time."

"But he is dead—he is drowned!"

"Folk are brought round after they're dead-drowned. Whatten was I thinking of, to sit still when I should be stirring mysel? Here, whisth thee, child—whisth thee! tak' this, tak' aught to play wi', but dunnot cry while my heart's breaking! Oh, where is my strength gone to? Oh John—husband!"

Margaret saved her from falling by catching her in her arms. She sat down in the rocking chair, and held the woman upon her knees, her head lying on Margaret's shoulder. The other children, clustered together in affright, began to understand the mystery of the scene; but the ideas came slowly, for their brains were dull and languid of perception. They set up such a cry of despair as they guessed the truth, that Margaret knew not how to bear it. Johnny's cry was loudest of them all, though he knew not why he cried, poor little fellow.

The mother quivered as she lay in Margaret's arms. Margaret heard a noise at the door.

"Open it. Open it quick," said she to the eldest child. "It's bolted; make no noise—be very still. Oh, papa, let them go upstairs very softly and carefully, and perhaps she will not hear them. She has fainted—that's all."

"It's as well for her, poor creature," said a woman following in the wake of the bearers of the dead. "But yo're not fit to hold her. Stay, I'll run fetch a pillow, and we'll let her down easy on the floor."

This helpful neighbour was a great relief to Margaret; she was evidently a stranger to the house, a new-comer in the district, indeed; but she was so kind and thoughtful that Margaret felt she was no longer needed; and that it would be better, perhaps, to set an example of clearing the house, which was filled with idle, if sympathising gazers.

She looked round for Nicholas Higgins. He was not there. So she spoke to the woman who had taken the lead in placing Mrs. Boucher on the floor.

"Can you give all these people a hint that they had better leave in quietness? So that when she comes round, she should only find one or two that she knows about her. Papa, will you speak to the men, and get them to go away. She cannot breathe, poor thing, with this crowd about her."

Margaret was kneeling down by Mrs. Boucher and bathing her

face with vinegar; but in a few minutes she was surprised at the gush
of fresh air. She looked round, and saw a smile pass between her
father and the woman.

"What is it?" asked she.

"Only our good friend here," replied her father, "hit on a capital
expedient for clearing the place."

"I bid 'em begone, and each take a child with 'em, and to mind
that they were orphans, and their mother a widow. It was who could
do most, and the childer are sure of a bellyful to-day, and of kindness
too. Does hoo know how he died?"

"No," said Margaret; "I could not tell her all at once."

"Hoo mun be told because of th' Inquest, See! Hoo's coming
round; shall you or I do it? Or mappen your father would be best?"

"No; you, you," said Margaret.

They awaited her perfect recovery in silence. Then the neighbour
woman sat down on the floor, and took Mrs. Boucher's head and
shoulders on her lap.

"Neighbour," said she, "your man is dead. Guess yo' how he died?"

"He were drowned," said Mrs. Boucher, feebly, beginning to cry
for the first time, at this rough probing of her sorrows.

"He were found drowned. He were coming home very hopeless o'
aught on earth. He thought God could na be harder than men; mappen not so hard; mappen as tender as a mother; mappen tenderer.
I'm not saying he did right, and I'm not saying he did wrong. All I
say is, may neither me nor mine ever have his sore heart, or we may
do like things."

"He has left me alone wi' a' these children!" moaned the widow,
less distressed at the manner of the death than Margaret expected;
but it was of a piece with her helpless character to feel his loss as
principally affecting herself and her children.

"Not alone," said Mr. Hale, solemnly. "Who is with you? Who will
take up your cause?" The widow opened her eyes wide, and looked
at the new speaker, of whose presence she had not been aware till
then.

"Who has promised to be a father to the fatherless?" continued
he.

"But I've getten six children, sir, and the eldest not eight years of
age. I'm not meaning for to doubt His power, sir,—only it needs a
deal o' trust;" and she began to cry afresh.

"Hoo'll be better able to talk to-morrow, sir," said the neighbour.
"Best comfort now would be the feel of a child at her heart. I'm sorry
they took the babby."

"I'll go for it," said Margaret. And in a few minutes she returned,
carrying Johnnie, his face all smeared with eating, and his hands

loaded with treasures in the shape of shells, and bits of crystal, and the head of a plaster figure. She placed him in his mother's arms.

"There!" said the woman, "now you go. They'll cry together, and comfort together, better nor any one but a child can do. I'll stop with her as long as I'm needed, and if yo' come to-morrow, yo' can have a deal o' wise talk with her, that she's not up to to-day."

As Margaret and her father went slowly up the street, she paused at Higgins's closed door.

"Shall we go in?" asked her father. "I was thinking of him too."

They knocked. There was no answer, so they tried the door. It was bolted, but they thought they heard him moving within.

"Nicholas!" said Margaret. There was no answer, and they might have gone away, believing the house to be empty, if there had not been some accidental fall, as of a book, within.

"Nicholas!" said Margaret, again. "It is only us. Won't you let us come in?"

"No," said he. "I spoke as plain as I could, 'bout using words, when I bolted th' door. Let me be, this day."

Mr. Hale would have urged their desire, but Margaret placed her finger on his lips.

"I don't wonder at it," said she. "I myself long to be alone. It seems the only thing to do one good after a day like this."

Chapter XII.

Looking South.

"A spade! a rake! a hoe!
A pickaxe or a bill!
A hook to reap, or a scythe to mow,
A flail, or what ye will—
And here's a ready hand
To ply the needful tool,
And skill'd enough, by lessons rough,
In Labour's rugged school."

HOOD.[1]

Higgins's door was locked the next day, when they went to pay their call on the widow Boucher: but they learnt this time from an officious neighbour, that he was really from home. He had, however, been in to see Mrs. Boucher, before starting on his day's business,

---

1. Thomas Hood (1799–1845), a popular and prolific poet who was well known both for his comic verse and for his poetry on social themes. These lines are the opening stanza of "The Lay of the Labourer" (1844), which describes the plight of the agricultural laborer, as does Margaret to Higgins in this chapter.

whatever that was. It was but an unsatisfactory visit to Mrs. Boucher; she considered herself as an ill-used woman by her poor husband's suicide; and there was quite germ of truth enough in this idea to make it a very difficult one to refute. Still, it was unsatisfactory to see how completely her thoughts were turned upon herself and her own position, and this selfishness extended even to her relations with her children, whom she considered as incumbrances, even in the very midst of her somewhat animal affection for them. Margaret tried to make acquaintances with one or two of them, while her father strove to raise the widow's thoughts into some higher channel than that of mere helpless querulousness. She found that the children were truer and simpler mourners than the widow. Daddy had been a kind daddy to them; each could tell, in their eager stammering way, of some tenderness shown, some indulgence granted by the lost father.

"Is yon thing upstairs really him? it doesna look like him. I'm feared on it, and I never was feared o' daddy."

Margaret's heart bled to hear that the mother, in her selfish requirement of sympathy, had taken her children upstairs to see their disfigured father. It was intermingling the coarseness of horror with the profoundness of natural grief. She tried to turn their thoughts in some other direction; on what they could do for mother; on what—for this was a more efficacious way of putting it—what father would have wished them to do. Margaret was more successful than Mr. Hale in her efforts. The children seeing their little duties lie in action close around them, began to try each one to do something that she suggested towards redding up[2] the slatternly room. But her father set too high a standard, and too abstract a view, before the indolent invalid. She could not rouse her torpid mind into any vivid imagination of what her husband's misery might have been, before he had resorted to the last terrible step; she could only look upon it as it affected herself; she could not enter into the enduring mercy of the God who had not specially interposed to prevent the water from drowning her prostrate husband; and although she was secretly blaming her husband for having fallen into such drear despair, and denying that he had any excuse for his last rash act, she was inveterate in her abuse of all who could by any possibility be supposed to have driven him to such desperation. The masters—Mr. Thornton in particular, whose mill had been attacked by Boucher, and who, after the warrant had been issued for his apprehension on the charge of rioting, had caused it to be withdrawn,—the Union, of which Higgins was the representative to the poor woman,—the children so numerous, so hungry, and so noisy—all made up one great army of

2. Cleaning up.

personal enemies, whose fault it was that she was now a helpless widow.

Margaret heard enough of this unreasonableness to dishearten her; and when they came away she found it impossible to cheer her father.

"It is the town life," said she. "Their nerves are quickened by the haste and bustle and speed of everything around them, to say nothing of the confinement in these pent-up houses, which of itself is enough to induce depression and worry of spirits. Now in the country, people live so much more out of doors, even children, and even in the winter."

"But people must live in towns. And in the country some get such stagnant habits of mind that they are almost fatalists."

"Yes; I acknowledge that. I suppose each mode of life produces its own trials and its own temptations. The dweller in towns must find it as difficult to be patient and calm, as the country-bred man must find it to be active, and equal to unwonted emergencies. Both must find it hard to realise a future of any kind; the one because the present is so living and hurrying and close around him; the other because his life tempts him to revel in the mere sense of animal existence, not knowing of, and consequently not caring for any pungency of pleasure, for the attainment of which he can plan, and deny himself and look forward."

"And thus both the necessity for engrossment, and the stupid content in the present, produce the same effects. But this poor Mrs. Boucher! how little we can do for her."

"And yet we dare not leave her without our efforts, although they may seem so useless. Oh papa! it's a hard world to live in!"

"So it is, my child. We feel it so just now, at any rate; but we have been very happy, even in the midst of our sorrow. What a pleasure Frederick's visit was!"

"Yes, that it was," said Margaret, brightly. "It was such a charming, snatched, forbidden thing." But she suddenly stopped speaking. She had spoiled the remembrance of Frederick's visit to herself by her own cowardice. Of all faults the one she most despised in others was the want of bravery; the meanness of heart which leads to untruth. And here had she been guilty of it! Then came the thought of Mr. Thornton's cognisance of her falsehood. She wondered if she should have minded detection half so much from any one else. She tried herself in imagination with her Aunt Shaw and Edith; with her father; with Captain and Mr. Lennox; with Frederick. The thought of the last knowing what she had done, even in his own behalf, was the most painful, for the brother and sister were in the first flush of their mutual regard and love; but even any fall in Frederick's opinion was as nothing to the shame, the shrinking shame she felt at the thought of meeting Mr. Thornton again. And yet she longed to see him, to get it over; to understand where she stood in his opinion. Her cheeks burnt as she recollected how proudly she had implied an objection to trade (in the early days of their acquaintance), because it too often led to the deceit of passing off inferior for superior goods, in the one branch; of assuming credit for wealth and resources not possessed, in the other. She remembered Mr. Thornton's look of calm disdain, as in few words he gave her to understand that, in the great scheme of commerce, all dishonourable ways of acting were sure to prove injurious in the long run, and that, testing such actions simply according to the poor standard of success, there was folly and not wisdom in all such, and every kind of deceit in trade, as well as in other things. She remembered—she, then strong in her own untempted truth—asking him, if he did not think that buying in the cheapest and selling in the dearest market proved some want of the transparent justice which is so intimately connected with the idea of truth: and she had used the word chivalric—and her father had corrected her with the higher word, Christian; and so drawn the argument upon himself, while she sat silent by with a slight feeling of contempt.

No more contempt for her!—no more talk about the chivalric! Henceforward she must feel humiliated and disgraced in his sight. But when should she see him? Her heart leaped up in apprehension at every ring of the door-bell; and yet when it fell down to calmness, she felt strangely saddened and sick at heart at each disappointment. It was very evident that her father expected to see him, and was surprised that he did not come. The truth was, that there were points in their conversation the other night on which they had no time then to enlarge; but it had been understood that if possible on the succeeding evening—if not then, at least the very first evening that Mr. Thornton could command,—they should meet for further discussion. Mr. Hale had looked forward to this meeting ever since they had parted. He had not yet resumed the instruction to his pupils, which he had relinquished at the commencement of his wife's more serious illness, so he had fewer occupations than usual; and the great interest of the last day or so (Boucher's suicide) had driven him back with more eagerness than ever upon his speculations. He was restless all evening. He kept saying, "I quite expected to have seen Mr. Thornton. I think the messenger who brought the book last night must have had some note, and forgot to deliver it. Do you think there has been any message left to-day?"

"I will go and inquire, papa," said Margaret, after the changes on these sentences had been rung once or twice. "Stay, there's a ring!" She sat down instantly, and bent her head attentively over her work. She heard a step on the stairs, but it was only one, and she knew it was Dixon's. She lifted up her head and sighed, and believed she felt glad.

"It's that Higgins, sir. He wants to see you, or else Miss Hale. Or it might be Miss Hale first, and then you, sir; for he's in a strange kind of way."

"He had better come up here, Dixon; and then he can see us both, and choose which he likes for his listener."

"Oh! very well, sir. I've no wish to hear what he's got to say, I'm sure; only, if you could see his shoes, I'm sure you'd say the kitchen was the fitter place."

"He can wipe them, I suppose," said Mr. Hale. So Dixon flung off, to bid him walk up-stairs. She was a little mollified, however, when he looked at his feet with a hesitating air; and then, sitting down on the bottom stair, he took off the offending shoes, and without a word walked up-stairs.

"Sarvant, sir!" said he, slicking his hair down when he came into the room: "If hoo'l excuse me (looking at Margaret) for being i' my stockings; I'se been tramping a' day, and streets is none o' th' cleanest."

Margaret thought that fatigue might account for the change in his manner, for he was unusually quiet and subdued; and he had evidently some difficulty in saying what he came to say.

Mr. Hale's ever-ready sympathy with anything of shyness or hesitation, or want of self-possession, made him come to his aid.

"We shall have tea up directly, and then you'll take a cup with us, Mr. Higgins. I am sure you are tired, if you've been out much this wet relaxing day. Margaret, my dear, can't you hasten tea?"

Margaret could only hasten tea by taking the preparation of it into her own hands, and so offending Dixon, who was emerging out of her sorrow for her late mistress into a very touchy, irritable state. But Martha, like all who came in contact with Margaret—even Dixon herself, in the long run—felt it a pleasure and an honour to forward any of her wishes; and her readiness, and Margaret's sweet forbearance, soon made Dixon ashamed of herself.

"Why master and you must always be asking the lower classes upstairs, since we came to Milton, I cannot understand. Folk at Helstone were never brought higher than the kitchen; and I've let one or two of them know before now that they might think it an honour to be even there."

Higgins found it easier to unburden himself to one than to two. After Margaret left the room, he went to the door and assured himself that it was shut. Then he came and stood close to Mr. Hale.

"Master," said he, "yo'd not guess easy what I've been tramping after to-day. Special if yo' remember my manner o' talk yesterday. I've been a seeking work. I have," said he. "I said to mysel', I'd keep a civil tongue in my head, let who would say what 'em would. I'd set my teeth into my tongue sooner nor speak i' haste. For that man's sake—yo' understand," jerking his thumb back in some unknown direction.

"No, I don't," said Mr. Hale, seeing he waited for some kind of assent, and completely bewildered as to who "that man" could be.

"That chap as lies theer," said he, with another jerk. "Him as went and drownded himself, poor chap! I did na' think he'd got it in him to lie still and let th' water creep o'er him till he died. Boucher, yo' know."

"Yes, I know now," said Mr. Hale. "Go back to what you were saying: you'd not speak in haste——"

"For his sake. Yet not for his sake; for where'er he is, and whate'er, he'll ne'er know other clemming or cold again; but for the wife's sake, and the bits o' childer."

"God bless you!" said Mr. Hale, starting up; then, calming down, he said breathlessly, "What do you mean? Tell me out."

"I have telled yo'," said Higgins, a little surprised at Mr. Hale's agitation. "I would na ask for work for mysel'; but them's left as a charge on me. I reckon, I would ha guided Boucher to a better end; but I set him off o' th' road, and so I mun answer for him."

Mr. Hale got hold of Higgins's hand and shook it heartily, without speaking. Higgins looked awkward and ashamed.

"Theer, theer, master! Theer's ne'er a man, to call a man, amongst us, but what would do th' same; ay, and better too; for, belie' me, Is'e ne'er got a stroke o' work, nor yet a sight of any. For all I telled Hamper that, let alone his pledge—which I would not sign—no, I could na, not e'en for this—he'd ne'er ha' such a worker on his mill as I would be—he'd ha' none o' me—no more would none o' th' others. I'm a poor black feckless sheep—childer may clem for aught I can do, unless, parson, yo'd help me?"

"Help you! How? I would do anything,—but what can I do?"

"Miss there"—for Margaret had re-entered the room, and stood silent, listening—"has often talked grand o' the South, and the ways down there. Now I dunnot know how far off it is, but I've been thinking if I could get 'em down theer, where food is cheap and wages good, and all the folk, rich and poor, master and man, friendly like; yo' could, may be, help me to work. I'm not forty-five, and I've a deal o' strength in me, measter."

"But what kind of work could you do, my man?"

"Well, I reckon I could spade a bit——"

"And for that," said Margaret, stepping forwards, "for anything you could do, Higgins, with the best will in the world, you would, may be, get nine shillings a week; may be ten, at the outside. Food is much the same as here, except that you might have a little garden——"

"The childer could work at that," said he. "I'm sick o' Milton any-ways, and Milton is sick o' me."

"You must not go to the South," said Margaret, "for all that. You could not stand it. You would have to be out all weathers. It would kill you with rheumatism. The mere bodily work at your time of life would break you down. The fare is far different to what you have been accustomed to."

"I'se nought particular about my meat," said he, as if offended.

"But you've reckoned on having butcher's meat once a day, if you're in work; pay for that out of your ten shillings, and keep those poor children if you can. I owe it to you—since it's my way of talking that has set you off on this idea—to put it all clear before you. You would not bear the dulness of the life; you don't know what it is; it would eat you away like rust. Those that have lived there all their lives, are used to soaking in the stagnant waters. They labour on, from day to day, in the great solitude of steaming fields—never speaking or lifting up their poor, bent, downcast heads. The hard spade-work robs their brain of life; the sameness of their toil deadens their imagination; they don't care to meet to talk over thoughts and speculations, even of the weakest, wildest kind, after their work is done; they go home brutishly tired, poor creatures! caring for nothing but food and rest. You could not stir them up into any companion-ship, which you get in a town as plentiful as the air you breathe, whether it be good or bad—and that I don't know; but I do know, that you of all men are not one to bear a life among such labourers. What would be peace to them, would be eternal fretting to you. Think no more of it, Nicholas, I beg. Besides, you could never pay to get mother and children all there—that's one good thing."

"I've reckoned for that. One house mun do for us a', and the fur-niture o' t'other would go a good way. And men theer mun have their families to keep—mappen six or seven childer. God help 'em!" said he, more convinced by his own presentation of the facts than by all Margaret had said, and suddenly renouncing the idea, which had but recently formed itself in a brain worn out by the day's fatigue and anxiety. "God help 'em! North an' South have each getten their own troubles. If work's sure and steady theer, labour's paid at star-vation prices; while here we'n rucks o' money coming in one quarter, and ne'er a farthing th' next. For sure, th' world is in a confusion that passes me or any other man to understand; it needs fettling,[3] and who's to fettle it, if it's as yon folks say, and there's nought but what we see?"

Mr. Hale was busy cutting bread and butter; Margaret was glad of this, for she saw that Higgins was better left to himself: that if her

3. Putting in order.

father began to speak ever so mildly on the subject of Higgins's thoughts, the latter would consider himself challenged to an argument, and would feel himself bound to maintain his own ground. She and her father kept up an indifferent conversation until Higgins, scarcely aware whether he ate or not, had made a very substantial meal. Then he pushed his chair away from the table, and tried to take an interest in what they were saying; but it was of no use; and he fell back into dreamy gloom. Suddenly, Margaret said (she had been thinking of it for some time, but the words had stuck in her throat), "Higgins, have you been to Marlborough Mills to seek for work?"

"Thornton's?" asked he. "Ay, I've been at Thornton's."

"And what did he say?"

"Such a chap as me is not like to see the measter. Th' o'erlooker bid me go and be d——d."

"I wish you had seen Mr. Thornton," said Mr. Hale. "He might not have given you work, but he would not have used such language."

"As to th' language, I'm welly used to it; it dunnot matter to me. I'm not nesh[4] mysel' when I'm put out. It were th' fact that I were na wanted theer, no more nor ony other place, as I minded."

"But I wish you had seen Mr. Thornton," repeated Margaret. "Would you go again—it's a good deal to ask, I know—but would you go to-morrow and try him? I should be so glad if you would."

"I'm afraid it would be of no use," said Mr. Hale, in a low voice. "It would be better to let me speak to him." Margaret still looked at Higgins for his answer. Those grave soft eyes of hers were difficult to resist. He gave a great sigh.

"It would tax my pride above a bit; if it were for mysel', I could stand a deal o' clemming first; I'd sooner knock him down than ask a favour from him. I'd a deal sooner be flogged mysel'; but yo're not a common wench, axing yo'r pardon, nor yet have yo' common ways about yo'. I'll e'en make a wry face, and go at it to-morrow. Dunna yo' think that he'll do it. That man has it in him to be burnt at the stake afore he'll give in. I do it for yo'r sake, Miss Hale, and it's first time in my life as e'er I give way to a woman. Neither my wife nor Bess could e'er say that much again me."

"All the more do I thank you," said Margaret, smiling. "Though I don't believe you: I believe you have just given way to wife and daughter as much as most men."

"And as to Mr. Thornton," said Mr. Hale, "I'll give you a note to him, which, I think I may venture to say, will ensure you a hearing."

"I thank yo' kindly, sir, but I'd as lief stand on my own bottom. I dunnot stomach the notion of having favour curried for me, by one

4. Dainty, particular.

as doesn't know the ins and outs of the quarrel. Meddling 'twixt master and man is liker meddling 'twixt husband and wife than aught else: it takes a deal o' wisdom for to do ony good. I'll stand guard at the lodge door. I'll stand there fro' six in the morning till I get speech on him. But I'd liefer sweep th' streets, if paupers had na' got hold on that work. Dunna yo' hope, miss. There'll be more chance o' getting milk out of a flint. I wish yo' a very good night, and many thanks to yo'."

"You'll find your shoes by the kitchen fire; I took them there to dry," said Margaret.

He turned round and looked at her steadily, and then he brushed his lean hand across his eyes and went his way.

"How proud that man is!" said her father, who was a little annoyed at the manner in which Higgins had declined his intercession with Mr. Thornton.

"He is," said Margaret; "but what grand makings of a man there are in him, pride and all."

"It's amusing to see how he evidently respects the part in Mr. Thornton's character which is like his own."

"There's granite in all these northern people, papa, is there not?"

"There was none in poor Boucher, I am afraid; none in his wife either."

"I should guess from their tones that they had Irish blood in them. I wonder what success he'll have to-morrow. If he and Mr. Thornton would speak out together as man to man—if Higgins would forget that Mr. Thornton was a master, and speak to him as he does to us—and if Mr. Thornton would be patient enough to listen to him with his human heart, not with his master's ears—"

"You are getting to do Mr. Thornton justice at last, Margaret," said her father, pinching her ear.

Margaret had a strange choking at her heart, which made her unable to answer. "Oh!" thought she, "I wish I were a man, that I could go and force him to express his disapprobation, and tell him honestly that I knew I deserved it. It seems hard to lose him as a friend just when I had begun to feel his value. How tender he was with dear mamma! If it were only for her sake, I wish he would come, and then at least I should know how much I was abased in his eyes."

Chapter XIII.

Promises Fulfilled.

"Then proudly, proudly up she rose,
  Tho' the tear was in her e'e,
"Whate'er ye say, think what ye may,
  Ye's get nae word frae me!"
              SCOTCH BALLAD.

It was not merely that Margaret was known to Mr. Thornton to have spoken falsely,—though she imagined that for this reason only was she so turned in his opinion,—but that this falsehood of hers bore a distinct reference in his mind to some other lover. He could not forget the fond and earnest look that had passed between her and some other man—the attitude of familiar confidence, if not of positive endearment. The thought of this perpetually stung him; it was a picture before his eyes, wherever he went and whatever he was doing. In addition to this (and he ground his teeth as he remembered it), was the hour, dusky twilight; the place, so far away from home, and comparatively unfrequented. His nobler self had said at first, that all this last might be accidental, innocent, justifiable; but once allow her right to love and be beloved (and had he any reason to deny her right?—had not her words been severely explicit when she cast his love away from her?), she might easily have been beguiled into a longer walk, on to a later hour than she had anticipated. But that falsehood! which showed a fatal consciousness of something wrong, and to be concealed, which was unlike her. He did her that justice, though all the time it would have been a relief to believe her utterly unworthy of his esteem. It was this that made the misery—that he passionately loved her, and thought her, even with all her faults, more lovely and more excellent than any other woman; yet he deemed her so attached to some other man, so led away by her affection for him, as to violate her truthful nature. The very falsehood that stained her, was a proof how blindly she loved another—this dark, slight, elegant, handsome man—while he himself was rough, and stern, and strongly made. He lashed himself into an agony of fierce jealousy. He thought of that look, that attitude!—how he would have laid his life at her feet for such tender glances, such fond detention! He mocked at himself, for having valued the mechanical way in which she had protected him from the fury of the mob; now he had seen how soft and bewitching she looked when with a man she really loved. He remembered, point by point, the sharpness of her words—"There was not a man in all that crowd for whom she would not have done as much, far more readily than for him." He shared with the mob, in her desire of averting bloodshed from them;

but this man, this hidden lover, shared with nobody; he had looks, words, hand-cleavings, lies, concealment, all to himself.

Mr. Thornton was conscious that he had never been so irritable as he was now, in all his life long; he felt inclined to give a short abrupt answer, more like a bark than a speech, to every one that asked him a question; and this consciousness hurt his pride: he had always piqued himself on his self-control, and control himself he would. So the manner was subdued to a quiet deliberation, but the matter was even harder and sterner than common. He was more than usually silent at home; employing his evenings in a continual pace backwards and forwards, which would have annoyed his mother exceedingly if it had been practised by any one else; and did not tend to promote any forbearance on her part even to this beloved son.

"Can you stop—can you sit down for a moment? I have something to say to you, if you would give up that everlasting walk, walk, walk."

He sat down instantly, on a chair against the wall.

"I want to speak to you about Betsy. She says she must leave us; that her lover's death has so affected her spirits she can't give her heart to her work."

"Very well. I suppose other cooks are to be met with."

"That's so like a man. It's not merely the cooking, it is that she knows all the ways of the house. Besides, she tells me something about your friend Miss Hale."

"Miss Hale is no friend of mine. Mr. Hale is my friend."

"I am glad to hear you say so, for if she had been your friend, what Betsy says would have annoyed you."

"Let me hear it," said he, with the extreme quietness of manner he had been assuming for the last few days.

"Betsy says, that the night on which her lover—I forget his name—for she always calls him 'he'——"

"Leonards."

"The night on which Leonards was last seen at the station—when he was last seen on duty, in fact—Miss Hale was there, walking about with a young man who, Betsy believes, killed Leonards by some blow or push."

"Leonards was not killed by any blow or push."

"How do you know?"

"Because I distinctly put the question to the surgeon of the Infirmary. He told me there was an internal disease of long standing, caused by Leonards' habit of drinking to excess; that the fact of his becoming rapidly worse while in a state of intoxication, settled the question as to whether the last fatal attack was caused by excess of drinking, or the fall."

"The fall! What fall?"

"Caused by the blow or push of which Betsy speaks."

"Then there was a blow or push?"

"I believe so."

"And who did it?"

"As there was no inquest, in consequence of the doctor's opinion, I cannot tell you."

"But Miss Hale was there?"

No answer.

"And with a young man?"

Still no answer. At last he said: "I tell you, mother, that there was no inquest—no inquiry. No judicial inquiry, I mean."

"Betsy says that Woolmer (some man she knows, who is in a grocer's shop out at Crampton) can swear that Miss Hale was at the station at that hour, walking backwards and forwards with a young man."

"I don't see what we have to do with that. Miss Hale is at liberty to please herself."

"I'm glad to hear you say so," said Mrs. Thornton, eagerly. "It certainly signifies very little to us—not at all to you, after what has passed! but I—I made a promise to Mrs. Hale, that I would not allow her daughter to go wrong without advising and remonstrating with her. I shall certainly let her know my opinion of such conduct."

"I do not see any harm in what she did that evening," said Mr. Thornton, getting up, and coming near to his mother; he stood by the chimney-piece with his face turned away from the room.

"You would not have approved of Fanny's being seen out, after dark, in rather a lonely place, walking about with a young man. I say nothing of the taste which could choose the time, when her mother lay unburied, for such a promenade. Should you have liked your sister to have been noticed by a grocer's assistant for doing so?"

"In the first place, as it is not many years since I myself was a draper's assistant, the mere circumstance of a grocer's assistant noticing any act does not alter the character of the act to me. And in the next place, I see a great deal of difference between Miss Hale and Fanny. I can imagine that the one may have weighty reasons, which may and ought to make her overlook any seeming impropriety in her conduct. I never knew Fanny have weighty reasons for anything. Other people must guard her. I believe Miss Hale is a guardian to herself."

"A pretty character of your sister, indeed! Really, John, one would have thought Miss Hale had done enough to make you clear-sighted. She drew you on to an offer, by a bold display of pretended regard for you,—to play you off against this very young man, I've no doubt. Her whole conduct is clear to me now. You believe he is her lover, I suppose—you agree to that."

He turned round to his mother; his face was very gray and grim.

"Yes, mother. I do believe he is her lover." When he had spoken, he turned round again; he writhed himself about, like one in bodily pain. He leant his face against his hand. Then before she could speak, he turned sharp again:

"Mother. He is her lover, whoever he is; but she may need help and womanly counsel;—there may be difficulties or temptations which I don't know. I fear there are. I don't want to know what they are; but as you have ever been a good—ay! and a tender mother to me, go to her, and gain her confidence, and tell her what is best to be done. I know that something is wrong; some dread, must be a terrible torture to her."

"For God's sake, John!" said his mother, now really shocked, "what do you mean? What do you mean? What do you know?"

He did not reply to her.

"John! I don't know what I shan't think unless you speak. You have no right to say what you have done against her."

"Not against her, mother! I *could* not speak against her."

"Well! you have no right to say what you have done, unless you say more. These half-expressions are what ruin a woman's character."

"Her character! Mother, you do not dare—" he faced about, and looked into her face with his flaming eyes. Then, drawing himself up into determined composure and dignity, he said, "I will not say any more than this, which is neither more nor less than the simple truth, and I am sure you believe me,—I have good reason to believe, that Miss Hale is in some strait and difficulty connected with an attachment which, of itself, from my knowledge of Miss Hale's character, is perfectly innocent and right. What my reason is, I refuse to tell. But never let me hear any one say a word against her, implying any more serious imputation than that she now needs the counsel of some kind and gentle woman. You promised Mrs. Hale to be that woman!"

"No!" said Mrs. Thornton. "I am happy to say, I did not promise kindness and gentleness, for I felt at the time that it might be out of my power to render these to one of Miss Hale's character and disposition. I promised counsel and advice, such as I would give to my own daughter; I shall speak to her as I would do to Fanny, if she had gone gallivanting with a young man in the dusk. I shall speak with relation to the circumstances I know, without being influenced either one way or another by the 'strong reasons' which you will not confide to me. Then I shall have fulfilled my promise, and done my duty."

"She will never bear it," said he passionately.

"She will have to bear it, if I speak in her dead mother's name."

"Well!" said he, breaking away, "don't tell me any more about it. I cannot endure to think of it. It will be better that you should speak to her any way, than that she should not be spoken to at all.—Oh! that look of love!" continued he, between his teeth, as he bolted himself into his own private room. "And that cursed lie; which showed some terrible shame in the background, to be kept from the light in which I thought she lived perpetually! Oh, Margaret, Margaret! Mother, how you have tortured me! Oh! Margaret, could you not have loved me? I am but uncouth and hard, but I would never have led you into any falsehood for me."

The more Mrs. Thornton thought over what her son had said, in pleading for a merciful judgment for Margaret's indiscretion, the more bitterly she felt inclined towards her. She took a savage pleasure in the idea of "speaking her mind" to her, in the guise of fulfilment of a duty. She enjoyed the thought of showing herself untouched by the "glamour," which she was well aware Margaret had the power of throwing over many people. She snorted scornfully over the picture of the beauty of her victim; her jet black hair, her clear smooth skin, her lucid eyes would not help to save her one word of the just and stern reproach which Mrs. Thornton spent half the night in preparing to her mind.

"Is Miss Hale within?" She knew she was, for she had seen her at the window, and she had her feet inside the little hall before Martha had half answered her question.

Margaret was sitting alone, writing to Edith, and giving her many particulars of her mother's last days. It was a softening employment, and she had to brush away the unbidden tears as Mrs. Thornton was announced.

She was so gentle and ladylike in her mode of reception that her visitor was somewhat daunted; and it became impossible to utter the speech, so easy of arrangement with no one to address it to. Margaret's low rich voice was softer than usual; her manner more gracious, because in her heart she was feeling very grateful to Mrs. Thornton for the courteous attention of her call. She exerted herself to find subjects of interest for conversation; praised Martha, the servant whom Mrs. Thornton had found for them; had asked Edith for a little Greek air, about which she had spoken to Miss Thornton. Mrs. Thornton was fairly discomfited. Her sharp Damascus blade[1] seemed out of place, and useless among rose-leaves. She was silent, because she was trying to task herself up to her duty. At last, she stung herself into its performance by a suspicion which, in spite of all probability, she allowed to cross her mind, that all this sweetness was put on with a view of propitiating Mr. Thornton; that, somehow, the other attachment had fallen through, and that it suited Miss

1. The ancient Syrian city of Damascus was famous for its steel: the term "Damascus blade" was a common coinage for a high-quality weapon. Here, of course, used metaphorically.

Hale's purpose to recall her rejected lover. Poor Margaret! there was perhaps so much truth in the suspicion as this: that Mrs. Thornton was the mother of one whose regard she valued, and feared to have lost; and this thought unconsciously added to her natural desire of pleasing one who was showing her kindness by her visit. Mrs. Thornton stood up to go, but yet she seemed to have something more to say. She cleared her throat and began:

"Miss Hale, I have a duty to perform. I promised your poor mother that, as far as my poor judgment went, I would not allow you to act in any way wrongly, or (she softened her speech down a little here) inadvertently, without remonstrating; at least, without offering advice, whether you took it or not."

Margaret stood before her, blushing like any culprit, with her eyes dilating as she gazed at Mrs. Thornton. She thought she had come to speak to her about the falsehood she had told—that Mr. Thornton had employed her to explain the danger she had exposed herself to, of being confuted in full court! and although her heart sank to think he had not rather chosen to come himself, and upbraid her, and receive her penitence, and restore her again to his good opinion, yet she was too much humbled not to bear any blame on this subject patiently and meekly.

Mrs. Thornton went on:

"At first, when I heard from one of my servants, that you had been seen walking about with a gentleman, so far from home as the Outwood station, at such a time of the evening, I could hardly believe it. But my son, I am sorry to say, confirmed her story. It was indiscreet, to say the least; many a young woman has lost her character before now——"

Margaret's eyes flashed fire. This was a new idea—this was too insulting. If Mrs. Thornton had spoken to her about the lie she had told, well and good—she would have owned it, and humiliated herself. But to interfere with her conduct—to speak of her character! she—Mrs. Thornton, a mere stranger—it was too impertinent! She would not answer her—not one word. Mrs. Thornton saw the battle-spirit in Margaret's eyes, and it called up her combativeness also.

"For your mother's sake, I have thought it right to warn you against such improprieties; they must degrade you in the long run in the estimation of the world, even if in fact they do not lead you to positive harm."

"For my mother's sake," said Margaret, in a tearful voice, "I will bear much; but I cannot bear everything. She never meant me to be exposed to insult, I am sure."

"Insult, Miss Hale!"

"Yes, madam," said Margaret more steadily, "it is insult. What do you know of me that should lead you to suspect—Oh!" said she, breaking down, and covering her face with her hands—"I know now, Mr. Thornton has told you——"

"No, Miss Hale," said Mrs. Thornton, her truthfulness causing her to arrest the confession Margaret was on the point of making, though her curiosity was itching to hear it. "Stop. Mr. Thornton has told me nothing. You do not know my son. You are not worthy to know him. He said this. Listen, young lady, that you may understand, if you can, what sort of a man you rejected. This Milton manufacturer, his great tender heart scorned as it was scorned, said to me only last night, 'Go to her. I have good reason to know that she is in some strait, arising out of some attachment; and she needs womanly counsel.' I believe those were his very words. Farther than that—beyond admitting the fact of your being at the Outwood station with a gentleman, on the evening of the twenty-sixth—he has said nothing—not one word against you. If he has knowledge of anything which should make you sob so, he keeps it to himself."

Margaret's face was still hidden in her hands, the fingers of which were wet with tears. Mrs. Thornton was a little mollified.

"Come, Miss Hale. There may be circumstances, I'll allow, that, if explained, may take off from the seeming impropriety."

Still no answer. Margaret was considering what to say; she wished to stand well with Mrs. Thornton; and yet she could not, might not, give any explanation. Mrs. Thornton grew impatient.

"I shall be sorry to break off an acquaintance; but for Fanny's sake—as I told my son, if Fanny had done so we should consider it a great disgrace—and Fanny might be led away——"

"I can give you no explanation," said Margaret, in a low voice. "I have done wrong, but not in the way you think or know about. I think Mr. Thornton judges me more mercifully than you;"—she had hard work to keep herself from choking with her tears—"but, I believe, madam, you mean to do rightly."

"Thank you," said Mrs. Thornton, drawing herself up; "I was not aware that my meaning was doubted. It is the last time I shall interfere. I was unwilling to consent to do it, when your mother asked me. I had not approved of my son's attachment to you, while I only suspected it. You did not appear to me worthy of him. But when you compromised yourself as you did at the time of the riot, and exposed yourself to the comments of servants and workpeople, I felt it was no longer right to set myself against my son's wish of proposing to you—a wish, by the way, which he had always denied entertaining until the day of the riot." Margaret winced, and drew in her breath with a long, hissing sound; of which, however, Mrs. Thornton took no notice. "He came; you had apparently changed your mind. I told my son yesterday, that I thought it possible, short as was the interval, you might have heard or learnt something of this other lover——"

"What must you think of me, madam?" asked Margaret, throwing her head back with proud disdain, till her throat curved outwards like a swan's. "You can say nothing more, Mrs. Thornton. I decline every attempt to justify myself for anything. You must allow me to leave the room."

And she swept out of it with the noiseless grace of an offended princess. Mrs. Thornton had quite enough of natural humour to make her feel the ludicrousness of the position in which she was left. There was nothing for it but to show herself out. She was not particularly annoyed at Margaret's way of behaving. She did not care enough for her for that. She had taken Mrs. Thornton's remonstrance to the full as keenly to heart as that lady expected; and Margaret's passion at once mollified her visitor, far more than any silence or reserve could have done. It showed the effect of her words. "My young lady," thought Mrs. Thornton to herself; "you've a pretty good temper of your own. If John and you had come together, he would have had to keep a tight hand over you, to make you know your place. But I don't think you will go a-walking again with your beau, at such an hour of the day, in a hurry. You've too much pride and spirit in you for that. I like to see a girl fly out at the notion of being talked about. It shows they're neither giddy, nor bold by nature. As for that girl, she might be bold, but she'd never be giddy. I'll do her that justice. Now as to Fanny, she'd be giddy, and not bold. She's no courage in her, poor thing!"

Mr. Thornton was not spending the morning so satisfactorily as his mother. She, at any rate, was fulfilling her determined purpose. He was trying to understand where he stood; what damage the strike had done him. A good deal of his capital was locked up in new and expensive machinery; and he had also bought cotton largely, with a view to some great orders which he had in hand. The strike had thrown him terribly behindhand, as to the completion of these orders. Even with his own accustomed and skilled workpeople, he would have had some difficulty in fulfilling his engagements; as it was, the incompetence of the Irish hands, who had to be trained to their work, at a time requiring unusual activity, was a daily annoyance.

It was not a favourable hour for Higgins to make his request. But he had promised Margaret to do it at any cost. So, though every moment added to his repugnance, his pride, and his sullenness of temper, he stood leaning against the dead wall, hour after hour, first on one leg, then on the other. At last the latch was sharply lifted, and out came Mr. Thornton.

"I want for to speak to yo', sir."

"Can't stay now, my man. I'm too late as it is."

"Well, sir, I reckon I can wait till yo' come back."

Mr. Thornton was half way down the street. Higgins sighed. But it was no use. To catch him in the street, was his only chance of seeing "the measter;" if he had rung the lodge bell or even gone up to the house to ask for him, he would have been referred to the overlooker. So he stood still again, vouchsafing no answer, but a short nod of recognition to the few men who knew and spoke to him, as the crowd drove out of the millyard at dinner-time, and scowling with all his might at the Irish "knobsticks" who had just been imported. At last Mr. Thornton returned.

"What! you there still!"

"Ay, sir. I mun speak to yo'."

"Come in here, then. Stay, we'll go across the yard; the men are not come back, and we shall have it to ourselves. These good people, I see, are at dinner;" said he, closing the door of the porter's lodge.

He stopped to speak to the overlooker. The latter said in a low tone:

"I suppose you know, sir, that that man is Higgins, one of the leaders of the Union; he that made that speech in Hurstfield."

"No, I didn't," said Mr. Thornton, looking round sharply at his follower. Higgins was known to him by name as a turbulent spirit.

"Come along," said he, and his tone was rougher than before. "It is men such as this," thought he, "who interrupt commerce and injure the very town they live in: mere demagogues, lovers of power, at whatever cost to others."

"Well, sir! what do you want with me?" said Mr. Thornton, facing round at him, as soon as they were in the counting-house of the mill.

"My name is Higgins"—

"I know that," broke in Mr. Thornton. "What do you want, Mr. Higgins? That's the question."

"I want work."

"Work! You're a pretty chap to come asking me for work. You don't want impudence, that's very clear."

"I've getten enemies and backbiters, like my betters; but I ne'er heerd o' ony of them calling me o'er-modest," said Higgins. His blood was a little roused by Mr. Thornton's manner, more than by his words.

Mr. Thornton saw a letter addressed to himself on the table. He took it up and read it through. At the end, he looked up and said, "What are you waiting for?"

"An answer to th' question I axed."

"I gave it you before. Don't waste any more of your time."

"Yo' made a remark, sir, on my impudence: but I were taught that it was manners to say either 'yes' or 'no,' when I were axed a civil question. I should be thanfu' to yo' if yo'd give me work. Hamper will speak to my being a good hand."

"I've a notion you'd better not send me to Hamper to ask for a character, my man. I might hear more than you'd like."

"I'd take th' risk. Worst they could say of me is, that I did what I thought best, even to my own wrong."

"You'd better go and try them, then, and see whether they'll give you work. I've turned off upwards of a hundred of my best hands, for no other fault than following you, and such as you; and d'ye think I'll take you on? I might as well put a firebrand into the midst of the cotton-waste."

Higgins turned away; then the recollection of Boucher came over him, and he faced round with the greatest concession he could persuade himself to make.

"I'd promise yo', measter, I'd not speak a word as could do harm, if so be yo' did right by us; and I'd promise more: I'd promise that when I seed yo' going wrong, and acting unfair, I'd speak to yo' in private first; and that would be a fair warning. If yo' and I did na agree in our opinion o' your conduct, yo' might turn me off at an hour's notice."

"Upon my word, you don't think small beer of yourself! Hamper has had a loss of you. How came he to let you and your wisdom go?"

"Well, we parted wi' mutual dissatisfaction. I wouldn't gi'e the pledge they were asking; and they wouldn't have me at no rate. So I'm free to make another engagement; and as I said before, though I should na' say it, I'm a good hand, measter, and a steady man—specially when I can keep fro' drink; and that I shall do now, if I ne'er did afore."

"That you may have more money laid up for another strike, I suppose?"

"No! I'd be thankful if I was free to do that; it's for to keep th' widow and childer of a man who was drove mad by them knobsticks o' yourn; put out of his place by a Paddy that did na know weft fro' warp."

"Well! you'd better turn to something else, if you've any such good intention in your head. I shouldn't advise you to stay in Milton: you're too well known here."

"If it were summer," said Higgins, "I'd take to Paddy's work,[2] and go as a navvy, or haymaking, or summut, and ne'er see Milton again. But it's winter, and th' childer will clem."

"A pretty navvy you'd make! why, you couldn't do half a day's work at digging against an Irishman."

2. Irishman's work. Unskilled laboring work was often done by Irish immigrants.

"I'd only charge half-a-day for th' twelve hours, if I could only do half-a-day's work in th' time. Yo're not knowing of any place, where they could gi' me a trial, away fro' the mills, if I'm such a firebrand? I'd take any wage they thought I was worth, for the sake of those childer.'"

"Don't you see what you would be? You'd be a knobstick. You'd be taking less wages than the other labourers—all for the sake of another man's children. Think how you'd abuse any poor fellow who was willing to take what he could get to keep his own children. You and your Union would soon be down upon him. No! no! if it's only for the recollection of the way in which you've used the poor knob-sticks before now, I say No! to your question. I'll not give you work. I won't say, I don't believe your pretext for coming and asking for work; I know nothing about it. It may be true, or it may not. It's a very unlikely story, at any rate. Let me pass. I'll not give you work. There's your answer."

"I hear, sir. I would na ha' troubled yo', but that I were bid to come, by one as seemed to think yo'd gotten some soft place in yo'r heart. Hoo were mistook, and I were misled. But I'm not the first man as is misled by a woman."

"Tell her to mind her own business the next time, instead of taking up your time and mine too. I believe women are at the bottom of every plague in this world. Be off with you."

"I'm obleeged to yo' for a' yo'r kindness, measter, and most of a' for yo'r civil way o' saying good-bye."

Mr. Thornton did not deign a reply. But, looking out of the window a minute after, he was struck with the lean, bent figure going out of the yard: the heavy walk was in strange contrast with the resolute, clear determination of the man to speak to him. He crossed to the porter's lodge:

"How long has that man Higgins been waiting to speak to me?"

"He was outside the gate before eight o'clock, sir. I think he's been there ever since."

"And it is now—?"

"Just one, sir."

"Five hours," thought Mr. Thornton; "it's a long time for a man to wait, doing nothing but first hoping and then fearing."

Chapter XIV.

Making Friends.

"Nay, I have done; you get no more of me:
And I am glad, yea glad with all my heart,
That thus so clearly I myself am free."
                                    DRAYTON.[1]

Margaret shut herself up in her own room, after she had quitted Mrs. Thornton. She began to walk backwards and forwards, in her old habitual way of showing agitation; but, then, remembering that in that slightly-built house every step was heard from one room to another, she sat down until she heard Mrs. Thornton go safely out of the house. She forced herself to recollect all the conversation that had passed between them; speech by speech, she compelled her memory to go through with it. At the end, she rose up, and said to herself, in a melancholy tone:

"At any rate, her words do not touch me; they fall off from me; for I am innocent of all the motives she attributes to me. But still, it is hard to think that any one—any woman—can believe all this of another so easily. It is hard and sad. Where I have done wrong, she does not accuse me—she does not know. He never told her: I might have known he would not!"

She lifted up her head, as if she took pride in any delicacy of feeling which Mr. Thornton had shown. Then, as a new thought came across her, she pressed her hands tightly together:

"He, too, must take poor Frederick for some lover." (She blushed as the word passed through her mind.) "I see it now. It is not merely that he knows of my falsehood, but he believes that some one else cares for me; and that I——Oh dear!—oh dear! What shall I do? What do I mean? Why do I care what he thinks, beyond the mere loss of his good opinion as regards my telling the truth or not? I cannot tell. But I am very miserable! Oh, how unhappy this last year has been! I have passed out of childhood into old age. I have had no youth—no womanhood; the hopes of womanhood have closed for me—for I shall never marry; and I anticipate cares and sorrows just as if I were an old woman, and with the same fearful spirit. I am weary of this continual call upon me for strength. I could bear up for papa; because that is a natural, pious duty. And I think I could bear up against—at any rate, I could have the energy to resent, Mrs. Thornton's unjust, impertinent suspicions. But it is hard to feel how completely he must misunderstand me. What has happened to make

---

1. Michael Drayton, poet and dramatist (1563–1631). The lines are from his sonnet "Since there's no help, come let us kiss and part."

me so morbid to-day? I do not know. I only know I cannot help it. I must give way sometimes. No, I will not though," said she, springing to her feet. "I will not—I *will* not think of myself and my own position. I won't examine into my own feelings. It would be of no use now. Some time, if I live to be an old woman, I may sit over the fire, and, looking into the embers, see the life that might have been."

All this time, she was hastily putting on her things to go out, only stopping from time to time to wipe her eyes, with an impatience of gesture at the tears that would come, in spite of all her bravery.

"I dare say, there's many a woman makes as sad a mistake as I have done, and only finds it out too late. And how proudly and impertinently I spoke to him that day! But I did not know then. It has come upon me little by little, and I don't know where it began. Now I won't give way. I shall find it difficult to behave in the same way to him, with this miserable consciousness upon me; but I will be very calm and very quiet, and say very little. But, to be sure, I may not see him; he keeps out of our way evidently. That would be worse than all. And yet no wonder that he avoids me, believing what he must about me."

She went out, going rapidly towards the country, and trying to drown reflection by swiftness of motion.

As she stood on the door-step, at her return, her father came up:

"Good girl!" said he. "You've been to Mrs. Boucher's. I was just meaning to go there, if I had time, before dinner."

"No, papa; I have not," said Margaret, reddening. "I never thought about her. But I will go directly after dinner; I will go while you are taking your nap."

Accordingly Margaret went. Mrs. Boucher was very ill; really ill—not merely ailing. The kind and sensible neighbour, who had come in the other day, seemed to have taken charge of everything. Some of the children were gone to the neighbours. Mary Higgins had come for the three youngest at dinner-time; and since then Nicholas had gone for the doctor. He had not come as yet; Mrs. Boucher was dying; and there was nothing to do but to wait. Margaret thought that she should like to know his opinion, and that she could not do better than go and see the Higginses in the meantime. She might then possibly hear whether Nicholas had been able to make his application to Mr. Thornton.

She found Nicholas busily engaged in making a penny spin on the dresser, for the amusement of three little children, who were clinging to him in a fearless manner. He, as well as they, was smiling at a good long spin; and Margaret thought, that the happy look of interest in his occupation was a good sign. When the penny stopped spinning, "lile Johnnie" began to cry.

"Come to me," said Margaret, taking him off the dresser, and holding him in her arms; she held her watch to his ear, while she asked Nicholas if he had seen Mr. Thornton.

The look on his face changed instantly.

"Ay!" said he. "I've seen and heerd too much on him."

"He refused you, then?" said Margaret, sorrowfully.

"To be sure. I knew he'd do it all long. It's no good expecting marcy at the hands o' them measters. Yo're a stranger' and a foreigner, and aren't likely to know their ways; but I knowed it."

"I am sorry I asked you. Was he angry? He did not speak to you as Hamper did, did he?"

"He weren't o'er-civil!" said Nicholas, spinning the penny again, as much for his own amusement as for that of the children. "Never yo' fret, I'm only where I was. I'll go on tramp to-morrow. I gave him as good as I got. I told him, I'd not that good opinion on him that I'd ha' come a second time of mysel'; but yo'd advised me for to come, and I were beholden to yo'."

"You told him I sent you?"

"I dunno if I ca'd yo' by your name. I dunnot think I did. I said, a woman who knew no better had advised me for to come and see if there was a soft place in his heart."

"And he—?" asked Margaret.

"Said I were to tell yo' to mind yo'r own business.—That's the longest spin yet, my lads.—And them's civil words to what he used to me. But ne'er mind. We're but where we was; and I'll break stones on th' road afore I let these little uns clem."

Margaret put the struggling Johnnie out of her arms, back into his former place on the dresser.

"I am sorry I asked you to go to Mr. Thornton's. I am disappointed in him."

There was a slight noise behind her. Both she and Nicholas turned round at the same moment, and there stood Mr. Thornton, with a look of displeased surprise upon his face. Obeying her swift impulse, Margaret passed out before him, saying not a word, only bowing low to hide the sudden paleness that she felt had come over her face. He bent equally low in return, and then closed the door after her. As she hurried to Mrs. Boucher's, she heard the clang, and it seemed to fill up the measure of her mortification. He too was annoyed to find her there. He had tenderness in his heart—"a soft place," as Nicholas Higgins called it; but he had some pride in concealing it; he kept it very sacred and safe, and was jealous of every circumstance that tried to gain admission. But if he dreaded exposure of his tenderness, he was equally desirous that all men should recognise his justice; and he felt that he had been unjust, in giving so scornful a hearing to any one who had waited, with humble patience, for five hours, to speak to him. That the man had spoken saucily to him when he had the opportunity, was nothing to Mr. Thornton. He rather liked him for it; and he was conscious of his own irritability of temper at the time, which probably made them both quits. It was the five hours of waiting that struck Mr. Thornton. He had not five hours to spare himself; but one hour—two hours, of his hard penetrating intellectual, as well as bodily labour, did he give up to going about collecting evidence as to the truth of Higgins's story, the nature of his character, the tenor of his life. He tried not to be, but was convinced that all that Higgins had said was true. And then the conviction went in, as if by some spell, and touched the latent tenderness of his heart; the patience of the man, the simple generosity of the motive (for he had learnt about the quarrel between Boucher and Higgins), made him forget entirely the mere reasonings of justice, and overleap them by a diviner instinct. He came to tell Higgins he would give him work; and he was more annoyed to find Margaret there than by hearing her last words; for then he understood that she was the woman who had urged Higgins to come to him; and he dreaded the admission of any thought of her, as a motive to what he was doing solely because it was right.

"So that was the lady you spoke of as a woman?" said he indignantly to Higgins. "You might have told me who she was."

"And then, maybe, yo'd ha' spoken of her more civil than yo' did; yo'd getten a mother who might ha' kept yo'r tongue in check when yo' were talking o' women being at the root of all the plagues."

"Of course you told that to Miss Hale?"

"In coorse I did. Leastways, I reckon I did. I telled her she weren't to meddle again in aught that concerned yo'."

"Whose children are those—yours?" Mr. Thornton had a pretty good notion whose they were, from what he had heard; but he felt awkward in turning the conversation round from this unpromising beginning.

"They're not mine, and they are mine."

"They are the children you spoke of to me this morning?"

"When yo' said," replied Higgins, turning round, with ill-smothered fierceness, "that my story might be true or might not, but it were a very unlikely one. Measter, I've not forgotten."

Mr. Thornton was silent for a moment; then he said: "No more have I. I remember what I said. I spoke to you about those children in a way I had no business to do. I did not believe you. I could not have taken care of another man's children myself, if he had acted towards me as I hear Boucher did towards you. But I know now that you spoke truth. I beg your pardon."

Higgins did not turn round, or immediately respond to this. But when he did speak, it was in a softened tone, although the words were gruff enough.

"Yo've no business to go prying into what happened between Boucher and me. He's dead, and I'm sorry. That's enough."

"So it is. Will you take work with me? That's what I came to ask."

Higgins's obstinacy wavered, recovered strength, and stood firm. He would not speak. Mr. Thornton would not ask again. Higgins's eye fell on the children.

"Yo've called me impudent, and a liar, and a mischief-maker, and yo' might ha' said wi' some truth, as I were now and then given to drink. An' I ha' called you a tyrant, an' an oud bull-dog, and a hard, cruel master; that's where it stands. But for th' childer. Measter, do yo' think we can e'er get on together?"

"Well!" said Mr. Thornton, half-laughing, "it was not my proposal that we should go together. But there's one comfort, on your own showing. We neither of us can think much worse of the other than we do now."

"That's true," said Higgins, reflectively. "I've been thinking, ever sin' I saw you, what a marcy it were yo' did na take me on, for that I ne'er saw a man whom I could less abide. But that's maybe been a hasty judgment; and work's work to such as me. So, measter, I'll come; and what's more, I thank yo'; and that's a deal fro' me," said he, more frankly, suddenly turning round and facing Mr. Thornton fully for the first time.

"And this is a deal from me," said Mr. Thornton, giving Higgins's hand a good grip. "Now mind you come sharp to your time," continued he, resuming the master. "I'll have no laggards at my mill. What fines we have, we keep pretty sharply. And the first time I catch you making mischief, off you go. So now you know where you are."

"Yo' spoke of my wisdom this morning. I reckon I may bring it wi' me; or would yo' rayther have me 'bout my brains?"

" 'Bout your brains if you use them for meddling with my business; with your brains if you can keep them to your own."

"I shall need a deal o' brains to settle where my business ends and yo'rs begins."

"Your business has not begun yet, and mine stands still for me. So good afternoon."

Just before Mr. Thornton came up to Mrs. Boucher's door, Margaret came out of it. She did not see him; and he followed her for several yards, admiring her light and easy walk, and her tall and graceful figure. But, suddenly, this simple emotion of pleasure was tainted, poisoned by jealousy. He wished to overtake her, and speak to her, to see how she would receive him, now she must know he was aware of some other attachment. He wished too, but of this wish he was rather ashamed, that she should know that he had justified her wisdom in sending Higgins to him to ask for work, and had repented him of his morning's decision. He came up to her. She started.

"Allow me to say, Miss Hale, that you were rather premature in expressing your disappointment. I have taken Higgins on."

"I am glad of it," said she, coldly.

"He tells me, he repeated to you, what I said this morning about—." Mr. Thornton hesitated. Margaret took it up:

"About women not meddling. You had a perfect right to express your opinion, which was a very correct one, I have no doubt. But" she went on a little more eagerly, "Higgins did not quite tell you the exact truth." The word "truth," reminded her of her own untruth, and she stopped short, feeling exceedingly uncomfortable.

Mr. Thornton at first was puzzled to account for her silence; and then he remembered the lie she had told, and all that was foregone. "The exact truth!" said he. "Very few people do speak the exact truth. I have given up hoping for it. Miss Hale, have you no explanation to give me? You must perceive what I cannot but think."

Margaret was silent. She was wondering whether an explanation of any kind would be consistent with her loyalty to Frederick.

"Nay," said he, "I will ask no farther. I may be putting temptation in your way. At present, believe me, your secret is safe with me. But you run great risks, allow me to say, in being so indiscreet. I am now only speaking as a friend of your father's: if I had any other thought or hope, of course that is at an end. I am quite disinterested."

"I am aware of that," said Margaret, forcing herself to speak in an indifferent, careless way. "I am aware of what I must appear to you, but the secret is another person's, and I cannot explain it without doing him harm."

"I have not the slightest wish to pry into the gentleman's secrets," he said, with growing anger. "My own interest in you is—simply that of a friend. You may not believe me, Miss Hale, but it is—in spite of the persecution I'm afraid I threatened you with at one time—but that is all given up; all passed away. You believe me, Miss Hale?"

"Yes," said Margaret, quietly and sadly.

"Then, really, I don't see any occasion for us to go on walking together. I thought, perhaps you might have had something to say, but I see we are nothing to each other. If you're quite convinced, that any foolish passion on my part is entirely over, I will wish you good afternoon." He walked off very hastily.

"What can he mean?" thought Margaret,—"what could he mean by speaking so, as if I were always thinking that he cared for me, when I know he does not; he cannot. His mother will have said all those cruel things about me to him. But I won't care for him. I surely am mistress enough of myself to control this wild, strange, miserable feeling, which tempted me even to betray my own dear Frederick, so that I might but regain his good opinion—the good opinion of a man who takes such pains to tell me that I am nothing to him. Come! poor little heart! be cheery and brave. We'll be a great deal to one another, if we are thrown off and left desolate."

Her father was almost startled by her merriment this morning. She talked incessantly, and forced her natural humour to an unusual pitch; and if there was a tinge of bitterness in much of what she said; if her accounts of the old Harley Street set were a little sarcastic, her father could not bear to check her, as he would have done at another time—for he was glad to see her shake off her cares. In the middle of the evening, she was called down to speak to Mary Higgins; and when she came back, Mr. Hale imagined that he saw traces of tears on her cheeks. But that could not be, for she brought good news—that Higgins had got work at Mr. Thornton's mill. Her spirits were damped, at any rate, and she found it very difficult to go on talking at all, much more in the wild way that she had done. For some days her spirits varied strangely; and her father was beginning to be anxious about her, when news arrived from one or two quarters that promised some change and variety for her. Mr. Hale received a letter from Mr. Bell, in which that gentleman volunteered a visit to them; and Mr. Hale imagined that the promised society of his old Oxford friend would give as agreeable a turn to Margaret's ideas as it did to his own. Margaret tried to take an interest in what pleased her father; but she was too languid to care about any Mr. Bell, even though he were twenty times her godfather. She was more roused by a letter from Edith, full of sympathy about her aunt's death; full of details about herself, her husband, and child; and at the end saying, that as the climate did not suit the baby, and as Mrs. Shaw was talking of returning to England, she thought it probable that Captain Lennox might sell out, and that they might all go and live again in the old Harley Street house; which, however, would seem very incomplete without Margaret. Margaret yearned after that old house, and the placid tranquillity of that old well-ordered, monotonous life. She had found it occasionally tiresome while it lasted; but since then she had been buffeted about, and felt so exhausted by this recent struggle with herself, that she thought that even stagnation would be a rest and a refreshment. So she began to look towards a long visit to the Lennoxes, on their return to England, as to a point—no, not of hope—but of leisure, in which she could regain her power and command over herself. At present it seemed to her as if all subjects tended towards Mr. Thornton; as if she could not forget him with all her endeavours. If she went to see the Higginses, she heard of him there; her father had resumed their readings together, and quoted his opinions perpetually; even Mr. Bell's visit brought his tenant's name upon the tapis;[2] for he wrote word, that he believed he must be occupied some great part of his time with Mr. Thornton, as a new lease was in preparation, and the terms of it must be agreed upon.

Chapter XV.

Out of Tune.

> "I have no wrong, where I can claim no right,
>   Naught ta'en me fro, where I have nothing had,
>   Yet of my woe I cannot so be quite;
>   Namely, since that another may be glad
>   With that, that thus in sorrow makes me sad."
>   WYATT.[1]

Margaret had not expected much pleasure to herself from Mr. Bell's visit—she had only looked forward to it on her father's account, but when her godfather came, she at once fell into the most natural position of friendship in the world. He said she had no merit in being what she was, a girl so entirely after his own heart; it was an hereditary power which she had, to walk in and take possession of his regard; while she, in reply, gave him much credit for being so fresh and young under his Fellow's cap and gown.

"Fresh and young in warmth and kindness, I mean. I'm afraid I must own, that I think your opinions are the oldest and mustiest I have met with this long time."

"Hear this daughter of yours, Hale! Her residence in Milton has quite corrupted her. She's a democrat, a red republican, a member of the Peace Society, a socialist—"

"Papa, it's all because I'm standing up for the progress of commerce. Mr. Bell would have had it keep still at exchanging wild-beast skins for acorns."

"No, no. I'd dig the ground and grow potatoes. And I'd shave the wild-beast skins and make the wool into broad cloth. Don't exaggerate, missy. But I'm tired of this bustle. Everybody rushing over everybody, in their hurry to get rich."

"It is not every one who can sit comfortably in a set of college rooms, and let his riches grow without any exertion of his own. No doubt there is many a man here who would be thankful if his prop-

2. Literally, a carpet (French). Thus, "on the carpet"; "under consideration."
1. Sir Thomas Wyatt (c. 1503–1542) poet and diplomat. The lines are from his poem "Th' answere that ye made to me, my dere" on the subject of a rejected suitor's belief that another lover has been preferred. It is thus appropriate to the content of the chapter.

erty would increase as yours has done, without his taking any trouble about it," said Mr. Hale.

"I don't believe they would. It's the bustle and the struggle they like. As for sitting still, and learning from the past, or shaping out the future by faithful work done in a prophetic spirit—Why! Pooh! I don't believe there's a man in Milton who knows how to sit still; and it is a great art."

"Milton people, I suspect, think Oxford men don't know how to move. It would be a very good thing if they mixed a little more."

"It might be good for the Miltoners. Many things might be good for them which would be very disagreeable for other people."

"Are you not a Milton man yourself?" asked Margaret. "I should have thought you would have been proud of your town."

"I confess, I don't see what there is to be proud of. If you'll only come to Oxford, Margaret, I will show you a place to glory in."

"Well!" said Mr. Hale, "Mr. Thornton is coming to drink tea with us to-night, and he is as proud of Milton as you of Oxford. You two must try and make each other a little more liberal-minded."

"I don't want to be more liberal-minded, thank you," said Mr. Bell.

"Is Mr. Thornton coming to tea, papa?" asked Margaret in a low voice.

"Either to tea or soon after. He could not tell. He told us not to wait."

Mr. Thornton had determined that he would make no inquiry of his mother as to how far she had put her project into execution of speaking to Margaret about the impropriety of her conduct. He felt pretty sure that, if this interview took place, his mother's account of what passed at it would only annoy and chagrin him, though he would all the time be aware of the colouring which it received by passing though her mind. He shrank from hearing Margaret's very name mentioned; he, while he blamed her—while he was jealous of her—while he renounced her—he loved her sorely, in spite of himself. He dreamt of her; he dreamt she came dancing towards him with outspread arms, and with a lightness and gaiety which made him loathe her, even while it allured him. But the impression of this figure of Margaret—with all Margaret's character taken out of it, as completely as if some evil spirit had got possession of her form—was so deeply stamped upon his imagination, that when he wakened he felt hardly able to separate the Una from the Duessa,[2] and the dislike he had to the latter seemed to envelope and disfigure the former. Yet

---

2. The contrasted images of woman in Spenser's *Faerie Queene*, bk. 1. They have multiple allegorical significance: Una, who is indivisible, represents truth; Duessa, duality and false-hood. In Spenser's poem Duessa appears to the Red Cross Knight in the image of Una, thus deceiving him.

he was too proud to acknowledge his weakness by avoiding the sight of her. He would neither seek an opportunity of being in her company nor avoid it. To convince himself of his power of self-control, he lingered over every piece of business this afternoon; he forced every movement into unnatural slowness and deliberation; and it was consequently past eight o'clock before he reached Mr. Hale's. Then there were business arrangements to be transacted in the study with Mr. Bell; and the latter kept on, sitting over the fire, and talking wearily, long after all business was transacted, and when they might just as well have gone upstairs. But Mr. Thornton would not say a word about moving their quarters; he chafed and chafed, and thought Mr. Bell a most prosy companion; while Mr. Bell returned the compliment in secret, by considering Mr. Thornton about as brusque and curt a fellow as he had ever met with, and terribly gone off both in intelligence and manner. At last, some slight noise in the room above suggested the desirableness of moving there. They found Margaret with a letter open before her, eagerly discussing its contents with her father. On the entrance of the gentlemen, it was immediately put aside; but Mr. Thornton's eager senses caught some few words of Mr. Hale's to Mr. Bell.

"A letter from Henry Lennox. It makes Margaret very hopeful."

Mr. Bell nodded. Margaret was red as a rose[3] when Mr. Thornton looked at her. He had the greatest mind in the world to get up and go out of the room that very instant, and never set foot in the house again.

"We were thinking," said Mr. Hale, "that you and Mr. Thornton had taken Margaret's advice, and were each trying to convert the other, you were so long in the study."

"And you thought there would be nothing left of us but an opinion, like the Kilkenny cat's tail.[4] Pray whose opinion did you think would have the most obstinate vitality?"

Mr. Thornton had not a notion what they were talking about, and disdained to inquire. Mr. Hale politely enlightened him.

"Mr. Thornton, we were accusing Mr. Bell this morning of a kind of Oxonian mediæval bigotry[5] against his native town; and we—Margaret, I believe—suggested that it would do him good to associate a little with Milton manufacturers."

"I beg your pardon. Margaret thought it would do the Milton man-

---

3. The echo is of Coleridge's *Rime of the Ancient Mariner*, stanza 9: "The bride hath paced into the hall, / Red as a rose is she."
4. A reference to a popular story of two cats from Kilkenny, Ireland, who fought until their tails and claws were all that was left of them.
5. "Oxonian" means associated with Oxford University. In the Victorian period the university was often associated with medievalism, a charge that was accepted, even welcomed, by members of the university themselves.

ufacturers good to associate a little more with Oxford men. Now wasn't it so, Margaret?"

"I believe I thought it would do both good to see a little more of the other,—I did not know it was my idea any more than papa's."

"And so you see, Mr. Thornton, we ought to have been improving each other down-stairs, instead of talking over vanished families of Smiths and Harrisons. However, I am willing to do my part now. I wonder when you Milton men intend to live. All your lives seem to be spent in gathering together the materials for life."

"By living, I suppose you mean enjoyment."

"Yes, enjoyment,—I don't specify of what, because I trust we should both consider mere pleasure as very poor enjoyment."

"I would rather have the nature of the enjoyment defined."

"Well! enjoyment of leisure—enjoyment of the power and influence which money gives. You are all striving for money. What do you want it for?"

Mr. Thornton was silent. Then he said, "I really don't know. But money is not what I strive for."

"What then?"

"It is a home question.[6] I shall have to lay myself open to such a catechist, and I am not sure that I am prepared to do it."

"No!" said Mr. Hale; "don't let us be personal in our catechism. You are neither of you representative men; you are each of you too individual for that."

"I am not sure whether to consider that as a compliment or not. I should like to be the representative of Oxford, with its beauty and its learning, and its proud old history. What do you say, Margaret; ought I to be flattered?"

"I don't know Oxford. But there is a difference between being the representative of a city and the representative man of its inhabitants."

"Very true, Miss Margaret. Now I remember, you were against me this morning, and were quite Miltonian and manufacturing in your preferences." Margaret saw the quick glance of surprise that Mr. Thornton gave her, and she was annoyed at the construction which he might put on this speech of Mr. Bell's. Mr. Bell went on—

"Ah! I wish I could show you our High Street—our Radcliffe Square. I am leaving out our colleges, just as I give Mr. Thornton leave to omit his factories in speaking of the charms of Milton. I have a right to abuse my birth-place. Remember I am a Milton man."

Mr. Thornton was annoyed more than he ought to have been at all that Mr. Bell was saying. He was not in a mood for joking. At

6. I.e., a personal matter.

another time, he could have enjoyed Mr. Bell's half testy condemnation of a town where the life was so at variance with every habit he had formed; but now, he was galled enough to attempt to defend what was never meant to be seriously attacked.

"I don't set up Milton as a model of a town."

"Not in architecture?" slyly asked Mr. Bell.

"No! We've been too busy to attend to mere outward appearances."

"Don't say *mere* outward appearances," said Mr. Hale, gently. "They impress us all, from childhood upward—every day of our life."

"Wait a little while," said Mr. Thornton. "Remember, we are of a different race from the Greeks, to whom beauty was everything, and to whom Mr. Bell might speak of a life of leisure and serene enjoyment, much of which entered in through their outward senses. I don't mean to despise them, any more than I would ape them. But I belong to Teutonic blood; it is little mingled in this part of England to what it is in others; we retain much of their language; we retain more of their spirit; we do not look upon life as a time for enjoyment, but as a time for action and exertion. Our glory and our beauty arise out of our inward strength, which makes us victorious over material resistance, and over greater difficulties still. We are Teutonic up here in Darkshire in another way. We hate to have laws made for us at a distance. We wish people would allow us to right ourselves, instead of continually meddling, with their imperfect legislation. We stand up for self-government, and oppose centralisation."

"In short, you would like the Heptarchy[7] back again. Well, at any rate, I revoke what I said this morning—that you Milton people did not reverence the past. You are regular worshippers of Thor."[8]

"If we do not reverence the past as you do in Oxford, it is because we want something which can apply to the present more directly. It is fine when the study of the past leads to a prophecy of the future. But to men groping in new circumstances, it would be finer if the words of experience could direct us how to act in what concerns us most intimately and immediately; which is full of difficulties that must be encountered; and upon the mode in which they are met and conquered—not merely pushed aside for the time—depends our future. Out of the wisdom of the past, help us over the present. But no! People can speak of Utopia much more easily than of the next day's duty; and yet when that duty is all done by others, who so ready to cry, 'Fie, for shame!' "

"And all this time I don't see what you are talking about. Would

---

7. The seven ancient kingdoms of Anglo-Saxon England, which preserved their individual rights within a system of loosely associated government. Thornton's arguments are against centralized government and reflect a view prevalent among northern manufacturers at the time.

8. The Norse god of thunder; thus "worshippers of power."

you Milton men condescend to send up your to-day's difficulty to Oxford? You have not tried us yet."

Mr. Thornton laughed outright at this. "I believe I was talking with reference to a good deal that has been troubling us of late; I was thinking of the strikes we have gone through, which are troublesome and injurious things enough, as I am finding to my cost. And yet this last strike, under which I am smarting, has been respectable."

"A respectable strike!" said Mr. Bell. "That sounds as if you were far gone in the worship of Thor."

Margaret felt, rather than saw, that Mr. Thornton was chagrined by the repeated turning into jest of what he was feeling as very serious. She tried to change the conversation from a subject about which one party cared little, while, to the other, it was deeply, because personally, interesting. She forced herself to say something.

"Edith says she finds the printed calicoes in Corfu better and cheaper than in London."

"Does she?" said her father. "I think that must be one of Edith's exaggerations. Are you sure of it, Margaret?"

"I am sure she says so, papa."

"Then I am sure of the fact," said Mr. Bell. "Margaret, I go so far in my idea of your truthfulness, that it shall cover your cousin's character. I don't believe a cousin of yours could exaggerate."

"Is Miss Hale so remarkable for truth?" said Mr. Thornton, bitterly. The moment he had done so, he could have bitten his tongue out. What was he? And why should he stab her with her shame in this way? How evil he was to-night; possessed by ill-humour at being detained so long from her; irritated by the mention of some name, because he thought it belonged to a more successful lover; now ill-tempered because he had been unable to cope, with a light heart, against one who was trying, by gay and careless speeches, to make the evening pass pleasantly away,—the kind old friend to all parties, whose manner by this time might be well known to Mr. Thornton, who had been acquainted with him for many years. And then to speak to Margaret as he had done! She did not get up and leave the room, as she had done in former days, when his abruptness or his temper had annoyed her. She sat quite still, after the first momentary glance of grieved surprise, that made her eyes look like some child's who has met with an unexpected rebuff; they slowly dilated into mournful, reproachful sadness; and then they fell, and she bent over her work, and did not speak again. But he could not help looking at her, and he saw a sigh tremble over her body, as if she quivered in some unwonted chill. He felt as the mother would have done in the midst of "her rocking it, and rating it,"[9] had she been called away

9. Rocking and reproving it. The allusion is to a poem by Richard Edwards (c. 1523–1566), "In going to my naked bed," from *Paradise of Dainty Devices* (1576). The poem draws an

before her slow confiding smile, implying perfect trust in mother's love, had proved the renewing of its love. He gave short sharp answers; he was uneasy and cross, unable to discern between jest and earnest; anxious only for a look, a word of hers, before which to prostrate himself in penitent humility. But she neither looked nor spoke. Her round taper fingers flew in and out of her sewing, as steadily and swiftly as if that were the business of her life. She could not care for him, he thought, or else the passionate fervour of his wish would have forced her to raise those eyes, if but for an instant, to read the late repentance in his. He could have struck her before he left, in order that by some strange overt act of rudeness, he might earn the privilege of telling her the remorse that gnawed at his heart. It was well that the long walk in the open air wound up this evening for him. It sobered him back into grave resolution, that henceforth he would see as little of her as possible,—since the very sight of that face and form, the very sounds of that voice (like the soft winds of pure melody) had such power to move him from his balance. Well! He had known what love was—a sharp pang, a fierce experience, in the midst of whose flames he was struggling! but, through that furnace he would fight his way out into the serenity of middle age,— all the richer and more human for having known this great passion.

When he had somewhat abruptly left the room, Margaret rose from her seat, and began silently to fold up her work. The long seams were heavy, and had an unusual weight for her languid arms. The round lines in her face took a lengthened, straighter form, and her whole appearance was that of one who had gone through a day of great fatigue. As the three prepared for bed; Mr. Bell muttered forth a little condemnation of Mr. Thornton.

"I never saw a fellow so spoiled by success. He can't bear a word; a jest of any kind. Everything seems to touch on the soreness of his high dignity. Formerly, he was as simple and noble as the open day; you could not offend him, because he had no vanity."

"He is not vain now," said Margaret, turning round from the table, and speaking with quiet distinctness. "To-night he has not been like himself. Something must have annoyed him before he came here."

Mr. Bell gave her one of his sharp glances from above his spectacles. She stood it quite calmly; but, after she had left the room, he suddenly asked,—

"Hale! did it ever strike you that Thornton and your daughter have what the French call a tendresse for each other?"

"Never!" said Mr. Hale, first startled and then flurried by the new

---

analogy between a mother's love for a child she has nursed to sleep and reconciliation between friends who have had a disagreement: "She rocked and rated it till that it on her smiled / . . . / The falling out of faithful friends, renewing is of love." It thus has a wider application to the theme of Thornton's love for Margaret.

idea. "No, I am sure you are wrong. I am almost certain you are mistaken. If there is anything, it is all on Mr. Thornton's side. Poor fellow! I hope and trust he is not thinking of her, for I am sure she would not have him."

"Well! I'm a bachelor, and have steered clear of love affairs all my life; so perhaps my opinion is not worth having. Or else I should say there were very pretty symptoms about her!"

"Then I am sure you are wrong," said Mr. Hale. "He may care for her, though she really has been almost rude to him at times. But she!—why, Margaret would never think of him, I'm sure! Such a thing has never entered her head."

"Entering her heart would do. But I merely threw out a suggestion of what might be. I dare say I was wrong. And whether I was wrong or right, I'm very sleepy; so, having disturbed your night's rest (as I can see) with my untimely fancies, I'll betake myself with an easy mind to my own."

But Mr. Hale resolved that he would not be disturbed by any such nonsensical idea; so he lay awake, determining not to think about it.

Mr. Bell took his leave the next day, bidding Margaret look to him as one who had a right to help and protect her in all her troubles, of whatever nature they might be. To Mr. Hale he said,—

"That Margaret of yours has gone deep into my heart. Take care of her, for she is a very precious creature,—a great deal too good for Milton,—only fit for Oxford, in fact. The town, I mean; not the men. I can't match her yet. When I can, I shall bring my young man to stand side by side with your young woman, just as the genie in the Arabian nights brought Prince Caralmazan to match with the fairy's Princess Badoura."[1]

"I beg you'll do no such thing. Remember the misfortunes that ensued; and besides, I can't spare Margaret."

"No; on second thoughts, we'll have her to nurse us ten years hence, when we shall be two cross old invalids. Seriously, Hale! I wish you'd leave Milton; which is a most unsuitable place for you, though it was my recommendation in the first instance. If you would, I'd swallow my shadows of doubts, and take a college living; and you and Margaret should come and live at the parsonage—you to be a sort of lay curate, and take the unwashed off my hands; and she to be our housekeeper—the village Lady Bountiful—by day; and read us to sleep in the evenings. I could be very happy in such a life. What do you think of it?"

"Never!" said Mr. Hale, decidedly. "My one great change has been made and my price of suffering paid. Here I stay out my life; and here will I be buried, and lost in the crowd."

1. In the story referred to, the prince and the princess are brought together, separated, and then united by magical means.

"I don't give up my plan yet. Only I won't bait you with it any more just now. Where's the Pearl?[2] Come, Margaret, give me a farewell kiss; and remember, my dear, where you may find a true friend, as far as his capability goes. You are my child, Margaret. Remember that, and God bless you!"

So they fell back into the monotony of the quiet life they would henceforth lead. There was no invalid to hope and fear about; even the Higginses—so long a vivid interest—seemed to have receded from any need of immediate thought. The Boucher children, left motherless orphans, claimed what of Margaret's care she could bestow; and she went pretty often to see Mary Higgins, who had charge of them. The two families were living in one house: the elder children were at humble schools, the younger ones were tended, in Mary's absence at her work, by the kind neighbour whose good sense had struck Margaret at the time of Boucher's death. Of course she was paid for her trouble; and indeed, in all his little plans and arrangements for these orphan children, Nicholas showed a sober judgment, and regulated method of thinking, which were at variance with his former more eccentric jerks of action. He was so steady at his work, that Margaret did not often see him during these winter months; but when she did, she saw that he winced away from any reference to the father of those children, whom he had so fully and heartily taken under his care. He did not speak easily of Mr. Thornton.

"To tell the truth," said he, "he fairly bamboozles me. He's two chaps. One chap I knowed of old as were measter all o'er. T'other chap hasn't an ounce of measter's flesh about him. How them two chaps is bound up in one body, is a craddy[3] for me to find out. I'll not be beat by it, though. Meanwhile he comes here pretty often; that's how I know the chap that's a man, not a measter. And I reckon he's taken aback by me pretty much as I am by him; for he sits and listens and stares, as if I were some strange beast newly caught in some of the zones. But I'm none daunted. It would take a deal to daunt me in my own house, as he sees. And I tell him some of my mind that I reckon he'd ha' been the better of hearing when he were a younger man."

"And does he not answer you?" asked Mr. Hale.

"Well! I'll not say th' advantage is all on his side, for all I take credit for improving him above a bit. Sometimes he says a rough thing or two, which is not agreeable to look at at first, but has a queer smack o' truth in it when yo' come to chew it. He'll be coming

2. The name Margaret is derived from the Greek for "pearl": the two Oxford scholars would understand the allusion.
3. A puzzle.

to-night, I reckon, about them childer's schooling. He's not satisfied wi' the make of it, and wants for t' examine 'em."

"What are they"—began Mr. Hale; but Margaret, touching his arm, showed him her watch.

"It is nearly seven," she said. "The evenings are getting longer now. Come, papa." She did not breathe freely till they were some distance from the house. Then, as she became more calm, she wished that she had not been in so great a hurry; for, somehow, they saw Mr. Thornton but very seldom now; and he might have come to see Higgins, and for the old friendship's sake she should like to have seen him to-night.

Yes! he came very seldom, even for the dull cold purpose of lessons. Mr. Hale was disappointed in his pupil's lukewarmness about Greek literature, which had but a short time ago so great an interest for him. And now it often happened that a hurried note from Mr. Thornton would arrive, just at the last moment, saying that he was so much engaged that he could not come to read with Mr. Hale that evening. And though other pupils had taken more than his place as to time, no one was like his first scholar in Mr. Hale's heart. He was depressed and sad at this partial cessation of an intercourse which had become dear to him; and he used to sit pondering over the reason that could have occasioned this change.

He startled Margaret, one evening as she sat at her work, by suddenly asking:

"Margaret! had you ever any reason for thinking that Mr. Thornton cared for you?"

He almost blushed as he put this question; but Mr. Bell's scouted idea recurred to him, and the words were out of his mouth before he well knew what he was about.

Margaret did not answer immediately; but by the bent drooping of her head, he guessed what her reply would be.

"Yes; I believe—oh papa, I should have told you." And she dropped her work, and hid her face in her hands.

"No, dear; don't think that I am impertinently curious. I am sure you would have told me if you had felt that you could return his regard. Did he speak to you about it?"

No answer at first; but by-and-by a little gentle reluctant "Yes."

"And you refused him?"

A long sigh; a more helpless, nerveless attitude, and another "Yes." But before her father could speak, Margaret lifted up her face, rosy with some beautiful shame, and, fixing her eyes upon him, said:

"Now, papa, I have told you this, and I cannot tell you more; and then the whole thing is so painful to me; every word and action connected with it is so unspeakably bitter, that I cannot bear to think of it. Oh, papa, I am sorry to have lost you this friend, but I could not help it—but oh! I am very sorry." She sat down on the ground, and laid her head on his knees.

"I too, am sorry, my dear. Mr. Bell quite startled me when he said, some idea of the kind—"

"Mr. Bell! Oh did Mr. Bell see it?"

"A little; but he took it into his head that you—how shall I say it?—that you were not ungraciously disposed towards Mr. Thornton, I knew that could never be. I hoped the whole thing was but an imagination; but I knew too well what your real feelings were to suppose that you could ever like Mr. Thornton in that way. But I am very sorry."

They were very quiet and still for some minutes. But, on stroking her cheek in a caressing way soon after, he was almost shocked to find her face wet with tears. As he touched her, she sprang up, and smiling with forced brightness, began to talk of the Lennoxes with such a vehement desire to turn the conversation, that Mr. Hale was too tender-hearted to try to force it back into the old channel.

"To-morrow—yes, to-morrow they will be back in Harley Street. Oh, how strange it will be! I wonder what room they will make into the nursery? Aunt Shaw will be happy with the baby. Fancy Edith a mamma! And Captain Lennox—I wonder what he will do with himself now he has sold out!"

"I'll tell you what," said her father, anxious to indulge her in this fresh subject of interest, "I think I must spare you for a fortnight just to run up to town and see the travellers. You could learn more, by half an hour's conversation with Mr. Henry Lennox, about Frederick's chances, than in a dozen of these letters of his; so it would, in fact, be uniting business with pleasure."

"No, papa, you cannot spare me, and what's more, I won't be spared." Then after a pause, she added: "I am losing hope sadly about Frederick; he is letting us down gently, but I can see that Mr. Lennox himself has no hope of hunting up the witnesses under years and years of time. No," said she, "that bubble was very pretty, and very dear to our hearts; but it has burst like many another; and we must console ourselves with being glad that Frederick is so happy, and with being a great deal to each other. So don't offend me by talking of being able to spare me, papa, for I assure you you can't."

But the idea of a change took root and germinated in Margaret's heart, although not in the way in which her father proposed it at first. She began to consider how desirable something of the kind would be to her father, whose spirits, always feeble, now became too frequently depressed, and whose health, though he never complained, had been seriously affected by his wife's illness and death. There were the regular hours of reading with his pupils, but that all giving and no receiving could no longer be called companionship, as in the old days when Mr. Thornton came to study under him. Margaret was conscious of the want under which he was suffering, unknown to himself; the want of a man's intercourse with men. At Helstone there had been perpetual occasion for an interchange of visits with neighbouring clergymen; and the poor labourers in the fields, or leisurely tramping home at eve, or tending their cattle in the forest, were always at liberty to speak or be spoken to. But in Milton every one was too busy for quiet speech, or any ripened intercourse of thought; what they said was about business, very present and actual; and when the tension of mind relating to their daily affairs was over, they sunk into fallow rest until next morning. The workman was not to be found after the day's work was done; he had gone away to some lecture, or some club, or some beer-shop, according to his degree of character. Mr. Hale thought of trying to deliver a course of lectures at some of the institutions, but he contemplated doing this so much as an effort of duty, and with so little of the genial impulse of love towards his work and its end, that Margaret was sure that it would not be well done until he could look upon it with some kind of zest.

Chapter XVI.

The Journey's End.

> I see my way as birds their trackless way—
> I shall arrive! what time, what circuit first,
> I ask not; but unless God send his hail
> Or blinding fire-balls, sleet, or stifling snow,
> In some time—his good time—I shall arrive;
> He guides me and the bird. In His good time!
>   BROWNING'S PARACELSUS.[1]

So the winter was getting on, and the days were beginning to lengthen, without bringing with them any of the brightness of hope which usually accompanies the rays of a February sun. Mrs. Thornton had of course entirely ceased to come to the house. Mr. Thornton came occasionally, but his visits were addressed to her father, and were confined to the study. Mr. Hale spoke of him as always the same; indeed, the very rarity of their intercourse seemed to make Mr. Hale set only the higher value on it. And from what Margaret could gather of what Mr. Thornton had said, there was nothing in the cessation of his visits which could arise from any umbrage or

---

1. The quotation, from Browning's early poem *Paracelsus* (1835), relates to the content of the chapter in that it anticipates the conclusion of Hale's spiritual quest.

vexation. His business affairs had become complicated during the strike, and required closer attention than he had given to them last winter. Nay, Margaret could even discover that he spoke from time to time of her, and always, as far as she could learn, in the same calm friendly way, never avoiding and never seeking any mention of her name.

She was not in spirits to raise her father's tone of mind. The dreary peacefulness of the present time had been preceded by so long a period of anxiety and care—even intermixed with storms—that her mind had lost its elasticity. She tried to find herself occupation in teaching the two younger Boucher children, and worked hard at goodness; hard, I say most truly, for her heart seemed dead to the end of all her efforts; and though she made them punctually and painfully, yet she stood as far off as ever from any cheerfulness; her life seemed still bleak and dreary. The only thing she did well, was what she did out of unconscious piety, the silent comforting and consoling of her father. Not a mood of his but what found a ready sympathiser in Margaret; not a wish of his that she did not strive to forecast, and to fulfil. They were quiet wishes to be sure, and hardly named without hesitation and apology. All the more complete and beautiful was her meek spirit of obedience. March brought the news of Frederick's marriage. He and Dolores wrote; she in Spanish-English, as was but natural, and he with little turns and inversions of words which proved how far the idioms of his bride's country were infecting him.

On the receipt of Henry Lennox's letter, announcing how little hope there was of his ever clearing himself at a court-martial, in the absence of the missing witnesses, Frederick had written to Margaret a pretty vehement letter, containing his renunciation of England as his country; he wished he could unnative himself, and declared that he would not take his pardon if it were offered him, nor live in the country if he had permission to do so. All of which made Margaret cry sorely, so unnatural did it seem to her at the first opening; but on consideration, she saw rather in such expression the poignancy of the disappointment which had thus crushed his hopes; and she felt that there was nothing for it but patience. In the next letter, Frederick spoke so joyfully of the future that he had no thought for the past; and Margaret found a use in herself for the patience she had been craving for him. She would have to be patient. But the pretty, timid, girlish letters of Dolores were beginning to have a charm for both Margaret and her father. The young Spaniard was so evidently anxious to make a favourable impression upon her lover's English relations, that her feminine care peeped out at every erasure; and the letters announcing the marriage, were accompanied by a splendid black lace mantilla, chosen by Dolores herself for her

unseen sister-in-law, whom Frederick had represented as a paragon
of beauty, wisdom and virtue. Frederick's worldly position was raised
by this marriage on to as high a level as they could desire. Barbour
and Co. was one of the most extensive Spanish houses, and into it
he was received as a junior partner. Margaret smiled a little, and
then sighed as she remembered afresh her old tirades against trade.
Here was her preux chevalier[2] of a brother turned merchant, trader!
But then she rebelled against herself, and protested silently against
the confusion implied between a Spanish merchant and a Milton
millowner. Well! trade or no trade, Frederick was very, very happy.
Dolores must be charming, and the mantilla was exquisite! And then
she returned to the present life.

Her father had occasionally experienced a difficulty in breathing
this spring, which had for the time distressed him exceedingly. Margaret was less alarmed, as this difficulty went off completely in the
intervals; but she still was so desirous of his shaking off the liability
altogether, as to make her very urgent that he should accept Mr.
Bell's invitation to visit him at Oxford this April. Mr. Bell's invitation
included Margaret. Nay more, he wrote a special letter commanding
her to come; but she felt as if it would be a greater relief to her to
remain quietly at home, entirely free from any responsibility whatever, and so to rest her mind and heart in a manner which she had
not been able to do for more than two years past.

When her father had driven off on his way to the railroad, Margaret felt how great and long had been the pressure on her time and
her spirits. It was astonishing, almost stunning, to feel herself so
much at liberty; no one depending on her for cheering care, if not
for positive happiness; no invalid to plan and think for; she might be
idle, and silent, and forgetful,—and what seemed worth more than
all the other privileges—she might be unhappy if she liked. For
months past, all her own personal cares and troubles had had to be
stuffed away into a dark cupboard; but now she had leisure to take
them out, and mourn over them, and study their nature, and seek
the true method of subduing them into the elements of peace. All
these weeks she had been conscious of their existence in a dull kind
of way, though they were hidden out of sight. Now, once for all she
would consider them, and appoint to each of them its right work in
her life. So she sat almost motionless for hours in the drawing-room,
going over the bitterness of every remembrance with an unwincing
resolution. Only once she cried aloud, at the stinging thought of the
faithlessness which gave birth to that abasing falsehood.

She now would not even acknowledge the force of the temptation;
her plans for Frederick had all failed, and the temptation lay there

2. Valiant knight (French).

a dead mockery,—a mockery which had never had life in it; the lie
had been so despicably foolish, seen by the light of the ensuing
events, and faith in the power of truth so infinitely the greater wisdom!

In her nervous agitation, she unconsciously opened a book of her
father's that lay upon the table,—the words that caught her eye
in it, seemed almost made for her present state of acute self-
abasement:—

> "Je ne voudrois pas reprendre mon cœur en ceste sorte: meurs
> de honte, aveugle, impudent, traistre et desloyal à ton Dieu, et
> sembables choses; mais je voudrois le corriger par voye de com-
> passion. Or sus, mon pauvre cœur, nous voilà tombez dans la
> fosse, laquelle nous avions tant resolu d'eschapper. Ah!
> relevons-nous, et quittons-la pour jamais, reclamons la miseri-
> corde de Dieu, et esperons en elle qu'elle nous assistera pour
> desormais estre plus fermes; et remettons-nous au chemin de
> l'humilitè. Courage, soyons meshuy sur nos gardes, Dieu nous
> aydera."[3]

"The way of humility. Ah," thought Margaret, "that is what I have
missed! But courage, little heart. We will turn back, and by God's
help we may find the lost path."

So she rose up, and determined at once to set to on some work
which should take her out of herself. To begin with, she called in
Martha, as she passed the drawing-room door in going up-stairs, and
tried to find out what was below the grave, respectful, servant-like
manner, which crusted over her individual character with an obedience that was almost mechanical. She found it difficult to induce
Martha to speak of any of her personal interests; but at last she
touched the right chord, in naming Mrs. Thornton. Martha's whole
face brightened, and, on a little encouragement, out came a long
story, of how her father had been in early life connected with Mrs.
Thornton's husband—nay, had even been in a position to show him
some kindness; what, Martha hardly knew, for it had happened when
she was quite a little child; and circumstances had intervened to
separate the two families until Martha was nearly grown up, when,
her father having sunk lower and lower from his original occupation
as clerk in a warehouse, and her mother being dead, she and her

---

3. "I should not like to chide my heart in this manner, saying, 'Die of shame in your blind,
insolent and treacherous disloyalty to your God,' and suchlike things; but I would wish to
set it right by means of compassion, saying, 'Now then, my poor heart, here we are fallen
into the pit which we had so determined to avoid. Ah! let us seek the light and leave this
pit for ever; let us crave the mercy of God and hope that it will help us henceforth to be
more resolute; let us seek once more the way of humility. Courage, may we be henceforth
on our guard. God will help us!' " (French). From *An Introduction to the Devout Life* (1608)
III. 9, by the mystic, St. Francis de Sales (1567–1622), trans. Elfrieda Dubois for *Easson
1973*. The quotation retains the original seventeenth-century French. An English translation of the work was published in 1848.

sister, to use Martha's own expression, would have been "lost" but
for Mrs. Thornton; who sought them out, and thought for them, and
cared for them.

"I had had the fever, and was but delicate; and Mrs. Thornton,
and Mr. Thornton too, they never rested till they had nursed me up
in their own house, and sent me to the sea and all. The doctors said
the fever was catching, but they cared none for that—only Miss
Fanny, and she went a-visiting these folk that she is going to marry
into. So, though she was afraid at the time, it has all ended well."

"Miss Fanny going to be married!" exclaimed Margaret.

"Yes; and to a rich gentleman, too, only he's a deal older than she
is. His name is Watson; and his mills are somewhere out beyond
Hayleigh; it's a very good marriage, for all he's got such gray hair."

At this piece of information, Margaret was silent long enough for
Martha to recover her propriety, and, with it, her habitual shortness
of answer. She swept up the hearth, asked at what time she should
prepare tea, and quitted the room with the same wooden face with
which she had entered it. Margaret had to pull herself up from
indulging a bad trick, which she had lately fallen into, of trying to
imagine how every event that she heard of in relation to Mr. Thornton would affect him: whether he would like it or dislike it.

The next day she had the little Boucher children for their lessons,
and took a long walk, and ended by a visit to Mary Higgins. Somewhat to Margaret's surprise, she found Nicholas already come home
from his work; the lengthening light had deceived her as to the late-
ness of the evening. He too seemed, by his manners, to have entered
a little more on the way of humility; he was quieter, and less self-
asserting.

"So th' oud gentleman's away on his travels, is he?" said he. "Little
'uns told me so. Eh! but the're sharp 'uns, they are; I a'most think
they beat my own wenches for sharpness, though mappen it's wrong
to say so, and one on 'em in her grave. There's summut in th' weather,
I reckon, as sets folk a-wandering. My measter, him at th' shop yonder, is spinning about th' world somewhere."

"Is that the reason you're so soon at home to-night?" asked Margaret innocently.

"Thou know'st nought about it, that's all," said he, contemptuously. "I'm not one wi' two faces—one for my measter, and t'other
for his back. I counted a' th' clocks in the town striking afore I'd
leave my work. No! yon Thornton's good enough for to fight wi', but
too good for to be cheated. It were you as getten me the place, and
I thank yo' for it. Thornton's is not a bad mill, as times go. Stand
down, lad, and say yo'r pretty hymn to Miss Marget. That's right;
steady on thy legs, and right arm out as straight as a skewer. One to
stop, two to stay, three mak' ready, and four away!"

The little fellow repeated a Methodist hymn, far above his comprehension in point of language, but of which the swinging rhythm had caught his ear, and which he repeated with all the developed cadence of a member of parliament. When Margaret had duly applauded, Nicholas called for another, and yet another, much to her surprise, as she found him thus oddly and unconsciously led to take an interest in the sacred things which he had formerly scouted.

It was past the usual tea-time when she reached home; but she had the comfort of feeling that no one had been kept waiting for her; and of thinking her own thoughts while she rested, instead of anxiously watching another person to learn whether to be grave or gay. After tea she resolved to examine a large packet of letters, and pick out those that were to be destroyed.

Among them she came to four or five of Mr. Henry Lennox's, relating to Frederick's affairs; and she carefully read them over again, with the sole intention, when she began, to ascertain exactly on how fine a chance the justification of her brother hung. But when she had finished the last, and weighed the pros and cons, the little personal revelation of character contained in them forced itself on her notice. It was evident enough, from the stiffness of the wording, that Mr. Lennox had never forgotten his relation to her in any interest he might feel in the subject of the correspondence. They were clever letters; Margaret saw that in a twinkling; but she missed out of them all hearty and genial atmosphere. They were to be preserved, however, as valuable; so she laid them carefully on one side. When this little piece of business was ended, she fell into a reverie; and the thought of her absent father ran strangely in Margaret's head this night. She almost blamed herself for having felt her solitude (and consequently his absence) as a relief; but these two days had set her up afresh, with new strength and brighter hope. Plans which had lately appeared to her in the guise of tasks, now appeared like pleasures. The morbid scales had fallen from her eyes, and she saw her position and her work more truly. If only Mr. Thornton would restore her the lost friendship,—nay, if he would only come from time to time to cheer her father as in former days,—though she should never see him, she felt as if the course of her future life, though not brilliant in prospect, might lie clear and even before her. She sighed as she rose up to go to bed. In spite of the "One step's enough for me,"[4]—in spite of the one plain duty of devotion to her father,— there lay at her heart an anxiety and a pang of sorrow.

And Mr. Hale thought of Margaret, that April evening, just as

---

4. A slight misquotation of Cardinal Newman's poem "The Pillar of the Cloud," better known as the hymn "Lead kindly light," written in 1833: "I do not ask to see / The distant scene; one step enough for me." Newman's poem is about his own spiritual journey, and the quotation thus reinforces the chapter motto. (See n.1 above.)

strangely and as persistently as she was thinking of him. He had been fatigued by going about among his old friends and old familiar places. He had had exaggerated ideas of the change which his altered opinions might make in his friends' reception of him; but although some of them might have felt shocked or grieved, or indignant at his falling off in the abstract, as soon as they saw the face of the man whom they had once loved, they forgot his opinions in himself; or only remembered them enough to give an additional tender gravity to their manner. For Mr. Hale had not been known to many; he had belonged to one of the smaller colleges, and had always been shy and reserved; but those who in youth had cared to penetrate to the delicacy of thought and feeling that lay below his silence and indecision, took him to their hearts, with something of the protecting kindness which they would have shown to a woman. And the renewal of this kindliness, after the lapse of years, and an interval of so much change, overpowered him more than any roughness or expression of disapproval could have done.

"I'm afraid we've done too much," said Mr. Bell. "You're suffering now from having lived so long in that Milton air."

"I am tired," said Mr. Hale. "But it is not Milton air. I'm fifty-five years of age, and that little fact of itself accounts for any loss of strength."

"Nonsense! I'm upwards of sixty, and feel no loss of strength, either bodily or mental. Don't let me hear you talking so. Fifty-five! why, you're quite a young man."

Mr. Hale shook his head. "These last few years!" said he. But after a minute's pause, he raised himself from his half recumbent position, in one of Mr. Bell's luxurious easy-chairs, and said with a kind of trembling earnestness:

"Bell! you're not to think, that if I could have foreseen all that would come of my change of opinion, and my resignation of my living—no! not even if I could have known how *she* would have suffered,—that I would undo it—the act of open acknowledgment that I no longer held the same faith as the church in which I was a priest. As I think now, even if I could have foreseen that cruellest martyrdom of suffering, through the sufferings of one whom I loved, I would have done just the same as far as that step of openly leaving the church went. I might have done differently, and acted more wisely, in all that I subsequently did for my family. But I don't think God endued me with over-much wisdom or strength," he added, falling back into his old position.

Mr. Bell blew his nose ostentatiously before answering. Then he said:

"He gave you strength to do what your conscience told you was right; and I don't see that we need any higher or holier strength than that; or wisdom either. I know I have not that much; and yet men set me down in their fool's books as a wise man; an independent character; strong-minded, and all that cant. The veriest idiot who obeys his own simple law of right, if it be but in wiping his shoes on a door-mat, is wiser and stronger than I. But what gulls men are!"

There was a pause. Mr. Hale spoke first, in continuation of his thought:

"About Margaret."

"Well! about Margaret. What then?"

"If I die——"

"Nonsense!"

"What will become of her—I often think? I suppose the Lennoxes will ask her to live with them. I try to think they will. Her aunt Shaw loved her well in her own quiet way; but she forgets to love the absent."

"A very common fault. What sort of people are the Lennoxes?"

"He, handsome, fluent, and agreeable. Edith, a sweet little spoiled beauty. Margaret loves her with all her heart, and Edith with as much of her heart as she can spare."

"Now, Hale; you know that girl of yours has got pretty nearly all my heart. I told you that before. Of course, as your daughter, as my god-daughter, I took great interest in her before I saw her the last time. But this visit that I paid to you at Milton made me her slave. I went, a willing old victim, following the car of the conqueror. For, indeed, she looks as grand and serene as one who has struggled, and may be struggling, and yet has the victory secure in sight. Yes, in spite of all her present anxieties, that was the look on her face. And so, all I have is at her service, if she needs it; and will be hers, whether she will or no, when I die. Moreover, I myself, will be her preux chevalier, sixty and gouty though I be. Seriously, old friend, your daughter shall be my principal charge in life, and all the help that either my wit or my wisdom or my willing heart can give, shall be hers. I don't choose her out as a subject for fretting. Something, I know of old, you must have to worry yourself about, or you wouldn't be happy. But you're going to outlive me by many a long year. You, spare, thin men are always tempting and always cheating Death! It's the stout, florid fellows like me, that always go off first."

If Mr. Bell had had a prophetic eye he might have seen the torch all but inverted, and the angel with the grave and composed face standing very nigh, beckoning to his friend. That night Mr. Hale laid his head down on the pillow on which it never more should stir with life. The servant who entered his room in the morning, received no answer to his speech; drew near the bed, and saw the calm, beautiful face lying white and cold under the ineffaceable seal of death. The attitude was exquisitely easy; there had been no pain—no struggle. The action of the heart must have ceased as he lay down.

Mr. Bell was stunned by the shock; and only recovered when the time came for being angry at every suggestion of his man's.

"A coroner's inquest? Pooh. You don't think I poisoned him! Dr. Forbes says it is just the natural end of a heart complaint. Poor old Hale! You wore out that tender heart of yours before its time. Poor old friend! how he talked of his——Wallis, pack up a carpet-bag for me in five minutes. Here have I been talking. Pack it up, I say. I must go to Milton by the next train."

The bag was packed, the cab ordered, the railway reached, in twenty minutes from the moment of this decision. The London train whizzed by, drew back some yards, and in Mr. Bell was hurried by the impatient guard. He threw himself back in his seat, to try, with closed eyes, to understand how one in life yesterday could be dead to-day; and shortly tears stole out between his grizzled eye-lashes, at the feeling of which he opened his keen eyes, and looked as severely cheerful as his set determination could make him. He was not going to blubber before a set of strangers. Not he!

There was no set of strangers, only one sitting far from him on the same side. By and bye Mr. Bell peered at him, to discover what manner of man it was that might have been observing his emotion; and behind the great sheet of the outspread "Times," he recognised Mr. Thornton.

"Why, Thornton! is that you?" said he, removing hastily to a closer proximity. He shook Mr. Thornton vehemently by the hand, until the grip ended in a sudden relaxation, for the hand was wanted to wipe away tears. He had last seen Mr. Thornton in his friend Hale's company.

"I'm going to Milton, bound on a melancholy errand. Going to break to Hale's daughter the news of his sudden death!"

"Death! Mr. Hale dead!"

"Ay; I keep saying it to myself, 'Hale is dead!' but it doesn't make it any the more real. Hale is dead for all that. He went to bed well, to all appearance, last night, and was quite cold this morning when my servant went to call him."

"Where? I don't understand!"

"At Oxford. He came to stay with me; hadn't been in Oxford this seventeen years—and this is the end of it."

Not one word was spoken for above a quarter of an hour. Then Mr. Thornton said:

"And she!" and stopped full short.

"Margaret you mean. Yes! I am going to tell her. Poor fellow! how full his thoughts were of her all last night! Good God! Last night only. And how immeasurably distant he is now! But I take Margaret as my child for his sake. I said last night I would take her for her own sake. Well, I take her for both."

Mr. Thornton made one or two fruitless attempts to speak, before he could get out the words:

"What will become of her!"

"I rather fancy there will be two people waiting for her: myself for one. I would take a live dragon into my house to live, if, by hiring such a chaperon, and setting up an establishment of my own, I could make my old age happy with having Margaret for a daughter. But there are those Lennoxes!"

"Who are they?" asked Mr. Thornton with trembling interest.

"Oh, smart London people, who very likely will think they've the best right to her. Captain Lennox married her cousin—the girl she was brought up with. Good enough people, I dare say. And there's her aunt, Mrs. Shaw. There might be a way open, perhaps, by my offering to marry that worthy lady! but that would be quite a pis aller.[5] And then there's that brother!"

"What brother? A brother of her aunt's?"

"No, no; a clever Lennox, (the captain's a fool, you must understand); a young barrister, who will be setting his cap at Margaret. I know he has had her in his mind this five years or more; one of his chums told me as much; and he was only kept back by her want of fortune. Now that will be done away with."

"How?" asked Mr. Thornton, too earnestly curious to be aware of the impertinence of his question.

"Why, she'll have my money at my death. And if this Henry Lennox is half good enough for her, and she likes him—well! I might find another way of getting a home through a marriage. I'm dreadfully afraid of being tempted, at an unguarded moment, by the aunt."

Neither Mr. Bell nor Mr. Thornton was in a laughing humour; so the oddity of any of the speeches which the former made was unnoticed by them. Mr. Bell whistled, without emitting any sound beyond a long hissing breath; changed his seat, without finding comfort or rest; while Mr. Thornton sat immoveably still, his eyes fixed on one spot in the newspaper, which he had taken up in order to give himself leisure to think.

"Where have you been?" asked Mr. Bell, at length.

"To Havre. Trying to detect the secret of the great rise in the price of cotton."

"Ugh! Cotton, and speculations, and smoke, well-cleansed and well-cared-for machinery, and unwashed and neglected hands. Poor

5. A makeshift solution (French).

old Hale! Poor old Hale! If you could have known the change which it was to him from Helstone. Do you know the New Forest at all?"

"Yes." (Very shortly).

"Then you can fancy the difference between it and Milton. What part were you in? Were you ever at Helstone? a little picturesque village, like some in the Odenwald?[6] You know Helstone?"

"I have seen it. It was a great change to leave it and come to Milton."

He took up his newspaper with a determined air, as if resolved to avoid further conversation; and Mr. Bell was fain to resort to his former occupation of trying to find out how he could best break the news to Margaret.

She was at an upstairs window; she saw him alight; she guessed the truth with an instinctive flash. She stood in the middle of the drawing-room, as if arrested in her first impulse to rush down stairs, and as if by the same restraining thought she had been turned to stone; so white and immoveable was she.

"Oh! don't tell me! I know it from your face! You would have sent—you would not have left him—if he were alive! Oh papa, papa!"

Chapter XVII.

Alone! Alone![1]

"When some beloved voice that was to you
Both sound and sweetness, faileth suddenly,
And silence, against which you dare not cry,
Aches round you like a strong disease and new—
What hope? what help? what music will undo
That silence to your sense?"[2]

MRS. BROWNING.

The shock had been great. Margaret fell into a state of prostration, which did not show itself in sobs and tears, or even find the relief of words. She lay on the sofa, with her eyes shut, never speaking but when spoken to, and then replying in whispers. Mr. Bell was perplexed. He dared not leave her; he dared not ask her to accompany him back to Oxford, which had been one of the plans he had formed on the journey to Milton, her physical exhaustion was evidently too complete for her to undertake any such fatigue—putting the sight

6. A wooded region of Germany.
1. Echoing Coleridge's *Rime of the Ancient Mariner*: "Alone, alone, all, all alone / Alone on a wide wide sea!" (part 4, stanza 3).
2. The opening lines of Elizabeth Barrett Browning's sonnet "Substitution," on the subject of a sudden death.

that she would have to encounter out of the question. Mr. Bell sat over the fire, considering what he had better do. Margaret lay motionless, and almost breathless by him. He would not leave her, even for the dinner which Dixon had prepared for him down-stairs, and, with sobbing hospitality, would fain have tempted him to eat. He had a plateful of something brought up to him. In general, he was particular and dainty enough, and knew well each shade of flavour in his food, but now the devilled chicken tasted like sawdust. He minced up some of the fowl for Margaret, and peppered and salted it well; but when Dixon, following his directions, tried to feed her, the languid shake of head, proved that in such a state as Margaret was in, food would only choke, not nourish her.

Mr. Bell gave a great sigh; lifted up his stout old limbs (stiff with travelling) from their easy position, and followed Dixon out of the room.

"I can't leave her. I must write to them at Oxford, to see that the preparations are made: they can be getting on with these till I arrive. Can't Mrs. Lennox come to her? I'll write and tell her she must. The girl must have some woman-friend about her, if only to talk her into a good fit of crying."

Dixon was crying—enough for two; but, after wiping her eyes and steadying her voice, she managed to tell Mr. Bell, that Mrs. Lennox was too near her confinement to be able to undertake any journey at present.

"Well! I suppose we must have Mrs. Shaw; she's come back to England, isn't she?

"Yes, sir, she's come back; but I don't think she will like to leave Mrs. Lennox at such an interesting time," said Dixon, who did not much approve of a stranger entering the household, to share with her in her ruling care of Margaret.

"Interesting time be—" Mr. Bell restricted himself to coughing over the end of his sentence. "She could be content to be at Venice or Naples, or some of those Popish places, at the last 'interesting time,' which took place in Corfu, I think. And what does that little prosperous woman's interesting time' signify, in comparison with that poor creature there,—that helpless, homeless, friendless, Margaret—lying as still on that sofa as if it were an altar-tomb, and she the stone statue on it. I tell you, Mrs. Shaw shall come. See that a room, or whatever she wants, is got ready for her by to-morrow night. I'll take care she comes."

Accordingly Mr. Bell wrote a letter, which Mrs. Shaw declared, with many tears, to be so like one of the dear general's when he was going to have a fit of the gout, that she should always value and preserve it. If he had given her the option, by requesting or urging her, as if a refusal were possible, she might not have come—true and sincere as was her sympathy with Margaret. It needed the sharp uncourteous command to make her conquer her vis inertiæ, and allow herself to be packed by her maid, after the latter had completed the boxes. Edith, all cap, shawls, and tears, came out to the top of the stairs, as Captain Lennox was taking her mother down to the carriage:

"Don't forget, mamma; Margaret must come and live with us. Sholto[3] will go to Oxford on Wednesday, and you must send word by Mr. Bell to him when we're to expect you. And if you want Sholto, he can go on from Oxford to Milton. Don't forget, mamma; you are to bring back Margaret."

Edith re-entered the drawing-room. Mr. Henry Lennox was there, cutting open the pages of a new Review. Without lifting his head, he said, "If you don't like Sholto to be so long absent from you, Edith, I hope you will let me go down to Milton, and give what assistance I can."

"Oh, thank you," said Edith, "I dare say old Mr. Bell will do everything he can, and more help may not be needed. Only one does not look for much savoir-faire[4] from a resident Fellow. Dear, darling Margaret! won't it be nice to have her here, again? You were both great allies, years ago."

"Were we?" asked he indifferently, with an appearance of being interested in a passage in the Review.

"Well, perhaps not—I forget. I was so full of Sholto. But doesn't it fall out well, that if my uncle was to die, it should be just now, when we are come home, and settled in the old house, and quite ready to receive Margaret? Poor thing! what a change it will be to her from Milton! I'll have new chintz for her bedroom, and make it look new and bright, and cheer her up a little."

In the same spirit of kindness, Mrs. Shaw journeyed to Milton, occasionally dreading the first meeting, and wondering how it would be got over; but more frequently planning how soon she could get Margaret away from "that horrid place," and back into the pleasant comforts of Harley Street.

"Oh dear!" she said to her maid; "look at those chimneys! My poor sister Hale! I don't think I could have rested at Naples, if I had known what it was! I must have come and fetched her and Margaret away." And to herself she acknowledged, that she had always thought her brother-in-law rather a weak man, but never so weak as now, when she saw for what a place he had exchanged the lovely Helstone home.

Margaret had remained in the same state; white, motionless, speechless, tearless. They had told her that her aunt Shaw was com-

---

3. Gaskell seems to have forgotten that Captain Lennox has earlier been identified as "Cosmo" (vol. II, chap. 4, n. 3). I have retained her error.
4. Knowledge of the world, practical knowledge (French).

ing; but she had not expressed either surprise or pleasure, or dislike to the idea. Mr. Bell, whose appetite had returned, and who appreciated Dixon's endeavours to gratify it, in vain urged upon her to taste some sweetbreads stewed with oysters; she shook her head with the same quiet obstinacy as on the previous day; and he was obliged to console himself for her rejection, by eating them all himself. But Margaret was the first to hear the stopping of the cab that brought her aunt from the railway station. Her eyelids quivered, her lips coloured and trembled. Mr. Bell went down to meet Mrs. Shaw; and when they came up, Margaret was standing, trying to steady her dizzy self; and when she saw her aunt, she went forward to the arms open to receive her, and first found the passionate relief of tears on her aunt's shoulder. All thoughts of quiet habitual love, of tenderness for years, of relationship to the dead,—all that inexplicable likeness in look, tone, and gesture, that seem to belong to one family, and which reminded Margaret so forcibly at this moment of her mother,—came in to melt and soften her numbed heart into the overflow of warm tears.

Mr. Bell stole out of the room, and went down into the study, where he ordered a fire, and tried to divert his thoughts by taking down and examining the different books. Each volume brought a remembrance or a suggestion of his dead friend. It might be a change of employment from his two days' work of watching Margaret, but it was no change of thought. He was glad to catch the sound of Mr. Thornton's voice, making enquiry at the door. Dixon was rather cavalierly dismissing him; for with the appearance of Mrs. Shaw's maid, came visions of former grandeur, of the Beresford blood, of the "station" (so she was pleased to term it) from which her young lady had been ousted, and to which she was now, please God, to be restored. These visions, which she had been dwelling on with complacency in her conversation with Mrs. Shaw's maid (skilfully eliciting meanwhile all the circumstances of state and consequence connected with the Harley Street establishment, for the edification of the listening Martha), made Dixon rather inclined to be supercilious in her treatment of any inhabitant of Milton; so, though she always stood rather in awe of Mr. Thornton, she was as curt as she durst be in telling him that he could see none of the inmates of the house that night. It was rather uncomfortable to be contradicted in her statement by Mr. Bell's opening the study-door, and calling out:

"Thornton! is that you? Come in for a minute or two; I want to speak to you." So Mr. Thornton went into the study, and Dixon had to retreat into the kitchen, and reinstate herself in her own esteem by a prodigious story of Sir John Beresford's coach and six, when he was high sheriff.

"I don't know what I wanted to say to you after all. Only it's dull enough to sit in a room where everything speaks to you of a dead friend. Yet Margaret and her aunt must have the drawing-room to themselves!"

"Is Mrs.—is her aunt come?" asked Mr. Thornton.

"Come? Yes! maid and all. One would have thought she might have come by herself at such a time! And now I shall have to turn out and find my way to the Clarendon."

"You must not go to the Clarendon. We have five or six empty bed-rooms at home."

"Well aired?"

"I think you may trust my mother for that."

"Then I'll only run up-stairs and wish that wan girl good-night, and make my bow to her aunt, and go off with you straight."

Mr. Bell was some time up-stairs. Mr. Thornton began to think it long, for he was full of business, and had hardly been able to spare the time for running up to Crampton, and enquiring how Miss Hale was.

When they had set out upon their walk, Mr. Bell said:

"I was kept by those women in the drawing-room. Mrs. Shaw is anxious to get home—on account of her daughter, she says—and wants Margaret to go off with her at once. Now she is no more fit for travelling than I am for flying. Besides, she says, and very justly, that she has friends she must see—that she must wish good-bye to several people; and then her aunt worried her about old claims, and was she forgetful of old friends? And she said, with a great burst of crying, she should be glad enough to go from a place where she had suffered so much. Now I must return to Oxford to-morrow, and I don't know on which side of the scale to throw in my voice."

He paused, as if asking a question; but he received no answer from his companion, the echo of whose thoughts kept repeating—

"Where she had suffered so much." Alas! and that was the way in which this eighteen months in Milton—to him so unspeakably pre-cious, down to its very bitterness, which was worth all the rest of life's sweetness—would be remembered. Neither loss of father, nor loss of mother, dear as she was to Mr. Thornton, could have poisoned the remembrance of the weeks, the days, the hours, when a walk of two miles, every step of which was pleasant, as it brought him nearer and nearer to her, took him to her sweet presence—every step of which was rich, as each recurring moment that bore him away from her made him recall some fresh grace in her demeanour, or pleasant pungency in her character. Yes! whatever had happened to him, external to his relation to her, he could never have spoken of that time, when he could have seen her every day—when he had her within his grasp, as it were—as a time of suffering. It had been a royal time of luxury to him, with all its stings and contumelies,[5] compared to the poverty that crept round and clipped the anticipation of the future down to sordid fact, and life without an atmosphere of either hope or fear.

Mrs. Thornton and Fanny were in the dining-room; the latter in a flutter of small exultation, as the maid held up one glossy material after another, to try the effect of the wedding-dresses by candlelight. Her mother really tried to sympathise with her, but could not. Neither taste nor dress were in her line of subjects, and she heartily wished that Fanny had accepted her brother's offer of having the wedding clothes provided by some first-rate London dressmaker, without the endless troublesome discussions, and unsettled wavering, that arose out of Fanny's desire to choose and superintend everything herself. Mr. Thornton was only too glad to mark his grateful approbation of any sensible man, who could be captivated by Fanny's second-rate airs and graces, by giving her ample means for providing herself with the finery, which certainly rivalled, if it did not exceed, the lover in her estimation. When her brother and Mr. Bell came in, Fanny blushed and simpered, and fluttered over the signs of her employment, in a way which could not have failed to draw attention from any one else but Mr. Bell. If he thought about her and her silks and satins at all, it was to compare her and them with the pale sorrow he had left behind him, sitting motionless, with bent head and folded hands, in a room where the stillness was so great that you might almost fancy the rush in your straining ears was occasioned by the spirits of the dead, yet hovering round their beloved. For, when Mr. Bell had first gone up-stairs, Mrs. Shaw lay asleep on the sofa; and no sound broke the silence.

Mrs. Thornton gave Mr. Bell her formal, hospitable welcome. She was never so gracious as when receiving her son's friends in her son's house; and the more unexpected they were, the more honour to her admirable housekeeping preparations for comfort.

"How is Miss Hale?" she asked.

"About as broken down by this last stroke as she can be."

"I am sure it is very well for her that she has such a friend as you."

"I wish I were her only friend, madam. I daresay it sounds very brutal; but here have I been displaced, and turned out of my post of comforter and adviser by a fine lady aunt; and there are cousins and what not claiming her in London, as if she were a lap-dog belonging to them. And she is too weak and miserable to have a will of her own."

"She must indeed be weak," said Mrs. Thornton, with an implied

5. Insults, reproaches.

meaning which her son understood well. "But where," continued
Mrs. Thornton, "have these relations been all this time that Miss
Hale has appeared almost friendless, and has certainly had a good
deal of anxiety to bear?" But she did not feel interest enough in the
answer to her question to wait for it. She left the room to make her
household arrangements.

"They have been living abroad. They have some some kind of claim
upon her. I will do them that justice. The aunt brought her up, and
she and the cousin have been like sisters. The thing vexing me, you
see, is that I wanted to take her for a child of my own; and I am
jealous of these people, who don't seem to value the privilege of their
right. Now it would be different if Frederick claimed her."

"Frederick!" exclaimed Mr. Thornton, "Who is he? What
right—?" He stopped short in his vehement question.

"Frederick," said Mr. Bell in surprise. "Why don't you know? He's
her brother. Have you not heard—"

"I never heard his name before. Where is he? Who is he?"

"Surely I told you about him, when the family first came to Milton—the son who was concerned in that mutiny."

"I never heard of him till this moment. Where does he live?"

"In Spain. He's liable to be arrested the moment he sets foot on
English ground. Poor fellow! he will grieve at not being able to attend
his father's funeral. We must be content with Captain Lennox; for I
don't know of any other relation to summon."

"I hope I may be allowed to go?"

"Certainly; thankfully. You're a good fellow, after all, Thornton.
Hale liked you. He spoke to me, only the other day, about you at
Oxford. He regretted he had seen so little of you lately. I am obliged
to you for wishing to show him respect."

"But about Frederick. Does he never come to England?"

"Never."

"He was not over here about the time of Mrs. Hale's death?"

"No. Why, I was here then. I had'nt seen Hale for years and years:
and, if you remember, I came— No, it was some time after that that
I came. But poor Frederick Hale was not here then. What made you
think he was?"

"I saw a young man walking with Miss Hale one day," replied Mr.
Thornton, "and I think it was about that time."

"Oh, that would be this young Lennox, the Captain's brother. He's
a lawyer, and they were in pretty constant correspondence with him;
and I remember Mr. Hale told me he thought he would come down.
Do you know," said Mr. Bell, wheeling round, and shutting one eye,
the better to bring the forces of the other to bear with keen scrutiny
on Mr. Thornton's face, "that I once fancied you had a little tenderness for Margaret?"

No answer. No change of countenance.

"And so did poor Hale. Not at first, and not till I had put it into his head."

"I admired Miss Hale. Every one must do so. She is a beautiful creature," said Mr. Thornton, driven to bay by Mr. Bell's pertinacious questioning.

"Is that all! You can speak of her in that measured way, as simply a 'beautiful creature'—only something to catch the eye. I did hope you had had nobleness enough in you to make you pay her the homage of the heart. Though I believe—in fact I know, she would have rejected you, still to have loved her without return would have lifted you higher than all those, be they who they may, that have never known her to love. 'Beautiful creature' indeed! Do you speak of her as you would of a horse or a dog?"

Mr. Thornton's eyes glowed like red embers.

"Mr. Bell," said he, "before you speak so, you should remember that all men are not as free to express what they feel as you are. Let us talk of something else." For though his heart leaped up, as at a trumpet-call, to every word that Mr. Bell had said, and though he knew that what he had said would henceforward bind the thought of the old Oxford Fellow closely up with the most precious things of his heart, yet he would not be forced into any expression of what he felt towards Margaret. He was no mocking-bird of praise, to try because another extolled what he reverenced and passionately loved, to outdo him in laudation. So he turned to some of the dry matters of business that lay between Mr. Bell and him, as landlord and tenant.

"What is that heap of brick and mortar we came against in the yard? Any repairs wanted?"

"No, none, thank you."

"Are you building on your own account? If you are, I'm very much obliged to you."

"I'm building a dining-room—for the men I mean—the hands."

"I thought you were hard to please, if this room wasn't good enough to satisfy you, a bachelor."

"I've got acquainted with a strange kind of chap, and I put one or two children in whom he is interested to school. So, as I happened to be passing near his house one day, I just went there about some trifling payment to be made; and I saw such a miserable black frizzle of a dinner—a greasy cinder of meat, as first set me a-thinking. But it was not till provisions grew so high this winter that I bethought me how, by buying things wholesale, and cooking a good quantity of provisions together, much money might be saved, and much comfort gained. So I spoke to my friend—or my enemy—the man I told you of—and he found fault with every detail of my plan; and in consequence I laid it aside, both as impracticable, and also because if I forced it into operation I should be interfering with the independence of my men; when, suddenly, this Higgins came to me and graciously signified his approval of a scheme so nearly the same as mine, that I might fairly have claimed it; and, moreover, the approval of several of his fellow-workmen, to whom he had spoken. I was a little 'riled,' I confess, by his manner, and thought of throwing the whole thing overboard to sink or swim. But it seemed childish to relinquish a plan which I had once thought wise and well-laid, just because I myself did not receive all the honour and consequence due to the originator. So I coolly took the part assigned to me, which is something like that of steward to a club. I buy in the provisions wholesale, and provide a fitting matron or cook."

"I hope you give satisfaction in your new capacity. Are you a good judge of potatoes and onions? But I suppose Mrs. Thornton assists you in your marketing."

"Not a bit," replied Mr. Thornton. "She disapproves of the whole plan, and now we never mention it to each other. But I manage pretty well, getting in great stocks from Liverpool, and being served in butcher's meat by our own family butcher. I can assure you, the hot dinners the matron turns out are by no means to be despised."

"Do you taste each dish as it goes in, in virtue of your office? I hope you have a white wand."

"I was very scrupulous, at first, in confining myself to the mere purchasing part, and even in that I rather obeyed the men's orders, conveyed through the housekeeper, than went by my own judgment. At one time, the beef was too large, at another the mutton was not fat enough. I think they saw how careful I was to leave them free, and not to intrude my own ideas upon them; so, one day, two or three of the men—my friend Higgins among them—asked me if I would not come in and take a snack. It was a very busy day, but I saw that the men would be hurt if, after making the advance, I didn't meet them half-way, so I went in, and I never made a better dinner in my life. I told them (my next neighbours I mean, for I'm no speech-maker) how much I'd enjoyed it; and for some time, whenever that especial dinner recurred in their dietary, I was sure to be met by these men, with a 'Master, there's hot-pot[6] for dinner to-day, win yo' come?' If they had not asked me, I would no more have intruded on them than I'd have gone to the mess at the barracks without invitation."

"I should think you were rather a restraint on your hosts' conversation. They can't abuse the masters while you're there. I suspect they take it out on non-hot-pot days."

6. A stew of meat and vegetables, popular in Lancashire.

"Well! hitherto we've steered clear of all vexed questions. But if any of the old disputes came up again, I would certainly speak out my mind next hot-pot day. But you are hardly acquainted with our Darkshire fellows, for all you're a Darkshire man yourself. They have such a sense of humour, and such a racy mode of expression! I am getting really to know some of them now, and they talk pretty freely before me."

"Nothing like the act of eating for equalising men. Dying is nothing to it. The philosopher dies sententiously—the pharisee ostentatiously—the simple-hearted humbly—the poor idiot blindly, as the sparrow falls to the ground; the philosopher and idiot, publican and pharisee, all eat after the same fashion—given an equally good digestion. There's theory for theory for you!"

"Indeed I have no theory; I hate theories."

"I beg your pardon. To show my penitence, will you accept a ten pound note towards your marketing, and give the poor fellows a feast?"

"Thank you; but I'd rather not. They pay me rent for the oven and cooking-places at the back of the mill: and will have to pay more for the new dining-room. I don't want it to fall into a charity. I don't want donations. Once let in the principle, and I should have people going, and talking, and spoiling the simplicity of the whole thing."

"People will talk about any new plan. You can't help that."

"My enemies, if I have any, may make a philanthropic fuss about this dinner-scheme; but you are a friend, and I expect you will pay my experiment the respect of silence. It is but a new broom at present, and sweeps clean enough. But by-and-by we shall meet with plenty of stumbling-blocks, no doubt."

Chapter XVIII.

Margaret's Flittin'.[1]

"The meanest thing to which we bid adieu,
Loses its meanness in the parting hour."

ELLIOTT.[2]

Mrs. Shaw took as vehement a dislike as it was possible for one of her gentle nature to do, against Milton. It was noisy, and smoky, and the poor people whom she saw in the streets were dirty, and the rich ladies over-dressed, and not a man that she saw, high or low, had

1. Flight, sudden departure (dialect). The term was usually used for working-class people who left their accommodations while still owing rent; Gaskell's application of it to Margaret here is thus jocular.
2. The lines are from his poem *The Village Patriarch*, IX, section iv, lines 1–2 (1831).

his clothes made to fit him. She was sure Margaret would never regain her lost strength while she stayed in Milton; and she herself was afraid of one of her old attacks of the nerves. Margaret must return with her, and that quickly. This, if not the exact force of her words, was at any rate the spirit of what she urged on Margaret, till the latter, weak, weary, and broken-spirited, yielded a reluctant promise that, as soon as Wednesday was over, she would prepare to accompany her aunt back to town, leaving Dixon in charge of all the arrangements for paying bills, disposing of furniture, and shutting up the house. Before that Wednesday—that mournful Wednesday, when Mr. Hale was to be interred, far away from either of the homes he had known in life, and far away from the wife who lay lonely among strangers (and this last was Margaret's great trouble, for she thought that if she had not given way to that overwhelming stupor during the first sad days, she could have arranged things otherwise)—before that Wednesday, Margaret received a letter from Mr. Bell.

"MY DEAR MARGARET:—I did mean to have returned to Milton on Thursday, but unluckily it turns out to be one of the rare occasions when we, Plymouth Fellows, are called upon to perform any kind of duty, and I must not be absent from my post. Captain Lennox and Mr. Thornton are here. The former seems a smart, well-meaning man; and has proposed to go over to Milton, and assist you in any search for the will; of course there is none, or you would have found it by this time, if you followed my directions. Then the Captain declares he must take you and his mother-in-law home; and, in his wife's present state, I don't see how you can expect him to remain away longer than Friday. However, that Dixon of yours is trusty; and can hold her, or your own, till I come. I will put matters into the hands of my Milton attorney if there is no will; for I doubt this smart captain is no great man of business. Nevertheless, his moustachios are splendid. There will have to be a sale, so select what things you wish reserved. Or you can send a list afterwards. Now two things more, and I have done. You know, or if you don't, your poor father did, that you are to have my money and goods when I die. Not that I mean to die yet; but I name this just to explain what is coming. These Lennoxes seem very fond of you now; and perhaps may continue to be; perhaps not. So it is best to start with a formal agreement; namely, that you are to pay them two hundred and fifty pounds a year, as long as you and they find it pleasant to live together. (This, of course, includes Dixon; mind you don't be cajoled into paying any more for her.) Then you won't be thrown adrift, if some day the captain wishes to have his house to himself, but you can carry yourself and your two hundred and fifty pounds off somewhere else; if, indeed, I have not claimed you to come and keep house for me first. Then as to dress, and Dixon, and personal expenses, and confectionery (all young ladies eat confectionery till wisdom comes by age), I shall consult some lady of my acquaintance, and see how much you will have from your father before fixing this. Now, Margaret, have you flown out before you have read this far, and wondered what right the old man has to settle your affairs for you so cavalierly? I make no doubt you have. Yet the old man has a right. He has loved your father for five and thirty years; he stood beside him on his wedding-day; he closed his eyes in death. Moreover, he is your godfather; and as he cannot do you much good spiritually, having a hidden consciousness of your superiority in such things, he would fain do you the poor good of endowing you materially. And the old man has not a known relation on earth; 'who is there to mourn for Adam Bell?' and his whole heart is set and bent upon this one thing, and Margaret Hale is not the girl to say him nay. Write by return, if only two lines, to tell me your answer. But *no thanks*."

Margaret took up a pen and scrawled with trembling hand, "Margaret Hale is not the girl to say him nay." In her weak state she could not think of any other words, and yet she was vexed to use these. But she was so much fatigued even by this slight exertion, that if she could have thought of another form of acceptance, she could not have sat up to write a syllable of it. She was obliged to lie down again, and try not to think.

"My dearest child! Has that letter vexed or troubled you?"

"No!" said Margaret feebly. "I shall be better when to-morrow is over."

"I feel sure, darling, you won't be better till I get you out of this horrid air. How you can have borne it this two years I can't imagine."

"Where could I go to? I could not leave papa and mamma."

"Well! don't distress yourself, my dear. I dare say it was all for the best, only I had no conception of how you were living. Our butler's wife lives in a better house than this."

"It is sometimes very pretty—in summer; you can't judge by what it is now. I have been very happy here," and Margaret closed her eyes by way of stopping the conversation.

The house teemed with comfort now, compared to what it had done. The evenings were chilly, and by Mrs. Shaw's directions fires were lighted in every bedroom. She petted Margaret in every possible way, and bought every delicacy, or soft luxury in which she herself would have burrowed and sought comfort. But Margaret was indifferent to all these things; or, if they forced themselves upon her attention, it was simply as causes for gratitude to her aunt, who was putting herself so much out of her way to think of her. She was restless, though so weak. All the day long, she kept herself from thinking of the ceremony which was going on at Oxford, by wandering from room to room, and languidly setting aside such articles as she wished to retain. Dixon followed her by Mrs. Shaw's desire, ostensibly to receive instructions, but with a private injunction to soothe her into repose as soon as might be.

"These books, Dixon, I will keep. All the rest will you send to Mr. Bell? They are of a kind that he will value for themselves, as well as for papa's sake. This——I should like you to take this to Mr. Thornton, after I am gone. Stay; I will write a note with it." And she sat down hastily, as if afraid of thinking, and wrote:

"DEAR SIR,—The accompanying book I am sure will be valued by you for the sake of my father, to whom it belonged.
"Yours sincerely,
"MARGARET HALE."

She set out again upon her travels through the house, turning over articles, known to her from her childhood, with a sort of caressing reluctance to leave them—old-fashioned, worn and shabby, as they might be. But she hardly spoke again; and Dixon's report to Mrs. Shaw was, that "she doubted whether Miss Hale heard a word of what she said, though she talked the whole time, in order to divert her intention." The consequence of being on her feet all day was excessive bodily weariness in the evening, and a better night's rest than she had had since she had heard of Mr. Hale's death.

At breakfast time the next day, she expressed her wish to go and bid one or two friends good-bye. Mrs. Shaw objected:

"I am sure, my dear, you can have no friends here with whom you are sufficiently intimate to justify you in calling upon them so soon; before you have been at church."

"But to-day is my only day; if Captain Lennox comes this afternoon, and if we must—if I must really go to-morrow——"

"Oh, yes; we shall go to-morrow. I am more and more convinced that this air is bad for you, and makes you look so pale and ill; besides, Edith expects us; and she may be waiting me; and you cannot be left alone, my dear, at your age. No; if you must pay these calls, I will go with you. Dixon can get us a coach, I suppose?"

So Mrs. Shaw went to take care of Margaret, and took her maid with her to take care of the shawls and air-cushions. Margaret's face was too sad to lighten up into a smile at all this preparation for paying two visits, that she had often made by herself at all hours of the day. She was half afraid of owning that one place to which she was going was Nicholas Higgins'; all she could do was to hope her aunt would be indisposed to get out of the coach, and walk up the court, and at every breath of wind have her face slapped by wet clothes, hanging out to dry on ropes stretched from house to house.

There was a little battle in Mrs. Shaw's mind between ease and a sense of matronly propriety; but the former gained the day; and with many an injunction to Margaret to be careful of herself, and not to catch any fever, such as was always lurking in such places, her aunt permitted her to go where she had often been before without taking any precaution or requiring any permission.

Nicholas was out; only Mary and one or two of the Boucher children at home. Margaret was vexed with herself for not having timed her visit better. Mary had a very blunt intellect, although her feelings were warm and kind; and the instant she understood what Margaret's purpose was in coming to see them, she began to cry and sob with so little restraint that Margaret found it useless to say any of the thousand little things which had suggested themselves to her as she was coming along in the coach. She could only try to comfort her a little by suggesting the vague chance of their meeting again, at some possible time, in some possible place, and bid her tell her father how much she wished, if he could manage it, that he should come to see her when he had done his work in the evening.

As she was leaving the place, she stopped and looked round; then hesitated a little before she said:

"I should like to have some little thing to remind me of Bessy."

Instantly Mary's generosity was keenly alive. What could they give? And on Margaret's singling out a little common drinking-cup, which she remembered as the one always standing by Bessy's side with drink for her feverish lips, Mary said:

"Oh, take summut better; that only cost four-pence!"

"That will do, thank you," said Margaret; and she went quickly away, while the light caused by the pleasure of having something to give yet lingered on Mary's face.

"Now to Mrs. Thornton's," thought she to herself. "It must be done." But she looked rather rigid and pale at the thoughts of it, and had hard work to find the exact words in which to explain to her aunt who Mrs. Thornton was, and why she should go to bid her farewell.

They (for Mrs. Shaw alighted here) were shown into the drawing-room, in which a fire had only just been kindled. Mrs. Shaw huddled herself up in her shawl, and shivered.

"What an icy room!" she said.

They had to wait for some time before Mrs. Thornton entered. There was some softening in her heart towards Margaret, now that she was going away out of her sight. She remembered her spirit, as shown at various times and places, even more than the patience with which she had endured long and wearing cares. Her countenance was blander than usual, as she greeted her; there was even a shade of tenderness in her manner, as she noticed the white, tear-swollen face, and the quiver in the voice which Margaret tried to make so steady.

"Allow me to introduce my aunt, Mrs. Shaw. I am going away from Milton to-morrow; I do not know if you are aware of it; but I wanted to see you once again, Mrs. Thornton, to—to apologise for my manner the last time I saw you; and to say that I am sure you meant kindly—however much we may have misunderstood each other."

Mrs. Shaw looked extremely perplexed by what Margaret had said. Thanks for kindness! and apologies for failure in good manners! But Mrs. Thornton replied:

"Miss Hale, I am glad you do me justice. I did no more than I believed to be my duty in remonstrating with you as I did. I have always desired to act the part of a friend to you. I am glad you do me justice."

"And," said Margaret, blushing excessively as she spoke, "will you do me justice, and believe that though I cannot—I do not choose—to give explanations of my conduct, I have not acted in the unbecoming way you apprehended?"

Margaret's voice was so soft, and her eyes so pleading, that Mrs. Thornton was for once affected by the charm of manner to which she had hitherto proved herself invulnerable.

"Yes, I do believe you. Let us say no more about it. Where are you going to reside, Miss Hale? I understood from Mr. Bell that you were going to leave Milton. You never liked Milton, you know," said Mrs. Thornton, with a sort of grim smile; "but for all that, you must not expect me to congratulate you on quitting it. Where shall you live?"

"With my aunt," replied Margaret, turning towards Mrs. Shaw.

"My niece will reside with me in Harley Street. She is almost like a daughter to me," said Mrs. Shaw, looking fondly at Margaret; "and I am glad to acknowledge my own obligation for any kindness that has been shown to her. If you and your husband ever come to town, my son and daughter, Captain and Mrs. Lennox, will, I am sure, join with me in wishing to do anything in our power to show you attention."

Mrs. Thornton thought in her own mind, that Margaret had not taken much care to enlighten her aunt as to the relationship between the Mr. and Mrs. Thornton, towards whom the fine-lady aunt was extending her soft patronage; so she answered shortly,

"My husband is dead. Mr. Thornton is my son. I never go to London; so I am not likely to be able to avail myself of your polite offers."

At this instant Mr. Thornton entered the room; he had only just returned from Oxford. His mourning suit spoke of the reason that had called him there.

"John," said his mother, "this lady is Mrs. Shaw, Miss Hale's aunt. I am sorry to say, that Miss Hale's call is to wish us good-bye."

"You are going then!" said he, in a low voice.

"Yes," said Margaret. "We leave to-morrow."

"My son-in-law comes this evening to escort us," said Mrs. Shaw.

Mr. Thornton turned away. He had not sat down, and now he seemed to be examining something on the table, almost as if he had discovered an unopened letter, which had made him forget the present company. He did not even seem to be aware when they got up to take leave. He started forwards, however, to hand Mrs. Shaw down to the carriage. As it drove up, he and Margaret stood close together on the door-step, and it was impossible but that the recollection of the day of the riot should force itself into both their minds. Into his it came associated with the speeches of the following day; her passionate declaration that there was not a man in all that violent and desperate crowd, for whom she did not care as much as for him. And at the remembrance of her taunting words, his brow grew stern, though his heart beat thick with longing love. "No!" said he, "I put it to the touch once, and I lost it all. Let her go,—with her stony heart, and her beauty;—how set and terrible her look is now, for all her loveliness of feature! She is afraid I shall speak what will require some stern repression. Let her go. Beauty and heiress as she may be, she will find it hard to meet with a truer heart than mine. Let her go!"

And there was no tone of regret, or emotion of any kind in the voice with which he said good-bye; and the offered hand was taken with a resolute calmness, and dropped as carelessly as if it had been a dead and withered flower. But none in his household saw Mr. Thornton again that day. He was busily engaged; or so he said.

Margaret's strength was so utterly exhausted by these visits, that she had to submit to much watching, and petting, and sighing "I-told-you-so's," from her aunt. Dixon said she was quite as bad as she had been on the first day she heard of her father's death; and she and Mrs. Shaw consulted as to the desirableness of delaying the morrow's journey. But when her aunt reluctantly proposed a few days' delay to Margaret, the latter writhed her body as if in acute suffering, and said:

"Oh! let us go. I cannot be patient here. I shall not get well here. I want to forget."

So the arrangements went on; and Captain Lennox came, and with him news of Edith and the little boy; and Margaret found that the indifferent, careless conversation of one who, however kind, was not too warm and anxious a sympathiser, did her good. She roused up; and by the time that she knew she might expect Higgins, she was able to leave the room quietly, and await in her own chamber the expected summons.

"Eh!" said he, as she came in, "to think of th' oud gentleman dropping off as he did! Yo' might ha' knocked me down wi' a straw when
they told me. 'Mr. Hale?' said I; 'him as was th' parson?' 'Ay,' said
they. 'Then,' said I, 'there's as good a man gone as ever lived on this
earth, let who will be t' other!' And I came to see yo', and tell yo' how
grieved I were, but them women in th' kitchen wouldn't tell yo' I
were there. They said yo' were ill,—and butter[3] me, but yo' dunnot
look like th' same wench. And yo're going to be a grand lady up i'
Lunnon, aren't yo'?"

"Not a grand lady," said Margaret, half smiling.

"Well! Thornton said—says he, a day or two ago, 'Higgins, have
yo' seen Miss Hale?' 'No,' says I; 'there's a pack o' women who won't
let me at her. But I can bide my time, if she's ill. She and I knows
each other pretty well; and hoo'l not go doubting that I'm main sorry
for th' oud gentleman's death, just because I can't get at her and tell
her so.' And says he, 'Yo'll not have much time for to try and see her,
my fine chap. She's not for staying with us a day longer nor she can
help. She's got grand relations, and they're carrying her off; and we
sha'n't see her no more.' 'Measter,' said I, 'if I dunnot see her afore
hoo goes, I'll strive to get up to Lunnun next Whissuntide, that I
will. I'll not be baulked of saying her good-bye by any relations what-
somdever.' But, bless yo', I knowed yo'd come. It were only for to
humour the measter, I let on as if I thought yo'd mappen leave Milton without seeing me."

"You're quite right," said Margaret. "You only do me justice. And
you'll not forget me, I'm sure. If no one else in Milton remembers
me, I'm certain you will; and papa too. You know how good and how
tender he was. Look, Higgins! here is his bible. I have kept it for you.
I can ill spare it; but I know he would have liked you to have it. I'm
sure you'll care for it, and study what is in it, for his sake."

"Yo' may say that. If it were the deuce's own scribble, and yo' axed
me to read in it for yo'r sake, and th' oud gentleman's, I'd do it.
Whatten's this, wench? I'm not going for to take yo'r brass, so dunnot
think it. We've been great friends, 'bout the sound o' money passing
between us,"

"For the children—for Boucher's children," said Margaret, hurriedly. "They may need it. You've no right to refuse it for them. I
would not give you a penny," she said, smiling; "don't think there's
any of it for you."

"Well, wench! I can nobbut say, Bless yo'! and bless yo'!—and
amen."

---

3. Normally, compliment, flatter, in the sense of "get round me," but here more of a general
    exclamation.

Chapter XIX.[1]

Ease Not Peace.

"A dull rotation, never at a stay,
Yesterday's face twin image of to-day."
COWPER.[2]

"Of what each one should be, he sees the form and rule,
And till he reach to that, his joy can ne'er be full."
RÜCKERT.[3]

It was very well for Margaret that the extreme quiet of the Harley Street house, during Edith's recovery from her confinement, gave her the natural rest which she needed. It gave her time to comprehend the sudden change which had taken place in her circumstances within the last two months. She found herself at once an inmate of a luxurious house, where the bare knowledge of the existence of every trouble or care seemed scarcely to have penetrated. The wheels of the machinery of daily life were well oiled, and went along with delicious smoothness. Mrs. Shaw and Edith could hardly make enough of Margaret, on her return to what they persisted in calling her home. And she felt that it was almost ungrateful in her to have a secret feeling that the Helstone vicarage—nay, even the poor little house at Milton, with her anxious father and her invalid mother, and all the small household cares of comparative poverty, composed her idea of home. Edith was impatient to get well, in order to fill Margaret's bed-room with all the soft comforts, and pretty nick-knacks, with which her own abounded. Mrs. Shaw and her maid found plenty of occupation in restoring Margaret's wardrobe to a state of elegant variety. Captain Lennox was easy, kind, and gentlemanly; sat with his wife in her dressing-room an hour or two every day; played with his little boy for another hour, and lounged away the rest of his time at his club, when he was not engaged out to dinner. Just before Margaret had recovered from her necessity for quiet and repose—before she had begun to feel her life wanting and dull—Edith came

---

1. For the first volume edition of *North and South* Gaskell redrafted the concluding chapters of the novel as they appeared in *Household Words* from this point, introducing new chapter divisions and also new material. The changes that she made delayed the death of Mr. Bell and allowed for Margaret's return with him to Helstone (vol. II, chaps. 20, 21). They also allowed for fuller treatment of Frederick Hale's situation, an issue on which she was anxious to be absolutely clear.
2. William Cowper (1737–1800). The lines are from his poem "Hope," published in his *Poems* (1782). The poem argues that worldly hopes and ambitions are illusory; the only meaningful form of hope that we have lies in "recompense divine."
3. Friedrich Rückert (1781–1866), German poet admired by Gaskell's friend Catherine Winkworth. The lines are from his poem "Angereihte Perlen," *Pantheon* Part 5 (*Collected Poems*, 1834–38), vol. 6. The poem is made up of a sequence of epigrammatic couplets. There is a mistranslation in the second line where in the original the poem reads "Friede" (peace), not "Freude" (joy).

down-stairs and resumed her usual part in the household; and Margaret fell into the old habit of watching, and admiring, and ministering to her cousin. She gladly took all charge of the semblances of duties off Edith's hands; answered notes, reminded her of engagements, tended her when no gaiety was in prospect, and she was consequently rather inclined to fancy herself ill. But all the rest of the family were in the full business of the London season, and Margaret was often left alone. Then her thoughts went back to Milton, with a strange sense of the contrast between the life there, and here. She was getting surfeited of the eventless ease in which no struggle or endeavour was required. She was afraid lest she should even become sleepily deadened into forgetfulness of anything beyond the life which was lapping her round with luxury. There might be toilers and moilers there in London, but she never saw them; the very servants lived in an underground world of their own, of which she knew neither the hopes nor the fears; they only seemed to start into existence when some want or whim of their master and mistress needed them. There was a strange unsatisfied vacuum in Margaret's heart and mode of life; and, once when she had dimly hinted this to Edith, the latter, wearied with dancing the night before, languidly stroked Margaret's cheek as she sat by her in the old attitude,—she on a footstool by the sofa where Edith lay.

"Poor child!" said Edith. "It is a little sad for you to be left, night after night, just at this time when all the world is so gay. But we shall be having our dinner-parties soon—as soon as Henry comes back from circuit—and then there will be a little pleasant variety for you. No wonder it is moped, poor darling!"

Margaret did not feel as if the dinner-parties would be a panacea. But Edith piqued herself on her dinner-parties; "so different," as she said, "from the old dowager dinners under mamma's régime;" and Mrs. Shaw herself seemed to take exactly the same kind of pleasure in the very different arrangements and circle of acquaintances which were to Captain and Mrs. Lennox's taste, as she did in the more formal and ponderous entertainments which she herself used to give. Captain Lennox was always extremely kind and brotherly to Margaret. She was really very fond of him, excepting when he was anxiously attentive to Edith's dress and appearance, with a view to her beauty making a sufficient impression on the world. Then all the latent Vashti[4] in Margaret was roused, and she could hardly keep herself from expressing her feelings.[5]

---

4. An independently minded woman. In the Old Testament, Vashti was the wife of King Ahasuerus: when she refused to come to his feast he sent his chamberlains to fetch her. The king replaced Vashti as his queen by Esther (Esther 1).

5. In the first edition this paragraph, with the exception of the first sentence ("Margaret did not feel as if the dinner-parties would be a panacea.") and the following paragraph were both inserted, with minor adjustments, by mistake and at separate points in volume II,

The course of Margaret's day was this: a quiet hour or two before a late breakfast; an unpunctual meal, lazily eaten by weary and half-awake people, but yet at which, in all its dragged-out length, she was expected to be present, because, directly afterwards, came a discussion of plans, at which, although they none of them concerned her, she was expected to give her sympathy, if she could not assist with her advice; an endless number of notes to write, which Edith invariably left to her, with many caressing compliments as to her eloquence du billet;[6] a little play with Sholto as he returned from his morning's walk; besides the care of the children during the servants' dinner; a drive or callers; and some dinner or morning engagement for her aunt and cousins, which left Margaret free, it is true, but rather wearied with the inactivity of the day, coming upon depressed spirits and delicate health.

She looked forward with longing, though unspoken interest to the homely object of Dixon's return from Milton; where, until now, the old servant had been busily engaged in winding up all the affairs of the Hale family. It had appeared a sudden famine to her heart, this entire cessation of any news respecting the people amongst whom she had lived so long. It was true, that Dixon, in her business-letters, quoted, every now and then, an opinion of Mr. Thornton's as to what she had better do about the furniture, or how act in regard to the landlord of the Crampton Terrace house. But it was only here and there that the name came in, or any Milton name, indeed; and Margaret was sitting one evening, all alone in the Lennox's drawing-room, not reading Dixon's letters, which yet she held in her hand, but thinking over them, and recalling the days which had been, and picturing the busy life out of which her own had been taken and never missed; wondering if all went on in that whirl just as if she and her father had never been; questioning within herself, if no one in all the crowd missed her, (not Higgins, she was not thinking of him,) when, suddenly, Mr. Bell was announced; and Margaret hurried the letters into her work-basket, and started up, blushing as if she had been doing some guilty thing.

"Oh, Mr. Bell! I never thought of seeing you!"

"But you give me a welcome, I hope, as well as that very pretty start of surprise."

"Have you dined? How did you come? Let me order you some dinner."

"If you're going to have any. Otherwise, you know, there is no one

---

chapter 22. See p. 368, nn. 3 and 4 below. Both of these errors were corrected in the second edition of the novel, published in 1855.

6. At letter-writing (French).

who cares less for eating than I do. But where are the others? Gone out to dinner? Left you alone?"

"Oh yes! and it is such a rest. I was just thinking—But will you run the risk of dinner? I don't know if there is anything in the house."

"Why, to tell you the truth, I dined at my club. Only they don't cook as well as they did, so I thought, if you were going to dine, I might try and make out my dinner. But never mind, never mind! There aren't ten cooks in England to be trusted at impromptu dinners. If their skill and their fires will stand it, their tempers won't. You shall make me some tea, Margaret. And now, what were you thinking of? you were going to tell me. Whose letters were those, god-daughter, that you hid away so speedily?"

"Only Dixon's," replied Margaret, growing very red.

"Whew! is that all? Who do you think came up in the train with me?"

"I don't know," said Margaret, resolved against making a guess.

"Your what d'ye call him? What's the right name for a cousin-in-law's brother?"

"Mr. Henry Lennox?" asked Margaret.

"Yes," replied Mr. Bell. "You knew him formerly, didn't you? What sort of a person is he, Margaret?"

"I liked him long ago," said Margaret, glancing down for a moment. And then she looked straight up and went on in her natural manner. "You know we have been corresponding about Frederick since; but I have not seen him for nearly three years, and he may be changed. What did you think of him?"

"I don't know. He was so busy trying to find out who I was, in the first instance, and what I was in the second, that he never let out what he was; unless indeed that veiled curiosity of his as to what manner of man he had to talk to was not a good piece, and a fair indication of his character. Do you call him good looking, Margaret?"

"No! certainly not. Do you?"

"Not I. But I thought, perhaps you might. Is he a great deal here?"

"I fancy he is when he is in town. He has been on circuit now since I came. But—Mr. Bell—have you come from Oxford or from Milton?"

"From Milton. Don't you see I'm smoke-dried?"

"Certainly. But I thought that it might be the effect of the antiquities of Oxford."

"Come now, be a sensible woman! In Oxford, I could have managed all the landlords in the place, and had my own way, with half the trouble your Milton landlord has given me, and defeated me after all. He won't take the house off our hands till next June twelvemonth. Luckily, Mr. Thornton found a tenant for it. Why don't you ask after

Mr. Thornton, Margaret? He has proved himself a very active friend of yours, I can tell you. Taken more than half the trouble off my hands."

"And how is he? How is Mrs. Thornton?" asked Margaret hurriedly and below her breath, though she tried to speak out.

"I suppose they're well. I've been staying at their house till I was driven out of it by the perpetual clack about that Thornton girl's marriage. It was too much for Thornton himself, though she was his sister. He used to go and sit in his own room perpetually. He's getting past the age for caring for such things, either as principal or accessory. I was surprised to find the old lady falling into the current, and carried away by her daughter's enthusiasm for orange-blossoms and lace. I thought Mrs. Thornton had been made of sterner stuff."

"She would put on any assumption of feeling to veil her daughter's weakness," said Margaret in a low voice.

"Perhaps so. You've studied her, have you? She doesn't seem over fond of you, Margaret."

"I know it," said Margaret. "Oh, here is tea at last!" exclaimed she, as if relieved. And with tea came Mr. Henry Lennox, who had walked up to Harley Street after a late dinner, and had evidently expected to find his brother and sister-in-law at home. Margaret suspected him of being as thankful as she was at the presence of a third party, on this their first meeting since the memorable day of his offer, and her refusal at Helstone. She could hardly tell what to say at first, and was thankful for all the tea-table occupations, which gave her an excuse for keeping silence, and him an opportunity of recovering himself. For, to tell the truth, he had rather forced himself up to Harley Street this evening, with a view of getting over an awkward meeting, awkward even in the presence of Captain Lennox and Edith, and doubly awkward now that he found her the only lady there, and the person to whom he must naturally and perforce address a great part of his conversation. She was the first to recover her self-possession. She began to talk on the subject which came uppermost in her mind, after the first flush of awkward shyness.

"Mr. Lennox, I have been so much obliged to you for all you have done about Frederick."

"I am only sorry it has been so unsuccessful," replied he, with a quick glance towards Mr. Bell, as if reconnoitring how much he might say before him. Margaret, as if she read his thought, addressed herself to Mr. Bell, both including him in the conversation, and implying that he was perfectly aware of the endeavours that had been made to clear Frederick.

"That Horrocks—that very last witness of all, has proved as unavailing as all the others. Mr. Lennox has discovered that he sailed for Australia only last August; only two months before Frederick was in England, and gave us the names of——"

"Frederick in England! you never told me that!" exclaimed Mr. Bell in surprise.

"I thought you knew. I never doubted you had been told. Of course, it was a great secret, and perhaps I should not have named it now," said Margaret, a little dismayed.

"I have never named it to either my brother or your cousin," said Mr. Lennox, with a little professional dryness of implied reproach.

"Never mind, Margaret. I am not living in a talking, babbling world, nor yet among people who are trying to worm facts out of me; you needn't look so frightened because you have let the cat out of the bag to a faithful old hermit like me. I shall never name his having been in England; I shall be out of temptation, for no one will ask me. Stay!" (interrupting himself rather abruptly) "was it at your mother's funeral?"

"He was with mamma when she died," said Margaret, softly.

"To be sure! To be sure! Why, some one asked me if he had not been over then, and I denied it stoutly—not many weeks ago—who could it have been? Oh! I recollect!"

But he did not say the name; and although Margaret would have given much to know if her suspicions were right, and it had been Mr. Thornton who had made the enquiry, she could not ask the question of Mr. Bell, much as she longed to do so.

There was a pause for a moment or two. Then Mr. Lennox said, addressing himself to Margaret, "I suppose as Mr. Bell is now acquainted with all the circumstances attending your brother's unfortunate dilemma, I cannot do better than inform him exactly how the research into the evidence we once hoped to produce in his favour stands at present. So, if he will do me the honour to breakfast with me to-morrow, we will go over the names of these missing gentry."

"I should like to hear all the particulars, if I may. Cannot you come here? I dare not ask you both to breakfast, though I am sure you would be welcome. But let me know all I can about Frederick, even though there may be no hope at present."

"I have an engagement at half-past eleven. But I will certainly come if you wish it," replied Mr. Lennox with a little after-thought of extreme willingness, which made Margaret shrink into herself, and almost wish that she had not proposed her natural request. Mr. Bell got up and looked around him for his hat, which had been removed to make room for tea.

"Well!" said he, "I don't know what Mr. Lennox is inclined to do, but I'm disposed to be moving off homewards. I've been a journey to-day, and journeys begin to tell upon my sixty and odd years."

"I believe I shall stay and see my brother and sister," said Mr. Lennox, making no movement of departure. Margaret was seized with a shy awkward dread of being left alone with him. The scene on the little terrace in the Helstone garden was so present to her, that she could hardly help believing it was so with him.

"Don't go yet, please Mr. Bell," said she, hastily. "I want you to see Edith; and I want Edith to know you. Please!" said she, laying a light but determined hand on his arm. He looked at her, and saw the confusion stirring in her countenance; he sat down again, as if her little touch had been possessed of resistless strength.

"You see how she overpowers me, Mr. Lennox," said he. "And I hope you noticed the happy choice of her expressions; she wants me to 'see' this cousin Edith, who, I am told, is a great beauty; but she has the honesty to change her word when she comes to me—Mrs. Lennox is to 'know' me. I suppose I am not much to 'see,' eh, Margaret?"

He joked, to give her time to recover from the slight flutter which he had detected in her manner on his proposal to leave; and she caught the tone, and threw the ball back. Mr. Lennox wondered how his brother, the Captain, could have reported her as having lost all her good looks. To be sure, in her quiet black dress, she was a contrast to Edith, dancing in her white crape mourning, and long floating golden hair, all softness and glitter. She dimpled and blushed most becomingly when introduced to Mr. Bell, conscious that she had her reputation as a beauty to keep up, and that it would not do to have a Mordecai[7] refusing to worship and admire, even in the shape of an old Fellow of a College, which nobody had ever heard of. Mrs. Shaw and Captain Lennox, each in their separate way, gave Mr. Bell a kind and sincere welcome, winning him over to like them almost in spite of himself, especially when he saw how naturally Margaret took her place as sister and daughter of the house.

"What a shame that we were not at home to receive you," said Edith. "You, too, Henry! though I don't know that we should have stayed at home for you. And for Mr. Bell! for Margaret's Mr. Bell——"

"There is no knowing what sacrifices you would not have made," said her brother-in-law. "Even a dinner-party! and the delight of wearing this very becoming dress."

Edith did not know whether to frown or to smile. But it did not suit Mr. Lennox to drive her to the first of these alternatives; so he went on.

"Will you show your readiness to make sacrifices to-morrow morn-

---

7. Esther 3:2: "Mordecai bowed not, nor did him reverence." Mordecai refused the command of King Ahasuerus to bow to Haman. This extends the reference to the story of Esther and Vashti referred to above.

ing, first by asking me to breakfast, to meet Mr. Bell, and secondly, by being so kind as to order it at half-past nine, instead of ten o'clock? I have some letters and papers that I want to show to Miss Hale and Mr. Bell."

"I hope Mr. Bell will make our house his own during his stay in London," said Captain Lennox. "I am only so sorry we cannot offer him a bed-room."

"Thank you. I am much obliged to you. You would only think me a churl if you had, for I should decline it, I believe, in spite of all the temptations of such agreeable company," said Mr. Bell, bowing all round, and secretly congratulating himself on the neat turn he had given to his sentence, which, if put into plain language, would have been more to this effect: "I couldn't stand the restraints of such a proper-behaved and civil-spoken set of people as these are: it would be like meat without salt. I'm thankful they haven't a bed. And how well I rounded my sentence! I'm absolutely catching the trick of good manners."

His self-satisfaction lasted him till he was fairly out in the streets, walking side by side with Henry Lennox. Here he suddenly remembered Margaret's little look of entreaty as she urged him to stay longer, and he also recollected a few hints given him long ago by an acquaintance of Mr. Lennox's, as to his admiration of Margaret. It gave a new direction to his thoughts. "You have known Miss Hale[8] for a long time, I believe. How do you think her looking? She strikes me as pale and ill."

"I thought her looking remarkably well. Perhaps not when I first came in—now I think of it. But certainly, when she grew animated, she looked as well as ever I saw her do."

"She has had a great deal to go through," said Mr. Bell.

"Yes! I have been sorry to hear of all she has had to bear; not merely the common and universal sorrow arising from death, but all the annoyance which her father's conduct must have caused her, and then——"

"Her father's conduct!" said Mr. Bell, in an accent of surprise. "You must have heard some wrong statement. He behaved in the most conscientious manner. He showed more resolute strength than I should ever have given him credit for formerly."

"Perhaps I have been wrongly informed. But I have been told, by his successor in the living—a clever, sensible man, and a thoroughly active clergyman—that there was no call upon Mr. Hale to do what he did, relinquish the living, and throw himself and his family on the tender mercies of private teaching in a manufacturing town; the bishop had offered him another living, it is true, but if he had come

8. First edition reads "Miss Lennox," in error. Corrected in 2nd edition.

to entertain certain doubts, he could have remained where he was, and so had no occasion to resign. But the truth is, these country clergymen live such isolated lives—isolated, I mean, from all inter-course with men of equal cultivation with themselves, by whose minds they might regulate their own, and discover when they were going either too fast or too slow—that they are very apt to disturb themselves with imaginary doubts as to the articles of faith, and throw up certain opportunities of doing good for very uncertain fancies of their own."

"I differ from you. I do not think they are very apt to do as my poor friend Hale did." Mr. Bell was inwardly chafing.

"Perhaps I used too general an expression, in saying 'very apt.' But certainly, their lives are such as very often to produce either inor-dinate self-sufficiency, or a morbid state of conscience," replied Mr. Lennox with perfect coolness.

"You don't meet with any self-sufficiency among the lawyers, for instance?" asked Mr. Bell. "And seldom, I imagine, any cases of mor-bid conscience." He was becoming more and more vexed, and for-getting his lately-caught trick of good manners. Mr. Lennox saw now that he had annoyed his companion; and as he had talked pretty much for the sake of saying something, and so passing the time while their road lay together, he was very indifferent as to the exact side he took upon the question, and quietly came round by saying: "To be sure, there is something fine in a man of Mr. Hale's age leaving his home of twenty years, and giving up all settled habits, for an idea which was probably erroneous—but that does not matter—an untangible thought. One cannot help admiring him, with a mixture of pity in one's admiration, something like what one feels for Don Quixote.[9] Such a gentleman as he was too! I shall never forget the refined and simple hospitality he showed to me that last day at Hel-stone."

Only half mollified, and yet anxious, in order to lull certain qualms of his own conscience, to believe that Mr. Hale's conduct had a tinge of Quixotism in it, Mr. Bell growled out—"Aye! And you don't know Milton. Such a change from Helstone! It is years since I have been at Helstone—but I'll answer for it, it is standing there yet—every stick and every stone as it has done for the last century, while Milton! I go there every four or five years—and I was born there—yet I do assure you, I often lose my way—aye, among the very piles of ware-houses that are built upon my father's orchard. Do we part here? Well, good night, sir; I suppose we shall meet in Harley Street to-morrow morning."

9. The hero of Miguel Cervantes's novel of the same name who was famous for stubbornly pursuing lost or ridiculous causes.

Chapter XX.[1]

Not All A Dream.

"Where are the sounds that swam along
The buoyant air when I was young?
The last vibration now is o'er,
And they who listened are no more;
Ah! let me close my eyes and dream."

W. S. LANDOR.[2]

The idea of Helstone had been suggested to Mr. Bell's waking mind
by his conversation with Mr. Lennox, and all night long it ran riot
through his dreams. He was again the tutor in the college where he
now held the rank of Fellow; it was again a long vacation, and he
was staying with his newly married friend, the proud husband, and
happy Vicar of Helstone. Over babbling brooks they took impossible
leaps, which seemed to keep them whole days suspended in the air.
Time and space were not, though all other things seemed real. Every
event was measured by the emotions of the mind, not by its actual
existence, for existence it had none. But the trees were gorgeous in
their autumnal leafiness—the warm odours of flower and herb came
sweet upon the sense—the young wife moved about her house with
just that mixture of annoyance at her position, as regarded wealth,
with pride in her handsome and devoted husband, which Mr. Bell
had noticed in real life a quarter of a century ago. The dream was
so like life that, when he awoke, his present life seemed like a dream.
Where was he? In the close, handsomely furnished room of a London
hotel! Where were those who spoke to him, moved around him,
touched him, not an instant ago? Dead! buried! lost for evermore, as
far as earth's[3] for evermore would extend. He was an old man, so
lately exultant in the full strength of manhood. The utter loneliness
of his life was insupportable to think about. He got up hastily, and
tried to forget what never more might be, in a hurried dressing for
the breakfast in Harley Street.

He could not attend to all the lawyer's details, which, as he saw,
made Margaret's eyes dilate, and her lips grow pale, as one by one
fate decreed, or so it seemed, every morsel of evidence which would
exonerate Frederick, should fall from beneath her feet and disappear.
Even Mr. Lennox's well-regulated professional voice took a softer,

---

1. This and the following chapter do not appear in the *Household Words* text. They appeared
for the first time in the first edition.
2. Walter Savage Landor (1775–1864). The lines are from "Epigram 24," *The Last Fruit off
an Old Tree* (1853). A final line was omitted.
3. A word is obviously omitted here ("boundaries"), but no edition I have consulted supplies
it.

tenderer tone, as he drew near to the extinction of the last hope. It was not that Margaret had not been perfectly aware of the result before. It was only that the details of each successive disappointment came with such relentless minuteness to quench all hope, that she at last fairly gave way to tears. Mr. Lennox stopped reading.

"I had better not go on," said he, in a concerned voice. "It was a foolish proposal of mine. Lieutenant Hale," and even this giving him the title of the service from which he had so harshly been expelled, was soothing to Margaret. "Lieutenant Hale is happy now; more secure in fortune and future prospects than he could ever have been in the navy; and has, doubtless, adopted his wife's country as his own."

"That is it," said Margaret. "It seems so selfish in me to regret it," trying to smile, "and yet he is lost to me, and I am so lonely." Mr. Lennox turned over his papers, and wished that he were as rich and prosperous as he believed he should be some day. Mr. Bell blew his nose, but, otherwise, he also kept silence; and Margaret, in a minute or two, had apparently recovered her usual composure. She thanked Mr. Lennox very courteously for his trouble; all the more courteously and graciously because she was conscious that, by her behaviour, he might have probably been led to imagine that he had given her needless pain. Yet it was pain she would not have been without.

Mr. Bell came up to wish her good-bye.

"Margaret!" said he, as he fumbled with his gloves. "I am going down to Helstone to-morrow, to look at the old place. Would you like to come with me? Or would it give you too much pain? Speak out, don't be afraid."

"Oh, Mr. Bell," said she—and could say no more. But she took his old gouty hand, and kissed it.

"Come, come; that's enough," said he, reddening with awkwardness. "I suppose your aunt Shaw will trust you with me. We'll go to-morrow morning, and we shall get there about two o'clock, I fancy. We'll take a snack, and order dinner at the little inn—the Lennard Arms, it used to be,—and go and get an appetite in the forest. Can you stand it, Margaret? It will be a trial, I know, to both of us, but it will be a pleasure to me, at least. And there we'll dine—it will be but doe-venison, if we can get it at all—and then I'll take my nap while you go out and see old friends. I'll give you back safe and sound, barring railway accidents, and I'll insure your life for a thousand pounds before starting, which may be some comfort to your relations; but otherwise, I'll bring you back to Mrs. Shaw by lunch-time on Friday. So, if you say yes, I'll just go up-stairs and propose it."

"It's no use my trying to say how much I shall like it," said Margaret, through her tears.

"Well, then, prove your gratitude by keeping those fountains of yours dry for the next two days. If you don't, I shall feel queer myself about the lachrymal ducts, and I don't like that."

"I won't cry a drop," said Margaret, winking her eyes to shake the tears off her eye-lashes, and forcing a smile.

"There's my good girl. Then we'll go up-stairs and settle it all." Margaret was in a state of almost trembling eagerness, while Mr. Bell discussed his plan with her aunt Shaw, who was first startled, then doubtful and perplexed, and in the end, yielding rather to the rough force of Mr. Bell's words than to her own conviction; for to the last, whether it was right or wrong, proper or improper, she could not settle to her own satisfaction, till Margaret's safe return, the happy fulfilment of the project, gave her decision enough to say, "she was sure it had been a very kind thought of Mr. Bell's, and just what she herself had been wishing for Margaret, as giving her the very change which she required, after all the anxious time she had had."

Chapter XXI.

Once and Now.

"So on those happy days of yore
Oft as I dare to dwell once more,
Still must I miss the friends so tried,
Whom Death has severed from my side.

But ever when true friendship binds,
Spirit it is that spirit finds;
In spirit then our bliss we found,
In spirit yet to them I'm bound."

UHLAND.[1]

Margaret was ready long before the appointed time, and had leisure enough to cry a little, quietly, when unobserved, and to smile brightly when any one looked at her. Her last alarm was lest they should be too late and miss the train; but no! they were all in time; and she breathed freely and happily at length, seated in the carriage opposite to Mr. Bell, and whirling away past the well-known stations; seeing the old south country-towns and hamlets sleeping in the warm light of the pure sun, which gave a yet ruddier colour to their tiled roofs, so different to the cold slates of the north. Broods of pigeons hovered around these peaked quaint gables, slowly settling here and there, and ruffling their soft, shiny feathers, as if exposing every fibre to the delicious warmth. There were few people about at the stations,

---

1. Johann Ludwig Uhland (1787–1862), German poet. The poem from which Gaskell quotes (in English, "Crossing the Stream,") had personal associations for her, relating to the deaths of two infant children. She prefixed lines from it to her first novel, *Mary Barton* (1848).

it almost seemed as if they were too lazily content to wish to travel;
none of the bustle and stir that Margaret had noticed in her two
journeys on the London and North-Western line. Later on in the
year, this line of railway should be stirring and alive with rich
pleasure-seekers; but as to the constant going to and fro of busy
tradespeople it would always be widely different from the northern
lines. Here a spectator or two stood lounging at nearly every station,
with his hands in his pockets, so absorbed in the simple act of watching, that it made the travellers wonder what he could find to do when
the train whirled away, and only the blank of a railway, some sheds,
and a distant field or two were left for him to gaze upon. The hot air
danced over the golden stillness of the land, farm after farm was left
behind, each reminding Margaret of German Idylls—of Herman and
Dorothea—of Evangeline.[2] From this waking dream she was roused.
It was the place to leave the train and take the fly to Helstone. And
now sharper feelings came shooting through her heart, whether pain
or pleasure she could hardly tell. Every mile was redolent of associations, which she would not have missed for the world, but each
of which made her cry upon "the days that are no more,"[3] with inef-
fable longing. The last time she had passed along this road was when
she had left it with her father and mother—the day, the season, had
been gloomy, and she herself hopeless, but they were there with her.
Now she was alone, an orphan, and they, strangely, had gone away
from her, and vanished from the face of the earth. It hurt her to see
the Helstone road so flooded in the sun-light, and every turn and
every familiar tree so precisely the same in its summer glory as it had
been in former years. Nature felt no change, and was ever young.

   Mr. Bell knew something of what would be passing through her
mind, and wisely and kindly held his tongue. They drove up to the
Lennard Arms; half farm-house, half-inn, standing a little apart from
the road, as much as to say, that the host did not so depend on the
custom of travellers, as to have to court it by any obtrusiveness; they,
rather, must seek him out. The house fronted the village green; and
right before it stood an immemorial lime-tree benched all round, in
some hidden recesses of whose leafy wealth hung the grim escutch-
eon of the Lennards. The door of the inn stood wide open, but there
was no hospitable hurry to receive the travellers. When the landlady
did appear—and they might have abstracted many an article first—
she gave them a kind welcome, almost as if they had been invited
guests, and apologised for her coming having been so delayed, by
saying, that it was hay-time, and the provisions for the men had to

2. "Herman and Dorothea" (1797) is a poem by Johann Wolfgang von Goethe; "Evangeline,"
   however, is probably the narrative poem (1847) by Henry Wadsworth Longfellow. (First
   and subsequent editions read "Idyls"; I have amended to the more common spelling.)
3. The final words of each stanza of Tennyson's poem "Tears, idle tears," written in 1834
   and included in The Princess (1847).

be sent a-field, and she had been too busy packing up the baskets to hear the noise of wheels over the road, which, since they had left the highway, ran over soft short turf.

"Why, bless me!" exclaimed she, as at the end of her apology, a glint of sunlight showed her Margaret's face, hitherto unobserved in that shady parlour. "It's Miss Hale, Jenny," said she, running to the door, and calling to her daughter. "Come here, come directly, it's Miss Hale!" And then she went up to Margaret, and shook her hands with motherly fondness.

"And how are you all? How's the Vicar and Miss Dixon? The Vicar above all! God bless him! We've never ceased to be sorry that he left."

Margaret tried to speak and tell her of her father's death; of her mother's it was evident that Mrs. Purkis was aware, from her omission of her name. But she choked in the effort, and could only touch her deep mourning, and say the one word, "Papa."

"Surely, sir, it's never so!" said Mrs. Purkis, turning to Mr. Bell for confirmation of the sad suspicion that now entered her mind. "There was a gentleman here in the spring—it might have been as long ago as last winter—who told us a deal of Mr. Hale and Miss Margaret; and he said Mrs. Hale was gone, poor lady. But never a word of the Vicar's being ailing!"

"It is so, however," said Mr. Bell. "He died quite suddenly, when on a visit to me at Oxford. He was a good man, Mrs. Purkis, and there's many of us that might be thankful to have as calm an end as his. Come Margaret, my dear! Her father was my oldest friend, and she's my god-daughter, so I thought we would just come down together and see the old place; and I know of old you can give us comfortable rooms and a capital dinner. You don't remember me I see, but my name is Bell, and once or twice when the parsonage has been full, I've slept here, and tasted your good ale."

"To be sure; I ask your pardon; but you see I was taken up with Miss Hale. Let me show you to a room, Miss Margaret, where you can take off your bonnet, and wash your face. It's only this very morning I plunged some fresh-gathered roses head downward in the water-jug, for, thought I, perhaps some one will be coming, and there's nothing so sweet as spring-water scented by a musk rose or two. To think of the Vicar being dead! Well, to be sure, we must all die; only that gentleman said, he was quite picking up after his trouble about Mrs. Hale's death."

"Come down to me, Mrs. Purkis, after you have attended to Miss Hale. I want to have a consultation with you about dinner."

The little casement window in Margaret's bed-chamber was almost filled up with rose and vine branches; but pushing them aside, and stretching a little out, she could see the tops of the parsonage chim-

neys above the trees; and distinguish many a well-known line
through the leaves.

"Aye!" said Mrs. Purkis, smoothing down the bed, and despatching
Jenny for an armful of lavender-scented towels, "times is changed,
miss; our new Vicar has seven children, and is building a nursery
ready for more, just out where the arbour and tool-house used to be
in old times. And he has had new grates put in, and a plate-glass
window in the drawing-room. He and his wife are stirring people,
and have done a deal of good; at least they say it's doing good; if it
were not, I should call it turning things upside down for very little
purpose. The new Vicar is a teetotaller, miss, and a magistrate, and
his wife has a deal of receipts for economical cooking, and is for
making bread without yeast; and they both talk so much, and both
at a time, that they knock one down as it were, and it's not till they're
gone, and one's a little at peace, that one can think that there were
things one might have said on one's own side of the question. He'll
be after the men's cans in the hay-field, and peeping in; and then
there'll be an ado because it's not ginger beer, but I can't help it. My
mother and my grandmother before me sent good malt liquor to
haymakers, and took salts and senna when anything ailed them; and
I must e'en go on in their ways, though Mrs. Hepworth does want
to give me comfits instead of medicine, which, as she says, is a deal
pleasanter, only I've no faith in it. But I must go, miss, though I'm
wanting to hear many a thing; I'll come back to you before long."

Mr. Bell had strawberries and cream, a loaf of brown bread,
and a jug of milk, (together with a Stilton cheese and a bottle of port
for his own private refreshment,) ready for Margaret on her coming down stairs; and after this rustic luncheon they set out to walk,
hardly knowing in what direction to turn, so many old familiar
inducements were there in each.

"Shall we go past the vicarage?" asked Mr. Bell.

"No, not yet. We will go this way, and make a round so as to come
back by it," replied Margaret.

Here and there old trees had been felled the autumn before; or a
squatter's roughly-built and decaying cottage had disappeared. Margaret missed them each and all, and grieved over them like old
friends. They came past the spot where she and Mr. Lennox had
sketched. The white, lightning-scarred trunk of the venerable beech,
among whose roots they had sat down was there no more; the old
man, the inhabitant of the ruinous cottage, was dead; the cottage
had been pulled down, and a new one, tidy and respectable, had
been built in its stead. There was a small garden on the place where
the beech-tree had been.

"I did not think I had been so old," said Margaret after a pause of
silence; and she turned away sighing.

"Yes!" said Mr. Bell. "It is the first changes among familiar things that make such a mystery of time to the young, afterwards we lose the sense of the mysterious. I take changes in all I see as a matter of course. The instability of all human things is familiar to me, to you it is new and oppressive."

"Let us go on to see little Susan," said Margaret, drawing her companion up a grassy road-way, leading under the shadow of a forest glade.

"With all my heart, though I have not an idea who little Susan may be. But I have a kindness for all Susans, for simple Susan's sake."[4]

"My little Susan was disappointed when I left without wishing her goodbye; and it has been on my conscience ever since, that I gave her pain which a little more exertion on my part might have prevented. But it is a long way. Are you sure you will not be tired?"

"Quite sure. That is, if you don't walk so fast. You see, here there are no views that can give one an excuse for stopping to take breath. You would think it romantic to be walking with a person 'fat and scant o' breath'[5] if I were Hamlet, Prince of Denmark. Have compassion on my infirmities for his sake."

"I will walk slower for your own sake. I like you twenty times better than Hamlet."

"On the principle that a living ass is better than a dead lion?"

"Perhaps so. I don't analyse my feelings."

"I am content to take your liking me, without examining too curiously into the materials it is made of. Only we need not walk at a snail's pace."

"Very well. Walk at your own pace, and I will follow. Or stop still and meditate, like the Hamlet you compare yourself to, if I go too fast."

"Thank you. But as my mother has not murdered my father, and afterwards married my uncle, I shouldn't know what to think about, unless it were balancing the chances of our having a well-cooked dinner or not. What do you think?"

"I am in good hopes. She used to be considered a famous cook as far as Helstone opinion went."

"But have you considered the distraction of mind produced by all this haymaking?"

Margaret felt all Mr. Bell's kindness in trying to make cheerful talk about nothing, to endeavour to prevent her from thinking too curiously about the past. But she would rather have gone over these dear-

4. The story of "Simple Susan," by Maria Edgeworth (1767–1849), first appeared in her volume of children's stories, *The Parent's Assistant*, in 1800. Edgeworth's stories, which combined simple narratives with a moral message, were a popular educational aid throughout the nineteenth century.
5. *Hamlet* V.2.

loved walks in silence, if indeed she were not ungrateful enough to wish that she might have been alone.

They reached the cottage where Susan's widowed mother lived. Susan was not there. She was gone to the parochial school. Margaret was disappointed, and the poor woman saw it, and began to make a kind of apology.

"Oh! it is quite right," said Margaret. "I am very glad to hear it. I might have thought of it. Only she used to stop at home with you."

"Yes, she did; and I miss her sadly. I used to teach her what little I knew at nights. It were not much to be sure. But she were getting such a handy girl, that I miss her sore. But she's a deal above me in learning now." And the mother sighed.

"I'm all wrong," growled Mr. Bell. "Don't mind what I say. I'm a hundred years behind the world. But I should say, that the child was getting a better and simpler, and more natural education stopping at home, and helping her mother, and learning to read a chapter in the New Testament every night by her side, than from all the schooling under the sun."

Margaret did not want to encourage him to go on by replying to him, and so prolonging the discussion before the mother. So she turned to her and asked,

"How is old Betty Barnes?"

"I don't know," said the woman rather shortly. "We'se not friends."

"Why not?" asked Margaret, who had formerly been the peacemaker of the village.

"She stole my cat."

"Did she know it was yours?"

"I don't know. I reckon not."

"Well! could not you get it back again when you told her it was yours?"

"No! for she'd burnt it."

"Burnt it!" exclaimed both Margaret and Mr. Bell.

"Roasted it!" explained the woman.

It was no explanation. By dint of questioning, Margaret extracted from her the horrible fact that Betty Barnes, having been induced by a gypsy fortune-teller to lend the latter her husband's Sunday clothes, on promise of having them faithfully returned on the Saturday night before Goodman Barnes should have missed them, became alarmed by their non-appearance, and her consequent dread of her husband's anger, and as, according to one of the savage country superstitions, the cries of a cat, in the agonies of being boiled or roasted alive, compelled (as it were) the powers of darkness to fulfil the wishes of the executioner, resort had been had to the charm. The poor woman evidently believed in its efficacy; her only feeling was indignation that her cat had been chosen out from all others for a sacrifice. Margaret listened in horror; and endeavoured in vain to enlighten the woman's mind; but she was obliged to give it up in despair. Step by step she got the woman to admit certain facts, of which the logical connexion and sequence was perfectly clear to Margaret; but at the end, the bewildered woman simply repeated her first assertion, namely, that "it were very cruel for sure, and she should not like to do it; but that there were nothing like it for giving a person what they wished for; she had heard it all her life; but it were very cruel for all that." Margaret gave it up in despair, and walked away sick at heart.

"You are a good girl not to triumph over me," said Mr. Bell.

"How? What do you mean?"

"I own, I am wrong about schooling. Anything rather than have that child brought up in such practical paganism."

"Oh! I remember. Poor little Susan! I must go and see her; would you mind calling at the school?"

"Not a bit. I am curious to see something of the teaching she is to receive."

They did not speak much more, but thridded their way through many a bosky dell, whose soft green influence could not charm away the shock and the pain in Margaret's heart, caused by the recital of such cruelty; a recital too, the manner of which betrayed such utter want of imagination, and therefore of any sympathy with the suffering animal.

The buzz of voices, like the murmur of a hive of busy human bees, made itself heard as soon as they emerged from the forest on the more open village-green on which the school was situated. The door was wide open, and they entered. A brisk lady in black, here, there, and everywhere, perceived them, and bade them welcome with somewhat of the hostess-air which, Margaret remembered, her mother was wont to assume, only in a more soft and languid manner, when any rare visitors strayed in to inspect the school. She knew at once it was the present Vicar's wife, her mother's successor; and she would have drawn back from the interview had it been possible; but in an instant she had conquered this feeling, and modestly advanced, meeting many a bright glance of recognition, and hearing many a half-suppressed murmur of "It's Miss Hale." The Vicar's lady heard the name, and her manner at once became more kindly. Margaret wished she could have helped feeling that it also became more patronizing. The lady held out a hand to Mr. Bell, with—

"Your father, I presume, Miss Hale. I see it by the likeness. I am sure I am very glad to see you, sir, and so will the Vicar be."

Margaret explained that it was not her father, and stammered out the fact of his death; wondering all the time how Mr. Hale could have borne coming to revisit Helstone, if it had been as the Vicar's

lady supposed. She did not hear what Mrs. Hepworth was saying,
and left it to Mr. Bell to reply, looking round, meanwhile, for her old
acquaintances.

"Ah! I see you would like to take a class, Miss Hale. I know it by
myself. First class stand up for a parsing lesson[6] with Miss Hale."

Poor Margaret, whose visit was sentimental, not in any degree
inspective, felt herself taken in; but as in some way bringing her in
contact with little eager faces, once well-known, and who had
received the solemn rite of baptism from her father, she sat down,
half losing herself in tracing out the changing features of the girls,
and holding Susan's hand for a minute or two, unobserved by all,
while the first class sought for their books, and the Vicar's lady went
as near as a lady could towards holding Mr. Bell by the button, while
she explained the Phonetic system to him, and gave him a conversation she had had with the Inspector about it.

Margaret bent over her book, and seeing nothing but that—hearing the buzz of children's voices, old times rose up, and she thought
of them, and her eyes filled with tears, till all at once there was a
pause—one of the girls was stumbling over the apparently simple
word "a," uncertain what to call it.

"A, an indefinite article," said Margaret, mildly.

"I beg your pardon," said the Vicar's wife, all eyes and ears; "but
we are taught by Mr. Milsome to call 'a' an—who can remember?"

"An adjective absolute," said half-a-dozen voices at once. And Margaret sat abashed. The children knew more than she did. Mr. Bell
turned away, and smiled.

Margaret spoke no more during the lesson. But after it was over,
she went quietly round to one or two old favourites, and talked to
them a little. They were growing out of children into great girls;
passing out of her recollection in their rapid development, as she, by
her three years' absence, was vanishing from theirs. Still she was
glad to have seen them all again, though a tinge of sadness mixed
itself with her pleasure. When school was over for the day, it was yet
early in the summer afternoon; and Mrs. Hepworth proposed to Margaret that she and Mr. Bell should accompany her to the parsonage,
and see the—the word "improvements" had half slipped out of her
mouth, but she substituted the more cautious term "alterations"
which the present Vicar was making. Margaret did not care a straw
about seeing the alterations, which jarred upon her fond recollection
of what her home had been; but she longed to see the old place once
more, even though she shivered away from the pain which she knew
she should feel.

6. A grammar lesson in which children were required to identify parts of speech.

The parsonage was so altered, both inside and out, that the real pain was less than she had anticipated. It was not like the same place. The garden, the grass-plat, formerly so daintily trim that even a stray rose-leaf seemed like a fleck on its exquisite arrangement and propriety, was strewed with children's things; a bag of marbles here, a hoop there; a straw-hat forced down upon a rose-tree as on a peg, to the destruction of a long beautiful tender branch laden with flowers, which in former days would have been trained up tenderly, as if beloved. The little square matted hall was equally filled with signs of merry healthy rough childhood.

"Ah!" said Mrs. Hepworth, "you must excuse this untidiness, Miss Hale. When the nursery is finished, I shall insist upon a little order. We are building a nursery out of your room, I believe. How did you manage, Miss Hale, without a nursery?"

"We were but two," said Margaret. "You have many children, I presume?"

"Seven. Look here! we are throwing out a window to the road on this side. Mr. Hepworth is spending an immense deal of money on this house; but really it was scarcely habitable when we came—for so large a family as ours I mean, of course." Every room in the house was changed, besides the one of which Mrs. Hepworth spoke, which had been Mr. Hale's study formerly; and where the green gloom and delicious quiet of the place had conduced, as he had said, to a habit of meditation, but, perhaps, in some degree to the formation of a character more fitted for thought than action. The new window gave a view of the road, and had many advantages, as Mrs. Hepworth pointed out. From it the wandering sheep of her husband's flock might be seen, who straggled to the tempting beer-house, unobserved as they might hope, but not unobserved in reality; for the active Vicar kept his eye on the road, even during the composition of his most orthodox sermons, and had a hat and stick hanging ready at hand to seize, before sallying out after his parishioners, who had need of quick legs if they could take refuge in the "Jolly Forester" before the teetotal Vicar had arrested them. The whole family were quick, brisk, loud-talking, kind-hearted, and not troubled with much delicacy of perception. Margaret feared that Mrs. Hepworth would find out that Mr. Bell was playing upon her, in the admiration he thought fit to express for everything that especially grated on his taste. But no! she took it all literally, and with such good faith, that Margaret could not help remonstrating with him as they walked slowly away from the parsonage back to their inn.

"Don't scold, Margaret. It was all because of you. If she had not shown you every change with such evident exultation in their superior sense, in perceiving what an improvement this and that would

be, I could have behaved well. But if you must go on preaching, keep
it till after dinner, when it will send me to sleep, and help my digestion."

They were both of them tired, and Margaret herself so much so,
that she was unwilling to go out as she had proposed to do, and have
another ramble among the woods and fields so close to the home of
her childhood. And, somehow, this visit to Helstone had not been
all—had not been exactly what she had expected. There was change
everywhere; slight, yet pervading all. Households were changed by
absence, or death, or marriage, or the natural mutations brought by
days and months and years, which carry us on imperceptibly from
childhood to youth, and thence through manhood to age, whence
we drop like fruit, fully ripe, into the quiet mother earth. Places were
changed—a tree gone here, a bough there, bringing in a long ray of
light where no light was before—a road was trimmed and narrowed,
and the green straggling pathway by its side enclosed and cultivated.
A great improvement it was called; but Margaret sighed over the old
picturesqueness, the old gloom, and the grassy wayside of former
days. She sat by the window on the little settle, sadly gazing out upon
the gathering shades of night, which harmonised well with her pensive thought. Mr. Bell slept soundly, after his unusual exercise
through the day. At last he was roused by the entrance of the tea-
tray, brought in by a flushed-looking country-girl, who had evidently
been finding some variety from her usual occupation of waiter, in
assisting this day in the hay-field.

"Hallo! Who's there! Where are we? Who's that,—Margaret? Oh,
now I remember all. I could not imagine what woman was sitting
there in such a doleful attitude, with her hands clasped straight out
upon her knees, and her face looking so steadfastly before her. What
were you looking at?" asked Mr. Bell, coming to the window, and
standing behind Margaret.

"Nothing," said she, rising up quickly, and speaking as cheerfully
as she could at a moment's notice.

"Nothing indeed! A bleak back-ground of trees, some white linen
hung out on the sweet-briar hedge, and a great waft of damp air.
Shut the window, and come in and make tea."

Margaret was silent for some time. She played with her teaspoon,
and did not attend particularly to what Mr. Bell said. He contradicted
her, and she took the same sort of smiling notice of his opinion as
if he had agreed with her. Then she sighed, and putting down her
spoon, she began, apropos of nothing at all, and in the high-pitched
voice which usually shows that the speaker has been thinking for
some time on the subject that they wish to introduce—"Mr. Bell,
you remember what we were saying about Frederick last night, don't
you?"

"Last night. Where was I? Oh, I remember! Why it seems a week ago. Yes, to be sure, I recollect we talked about him, poor fellow."

"Yes—and do you not remember that Mr. Lennox spoke about his having been in England about the time of dear mamma's death?" asked Margaret, her voice now lower than usual.

"I recollect. I hadn't heard of it before."

"And I thought—I always thought that papa had told you about it."

"No! he never did. But what about it, Margaret?"

"I want to tell you of something I did that was very wrong, about that time," said Margaret, suddenly looking up at him with her clear honest eyes. "I told a lie;" and her face became scarlet.

"True, that was bad I own; not but what I have told a pretty round number in my life, not all in downright words, as I suppose you did, but in actions, or in some shabby circumlocutory way, leading people either to disbelieve the truth, or believe a falsehood. You know who is the father of lies, Margaret? Well! a great number of folk, thinking themselves very good, have odd sorts of connexion with lies, left-hand marriages,[7] and second cousins-once-removed. The tainting blood of falsehood runs through us all. I should have guessed you as far from it as most people. What! crying, child? Nay, now we'll not talk of it, if it ends in this way. I dare say you have been sorry for it, and that you won't do it again, and it's long ago now, and in short I want you to be very cheerful, and not very sad, this evening."

Margaret wiped her eyes, and tried to talk about something else, but suddenly she burst out afresh.

"Please, Mr. Bell, let me tell you about it—you could perhaps help me a little; no, not help me, but if you knew the truth, perhaps you could put me to rights—that is not it, after all," said she, in despair at not being able to express herself more exactly as she wished.

Mr. Bell's whole manner changed. "Tell me all about it, child," said he.

"It's a long story; but when Fred came, mamma was very ill, and I was undone with anxiety, and afraid, too, that I might have drawn him into danger; and we had an alarm just after her death, for Dixon met some one in Milton—a man called Leonards—who had known Fred, and who seemed to owe him a grudge, or at any rate to be tempted by the recollection of the reward offered for his apprehension; and with this new fright, I thought I had better hurry off Fred to London, where, as you would understand from what we said the

---

7. Morganatic marriages, i.e., marriages in which the wife and children were not entitled to any share of the husband's assets. The term came to be used generally for marriages involving a wealthy man and a wife of substantially lower status, or more specifically of the servant classes. Such marriages were often hushed up.

other night, he was to go to consult Mr. Lennox as to his chances if he stood the trial. So we—that is, he and I,—went to the railway station; it was one evening, and it was just getting rather dusk, but still light enough to recognize and be recognized, and we were too early, and went out to walk in a field just close by; I was always in a panic about this Leonards, who was, I knew, somewhere in the neighbourhood; and then, when we were in the field, the low red sunlight just in my face, some one came by on horseback in the road just below the field-style by which we stood. I saw him look at me, but I did not know who it was at first, the sun was so in my eyes, but in an instant the dazzle went off, and I saw it was Mr. Thornton, and we bowed,"——

"And he saw Frederick of course," said Mr. Bell, helping her on with her story, as he thought.

"Yes; and then at the station a man came up—tipsy and reeling— and he tried to collar Fred, and over-balanced himself as Fred wrenched himself away, and fell over the edge of the platform; not far, not deep; not above three feet; but oh! Mr. Bell, somehow that fall killed him!"

"How awkward. It was this Leonards, I suppose. And how did Fred get off?"

"Oh! he went off immediately after the fall, which we never thought could have done the poor fellow any harm, it seemed so slight an injury."

"Then he did not die directly?"

"No! not for two or three days. And then—oh, Mr. Bell! now comes the bad part," said she, nervously twining her fingers together. "A police inspector came and taxed me with having been the companion of the young man, whose push or blow had occasioned Leonards' death; that was a false accusation, you know, but we had not heard that Fred had sailed, he might still be in London and liable to be arrested on this false charge, and his identity with the Lieutenant Hale, accused of causing that mutiny, discovered, he might be shot; all this flashed through my mind, and I said it was not me. I was not at the railway station that night. I knew nothing about it. I had no conscience or thought but to save Frederick."

"I say it was right. I should have done the same. You forgot yourself in thought for another. I hope I should have done the same."

"No, you would not. It was wrong, disobedient, faithless. At that very time Fred was safely out of England, and in my blindness I forgot that there was another witness who could testify to my being there."

"Who?"

"Mr. Thornton. You know he had seen me close to the station; we had bowed to each other."

"Well! he would know nothing of this riot about the drunken fellow's death. I suppose the inquiry never came to anything."

"No! the proceedings they had begun to talk about on the inquest were stopped. Mr. Thornton did know all about it. He was a magistrate, and he found out that it was not the fall that had caused the death. But not before he knew what I had said. Oh, Mr. Bell!" She suddenly covered her face with her hands, as if wishing to hide herself from the presence of the recollection.

"Did you have any explanation with him? Did you ever tell him the strong, instinctive motive?"

"The instinctive want of faith, and clutching at a sin to keep myself from sinking," said she bitterly. "No! How could I? He knew nothing of Frederick. To put myself to rights in his good opinion, was I to tell him of the secrets of our family, involving, as they seemed to do, the chances of poor Frederick's entire exculpation? Fred's last words had been to enjoin me to keep his visit a secret from all. You see, papa never told, even you. No! I could bear the shame—I thought I could at least. I did bear it. Mr. Thornton has never respected me since."

"He respects you, I am sure," said Mr. Bell. "To be sure, it accounts a little for——. But he always speaks of you with regard and esteem, though now I understand certain reservations in his manner."

Margaret did not speak; did not attend to what Mr. Bell went on to say; lost all sense of it. By-and-bye she said:

"Will you tell me what you refer to about 'reservations' in his manner of speaking of me?"

"Oh! simply he has annoyed me by not joining in my praises of you. Like an old fool, I thought that everyone would have the same opinions as I had; and he evidently could not agree with me. I was puzzled at the time. But he must be perplexed, if the affair has never been in the least explained. There was first your walking out with a young man in the dark—"

"But it was my brother!" said Margaret, surprised.

"True. But how was he to know that?"

"I don't know. I never thought of any thing of that kind," said Margaret, reddening, and looking hurt and offended.

"And perhaps he never would, but for the lie,—which, under the circumstances, I maintain, was necessary."

"It was not. I know it now. I bitterly repent it."

There was a long pause of silence. Margaret was the first to speak.

"I am not likely ever to see Mr. Thornton again,"—and there she stopped.

"There are many things more unlikely, I should say," replied Mr. Bell.

"But I believe I never shall. Still, somehow one does not like to have sunk so low in—in a friend's opinion as I have done in his." Her eyes were full of tears, but her voice was steady, and Mr. Bell was not looking at her. "And now that Frederick has given up all hope, and almost all wish of ever clearing himself, and returning to England, it would be only doing myself justice to have all this explained. If you please, and if you can, if there is a good opportunity, (don't force an explanation upon him, pray,) but if you can, will you tell him the whole circumstances, and tell him also that I gave you leave to do so, because I felt that for papa's sake I should not like to lose his respect, though we may never be likely to meet again?"

"Certainly. I think he ought to know. I do not like you to rest even under the shadow of an impropriety; he would not know what to think of seeing you alone with a young man."

"As for that," said Margaret, rather haughtily, "I hold it is 'Honi soit qui mal y pense.'[8] Yet still I should choose to have it explained, if any natural opportunity for easy explanation occurs. But it is not to clear myself of any suspicion of improper conduct that I wish to have him told—if I thought that he had suspected me, I should not care for his good opinion—no! it is that he may learn how I was tempted, and how I fell into the snare; why I told that falsehood, in short."

"Which I don't blame you for. It is no partiality of mine, I assure you."

"What other people may think of the rightness or wrongness is nothing in comparison to my own deep knowledge, my innate conviction that it was wrong. But we will not talk of that any more, if you please. It is done—my sin is sinned. I have now to put it behind me, and be truthful for evermore, if I can."

"Very well. If you like to be uncomfortable and morbid, be so. I always keep my conscience as tight shut up as a jack-in-a-box, for when it jumps into existence it surprises me by its size. So I coax it down again, as the fisherman coaxed the genie.[9] 'Wonderful,' say I, 'to think that you have been concealed so long; and in so small a compass, that I really did not know of your existence. Pray, sir, instead of growing larger and larger every instant, and bewildering me with your misty outlines, would you once more compress yourself into your former dimensions?' And when I've got him down, don't I clap the seal on the vase, and take good care how I open it again, and how I go against Solomon, wisest of men, who confined him there."

8. "Evil be to him who evil thinks": traditionally the motto of the Order of the Garter.
9. In the story in the *Arabian Nights*.

But it was no smiling matter to Margaret. She hardly attended to what Mr. Bell was saying. Her thoughts ran upon the idea, before entertained, but which now had assumed the strength of a conviction, that Mr. Thornton no longer held his former good opinion of her—that he was disappointed in her. She did not feel as if any explanation could ever reinstate her—not in his love, for that and any return on her part she had resolved never to dwell upon, and she kept rigidly to her resolution—but in the respect and high regard which she had hoped would have ever made him willing, in the spirit of Gerald Griffin's beautiful lines,

> "To turn and look back when thou hearest
>   The sound of my name."[1]

She kept choking and swallowing all the time that she thought about it. She tried to comfort herself with the idea, that what he imagined her to be, did not alter the fact of what she was. But it was a truism, a phantom, and broke down under the weight of her regret. She had twenty questions on the tip of her tongue to ask Mr. Bell, but not one of them did she utter. Mr. Bell thought that she was tired, and sent her early to her room, where she sat long hours by the open window, gazing out on the purple dome above, where the stars arose, and twinkled and disappeared behind the great umbrageous trees before she went to bed. All night long too, there burnt a little light on earth; a candle in her old bedroom, which was the nursery with the present inhabitants of the parsonage, until the new one was built. A sense of change, of individual nothingness, of perplexity and disappointment, overpowered Margaret. Nothing had been the same; and this slight, all-pervading instability, had given her greater pain than if all had been too entirely changed for her to recognise it.

"I begin to understand now what heaven must be—and, oh! the grandeur and repose of the words—'The same yesterday, to-day, and for ever.' Everlasting! 'From everlasting to everlasting, Thou art God.'[2] That sky above me looks as though it could not change, and yet it will. I am so tired—so tired of being whirled on through all these phases of my life, in which nothing abides by me, no creature, no place; it is like the circle in which the victims of earthly passion eddy continually. I am in the mood in which women of another religion take the veil. I seek heavenly steadfastness in earthly monotony. If I were a Roman Catholic and could deaden my heart, stun it with some great blow, I might become a nun. But I should pine after my

---

1. Gerald Griffin (1803–1840), a nineteenth-century Irish poet. The poem from which the lines are taken is "A place in thy memory, dearest."
2. A conflation of Hebrews 13:8 and Psalms 90:2.

kind; no, not my kind, for love for my species could never fill my heart to the utter exclusion of love for individuals. Perhaps it ought to be so, perhaps not; I cannot decide to-night."

Wearily she went to bed, wearily she arose in four or five hours' time. But with the morning came hope, and a brighter view of things.

"After all it is right," said she, hearing the voices of children at play while she was dressing. "If the world stood still, it would retrograde and become corrupt, if that is not Irish. Looking out of myself, and my own painful sense of change, the progress all around me is right and necessary. I must not think so much of how circumstances affect me myself, but how they affect others, if I wish to have a right judgment, or a hopeful trustful heart." And with a smile ready in her eyes to quiver down to her lips, she went into the parlour and greeted Mr. Bell.

"Ah, Missy! you were up late last night, and so you're late this morning. Now I've got a little piece of news for you. What do you think of an invitation to dinner? a morning call, literally in the dewy morning. Why, I've had the Vicar here already, on his way to the school. How much the desire of giving our hostess a teetotal lecture for the benefit of the haymakers, had to do with his earliness, I don't know; but here he was, when I came down just before nine; and we are asked to dine there to-day."

"But Edith expects me back—I cannot go," said Margaret, thankful to have so good an excuse.

"Yes! I know; so I told him. I thought you would not want to go. Still it is open, if you would like it."

"Oh, no!" said Margaret. "Let us keep to our plan. Let us start at twelve. It is very good and kind of them; but indeed I could not go."

"Very well. Don't fidget yourself, and I'll arrange it all."

Before they left Margaret stole round to the back of the Vicarage garden, and gathered a little straggling piece of honeysuckle. She would not take a flower the day before, for fear of being observed, and her motives and feelings commented upon. But as she returned across the common, the place was reinvested with the old enchanting atmosphere. The common sounds of life were more musical there than anywhere else in the whole world, the light more golden, the life more tranquil and full of dreamy delight. As Margaret remembered her feelings yesterday, she said to herself:

"And I too change perpetually—now this, now that—now disappointed and peevish because all is not exactly as I had pictured it, and now suddenly discovering that the reality is far more beautiful than I had imagined it. Oh, Helstone! I shall never love any place like you."

A few days afterwards, she had found her level, and decided that she was very glad to have been there, and that she had seen it again, and that to her it would always be the prettiest spot in the world, but that it was so full of associations with former days, and especially with her father and mother, that if it were all to come over again, she should shrink back from such another visit as that which she had paid with Mr. Bell.

Chapter XXII.

Something Wanting.

> "Experience, like a pale musician, holds
> A dulcimer of patience in his hand;
> Whence harmonies we cannot understand,
> Of God's will in His worlds, the strain unfolds
> In sad, perplexed minors."
>
> MRS. BROWNING.[1]

About this time Dixon returned from Milton, and assumed her post as Margaret's maid. She brought endless pieces of Milton gossip: How Martha had gone to live with Miss Thornton, on the latter's marriage; with an account of the bridesmaids, dresses and break-fasts, at that interesting ceremony; how people thought that Mr. Thornton had made too grand a wedding of it, considering he had lost a deal by the strike, and had had to pay so much for the failure of his contracts; how little money articles of furniture—long cher-ished by Dixon—had fetched at the sale, which was a shame con-sidering how rich folks were at Milton; how Mrs. Thornton had come one day and got two or three good bargains, and Mr. Thornton had come the next, and in his desire to obtain one or two things, had bid against himself, much to the enjoyment of the bystanders, so as Dixon observed, that made things even; if Mrs. Thornton paid too little, Mr. Thornton paid too much. Mr. Bell had sent all sorts of orders about the books; there was no understanding him, he was so particular; if he had come himself it would have been all right, but letters always were and always will be more puzzling than they are worth. Dixon had not much to tell about the Higginses. Her memory had an aristocratic bias, and was very treacherous whenever she tried to recall any circumstance connected with those below her in life. Nicholas was very well she believed. He had been several times at the house asking for news of Miss Margaret—the only person who ever did ask, except once Mr. Thornton. And Mary? oh! of course she was very well, a great, stout, slatternly thing! She did hear, or perhaps it was only a dream of hers, though it would be strange if

---

1. The opening lines of Elizabeth Barrett Browning's sonnet "Perplexed Music," on the sub-ject of mental frustration.

she had dreamt of such people as the Higginses, that Mary had gone
to work at Mr. Thornton's mill, because her father wished her to
know how to cook; but what nonsense that could mean she didn't
know. Margaret rather agreed with her that the story was incoherent
enough to be like a dream. Still it was pleasant to have some one
now with whom she could talk of Milton, and Milton people. Dixon
was not over-fond of the subject, rather wishing to leave that part of
her life in shadow. She liked much more to dwell upon speeches of
Mr. Bell's, which had suggested an idea to her of what was really his
intention—making Margaret his heiress. But her young lady gave
her no encouragement, nor in any way gratified her insinuating
enquiries, however disguised in the form of suspicions or assertions.

All this time, Margaret had a strange undefined longing to hear
that Mr. Bell had gone to pay one of his business visits to Milton;
for it had been well understood between them, at the time of their
conversation at Helstone, that the explanation she had desired
should only be given to Mr. Thornton by word of mouth, and even
in that manner should be in nowise forced upon him. Mr. Bell was
no great correspondent, but he wrote from time to time long or short
letters, as the humour took him, and although Margaret was not
conscious of any definite hope, on receiving them, yet she always
put away his notes with a little feeling of disappointment. He was
not going to Milton; he said nothing about it at any rate. Well! she
must be patient. Sooner or later the mists would be cleared away.
Mr. Bell's letters were hardly like his usual self; they were short, and
complaining, with every now and then a little touch of bitterness
that was unusual. He did not look forward to the future; he rather
seemed to regret the past, and be weary of the present. Margaret
fancied that he could not be well; but in answer to some enquiry of
hers as to his health, he sent her a short note, saying there was an
old-fashioned complaint called the spleen; that he was suffering
from that, and it was for her to decide if it was more mental or
physical; but that he should like to indulge himself in grumbling,
without being obliged to send a bulletin every time.

In consequence of this note, Margaret made no more enquiries
about his health. One day Edith let out accidentally a fragment of a
conversation which she had had with Mr. Bell, when he was last in
London, which possessed Margaret with the idea that he had some
notion of taking her to pay a visit to her brother and new sister-in-
law, at Cadiz, in the autumn. She questioned and cross-questioned
Edith, till the latter was weary, and declared that there was nothing
more to remember; all he had said was that he half-thought he
should go, and hear for himself what Frederick had to say about the
mutiny; and that it would be a good opportunity for Margaret to
become acquainted with her new sister-in-law; that he always went

somewhere during the long vacation, and did not see why he should not go to Spain as well as anywhere else. That was all. Edith hoped Margaret did not want to leave them, that she was so anxious about all this. And then, having nothing else particular to do, she cried, and said that she knew she cared much more for Margaret than Margaret did for her. Margaret comforted her as well as she could, but she could hardly explain to her how this idea of Spain, mere Chateau en Espagne[2] as it might be, charmed and delighted her. Edith was in the mood to think that any pleasure enjoyed away from her was a tacit affront, or at best a proof of indifference. So Margaret had to keep her pleasure to herself, and could only let it escape by the safety-valve of asking Dixon, when she dressed for dinner, if she would not like to see Master Frederick and his new wife very much indeed?

"She's a Papist, Miss, isn't she?"

"I believe—oh yes, certainly!" said Margaret, a little damped for an instant at this recollection.

"And they live in a Popish country?"

"Yes."

"Then I'm afraid I must say, that my soul is dearer to me than even Master Frederick, his own dear self. I should be in a perpetual terror, Miss, lest I should be converted."

"Oh," said Margaret, "I do not know that I am going; and if I go, I am not such a fine lady as to be unable to travel without you. No! dear old Dixon, you shall have a long holiday, if we go. But I'm afraid it is a long 'if.' "

Now Dixon did not like this speech. In the first place, she did not like Margaret's trick of calling her 'dear old Dixon' whenever she was particularly demonstrative. She knew that Miss Hale was apt to call all people that she liked "old," as a sort of term of endearment; but Dixon always winced away from the application of the word to herself, who, being not much past fifty, was, she thought, in the very prime of life. Secondly, she did not like being so easily taken at her word; she had, with all her terror, a lurking curiosity about Spain, the Inquisition, and Popish mysteries. So, after clearing her throat, as if to show her willingness to do away with difficulties, she asked Miss Hale, whether she thought if she took care never to see a priest, or enter into one of their churches, there would be so very much danger of her being converted? Master Frederick, to be sure, had gone over unaccountable.

"I fancy it was love that first predisposed him to conversion," said Margaret, sighing.

"Indeed, Miss!" said Dixon; "well! I can preserve myself from

---

2. Castle in Spain, metaphorically, a fantasy (French).

priests, and from churches; but love steals in unawares! I think it's
as well I should not go."

Margaret was afraid of letting her mind run too much upon this
Spanish plan. But it took off her thoughts from too impatiently dwelling upon her desire to have all explained to Mr. Thornton. Mr. Bell
appeared for the present to be stationary at Oxford, and to have no
immediate purpose of going to Milton, and some secret restraint
seemed to hang over Margaret, and prevent her from even asking,
or alluding again to any probability of such a visit on his part. Nor
did she feel at liberty to name what Edith had told her of the idea
he had entertained,—it might be but for five minutes,—of going to
Spain. He had never named it at Helstone, during all that sunny day
of leisure; it was very probably but the fancy of a moment,—but if
it were true, what a bright outlet it would be from the monotony of
her present life, which was beginning to fall upon her.[3]

One of the great pleasures of Margaret's life at this time, was in
Edith's boy. He was the pride and plaything of both father and
mother, as long as he was good; but he had a strong will of his own,
and as soon as he burst out into one of his stormy passions, Edith
would throw herself back in despair and fatigue, and sigh out, "Oh
dear, what shall I do with him! Do, Margaret, please ring the bell for
Hanley."

But Margaret almost liked him better in these manifestations of
character than in his good blue-sashed moods. She would carry him
off into a room, where they two alone battled it out; she with a firm
power which subdued him into peace, while every sudden charm and
wile she possessed, was exerted on the side of right, until he would
rub his little hot and tear-smeared face all over hers, kissing and
caressing till he often fell asleep in her arms or on her shoulder.
Those were Margaret's sweetest moments. They gave her a taste of
the feeling that she believed would be denied to her for ever.[4]

Mr. Henry Lennox added a new and not disagreeable element to
the course of the household life by his frequent presence. Margaret
thought him colder, if more brilliant than formerly; but there were
strong intellectual tastes, and much and varied knowledge, which
gave flavour to the otherwise rather insipid conversation. Margaret
saw glimpses in him of a slight contempt for his brother and sister-
in-law, and for their mode of life, which he seemed to consider as
frivolous and purposeless. He once or twice spoke to his brother, in
Margaret's presence, in a pretty sharp tone of enquiry, as to whether

3. At this point in the text of the first edition a paragraph from vol. II, chap. 19 beginning
"The course of Margaret's day was this:" (p. 340 above) was erroneously repeated. I have
deleted it at this point. See p. 340, n. 5 above.
4. At this point in the text of the first edition a further paragraph from vol. II, chap. 19 was
repeated. Slightly adjusted, it begins, "Edith piqued herself on her dinner-parties";
(p. 339–40 above). Again I have deleted the paragraph at this point. See p. 340, n. 5 above.

he meant entirely to relinquish his profession; and on Captain Lennox's reply, that he had quite enough to live upon, she had seen Mr. Lennox's curl of the lip as he said, "And is that all you live for?"

But the brothers were much attached to each other, in the way that any two persons are, when the one is cleverer and always leads the other, and this last is patiently content to be led. Mr. Lennox was pushing on in his profession; cultivating, with profound calculation, all those connections that might eventually be of service to him; keen-sighted, far-seeing, intelligent, sarcastic, and proud. Since the one long conversation relating to Frederick's affairs, which she had with him the first evening in Mr. Bell's presence, she had had no great intercourse with him, further than that which arose out of their close relations with the same household. But this was enough to wear off the shyness on her side, and any symptoms of mortified pride and vanity on his. They met continually, of course, but she thought that he rather avoided being alone with her; she fancied that he, as well as she, perceived that they had drifted strangely apart from their former anchorage, side by side, in many of their opinions, and all their tastes.

And yet, when he had spoken unusually well, or with remarkable epigrammatic point, she felt that his eye sought the expression of her countenance first of all, if but for an instant; and that, in the family intercourse which constantly threw them together, her opinion was the one to which he listened with a deference,—the more complete, because it was reluctantly paid, and concealed as much as possible.

Chapter XXIII.

"Ne'er to be found again."

"My own, my father's friend!
I cannot part with thee!
I ne'er have shown, thou ne'er hast known,
How dear thou art to me."

ANON.

The elements of the dinner-parties which Mrs. Lennox gave, were these; her friends contributed the beauty, Captain Lennox the easy knowledge of the subjects of the day; and Mr. Henry Lennox and the sprinkling of rising men who were received as his friends, brought the wit, the cleverness, the keen and extensive knowledge of which they knew well enough how to avail themselves without seeming pedantic, or burdening the rapid flow of conversation.

These dinners were delightful; but even here Margaret's dissatisfaction found her out. Every talent, every feeling, every acquirement; nay, even every tendency towards virtue, was used up as materials for fireworks; the hidden, sacred fire, exhausted itself in sparkle and crackle. They talked about art in a merely sensuous way, dwelling on outside effects, instead of allowing themselves to learn what it has to teach. They lashed themselves up into an enthusiasm about high subjects in company, and never thought about them when they were alone; they squandered their capabilities of appreciation into a mere flow of appropriate words. One day, after the gentlemen had come up into the drawing-room, Mr. Lennox drew near to Margaret, and addressed her in almost the first voluntary words he had spoken to her since she had returned to live in Harley Street.

"You did not look pleased at what Shirley was saying at dinner."

"Didn't I? My face must be very expressive," replied Margaret.

"It always was. It has not lost the trick of being eloquent."

"I did not like," said Margaret, hastily, "his way of advocating what he knew to be wrong—so glaringly wrong—even in jest."

"But it was very clever. How every word told! Do you remember the happy epithets?"

"Yes."

"And despise them, you would like to add. Pray don't scruple, though he is my friend."

"There! that is the exact tone in you, that"—she stopped short.

He listened for a moment to see if she would finish her sentence; but she only reddened, and turned away; before she did so, however, she heard him say, in a very low, clear voice,—

"If my tones, or modes of thought, are what you dislike, will you do me the justice to tell me so, and so give me the chance of learning to please you?"

All these weeks there was no intelligence of Mr. Bell's going to Milton. He had spoken of it at Helstone as of a journey which he might have to take in a very short time from then; but he must have transacted his business by writing, Margaret thought, ere now, and she knew that if he could, he would avoid going to a place which he disliked, and moreover would little understand the secret importance which she affixed to the explanation that could only be given by word of mouth. She knew that he would feel that it was necessary that it should be done; but whether in summer, autumn, or winter, it would signify very little. It was now August, and there had been no mention of the Spanish journey to which he had alluded to Edith, and Margaret tried to reconcile herself to the fading away of this illusion.

But one morning she received a letter, saying that next week he meant to come up to town; he wanted to see her about a plan which he had in his head; and, moreover, he intended to treat himself to a little doctoring, as he had begun to come round to her opinion, that it would be pleasanter to think that his health was more in fault than he, when he found himself irritable and cross. There was altogether a tone of forced cheerfulness in the letter, as Margaret noticed afterwards; but at the time her attention was taken up by Edith's exclamations.

"Coming up to town! Oh dear! and I am so worn out by the heat that I don't believe I have strength enough in me for another dinner. Besides, everybody has left but our dear stupid selves, who can't settle where to go to. There would be nobody to meet him."

"I'm sure he would much rather come and dine with us quite alone than with the most agreeable strangers you could pick up. Besides, if he is not well he won't wish for invitations. I am glad he has owned it at last. I was sure he was ill from the whole tone of his letters, and yet he would not answer me when I asked him, and I had no third person to whom I could apply for news."

"Oh! he is not very ill, or he would not think of Spain."

"He never mentions Spain."

"No! but his plan that is to be proposed evidently relates to that. But would you really go in such weather as this?"

"Oh! it will get cooler every day. Yes! Think of it! I am only afraid I have thought and wished too much—in that absorbing wilful way which is sure to be disappointed—or else gratified, to the letter, while in the spirit it gives no pleasure."

"But that's superstitious, I'm sure, Margaret."

"No, I don't think it is. Only it ought to warn me, and check me from giving way to such passionate wishes. It is a sort of 'Give me children, or else I die.'[1] I'm afraid my cry is, 'Let me go to Cadiz, or else I die.'"

"My dear Margaret! You'll be persuaded to stay there; and then what shall I do? Oh! I wish I could find somebody for you to marry here, that I could be sure of you!"

"I shall never marry."

"Nonsense, and double nonsense! Why, as Sholto says, you're such an attraction to the house, that he knows ever so many men who will be glad to visit here next year for your sake."

Margaret drew herself up haughtily. "Do you know, Edith, I sometimes think your Corfu life has taught you——"

"Well!"

"Just a shade or two of coarseness."

Edith began to sob so bitterly, and to declare so vehemently that Margaret had lost all love for her, and no longer looked upon her as a friend, that Margaret came to think that she had expressed too harsh an opinion for the relief of her own wounded pride, and ended

1. The cry of Rachel, who was barren, to Jacob, her husband (Genesis 30:1).

by being Edith's slave for the rest of the day; while that little lady, overcome by wounded feeling, lay like a victim on the sofa, heaving occasionally a profound sigh, till at last she fell asleep.

Mr. Bell did not make his appearance even on the day to which he had for a second time deferred his visit. The next morning there came a letter from Wallis, his servant, stating that his master had not been feeling well for some time, which had been the true reason of his putting off his journey; and that at the very time when he should have set out for London, he had been seized with an apoplectic fit; it was, indeed, Wallis added, the opinion of the medical men—that he could not survive the night; and more than probable, that by the time Miss Hale received this letter his poor master would be no more.

Margaret received this letter at breakfast-time, and turned very pale as she read it; then silently putting it into Edith's hands, she left the room.

Edith was terribly shocked as she read it, and cried in a sobbing, frightened, childish way, much to her husband's distress. Mrs. Shaw was breakfasting in her own room, and upon him devolved the task of reconciling his wife to the near contact into which she seemed to be brought with death, for the first time that she could remember in her life. Here was a man who was to have dined with them to-day lying dead or dying instead! It was some time before she could think of Margaret. Then she started up, and followed her upstairs into her room. Dixon was packing up a few toilette articles, and Margaret was hastily putting on her bonnet, shedding tears all the time, and her hands trembling so that she could hardly tie the strings.

"Oh, dear Margaret! how shocking! What are you doing? Are you going out? Sholto would telegraph or do anything you like."

"I am going to Oxford. There is a train in half-an-hour. Dixon has offered to go with me, but I could have gone by myself. I must see him again. Besides, he may be better, and want some care. He has been like a father to me. Don't stop me, Edith."

"But I must. Mamma won't like it at all. Come and ask her about it, Margaret. You don't know where you're going. I should not mind if he had a house of his own; but in his Fellow's rooms! Come to mamma, and do ask her before you go. It will not take a minute."

Margaret yielded, and lost her train. In the suddenness of the event, Mrs. Shaw became bewildered and hysterical, and so the precious time slipped by. But there was another train in a couple of hours; and after various discussions on propriety and impropriety, it was decided that Captain Lennox should accompany Margaret, as the one thing to which she was constant was her resolution to go, alone or otherwise, by the next train, whatever might be said of the propriety or impropriety of the step. Her father's friend, her own friend, was lying at the point of death; and the thought of this came upon her with such vividness, that she was surprised herself at the firmness with which she asserted something of her right to independence of action; and five minutes before the time for starting, she found herself sitting in a railway-carriage opposite to Captain Lennox.

It was always a comfort to her to think that she had gone, though it was only to hear that he had died in the night. She saw the rooms that he had occupied, and associated them ever after most fondly in her memory with the idea of her father, and his one cherished and faithful friend.

They had promised Edith before starting, that if all had ended as they feared, they would return to dinner; so that long, lingering look around the room in which her father had died, had to be interrupted, and a quiet farewell taken of the kind old face that had so often come out with pleasant words, and merry quips and cranks.

Captain Lennox fell asleep on their journey home; and Margaret could cry at leisure, and bethink her of this fatal year, and all the woes it had brought to her. No sooner was she fully aware of one loss than another came—not to supersede her grief for the one before, but to re-open wounds and feelings scarcely healed. But at the sound of the tender voices of her aunt and Edith, of merry little Sholto's glee at her arrival, and at the sight of the well-lighted rooms, with their mistress pretty in her paleness and her eager sorrowful interest, Margaret roused herself from her heavy trance of almost superstitious hopelessness, and began to feel that even around her joy and gladness might gather. She had Edith's place on the sofa; Sholto was taught to carry aunt Margaret's cup of tea very carefully to her; and by the time she went up to dress, she could thank God for having spared her dear old friend a long or a painful illness.[2]

2. In the second English edition, the following paragraph was added to conclude this chapter:

But when night came—solemn night, and all the house was quiet, Margaret still sate [sic] watching the beauty of a London sky at such an hour, on such a summer evening; the faint pink reflection of earthly lights on the soft clouds that float tranquilly into the white moonlight, out of the warm gloom which lies motionless around the horizon. Margaret's room had been the day nursery of her childhood, just when it merged into girlhood, and when the feelings and conscience had been first awakened into full activity. On some such night as this she remembered promising to herself to live as brave and noble a life as any heroine she ever read or heard of in romance, a life sans peur et sans reproche; it had seemed to her then that she had only to will, and such a life would be accomplished. And now she had learnt that not only to will, but also to pray, was a necessary condition in the truly heroic. Trusting to herself, she had fallen. It was a just consequence of her sin, that all excuses for it, all temptation to it, should remain for ever unknown to the person in whose opinion it had sunk her lowest. She stood face to face at last with her sin. She knew it for what it was; Mr. Bell's kindly sophistry that nearly all men were guilty of equivocal actions, and that the motive ennobled the evil, had never had much real weight with her. Her own first thought of how, if she had known all, she might have fearlessly told the truth, seemed low and poor. Nay, even now, her anxiety to have her character for truth partially excused in Mr. Thornton's eyes, as Mr. Bell had promised to do, was a very small and petty consideration, now

Chapter XXIV.

Breathing Tranquillity.

> "And down the sunny beach she paces slowly,
> With many doubtful pauses by the way;
> Grief hath an influence so hush'd and holy."
>
> HOOD.[1]

"Is not Margaret the heiress?" whispered Edith to her husband, as they were in their room alone at night after the sad journey to Oxford. She had pulled his tall head down, and stood upon tiptoe, and implored him not to be shocked, before she had ventured to ask this question. Captain Lennox was, however, quite in the dark; if he had ever heard, he had forgotten; it could not be much that a Fellow of a small college had to leave; but he had never wanted her to pay for her board; and two hundred and fifty pounds a year was something ridiculous, considering that she did not take wine. Edith came down upon her feet a little bit sadder; with a romance blown to pieces.

A week afterwards, she came prancing towards her husband, and made him a low curtsey:

"I am right, and you are wrong, most noble Captain. Margaret has had a lawyer's letter, and she is residuary legatee—the legacies being about two thousand pounds, and the remainder about forty thousand, at the present value of property in Milton.

"Indeed! and how does she take her good fortune?"

"Oh, it seems she knew she was to have it all along; only she had no idea it was so much. She looks very white and pale, and says she's afraid of it; but that's nonsense, you know, and will soon go off. I left mamma pouring congratulations down her throat, and stole away to tell you."

It seemed to be supposed, by general consent, that the most natural thing was to consider Mr. Lennox henceforward as Margaret's legal adviser. She was so entirely ignorant of all forms of business that in nearly everything she had to refer to him. He chose out her attorney; he came to her with papers to be signed. He was never so happy as when teaching her of what all these mysteries of the law were the signs and types.

"Henry," said Edith, one day, archly; "do you know what I hope and expect all these long conversations with Margaret will end in?"

---

that she was afresh taught by death what life should be. If all the world spoke, acted, or kept silence with intent to deceive,—if dearest interests were at stake, and dearest lives in peril,—if no one should ever know of her truth or her falsehood to measure out their honour or contempt for her by, straight alone where she stood, in the presence of God, she prayed that she might have strength to speak and act the truth for evermore.

1. The lines quoted are from Thomas Hood's poem "Hero and Leander" (1827), stanza 114.

"No, I don't," said he, reddening. "And I desire you not to tell me."

"Oh, very well; then I need not tell Sholto not to ask Mr. Montagu so often to the house."

"Just as you choose," said he with forced coolness. "What you are thinking of, may or may not happen; but this time, before I commit myself, I will see my ground clear. Ask whom you choose. It may not be very civil, Edith, but if you meddle in it you will mar it. She has been very farouche with me for a long time; and is only just beginning to thaw a little from her Zenobia ways. She has the making of a Cleopatra[2] in her, if only she were a little more pagan."

"For my part," said Edith, a little maliciously, "I am very glad she is a Christian. I know so very few!"

There was no Spain for Margaret that autumn; although to the last she hoped that some fortunate occasion would call Frederick to Paris, whither she could easily have met with a convoy. Instead of Cadiz, she had to content herself with Cromer.[3] To that place her aunt Shaw and the Lennoxes were bound. They had all along wished her to accompany them, and, consequently, with their characters, they made but lazy efforts to forward her own separate wish. Perhaps Cromer was, in one sense of the expression, the best for her. She needed bodily strengthening and bracing as well as rest.

Among other hopes that had vanished, was the hope, the trust she had had, that Mr. Bell would have given Mr. Thornton the simple facts of the family circumstances which had preceded the unfortunate accident that led to Leonards' death. Whatever opinion—however changed it might be from what Mr. Thornton had once entertained, she had wished it to be based upon a true understanding of what she had done; and why she had done it. It would have been a pleasure to her; would have given her rest on a point on which she should now all her life be restless, unless she could resolve not to think upon it. It was now so long after the time of these occurrences, that there was no possible way of explaining them save the one which she had lost by Mr. Bell's death. She must just submit, like many another, to be misunderstood; but, though reasoning herself into the belief that in this hers was no uncommon lot, her heart did not ache the less with longing that some time—years and years hence—before he died at any rate, he might know how much she had been tempted. She thought that she did not want to hear that all was explained to him, if only she could be sure that he would know. But this wish was vain, like so many others; and when she had schooled herself into this conviction, she turned with all her heart and strength to

2. Zenobia and Cleopatra provide contrasting examples of female rulers. Zenobia, Queen of Palmyra, governed her country and fought unsuccessfully against the Romans in the third century C.E. Cleopatra, Queen of Egypt, by contrast, was an example of seductive languor, who famously distracted both Julius Caesar and Mark Antony from their responsibilities.
3. A seaside town in Norfolk on the east coast of England. It is known for its bracing climate.

the life that lay immediately before her, and resolved to strive and make the best of that.

She used to sit long hours upon the beach, gazing intently on the waves as they chafed with perpetual motion against the pebbly shore,—or she looked out upon the more distant heave, and sparkle against the sky, and heard, without being conscious of hearing, the eternal psalm, which went up continually. She was soothed without knowing how or why. Listlessly she sat there, on the ground, her hands clasped round her knees, while her aunt Shaw did small shoppings, and Edith and Captain Lennox rode far and wide on shore and inland. The nurses, sauntering on with their charges, would pass and repass her, and wonder in whispers what she could find to look at so long, day after day. And when the family gathered at dinner-time, Margaret was so silent and absorbed that Edith voted her moped, and hailed a proposal of her husband's with great satisfaction, that Mr. Henry Lennox should be asked to take Cromer for a week, on his return from Scotland in October.

But all this time for thought enabled Margaret to put events in their right places, as to origin and significance, both as regarded her past life and her future. Those hours by the sea-side were not lost, as any one might have seen who had had the perception to read, or the care to understand, the look that Margaret's face was gradually acquiring. Mr. Henry Lennox was excessively struck by the change.

"The sea has done Miss Hale an immense deal of good, I should fancy," said he, when she first left the room after his arrival in their family circle. "She looks ten years younger than she did in Harley Street."

"That's the bonnet I got her!" said Edith, triumphantly. "I knew it would suit her the moment I saw it."

"I beg your pardon," said Mr. Lennox, in the half-contemptuous, half-indulgent tone he generally used to Edith. "But I believe I know the difference between the charms of a dress and the charms of a woman. No mere bonnet would have made Miss Hale's eyes so lustrous and yet so soft, or her lips so ripe and red—and her face altogether so full of peace and light.—She is like, and yet more,"—he dropped his voice,—"like the Margaret Hale of Helstone."

From this time the clever and ambitious man bent all his powers to gaining Margaret. He loved her sweet beauty. He saw the latent sweep of her mind, which could easily (he thought) be led to embrace all the objects on which he had set his heart. He looked upon her fortune only as a part of the complete and superb character of herself and her position: yet he was fully aware of the rise which it would immediately enable him, the poor barrister, to take. Eventually he would earn such success, and such honours, as would enable him to pay her back, with interest, that first advance in wealth which he should owe to her. He had been to Milton on business connected with her property, on his return from Scotland; and with the quick eye of a skilled lawyer, ready ever to take in and weigh contingencies, he had seen that much additional value was yearly accruing to the lands and tenements which she owned in that prosperous and increasing town. He was glad to find that the present relationship between Margaret and himself, of client and legal adviser, was gradually superseding the recollection of that unlucky, mismanaged day at Helstone. He had thus unusual opportunities of intimate intercourse with her, besides those that arose from the connection between the families.

Margaret was only too willing to listen as long as he talked of Milton, though he had seen none of the people whom she more especially knew. It had been the tone with her aunt and cousin to speak of Milton with dislike and contempt; just such feelings as Margaret was ashamed to remember she had expressed and felt on first going to live there. But Mr. Lennox almost exceeded Margaret in his appreciation of the character of Milton and its inhabitants. Their energy, their power, their indomitable courage in struggling and fighting; their lurid vividness of existence, captivated and arrested his attention. He was never tired of talking about them; and had never perceived how selfish and material were too many of the ends they proposed to themselves as the result of all their mighty, untiring endeavour, till Margaret, even in the midst of her gratification, had the candour to point this out, as the tainting sin in so much that was noble, and to be admired. Still, when other subjects palled upon her, and she gave but short answers to many questions, Henry Lennox found out that an enquiry as to some Darkshire peculiarity of character, called back the light into her eye, the glow into her cheek.

When they returned to town, Margaret fulfilled one of her seaside resolves, and took her life into her own hands. Before they went to Cromer, she had been as docile to her aunt's laws as if she were still the scared little stranger who cried herself to sleep that first night in the Harley Street nursery. But she had learnt, in those solemn hours of thought, that she herself must one day answer for her own life, and what she had done with it; and she tried to settle that most difficult problem for women, how much was to be utterly merged in obedience to authority, and how much might be set apart for freedom in working. Mrs. Shaw was as good-tempered as could be; and Edith had inherited this charming domestic quality; Margaret herself had probably the worst temper of the three, for her quick perceptions, and over-lively imagination made her hasty, and her early isolation from sympathy had made her proud; but she had an indescribable childlike sweetness of heart, which made her manners, even in her rarely wilful moods, irresistible of old; and now, chastened even by what the world called her good fortune, she charmed her reluctant aunt into acquiescence with her will. So Margaret gained the acknowledgment of her right to follow her own ideas of duty.

"Only don't be strong-minded," pleaded Edith. "Mamma wants you to have a footman of your own; and I'm sure you're very welcome, for they're great plagues. Only to please me, darling, don't go and have a strong mind; it's the only thing I ask. Footman or no footman, don't be strong-minded."

"Don't be afraid, Edith. I'll faint on your hands at the servant's dinner-time, the very first opportunity; and then, what with Sholto playing with the fire, and the baby crying, you'll begin to wish for a strong-minded woman, equal to any emergency."

"And you'll not grow too good to joke and be merry?"

"Not I. I shall be merrier than I have ever been, now I have got my own way."

"And you'll not go a figure,[4] but let me buy your dresses for you?"

"Indeed I mean to buy them for myself. You shall come with me if you like; but no one can please me but myself."

"Oh! I was afraid you'd dress in brown and dust-colour, not to show the dirt you'll pick up in all those places. I'm glad you're going to keep one or two vanities, just by way of specimens of the old Adam."

"I'm going to be just the same, Edith, if you and my aunt could but fancy so. Only as I have neither husband nor child to give me natural duties, I must make myself some, in addition to ordering my gowns."

In the family conclave, which was made up of Edith, her mother, and her husband, it was decided that perhaps all these plans of hers would only secure her the more for Henry Lennox. They kept her out of the way of other friends who might have eligible sons or brothers; and it was also agreed that she never seemed to take much pleasure in the society of any one but Henry, out of their own family. The other admirers, attracted by her appearance or the reputation of her fortune, were swept away, by her unconscious smiling disdain, into the paths frequented by other beauties less fastidious, or other heiresses with a larger amount of gold. Henry and she grew slowly into closer intimacy; but neither he nor she were people to brook the slightest notice of their proceedings.

---

4. "Make yourself look conspicuous," perhaps in a negative sense. The fashionable Edith doubts Margaret's capacity to dress elegantly.

Chapter XXV.

Changes at Milton.

"Here we go up, up, up;
And here we go down, down, downee!"
NURSERY SONG.

Meanwhile, at Milton the chimneys smoked, the ceaseless roar and mighty beat, and dizzying whirl of machinery, struggled and strove perpetually. Senseless and purposeless were wood and iron and steam in their endless labours; but the persistence of their monotonous work was rivalled in tireless endurance by the strong crowds, who, with sense and with purpose, were busy and restless in seeking after—What? In the streets there were few loiterers,—none walking for mere pleasure; every man's face was set in lines of eagerness or anxiety; news was sought for with fierce avidity; and men jostled each other aside in the Mart and in the Exchange, as they did in life, in the deep selfishness of competition. There was gloom over the town. Few came to buy, and those who did were looked at suspiciously by the sellers; for credit was insecure, and the most stable might have their fortunes affected by the sweep in the great neighbouring port among the shipping houses. Hitherto there had been no failures in Milton; but, from the immense speculations that had come to light in making a bad end in America,[1] and yet nearer home, it was known that some Milton houses of business must suffer so severely that every day men's faces asked, if their tongues did not, "What news? Who is gone? How will it affect me?" And if two or three spoke together, they dwelt rather on the names of those who were safe than dared to hint at those likely, in their opinion, to go; for idle breath may, at such times, cause the downfall of some who might otherwise weather the storm; and one going down drags many after. "Thornton is safe," say they. "His business is large—extending every year; but such a head as he has, and so prudent with all his daring!" Then one man draws another aside, and walks a little apart, and, with head inclined into his neighbour's ear, he says, "Thornton's business is large; but he has spent his profits in extending it; he has no capital laid by; his machinery is new within these two years, and

---

1. This seems to refer to an event of which Gaskell assumes common knowledge. Peter Mathias records that in the late 1830s British loans were used by United States financiers in an attempt to rig the cotton market: "Falling trade values in 1839 then set off a general financial panic in the United States. By 1841 nine states were defaulting on loans and it was embarrassing to be an American in London. The flow of capital from London to the States did not revive much until after 1850; nor did trade with America" (Peter Mathias, *The First Industrial Nation*, London: Methuen, 1969, p. 324). If Gaskell's reference is to this sequence of events, however, it is anachronistic: the action of *North and South* is usually assumed to be roughly contemporary with the time of her writing of the novel.

has cost him—we won't say what!—a word to the wise!" But that Mr. Harrison was a croaker,—a man who had succeeded to his father's trade-made fortune, which he had feared to lose by altering his mode of business to any having a larger scope; yet he grudged every penny made by others more daring and far-sighted.

But the truth was, Mr. Thornton was hard pressed. He felt it acutely in his vulnerable point—his pride in the commercial character which he had established for himself. Architect of his own fortunes, he attributed this to no special merit or qualities of his own, but to the power, which he believed that commerce gave to every brave, honest, and persevering man, to raise himself to a level from which he might see and read the great game of worldly success, and honestly, by such far-sightedness, command more power and influence than in any other mode of life. Far away, in the East and in the West, where his person would never be known, his name was to be regarded, and his wishes to be fulfilled, and his word pass like gold. That was the idea of merchant-life with which Mr. Thornton had started. "Her merchants be like princes,"[2] said his mother, reading the text aloud, as if it were a trumpet-call to invite her boy to the struggle. He was but like many others—men, women, and children— alive to distant, and dead to near things. He sought to possess the influence of a name in foreign countries and far-away seas,—to become the head of a firm that should be known for generations; and it had taken him long silent years to come even to a glimmering of what he might be now, to-day, here in his own town, his own factory, among his own people. He and they had led parallel lives— very close, but never touching—till the accident (or so it seemed) of his acquaintance with Higgins. Once brought face to face, man to man, with an individual of the masses around him, and (take notice) out of the character of master and workman, in the first instance, they had each begun to recognise that "we have all of us one human heart."[3] It was the fine point of the wedge; and until now, when the apprehension of losing his connection with two or three of the workmen whom he had so lately begun to know as men,—of having a plan or two, which were experiments lying very close to his heart, roughly nipped off without trial,—gave a new poignancy to the subtle fear that came over him from time to time; until now, he had never recognised how much and how deep was the interest he had grown of late to feel in his position as manufacturer, simply because it led him into such close contact, and gave him the opportunity of so much power, among a race of people strange, shrewd, ignorant; but, above all, full of character and strong human feeling.

2. Isaiah 23:8, slightly misquoted.
3. From William Wordsworth's poem "The Old Cumberland Beggar," line 146, in *Lyrical Ballads* (second edition, 1800).

He reviewed his position as a Milton manufacturer. The strike a year and a half ago,—or more, for it was now untimely wintry weather, in a late spring,—that strike, when he was young, and he now was old—had prevented his completing some of the large orders he had then on hand. He had locked up a good deal of his capital in new and expensive machinery, and he had also bought cotton largely, for the fulfilment of these orders, taken under contract. That he had not been able to complete them, was owing in some degree to the utter want of skill on the part of the Irish hands whom he had imported; much of their work was damaged and unfit to be sent forth by a house which prided itself on turning out nothing but first-rate articles. For many months, the embarrassment caused by the strike had been an obstacle in Mr. Thornton's way; and often, when his eye fell on Higgins, he could have spoken angrily to him without any present cause, just from feeling how serious was the injury that had arisen from this affair in which he was implicated. But when he became conscious of this sudden, quick resentment, he resolved to curb it. It would not satisfy him to avoid Higgins; he must convince himself that he was master over his own anger, by being particularly careful to allow Higgins access to him, whenever the strict rules of business, or Mr. Thornton's leisure permitted. And by-and-bye, he lost all sense of resentment in wonder how it was, or could be, that two men like himself and Higgins, living by the same trade, working in their different ways at the same object, could look upon each other's position and duties in so strangely different a way. And thence arose that intercourse, which though it might not have the effect of preventing all future clash of opinion and action, when the occasion arose, would, at any rate, enable both master and man to look upon each other with far more charity and sympathy, and bear with each other more patiently and kindly. Besides this improvement of feeling, both Mr. Thornton and his workmen found out their ignorance as to positive matters of fact, known heretofore to one side, but not to the other.

But now had come one of those periods of bad trade, when the market falling brought down the value of all large stocks; Mr. Thornton's fell to nearly half. No orders were coming in; so he lost the interest of the capital he had locked up in machinery; indeed, it was difficult to get payment for the orders completed; yet there was the constant drain of expenses for working the business. Then the bills became due for the cotton he had purchased; and money being scarce, he could only borrow at exorbitant interest, and yet he could not realise any of his property. But he did not despair; he exerted himself day and night to foresee and to provide for all emergencies; he was as calm and gentle to the women in his home as ever; to the workmen in his mill he spoke not many words, but they knew him by this time; and many a curt, decided answer was received by them rather with sympathy for the care they saw pressing upon him, than with the suppressed antagonism which had formerly been smouldering, and ready for hard words and hard judgments on all occasions. "Th' measter's a deal to potter[4] him," said Higgins, one day, as he heard Mr. Thornton's short, sharp inquiry, why such a command had not been obeyed; and caught the sound of the suppressed sigh which he heaved in going past the room where some of the men were working. Higgins and another man stopped over-hours that night, unknown to any one, to get the neglected piece of work done; and Mr. Thornton never knew but that the overlooker, to whom he had given the command in the first instance, had done it himself.

"Eh! I reckon I know who'd ha' been sorry for to see our measter sitting so like a piece o' grey calico! Th'ou'd parson would ha' fretted his woman's heart out, if he'd seen the woeful looks I have seen on our measter's face," thought Higgins, one day, as he was approaching Mr. Thornton in Marlborough Street.

"Measter," said he, stopping his employer in his quick resolved walk, and causing that gentleman to look up with a sudden annoyed start, as if his thoughts had been far away.

"Have yo' heerd aught of Miss Marget lately?"

"Miss—who?" replied Mr. Thornton.

"Miss Marget—Miss Hale—th' oud parson's daughter—yo' known who I mean well enough, if yo'll only think a bit—" (there was nothing disrespectful in the tone in which this was said).

"Oh yes!" and suddenly, the wintry frost-bound look of care had left Mr. Thornton's face, as if some soft summer gale had blown all anxiety away from his mind; and though his mouth was as much compressed as before, his eyes smiled out benignly on his questioner.

"She's my landlord now, you know, Higgins. I hear of her through her agent here, every now and then. She's well and among friends—thank you, Higgins." That "thank you" that lingered after the other words, and yet came with so much warmth of feeling, let in a new light to the acute Higgins. It might be but a will-o'-th'-wisp, but he thought he would follow it and ascertain whither it would lead him.

"And she's not getten married, measter?"

"Not yet." The face was cloudy once more. "There is some talk of it, as I understand, with a connection of the family."

"Then she'll not be for coming to Milton again, I reckon."

"No!"

"Stop a minute, measter." Then going up confidentially close, he said, "Is th' young gentleman cleared?" He enforced the depth of his

4. Bother.

intelligence by a wink of the eye, which only made things more mysterious to Mr. Thornton.

"Th' young gentleman, I mean—Master Frederick, they ca'ad him—her brother as was over here, yo' known."

"Over here."

"Ay, to be sure, at th' missus's death. Yo' need na be feared of my telling; for Mary and me, we knowed it all along, only we held our peace, for we got it through Mary working in th' house."

"And he was over. It was her brother!"

"Sure enough, and I reckoned yo' knowed it, or I'd never ha' let on. Yo' knowed she had a brother?"

"Yes, I know all about him. And he was over at Mrs. Hale's death?"

"Nay! I'm not going for to tell more. I've maybe getten them into mischief already, for they kept it very close. I nobbut wanted to know if they'd getten him cleared?"

"Not that I know of. I know nothing. I only hear of Miss Hale, now, as my landlord, and through her lawyer."

He broke off from Higgins, to follow the business on which he had been bent when the latter first accosted him; leaving Higgins baffled in his endeavour.

"It was her brother," said Mr. Thornton to himself. "I am glad. I may never see her again; but it is a comfort—a relief—to know that much. I knew she could not be unmaidenly; and yet I yearned for conviction. Now I am glad!"

It was a little golden thread running through the dark web of his present fortunes; which were growing ever gloomier and more gloomy. His agent had largely trusted a house in the American trade, which went down, along with several others, just at this time, like a pack of cards, the fall of one compelling other failures. What were Mr. Thornton's engagements? Could he stand?

Night after night he took books and papers into his own private room, and sat up there long after the family were gone to bed. He thought that no one knew of this occupation of the hours he should have spent in sleep. One morning, when daylight was stealing in through the crevices of his shutters, and he had never been in bed, and, in hopeless indifference of mind, was thinking that he could do without the hour or two of rest, which was all that he should be able to take before the stir of daily labour began again, the door of his room opened, and his mother stood there, dressed as she had been the day before. She had never laid herself down to slumber any more than he. Their eyes met. Their faces were cold and rigid, and wan, from long watching.

"Mother! why are not you in bed?"

"Son John," said she, "do you think I can sleep with an easy mind, while you keep awake full of care? You have not told me what your trouble is; but sore trouble you have had these many days past."

"Trade is bad."

"And you dread——"

"I dread nothing," replied he, drawing up his head, and holding it erect. "I know now that no man will suffer by me. That was my anxiety."

"But how do you stand? Shall you—will it be a failure?" her steady voice trembling in an unwonted manner.

"Not a failure. I must give up business, but I pay all men. I might redeem myself—I am sorely tempted—"

"How? Oh, John! keep up your name—try all risks for that. How redeem it?"

"By a speculation offered to me, full of risk; but, if successful, placing me high above water-mark, so that no one need ever know the strait I am in. Still, if it fails—"

"And if it fails," said she, advancing, and laying her hand on his arm, her eyes full of eager light. She held her breath to hear the end of his speech.

"Honest men are ruined by a rogue," said he gloomily. "As I stand now, my creditors' money is safe—every farthing of it; but I don't know where to find my own—it may be all gone, and I penniless at this moment. Therefore, it is my creditors' money that I should risk."

"But if it succeeded, they need never know. Is it so desperate a speculation? I am sure it is not, or you would never have thought of it. If it succeeded—"

"I should be a rich man, and my peace of conscience would be gone!"

"Why! You would have injured no one."

"No; but I should have run the risk of ruining many for my own paltry aggrandisement. Mother, I have decided! You won't much grieve over our leaving this house, shall you, dear mother?"

"No! but to have you other than what you are will break my heart. What can you do?"

"Be always the same John Thornton in whatever circumstances; endeavouring to do right, and making great blunders; and then trying to be brave in setting to afresh. But it is hard, mother. I have so worked and planned. I have discovered new powers in my situation too late—and now all is over. I am too old to begin again with the same heart. It is hard, mother."

He turned away from her, and covered his face with his hands.

"I can't think," said she, with gloomy defiance in her tone, "how it comes about. Here is my boy—good son, just man, tender heart— and he fails in all he sets his mind upon: he finds a woman to love, and she cares no more for his affection than if he had been any common man; he labours, and his labour comes to nought. Other people prosper and grow rich, and hold their paltry names high and dry above shame."

"Shame never touched me," said he, in a low tone: but she went on.

"I sometimes have wondered where justice was gone to, and now I don't believe there is such a thing in the world,—now you are come to this; you, my own John Thornton, though you and I may be beggars together—my own dear son!"

She fell upon his neck, and kissed him through her tears.

"Mother!" said he, holding her gently in his arms, "Who has sent me my lot in life, both of good and of evil?"

She shook her head. She would have nothing to do with religion just then.

"Mother," he went on, seeing that she would not speak, "I, too, have been rebellious; but I am striving to be so no longer. Help me, as you helped me when I was a child. Then you said many good words—when my father died, and we were sometimes sorely short of comforts—which we shall never be now; you said brave, noble, trustful words then, mother, which I have never forgotten, though they may have lain dormant. Speak to me again in the old way, mother. Do not let us have to think that the world has too much hardened our hearts. If you would say the old good words, it would make me feel something of the pious simplicity of my childhood. I say them to myself, but they would come differently from you, remembering all the cares and trials you have had to bear."

"I have had a many," said she, sobbing, "but none so sore as this. To see you cast down from your rightful place! I could say it for myself, John, but not for you. Not for you! God has seen fit to be very hard on you, very."

She shook with the sobs that come so convulsively when an old person weeps. The silence around her struck her at last; and she quieted herself to listen. No sound. She looked. Her son sat by the table, his arms thrown half across it, his head bent face downwards.

"Oh, John!" she said, and she lifted his face up. Such a strange, pallid look of gloom was on it, that for a moment it struck her that this look was the forerunner of death; but, as the rigidity melted out of the countenance and the natural colour returned, and she saw that he was himself once again, all worldly mortification sank to nothing before the consciousness of the great blessing that he himself by his simple existence was to her. She thanked God for this, and this alone, with a fervour that swept away all rebellious feelings from her mind.

He did not speak readily; but he went and opened the shutters, and let the ruddy light of dawn flood the room. But the wind was in the east; the weather was piercing cold, as it had been for weeks; there would be no demand for light summer goods this year. That hope for the revival of trade must utterly be given up.

It was a great comfort to have had this conversation with his mother; and to feel sure that, however they might henceforward keep silence on all these anxieties, they yet understood each other's feelings, and were, if not in harmony, at least not in discord with each other, in their way of viewing them. Fanny's husband was vexed at Thornton's refusal to take any share in the speculation which he had offered to him, and withdrew from any possibility of being supposed able to assist him with the ready money, which indeed the speculator needed for his own venture.

There was nothing for it at last, but that which Mr. Thornton had dreaded for many weeks; he had to give up the business in which he had been so long engaged with so much honour and success; and look out for a subordinate situation. Marlborough Mills and the adjacent dwelling were held under a long lease; they must, if possible, be relet. There was an immediate choice of situations offered to Mr. Thornton. Mr. Hamper would have been only too glad to have secured him as a steady and experienced partner for his son, whom he was setting up with a large capital in a neighbouring town; but the young man was half-educated as regarded information, and wholly uneducated as regarded any other responsibility than that of getting money, and brutalised both as to his pleasures and his pains. Mr. Thornton declined having any share in a partnership, which would frustrate what few plans he had that survived the wreck of his fortunes. He would sooner consent to be only a manager, where he could have a certain degree of power beyond the mere money-getting part, than have to fall in with the tyrannical humours of a moneyed partner with whom he felt sure that he should quarrel in a few months.

So he waited, and stood on one side with profound humility, as the news swept through the Exchange, of the enormous fortune which his brother-in-law had made by his daring speculation. It was a nine days' wonder. Success brought with it its worldly consequence of extreme admiration. No one was considered so wise and far-seeing as Mr. Watson.

Chapter XXVI.

Meeting Again.

"Bear up, brave heart! we will be calm and strong;
Sure, we can master eyes, or cheek, or tongue,
Nor let the smallest tell-tale sign appear
She ever was, and is, and will be dear."

RHYMING PLAY.

It was a hot summer's evening. Edith came into Margaret's bedroom, the first time in her habit, the second ready dressed for dinner. No one was there at first; the next time Edith found Dixon laying out Margaret's dress on the bed; but no Margaret. Edith remained to fidget about.

"Oh, Dixon! not those horrid blue flowers to that dead gold-coloured gown. What taste! Wait a minute, and I will bring you some pomegranate blossoms."

"It's not a dead gold-colour, ma'am. It's a straw-colour. And blue always goes with straw-colour." But Edith had brought the brilliant scarlet flowers before Dixon had got half through her remonstrance.

"Where is Miss Hale?" asked Edith, as soon as she had tried the effect of the garniture. "I can't think," she went on, pettishly, "how my aunt allowed her to get into such rambling habits in Milton! I'm sure I'm always expecting to hear of her having met with something horrible among all those wretched places she pokes herself into. I should never dare to go down some of those streets without a servant. They're not fit for ladies."

Dixon was still huffed about her despised taste; so she replied, rather shortly:

"It's no wonder to my mind, when I hear ladies talk such a deal about being ladies—and when they're such fearful, delicate, dainty ladies too—I say it's no wonder to me that there are no longer any saints on earth——"

"Oh, Margaret! here you are! I have been so wanting you. But how your cheeks are flushed with the heat, poor child! But only think what that tiresome Henry has done; really, he exceeds brother-in-law's limits. Just when my party was made up so beautifully—fitted in so precisely for Mr. Colthurst—there has Henry come, with an apology it is true, and making use of your name for an excuse, and asked me if he may bring that Mr. Thornton of Milton—your tenant, you know—who is in London about some law business. It will spoil my number, quite."

"I don't mind dinner. I don't want any," said Margaret, in a low voice. "Dixon can get me a cup of tea here, and I will be in the drawing-room by the time you come up. I shall really be glad to lie down."

"No, no! that will never do. You do look wretchedly white, to be sure; but that is just the heat, and we can't do without you possibly. (Those flowers a little lower, Dixon. They look glorious flames, Margaret, in your black hair.) You know we planned you to talk about Milton to Mr. Colthurst. Oh! to be sure! and this man comes from Milton. I believe it will be capital, after all. Mr. Colthurst can pump him well on all the subjects in which he is interested, and it will be great fun to trace out your experiences, and this Mr. Thornton's wisdom, in Mr. Colthurst's next speech in the House. Really, I think it is a happy hit of Henry's. I asked him if he was a man one would be ashamed of; and he replied, 'Not if you've any sense in you, my little sister.' So I suppose he is able to sound his h's, which is not a common Darkshire accomplishment—eh, Margaret?"

"Mr. Lennox did not say why Mr. Thornton was come up to town? Was it law business connected with the property?" asked Margaret, in a constrained voice.

"Oh! he's failed, or something of the kind, that Henry told you of that day you had such a headache,—what was it? (There, that's capital, Dixon. Miss Hale does us credit, does she not?) I wish I was as tall as a queen, and as brown as a gipsy, Margaret."

"But about Mr. Thornton?"

"Oh! I really have such a terrible head for law business. Henry will like nothing better than to tell you all about it. I know the impression he made upon me was, that Mr. Thornton is very badly off, and a very respectable man, and that I'm to be very civil to him; and as I did not know how, I came to you to ask you to help me. And now come down with me, and rest on the sofa for a quarter of an hour."

The privileged brother-in-law came early; and Margaret, reddening as she spoke, began to ask him the questions she wanted to hear answered about Mr. Thornton.

"He came up about this sub-letting the property—Marlborough Mills, and the house and premises adjoining, I mean. He is unable to keep it on; and there are deeds and leases to be looked over, and agreements to be drawn up. I hope Edith will receive him properly; but she was rather put out, as I could see, by the liberty I had taken in begging for an invitation for him. But I thought you would like to have some attention shown him: and one would be particularly scrupulous in paying every respect to a man who is going down in the world." He had dropped his voice to speak to Margaret, by whom he was sitting; but as he ended he sprang up, and introduced Mr. Thornton, who had that moment entered, to Edith and Captain Lennox.

Margaret looked with an anxious eye at Mr. Thornton while he was thus occupied. It was considerably more than a year since she had seen him; and events had occurred to change him much in that time. His fine figure yet bore him above the common height of men; and gave him a distinguished appearance, from the ease of motion which arose out of it, and was natural to him; but his face looked older and care-worn; yet a noble composure sat upon it, which impressed those who had just been hearing of his changed position, with a sense of inherent dignity and manly strength. He was aware, from the first glance he had given round the room, that Margaret was there; he had seen her intent look of occupation as she listened to Mr. Henry Lennox; and he came up to her with the perfectly regulated manner of an old friend. With his first calm words a vivid colour flashed into her cheeks, which never left them again during the evening. She did not seem to have much to say to him. She disappointed him by the quiet way in which she asked what seemed to him to be the merely necessary questions respecting her old acquaintances, in Milton; but others came in—more intimate in the house than he—and he fell into the background, where he and Mr. Lennox talked together from time to time.

"You think Miss Hale looking well," said Mr. Lennox, "don't you? Milton didn't agree with her, I imagine; for when she first came to London, I thought I had never seen any one so much changed. To-night she is looking radiant. But she is much stronger. Last autumn she was fatigued with a walk of a couple of miles. On Friday evening we walked up to Hampstead and back. Yet on Saturday she looked as well as she does now."

"We!" Who? They two alone?

Mr. Colthurst was a very clever man, and a rising member of parliament. He had a quick eye at discerning character, and was struck by a remark which Mr. Thornton made at dinner-time. He enquired from Edith who that gentleman was; and, rather to her surprise, she found, from the tone of his "Indeed!" that Mr. Thornton of Milton was not such an unknown name to him as she had imagined it would be. Her dinner was going off well. Henry was in good humour, and brought out his dry caustic wit admirably. Mr. Thornton and Mr. Colthurst found one or two mutual subjects of interest, which they could only touch upon then, reserving them for more private after-dinner talk. Margaret looked beautiful in the pomegranate flowers; and if she did lean back in her chair and speak but little, Edith was not annoyed, for the conversation flowed on smoothly without her. Margaret was watching Mr. Thornton's face. He never looked at her; so she might study him unobserved, and note the changes which even this short time had wrought in him. Only at some unexpected mot of Mr. Lennox's, his face flashed out into the old look of intense enjoyment; the merry brightness returned to his eyes, the lips just parted to suggest the brilliant smile of former days; and for an instant, his glance instinctively sought hers, as if he wanted her sympathy. But when their eyes met, his whole countenance changed; he was grave and anxious once more; and he resolutely avoided even looking near her again during dinner.

There were only two ladies besides their own party, and as these were occupied in conversation by her aunt and Edith, when they went up into the drawing-room, Margaret languidly employed herself about some work. Presently the gentlemen came up, Mr. Colthurst and Mr. Thornton in close conversation. Mr. Lennox drew near to Margaret, and said in a low voice:

"I really think Edith owes me thanks for my contribution to her party. You've no idea what an agreeable, sensible fellow this tenant of yours is. He has been the very man to give Colthurst all the facts he wanted coaching in. I can't conceive how he contrived to mismanage his affairs."

"With his powers and opportunities you would have succeeded," said Margaret. He did not quite relish the tone in which she spoke, although the words but expressed a thought which had passed through his own mind. As he was silent, they caught a swell in the sound of conversation going on near the fire-place between Mr. Colthurst and Mr. Thornton.

"I assure you, I heard it spoken of with great interest—curiosity as to its result, perhaps I should rather say. I heard your name frequently mentioned during my short stay in the neighbourhood." Then they lost some words; and when next they could hear Mr. Thornton was speaking.

"I have not the elements for popularity—if they spoke of me in that way, they were mistaken. I fall slowly into new projects; and I find it difficult to let myself be known, even by those whom I desire to know, and with whom I would fain have no reserve. Yet, even with all these drawbacks, I felt that I was on the right path, and that, starting from a kind of friendship with one, I was becoming acquainted with many. The advantages were mutual: we were both unconsciously and consciously teaching each other."

"You say 'were.' I trust you are intending to pursue the same course?"

"I must stop Colthurst," said Henry Lennox, hastily. And by an abrupt, yet apropos question, he turned the current of the conversation, so as not to give Mr. Thornton the mortification of acknowledging his want of success and consequent change of position. But as soon as the newly-started subject had come to a close, Mr. Thornton resumed the conversation just where it had been interrupted, and gave Mr. Colthurst the reply to his inquiry.

"I have been unsuccessful in business, and have had to give up my position as a master. I am on the look out for a situation in

Milton, where I may meet with employment under some one who will be willing to let me go along my own way in such matters as these. I can depend upon myself for having no go-ahead theories that I would rashly bring into practice. My only wish is to have the opportunity of cultivating some intercourse with the hands beyond the mere 'cash nexus.'[1] But it might be the point Archimedes sought from which to move the earth,[2] to judge from the importance attached to it by some of our manufacturers, who shake their heads and look grave as soon as I name the one or two experiments that I should like to try."

"You call them 'experiments' I notice," said Mr. Colthurst, with a delicate increase of respect in his manner.

"Because I believe them to be such. I am not sure of the consequences that may result from them. But I am sure they ought to be tried. I have arrived at the conviction that no mere institutions, however wise, and however much thought may have been required to organise and arrange them, can attach class to class as they should be attached, unless the working out of such institutions bring the individuals of the different classes into actual personal contact. Such intercourse is the very breath of life. A working man can hardly be made to feel and know how much his employer may have laboured in his study at plans for the benefit of his workpeople. A complete plan emerges like a piece of machinery, apparently fitted for every emergency. But the hands accept it as they do machinery, without understanding the intense mental labour and forethought required to bring it to such perfection. But I would take an idea, the working out of which would necessitate personal intercourse; it might not go well at first, but at every hitch interest would be felt by an increasing number of men, and at last its success in working come to be desired by all, as all had borne a part in the formation of the plan; and even then I am sure that it would lose its vitality, cease to be living, as soon as it was no longer carried on by that sort of common interest which invariably makes people find means and ways of seeing each other, and becoming acquainted with each others' characters and persons, and even tricks of temper and modes of speech. We should understand each other better, and I'll venture to say we should like each other more."

"And you think they may prevent the recurrence of strikes?"

"Not at all. My utmost expectation only goes so far as this—that

---

1. A term sometimes attributed to Karl Marx; in fact, Marx was anticipated by Thomas Carlyle, notably in *Chartism* (1839), where he referred to "epochs when cash payment has become the sole nexus of man to man" (chap. 2).
2. The idea attributed to Archimedes, the Greek thinker, that if one could find a position outside the earth on which to stand, the earth itself could be moved on the principle of leverage, had become a metaphor for something possible in theory but impossible in practice.

they may render strikes not the bitter, venomous sources of hatred they have hitherto been. A more hopeful man might imagine that a closer and more genial intercourse between classes might do away with strikes. But I am not a hopeful man."

Suddenly, as if a new idea had struck him, he crossed over to where Margaret was sitting, and began, without preface, as if he knew she had been listening to all that had passed:

"Miss Hale, I had a round-robin from some of my men—I suspect in Higgins' handwriting—stating their wish to work for me, if ever I was in a position to employ men again on my own behalf. That was good, wasn't it?"

"Yes. Just right. I am glad of it," said Margaret, looking up straight into his face with her speaking eyes, and then dropping them under his eloquent glance. He gazed back at her for a minute, as if he did not know exactly what he was about. Then sighed; and saying, "I knew you would like it," he turned away, and never spoke to her again until he bid her a formal "good night."

As Mr. Lennox took his departure, Margaret said, with a blush that she could not repress, and with some hesitation,

"Can I speak to you to-morrow? I want your help about—something."

"Certainly. I will come at whatever time you name. You cannot give me a greater pleasure than by making me of any use. At eleven? Very well."

His eye brightened with exultation. How she was learning to depend upon him! It seemed as if any day now might give him the certainty, without having which he had determined never to offer to her again.

Chapter XXVII.

"Pack Clouds Away."

> "For joy or grief, for hope or fear,
> For all hereafter, as for here,
> In peace or strife, in storm or shine."
> ANON.

Edith went about on tip-toe, and checked Sholto in all loud speaking that next morning, as if any sudden noise would interrupt the conference that was taking place in the drawing-room. Two o'clock came; and they still sat there with closed doors. Then there was a man's footstep running down stairs; and Edith peeped out of the drawing-room.

"Well, Henry?" said she, with a look of interrogation.

"Well!" said he, rather shortly.

"Come in to lunch!"

"No, thank you, I can't. I've lost too much time here already."

"Then it's not all settled," said Edith despondingly.

"No! not at all. It never will be settled, if the 'it' is what I conjecture you mean. That will never be, Edith, so give up thinking about it."

"But it would be so nice for us all," pleaded Edith. "I should always feel comfortable about the children, if I had Margaret settled down near me. As it is, I am always afraid of her going off to Cadiz."

"I will try, when I marry, to look out for a young lady who has a knowledge of the management of children. That is all I can do. Miss Hale would not have me. And I shall not ask her."

"Then, what have you been talking about?"

"A thousand things you would not understand: investments, and leases, and value of land."

"Oh, go away if that's all. You and she will be unbearably stupid, if you've been talking all this time about such weary things."

"Very well. I'm coming again to-morrow, and bringing Mr. Thornton with me, to have some more talk with Miss Hale."

"Mr. Thornton! What has he to do with it?"

"He is Miss Hale's tenant," said Mr. Lennox, turning away. "And he wishes to give up his lease."

"Oh! very well. I can't understand details, so don't give them me."

"The only detail I want you to understand is, to let us have the back drawing-room undisturbed, as it was to-day. In general, the children and servants are so in and out, that I can never get any business satisfactorily explained; and the arrangements we have to make to-morrow are of importance."

No one ever knew why Mr. Lennox did not keep to his appointment on the following day. Mr. Thornton came true to his time; and, after keeping him waiting for nearly an hour, Margaret came in looking very white and anxious.

She began hurriedly:

"I am so sorry Mr. Lennox is not here,—he could have done it so much better than I can. He is my adviser in this"——

"I am sorry that I came, if it troubles you. Shall I go to Mr. Lennox's chambers and try and find him?"

"No, thank you. I wanted to tell you, how grieved I was to find that I am to lose you as a tenant. But, Mr. Lennox says, things are sure to brighten"——

"Mr. Lennox knows little about it," said Mr. Thornton quietly. "Happy and fortunate in all a man cares for, he does not understand what it is to find oneself no longer young—yet thrown back to the starting-point which requires the hopeful energy of youth—to feel one half of life gone, and nothing done—nothing remaining of wasted opportunity, but the hitter recollection that it has been. Miss Hale, I would rather not hear Mr. Lennox's opinion of my affairs. Those who are happy and successful themselves are too apt to make light of the misfortunes of others."

"You are unjust," said Margaret, gently. "Mr. Lennox has only spoken of the great probability which he believes there to be of your redeeming—your more than redeeming what you have lost—don't speak till I have ended—pray don't!" And collecting herself once more, she went on rapidly, turning over some law papers, and statements of accounts in a trembling hurried manner. "Oh! here it is! and—he drew me out a proposal—I wish he was here to explain it— showing that if you would take some money of mine, eighteen hundred and fifty-seven pounds,[1] lying just at this moment unused in the bank, and bringing me in only two and a half per cent—you could pay me much better interest, and might go on working Marlborough Mills." Her voice had cleared itself and become more steady. Mr. Thornton did not speak, and she went on looking for some paper on which were written down the proposals for security; for she was most anxious to have it all looked upon in the light of a mere business arrangement, in which the principal advantage would be on her side. While she sought for this paper, her very heart-pulse was arrested by the tone in which Mr. Thornton spoke. His voice was hoarse, and trembling with tender passion, as he said:—

"Margaret!"

For an instant she looked up; and then sought to veil her luminous eyes by dropping her forehead on her hands. Again, stepping nearer, he besought her with another tremulous eager call upon her name.

"Margaret!"

Still lower went the head; more closely hidden was the face, almost resting on the table before her. He came close to her. He knelt by her side, to bring his face to a level with her ear; and whispered— panted out the words:—

"Take care.—If you do not speak—I shall claim you as my own in some strange presumptuous way.—Send me away at once, if I must go;—Margaret!—"

At that third call she turned her face, still covered with her small white hands, towards him, and laid it on his shoulder, hiding it even there; and it was too delicious to feel her soft cheek against his, for him to wish to see either deep blushes or loving eyes. He clasped her close. But they both kept silence. At length she murmured in a broken voice:

"Oh, Mr. Thornton, I am not good enough!"

1. Easson notes the inadequacy of this sum as it stands; it was changed to "eighteen thousand and fifty-seven pounds" in the second edition (*Easson 1973*, p. 448).

"Not good enough! Don't mock my own deep feeling of unworthiness."

After a minute or two, he gently disengaged her hands from her face, and laid her arms as they had once before been placed to protect him from the rioters.

"Do you remember, love?" he murmured. "And how I requited you with my insolence the next day?"

"I remember how wrongly I spoke to you,—that is all."

"Look here! Lift up your head. I have something to show you!" She slowly faced him, glowing with beautiful shame.

"Do you know these roses?" he said, drawing out his pocket-book, in which were treasured up some dead flowers.

"No!" she replied, with innocent curiosity. "Did I give them to you?"

"No! Vanity; you did not. You may have worn sister roses very probably."

She looked at them, wondering for a minute, then she smiled a little as she said—

"They are from Helstone, are they not? I know the deep indentations round the leaves. Oh! have you been there? When were you there?"

"I wanted to see the place where Margaret grew to what she is, even at the worst time of all, when I had no hope of ever calling her mine. I went there on my return from Havre."

"You must give them to me," she said, trying to take them out of his hand with gentle violence.

"Very well. Only you must pay me for them!"

"How shall I ever tell Aunt Shaw?" she whispered, after some time of delicious silence.

"Let me speak to her."

"Oh, no! I owe to her,—but what will she say?"

"I can guess. Her first exclamation will be, 'That man!' "

"Hush!" said Margaret, "or I shall try and show you your mother's indignant tones as she says, 'That woman!' "

THE END.

CONTEXTS
1850–1900

Letters

ELIZABETH GASKELL

From Letters†

To Lady Kay-Shuttleworth[1]

Silverdale, near Lancaster / July 16. [?1850]
* * * I believe what I have said in Mary Barton to be perfectly true,
but by no means the whole truth; and I have always felt deeply
annoyed at anyone, or any set of people who chose to consider that
I had manifested the whole truth; I do not think it possible to do
this in any *one* work of fiction. You say 'I think there are good mill-
owners; I think the factory system might be made a great engine for
good'; and in this no one can more earnestly and heartily agree with
you than I do. I can not imagine a nobler scope for a thoughtful
energetic man, desirous of doing good to his kind, than that presented to his powers as the master of a factory. But I believe that
there is much to be discovered yet as to the right position and mutual
duties of employer, and employed; * * * I think the best and most
benevolent employers would say how difficult they, with all their
experience, found it to unite theory and practice. * * * It would
require a wise man, practical and full of experience, one able to
calculate consequences, to choose out the best among the many
systems which are being tried by the benevolent mill-owners. * * *
And I should like some *man*, who had a man's correct knowledge, to
write on this subject, and make the poor intelligent work-people

---

† From *The Letters of Mrs Gaskell*, ed. J. A. V. Chapple and Arthur Pollard, Manchester,
U.K., 1966 (*Letters*), and *Further Letters of Mrs Gaskell*, ed. John Chapple and Alan Shelston, Manchester, U.K., 2000 (*Further Letters*). Reprinted by permission of the publisher.
This sequence of letters reveals a number of issues that arose in the writing and publication
process of *North and South*, notably over questions of serialization. It should be read in
conjunction with the sequence of letters by Dickens below. I have retained the conventions
of these editions with minor adjustments. Square brackets [ ] indicate conjectured readings
or dates. In most cases I have retained Gaskell's form of address to her correspondents
together with her signatures, since these indicate the level of her connection with them.
Of the addresses, Silverdale was Gaskell's summer house near the lake district; Plymouth
Grove was her Manchester home. Notes are the Editor's.
1. Friend of both Elizabeth Gaskell and Charlotte Brontë; she engineered their first meeting
in 1850. In this letter Gaskell responds to the criticism of her earlier industrial novel,
Mary Barton, to the effect that it was biased against the mill owners.

understand the infinite anxiety as to right and wrong-doing which I
believe that riches bring to many.

*   *   *

My dear lady, I am
Yours very faithfully, E. C. Gaskell.
(*Letters*, pp. 118–21)

To John Forster[2]

Sunday—[23 April 1854]
* * * Oh! I wrote to Mr Dickens, & he says he is not going to have
a strike[3],—altogether his answer sets me at ease. I have half wondered whether another character might not be introduced into Margaret,[4],—Mrs Thornton, the mother, to have taken as a sort of
humble companion & young housekeeper the orphan daughter of an
old friend in humble, retired country life on the borders of Lancashire,—& this girl to be in love with Mr Thornton in a kind of passionate despairing way,—but both jealous of Margaret, & yet angry
that she gives Mr Thornton pain—I know the kind of wild wayward
character that grows up in lonesome places, which has a sort of
Southern capacity of hating & loving. She shd not be what people
call *educated*, but with strong sense.

*   *   *

Yours most truly
E. C. Gaskell.
(*Letters*, pp. 279–81)

To Catherine Winkworth[5]

Wednesday Evening [11 to 14 Oct. 1854] /
½ p. 5 Lea-Hurst, Matlock Privatish
* * * And now the house is cleared; and I am established high up,
in two rooms opening one out of the other; the old nurseries; the
inner one—very barely furnished—is my bedroom now; but usually
Miss N's. It is curious how simple it is compared even to that of our
girls. The carpet does not cover the floor, is far from new. The furniture is painted wood; no easy chair, no sofa, a little curtainless bed;
a small glass not so large as mine at home. One of the windows opens

2. Friend and adviser of Gaskell, and also of Dickens. Forster was to become Dickens's first
   full-scale biographer.
3. I.e., in *Hard Times,* running in *Household Words* and preceding *North and South*.
4. Gaskell's working title for *North and South*.
5. Close friend of Gaskell. At this point Gaskell went to Lea Hurst, the Derbyshire home of
   the Nightingale family, in order to be able to devote herself exclusively to the writing of
   North and South. This letter describes the conditions in which this writing took place.

out on a battlement from which, high as Lea Hurst is, one can see the clouds careering round one.

*   *   *

It is getting dark. I am to have my tea, up in my turret—at 6.—And after that I shall lock my outer door & write. I am stocked with coals, and have candles up here; for I am a quarter of a mile of staircase & odd intricate passage away from every one else in the house. Could solitude be more complete! * * * So *ought* not M. Hale to stand a good chance. I do think she [i.e., "Margaret"] is going on well. I am satisfied. Not that I have written so much, but so *well*. There's modesty for you.

*   *   *

What do you think of a fire burning down Mr Thornton's mills *and house* as a *help* to failure? Then Margaret would rebuild them larger & better & need not go & live there when she's married. Tell me what you think: M H has just told the lie, & is gathering herself up after her dead faint; very meek & stunned & humble. One companion I have got—an *owl*.

Your very affec[tionate] Lily.[6]
(*Letters*, pp. 305–10)

To Emily Shaen[7]

Lea Hurst, / Oct. 27th, 1854
* * * I've got to (with Margaret * * *) when they've quarrelled, silently, after the lie and she knows she loves him, and he is trying not to love her; and Frederick is gone back to Spain and Mrs Hale is dead and Mr Bell has come to stay with the Hales, and Mr Thornton ought to be developing himself—and Mr Hale ought to die— and if I could get over this next piece I could swim through the London life beautifully into the sunset glory of the last scene. But hitherto Thornton is good; and I'm afraid of a touch marring him; and I want to keep his character consistent with itself, and large and strong and tender, and *yet a master*. That's my next puzzle. I am enough on not to hurry; and yet I don't know if waiting and thinking will bring any new ideas about him. * * *

Your own grateful and affectionate,
Lily.
(*Letters*, pp. 316–21)

6. A name Gaskell used among close friends.
7. Friend of Gaskell; her husband, William Shaen, was Gaskell's legal adviser and acted for her in literary matters. The letter is from the Nightingale home.

To ?Charles Dickens

Sunday [?17 December 1854]

My dear Sir,

I was very much gratified by your note the other day; *very* much indeed. I dare say I shall like my story, when I am a little further from it; at present I can only feel depressed about it, I meant it to have been so much better. I send what I am afraid you will think too large a batch of it by this post. What Mr Wills[8] has got already *fills up* the No for January 13, leaving me only two more numbers, Janry 20, & Janry 27th so what I send to-day is meant to be crammed & stuffed into Janry 20th; & I'm afraid I've nearly as much more for Jany 27.

It is 33 pages of my writing that I send to-day. I have tried to shorten & compress it, both because it was a dull piece, & to get it into reasonable length, but there were [sic] a whole catalogue of events to be got over: and what I want to tell you now is this,—Mr Gaskell has looked this piece well over, so I don't think there will be any carelessnesses left in it, & so there ought not to be any misprints; therefore I never wish to see it's [sic] face again; but, *if you will keep the MS for me, & shorten it as you think best for H W.* I shall be very glad. Shortened I see it must be.

I think a better title than N. & S. would have been 'Death & Variations'. There are 5 deaths, each beautifully suited to the character of the individual.

* * *

Yours most truly
E. C. Gaskell

I shall direct the batch of MS to the Office. Don't consult me as to the shortenings; only please yrself.

(*Letters*, pp. 323–24)

To Eliza Fox[9]

P[lymouth] Grove. / Monday, Dec. 24 [?25], 1854

My dearest Tottie,

Oh what a shameful time it is since I've written to you! and what a shame of me not to write, for yr last letter was such a nice one, though its [sic] been stinging me with reproaches this two months past, but I believe I've been as nearly dazed and crazed with this c—, d— be h— to it, story as can be. I've been sick of writing, and everything connected with literature or improvement of the mind; to say

---

8. Dickens's sub-editor at *Household Words*.
9. Eliza Fox, daughter of the Radical clergyman William Fox, painter in her own right and friend of Elizabeth Gaskell, to whom she was known by her pet name, "Tottie."

nothing of deep hatred to my species about whom I was obliged to write as if I loved 'em. Moreover I have had to write so hard that I have spoilt my hand, and forgotten all my spelling. Seriously it has been a terrible weight on me and has made me have some of the most felling headaches I ever had in my life * * *

(*Letters*, pp. 325–26)

To Anna Jameson[1]

Plymouth Grove / Sunday Evening [January 1855]:
My dear Mrs Jameson,

You can't think what pleasure your kind note of appreciation gave, and gives me. I made a half-promise (as perhaps I told you,) to Mr Dickens, which he understood as a whole one; and though I had the plot and characters in my head long ago, I have often been in despair about the working of them out; because of course, in this way of publishing it, I had to write pretty hard without waiting for the happy leisure hours. And then 20 numbers was, I found, my allowance; instead of the too scant 22, which I had fancied were included in 'five months'; and at last the story is huddled & hurried up; especially in the rapidity with which the sudden death of Mr Bell, succeeds to the sudden death of Mr Hale. But what could I do? Every page was grudged me, just at last, when I did certainly infringe all the bounds & limits they set me as to quantity. Just at the very last I was compelled to desperate compression. But now I am not sure if, when the barrier gives way between 2 such characters as Mr Thornton and Margaret it would not go all smash in a moment,—and I don't feel quite certain that I dislike the end as it now stands. But, it is being republished as a whole, in two vols;—and the question is shall I alter & enlarge what is already written, bad & hurried-up though it be? I can not insert small pieces here and there—I feel as if I must throw myself back a certain distance in the story, & re-write it from there; retaining the present incidents, but filling up intervals of time &c &c. Would you give me your *very* valuable opinion as to this? If I have taken to a book, or poem * * * the first time of reading I am like a child, and angry at every alteration even though it may be an improvement. I am going to follow your plan and run away from reviewers. * * * I shall send you a copy of N. & S. if you will kindly accept it. And I really shall be grateful to you for an answer to my question about the alterations.

Yours ever most truly
E. C. Gaskell
(*Letters*, pp.328–29)

1. Writer and art historian, at this time a warm friend of Gaskell.

To Anna Jameson

Plymouth Grove— / Tuesday, Jan 30. [1855]
My dear Mrs Jameson,
No! indeed, you have not been a bit too abrupt. I wanted just what
you tell me,—even more decidedly if need were; & truth is too precious & valuable a thing to need drapery,—you tell me just what I
wanted to know. If the story had been poured just warm out of the
mind, it would have taken a much larger mould. It was the cruel
necessity of compressing it that hampered me. And now I can't do
much; I may not even succeed when I try, but I will try for my own
satisfaction even if it does not answer, & I have to cancel what I am
now meaning to write, and all before the end of next week!

* * *

Ever dear Mrs Jameson
Yours most truly
E. C. Gaskell
(*Letters*, pp. 330–31)

To William Fairbairn[2]

Plymouth Grove / [?Summer 1855]
My dear Mr Fairbairn,—I am ashamed that I have been so long in
acknowledging your kind friendly note, and very just criticisms on
'North and South'.

* * *

I agree with you that there are a certain set of characters in 'North
and South', of no particular interest to any one in the tale, any more
than such people would be in real life; but they were wanted to fill
up unimportant places in the story, when otherwise there would have
been unsightly gaps.

Mr Hale is not a 'sceptic'; he has *doubts*, and can resolve greatly
about great things, and is capable of self-sacrifice in theory; but in
the details of practice he is weak and vacillating. I know a character
just like his, a clergyman who has left the Church from principle,
and in that did finely; but his daily life is a constant unspoken regret
that he did so, although he would do it again if need be.

* * *

2. Engineer and Manchester acquaintance of Gaskell; later Sir William Fairbairn and pres-
   ident of the British Association for the Advancement of Science.

Thank you again, dear Mr Fairbairn, for your note, which I shall always value, and believe me,

I am yours most truly,
E. C. Gaskell.
(*Letters*, pp. 352–53)

To Mrs Maria James[3]

Thursday / [?25 January 1855]

* * * Oh! I have been so cramped for room at the end of N & S! They objected to more than 20 numbers; said 'the public would expect me to keep my word' & c,—a word which *they* had passed, not I. I begged hard for the interpretation of 'five months' to include 22 nos and obtained the favour with a kind of Che sarà sarà resignation on their part, & a perpetual grumbling. So my poor story is like a pantomime figure, with a great large head, and very small trunk. And it might have been so good! I shall try to add something to the separate publication to make it less unnatural, & deformed. But I will never write for H. W. again.

* * *

Yours affectionately E. C. Gaskell
(*Further Letters*, p. 122)

To Verlag B. Tauchnitz[4]

Chez M. Mohl, / 120, Rue du Bac, Paris, /
February 20th [*1855*]:

Now *North and South* has appeared in *Household Words* (in 20 numbers extending from the beginning of last September to the end of January) . . . I may add that I am writing a good deal in addition to the last quarter of the story which had to be very much compressed, and spoilt to suit the purposes of *Household Words*. I think it certain that there will be a sixth part of additional matter. * * *

(*Further Letters*, p. 125)

---

3. Wife of Sir William James, a distinguished lawyer and friend of Gaskell.
4. German publisher who initiated and developed a paperback series of reprints of English and American fiction for railway travellers. This letter, of which only a fragment remains in a printed source, is in response to a request from them that *North and South* might be included in this series. It is written from the Paris home of Gaskell's friend Madame Mohl, whom she visited frequently.

CHARLES DICKENS

From Letters†

To Mrs Gaskell, 31 January 1850

Devonshire Terrace Thirty First January 1850

My Dear Mrs Gaskell,

You may perhaps have seen an announcement in the papers, of my intention to start a new cheap weekly journal of general literature?

I do not know what your literary vows of temperance or abstinence may be, but as I *do* honestly know that there is no living English writer whose aid I would desire to enlist, in preference to the authoress of Mary Barton (a book that most profoundly affected and impressed me) I venture to ask you whether you can give me any hope that you will write a *short* tale, or any number of tales, for the projected pages.

No writer's name will be used—neither my own, nor any others—every paper will be published without any signature; and all will seem to express the general mind and purpose of the Journal, which is, the raising up of those that are down, and the general improvement of our social condition. I should set a value on your help, which your modesty can hardly imagine; and I am perfectly sure that the least result of your reflection or observation in respect of the life around you, would attract attention and do good.[1] * * *

To Mrs Gaskell, [15] and 17 June, 1854

Tavistock House / Thursday Evening Sixteenth June / 1854

My Dear Mrs. Gaskell,

I have read the MS[2] you have had the kindness to send me, with all possible attention and care. I have shut myself up for the purpose, and allowed nothing to divide my thoughts. It opens an admirable story, is full of character and power, has a strong suspended interest in it (the end of which, I don't in the least foresee), and has the very best marks of your hand upon it. If I had had more to read, I certainly could not have stopped, but must have read on.

† The source for this selection from Dickens's letters is *The Letters of Charles Dickens* (The Pilgrim Edition), volume 6, 1850–1852, ed. Graham Storey, Kathleen Tillotson, and Nina Burgis; volume 7, 1853–1855, ed. Graham Storey, Kathleen Tillotson, and Angus Easson (Oxford: Clarendon Press, 1988, 1993). The conventions of this edition have been retained; a slash [/] indicates a line break. Some editorial notes have been edited or omitted and the notes re-numbered. Reprinted by permission of Oxford University Press [*Editor*].

1. *Lizzie Leigh* was written in response to this approach by Dickens. [*Editor*].

2. Corresponding to the first seven numbers of *North and South*, to be serialized in *HW* weekly from 2 Sep.

Now, addressing myself to the consideration of its being published in weekly portions, let me endeavour to shew you as distinctly as I can, the divisions into which it must fall. According to the best of my judgement and experience, if it were divided in any other way—reference being always had to the weekly space available for the purpose in Household Words—it would be mortally injured.

I would end No. 1—With the announcement of Mr. Lennox at the parsonage

I would end No. 2—With Mr. Hale's announcement to Margaret, that Milton-Northern is the place they are going to. This No. therefore would contain Lennox's proposal, and the father's communication to his daughter of his leaving the church.

I would end No. 3—With their fixing on the watering-place as their temporary sojourn.

I would end No. 4—With Margaret's sitting down at night in their new house, to read Edith's letter. This No. therefore, would contain the account of Milton, and the new house, and the Mill Owner's first visit.

I would end No. 5—With the Mill-Owner's leaving the house after the tea-visit. This No. therefore would contain the introduction of his mother, and also of the working father and daughter—the Higgins family.

I would end No. 6—With Margaret leaving their dwelling, after the interview with Bessy when she is lying down.[3]

These Nos. would sometimes require to be again divided into two chapters, and would sometimes want a word or two of conclusion. If you could be content to leave this to me, I could make those arrangements of the text without much difficulty.[4] The only place where I do not see my way, and where the story—always with a special eye to this form of publication—seems to me to flag unmanageably, without an amount of excision that I dare scarcely hint at, is between Nos. 2 and 3, where the Dialogue is long—is on a difficult and dangerous subject[5]—and where, to bring the murder out at once,[6] I think there is a necessity for fusing two Nos. into one. This is the only difficult place in the whole 114 sides of foolscap.[7]

---

3. The first three numbers end as CD suggests. Nos 4, 5, and 6 do not match exactly with Dickens's suggestions, and Margaret's talk with Bessy Higgins is not reached until the end of No 7 [Editor].

4. The MS of North and South does not survive, but we know from the MS of Gaskell's final novel, Wives and Daughters, that it was apparently not her practice to make chapter divisions in her manuscript [Editor].

5. Mr. Hale's explanation to Margaret as to why he must leave the Church of England; it occupies more than half of chap. 4.

6. I.e., to come to the unpleasant point at once.

7. Mrs. Gaskell apparently agreed to condense the two numbers, but in fact sent Wills the second number unaltered: see To Mrs Gaskell, 20 Aug 54 (p. 411 below).

As nearly as I can calculate, *about* 18 sides of your writing would make a weekly No. On *about* this calculation, the MS I have, would divide at the good points I have mentioned, and pretty equally. I do not apologize to you for laying so much stress on the necessity of its dividing well, because I am bound to put before you my perfect conviction that if it did not, the story would be wasted—would miss its effect as it went on—*and would not recover it when published complete*. The last consideration is strong with me, because it is based on my long comparison of the advantages and disadvantages of the periodical form of appearance.

I hope these remarks will not confuse you, but you will come out tolerably clear after a second reading, and will convey to you the means of looking at your whole story from the weekly point of view. It cannot, I repeat, be disregarded without injury to the book. All the MS that I have—with the exception I have mentioned and allowing a very reasonable margin indeed for a little compression here and there—might have been expressly written to meet the exigencies of the case.

                                        Saturday Seventeenth June.
That my calculations might be accurate, I thought it well to stop my note and send eighteen of your sides to the Printer's (I took them out at random) to be calculated. Their estimate exactly accords with mine. I have therefore no doubt of its correctness.

Is there is anything else I can tell you, or anything else you want to ask me? Pray do not entertain the idea that you can give me any trouble I shall not be delighted to encounter. * * *

Have you thought of a name?[8] I cannot suggest one without knowing more of the story. Then perhaps I might hit upon a good title if you did not.

                        Ever My Dear Mrs. Gaskell / Faithfully Yours
                                        Charles Dickens

To Mrs Gaskell, 2 July 1854:

Villa du Camp de droite, Boulogne[9] / Sunday Second July, 1854
My Dear Mrs. Gaskell

                              *   *   *

---

8. Mrs. Gaskell's original title was "Margaret Hale," after the heroine. On ?17 Dec 54, she wrote to CD: "I think a better title than N. & S. would have been 'Death & Variations'. There are 5 deaths, each beautifully suited to the character of the individual." [See p. 402 above.]

9. Between mid-June and the beginning of October 1854 Dickens was staying with his family at this address in France [*Editor*]

Margaret Hale is as good a name as any other; and I merely referred to its having a name at all, because books usually have names, and you had left the title of the story blank.[1]

Hard Times will be finished in Household Words, please God, either on Saturday the 12th. of August, or on Saturday the 19th. of August. I think its successor should begin not later than Saturday the 2nd. of September.

But I cannot so well give you the opinion you require (as to whether I should think the risk of beginning before the entire MS is in hand, too great), now, as when I shall have read some more of the story. If you will kindly let me have at the office in London by the 25th. of July what more of it you can then spare, I will read it at once, and write to you finally on the point.[2]

* * *

* * * I should propose to advertize the story, exactly as I allow my own stories to be advertised; and I assure you that I have a very considerable respect for my Art and a very considerable respect for myself.

Dear Mrs. Gaskell / Faithfully Yours always

Charles Dickens

To Mrs Gaskell, 26 July 1854:

Villa du Camp de droite, Boulogne
Wednesday Twenty Sixth July, 1854

My Dear Mrs. Gaskell.

Having finished my story[3] and got to London, a week earlier than I had expected, I brought back the continuation of your MS[4] to read here. Confining myself as in my last note, strictly to the business of the subject (that I may be the better understood), I proceed, first, to say how I would divide it.

I would make five weekly parts of it.[5] The first to close with the end of the strike conversation held by Margaret and her father with Mr Thornton. The second to close with the receipt of the dinner Invitation. The third to close with Margaret's leaving Higgins's house after Boucher has charged his miseries upon Higgins and the Union. The fourth to close with her being admitted into the Mill on the day of the Riot, and the porter's shutting the gate. The fifth to close with

1. Title settled by 26 July * * * though at whose suggestion is not clear.
2. CD had so far seen nearly to the end of volume I, chap. 13; the July portion of MS took him to the end of chap. 22. By mid-Oct, six weeks after publication began, Mrs. Gaskell had reached the end of chap. 3 (vol. II, chap. 9).
3. I.e., *Hard Times* [*Editor*]
4. Of *North and South*. This portion became vol. I, chaps 14–22 of the volume issue.
5. Published in *HW*, 21 Oct to 18 Nov 54, divided as CD suggests, except that the third part (chaps. 18–19) opens with the receipt of the dinner invitation.

the end of the Thornton declaration scene, and the end of the MS I have.

The fifth part would be a long one, but the interest and action are strong, and it would not be too long. It appears to me that the conversation in the first part is unnecessarily lengthy, and I think that portion—not only as a portion, but as a part of the book—would be very materially improved if you would not object to make some curtailment in the printed proof.[6]

North and South appears to me a better name than Margaret Hale. It implies more, and is expressive of the opposite people brought face to face by the story.

I should be happy to begin the publication at once, having so much MS in hand. I should advertize the tale as to be completed in about 20 weekly portions,[7] and as being by the Author of Mary Barton. These particulars, and its name, would be all that the announcement need state. By the expression "at once," I mean on Saturday the Second of September, nominally: but really on the preceding Wednesday—the No. being always actually published on Wednesday, though dated Saturday.

I do not understand whether you permit me to divide the story with chapters. But I believe you are aware that it will at least be necessary to begin every weekly portion as a new chapter.

May I ask you to be so good as to reply to me, as soon as you can, whether you are content to have the story announced as I have proposed. It is very important that early advantage should be taken of all the usual channels of literary advertisement. There is no time to spare.

My Dear Mrs. Gaskell / Faithfully Yours always
Charles Dickens

To Mrs Gaskell, 31 July 1854

Villa du Camp de droite, Boulogne
Monday Thirty First July 1854

My Dear Mrs. Gaskell.

I merely confined myself to the business-part of our communication, because you seemed a little to resent my doing anything else. Your pleasant letter blows all that seeming, away in a breath. * * *

I have given out the announcement in the manner we have agreed on, for beginning on Saturday the Second of September—that is (as I have already said) nominally: the real day being the Wednesday previous to that date. * * * But I have laid this injunction on them—

6. Either Mrs. Gaskell agreed to this or CD assumed she had, since on her failure to do so he reacted angrily.

7. It ran for 22 weeks (2 Sep 54–27 Jan 55). Though Mrs Gaskell later claimed that 20 weeks was all she was allowed (*Letters*, p. 328), CD gave her five full calendar months.

that the advertizing is in no case to be different from that of Hard Times *as I approved of it*. And I am sure you will find that to be as unobjectionable as such a thing can be.

Will you send up to London, addressed to Wills, the MS I had at first, and returned to you? We will have a quantity of it got into type, and I will merely divide it into chapters. If I ever have a suggestion to make, I will intimate it on the proof in pencil. You will take no notice of it, if you don't approve of it.

* * *

My Dear Mrs. Gaskell / Very faithfully Yours
Charles Dickens

To W. H. Wills, 19 August 1854

Boulogne Saturday Nineteenth August 1854
My Dear Wills.

* * *

I am alarmed by the quantity of North and South. It is not objectionable for a beginning, but would become so in the progress of a not compactly written and artfully devised story.[8]

* * *

Ever Faithfully
CD

To Mrs Gaskell, 20 August 1854

Villa du Camp de droite, Boulogne
Sunday Twentieth August 1854
My Dear Mrs. Gaskell

I have just received from Wills, in proof, our No. for the 9th. of September containing the Second Part of North and South, as it originally stood, and *unaltered by you*.

This is the place where we agreed that there should be a great condensation, and a considerable compression, where Mr Hale states his doubts to Margaret.[9] The mechanical necessities of Household Words oblige us to get to press with this No. *immediately*. In case you should not already have altered the proof and sent it to Wills (which very possibly you have: and in that case forgive my

8. The following day Dickens wrote to Wills: "It is perfectly plain to me that if we put in more, every week, of North and South than we did of Hard Times, we shall ruin Household Words. Therefore it must at all hazards be kept down." [*Editor*].
9. Although CD had proposed this to her on 15 June and she had apparently agreed to make cuts (see p. 409 above), vol. 1, chap. 4 makes it clear that she did not do so.

troubling you) will you be so kind as to do so at once. What I would recommend—and did recommend—is, to make the scene between Margaret and her father relative to his leaving the church and their destination being Milton-Northern, as short as you could find it in your heart to make it.

I have made a break at Lennox's going away, and begin a new chapter (*not* a weekly part, you understand) with "He was gone."[1]

*   *   *

My Dear Mrs. Gaskell / Always Very Faithfully Yours
CD

To W. H. Wills, 14 October 1854:

Boulogne, Saturday October Fourteenth / 1854
My Dear Wills.

*   *   *

I am sorry to hear of the Sale dropping, but I am not surprised.[2] Mrs Gaskell's story, so divided, is wearisome in the last degree. It would have had scant attraction enough if the casting in Whitefriars[3] had been correct; but thus wire-drawn it is a dreary business. Never mind! I am ready to come up to the scratch on my return, and to shoulder the wheel.

*   *   *

Ever Faithfully
CD

To Mrs Gaskell, 27 January 1855

Tavistock House / Twenty Seventh January 1855
My Dear Mrs. Gaskell.

Let me congratulate you on the conclusion of your story;[4] not because it is the end of a task to which you had conceived a dislike (for I imagine you to have got the better of that delusion by this time), but because it is the vigorous and powerful accomplishment of an anxious labor. It seems to me that you have felt the ground thoroughly firm under your feet, and have strided on with a force and purpose that MUST now give you pleasure.

1. The opening of vol. 1, chap. 4. After these words [i.e., on the letter itself—*Editor*] Mrs. Gaskell has written "I've not a notion what he means." Clearly she kept no draft of her MS.
2. I.e., of *Household Words*. Dickens associates this drop in sales with his misgivings about *North and South*. The editors of Dickens's letters suggest that the drop must have been temporary [*Editor*]
3. The original calculations for the novel's length, made by the printers [*Editor*].
4. The final instalment of *North and South* appeared in *HW*, 27 Jan 55, X, 561.

You will not, I hope, allow that non-lucid interval of dissatisfaction with yourself (and me?) which beset you for a minute or two once upon a time, to linger in the shape of any disagreeable association with Household Words. I shall still look forward to the large sides of paper, and shall soon feel disappointed if they don't begin to reappear.

I thought it best that Wills should write the business-letter[5] on the conclusion of the story, as that part of our communication had always previously rested with him. I trust you found it satisfactory? I refer to it, not as a matter of mere form, but because I sincerely wish everything between us to be beyond the possibility of misunderstanding or reservation.

Dear Mrs. Gaskell / Very faithfully Yours
Charles Dickens

Other Contemporary Correspondence

Charlotte Brontë to Elizabeth Gaskell

30 September 1854[1]

* * * What has appeared I like well, and better, each fresh number; best of all the last (to-days).[2] The Subject seems to me difficult: at first, I groaned over it: if you had any narrowness of views or bitterness of feeling towards the Church or her Clergy, I should groan over it still; but I think I see the ground you are about to take as far as the Church is concerned; not that of attack on her, but of defence of those who conscientiously differ from her, and feel it a duty to leave her fold. Well—it is good ground, but still rugged for the step of Fiction; stony—thorny will it prove at times—I fear. It seems to me that you understand well the Genius of the North. Where the Southern Lady and the Northern Mechanic are brought into contrast and contact I think Nature is well respected. Simple, true and good did I think the last number—clear of artificial trammels of style and thought. * * *

Parthenope Nightingale to Elizabeth Gaskell[3]

* * * By the bye, I must say what a deal of wisdom there seems to me in "N & S." It has instructed me exceedingly. You hold the bal-

5. The editors of Dickens's letters note that Wills forwarded a check for 200 guineas to Mrs. Gaskell and hoped "it will be satisfactory to you and will not indispose you to a preservation of your association with us" [Editor].

1. MS held in the John Rylands University Library of Manchester. Reprinted by permission of the director. All notes are the Editor's.

2. Charlotte Brontë is reading the novel as it appears in parts; the reference is to the third part, concluding with vol. 1, chapter 9.

3. Quoted, undated, in Elizabeth Haldane, *Mrs Gaskell and Her Friends* (London: Hodder

ance very evenly and it must be a hard task. I am quite sorry to part with it, and wish it had not ended so soon, or so abruptly, but I am afraid you are right, for I am afraid Margaret will not be happy, tho' she will make him so; he is too old to mould, and the poetry of her nature will suffer under the iron mark which has so compressed his so long. And then Mrs. Thornton will never forgive her for having reinstated her son, that hard, coarse, ungenerous woman will never consent to take an obligation as he does so beautifully (for I think that is one of the best things you have done—he is too proud to be annoyed at being obliged to his wife and loves her too deeply to know that it is a burthen). They (Mrs. T. and M.) cannot live together and be happy and yet she cannot be turned out of the house, but when do one's friends marriages satisfy one? They are the most melancholy things generally one goes through. * * *

John Forster to Elizabeth Gaskell

31 January 1855[4]

My dear Mrs Gaskell,

Though better, I am far from well—and my work makes me beg excuses—and you will forgive a very brief note. Indeed there is little to say beyond enclosing this letter—and one which Mr Chapman has sent me—back to you. For the whole case is before you, and no one can determine but yourself what is best to be done in it. I find the impression as to the hurried conclusion certainly prevailing however the story is named—and I am myself in favour of an attempt to rewrite the last chapter—I mean make such additions as would give a different character to the termination of the story—a more detailed and progressive character to the same incidents and the same close. But after all, it is easy to say this—and *you* must see whether so easy to do it—and do it effectively. I retain my opinion about Thornton. He suffers a little with me—but I must confess he is more my hero, after all, than she is my heroine, for with all my admiration of her, I don't think her quite entitled to reject him at first as she does— and therefore I don't altogether like her contriving to have the advantage in the end. In all this, however, I may be wrong—and my allegiance to her never swerved till you made me like and support *him* so much. So you are responsible for whatever may annoy you in this opinion.—I would not, if I decided on the change, restrict myself as

and Stoughton, 1930), p. 105. Parthenope Nightingale (1819–1890) was Florence Nightingale's older sister.

4. This previously unpublished letter is reprinted by permission of the Director, The John Rylands University Library of Manchester. John Forster (1812–1876). Man of letters, friend of Gaskell, and later, biographer of Dickens.

to time in doing it. I would take it and finish it in France—if you cannot do so here. Anything *I* can do in the way of hurrying proofs for you—or *anything*—you know you can depend upon. And so I close this my *in*definite note—but indeed, my dear Mrs Gaskell, this is a matter (I mean as to *how* the effect of hurry at the last is to be removed) which only you can yourself properly decide. May you resolve for the best. Indeed I am sure you will.

Yrs most truly
John Forster

Anna Jameson to Elizabeth Gaskell[5]

* * * Now, in regard to your charming Tale—I am so grateful to *it* and to *you* that criticism seems ungracious—but since you ask my opinion so distinctly you shall have it.[6] I *do* think the conclusion hurried—and what you call huddled up; there should be more gradation in effect, and the rapidity of the incidents at the close destroys the proportions of your story as a work of art—I mean the end is not in proportion with the beginning. This is a fault of *construction*—but what is done is so beautiful and complete that it is only in considering the work as a whole that we feel that too great compression—we want to know something more about the other characters. I do not know whether to advise you to alter it—what has once been thrown warm off the mind and has run into the mould seldom bears alteration—but do not, with your powers, engage to write periodically; it has had a mischievous effect, I think, on Dickens and Thackeray—and it enrages me to lose that beautiful picture of the gradual opening of the mutual mind and heart of the two beings you have created with such an intense vitality and which you would have given with such delicacy and power—so here you have my opinion most crudely and unceremoniously but most truly—and pray send me a copy—for I shall indeed value it.

W. R. Greg to Elizabeth Gaskell[7]

It is no compliment to say that your book has been my constant companion since I saw you; I only finished it last night. But I have been in society every day, and could only snatch time for a chapter before going to bed at night. Last night, however, I was home early and resolved upon a treat; so sat up until 1 o'clock, and came to an

5. Quoted, undated, Haldane, p. 113.
6. See Gaskell to Jameson above, p. 403.
7. Quoted, undated, in *The Works of Mrs Gaskell, with Introductions by A. W. Ward*, The "Knutsford" Edition, 8 vols. (London: John Murray, 1906), IV, p. xix. For details of Greg, see p. 462, n. below.

end, and was sorry when I had done it. I find no fault in it, which is a great thing for a critic to say, seeing that one inevitably gets the habit of reading in a somewhat critical spirit. I do not think it is as thorough a work of genius as 'Mary Barton'—nor the subject as interesting as 'Ruth'—but I like it better than either; and you know how, in spite of my indignation, I admired the first.[8] I think you have just taken the right tone, and the spirit and execution of the whole is excellent. The characters are all distinct, and kept distinct to the last, and the delineation is most delicate and just. Now you are, I know, so used to full and unmodified eulogy that I daresay my appreciation will appear faint, scanty, and grudging. Indeed it is not so; if you knew how painfully scrupulous I am (not as a matter of conscience, but of insuperable instinct) in matters of praise to keep within the truth—you would read more real admiration in my cold sentences than in the golden opinions of more demonstrative ones.

William Fairbairn to Elizabeth Gaskell[9]

* * * Poor old Higgins, with his weak consumptive daughter, is a true picture of a Manchester man. There are many like him in this town, and a better sample of Independent industry you could not have hit upon. Higgins is an excellent representative of a Lancashire operative—strictly independent—and one of the best characters in the place. * * *

Harriet Beecher Stowe to Elizabeth Gaskell, 24 May 1856[1]

* * * I must say in closing that I and my twin daughters read your North and South with so much enthusiasm that it was decreed at the time that mamma should write you an expression of thanks, but Time as he often does stole the pen till the memory of first love was past—but I will not deny myself the memory of it now. I *do hope* I may be permitted to see you this summer, I hope to be in England and *somewhere* we may meet—You have made me cry very unfairly over Mary Barton when I bought the book to amuse myself on a journey—but I bear no malice for that. * * *

8. Greg had previously reviewed *Mary Barton* in very critical terms in the *Edinburgh Review* (April 1849, lxxxix); *Ruth* (1853), Gaskell's second full-length novel, dealt with the dangerous subject of unmarried motherhood.
9. Quoted, undated, in Ward, IV, p. xx. Fairbairn was a Manchester engineer and employer known personally to Gaskell. See p. 404 above.
1. Reprinted in R. D. Waller, *Letters Addressed to Mrs Gaskell by Celebrated Contemporaries, Now in the possession of the John Rylands University Library of Manchester*: Manchester UP, 1935, pp. 164–65. Gaskell had met Stowe on the latter's visit to Britain in 1853.

Contemporary Reviews

THE SPECTATOR

From New Novels (31 March 1855)†

The author of "Mary Barton" displays that intellectual quality understood by the word power. She has power in conception, power in
depiction, power in expression. She has little or none of the larger
and loftier faculties implied by genius and imagination, which enable
their possessor to exhibit the spirit of things whereof only a glimpse
has been obtained. The life and its concomitants with which she is
familiar—the factory districts, and the society of a country town—
she delineates truthfully, though somewhat hardly. When she passes
into a higher sphere she is indebted to speculation for her ideas. Her
personae are rather abstractions than living beings; some of their
traits are ingeniously conceived, but exhibited more purely than is
ever the case in living beings. Other of their qualities partake of the
notions which the vulgar entertain about the aristocracy. Under the
most favourable circumstances there is a want of dramatic spirit and
geniality. Her persons as well as her scenes and dialogues want the
warmth of life.

In *North and South* the writer is for the most part on her strong
ground. The North is a manufacturing town with its inhabitants in
the cotton district. The South is chiefly represented by an amiable
ex-clergyman and his family. * * * The daughter is the heroine—and
an agreeable conception rather than creation—who stops short of
being charming by a slight touch of brusquerie, and a somewhat
overstrained contempt for trade and traders, though her own social
position is not really so high as that of many commercial people. The
North is characteristically represented by Mr. Thornton, a manufacturer of respectable family, but who has had to work his way through
difficulties and poverty in consequence of his father's extravagance
and reckless speculations; and by his mother, a woman of vigorous
mind, hard disposition, much pride in opposing the pride of gentility
or aristocracy, and with a somewhat stately bearing. Thornton is

† From *The Spectator*, XXVIII, 31 March 1855, pp. 341–42.

417

designed as a beau idéal of a Manchester manufacturer; straightforward in action, resolute in will, large-minded in what concerns the
manufacturing business abroad or at home, but a little sensitive with
refined people, and rather prejudiced against them. Though not personally hard-hearted, he seems so, from taking a large view of business life, and carrying to their extreme conclusions the modern
dogmas of political economy in relation to wages and capital. * * *

There are other persons and other interests than those directly
connected with Thornton and Margaret, where the North at least is
strongly represented. Among these are the workpeople, as well under
the varying circumstances of every-day life as during a strike. The
story is throughout of the present time, and contains scenes and
passages of remarkable vigour and considerable effect. Except in
occasional touches, there is a want of lifelike reality. The reader is
more moved to praise the power of the writer than to lose sight of
her in the work. * * *

North and South was originally published in "Household Words";
but it has been considerably extended since. This may have been of
advantage in giving more of smoothness than "Ruth" possessed. On
the other hand it has probably induced a tendency to make the tale
too much of a thread for over-development of everyday matters, and
to substitute successive scenes for a well-compacted story.

HENRY FOTHERGILL CHORLEY

The Athenaeum (7 April 1855)†

We imagine that this year of war[1] will produce few better tales than
'North and South,'—which its author has gathered from the columns
of a weekly contemporary, retouched and extended. The Author of
'Mary Barton'[2] possesses some of an artist's best qualities. She *will*
be attended to, having never as yet written without engaging the
reader's interest, whether he agrees with her or dissents from her
philosophies. Her dialogue is natural,—her eye for character is keen.
She enjoys humour, obviously,—she calls out pathos skilfully. Few
things have been met in modern fiction more touching than the fading away of the poor girl to whom Margaret Hale attaches herself on
removing from the South to a manufacturing town in Lancashire.
The poetical Methodism of this girl,—the homely, uncomplaining

† From *The Athenaeum*, 7 April 1855. Chorley (1808–1872), a reviewer and critic, was
   known to Gaskell and on friendly terms with her. Notes are the Editor's.
1. The Crimean War had begun the previous month.
2. The first edition of *North and South* was published as being by 'The Author of "Mary
   Barton," "Ruth," "Cranford," &c,' Gaskell remaining anonymous.

affection,—the mixture of rudeness and reverence with which she looks up to the delicately-nurtured Lady, make up an admirable picture. The Author of 'Mary Barton' seems bent on doing for Lancashire and the Lancashire dialect what Miss Edgeworth[3] did for Ireland and Scott for the land across the border. There has been no use of English *patois*[4] in English fiction comparable to hers. She has strong Lancashire sympathies too:—if they be class-sympathies such as propel her to a somewhat disproportionate exposure of the trials and sufferings of the poor, her excess is a generous one, and not accompanied by that offensive caricaturing of her more "conventional" heroes and heroines, which must always bring the sincerity of the caricaturist displaying it under question.

In another point the Author of 'North and South' is open to remonstrance. She deals with difficulties of morals needlessly, and too fearlessly, because, as we have again and again said, the riddle propounded cannot be solved in fiction; and because by all one-sided handling of such matters,—when passions become engaged and generous feelings are persuaded, and when the temptation must be dwelt upon as cruel, in apology for the offence,—there is always a danger of unmooring the eager and the inexperienced from their anchorage. The flat lie which Margaret Hale is made to tell in order to secure the escape of her brother, is gratuitous, painful,—staggering as an incident, and without useful result as a lesson. We cannot, in our hearts, blame Margaret; yet the author, by the sufferings which followed as a consequence, takes pains to show how blameworthy Margaret was. * * * In real, actual life, blameable, cowardly, and selfish is the man who turns away from dealing with difficulties so terrible. They must be faced, with such honour, such charity, such disposition to excuse, and such power to weigh good and evil as can be summoned; but to thrust them forward in Fiction (where only artistic truth is possible) amounts, in deed if not in purpose, to a wilful "playing with fire." It should be added, however, that the tenor and tissue of our author's writings are such as to satisfy us that no wilfulness has been in her mind, but an earnest, if a mistaken, desire to do good.

3. Maria Edgeworth (1767–1849), Irish novelist, author of a number of novels of Irish rural life. Sir Walter Scott himself acknowledged her influence on his Waverley novels.
4. I.e., native speech.

MANCHESTER WEEKLY ADVERTISER

From Unsigned Review (14 April 1855)†

"North and South" seems to us, both in conception and execution, the best of Mrs. Gaskell's fictions. It aims, nobly and generously, at reconciling two long-opposed sections of English society, by exhibiting to each the true worth and beauty of the other. The rugged industrial energy of the "north" is brought face to face with the culture and refinement of the "south," and after a little mutual misapprehension and hostility, there is established between them a firm friendship, based on the appreciation that arises out of better knowledge. The execution is extremely skilful. Mrs. Gaskell's style, naturally flowing and musical, has attained its maturity in "North and South," and it is wonderful by what quiet touches, she produces the most pathetic effects. The interest of the story, admirably sustained without any introduction of melodramatic incidents, will keep the mere novel-reader on the alert until the volumes are closed. Its masterly exhibition of character, in combination and in contrast; its sharp glances into the working of our social system, especially in the manufacturing districts; the spirit of hopefulness, cheerfulness and self-reliance which is breathed out from its deepest sadness, give it claims, moreover, to the attention of much more fastidious critics than the mere novel-reader. It is a very decided advance upon "Mary Barton;" it is a higher, wider, and clearer book than that celebrated performance. * * * In our district, where the scene is chiefly laid, it has a special title to be widely read, and the publication of "North and South" in *Household Words* may retrieve for the latter some of the popularity which it lost, by being made the vehicle of that unjust and untrue caricature of manufacturing life and character, Mr. Dickens's "Hard Times."

* * *

The character of Margaret, blending intellectuality and strength with womanly sweetness and playfulness, is admirably drawn. Whether her lover, Mr. Thornton, who reads "Homer" "in the intervals of business," would be accepted as the type of the manufacturer on Manchester 'Change,[1] may be doubted, but against his Homeric weakness must be set his blunt downrightness of speech and conduct, his pride of place, his scorn of government interference, and his determination not to be dictated to by his men. Not the least

† From *Manchester Weekly Advertiser*, 14 April 1855.
1. Shortening of "Exchange," i.e., the Manchester Cotton Exchange, where business was conducted.

successful portrait in the book is that of the lover's mother, Mrs. Thornton, a Lancashire lady of the old school, bound up in her son, and the deep, though quiet, affection of the stern parent and stern child is very finely brought out. If "south," on the whole, is painted throughout the work in favourable colours, and rather at the expense of "north," it must be allowed that querulous Mrs. Hale figures but poorly by the side of the stoical and business-like Mrs. Thornton, but she is made amends for by the fine sketch of her husband, the worn, thoughtful, mild, and guileless Mr. Hale, one of the best portraits of Mrs. Gaskell's gallery. Of course, a manufacturing novel would be nothing without a strike, and Mrs. Gaskell has introduced a fair proportion of the operative element, without giving it the undue predominance which fell to its share in "Mary Barton". Her operative hero, Stephen Higgins,[2] rails at masters, and asserts his rights with as much downrightness as Mr. Thornton, and all in the purest and raciest Lancashire dialect; and his dying daughter, Bessy, whose bodily agonies are mitigated by touches of heaven, expressed in the dialect of Methodism, touchingly contrasts with the religious unbelief of her rugged father. * * *

MARGARET OLIPHANT

Blackwood's Edinburgh Magazine (May 1855)†

* * * Ten years ago we professed an orthodox system of novel-making. Our lovers were humble and devoted—our ladies were beautiful and might be capricious if it pleased them; and we held it a very proper and most laudable arrangement * * * that the only true-love worth having was that reverent, knightly, chivalrous true-love which consecrated all womankind, and served one with fervour and enthusiasm. Such was our ideal, and such our system, in the old halcyon days of novel-writing; when suddenly there stole upon the scene, without either flourish of trumpets or public proclamation, a little fierce incendiary, doomed to turn the world of fancy upside down. She stole upon the scene—pale, small, by no means beautiful—something of a genius, something of a vixen—a dangerous little person, inimical to the peace of society. After we became acquainted

---

2. The reviewer mistakes the name of Gaskell's character, Nicholas Higgins.
† From "Modern Novelists—Great and Small," *Blackwood's Edinburgh Magazine*, LXXII, May 1855, pp. 554–68. Margaret Oliphant (1828–1897) was a prolific essayist and reviewer and a novelist in her own right. In this review she discusses the work of a number of novelists. The opening paragraph of this extract is part of her account of Charlotte Brontë's *Jane Eyre*, which, along with *Villette*, she sees as introducing radically innovative and egalitarian attitudes to sexual relationships in fiction.

with herself, we were introduced to her lover.[1] Such a lover! * * *
Such a wooing!—the lover is rude, brutal cruel. The little woman
fights against him with courage and spirit— * * *
* * * The old-fashioned deference and respect—the old-fashioned
wooing—what were they but so many proofs of the inferior position
of the woman. To whom the man condescended with the gracious
courtliness of his loftier elevation! * * * The man who presumed to
treat her with reverence was one who insulted her pretensions; while
the lover who struggled with her, as he would have struggled with
another man, only adding a certain amount of contemptuous brutality which no man would tolerate, was the only one who truly recognised her claims of equality.

*   *   *

These are the doctrines, startling and original, propounded by Jane
Eyre, and they are not Jane Eyre's opinions only, as we may guess
from the host of followers or imitators who have copied them.

*   *   *

Mrs Gaskell, a sensible and considerate woman, and herself rank-
ing high in her sphere, has just fallen subject to the same delusion.
North and South is extremely clever, as a story. * * * It is perhaps
better and livelier than any of Mrs Gaskell's previous works; yet here
are still the wide circles in the water, showing that not far off is the
identical spot where Jane Eyre and Lucy Snowe, in their wild sport,
have been casting stones; here again is the desperate, bitter quarrel
out of which love is to come; here is love itself, always in a fury, often
looking extremely like hatred, and by no means distinguished for its
good manners, or its graces of speech. Mrs Gaskell is perfect in all
the "properties" of her scene, and all her secondary people are well
drawn; but though her superb and stately Margaret is by no means
a perfect character, she does not seem to us a likely person to fall in
love with the churlish and ill-natured Thornton, whose "strong" qualities are not more amiable than are the dispositions of the other
members of his class whom we have before mentioned. Mrs Gaskell
lingers much upon the personal gifts of her grand beauty. Margaret
has glorious black hair, in which the pomegranate blossoms glow
like a flame; she has exquisite full lips, pouted with the breath of
wonder, or disdain, or resentment, as the case may be; she has beautiful rounded arms, hanging with a languid grace; she is altogether
a splendid and princely personage; and when, in addition to all this,
Margaret becomes an heiress, it is somewhat hard to see her delivered over to the impoverished Manchester man, who is as ready to

1. The references are to Jane Eyre and Mr. Rochester, in Charlotte Brontë's novel.

devour her as ever was an ogre in a fairy tale. The sober-minded who are readers of novels will feel Mrs Gaskell's desertion a serious blow. Shall all our love-stories be squabble after this? * * *

There is one feature of resemblance between Mrs Gaskell's last work and Mr Dickens' *Hard Times*. We are prepared in both for the discussion of an important social question; and in both, the story gradually slides off the public topic to pursue a course of its own. *North and South* has, of necessity, some good sketches of the "hands" and their homes; but it is Mr Thornton's fierce and rugged course of true love to which the author is most anxious to direct our attention; and we have little time to think of Higgins or his trades-union, in presence of this intermitting, but always lively warfare going on beside them. * * *

ÉMILE MONTÉGUT

From Revue des Deux Mondes (1 October 1855)†

North and South! Two very different societies, of which we have no conception in our France, where these two societies, though in complete opposition, exist alongside each other in the same places. In France, the society that I would call "historic" occupies the same areas as manufacturing society, and the latter is scattered throughout the whole country, in the north and the south, the east and the west. In France, Rouen, a town of old gothic remains, shelters modern textile palaces beneath its clock towers and abbeys, and the catholic town of Lyon mingles its factories and shops with its convents and its chapels. Industry in France has taken root everywhere, and our traditional society continues to a certain degree to take an interest in things which were dear to it in the old days and which are still familiar. On the other hand, in England industry is less widespread, but has conquered whole areas over which it holds sway. In the southern counties, traditional English life carries on. It is there that monuments and remains are to be found; it is there that farming communities have lived for a long time, controlled and shaped by the aristocracy; it is there that "gentlemen" are still all-powerful and "clergymen" are still respected by farmers as in the good old days of

† From "Le Roman de Moeurs Industrielles," *Revue des Deux Mondes*, 1 October 1855, XII (new period, second series), pp. 115–46. Translated for this Norton Critical Edition by Anne-Marie Hutchings. Montégut was a distinguished French literary commentator and critic who had previously reviewed Gaskell's *Ruth*. *North and South* was not translated into French until 1859, and it is clear that Montégut read it in English, but the discussion of *North and South* in this substantial review is a testimony to Gaskell's growing reputation overseas, while providing an interesting European perspective on her subject matter.

the Anglican church; it is there that the two universities continue to flourish in the midst of their classical culture. This is the area where the spirit of old England dwells with its mixture of liberalism and aristocracy; it is the homeland of the spirit of moderation amongst monarchists and Anglicans which is the basis of constitutional government as interpreted by Delolme—in a word, Anglo-Norman England. Go further north, and there is a strong chance that you will meet a different England, with a much more advanced way of interpreting the theory of the three powers. No more Anglo-Normans: Saxons through and through, untamed by the aristocracy and the morals of the cultured classes, brave, active, combative, lawless. They have a practical outlook, not an intellectual and leisurely culture: their education is acquired by familiarity with big business and their whole learning consists of an exact and complete knowledge of the state of all the markets in the world. There are no old towns with historic remains, but instead completely new towns which had long awaited the day when their seed would flower and which the nineteenth century has launched into the world. For their upper classes, they have firm, tireless and courageous bourgeois, always with a spyglass at their eye, like the general of an army, to observe the position or movement of the French, American or German market, always watching for the direction of the wind, like a sailor, to see why cotton is going up so high or wool is undergoing such a depreciation in value. The doctrines that are current in this land are no longer clever liberal theories, but radicalism at full strength, American-style democracy amongst the bourgeois and the bosses, socialist leanings amongst the proletariat. A political economy relying solely on trade and with trade alone in mind and a political philosophy of new human rights based on peace and with peace always in mind have been born and have prospered in this country, as everyone knows. Here as well, the Anglican church is less powerful than in the south, and there are more dissenters. It is a totally new England which finds itself face to face with the old England that does not give up and refuses to allow Great Britain to lose its distinctive character and become a new version of the United States. It is an England which has been created by industry, which has been freed by the Reform Bill, which the repeal of the Corn Laws has swollen with pride, and which the Crimean War has temporarily humbled and weakened.

* * *

Working in the fields comes naturally to man, and, however excessive it is, there is nothing to equal it. Although it can exhaust the body, it does not create any unhealthy feeling. Domestic work is natural to man, and it produces nothing but happiness and joy. Working for a trade, however tiring it may be, leads to sociability, companionship and partnership. Factory work alone, invention of science and the human spirit, perverts the soul even as it destroys the body. Oh! How vanquished nature takes its revenge, nature that breathes out health itself, the only true medicine, the one repairer of man's exhausted strength! Subjugated, it breeds only seeds of death. This compressed steam blinds and burns, this tamed strength strikes like thunder, these raw materials, originally harmless, release noxious gases. This thin cotton dust suffocates, these atoms of poison, glass and chemicals make their way surreptitiously into the lungs, this ceaseless noise of machines in motion leads to deafness. Have you noticed the implacable look of these machines, their cruel precision, their near-intelligence as deadly as mathematical calculations, and the absorbing and ravenous movements with which they bite into iron, wring thread, snatch cotton and lift weights? Well, eventually something of this mechanical toughness is shared by the people they employ. Through continual contact between man and machine, the heart becomes empty and is not refreshed. Work is the healthiest cure for vice, but, for this to happen, men have to be truly occupied, committing to it their intelligence and spirit. Here, there is no such thing: men gain from their efforts no satisfaction or joy; it is the machine alone that is truly productive. They gain none of those illusions that work can provide through its momentary absorption of the faculties. They experience nothing but a mechanical movement that allows thoughts to wander in emptiness and to brood, at first sadly and then angrily, on the gloomy events of life, misery, privation and sickness. Out of boredom, out of anger, men soon arrive at a violent hatred of work, which comes to seem a curse of life rather than its basic condition. This whole series of feelings follows on logically. In addition to these pains of hatred, boredom and tiredness, mechanical work gives rise to certain vices which perhaps will last for ever, however the relationship between master and worker may change: brutality, drunkenness and that other powerful vice that knows no subtler way of taking possession of a man than to feed his desire for violent destruction and a break from the common habits of life. If only they had air and light! But no, they have to toil in a workshop that is damp or stuffy, filthy, darkened by steam or the millions of atoms which escape from the materials they work on, and so physical ills are added to moral suffering. In truth, if one had to put up a sign on the doors of some centers of industry, it would be a group representing illness dragging its feet, but confident, holding hands with boredom, crouching sadly with lowered head, folded arms and doleful eyes, in the pose of a fatalistic Muslim.

So we are in no way surprised by the vices that we accuse the industrial populace of possessing. It would be more surprising if they

did not possess them. A whole series of psychological and physiolog-
ical observations demonstrate irrefutably, for those who are aware
of how easily men are corrupted, that these vices are the natural
result of this kind of work. Industrial labor corrupts. How we could
ever remedy it and turn this mass of people into a healthy populace
is a mystery, as the difficulties seem insurmountable. What is certain
is that something can and must be attempted to counter this scourge.

* * *

All the interest of the novel lies in these scenes of life in manufacturing towns. Mrs. Gaskell's aim was to show that these barbaric
and harsh physical conditions which prevail in the north and which
nobody thinks of fighting, because everyone has become inured to
them, would quickly disappear if by some means a little more of
southern civilization could be brought to the north. Here, the representative of the south is Margaret Hale, who, simply through the
influence of her femininity, is able to pacify many of the hatreds and
to heal many of the pains. This desirable union is symbolized by the
marriage of Margaret, the daughter of southern aristocratic civilization, to Mr. Thornton, the perfect type of the northern manufacturer. * * * [Mrs. Gaskell] in no way falls into the usual faults of
female authors. She views society in a wider and harsher light, without for all that giving up her feminine qualities. When her writings
are compared with those of English women who have had success
in recent years (with the exception of Currer Bell),[1] the huge gap
between her and them can at once be seen. For example, compare
Mary Barton with *Uncle Tom's Cabin*. The sympathy shown by Mrs.
Gaskell is not sentimental like that of the American novelist; she is
highly enlightened and impartial; she makes use of analysis and relies
on facts; she neither attacks nor defends masters and workers, but
puts both on trial and tells them the truth. In these social battles,
Mrs. Gaskell plays the role taken by Margaret Hale in the riot we
have quoted: according to her, that Mr. Thornton acts within his
rights is no reason to attribute wrong to the workers, or vice versa.
The grievances of both have a cause which neither party wants to
recognize, and Mrs. Gaskell, relying on the inviolable privileges of
her sex, points out the reasons for the misunderstanding. She plays
the role of judge by invoking, so to speak, her rights of woman. * * *

1. I.e., Charlotte Brontë.

GRAHAM'S MAGAZINE

From Review of New Books (June 1855)†

Mrs Gaskell, the authoress of this novel, has evinced in her previous writings so much depth of feeling, so strong a hold upon character, so keen a sympathy with the poor and wretched, and so fine a perception of the humorous as well as serious aspects of life, that the announcement of a new work from her pen excites something of the same pleasure that is experienced in the promise of a new volume from Thackeray or Miss Brontë. "North and South" does not disappoint this expectation. The characters are clearly and boldly drawn, and felicitously developed. Without sentimentality and without exaggeration, the inmost secrets of their hearts are laid before us. There is meaning and purpose in every page. Nothing is introduced merely to fill up. The interest centres in Thornton and Margaret; and the representation of the influence which love exerts on the tough heart and hard business-head of the former, is done with admirable power and with great knowledge of the workings of passion. The novel is so good that we wish the [*sic*] Harpers had issued it in a book, instead of pamphlet form.[1]

ELIZABETH GASKELL

Lizzie Leigh†

Chapter I.

When Death is present in a household on a Christmas Day, the very contrast between the time as it now is, and the day as it has often been, gives a poignancy to sorrow,—a more utter blankness to the desolation. James Leigh died just as the far-away bells of Rochdale[1] Church were ringing for morning service on Christmas Day, 1836.

---

† From "Review of New Books," *Graham's Magazine* [Philadelphia], XLVI, June 1855, p. 576.

1. *North and South* was first published in America on 14 February 1855 by Harper and Brothers in their "Library of Select Novels."

† *Lizzie Leigh* was the opening story of the first number of *Household Words* when it was published on 30 March 1850. It immediately followed Dickens's "A Preliminary Word," in which he introduced the magazine to its readers. It appeared in three installments from 30 March to 13 April, vol. 1, pp. 2–6; 32–35; 60–65. The *Household Words* text is reprinted here, with minor adjustments to spelling.

1. A mill town about ten miles northeast of Manchester and on the edge of the moors. Gaskell's choice of location is important: it enables her to balance the older farming culture of the area with the new industrial city.

A few minutes before his death, he opened his already glazing eyes, and made a sign to his wife, by the faint motion of his lips, that he had yet something to say. She stooped close down, and caught the broken whisper, 'I forgive her, Anne! May God forgive me.'

'Oh my love, my dear! only get well, and I will never cease showing my thanks for those words. May God in heaven bless thee for saying them. Thou'rt not so restless, my lad! may be—Oh God!'

For even while she spoke, he died.

They had been two-and-twenty years man and wife; for nineteen of those years their life had been as calm and happy, as the most perfect uprightness on the one side, and the most complete confidence and loving submission on the other, could make it. Milton's famous line[2] might have been framed and hung up as the rule of their married life, for he was truly the interpreter, who stood between God and her; she would have considered herself wicked if she had ever dared even to think him austere, though as certainly as he was an upright man, so surely was he hard, stern, and inflexible. But for three years the moan and the murmur had never been out of her heart; she had rebelled against her husband as against a tyrant, with a hidden sullen rebellion, which tore up the old land-marks of wifely duty and affection, and poisoned the fountains whence gentlest love and reverence had once been for ever springing.

But those last blessed words replaced him on his throne in her heart, and called out penitent anguish for all the bitter estrangement of later years. It was this which made her refuse all the entreaties of her sons, that she would see the kind-hearted neighbours, who called on their way from church, to sympathise and condole. No! she would stay with the dead husband that had spoken tenderly at last, if for three years he had kept silence; who knew but what, if she had only been more gentle and less angrily reserved he might have relented earlier—and in time!

She sat rocking herself to and fro by the side of the bed, while the footsteps below went in and out; she had been in sorrow too long to have any violent burst of deep grief now; the furrows were well worn in her cheeks, and the tears flowed quietly, if incessantly, all the day long. But when the winter's night drew on, and the neighbours had gone away to their homes, she stole to the window, and gazed out, long and wistfully, over the dark grey moors. She did not hear her son's voice, as he spoke to her from the door, nor his footstep as he drew nearer. She started when he touched her.

'Mother! come down to us. There's no one but Will and me. Dearest mother, we do so want you.' The poor lad's voice trembled, and

---

2. "He for God only, she for God in him": *Paradise Lost*, IV, 299. The reference would have been familiar to nineteenth-century readers.

he began to cry. It appeared to require an effort on Mrs. Leigh's part to tear herself away from the window, but with a sigh she complied with his request.

The two boys (for though Will was nearly twenty-one, she still thought of him as a lad) had done everything in their power to make the house-place comfortable for her. She herself, in the old days before her sorrow, had never made a brighter fire or a cleaner hearth, ready for her husband's return home, than now awaited her. The tea-things were all put out, and the kettle was boiling; and the boys had calmed their grief down into a kind of sober cheerfulness. They paid her every attention they could think of, but received little notice on her part; she did not resist—she rather submitted to all their arrangements; but they did not seem to touch her heart.

When tea was ended,—it was merely the form of tea that had been gone through,—Will moved the things away to the dresser. His mother leant back languidly in her chair.

'Mother, shall Tom read you a chapter? He's a better scholar than I.'

'Aye, lad!' said she, almost eagerly. 'That's it. Read me the Prodigal Son. Aye, aye, lad. Thank thee.'

Tom found the chapter, and read it in the high-pitched voice which is customary in village-schools. His mother bent forward, her lips parted, her eyes dilated; her whole body instinct with eager attention. Will sat with his head depressed, and hung down. He knew why that chapter had been chosen; and to him it recalled the family's disgrace. When the reading was ended, he still hung down his head in gloomy silence. But her face was brighter than it had been before for the day. Her eyes looked dreamy, as if she saw a vision; and by and by she pulled the bible towards her, and putting her finger underneath each word, began to read them aloud in a low voice to herself; she read again the words of bitter sorrow and deep humiliation; but most of all she paused and brightened over the father's tender reception of the repentant prodigal.

So passed the Christmas evening in the Upclose Farm.

The snow had fallen heavily over the dark waving moorland, before the day of the funeral. The black storm-laden dome of heaven lay very still and close upon the white earth, as they carried the body forth out of the house which had known his presence so long as its ruling power. Two and two the mourners followed, making a black procession, in their winding march over the unbeaten snow, to Milne-Row Church—now lost in some hollow of the bleak moors, now slowly climbing the heaving ascents. There was no long tarrying after the funeral, for many of the neighbours who accompanied the body to the grave had far to go, and the great white flakes which came slowly down, were the boding fore-runners of a heavy storm.

One old friend alone accompanied the widow and her sons to their home.

The Upclose Farm had belonged for generations to the Leighs; and yet its possession hardly raised them above the rank of labourers. There was the house and outbuildings, all of an old-fashioned kind, and about seven acres of barren unproductive land, which they had never possessed capital enough to improve; indeed they could hardly rely upon it for subsistence; and it had been customary to bring up the sons to some trade—such as a wheelwright's, or blacksmith's.

James Leigh had left a will, in the possession of the old man who accompanied them home. He read it aloud. James had bequeathed the farm to his faithful wife, Anne Leigh, for her life-time; and afterwards, to his son William. The hundred and odd pounds in the savings-bank was to accumulate for Thomas.

After the reading was ended, Anne Leigh sat silent for a time; and then she asked to speak to Samuel Orme alone. The sons went into the back-kitchen, and thence strolled out into the fields regardless of the driving snow. The brothers were dearly fond of each other, although they were very different in character. Will, the elder, was like his father, stern, reserved, and scrupulously upright. Tom (who was ten years younger) was gentle and delicate as a girl, both in appearance and character. He had always clung to his mother, and dreaded his father. They did not speak as they walked, for they were only in the habit of talking about facts, and hardly knew the more sophisticated language applied to the description of feelings.

Meanwhile their mother had taken hold of Samuel Orme's arm with her trembling hand.

'Samuel, I must let the farm—I must.'

'Let the farm! What's come o'er the woman?'

'Oh, Samuel!' said she, her eyes swimming in tears, 'I'm just fain to go and live in Manchester. I mun let the farm.'

Samuel looked, and pondered, but did not speak for some time. At last he said—

'If thou hast made up thy mind, there's no speaking again it; and thou must e'en go. Thou'lt be sadly pottered wi' Manchester ways; but that's not my look out. Why, thou'lt have to buy potatoes, a thing thou hast never done afore in all thy born life. Well! it's not my look out. It's rather for me than again me. Our Jenny is going to be married to Tom Higginbotham, and he was speaking of wanting a bit of land to begin upon. His father will be dying sometime, I reckon, and then he'll step into the Croft Farm. But meanwhile'—

'Then, thou'lt let the farm,' said she, stiff as eagerly as ever.

'Aye, aye, he'll take it fast enough, I've a notion. But I'll not drive a bargain with thee just now; it would not be right; we'll wait a bit.'

'No; I cannot wait, settle it out at once.'

'Well, well; I'll speak to Will about it. I see him out yonder. I'll step to him, and talk it over.'

Accordingly he went and joined the two lads, and without more ado, began the subject to them.

'Will, thy mother is fain to go live in Manchester, and covets to let the farm. Now, I'm willing to take it for Tom Higginbotham; but I like to drive a keen bargain, and there would be no fun chaffering with thy mother just now. Let thee and me buckle to, my lad! and try and cheat each other; it will warm us this cold day.'

'Let the farm!' said both the lads at once, with infinite surprise. 'Go live in Manchester!'

When Samuel Orme found that the plan had never before been named to either Will or Tom, he would have nothing to do with it, he said, until they had spoken to their mother; likely she was 'dazed' by her husband's death; he would wait a day or two, and not name it to any one; not to Tom Higginbotham himself, or may be he would set his heart upon it. The lads had better go in and talk it over with their mother. He bade them good day, and left them.

Will looked very gloomy, but he did not speak till they got near the house. Then he said,—

'Tom, go to th' shippon[3] and supper the cows. I want to speak to mother alone.'

When he entered the house-place, she was sitting before the fire, looking into its embers. She did not hear him come in; for some time she had lost her quick perception of outward things.

'Mother! what's this about going to Manchester?' asked he.

'Oh, lad!' said she, turning round, and speaking in a beseeching tone, 'I must go and seek our Lizzie. I cannot rest here for thinking on her. Many's the time I've left thy father sleeping in bed, and stole to th' window, and looked and looked my heart out towards Manchester, till I thought I must just set out and tramp over moor and moss straight away till I got there, and then lift up every downcast face till I came to our Lizzie. And often, when the south wind was blowing soft among the hollows, I've fancied (it could but be fancy, thou knowest) I heard her crying upon me; and I've thought the voice came closer and closer, till at last it was sobbing out "Mother" close to the door; and I've stolen down, and undone the latch before now, and looked out into the still black night, thinking to see her,—and turned sick and sorrowful when I heard no living sound but the sough of the wind dying away. Oh! speak not to me of stopping here, when she may be perishing for hunger, like the poor lad in the parable.' And now she lifted up her voice and wept aloud.

3. Cattle shed.

Will was deeply grieved. He had been old enough to be told the family shame when, more than two years before, his father had had his letter to his daughter returned by her mistress in Manchester, telling him that Lizzie had left her service some time—and why. He had sympathised with his father's stern anger; though he had thought him something hard, it is true, when he had forbidden his weeping, heart-broken wife to go and try to find her poor sinning child, and declared that henceforth they would have no daughter; that she should be as one dead, and her name never more be named at market or at meal time, in blessing or in prayer. He had held his peace, with compressed lips and contracted brow, when the neighbours had noticed to him how poor Lizzie's death had aged both his father and his mother; and how they thought the bereaved couple would never hold up their heads again. He himself had left as if that one event had made him old before his time; and had envied Tom the tears he had shed over poor, pretty, innocent, dead Lizzie. He thought about her sometimes, till he ground his teeth together, and could have struck her down in her shame. His mother had never named her to him until now.

'Mother!' said he at last. 'She may be dead. Most likely she is.'

'No, Will; she is not dead,' said Mrs. Leigh. 'God will not let her die till I've seen her once again. Thou dost not know how I've prayed and prayed just once again to see her sweet face, and tell her I've forgiven her, though she's broken my heart—she has, Will.' She could not go on for a minute or two for the choking sobs. 'Thou dost not know that, or thou wouldst not say she could be dead,—for God is very merciful, Will; He is,—He is much more pitiful than man,—I could never ha' spoken to thy father as I did to Him,—and yet thy father forgave her at last. The last words he said were that he forgave her. Thou'lt not be harder than thy father, Will? Do not try and hinder me going to seek her, for it's no use.'

Will sat very still for a long time before he spoke. At last he said, 'I'll not hinder you. I think she's dead, but that's no matter.'

'She is not dead,' said her mother, with low earnestness. Will took no notice of the interruption.

'We will all go to Manchester for a twelve-month, and let the farm to Tom Higginbotham. I'll get blacksmith's work; and Tom can have good schooling for awhile, which he's always craving for. At the end of the year you'll come back, mother, and give over fretting for Lizzie, and think with me that she is dead,—and, to my mind, that would be more comfort than to think of her living;' he dropped his voice as he spoke these last words. She shook her head, but made no answer. He asked again,—

'Will you, mother, agree to this?'

'I'll agree to it a-this-ns,' said she. 'If I hear and see nought of her for a twelvemonth, me being in Manchester looking out, I'll just ha' broken my heart fairly before the year's ended, and then I shall know neither love nor sorrow for her any more, when I'm at rest in the grave—I'll agree to that, Will.'

'Well, I suppose it must be so. I shall not tell Tom, mother, why we're flitting to Manchester. Best spare him.'

'As thou wilt,' said she, sadly, 'so that we go, that's all.'

Before the wild daffodils were in flower in the sheltered copses round Upclose Farm, the Leighs were settled in their Manchester home; if they could ever grow to consider that place as a home, where there was no garden, or outbuilding, no fresh breezy outlet, no far-stretching view, over moor and hollow,—no dumb animals to be tended, and, what more than all they missed, no old haunting memories, even though those remembrances told of sorrow, and the dead and gone.

Mrs. Leigh heeded the loss of all these things less than her sons. She had more spirit in her countenance than she had had for months, because now she had hope; of a sad enough kind, to be sure, but still it was hope. She performed all her household duties, strange and complicated as they were, and bewildered as she was with all the town-necessities of her new manner of life; but when her house was 'sided,'[4] and the boys come home from their work, in the evening, she would put on her things and steal out, unnoticed, as she thought, but not without many a heavy sigh from Will, after she had closed the house-door and departed. It was often past midnight before she came back, pale and weary, with almost a guilty look upon her face; but that face so full of disappointment and hope deferred, that Will had never the heart to say what he thought of the folly and hopelessness of the search. Night after night it was renewed, till days grew to weeks and weeks to months. All this time Will did his duty towards her as well as he could, without having sympathy with her. He staid at home in the evenings for Tom's sake, and often wished he had Tom's pleasure in reading, for the time hung heavy on his hands, as he sat up for his mother.

I need not tell you how the mother spent the weary hours. And yet I will tell you something. She used to wander out, at first as if without a purpose, till she rallied her thoughts, and brought all her energies to bear on the one point; then she went with earnest patience along the least known ways to some new part of the town, looking wistfully with dumb entreaty into people's faces; sometimes catching a glimpse of a figure which had a kind of momentary like-

4. Put in order, tidied.

ness to her child's, and following that figure with never wearying perseverance, till some light from shop or lamp showed the cold strange face which was not her daughter's. Once or twice a kind-hearted passer-by, struck by her look of yearning woe, turned back and offered help, or asked her what she wanted. When so spoken to, she answered only, 'You don't know a poor girl they call Lizzie Leigh, do you?' and when they denied all knowledge, she shook her head, and went on again. I think they believed her to be crazy. But she never spoke first to any one. She sometimes took a few minutes' rest on the door-steps, and sometimes (very seldom) covered her face and cried; but she could not afford to lose time and chances in this way; while her eyes were blinded with tears, the lost one might pass by unseen.

One evening, in the rich time of shortening autumn-days, Will saw an old man, who, without being absolutely drunk, could not guide himself rightly along the foot-path, and was mocked for his unsteadiness of gait by the idle boys of the neighbourhood. For his father's sake Will regarded old age with tenderness, even when most degraded and removed from the stern virtues which dignified that father; so he took the old man home, and seemed to believe his often-repeated assertions that he drank nothing but water. The stranger tried to stiffen himself up into steadiness as he drew nearer home, as if there were some one there, for whose respect he cared even in his half-intoxicated state, or whose feelings he feared to grieve. His home was exquisitely clean and neat even in outside appearance; threshold, window, and window-sill, were outward signs of some spirit of purity within. Will was rewarded for his attention by a bright glance of thanks, succeeded by a blush of shame, from a young woman of twenty or thereabouts. She did not speak, or second her father's hospitable invitations to him to be seated. She seemed unwilling that a stranger should witness her father's attempts at stately sobriety, and Will could not bear to stay and see her distress. But when the old man, with many a flabby shake of the hand, kept asking him to come again some other evening and see them, Will sought her down-cast eyes, and, though he could not read their veiled meaning, he answered timidly, 'If it's agreeable to everybody, I'll come—and thank ye.' But there was no answer from the girl to whom this speech was in reality addressed; and Will left the house liking her all the better for never speaking.

He thought about her a great deal for the next day or two; he scolded himself for being so foolish as to think of her, and then fell to with fresh vigour, and thought of her more than ever. He tried to depreciate her; he told himself she was not pretty, and then made indignant answer that he liked her looks much better than any beauty of them all. He wished he was not so country looking, so red-faced, so broad-shouldered; while she was like a lady, with her smooth colourless complexion, her bright dark hair and her spotless dress. Pretty, or not pretty, she drew his footsteps towards her; he could not resist the impulse that made him wish to see her once more, and find out some fault which should unloose his heart from her unconscious keeping. But there she was, pure and maidenly as before. He sat and looked, answering her father at cross-purposes, while she drew more and more into the shadow of the chimney-corner out of sight. Then the spirit that possessed him (it was not he himself, sure, that did so impudent a thing!) made him get up and carry the candle to a different place, under the pretence of giving her more light at her sewing, but, in reality, to be able to see her better; she could not stand this much longer, but jumped up, and said she must put her little niece to bed; and surely, there never was, before or since, so troublesome a child of two years old; for, though Will staid an hour and a half longer, she never came down again. He won the father's heart, though, by his capacity as a listener, for some people are not at all particular, and, so that they themselves may talk on undisturbed, are not so unreasonable as to expect attention to what they say.

Will did gather this much, however, from the old man's talk. He had once been quite in a genteel line of business, but had failed for more money than any greengrocer he had heard of; at least, any who did not mix up fish and game with greengrocery proper. This grand failure seemed to have been the event of his life, and one on which he dwelt with a strange kind of pride. It appeared as if at present he rested from his past exertions (in the bankrupt line), and depended on his daughter, who kept a small school for very young children. But all these particulars Will only remembered and understood, when he had left the house; at the time he heard them, he was thinking of Susan. After he had made good his footing at Mr. Palmer's, he was not long, you may be sure, without finding some reason for returning again and again. He listened to her father, he talked to the little niece, but he looked at Susan, both while he listened and while he talked. Her father kept on insisting upon his former gentility, the details of which would have appeared very questionable to Will's mind, if the sweet, delicate, modest Susan had not thrown an inexplicable air of refinement over all she came near. She never spoke much; she was generally diligently at work; but when she moved it was so noiselessly, and when she did speak, it was in so low and soft a voice, that silence, speech, motion and stillness, alike seemed to remove her high above Will's reach into some saintly and inaccessible air of glory—high above his reach, even as she knew him! And, if she were made acquainted with the dark secret behind, of his sister's shame, which was kept ever present to his mind by his mother's nightly search among the outcast and forsaken, would not Susan shrink away from him with loathing, as if he were tainted by the involuntary relationship? This was his dread; and thereupon followed a resolution that he would withdraw from her sweet company before it was too late. So he resisted internal temptation, and staid at home, and suffered and sighed. He became angry with his mother for her untiring patience in seeking for one who, he could not help hoping, was dead rather than alive. He spoke sharply to her, and received only such sad deprecatory answers as made him reproach himself, and still more lose sight of peace of mind. This struggle could not last long without affecting his health; and Tom, his sole companion through the long evenings, noticed his increasing languor, his restless irritability, with perplexed anxiety, and at last resolved to call his mother's attention to his brother's haggard, care-worn looks. She listened with a startled recollection of Will's claims upon her love. She noticed his decreasing appetite, and half-checked sighs.

'Will, lad! what's come o'er thee?' said she to him, as he sat listlessly gazing into the fire.

'There's nought the matter with me,' said he, as if annoyed at her remark.

'Nay, lad, but there is.' He did not speak again to contradict her; indeed she did not know if he had heard her, so unmoved did he look.

'Would'st like to go back to Upclose Farm?' asked she, sorrowfully.

'It's just blackberrying time,' said Tom.

Will shook his head. She looked at him awhile, as if trying to read that expression of despondency and trace it back to its source.

'Will and Tom could go,' said she; 'I must stay here till I've found her, thou know'st,' continued she, dropping her voice.

He turned quickly round, and with the authority he at all times exercised over Tom, bade him begone to bed.

When Tom had left the room he prepared to speak.

Chapter II.

'Mother,' then said Will, 'why will you keep on thinking she's alive? If she were but dead, we need never name her name again. We've never heard nought on her since father wrote her that letter; we never knew whether she got it or not. She'd left her place before then. Many a one dies is——"

'Oh my lad! dunnot speak so to me, or my heart will break outright,' said his mother, with a sort of cry. Then she calmed herself, for she yearned to persuade him to her own belief. 'Thou never asked, and thou'rt too like thy father for me to tell without asking—but it

were all to be near Lizzie's old place that I settled down on this side
o' Manchester; and the very day at after we came, I went to her old
missus, and asked to speak a word wi' her. I had a strong mind to
cast it up to her, that she should ha' sent my poor lass away without
telling on it to us first; but she were in black, and looked so sad I
could na' find in my heart to threep[1] it up. But I did ask her a bit
about our Lizzie. The master would have her turned away at a day's
warning, (he's gone to t'other place; I hope he'll meet wi' more mercy
there than he showed our Lizzie,—I do,—) and when the missus
asked her should she write to us, she says Lizzie shook her head; and
when she speered at her again, the poor lass went down on her knees,
and begged her not, for she said it would break my heart, (as it has
done, Will—God knows it has),' said the poor mother, choking with
her struggle to keep down her hard overmastering grief, 'and her
father would curse her—Oh, God, teach me to be patient.' She could
not speak for a few minutes,—'and the lass threatened, and said
she'd go drown herself in the canal, if the missus wrote home,—and
so—

'Well! I'd got a trace of my child,—the missus thought she'd gone
to th' workhouse to be nursed; and there I went—and there, sure
enough, she had been,—and they'd turned her out as soon as she
were strong, and told her she were young enough to work,—
but whatten kind o' work would be open to her, lad, and her baby to
keep?'

Will listened to his mother's tale with deep sympathy, not unmixed
with the old bitter shame. But the opening of her heart had unlocked
his, and after a while he spoke.

'Mother! I think I'd e'en better go home. Tom can stay wi' thee. I
know I should stay too, but I cannot stay in peace so near—her—
without craving to see her—Susan Palmer I mean.'

'Has the old Mr. Palmer thou told me on a daughter?' asked Mrs.
Leigh.

'Aye, he has. And I love her above a bit. And it's because I love
her I want to leave Manchester. That's all.'

Mrs. Leigh tried to understand this speech for some time, but
found it difficult of interpretation.

'Why should'st thou not tell her thou lov'st her? Thou'rt a likely
lad, and sure o' work. Thou 'lt have Upclose at my death; and as for
that I could let thee have it now, and keep myself by doing a bit of
charring.[2] It seems to me a very backwards sort o' way of winning
her to think of leaving Manchester.'

'Oh mother, she's so gentle and so good,—she's downright holy.

1. To contend with her. The woman is in mourning.
2. Cleaning.

She's never known a touch of sin; and can I ask her to marry me, knowing what we do about Lizzie, and fearing worse! I doubt if one like her could ever care for me; but if she knew about my sister, it would put a gulf between us, and she'd shudder up at the thought of crossing it. You don't know how good she is, mother!'

'Will, Will! if she's so good as thou say'st, she'll have pity on such as my Lizzie. If she has no pity for such, she's a cruel Pharisee, and thou'rt best without her.'

But he only shook his head, and sighed; and for the time the conversation dropped.

But a new idea sprang up in Mrs. Leigh's head. She thought that she would go and see Susan Palmer, and speak up for Will, and tell her the truth about Lizzie; and according to her pity for the poor sinner, would she be worthy or unworthy of him. She resolved to go the very next afternoon, but without telling any one of her plan. Accordingly she looked out the Sunday clothes she had never before had the heart to unpack since she came to Manchester, but which she now desired to appear in, in order to do credit to Will. She put on her old-fashioned black mode bonnet, trimmed with real lace; her scarlet cloth cloak, which she had had ever since she was married; and always spotlessly clean, she set forth on her unauthorised embassy. She knew the Palmers lived in Crown Street, though where she had heard it she could not tell; and modestly asking her way, she arrived in the street about a quarter to four o'clock. She stopped to inquire the exact number, and the woman whom she addressed told her that Susan Palmer's school would not be loosed till four, and asked her to step in and wait until then at her house.

'For,' said she, smiling, 'them that wants Susan Palmer wants a kind friend of ours; so we, in a manner, call cousins. Sit down, missus, sit down. I'll wipe the chair, so that it shanna dirty your cloak. My mother used to wear them bright cloaks, and they're right gradely things again a green field.'

'Han ye known Susan Palmer long?' asked Mrs. Leigh, pleased with the admiration of her cloak.

'Ever since they comed to live in our street. Our Sally goes to her school.'

'Whatten sort of a lass is she, for I ha' never seen her?'

'Well,—as for looks, I cannot say. It's so long since I first knowed her, that I've clean forgotten what I thought of her then. My master says he never saw such a smile for gladdening the heart. But may be it's not looks you're asking about. The best thing I can say of her looks is, that she's just one a stranger would stop in the street to ask help from if he needed it. All the little childer creeps as close as they can to her; she'll have as many as three or four hanging to her apron all at once.'

'Is she cocket[3] at all?'

'Cocket, bless you! you never saw a creature less set up in all your life. Her father's cocket enough. No! she's not cocket any way. You've not heard much of Susan Palmer, I reckon, if you think she's cocket. She's just one to come quietly in, and do the very thing most wanted; little things, maybe, that any one could do, but that few would think on, for another. She'll bring her thimble wi' her, and mend up after the childer o' nights,—and she writes all Betty Harker's letters to her grandchild out at service,—and she's in nobody's way, and that's a great matter, I take it. Here's the childer running past! School is loosed. You'll find her now, missus, ready to hear and to help. But we none on us frab[4] her by going near her in school-time.'

Poor Mrs. Leigh's heart began to beat, and she could almost have turned round and gone home again. Her country breeding had made her shy of strangers, and this Susan Palmer appeared to her like a real born lady by all accounts. So she knocked with a timid feeling at the indicated door, and when it was opened, dropped a simple curtsey without speaking. Susan had her little niece in her arms, curled up with fond endearment against her breast, but she put her gently down to the ground, and instantly placed a chair in the best corner of the room for Mrs. Leigh, when she told her who she was. 'It's not Will as has asked me to come,' said the mother, apologetically, 'I'd a wish just to speak to you myself!'

Susan coloured up to her temples, and stooped to pick up the little toddling girl. In a minute or two Mrs. Leigh began again.

'Will thinks you would na respect us if you knew all; but I think you could na help feeling for us in the sorrow God has put upon us; so I just put on my bonnet, and came off unknownst to the lads. Every one says you're very good, and that the Lord has keeped you from falling from his ways; but maybe you've never yet been tried and tempted as some is. I'm perhaps speaking too plain, but my heart's welly broken, and I can't be choice in my words as them who are happy can. Well now! I'll tell you the truth. Will dreads you to hear it but I'll just tell it you. You mun know,'—but here the poor woman's words failed her, and she could do nothing but sit rocking herself backwards and forwards, with sad eyes, straight-gazing into Susan's face, as if they tried to tell the tale of agony which the quivering lips refused to utter. Those wretched stony eyes forced the tears down Susan's cheeks, and, as if this sympathy gave the mother strength, she went on in a low voice, 'I had a daughter once, my heart's darling. Her father thought I made too much on her, and that she'd grow marred[5] staying at home; so he said she mun go among

3. Stuck up.
4. Harass.
5. Spoiled, peevish.

strangers, and learn to rough it. She were young, and liked the
thought of seeing a bit of the world; and her father heard on a place
in Manchester. Well! I'll not weary you. That poor girl were led
astray; and first thing we heard on it, was when a letter of her father's
was sent back by her missus, saying she'd left her place, or, to speak
right, the master had turned her into the street soon as he had heard
of her condition—and she not seventeen!'

She now cried aloud; and Susan wept too. The little child looked
up into their faces, and, catching their sorrow, began to whimper
and wail. Susan took it softly up, and hiding her face in its little
neck, tried to restrain her tears, and think of comfort for the mother.
At last she said:

'Where is she now?'

'Lass! I dunnot know,' said Mrs. Leigh, checking her sobs to communicate this addition to her distress. 'Mrs. Lomax told me she
went——

'Mrs. Lomax—what Mrs. Lomax?'

'Her as lives in Brabazon-street. She told me my poor wench
went to the workhouse fra there. I'll not speak again the dead; but
if her father would but ha' letten me,—but he were one who had no
notion—no, I'll not say that; best say nought. He forgave her on his
death-bed. I dare say I did na go th' right way to work.'

'Will you hold the child for me one instant?' said Susan.

"Ay, if it will come to me. Childer used to be fond on me till I got
the sad look on my face that scares them, I think.'

But the little girl clung to Susan; so she carried it upstairs with
her. Mrs. Leigh sat by herself—how long she did not know.

Susan came down with a bundle of far-worn baby-clothes.

'You must listen to me a bit, and not think too much about what
I'm going to tell you. Nanny is not my niece, nor any kin to me
that I know of. I used to go out working by the day. One night, as
I came home, I thought some woman was following me; I turned
to look. The woman, before I could see her face (for she turned it
to one side), offered me something. I held out my arms by instinct:
she dropped a bundle into them with a bursting sob that went
straight to my heart. It was a baby. I looked round again; but the
woman was gone. She had run away as quick as lightning. There
was a little packet of clothes—very few—and as if they were made
out of its mother's gowns, for they were large patterns to buy for a
baby. I was always fond of babies; and I had not my wits about me,
father says; for it was very cold, and when I'd seen as well as I
could (for it was past ten) that there was no one in the street, I
brought it in and warmed it. Father was very angry when he came,
and said he'd take it to the workhouse the next morning, and

flyted[6] me sadly about it. But when morning came I could not bear
to part with it; it had slept in my arms all night; and I've heard what
workhouse bringing up is. So I told father I'd give up going out working, and stay at home and keep school, if I might only keep the baby;
and after awhile, he said if I earned enough for him to have his
comforts, he'd let me; but he's never taken to her. Now, don't tremble
so,—I've but a little more to tell,—and maybe I'm wrong in telling
it; but I used to work next door to Mrs. Lomax's, in Brabazon-street,
and the servants were all thick together; and I heard about Bessy
(they called her) being sent away. I don't know that ever I saw her;
but the time would be about fitting to this child's age, and I've sometimes fancied it was her's. And now, will you look at the little clothes
that came with her—bless her!'

But Mrs. Leigh had fainted. The strange joy and shame, and gush-
ing love for the little child had overpowered her; it was some time
before Susan could bring her round. There she was all trembling,
sick impatience to look at the little frocks. Among them was a slip
of paper which Susan had forgotten to name, that had been pinned
to the bundle. On it was scrawled in a round stiff hand,

'Call her Anne. She does not cry much, and takes a deal of notice.
God bless you and forgive me.'

The writing was no clue at all; the name 'Anne,' common though
it was, seemed something to build upon. But Mrs. Leigh recognised
one of the frocks instantly, as being made out of part of a gown that
she and her daughter had bought together in Rochdale.

She stood up, and stretched out her hands in the attitude of blessing over Susan's bent head.

'God bless you, and show you His mercy in your need, as you have
shown it to this little child.'

She took the little creature in her arms, and smoothed away her
sad looks to a smile, and kissed it fondly, saying over and over again,
'Nanny, Nanny, my little Nanny.' At last the child was soothed, and
looked in her face and smiled back again.

'It has her eyes,' said she to Susan.

'I never saw her to the best of my knowledge. I think it must be
her's by the frock. But where can she be?'

'God knows,' said Mrs. Leigh; 'I dare not think she's dead. I'm sure
she isn't.'

'No! she's not dead. Every now and then a little packet is thrust
in under our door, with may be two half-crowns in it; once it was
half-a-sovereign. Altogether I've got seven-and-thirty shillings
wrapped up for Nanny. I never touch it, but I've often thought the

6. Scolded.

poor mother feels near to God when she brings this money. Father wanted to set the policeman to watch, but I said No, for I was afraid if she was watched she might not come, and it seemed such a holy thing to be checking her in, I could not find in my heart to do it.'

'Oh, if we could but find her! I'd take her in my arms, and we'd just lie down and die together.'

'Nay, don't speak so!' said Susan gently, 'for all that's come and gone, she may turn right at last. Mary Magdalen did, you know.'

'Eh! but I were nearer right about thee than Will. He thought you would never look on him again if you knew about Lizzie. But thou'rt not a Pharisee.'

'I'm sorry he thought I could be so hard,' said Susan in a low voice, and colouring up. Then Mrs. Leigh was alarmed, and in her motherly anxiety, she began to fear lest she had injured Will in Susan's estimation.

'You see Will thinks so much of you—gold would not be good enough for you to walk on, in his eye. He said you'd never look at him as he was, let alone his being brother to my poor wench. He loves you so, it makes him think meanly on everything belonging to himself, as not fit to come near ye,—but he's a good lad, and a good son—thou'lt be a happy woman if thou'lt have him,—so don't let my words go against him; don't!'

But Susan hung her head and made no answer. She had not known until now, that Will thought so earnestly and seriously about her; and even now she felt afraid that Mrs. Leigh's words promised her too much happiness, and that they could not be true. At any rate the instinct of modesty made her shrink from saying anything which might seem like a confession of her own feelings to a third person. Accordingly she turned the conversation on the child.

'I'm sure he could not help loving Nanny,' said she. 'There never was such a good little darling; don't you think she'd win his heart if he knew she was his niece, and perhaps bring him to think kindly on his sister?'

'I dunnot know,' said Mrs. Leigh, shaking her head. 'He has a turn in his eye like his father, that makes me——. He's right down good though. But you see I've never been a good one at managing folk; one severe look turns me sick, and then I say just the wrong thing, I'm so fluttered. Now I should like nothing better than to take Nanny home with me, but Tom knows nothing but that his sister is dead, and I've not the knack of speaking rightly to Will. I dare not do it, and that's the truth. But you mun not think badly of Will. He's so good hissel, that he can't understand how any one can do wrong; and, above all, I'm sure he loves you dearly.'

'I don't think I could part with Nanny,' said Susan, anxious to stop this revelation of Will's attachment to herself. 'He'll come round to her soon; he can't fail; and I'll keep a sharp look-out after the poor mother, and try and catch her the next time she comes with her little parcels of money.'

'Aye, lass! we mun get hold of her; my Lizzie. I love thee dearly for thy kindness to her child; but, if thou can'st catch her for me, I'll pray for thee when I'm too near my death to speak words; and while I live, I'll serve thee next to her,—she mun come first, thou know'st. God bless thee, lass. My heart is lighter by a deal than it was when I comed in. Them lads will be looking for me home, and I mun go, and leave this little sweet one,' kissing it. 'If I can take courage, I'll tell Will all that has come and gone between us two. He may come and see thee, mayn't he?'

'Father will be very glad to see him, I'm sure,' replied Susan. The way in which this was spoken satisfied Mrs. Leigh's anxious heart that she had done Will no harm by what she had said; and with many a kiss to the little one, and one more fervent tearful blessing on, Susan, she went homewards.

Chapter III.

That night Mrs. Leigh stopped at home; that only night for many months. Even Tom, the scholar, looked up from his books in amazement; but then he remembered that Will had not been well, and that his mother's attention having been called to the circumstance, it was only natural she should stay to watch him. And no watching could be more tender, or more complete. Her loving eyes seemed never averted from his face; his grave, sad, care-worn face. When Tom went to bed the mother left her seat, and going up to Will where he sat looking at the fire, but not seeing it, she kissed his forehead, and said,

'Will! lad, I've been to see Susan Palmer!'

She felt the start under her hand which was placed on his shoulder, but he was silent for a minute or two. Then he said,

'What took you there, mother?'

'Why, my lad, it was likely I should wish to see one you cared for; I did not put myself forward. I put on my Sunday clothes, and tried to behave as yo'd ha liked me. At least I remember trying at first; but after, I forgot all.'

She rather wished that he would question her as to what made her forget all. But he only said,

'How was she looking, mother?'

'Will, thou seest I never set eyes on her before; but she's a good gentle looking creature; and I love her dearly, as I've reason to.'

Will looked up with momentary surprise; for his mother was too shy to be usually taken with strangers. But after all it was natural in this case, for who could look at Susan without loving her? So still he did not ask any questions, and his poor mother had to take courage, and try again to introduce the subject near to her heart. But how?

'Will!' said she (jerking it out, in sudden despair of her own powers to lead to what she wanted to say), 'I told her all.'

'Mother! you've ruined me,' said he standing up, and standing opposite to her with a stern white look of affright on his face.

'No! my own dear lad; dunnot look so scared, I have not ruined you!' she exclaimed, placing her two hands on his shoulders and looking fondly into his face. 'She's not one to harden her heart against a mother's sorrow. My own lad, she's too good for that. She's not one to judge and scorn the sinner. She's too deep read in her New Testament for that. Take courage, Will; and thou mayst, for I watched her well, though it is not for one woman to let out another's secret. Sit thee down, lad, for thou look'st very white.'

He sat down. His mother drew a stool towards him, and sat at his feet.

'Did you tell her about Lizzie, then?' asked he, hoarse and low.

"I did, I told her all; and she fell a crying over my deep sorrow, and the poor wench's sin. And then a light comed into her face, trembling and quivering with some new glad thought; and what dost thou think it was, Will, lad? Nay, I'll not misdoubt but that thy heart will give thanks as mine did, afore God and His angels, for her great goodness. That little Nanny is not her niece, she's our Lizzie's own child, my little grandchild.' She could no longer restrain her tears, and they fell hot and fast, but still she looked into his face.

"Did she know it was Lizzie's child? I do not comprehend,' said he, flushing red.

'She knows now: she did not at first, but took the little helpless creature in, out of her own pitiful loving heart, guessing only that it was the child of shame, and she's worked for it, and kept it, and tended it ever sin' it were a mere baby, and loves it fondly. Will! won't you love it?' asked she beseechingly.

He was silent for an instant; then he said, 'Mother, I'll try. Give me time, for all these things startle me. To think of Susan having to do with such a child!'

'Aye, Will! and to think (as may be yet) of Susan having to do with the child's mother! For she is tender and pitiful, and speaks hopefully of my lost one, and will try and find her for me, when she comes, as she does sometimes, to thrust money under the door, for her baby. Think of that, Will. Here's Susan, good and pure as the angels in heaven, yet, like them, full of hope and mercy, and one who, like them, will rejoice over her as repents. Will, my lad, I'm not afeared of you now, and I must speak, and you must listen. I am your mother, and I dare to command you, because I know I am in the right and that God is on my side. If He should lead the poor wandering lassie to Susan's door, and she comes back crying and sorrowful, led by that good angel to us once more, thou shalt never say a casting-up word to her about her sin, but be tender and helpful towards one "who was lost and is found,"[1] so may God's blessing rest on thee, and so mayst thou lead Susan home as thy wife.'

She stood, no longer as the meek, imploring, gentle mother, but firm and dignified, as if the interpreter of God's will. Her manner was so unusual and solemn, that it overcame all Will's pride and stubbornness. He rose softly while she was speaking, and bent his head as if in reverence at her words, and the solemn injunction which they conveyed. When she had spoken, he said in so subdued a voice that she was almost surprised at the sound, 'Mother, I will.'

'I may be dead and gone,—but all the same,—thou wilt take home the wandering sinner, and heal up her sorrows, and lead her to her Father's house. My lad! I can speak no more; I'm turned very faint.'

He placed her in a chair; he ran for water. She opened her eyes and smiled.

'God bless you, Will. Oh! I am so happy. It seems as if she were found; my heart is so filled with gladness.'

That night Mr. Palmer stayed out late and long. Susan was afraid that he was at his old haunts and habits,—getting tipsy at some public-house; and this thought oppressed her, even though she had so much to make her happy, in the consciousness that Will loved her. She sat up long, and then she went to bed, leaving all arranged as well as she could for her father's return. She looked at the little rosy sleeping girl who was her bed-fellow, with redoubled tenderness, and with many a prayerful thought. The little arms entwined her neck as she lay down, for Nanny was a light sleeper, and was conscious that she, who was loved with all the power of that sweet child-ish heart, was near her, and by her, although she was too sleepy to utter any of her half-formed words.

And by-and-bye she heard her father come home, stumbling uncertain, trying first the windows, and next the door-fastenings, with many a loud incoherent murmur. The little Innocent twined around her seemed all the sweeter and more lovely, when she thought sadly of her erring father. And presently he called aloud for a light; she had left matches and all arranged as usual on the dresser, but, fearful of some accident from fire, in his unusually intoxicated state, she now got up softly, and putting on a cloak, went down to his assistance.

Alas! the little arms that were unclosed from her soft neck

1. A reference to the parable of the lost sheep, Luke 15:2–7.

belonged to a light, easily awakened sleeper. Nanny missed her darling Susy, and terrified at being left alone in the vast mysterious darkness, which had no bounds, and seemed infinite, she slipped out of bed, and tottered in her little night-gown towards the door. There was a light below, and there was Susy and safety! So she went onwards two steps towards the steep abrupt stairs; and then dazzled with sleepiness, she stood, she wavered, she fell! Down on her head on the stone floor she fell! Susan flew to her, and spoke all soft, entreating, loving words; but her white lids covered up the blue violets of eyes, and there was no murmur came out of the pale lips. The warm tears that rained down did not awaken her; she lay stiff, and weary with her short life, on Susan's knee. Susan went sick with terror. She carried her upstairs, and laid her tenderly in bed; she dressed herself most hastily, with her trembling fingers. Her father was asleep on the settle down stairs; and useless, and worse than useless if awake. But Susan flew out of the door, and down the quiet resounding street, towards the nearest doctor's house. Quickly she went; but as quickly a shadow followed, as if impelled by some sudden terror. Susan rung wildly at the night-bell,—the shadow crouched near. The doctor looked out from an upstairs window.

'A little child has fallen down stairs at No. 9, Crown-street, and is very ill,—dying I'm afraid. Please, for God's sake, sir, come directly. No. 9, Crown-street.'

'I'll be there directly,' said he, and shut the window.

'For that God you have just spoken about,—for His sake,—tell me are you Susan Palmer? Is it my child that lies a-dying?' said the shadow, springing forwards, and clutching poor Susan's arm.

'It is a little child of two years old,—I do not know whose it is; I love it as my own. Come with me, whoever you are; come with me.'

The two sped along the silent streets,—as silent as the night were they. They entered the house; Susan snatched up the light, and carried it upstairs. The other followed.

She stood with wild glaring eyes by the bedside, never looking at Susan, but hungrily gazing at the little white still child. She stooped down, and put her hand tight on her own heart, as if to still its beating, and bent her ear to the pale lips. Whatever the result was, she did not speak; but threw off the bed-clothes wherewith Susan had tenderly covered up the little creature, and felt its left side.

Then she threw up her arms with a cry of wild despair.

'She is dead! she is dead!'

She looked so fierce, so mad, so haggard, that for an instant Susan was terrified—the next, the holy God had put courage into her heart, and her pure arms were round that guilty wretched creature, and her tears were falling fast and warm upon her breast. But she was thrown off with violence.

'You killed her—you slighted her—you let her fall down those stairs! you killed her!'

Susan cleared off the thick mist before her, and gazing at the mother with her clear, sweet, angel-eyes, said mournfully—

'I would have laid down my own life for her.'

'Oh, the murder is on my soul!' exclaimed the wild bereaved mother, with the fierce impetuosity of one who has none to love her and to be beloved, regard to whom might teach self-restraint.

'Hush!' said Susan, her finger on her lips. 'Here is the doctor. God may suffer her to live.'

The poor mother turned sharp round. The doctor mounted the stair. Ah! that mother was right; the little child was really dead and gone.

And when he confirmed her judgment, the mother fell down in a fit. Susan, with her deep grief, had to forget herself, and forget her darling (her charge for years), and question the doctor what she must do with the poor wretch, who lay on the floor in such extreme of misery.

'She is the mother!' said she.

'Why did not she take better care of her child?' asked he, almost angrily.

But Susan only said, 'The little child slept with me; and it was I that left her.'

'I will go back and make up a composing draught; and while I am away you must get her to bed.'

Susan took out some of her own clothes, and softly undressed the stiff, powerless form. There was no other bed in the house but the one in which her father slept. So she tenderly lifted the body of her darling; and was going to take it down stairs, but the mother opened her eyes, and seeing what she was about, she said,

'I am not worthy to touch her, I am so wicked; I have spoken to you as I never should have spoken; but I think you are very good; may I have my own child to lie in my arms for a little while?'

Her voice was so strange a contrast to what it had been before she had gone into the fit that Susan hardly recognised it; it was now so unspeakably soft, so irresistibly pleading, the features too had lost their fierce expression and were almost as placid as death. Susan could not speak, but she carried the little child, and laid it in its mother's arms; then as she looked at them, something overpowered her, and she knelt down, crying aloud,

'Oh, my God, my God, have mercy on her, and forgive, and comfort her.'

But the mother kept smiling, and stroking the little face, murmuring soft tender words, as if it were alive; she was going mad, Susan thought; but she prayed on, and on, and ever still she prayed with streaming eyes.

The doctor came with the draught. The mother took it, with docile unconsciousness of its nature as medicine. The doctor sat by her; and soon she fell asleep. Then he rose softly, and beckoning Susan to the door, he spoke to her there.

'You must take the corpse out of her arms. She will not awake. That draught will make her sleep for many hours. I will call before noon again. It is now daylight. Good-bye.'

Susan shut him out; and then gently extricating the dead child from its mother's arms, she could not resist making her own quiet moan over her darling. She tried to learn off its little placid face, dumb and pale before her.

> "Not all the scalding tears of care
>   Shall wash away that vision fair;
> Not all the thousand thoughts that rise,
>   Not all the sights that dim her eyes,
>   Shall e'er usurp the place
>   Of that little angel-face."[2]

And then she remembered what remained to be done. She saw that all was right in the house; her father was still dead asleep on the settle, in spite of all the noise of the night. She went out through the quiet streets, deserted still although it was broad daylight, and to where the Leighs lived. Mrs. Leigh, who kept her country hours, was opening her window shutters. Susan took her by the arm, and, without speaking, went into the house-place. There she knelt down before the astonished Mrs. Leigh, and cried as she had never done before; but the miserable night had overpowered her, and she who had gone through so much calmly, now that the pressure seemed removed could not find the power to speak.

'My poor dear! What has made thy heart so sore as to come and cry a-this-ons. Speak and tell me. Nay, cry on, poor wench, if thou canst not speak yet. It will ease the heart, and then thou canst tell me.'

'Nanny is dead!' said Susan. 'I left her to go to father, and she fell down stairs, and never breathed again. Oh, that's my sorrow! but I've more to tell. Her mother is come—is in our house! Come and see if it's your Lizzie.' Mrs. Leigh could not speak, but, trembling, put on her things, and went with Susan in dizzy haste back to Crown-street.

<hr/>

2. The stanza is from a poem by "Barry Cornwall," "A year—an age shall fade," in his *English Songs* (1832). "Barry Cornwall" was the pseudonym of B. W. Proctor, a prolific popular poet and dramatist whom Gaskell met in 1849.

Chapter IV.

As they entered the house in Crown-street, they perceived that the door would not open freely on its hinges, and Susan instinctively looked behind to see the cause of the obstruction. She immediately recognised the appearance of a little parcel, wrapped in a scrap of newspaper, and evidently containing money. She stooped and picked it up. 'Look!' said she, sorrowfully, 'the mother was bringing this for her child last night.'

But Mrs. Leigh did not answer. So near to the ascertaining if it were her lost child or no, she could not be arrested, but pressed onwards with trembling steps and a beating, fluttering heart. She entered the bed-room, dark and still. She took no heed of the little corpse, over which Susan paused, but she went straight to the bed, and withdrawing the curtain, saw Lizzie,—but not the former Lizzie, bright, gay, buoyant, and undimmed. This Lizzie was old before her time; her beauty was gone; deep lines of care, and alas! of want (or thus the mother imagined) were printed on the cheek, so round, and fair, and smooth, when last she gladdened her mother's eyes. Even in her sleep she bore the look of woe and despair which was the prevalent expression of her face by day; even in her sleep she had forgotten how to smile. But all these marks of the sin and sorrow she had passed through only made her mother love her the more. She stood looking at her with greedy eyes, which seemed as though no gazing could satisfy their longing; and at last she stooped down and kissed the pale, worn hand that lay outside the bed-clothes. No touch disturbed the sleeper; the mother need not have laid the hand so gently down upon the counterpane. There was no sign of life, save only now and then a deep sob-like sigh. Mrs. Leigh sat down beside the bed, and, still holding back the curtain, looked on and on, as if she could never be satisfied.

Susan would fain have stayed by her darling one; but she had many calls upon her time and thoughts, and her will had now, as ever, to be given up to that of others. All seemed to devolve the burden of their cares on her. Her father, ill-humoured from his last night's intemperance, did not scruple to reproach her with being the cause of little Nanny's death; and when, after bearing his upbraiding meekly for some time, she could no longer restrain herself, but began to cry, he wounded her even more by his injudicious attempts at comfort: for he said it was as well the child was dead; it was none of theirs, and why should they be troubled with it? Susan wrung her hands at this, and came and stood before her father, and implored him to forbear. Then she had to take all requisite steps for the coroner's inquest; she had to arrange for the dismissal of her school; she had to summon a little neighbour, and send his willing feet on a message to William Leigh, who, she felt, ought to be informed of his mother's whereabouts, and of the whole state of affairs. She asked her messenger to tell him to come and speak to her,—that his mother was at her house. She was thankful that her father sauntered out to have a gossip at the nearest coach-stand, and to relate as many of the night's adventures as he knew; for as yet he was in ignorance of the watcher and the watched, who silently passed away the hours upstairs.

At dinner-time Will came. He looked red, glad, impatient, excited. Susan stood calm and white before him, her soft, loving eyes gazing straight into his.

'Will,' said she, in a low, quiet voice, 'your sister is upstairs.'

'My sister!' said he, as if affrighted at the idea, and losing his glad look in one of gloom. Susan saw it, and her heart sank a little, but she went on as calm to all appearance as ever.

'She was little Nanny's mother, as perhaps you know. Poor little Nanny was killed last night by a fall down stairs.' All the calmness was gone; all the suppressed feeling was displayed in spite of every effort. She sat down, and hid her face from him, and cried bitterly. He forgot everything but the wish, the longing to comfort her. He put his arm round her waist, and bent over her. But all he could say, was, 'Oh, Susan how can I comfort you! Don't take on so,—pray don't!' He never changed the words, but the tone varied every time he spoke. At last she seemed to regain her power over herself; and she wiped her eyes, and once more looked upon him with her own quiet, earnest, unfearing gaze.

'Your sister was near the house. She came in on hearing my words to the doctor. She is asleep now, and your mother is watching her. I wanted to tell you all myself. Would you like to see your mother?'

'No!' said he. 'I would rather see none but thee. Mother told me thou knew'st all.' His eyes were downcast in their shame.

But the holy and pure did not lower or veil her eyes.

She said, 'Yes, I know all—all but her sufferings. Think what they must have been!'

He made answer low and stern, 'She deserved them all; every jot.'

'In the eye of God, perhaps she does. He is the judge: we are not.'

'Oh!' she said with a sudden burst, 'Will Leigh! I have thought so well of you; don't go and make me think you cruel and hard. Goodness is not goodness unless there is mercy and tenderness with it. There is your mother who has been nearly heart-broken, now full of rejoicing over her child—think of your mother.'

'I do think of her,' said he. 'I remember the promise I gave her last night. Thou shouldst give me time. I would do right in time. I never think it o'er in quiet. But I will do what is right and fitting, never fear. Thou hast spoken out very plain to me; and misdoubted me,

Susan; I love thee so, that thy words cut me. If I did hang back a bit from making sudden promises, it was because not even for love of thee, would I say what I was not feeling; and at first I could not feel all at once as thou wouldst have me. But I'm not cruel and hard; for if I had been, I should na' have grieved as I have done.'

He made as if he were going away; and indeed he did feel he would rather think it over in quiet. But Susan, grieved at her incautious words, which had all the appearance of harshness, went a step or two nearer—paused—and then all over blushes, said in a low soft whisper—

'Oh Will! I beg your pardon. I am very sorry—won't you forgive me?'

She who had always drawn back, and been so reserved, said this in the very softest manner; with eyes now uplifted beseechingly, now dropped to the ground. Her sweet confusion told more than words could do; and Will turned back, all joyous in his certainty of being beloved, and took her in his arms and kissed her.

'My own Susan!' he said.

Meanwhile the mother watched her child in the room above.

It was late in the afternoon before she awoke; for the sleeping draught had been very powerful. The instant she awoke, her eyes were fixed on her mother's face with a gaze as unflinching as if she were fascinated. Mrs. Leigh did not turn away; nor move. For it seemed as if motion would unlock the stony command over herself which, while so perfectly still, she was enabled to preserve. But by-and-bye Lizzie cried out in a piercing voice of agony—

'Mother, don't look at me! I have been so wicked!' and instantly she hid her face, and grovelled among the bedclothes, and lay like one dead—so motionless was she.

Mrs. Leigh knelt down by the bed, and spoke in the most soothing tones.

'Lizzie, dear, don't speak so. I'm thy mother, darling; don't be afeard of me. I never left off loving thee, Lizzie. I was always a-thinking of thee. Thy father forgave thee afore he died.' (There was a little start here, but no sound was heard). 'Lizzie, lass, I'll do aught for thee; I'll live for thee; only don't be afeard of me. Whate'er thou art or hast been, we'll ne'er speak on't. We'll leave th' oud times behind us, and go back to the Upclose Farm. I but left it to find thee, my lass; and God has led me to thee. Blessed be His name. And God is good too, Lizzie. Thou hast not forgot thy Bible, I'll be bound, for thou wert always a scholar. I'm no reader, but I learnt off them texts to comfort me a bit, and I've said them many a time a day to myself. Lizzie, lass, don't hide thy head so, it's thy mother as is speaking to thee. Thy little child clung to me only yesterday; and if it's gone to be an angel, it will speak to God for thee. Nay, don't sob a that 'as;

thou shalt have it again in Heaven; I know thou'lt strive to get there, for thy little Nancy's sake—and listen! I'll tell thee God's promises to them that are penitent—only doan't be afeard.'

Mrs. Leigh folded her hands, and strove to speak very clearly, while she repeated every tender and merciful text she could remember. She could tell from the breathing that her daughter was listening; but she was so dizzy and sick herself when she had ended, that she could not go on speaking. It was all she could do to keep from crying aloud.

At last she heard her daughter's voice.

'Where have they taken her to?' she asked.

'She is down stairs. So quiet, and peaceful, and happy she looks.'

'Could she speak? Oh, if God—if I might but have heard her little voice! Mother, I used to dream of it. May I see her once again—Oh mother, if I strive very hard, and God is very merciful, and I go to heaven, I shall not know her—I shall not know my own again—she will shun me as a stranger and cling to Susan Palmer and to you. Oh woe! Oh woe!' She shook with exceeding sorrow.

In her earnestness of speech she had uncovered her face, and tried to read Mrs. Leigh's thoughts through her looks. And when she saw those aged eyes brimming full of tears, and marked the quivering lips, she threw her arms round the faithful mother's neck, and wept there as she had done in many a childish sorrow; but with a deeper, a more wretched grief.

Her mother hushed her on her breast; and lulled her as if she were a baby; and she grew still and quiet.

They sat thus for a long, long time. At last Susan Palmer came up with some tea and bread and butter for Mrs. Leigh. She watched the mother feed her sick, unwilling child, with every fond inducement to eat which she could devise; they neither of them took notice of Susan's presence. That night they lay in each other's arms; but Susan slept on the ground beside them.

They took the little corpse (the little unconscious sacrifice, whose early calling-home had reclaimed her poor wandering mother,) to the hills, which in her life-time she had never seen. They dared not lay her by the stern grand-father in Milne-Row churchyard, but they bore her to a lone moorland graveyard, where long ago the quakers used to bury their dead. They laid her there on the sunny slope, where the earliest spring-flowers blow.

Will and Susan live at the Upclose Farm. Mrs. Leigh and Lizzie dwell in a cottage so secluded that, until you drop into the very hollow where it is placed, you do not see it. Tom is a schoolmaster in Rochdale, and he and Will help to support their mother. I only know that, if the cottage be hidden in a green hollow of the hills, every sound of sorrow in the whole upland is heard there—every call of

suffering or of sickness for help is listened to, by a sad, gentle-looking
woman, who rarely smiles (and when she does, her smile is more sad
than other people's tears), but who comes out of her seclusion whenever there's a shadow in any household. Many hearts bless Lizzie
Leigh, but she—she prays always and ever for forgiveness—such
forgiveness as may enable her to see her child once more. Mrs. Leigh
is quiet and happy. Lizzie is to her eyes something precious,—as the
lost piece of silver[1] found once more. Susan is the bright one who
brings sunshine to all. Children grow around her and call her
blessed. One is called Nanny. Her, Lizzie often takes to the sunny
graveyard in the uplands, and while the little creature gathers the
daisies, and makes chains, Lizzie sits by a little grave, and weeps
bitterly.

FRIEDRICH ENGELS

[Manchester at Mid-Century]†

* * * Manchester proper lies on the left bank of the Irwell, between
that stream and the two smaller ones, the Irk and the Medlock,
which here empty into the Irwell. On the right bank of the Irwell,
bounded by a sharp curve of the river, lies Salford, and farther west-
ward Pendleton; northward from the Irwell lie Upper and Lower
Broughton; northward of the Irk, Cheetham Hill; south of the
Medlock lies Hulme; farther east Chorlton on Medlock; still farther,
pretty well to the east of Manchester, Ardwick. The whole assem-
blage of buildings is commonly called Manchester, and contains
about four hundred thousand inhabitants, rather more than less. The
town itself is peculiarly built, so that a person may live in it for years,
and go in and out daily without coming into contact with a working-
people's quarter or even with workers, that is, so long as he confines
himself to his business or to pleasure walks. This arises chiefly from
the fact, that by unconscious tacit agreement, as well as with out-
spoken conscious determination, the working-people's quarters are
sharply separated from the sections of the city reserved for the
middle-class; or, if this does not succeed, they are concealed with
the cloak of charity. Manchester contains, at its heart, a rather
extended commercial district, perhaps half a mile long and about as

1. Luke 15:8–9, following immediately on the parable of the lost sheep.
† From *The Condition of the Working Class in England in 1844*. Engels's work was first
published in Leipzig in 1845, in German as *Die Lage der Arbeitenden Klasse in England*.
The first English translation was published in Boston in 1887, and then in London in
1892. This translation is the one used for this extract, which describes how the class
divisions of industrial society were reflected in its organization of urban space.

broad, and consisting almost wholly of offices and warehouses. Nearly the whole district is abandoned by dwellers, and is lonely and deserted at night; only watchmen and policemen traverse its narrow lanes with their dark lanterns. This district is cut through by certain main thoroughfares upon which the vast traffic concentrates, and in which the ground level is lined with brilliant shops. In these streets the upper floors are occupied, here and there, and there is a good deal of life upon them until late at night. With the exception of this commercial district, all Manchester proper, all Salford and Hulme, a great part of Pendleton and Chorlton, two-thirds of Ardwick, and single stretches of Cheetham Hill and Broughton are all unmixed working-people's quarters, stretching like a girdle, averaging a mile and a half in breadth, around the commercial district. Outside, beyond this girdle, lives the upper and middle bourgeoisie, the middle bourgeoisie in regularly laid out streets in the vicinity of the working quarters, especially in Chorlton and the lower lying portions of Cheetham Hill; the upper bourgeoisie in remoter villas with gardens in Chorlton and Ardwick, or on the breezy heights of Cheetham Hill, Broughton, and Pendleton, in free, wholesome country air, in fine, comfortable homes, passed once every half or quarter hour by omnibuses going into the city. And the finest part of the arrangement is this, that the members of this money aristocracy can take the shortest road through the middle of all the labouring districts to their places of business, without ever seeing that they are in the midst of the grimy misery that lurks to the right and the left. For the thoroughfares leading from the Exchange in all directions out of the city are lined, on both sides, with an almost unbroken series of shops, and are so kept in the hands of the middle and lower bourgeoisie, which, out of self-interest, cares for a decent and cleanly external appearance and *can* care for it. True, these shops bear some relation to the districts which lie behind them, and are more elegant in the commercial and residential quarters than when they hide grimy working-men's dwellings; but they suffice to conceal from the eyes of the wealthy men and women of strong stomachs and weak nerves the misery and grime which form the complement of their wealth. So, for instance, Deansgate, which leads from the Old Church directly southward, is lined first with mills and warehouses, then with second-rate shops and ale-houses; farther south, when it leaves the commercial district, with less inviting shops, which grow dirtier and more interrupted by beerhouses and gin palaces the farther one goes, until at the southern end the appearance of the shops leaves no doubt that workers and workers only are their customers. So Market Street running south-east from the Exchange; at first brilliant shops of the best sort, with counting-houses or warehouses above; in the continuation, Piccadilly, immense hotels and warehouses; in the farther continuation, London Road, in the neighbourhood of the Medlock, factories, beerhouses, shops for the humbler bourgeoisie and the working population; and from this point onward, large gardens and villas of the wealthier merchants and manufacturers. In this way any one who knows Manchester can infer the adjoining districts, from the appearance of the thoroughfare, but one is seldom in a position to catch from the street a glimpse of the real labouring districts. I know very well that this hypocritical plan is more or less common to all great cities; I know, too, that the retail dealers are forced by the nature of their business to take possession of the great highways; I know that there are more good buildings than bad ones upon such streets everywhere, and that the value of land is greater near them than in remoter districts; but at the same time I have never seen so systematic a shutting out of the working-class from the thoroughfares, so tender a concealment of everything which might affront the eye and the nerves of the bourgeoisie, as in Manchester. And yet, in other respects, Manchester is less built according to a plan, after official regulations, is more an outgrowth of accident, than any other city; and when I consider in this connection the eager assurances of the middle-class, that the working-class is doing famously, I cannot help feeling that the liberal manufacturers, the "Big Wigs" of Manchester, are not so innocent after all, in the matter of this sensitive method of construction.

* * *

[The Preston Strike]†

At the adjourned meeting of the Masters' Association, held at the Bull Hotel on the 29th of December, the following resolutions were agreed to:—

"That inasmuch as no disposition has been as yet shown by the operatives generally to resume work, this meeting do adjourn to Thursday, the 26th of January, 1854.

"Should it, however, in the meantime be ascertained that many of

† From "Account of the strike and lock-out in the cotton trade at Preston in 1853 by James Lowe," *Trade Societies and Strikes. Report of the Committee on Trades' Societies, appointed by the National Association for the promotion of Social Science presented at the fourth annual meeting of the association at Glasgow. September, 1860.* The strike and lockout at Preston, Lancashire, from 1853 to 1854 was one of the most famous industrial disputes in the textile industry. It began when operatives at four mills struck over a wages dispute and were supported by workers from other mills throughout the town. The mill owners responded by closing down their mills to all workers, and then by introducing immigrant labor. On both sides the issue thus became one of "combination": the right to act as a body in support of individual members throughout the industry. Notes are the Editor's.

the operatives are desirous of returning to their work, immediate steps will be taken by the associated masters to open their mills."

It had, hitherto, been observed and had caused much comment and surprise, that the associated masters had preserved an unbroken silence upon all the questions in dispute between themselves and their operatives, and had avoided all reply to arguments directed to those questions, whether urged by the operatives or by independent observers. About this time, however, they saw fit to break this long silence; perhaps conceiving, and not without reason, that it damaged them in the minds of the unbiased, and certainly did not convince the operatives. Some few employers began now to combat the statements of the delegates as to their wages and lists of prices, by letters addressed to the newspapers, and placards posted upon the walls; and at length the Association issued a formal statement, explaining the case from the employers' point of view, and the motives which had led them to adopt the expedient of the lock-out. This document was as follows:—

"THE PRESTON STRIKE. TO THE PUBLIC. In consequence of the various misrepresentations which have been so unblushingly put forth by men who are the acknowledged leaders of the workpeople in the present struggle with their employers, we feel it to be a duty to ourselves and the public to make a few observations, and to state a few facts in reference thereto; and we offer these observations more especially to the attention of those who have only an imperfect acquaintance with the factory system, as well as to the factory operatives in this and other districts, whose sympathies and aid are solicited on behalf of the hands on strike in this town and neighbourhood, and who are liable to be misled by the *ex parte* statements of those whose interest it is indefinitely to prolong the strife.

We will not condescend to notice the various calumnies which are daily applied to the masters, believing that the great majority of the workpeople have no sympathy with such sentiments, and that the general character of the employers in Preston needs not fear a comparison with those of other districts. Neither do we think it necessary again to enter at large into the origin of the dispute further than to state our belief that the differences which in the first instance existed, would have been arranged and would not have resulted in a general stoppage of the mills, had it not been for the improper interference of strangers[1] between the masters and their hands.

"It is alleged that the workpeople are 'locked out,' and therefore unable to work, if disposed, and that the masters want 'to starve them into submission;' but it is not stated that the closing of the mills was only resorted to after the hands in several of them had struck work,

---

1. Agitators from outside the town.

or had given notice to that effect, although an advance of ten per cent. had been offered to them in August last upon the wages paid in 1852. The causes in which the strike originated were carefully investigated by the committee of the Masters' Association, and it was found that the differences between the demands of the operatives and the offers of their employers were so exceedingly small, that a more important question than that of wages was involved, and that these firms were to be made the victims of an organized combination, whose avowed object was to take the masters in succession, and compel them to accept the terms of the unionists.

"We now come to the question of wages, about which so much has been said with a view of misleading the public. The leaders of this agitation affirm that several reductions of wages have taken place from time to time, but they refer more particularly to that in 1847, and to a promise stated to have been made by the masters to give a corresponding advance when trade revived, as a justification of their demand for an advance of ten per cent. We at once admit that owing to the depressed state of trade in 1847 a general reduction of wages took place in the latter part of that year, or early in 1848. We deny, however, that any such promise was made by the masters generally, although this might have been done by some individual firms. Before proceeding further it is necessary to explain that most of the work done in factories is piecework, and that the prices paid are in all cases regulated by the quality of the raw material, and the state of the machinery. For instance—where the machinery is old, there may be a high rate of piecework and the weekly earnings low; and where the machinery is modern, and embraces all the recent improvements, there may be a lower rate of piecework and the earnings comparatively high, without any extra exertion on the part of the hands.

"Being anxious to ascertain the difference (if any) between the earnings of the various classes of operatives in 1847, before the above-mentioned reduction took place, and those in the summer of 1853, before the ten per cent. was demanded, we find, from the returns furnished us from the wages books of several large and influential firms, that instead of any decrease, there has been an actual increase, varying from five to thirty per cent., after making due allowance for the difference in the hours of labour from sixty-nine to sixty hours per week. We have not thought it necessary to extend these inquiries, not having the slightest doubt that, if the average of all the mills now closed had been taken, the result would have been the same. We take this opportunity of stating, for the information of those persons whose aid and contributions are solicited for the hands, that in a well-regulated spinning and weaving establishment, the weekly earnings of men employed therein vary from 12s. to 35s.;

women and young persons from 7s. 6d. to 15s.; and children from 4s. to 6s., according to the nature of the employment and the diligence and ability of the worker; and that the average of all classes of hands in such an establishment is about 10s. each.

"In reference to the statements so frequently made, that the wages paid in Preston are much lower than in other towns, the fact that this town has hitherto been well supplied with good hands sufficiently refutes these assertions, which are put forth without any proof whatever.

"In corroboration of the above, we would refer to the letters of three masters, in the *Preston Chronicle* of the 24th inst., respecting their own cases, and which, we feel assured, could be supported by many others of a similar kind; but these prove that wages are not generally lower here than elsewhere.

"After the continuance of this struggle for upwards of ten weeks, the operatives still persist in their demands, and evince the same indisposition to return to work, although the masters have declared their willingness to receive applications, and as soon as they were sufficiently numerous to enable them to open their mills, immediate steps would be taken to that effect. No applications of any consequence have been made, and the dispute appears as far off a settlement as ever.

(By order of the Committee,)
"JOHN HUMBER, Secretary, *pro tem*.
"PRESTON, *Dec.* 27, 1853."

To this statement the Weavers' Committee replied as follows:

"PRESTON LOCK-OUT.—TO THE BRITISH PUBLIC.—In consequence of the various misrepresentations which have been so unblushingly put forth by the 'Masters' Association;' we, the Weavers' Association, feel it to be a duty to ourselves and the public to publish the following answers:—

"1st.—In the document issued yesterday by the Masters' Committee, they say, 'that the differences which in the first instance existed would have been arranged, and would not have resulted in a general stoppage of the mills, had it not been for the improper interference of strangers between the masters and their hands.' We beg to say distinctly, that no *strangers* had, either properly or improperly, interfered in the disputes between the masters and their hands, previous to a notice being given for a general stoppage.

"2nd.—We repeat, that we have been 'locked out, in order to starve us into submission,' not because we objected to the advances made upon the price paid in 1852, for the great body of us were perfectly satisfied with the advances given, but because we thought fit to give our own money to support some four mills' hands that had disputes

with their employers, the primary cause of our sympathy being, that these workpeople had been denied the opportunity of explaining, or coming to an arrangement with their employers. It is false and without any foundation to say 'that these firms were to be made the victims of an organized combination, whose avowed object was to take the masters in succession, and compel them to accept the terms of the unionists.' We deny this statement, and challenge them to substantiate it. We, as a body, have never done or said anything to justify such a conclusion.

"3rd.—They say, 'We at once admit that, owing to the depressed state of trade in 1847, a general reduction of wages took place;' but with respect to the promise of restoring it when trade revived, they say, 'We deny, however, that any such promise was made by the masters generally, although this might have been done by some individual firms.' We are prepared to admit that every employer in the town did not make that promise: there were several firms where had the hands, or any portion of them, raised the shadow of an objection to the reduction, or solicited a promise of any description, they would have received summary ejectment; and such a process, in the state of the labour market at the time, would have been next to starvation and death; but the promise given at the firms where the masters allowed them some little 'freedom,' was justly considered applicable to all, and consequently, to those firms where the hands dare not ask, at that time, to be other than 'degraded slaves.'

"4th.—They say, 'Being anxious to ascertain the difference (if any) between the earnings of the various classes of operatives in 1847, *before* the above mentioned reduction took place, and those in the summer of 1853, *before* the 10 per cent. was demanded, we find, from the returns furnished us from the wages book of several large and influential firms, that instead of any decrease, there has been an actual increase, varying from 5 to 30 per cent., after making due allowance for the difference in the hours of labour, from sixty-nine to sixty hours per week.' Gentlemen, if your object had been to furnish statistical data of the benefit and blessings which have resulted from the passing of the Ten Hours' Bill[2] (that bill which you so long and so zealously opposed, and which you so often prophesied would be followed by ruinous and disastrous results—by the bye, we are told at the present time, that if you cannot succeed in reducing our wages ten per cent., it will be followed by disastrous ruin) we could have understood your motive; but because, by our untiring exertions, we have succeeded in doing as much work in sixty hours as we for-

---

2. The Ten Hours Bill of 1847 established a uniform working day in the textile mills, based on the principle of a ten-hour day and a fifty-eight hour week for all "protected persons"— i.e., women and young persons. The passing of the bill followed a long period of agitation by reformers and resistance by many of the employers.

merly did in sixty-nine hours, you are so ungenerous as to make this a justification for preventing us participating in the general prosperity which has followed; but you say, '*that in a well regulated spinning and weaving establishment,* the average earnings of all classes of hands are about 10*s.* each.' You forget to tell us whose well regulated establishment this is; but if all establishments where the average earnings are less than 10*s.* per week, are badly regulated establishments, we are prepared to prove from your own books, if you will furnish us with the facility, that the great body of establishments are anything but 'well regulated.'

"5th.—We repeat that the wages paid in Preston are less than what are paid in other districts, and this is the secret cause of the determination of the workpeople to improve their condition.

"6th.—We refer the public to the letters we have sent to the Preston papers, in answer to those which appeared in the *Chronicle* of Saturday last.

"7th.—We beg to say, that in this struggle the masters are the aggressors; we are on the defensive; we were (with the few exceptions referred to) satisfied with the wages given us before the 'Lock-out;' we understand that we must not resume work unless we will submit to a reduction of ten per cent.; we have offered to have the question settled upon reasonable terms, but 'no concession' is the terms of our employers; they have forced us to rely for an existence upon aid from other towns, and now tell us, that we can only resume work upon condition that we will degrade ourselves in the eyes of the world, by accepting a reduction, which must naturally be followed by a reduction in the wages of those who have so generously saved our children from starvation. Are these the only terms of honourable men? will it be the interest of the employers of Preston to see their workpeople both degraded and dishonest?—We think not; but if it be, we tell them that we will suffer much before we will submit to such depravity.

"In conclusion, we again reiterate, that we are prepared at any time to bring this dispute to an honourable and reasonable arrangement.

"By order of the Power-loom Weavers' Committee,
"JAMES WHALLEY, *Sec.*
"Committee Room, Preston, *Dec. 28th,* 1853."

It were needless to recapitulate the true facts of the case, already recorded in these pages, and to point out from them how far both these statements are erroneous.

✳   ✳   ✳

They took into their employ agents, who travelled about the country, especially in Ireland and in the agricultural counties of England,
inducing young people to come to Preston and learn the operations
of the cotton manufacture. It was charged against these agents at
the time that in the performance of their duty they were guilty of
deceiving the people whom they so induced; that they exaggerated
the average rate of earnings, and concealed the proportionate
expense of living, and that, when such a statement could be safely
hazarded, they even assured the recruits that the disputes at Preston
had been amicably concluded, and that only a few extra hands were
wanted to supply the vacancies in the mills. It is quite certain that
many of these immigrants, after their arrival in Preston, complained
bitterly of having been deceived, and expressed considerable surprise
on ascertaining the real position of affairs there. In opposition to
these tactics of the Masters' Association the delegates were not idle.
On the Monday after the issue of the foregoing placard, about sixty
persons were brought by train from Manchester, under the care of
one of the agents of the Masters' Association; but before they could
be got away from the station, and in their progress through the
streets of the town, most of them were induced to leave their con-
ductors, and accompany the emissaries of the unionists, by whom
they were led in triumph to the "Farmer's Arms," where they were
treated to meat and drink, and then sent back again to Manchester.
In order to prevent a repetition of this, the Association hired a house
closely approximating to the railway station, which they fitted up and
called "THE FACTORY IMMIGRANTS' HOME"—which title was painted
upon a sign-board and conspicuously fastened over the door of the
house. In its immediate results, the experiment was not very successful; for by far the larger proportion of the immigrants were
utterly useless to the masters. The correspondent of a London journal, writing from personal observation, gave the following picture of
the immigrants:—

"The Irish, who were the first to arrive, presented a picture of
wretchedness and squalor which it would be difficult, if desirable,
to realize. It is not easy to imagine how such a collection of filthy
unfortunates could be got together, and their state may be imagined
when it is known that forty of them are so bad that the masters can
make no use of them. An empty house opposite the railway station
has been converted into a sort of barracks for the reception of the
immigrants, and a policeman who entered this place on the morning
after the arrival of the Irish, left it immediately nauseated to sickness.
Some of the recruits from the north of England are more satisfactory,
and some families from Buckinghamshire seem clean, healthy, and
respectable. On Monday some amusement was created by the arrival
of a batch of female volunteers, rather gaily attired, and with veils;

they seemed very much amused at the adventure, and it is thought that they will not stick to weaving very long. Many stories are afloat about the conduct of the immigrants, especially the Irish. Some of those who fell to the lot of an associated master are said to have celebrated their advent by procuring a little whiskey, upon the strength of which they thrashed an overlooker; others said that they needn't expect them to get up at six o'clock in the morning; in another factory, the new comers are said to have run away in a fright directly the machinery was put in motion. At one mill, this morning, nine of the Irish turned out, on the ground that they had not been furnished with sufficient food, and certainly their condition seemed most deplorable. . . . The expense to the masters must be enormous."

Next week, the same correspondent wrote:—

"On Monday morning, thirty-five low Irish were brought from Manchester. I happened to be at the station when their effects were being removed from the train, and I saw bedding so full of vermin that the porters had to scald the trucks, and even the pavement of the station with boiling water. The railway officials are greatly to be blamed for permitting such filthy goods to be transported. Some of the Associated Masters meet the trains by which immigrants are expected, attended by a great posse of police, firemen, and specials. The polite manner with which these otherwise haughty gentlemen hand the females out of the carriages, inquiring after their bundles, and even dandling the babies, affords considerable amusement to the bystanders."

The importation of this mass of filth and pauperism into the town became a grave question with some of the middle-class inhabitants. * * *

WILLIAM RATHBONE GREG

The Claims of Labour†

* * *

* * * We have said that we think the author of the work we are reviewing, frequently confounds the duties which every man owes to all with whom he comes in contact, with those which arise out of

---

† William Rathbone Greg (1809–1881) was a writer on industrial issues and a member of a prominent northwestern family of mill owners. He was known personally to Gaskell. He severely criticized *Mary Barton*, arguing that its author was ignorant of economic theory. The article from which these extracts are taken is a review of *The Claims of Labour* (1844; 2nd edition, 1845) by Sir Arthur Helps (1813–1875) in the *Westminster Review*, no. 43, June 1845. All notes are the Editor's.

the relation between the employer and the employed; and assigns to the former many which belong to him no doubt, but which belong to him in common with every neighbour and every Christian, and which belong to him more especially in his capacity of member of the richer and the ruling classes. We shall endeavour to discriminate a little between these two sets of duties, for it appears to us of the very last importance, that, in the new relations between capital and labour, which have arisen from the advance of manufacturing industry, the collection of the artisan population into great *foci*,[1] and the system of working in large organized bodies under one head; the reciprocal claims of the two parties, and the principles which ought to regulate their mutual intercourse, should be fully understood. Every one will feel that at present this relation is not established on a sound basis, and does not work in a satisfactory manner.

It is impossible it should do so. We are now encountering the difficulties of a transition state, in which former rules and ties are loosened, and the new ones fitted to our changed condition are as yet unformed, or imperfectly recognised. Now there are three several positions in which capital and labour may relatively stand; the position of slavery, of feudal vassalage, and of free and simple bargain; the servile, the feudal, and the equal: and it is from not bearing in mind the distinction between them that our notions as to rights and duties are so misty and fluctuating. In the *first* of these relative positions, which is both the earliest and the simplest, perfect subjection is repaid by complete protection and subsistence; the master exacts from his slave all the duties of implicit obedience, and in return incurs towards him all the obligations consequent upon absolute power. In the *second*,—the position of vassalage—imperfect submission and occasional services are recompensed by partial protection, and aids in the procuring of a sustenance. In return for living on the land of his feudal superior, and under the shadow of his power, the vassal performs certain stipulated services without reward, and renders the willing homage of gratitude and reverence. In the *third* relation, that of bargain or mutual arrangement, simple service is balanced against simple payment. The capitalist *contracts* to pay a certain sum in return for a certain work which the labourer *contracts* to perform.

Now it is clear, that in this country we are passing from the second to the third of these relations. The second is almost abandoned, but the third is not yet fully established and recognised. Among the great manufacturing employers of labour, there is still some clinging to the feudal notions of bygone times, and among the great agricultural proprietors still more. The same may be said, *mutatis mutan-*

1. Centralized locations (Latin).

dis,[2] of the labourers in their respective districts. In the case of both capitalists and labourers (and for clearness we shall now confine our attention to the case of manufacturing industry) *they do not see clearly, or feel invariably, in which of the two previously mentioned relative positions they intend to stand. Each party borrows some of the* claims *of the preceding relation, but forgets the correlative* obligations. The artisan conceives that he is entitled to claim from his master the forbearance, the kindness, the assistance in difficulty and distress, which belong to the feudal relation; but he forgets to pay the corresponding duties of consideration, confidence, and respect. On the other hand, the master is too apt to forget that in the eye of the law his servants are now his equal fellow citizens, and to exact from them, not only the work he pays them for, but that deference, respect, and implicit obedience, to which only beneficence, justice, and consideration on his part, can fairly entitle him. We are convinced that it is the neglect of these simple reflections that has given rise to so much of the uneasy and unkindly feeling which unhappily prevails too extensively between the capitalist and the artisan; which gives rise to the charges of ingratitude and unreasonableness on the one side, and of unfeeling selfishness on the other. The simple fact is, that the relative position of the two classes is now more that of simple bargain than any other. We do not say it is desirable that it should be so, but it is fast becoming so, and everything tends to complete and consolidate this position; and it only requires to be fully understood that if one of the parties borrows anything from either of the previous conditions, the other must be held entitled to do the same. We cannot make society step back into feudalism, however modified; and, whatever Young England[3] may think, it would be as undesirable as it is impossible. The only matter for regret is that, owing to the want of statesmanlike foresight, and adequate preparation, *the third relation between capital and labour has come upon us before either capitalists or labourers are quite fitted to meet it.*

* * *

Let us now—putting aside for a moment the reciprocal claims of man upon man, of Christian upon Christian—and regarding the capitalist and the labourer simply in their mutual relation of two contracting parties—inquire briefly, what *are* the claims of Labour?

Labour has a right to claim justice, not charity—that is, it has a right to claim that, *in the great bargain to be struck between capital and labour, no advantage shall be given to capital, directly or indi-*

---

2. Making the necessary adjustments for circumstances (Latin).
3. A conservative political movement which called for a return to the values of a feudal society. Benjamin Disraeli was one of its leading figures.

rectly, by legislative enactments. It can claim nothing more; but this implies much.

It implies, in the *first* place, that legislature shall do nothing, or shall undo or equipoise what has been done, either to facilitate the education of capitalists, or to impede the education of labourers since there can be no fair or equal bargaining between ignorance and knowledge. Now it is notorious that not only has every facility and encouragement been given for centuries back by wealthy and privileged endowments, to the instruction of the upper classes, but that endowments originally designed for the instruction of the poor have been diverted from their purpose, or suffered to fall into disuse, by the neglect of those rulers whose duty it was to have watched over and enforced a sacred trust. It is notorious, also, that till the last few years legislature has done absolutely nothing to promote the education of the working classes; that its provision for that purpose even now is upon the most pitiful and niggard scale; and that it has suffered the narrow intolerance of sectaries and the domineering spirit of the hierarchy to thwart its first faint efforts to repair the injustice and neglect of centuries. If labour has one claim more sacred than another, it is that it shall be educated into a knowledge of its interests, its duties, and its rights.

The one great claim we have laid down implies, in the *second* place, that legislature shall have done nothing either to increase the numbers of the labourers or to restrict the field of their employment; since either proceeding will lessen the value of their labour, and of course the price they can obtain for it. In this matter, also, "we are verily guilty concerning our brother." The very ignorance in which we have allowed the people to remain, the mischievous and senseless principles on which our Poor Law was so long administered,[4] the anxiety of our great landed proprietors to increase the number of their political dependents, have all tended to stimulate the multiplication of the poor, while the whole tendency of our commercial policy for more than half a century has been to limit the field of employment, and thus defraud labour of its due demand; and it is only during the last *lustrum*[5] that the efforts of manufacturing capitalists have awakened the legislature to a sense of its errors and injustice, and induced it slowly to retrace its steps.

Thirdly, the admitted claim implies that legislature shall have done nothing, or shall undo what has been done, to enhance the price of the articles which the labourer has to buy, or of those which the

---

4. Under the "old" Poor Law paupers could receive relief and be provided with work under a parish-based system related to the price of bread and the size of their families. It was argued that this system imposed financial burdens on parishes and relieved the poor of the responsibility to limit their families. These provisions were eliminated in 1834 when the 'new' Poor Law came into force.

5. A five-year period following a census (Latin). There was a census in Britain in 1841.

capitalist has to sell; since this would be equivalent to a reduction of the earnings of the former, and to an augmentation of the profits of the latter. Unhappily this claim has been insolently and systematically set at nought. Legislature has done all in its power, has exhausted its ingenuity, to enhance the price of the principal article, which the labourer buys and the legislator sells; and this enormous injustice is still unremedied.[6]

Fourthly, it implies that in all matters of combination, either to keep up or keep down wages, the law should give equal liberty or equal restriction to each party. In this point the law is impartial; and in fact, the administration of the law is favourable rather to the artisan than to the capitalist.

These are the claims of labour—clear and unquestionable. If labour demands more than this, *it must give an equivalent*. The labourer gives labour to his employer in return for wages; if he expects his employer to give him more than wages, he must give his employer more than labour. If the employer is to give to the labourer protection, education, kindness, and assistance in hard times (which undoubtedly it is most desirable he should), the labourer, on his part, must render respect, obedience, and confidence to his employer. Without these it is *impossible* even for the best-intentioned employer effectually to serve him.

Now we are far from saying that we consider the most "meagre relation" between the parties as the best. On the contrary, we should wish that every large employer of labour should be a reverenced and valued friend in the midst of a circle of confiding and attached workmen. But the two positions are correlative; the one cannot exist without the other; and those are no true friends to the labourer or the artisan who would persuade him that the neglected duties are all on the part of his employer, and the denied or forgotten rights all on his own.

Before we conclude, let us add one word on a subject now rarely touched upon, but one to which attention occasionally requires to be recalled—the counter-claims of capital on labour. Passing over the simplest—a diligent and faithful performance of the work which the labourer has contracted to perform, the rest resolve themselves into one. Capital has a right to require from labour that it shall not, in a mistaken pursuit of its own exclusive interests, act fatally to the interests of both. Capital has a right to require not that labour shall neglect, but that it shall *understand* its own interests. When it has not understood them, as in the case of the sawyers and shipbuilders of Ireland, it has banished capital and ruined itself. In the manufac-

---

6. The reference is to the Corn Laws, by which the price of bread was kept at an artificially high level. After a long campaign led by the advocates of free trade, they were repealed in 1846.

turing districts of our own country we see among the operatives too much of the same misconception and want of thorough comprehension of the matter. Their own views are, naturally enough, limited and inaccurate; and unhappily they have too little confidence in their employers, even where that confidence has been deserved by a long course of unswerving justice and consideration, to listen to their exposition of the truth. In consequence, they allow themselves to be made the tools and the victims of men whose livelihood is derived from the misunderstandings they create and foster; and the amount of capital annually destroyed, and of wages annually foregone, owing to this cause alone, would astonish any one if fairly calculated out.

We have been led to speak of this by observing the numerous strikes for advance of wages, or redress of complaints, which, with returning prosperity, have been so rife during the last six months in the manufacturing districts, especially among the colliers, millwrights, and factory hands. We do not wish to express any opinion as to which party has justice on their side in these unfortunate disputes. We wish merely to call attention to the amount of capital which has thus been thrown idle, and therefore diminished or destroyed, and to the heavy loss which has been thus incurred by the operatives themselves. One case will suffice to put our meaning in a clear point of view. A large number of operatives employed in an establishment where extensive fixed capital was employed, left their work and demanded an advance of five per cent; but owing to some circumstances connected with the strike, and their conduct in the course of it, the demand was resisted, and they remained out six weeks. At the expiration of this time they returned to their work, having obtained nearly the whole advance they asked; but on coming to calculate the consequences, it appeared that the proprietor had lost by the stoppage a sum equal to five per cent on the capital employed, and that it *would take* 120 *weeks, or nearly two years and a half at the advanced rate of wages, before the workmen would have replaced the earnings they had foregone during the strike.* Nor is this all. In all probability, before the two years and a half have elapsed, trade may again have become unprosperous, and the advance now so dearly purchased will have to be relinquished. It is owing to injudicious struggles between capital and labour, such as the above, that the actual *earnings* of the operatives are sometimes actually *less* in prosperous than in dull and languid periods of trade. In other cases, as among the colliers, when the strike has lasted for months, no advance and no lapse of time can repay the losses which they have incurred.

The feudal age is gone; and neither its benefits nor its evils can now be brought back. We can no longer really serve the people, or ameliorate their condition, by *protecting* them as vassals, or *sup-*

porting them as slaves, or by *almsgiving*, as to paupers and beggars. The only plan which appears to us at once sound in its principle, and promising as to its prospects, is to spread instruction among the masses by every means in our power, and then leave them to "work out their own salvation;" to throw them on their own resources, but, at the same time, to give those resources full and free scope; to give them the means of rising, to show them the way of rising, and then leave them (with our best wishes and encouragements), to raise themselves. Any other elevation than one so achieved will be ill-founded, precarious, and temporary.

The second portion of the 'Claims of Labour,' which has just issued from the press, is chiefly devoted to the consideration of that class of remedies for the physical evils of our town population, which is suggested by the 'Health of Towns Report,'[7] such as ventilation, sewerage, building, supply of water, &c. The author has supplied nothing new, but has brought out in vivid relief, and placed before the public in an available form, the appalling facts brought to light by recent inquiries. We shall not quote any of his pictures, for we cannot abridge what is in itself a brief epitome, and we have no wish to supersede the necessity of referring to his pages. But we request attention to the following remarks, as peculiarly important at the present conjuncture.

> "If there is anything that requires thought and experience, it is the exercise of charity in such a complicated system as modern life. I do not know a more alarming sight than a number of people rushing to be benevolent without thought. In any general impulse there are at least as many thoughtless as wise persons excited by it; the latter may be saved from doing very foolish things by an instinct of sagacity; but for the great mass of mankind, the facts require to be clearly stated and the inferences carefully drawn for them, if they are to be prevented from wasting their benevolent impulses upon foolish or mischievous undertakings."—P. 219.

The author makes some most judicious and much-called-for observations upon a besetting sin of the philanthropic.

> "To alleviate the distress of the poor may be no gain, if in the process we aggravate the envies and jealousies which may be their especial temptation. The spirit to be wished for is sympathy; and that will not be produced by needless reproaches. Besides, it is such foolish injustice to lay the blame of the present state of things upon any class. If we must select any class,

---

7. There was a sequence of Parliamentary reports on urban conditions in the 1840s. This reference is probably to the *Second Report of the Commissioners for Inquiring into the State of Large Towns and Populous Districts* (1845).

do not let us turn to the wealthy, whom, perhaps, we think of first. They have, in no time that I am aware of, been the preeminent rulers of the world. The thinkers and writers, they are the governing class."

Several of our most popular writers of the present day have been guilty—one in particular[8]—of this encouragement of enmity.

"They should recollect that literature may fawn upon the masses as well as on the aristocracy; and in these days the temptation is in the former direction. But what is most grievous in this kind of writing is the mischief it may do to the working people themselves. If you have their true welfare at heart, you will not only care for their being fed and clothed, but you will be anxious not to encourage unreasonable expectations in them, not to make them ungrateful or greedy-minded. Above all, you will be solicitous to preserve some self-reliance in them. You will be careful not to let them think that their condition can be wholly changed without exertion of their own. . . . . . . *Depend upon it honest and bold things require to be said to the lower as well as to the higher classes*; and the former are, in these times, much less likely to have such things addressed to them."— P. 253.

W. E. FORSTER

Strikes and Lock-Outs†

* * * For weeks, if not months, the columns of our newspapers have contained almost daily records of the progress of a contest arresting attention even amid the noisier claims of "Our Paris or Vienna Correspondent," or the "Latest Telegraphic Despatch."[1] Whether regarded as a rebellion of the "men" against their "masters," as a struggle for power between two classes of the community, as a frantic and suicidal resistance to economic laws, or as their legitimate and natural result, there is indeed enough in this Lancashire "strike" to excite the interest of every Englishman; and in the oft-repeated questions: "What will be the end of this industrial conflict? can nothing

---

8. Almost certainly Dickens.
† William Edward Forster was Member of Parliament for Leeds. He wrote extensively on social issues. This essay was written in response to the Preston strike of 1854 (see pp. 455–62 above) and first published in the *Westminster Review* (new series, no. 5), Jan. 1854. Forster was later to become famous for his Elementary Education Bill of 1870. Unless indicated otherwise, notes are the Editor's.
1. Forster's article was written during the buildup to the Crimean War, hence the reference to the prominence of foreign news in the newspapers.

be done? must the mill-owners and their workpeople be left to fight it out?" we have proof that there is no lack of interest in the subject, baffling and disappointing as are its difficulties. These difficulties are so many, the causes of collision so far-reaching, and the effect of the evil so complicated and extensive, that he would be a bold man who should imagine himself provided with a remedy. Disclaiming any such presumption, yet believing that amidst all the discussion of this conflict, there is but little appreciation of its real meaning, or of the direction in which at least a remedy should be sought, we will attempt to examine the relation of the employers to the employed, in the light of the Lancashire "strikes and lock-outs."

Into the special details or merits of this particular struggle we do not intend to enter. Were we to try to do so, the whole of our space would be filled by statements and counter-statements, which, without the power of cross-examination, it would be vain for us to attempt to test. How far the "lock-out" has been forced upon the masters by partial "strikes" of the men, or how far it has been an attack on Trades-Unions, attempted at a time when such attack seemed comparatively easy;—what promises of an advance of wages were made in bad times, and to what extent they have been fulfilled;—whether the rate of wage in Preston and its neighbourhood was below the average of the cotton districts, and if so, for what reasons;—how far there is any truth in the assertion of the men, that the masters, or some of them, by "spurning" or "marking" those among their own hands who asked an advance, forced them to use the agency of the "central committee;"—and again, to what extent this "central committee" or its delegates have prevented or broken arrangements with which, without their interference, both parties would have been content;—whether all the associations of the operatives were in action before that of the employers, or whether any one of them could be considered a combination in self-defence;—what proportion of the workpeople have been victims rather than combatants "locked-out," even though they have neither struck themselves, nor aided those who have;—these are some among many much disputed points, to ascertain the truth respecting which is as difficult as it is desirable. But passing by all disputed incidents, there are facts and principles of the struggle admitted by both sides, the enumeration of which will suffice for our purpose.

No one disputes that, throughout an extensive manufacturing district, an immense majority of the labourers are idle, because they have agreed not to sell their labour at the only terms on which as large a majority of the capitalists have agreed that they will buy it; nor that these labourers are enabled thus to refrain from bargaining for their labour, by the contributions of those of their fellow-labourers who are still at work; nor, lastly, that the obstacle in the

way of this bargain consists in a difference not so much as to price
as to conditions of sale, in the attempt of the buyer to make it one
of these conditions that the seller shall cease from thus contributing
to his fellows.

This indeed is the lesson which the "hands" are told that they have
to learn—viz., that they are to have no "union" one with another.
"The miseries caused by the 'strike,' or 'lock-out,' call it which you
will,—the pinching want which accompanies it, the harassing debts,
and, worse than debts, the malignant feelings of suspicion, hatred,
revenge, which it leaves behind it,—all these effects are but a fit
punishment," it is said, "to those who combine to keep up the price
of labour by refusing to sell it, and a salutary warning to those who
might be tempted to contribute to their aid. Let but two or three
more of these lessons be repeated, and even our manufacturing operatives, with all their ignorance of the laws of political economy,
and with all their liability to be led by designing agitators, will learn
not to strike." It may be so; and yet these lessons seem to us too
costly. * * *

Descending for a moment from the platform of the masters, let us
go down amongst the men, and try to look at the struggle from their
point of view. How much on their side should we then see of virtue
under almost all its forms; of constancy under suffering, self-denial
against temptation, loyalty to their leaders, sacrifices for their fellows, devotion to their cause. When we consider the amount of the
contributions cheerfully paid by those in work, now when every
penny of wage is needed for food, we wonder what distress of their
fellows, what philanthropic project or political aim, what common
cause or even what common interest, would drag a proportionate
sum from the pockets of the rich. Men marvelled at the subscriptions
of the Lancashire cotton lords to the League;[2] there is as much need
to marvel at the subscriptions of their "hands" to the strikes. And
when we read in such documents as the letter of the Burnley guard-
ians to the Poor Law Board, how day after day hard-earned savings
are disappearing, and one article after another of furniture or dress is
going to the pawnshop; and how, spite of sacrifices which the classes
above them would consider the worst results of ruin, hunger and cold
yet creep into the desolate home, but do not drive its occupants to
submission, we can little wonder that those who thus feel themselves
the "forlorn hope" of their order, should put faith in their leaders,
inveigh against their masters as tyrants, and brand as traitors those of
their fellows who are too weak to hold out. But at this we do wonder,
that with every passion thus tempted and every feeling thus strained,

2. I.e., the Anti-Corn Law League, a group of business men and politicians led by the Manchester politicians Richard Cobden and John Bright, who were dedicated to the repeal of
the Corn Laws.

with their ideas of law and order, and even of right and wrong, confused and perverted as they must be, they still, with so few exceptions, obey the law and keep the peace, and refrain from attacks on
either persons or property. Surely our civilization and culture may
take shame to itself if it can find no easier method by which to teach
the laws of political economy to men and women such as these.

But what *are* these laws of political economy? It may be well,
before we go any further, to try to ascertain more precisely what they
decree upon these questions between labour and capital: for of this
we may be sure, that no constancy on their part, no pity on ours,
will ward off from those who break these laws the penalty for their
infraction. Strikes, it is said, and the combinations upon which they
are based, are attempts to give an artificial value to the article of
labour, higher than that which is naturally fixed by the relation of its
supply to its demand. If so, then it is but a truism to add, that all
such attempts to force nature must entail suffering on those who
make them. On the other hand, it may perhaps be objected, if the
rate of wages depends solely on the relation which the supply of
labour bears to the demand, then the natural tendency of strikes will
be to raise the rate because they diminish the supply. Granted; it is
so for a time, but only for a time, unless with the diminution of the
supply or labour there be also a permanent diminution in the supply
of labourers: otherwise, the demand not being increased, a higher
price will be given only until the deficiency of the supply be filled
up, and then the rate will be as before. And though the rate of wages
may for a time be higher, the actual amount of wage paid will not
be greater, because that which alone raises the rate is the fact that
many of the labourers get no wages at all. The utmost therefore that
a strike can do, is to force the capitalist to divide among the operatives at work the wages of those who are not at work; the labourers
as a body can gain nothing, but individuals may lose. This much a
strike can do, if the demand remains the same. But though a strike
cannot increase the demand for labour, it can and does diminish it;
in two ways, first, by suspending industry, it lessens the amount of
capital seeking investment; and secondly, by curtailing the purchasing powers of those who strike, it lessens the demand for the produce
of labour: for it cannot be too constantly borne in mind, that labour
is an article which does not admit of hoarding,—if the seller misses
his sale, he loses his commodity, and with it his power to purchase.
Moreover, a strike may succeed in driving away the capitalist, in
inducing him to take his money to a labour market which is not
confused by these artificial fluctuations. Therefore, to say nothing
of the bad effects of intimidation of "knob-sticks," or threats to masters,—too evident to dwell on,—or of the loss of power to work which

results from idleness, the Economists[3] are quite right when they assert that even a well conducted strike, a combination to refuse work without coercion, (if with human nature as it is there ever was or can be such an anomaly,) cannot even be to the pecuniary advantage of those who are engaged in it, though for a time it may seem to be so; must result in their losing more than they have gained, though it may end in other labourers stepping into their shoes and thriving on their ruin.

So much for the effects of strikes,—effects which even the "central committee" of operatives will hardly we think dispute. But to this statement they will reply, "Strikes, we confess, are an evil, but a necessary evil; it is the *fear of strikes* which does us good; and unless they took place, unless in certain contingencies they were expected to take place, this fear would not be felt, and it would be a long time before our employers would give us the fair market value of our labour, if they did not fear our refusal to sell it to them if they did not."

Now, in order to test the truth of this argument, we must consider a little more closely how the market value, not only of this article of labour but of articles generally, comes to vary: and in so doing we shall find that as a rule this value varies not simply in *consequence*, but also in *anticipation* of an alteration in the supply and demand. Men professing to be guided not by instinct but by reason, calculate what they will want themselves and what will be wanted by others; and whenever the majority of the dealers in a commodity agree in the calculation that the demand will be greater than the supply, the sellers quote a higher price for it, not merely after, nor at the time of, but before the increase of the consumption takes place. And so it is that if there be any fact which will widely influence trade, it is rarely that its effects are not anticipated. The harvest is bad; the price of corn rises, not because the scarcity has come—for the old stocks as yet far more than suffice—but because it is apprehended.

* * *

Very well then, value yourselves, is the reply: demand the advance if you please, do not wait for the offer; but demand it quietly, peaceably; do not "strike." Again the men say,—"What is the use of our demand, if you know that whether you accede to it or not, we shall continue to work? If we must sell you our labour, you would be fools not to buy it on your own terms, not ours." Very well then, make your work dependent on your pay; let each man make his own bar-

3. I.e., those economic theorists who argued for the unrestricted freedom of the market to determine wages and prices.

gain with his master, but let there be no combination or Trades-Union,—this, say the masters, is the very aim and object of our "lock-out," that in future the price of labour should be fixed like that of everything else by the "higgling of the market."

*　　*　　*

It is only by keeping constantly before us the real meaning of these combinations,[4] a meaning which perhaps even those who join them instinctively scarcely express to themselves, that we can understand the features of this present Lancashire conflict. Undoubtedly it began in a difference as to wages, and yet if you go to the masters they will tell you it is not so much a question of wages as of management. "We resort," they say, "to this fearful alternative of a 'lock-out,' in order that we may maintain our position as masters, and prevent a set of designing delegates or ignorant committee-men from interfering in our business. How can we dare to risk our capital, if a conclave of meddlers is to sit in consultation on the terms upon which it shall be employed? No man can serve two masters; our men shall choose between obeying the union committee and obeying us." On the other hand, the men fight as fiercely for their right to unite. We doubt not that, weeks since, finding that times were against them, and feeling indeed that the pitched battle was forced upon them—for partial strikes and skirmishes were all that they were then intending—the men would, in spite of the incitements of their leaders have drawn out of the dispute, had they not felt that the result of defeat would be not merely the loss of the ten per cent demanded, nor even the submission to a reduction, but the destruction of their Union, and thereby the inability to claim an advance in future. And hence it is, that the whole strength of the Union is now brought to bear upon Preston; contributions are paid to few of the other "turn-outs," and they are even recommended to turn in at a reduction, to free or to raise funds which may enable the Union cause to triumph in that district in which it has been most threatened. Both sides therefore are fighting about the same thing, and unlike many other combatants they know what it is; but their object in doing so is different. The men insist upon the interference of the "central committee," not because they desire such interference in itself, but because they believe that it is the only means by which they can get a fair share of the surplus produce of their labour. The masters, on the other hand, denounce such interference, not because they wish to cheat or to deprive the men of their fair share, but because they believe that the interference will diminish this surplus produce; and

4. Trade unions.

in holding such belief it can scarcely be denied that the masters are justified.

We have tried to sympathize with the men, because unless we do so we cannot understand them, and because they both suffer most, and their conduct jars most against our class prejudices; but we must not forget that our sympathy is due to the masters also. There are few positions more painful than that of a mill-owner, who, while seeking to do his duty to his workpeople so far as he can discover it, finds step in between him and them a third party, who, from ignorance of special difficulties, cannot but meddle, and who, very probably from intention, takes advantage of these difficulties to sow discord. To say that such a man hates a Trades-Union, and abhors its control, because he wants to be let alone to screw down his "hands" as low as he can, is an absurd slander; on the contrary, we generally find that the best masters, those whose consciences most acquit them of illiberality or injustice,—men who very often have employed their labourers at a loss, in order to make the burden of the bad times bear lighter on them,—are those who are the most determined opponents of the "union," the leaders of the "lock-outs" against the combinations which, had all the masters been like them, would never have existed. Nor would it be fair to deny, that as yet we have scarcely touched upon the chief evil of these combinations. It is vain to expect that they will ever be conducted without an attempt by the majority, who are willing to combine, to coerce the minority who are not. It is true that the present method of coercion is an improvement on that which was formerly adopted. * * * Nevertheless, while we rejoice in the progress of civilization thus exhibited, we question whether the coercion itself is much diminished. If the "unionists" are now becoming sufficiently enlightened to punish the "knobs-sticks" by help of ridicule, contempt, and exclusion, instead of by physical violence as of old, yet that same increase of moral sensitiveness which makes them prefer the new mode of punishment, also makes it to the victims as hard to bear.

The problem, then, which has to be solved we find to be this— how can the labourers believe that they will get, or rather, as their belief will have to be founded on a fact, how can they actually get their fair share in the produce of their labour? How can they be sure of participating in good times as soon, that is, as long, as does their employer, without the instrumentality of this costly, coercive, destructive system of "strikes?" or, in other words, how can they, without thus demanding it, get an advance in the value of their labour, as soon as the employers get an advance in the value of its product?

At first the solution of the problem thus put seems simple enough.

Let men and masters be what they should be, and the former would make a fitting and decorous demand, which the latter without demur would grant; nay, further, let but the labourers have been both industrious and economical, and the possession of the savings of their labour will back their demand as forcibly as does the power to levy a tax on the earnings of others; more forcibly indeed, because no association of employers could lock them out of the savings bank. Waiting, however, this millennium, when no labourers will be needy and no employers exacting, can no one suggest a substitution for strikes?

Arbitration is a suggestion which of late has been mooted; it is the lesson which the Manchester school proposes to teach all foreign potentates[5] and which therefore it may not unreasonably be asked to practise in its intestine quarrels, and certainly it is a lesson which at first sight seems altogether applicable to them. If, in order to escape the cost and anxiety and uncertainty of a law-suit, men can be found who will submit to the decision of arbitrators almost every kind of dispute which can be pleaded before a judge, what is there in these labour disputes which prevents their being thus settled, instead of by a process more harassing and expensive than any law-suit? * * *

Failing, however, such intermeddling law, we fear the mill-owner would continue to appeal to the law of the strongest, unless, indeed, he felt his operatives too strong for him, in which ease *they* would be likely to cry out, "Leave us alone to fight our own battles." Unless arbitration, therefore, be compulsory, there can be no security that it will be resorted to. Why then, many will say, not make it compulsory? For this reason, that the remedy would be little better than the disease. A compulsory arbitration would change the whole machinery of our manufacturing system, almost as much as do the present quarrels.

* * *

Nevertheless, though we disclaim all idea of compulsion as both unjust and inexpedient, does it therefore follow that we must dismiss all hope of voluntary arbitration? is there no way by which masters and men can be persuaded to stop fighting, and themselves to appoint arbiters to argue out the question before an umpire? We fear such persuasion both is and must be a hard task. It is the unfortunate characteristic of these industrial conflicts, that they so deeply involve not only the interests but the feelings and passions of the combat-

5. Members of the Anti-Corn Law League were then arguing that international disputes, in particular the situation in the Balkans leading up to the Crimean War, should be resolved by negotiation, not war.

ants, that if either side offer to arbitrate the other side will probably be too confident or angry or proud to accede. Moreover it is to be expected that the masters will, as in the case both of the engineer strike in 1852, and in that of the Preston lock-out now, refuse to submit to this mode of settlement, not because they doubt the justice of their cause, or wish to punish or revenge themselves on their opponents, but because such submission would be an acknowledgment of defeat, inasmuch as it would be a surrender of the very principle for which they are contending—viz., their right as masters to do their own mastership, and to manage their business without the meddling between them and their work people of any third parties. Therefore it is probable that they would not only not listen to any proposal for reference either made by the men, or pushed forward by bystanding peacemakers, but that they would also oppose any plan for permissive arbitration which the legislature might devise. Otherwise it might perhaps not be beyond the resources of parliamentary ingenuity to choose men, or rather to arrange a plan by which men might be chosen, who from their knowledge and character would be competent to act as arbitrators, if both parties agreed to employ them.

*　*　*

Parliament, however, can at the best do but little; the dispute is between the employers and the employed; and whatever difference of opinion there may be as to the propriety of any interference from without, legislative or other, there can be no question that such interference will be of little avail if the causes which lead to the dispute still remain in operation. Far better, then, that the disputants should settle their own disputes for themselves, if they can; for in so doing they may learn to avoid them in future. But can they, or will they? So long as the relation between employers and employed is defined by them both as one purely of bargain-making, we fear that they will not. "The value of labour," say the masters, quoting from the laws of political economy, "sooner or later must, like the value of every other article, rise or fall with its demand." "Granted," reply the men; "such are the first principles of political economy, and we believe them; but we also believe in the common law of that science—the custom and precedents of bargain—making—and they declare that, in the constant fluctuations of value, it is the place of the buyer to estimate the fall, but of the seller the rise. The difference between us and you is, that in bargains as to labour, but as to nothing else, you act only upon the first half of this rule. We believe and try to carry out the second also. You take care to offer less wage as trade becomes bad; if need be, you enter into an open combination to do so, but that rarely is necessary, inasmuch as, quoting from the old apostle of your science, Adam Smith, you have, as against us, a mutual understanding, which amounts to a tacit combination. We, therefore, will take care to demand more wage as trade becomes good; and we do so in company, because, individually, you would not attend to us. You say we are breaking the law of supply and demand by anticipating its operation; we reply, that we are carrying it out by giving it its customary interpretation. * * *

The conduct of the men, then, can scarcely be called inconsistent with the principles of bargain-making, though it may be so with the duties of mutual consideration and forbearance.

* * *

[Masters and Men]

In trying to define what manner of master is a mill owner, we shall find our best guide in the popular instinct as expressed in the phraseology of the day. When we designate those of whom he is master, we call them not slaves not serfs, nor even servants, but "men," sometimes "operatives" or "hands," to get rid of the distinction of sex; but if asked to give the history of the relation between employer and employed, most persons we think who care about the matter would say, that having been owners and slaves, then lords and villeins, then masters and servants, they are now masters and men. In other words, the relation, while quickly losing on the one hand the inferiority or degradation of service, does yet, on the other hand, keep the superiority and direction of mastership.[6] Address an assembly of factory workers as servants, and though generally the most attentive of audiences, your voice would be drowned in the resentment of the insult, but the speaker who followed you might talk of the "masters" without fear of offence. The Saxon instinct of these workers tells them that the common work in which they are engaged cannot get done without singleness of aim and of direction towards that aim, and therefore they feel that they ought to have a master as a manager. He is the manager of their joint undertaking, and if asked still more strictly to define his relation towards them, we should term him their managing partner.

What! the capitalist partner with the labourer! Why this is rank

6. True, the term "hands," giving the idea of mere machines, is a much more degrading one than that of servants, and we trust that the time may soon come when the heads and hearts of the factory workers will so assert themselves as to make it a term hardly possible to be used; nevertheless the degradation implied is not one of service. [Forster's note.]

socialism. Has not Mr. Ricardo[7] proved that they are necessary and natural antagonists one of another? that it is a general law that wages rise as profits diminish, and fall as they increase? and does not the *Times* tell us that any attempt or hope of the labourers to share the profits of the capitalist is the most Utopian of dreams? We have no space now to dispute the general law of Mr. Ricardo, but we are quite sure that had he been a practical manufacturer, he would have found his own case an exception, and have learnt from sad experience that if wages were falling so also were his profits; and so far from dreaming of the future, we are simply describing the present when we repeat, that in the factory system the present relation of employers and employed, however much either party may from ignorance or prejudice refuse to acknowledge it, actually *is* that of partners, with the employer as managing partner; and we add, that the conflicts between them will diminish just in proportion as the reality of this partnership is admitted, acted upon, and attempted to be made the most of.

Of course in thus using the word partnership, we do not give it its legal sense. The law, or rather the English law, limits its application to persons standing in a certain legal relation to one another and to the public. But disregarding the legal term, and looking merely at the fact, if we try to express the mutual relation of the individuals in a factory,—from the girl at her loom and the clerk at his ledger, to the manager who directs both, or the monied man who finds the capital,—we can find no better word than partners, because they are all engaged together in one undertaking, because in its success or failure they all must share, and because this success or failure depends not only upon their individual, but upon their joint exertion. They are partners in the work and in its reward, and according to the degree in which they fulfil the duties of partners, that is, according to their mutual good fellowship and continuous co-operation, must vary the amount of this reward. Undoubtedly between these partners there are and must be bargains as to the relative proportion of their shares in the reward, and this proportion will depend upon the relative value of their respective contributions, varying according to the law of supply and demand. But if we look upon them merely or solely as bargainmakers, we forget that in order that there should be any bargain to make, there must first have been a continuous co-operation, and if they in their bargains forget or disregard the conditions of this continuous co-operation, they also will quickly find that that about which they bargain will disappear.

7. David Ricardo (1772–1823), whose *Principles of Political Economy* (1817) was a key work in the foundations of nineteenth-century economic theory. His nephew, John Lewis Ricardo (1812–1862), was Member of Parliament for Stoke-upon-Trent and a prominent member of the Anti-Corn Law League.

This factory firm may indeed be considered as a corporate body, of which the manager is the brain, the capitalist the blood, and the operatives the muscles sinews and nerves, and, we may add, the good fellowship of them all the heart. Shame, then, upon the quarrels between the members of this body,—"Shall the head say to the hands, I have no need of you?" And shame, also, upon the false versions of scientific laws, which would set these members one against another, and would make their quarrels worse even than they are were it not that the harm which these false theories can do is limited in practice, for facts controvert them, and the instincts of the heads and hearts of men of business correct them. In the *esprit de corps* among the operatives of any well-managed factory, in the way in which they identify themselves with it and with their employer and with one another, speaking of "our mill," "cotton we have bought," "goods we have turned out," &c. &c.; in the sacrifices which the employer will make to keep his "people" about him, running his mill at a loss, and, reckless of all rules of bargain-making, buying labour when he does not want it; in the conviction of both, that if bad times come, both must suffer; in the claim of the employed, that as soon as good times come to the employer they also should come to them; and in the resistance of the employer to this claim, because it is so made as to interfere with the conditions of continuous co-operation; alike in the aspirations and demands of the one class, in the fears and indignation of the other, and in the actual circumstances of both, we see proof that their interests are identical, that their quarrels have arisen because the fact of identity is ignored, and will cease as soon as it is acknowledged. Let the master and the workpeople in each industrial undertaking, feel that because it is a joint undertaking it is an union of which they all are members, and this union will swallow up all other unions. There will then be no longer either wish or necessity in any of those who are within such union to combine with those without it, either to ask for an advance of wage or to refuse it.

* * * This feeling of union, or perception by the co-workers in an industrial undertaking that their individual interest depends on their continuous co-operation, can indeed only arise from their individual enlightenment, and must be the gradual work of time, strengthening their heads and warming their hearts by help of the interchange of opinion, and the inheritance of knowledge. No dictation from without, no law, or official order, can either produce this internal change, or force it forward. No Act of Parliament can develop this principle of partnership, or change the form under which it is expressed. But this much parliament can do; it can undo its own hindrances to the development, and abolish the restrictions by which it prevents society from feeling its way by experiment towards the new expression.

There are no labourers who talk more than do factory operatives about the feasibility and propriety of making their relation with the manager and capitalist one not only, as at present, of veiled, but also of professed partnership. They long to be called partners—to free themselves from the fetters of service,—to cast away all traces of its stigma,—to have a voice, if not in the direction of their labour, at least in the appointment of its directors,—to have their participation in profits with the capitalist defined by the very terms of their contract.

Doubtless it is for the fulfilment of the partnership idea that they are longing,—a fulfilment towards which the relation of employer and employed has been tending from the moment in which the latter ceased to be slave or serf of the former,—became in the eye of the law a freeman. But how far this idea can be fulfilled at present or in the immediate future, depends upon the freedom of both parties, but especially of the employed, from the tyranny of their own passions and prejudices; upon how far they have thrown off the fetters of sloth and ignorance, and what progress they have made in self-denial and self-government.

BESSIE RAYNER PARKES

The Condition of Working Women in England and France†

During the last two years we have seen a great public effort made towards relieving the difficulties of a special class of women—educated women who need a livelihood. And by dint of discussion the subject has been so thoroughly ventilated, and by dint of exertion so many plans have been tried with more or less success, that we may be fairly said to have attained to something like a reasonable hope of abolishing the evil in a due course of years, more particularly since public opinion is steadily directing itself to what is by far the truest remedy—a well-organized, widely-diffused, and persistent system of emigration.

Although, therefore, the necessity of action has not diminished, but still exists, and will do so for many years to come, we may consider the necessity for talking and writing in general terms about this particular class of the feminine community to be at an end. We must

† From *The English Woman's Home Journal*, vol. VIII, no. 43 (1 September 1861). Bessie Rayner Parkes (1829–1923) was a writer and activist in feminist causes. Notes are the Editor's.

all work, but those who are willing to help, now know where and how to apply.

Leaving, therefore, this difficult and much-vexed question wholly on one side for the time, I ask you to consider with me one which is much wider—which may indeed be said to include the first, and which I believe to be the most important social question of modern times, inasmuch as turn where we will it meets the social reformer on every side—I mean the change which the last century has brought about in the condition of the working women of England and France. I couple the two countries together because they essentially represent all that is implied in modern civilization, its benefits and its evils, in an almost equal degree; for if England has in some respects an advantage in the race, be sure that France is pursuing with giant strides, and that her capitalists and her workpeople are fast becoming the duplicates of our own.

Every one agrees, to judge by the incessant reference to it in the newspapers, that there is a certain phase of European life, peculiar to our generation and that of our fathers, which is so distinctly marked that it is indeed modern civilization. Some years ago, when Charles Mackay's songs were popular in the streets,[1] it was generally said to be the dawn of something quite new and splendid in the earth's history, the immediate herald of "the good time coming," but a strong reaction has taken place towards an appreciation of mediæval times; Mr. Ruskin, Mr. Froude, and a host of lesser men, have done battle for the Dark Ages,[2] and it is now generally conceded that Venice, Florence, and Holland, possessed in their palmy days a very respectable civilization of their own.

Whether, however, it be a marked growth, or only a marked change, it is evident that our ways are not as their ways, and that an immense increase of products, and a striking uniformity in what we produce, together with a constantly extending diffusion of material and intellectual goods, are the characteristics of the age of steam. England and France show them in every department of their public and private life, and the treaty of commerce, when once it comes fairly into play, is destined to increase them greatly, by stimulating each country to enormous production of its own specialities, so that all France, unless it goes to bed by gaslight, will probably adopt Birmingham candlesticks, and our Queen's subjects will more than ever be ruled in their costume by the fiats of Lyons and Paris for the year.

Now the point to which I am coming is the *price* at which this

1. Charles Mackay (1814–1889) was a popular poet. His *Songs for Music* (1856) marked the peak of his success; it contained a number of popular ballads which achieved instant popularity.
2. John Ruskin's *Stones of Venice*, championing Gothic architecture, was published in 1853. The writings of Richard Hurrell Froude (1803–1836) similarly offered a favorable view of the Middle Ages.

great European change has been accomplished: the price which has been silently levied in every manufacturing town in both kingdoms, the great revolution which has been so little noticed amidst the noise of politics and the clash of war—the withdrawal of women from the life of the household, and the suction of them by hundreds of thousands within the vortex of industrial life.

Perhaps you will attach more importance to what I say if I observe, that I have only very gradually become aware that this tendency pervades all the social economy of our time. Figures alone do not always impress the imagination; so many women in the cotton trade, so many in the woollen, the mind loses its track among the *oughts*, just as the savage gets bewildered beyond his own ten digits. But in thinking of governesses, and why there seemed to be such an inexplicable amount of suffering in that class, I have been brought face to face with these wider and deeper questions, and have seen that their actual destitution, though specially the result of overflowing numbers, is but part of a general tendency on the part of modern civilization to cast on women the responsibility of being their own breadwinners, and to say to them with a thousand tongues, "If thou wilt not work, neither shalt thou eat."

Look at the present constitution of Lancashire life; suppose the American war hinders the supply of cotton to such an extent that, before we can reckon on supplies from our Indian Empire or elsewhere, the mill hands are thrown out of employ, *who* will be thrown out of employ? Who are at least a majority of the total of the workpeople? Women and girls. You know what it is in Lancashire: those miles upon miles of dusky red dwellings, those acres of huge factories, those endless rows of spinning and weaving machines, each with its patient industrious female "hand." If a catastrophe falls on Yorkshire, and the chimneys of Bradford or Halifax cease to smoke, who are they that come upon the poor rates or hunger at home? Women and girls. I was told in Manchester, by one of the most eminent and thoughtful women in England,[3] that the outpouring of a mill in full work at the hour of dinner was such a torrent of living humanity that a lady could not walk against the stream: I was told the same thing at Bradford, by a female friend of my own. In both instances the quitting of the mill seemed to have struck their imaginations as a typical moment, and they spoke of it as something which once seen could not be forgotten.

At Nottingham and Leicester, which I have visited this spring, the women are so absorbed into the mills and warehouses that little is known of female destitution. In Birmingham, where vast numbers of women are employed in the lighter branches of the metal trade,

3. Almost certainly Gaskell herself, whom Parkes visited in Manchester in 1859.

they may be seen working in the button manufacture, in japanning, in pin and needle making. In Staffordshire they make nails, and unless you have seen them I cannot represent to your imagination the extraordinary figures they present—black with soot, muscular, brawny—undelightful to the last degree. In mines they are no longer allowed to work; but remember that they did work there not so long ago, taking with men an equal chance of fire-damp and drowning, even being sometimes harnessed to the carts if poor patient horses were too dear.

I read the other day of a whip makers' strike, which took place because women were being introduced into a branch of work for which men had hitherto been employed; but perhaps the most impressive thing which ever came to my immediate knowledge was the description in a small country paper of a factory strike, in which a prolonged irritation existed between the hands and the very excellent firm owning the works. There were letters and speeches to and fro; placards on the walls, and a liberal expenditure of forcible Saxon language. Now who were these hands "out on strike"? these people who made speeches, gathered together in angry knots at the corners of the streets?—Women!

After this, may I not say, that on no small body of ladies in London, on no committees or societies trying to struggle with the wants of the time, can rest the charge of unsexing women by advising them to follow new paths, away from household shelter and natural duties, when a mighty and all-pervading power, the power of trade, renders the workman's home empty of the housemother's presence for ten hours a day, and teaches English women the advantage of being "out on strike."

For it is clear, that, since modern society will have it so, women must work: "weeping," which Mr. Kingsley[4] regards as their appropriate employment, in fishing villages and elsewhere, being no longer to the purpose. I do not say that these myriads are, on the whole, ill paid, ill fed, sickly, or immoral; I only wish to point to the fact that they are actually working, and, for the most part, in non-domestic labor, a labor which cannot be carried on under a husband or a father's roof. And recognising this apparently hopeless necessity, I believe it to be just and advisable that printing and all such trades be fairly thrown open to them; for we have to do with hunger and thirst and cold; with an imperious need of meat and drink, and fire and clothing; and, moreover, as trade uses women up so freely whenever it finds them cheaper than men, they themselves have a just claim to the good along with the evil, and, being forced into industrial

4. Charles Kingsley (1819–1875), Christian Socialist and author of *The Water-Babies*. The line "For men must work and women must weep" is from his poem "The Three Fishers."

life, it is for them to choose, if possible, any work for which their tenderer, feebler, physical powers seem particularly adapted.

Let us now turn to France. It is two years since I was in Lyons, and with the introductions of M. Arles Dufours, one of the leading merchants and most enlightened economists of France, visited several of the *ateliers* (workshops) where not more than six women are employed in the silk-weaving, under a mistress, or where sometimes the family only work among themselves. The conditions of this manufacture are very peculiar, the silk being bought by the merchants and allotted to the weavers, who bring it to the warehouse in a finished state, so that there is a singular absence of the bustle of English trade; there is comparatively little speculation, and in many ways the work is conducted in a mode rendering it easy for the female workers.

Little by little there rises, however, a tendency to an industrial change. This subject is amply and eloquently discussed in those remarkable articles, from the pen of M. Jules Simon, which appeared in the *Revue des Deux Mondes*, and which are now gathered into a volume entitled "*L'Ouvrière*," the workwoman. He believes that the greater production which steam power creates will gradually tempt the Lyonese merchants to turn into master manufacturers, destroying the *ateliers* and the family work in common. At the time of my visit I only heard of one establishment actually in work on a large scale, and that was some miles out of the town, and had been created chiefly on a religious and charitable basis, that is to say, the young female apprentices are bound for three years, and are under charge of a community of religious women; but M. Simon mentions three principal houses of this kind, and alludes to others. Adult workmen are also received, being bound for eighteen months. The moral advantages of the surveillance exercised over the girls is apparent in the fact that they are more readily sought in marriage by respectable workmen than girls apprenticed in Lyons; yet the gathering together of numbers is surely, in itself, to be regretted, as paving the way for the adoption of the same principle for the mere sake of economical advantage. While families, however, eagerly seek the shelter for their daughters, the masters make no profits, because they are conducting business in a manner at variance with the habits of the surrounding trade; which instantly retrenches in an unfavorable season in a way which is impossible to a great establishment with an expensive plant.

The very same idea is being in this year of 1861 carried out in the French colony of Algiers for the first time. As I was an eye-witness of its commencement, in the month of January last, it may be of use for me to relate in what way—half-economical, half-charitable—the germ of a vast system of female industry may spring up. About three miles from the town of Algiers is a ravine of the most beautiful and romantic description, called from some local tradition *La Femme Sauvage*. It winds about among the steep hills, its sides clothed with the pine, the ilex, the olive, and with an underwood of infinite variety and loveliness. Wild flowers grow there in rich profusion, and under the bright blue sky of that almost tropical climate it seems as if anything so artificial and unnatural as our systems of industry could hardly exist for shame; yet in that very valley young female children are at this very moment, while I speak and you listen, winding silk for twelve clear hours a day!

The conditions of the case are as follows:—Considerably nearer the town is a large orphanage, containing about 400 children, under the care of the sisters of St. Vincent de Paul. Many of them are half-castes, others the poorest dregs as it were of the French population; and they are exactly the same material as in England or Ireland would be drifted into workhouses. Of course, in a place like Algiers, of limited colonial population and resources, it is no easy matter to find a profitable occupation for 400 orphan girls, and therefore when M. R——, (the very same gentleman who had organized M. B——'s factory near Lyons,) set up a silk-winding mill in *La Femme Sauvage*, the Algerine Government, which pays a considerable sum towards the support of the orphanage, were glad to apprentice thirty girls to M. R——, to be bound from the age of thirteen to that of twenty-one and to work, according to the usual conditions of French industry, twelve hours a day. The work consisted of winding the raw silk from the cocoon, by hand, aided by a slight machinery, and then in another part of the factory spinning it by means of the ordinary apparatus into skeins of silk ready for the market of the Lyons weavers. Three Sisters of Charity accompanied the children, and were to superintend them at all times, in the dormitory, the dining-room, and on Sundays, their only day of recreation. When the thirty apprentices were duly trained, M. R——was prepared to take seventy more, who were also to be accompanied by their devoted superintendents; so that if not at this moment, at all events before long, there will be 100 girls steadily training in that secluded valley, a thousand miles from here, the forerunners of a social change which may gradually develop Algiers into a manufacturing country, and absorb the lives of an untold number of women. I attended the little fête of installation, when a high ecclesiastical dignitary of Algiers came to perform divine service at the little chapel on the premises; he was accompanied by several of the civic functionaries of the town, whose carriages stood in the ravine, making quite a festive bustle. The two partners were gay and smiling—indeed, I believe them to have been good men, delighted not merely with the business aspects but with the benevolent side of their scheme; the sisters were radiantly pleased with the prospects of their charges; the dormitories were airy and wholesome, the dining-room and kitchen clean and commodious. The hundred girls, after being taught a respectable trade and enjoying careful moral superintendence during their youthful years, would be free at twenty-one, and would probably find respectable marriages without difficulty. Things being as they are in this modern life of ours it was undoubtedly a good and kind scheme, well and carefully carried out; careful for the welfare of the children in this world and the next; and yet, perhaps, you will not wonder that I could not help thinking of those poor children at their eternal spinnings whenever in after spring days I walked over the wild hills and through the scented glens of Algiers; and that they brought home to me, from the vivid contrast of the untrammelled nature around me, what perhaps in Europe might never strike the heart with equal vividness, that our modern civilization is in some respects a very singular thing when the kind hearts of a great nation can best show their kindness to orphan girls by shutting them up to spin silk at a machine for twelve hours a day from the age of thirteen to that of twenty-one.

Eight years of youthful girlhood with the smallest possibility during that time of sewing, cooking, sweeping, dusting, and with neither play nor instruction except the little they can pick up on Sunday. What will they be like in the year 1869!

So much for silk at Lyons and Algiers; and remembering that at Lyons the mode of industry is as yet very favorable to women, let us see how matters stand in regard to cotton and woollen at Rouen and at Lille, where, as a rule, the system of large factories already prevails. Referring to M. Simon's book we find that he starts on the first page of his preface with stating that he has passed more than a year in visiting the principal centres of industry in France, and that whereas the workman was once an intelligent force, he is now only an intelligence directing a force—that of steam; and that the immediate consequence of the change has been to replace men by women, because women are cheaper, and can direct the steam force with equal efficiency. "A few years ago," says he, "we had very little mechanical weaving, and, so to speak, no spinning by machinery; now, France has definitely and gloriously taken her place among the countries of large production," (*la grande industrie*.) He speaks of the men gathered together in regiments of labor presenting a firm and serried face to the powers of the State, no longer needing a rallying cry of opposition, since they are in mutual intercourse for twelve hours a day. "And what," he asks, "shall we say of the women? Formerly isolated in their households, now herded together in manufactories. When Colbert, the Minister of Louis XIV., was seeking how to regenerate the agricultural and industrial resources of France, he wished to collect the women into workshops, foreseeing the pecuniary advantages of such a concentration, but even his all-powerful will failed to accomplish this end; and France, which loves to live under a system of rigid administration, makes an exception in favor of domestic life, and would fain feel itself independent within four walls. But that which Colbert failed to achieve, even with the help of Louis the Great, a far more powerful monarch has succeeded in bringing to pass. From the moment when steam appeared in the industrial world, the wheel, the spindle, and the distaff broke in the hand, and the spinsters and weavers, deprived of their ancient livelihood, fled to the shadow of the tall factory chimney." "The mothers," says M. Simon, "have left the hearth and the cradle, and the young girls and the little children themselves have run to offer their feeble arms; whole villages are silent, while huge brick buildings swallow up thousands of living humanity from dawn of day until twilight shades."

Need I say more, except to point out that when once any new social or industrial principle has, so to speak, fairly set in, the last remains of the old system stand their ground with extreme difficulty against the advancing tide, and that trades by which solitary workers can earn a sufficient livelihood are every day decreasing in value, or being swept off into *la grande industrie*. Sewing will assuredly all be wrought in factories before long; the silk work, which formerly stretched down the valley of the Rhone as far as Avignon, has gradually drawn up to Lyons, leaving the city of the Popes empty and desolate within its vast walls. At Dijon, M. Maitre has gathered up the leather work of that ancient capital into his admirably organized *ateliers*, where he employs two hundred men and one hundred women, and binds prayer-books and photographic albums and *porte-monnaies*[5] enough to supply an immense retail trade in Paris. In England it is the same: we gather our people together and together, we cheapen and cheapen that which we produce. Did you ever, when children, play with quicksilver, and watch the tiny glittering balls attracted in larger and larger globules until they all rolled together into one? Such is the law of modern industry in England and France, and in all other countries according as they follow the lead of these two nations in the theoretic principles of life which lead to those results which are at once the triumph and the dark side of modern civilization.

Having thus pointed out the conditions under which so large a proportion of our national commercial prosperity is carried on, permit me to say a few words regarding the practical consequences and duties it entails. Nobody can doubt, that so vast a social change must be gradually inducing an equally great moral change, and that some

5. Purses.

of the consequences must be bad. I am careful to limit my expressions, because it must not be forgotten that I have not spoken to-day of the poor or of the degraded, but of the bulk of the factory workpeople of England and France, and of large classes in Scotland and Ireland, who earn their bread by respectable industry and are often the main support of their families. It is true, that I have heard and could tell grievous stories of the wild, half-savage state of the women and girls in some districts, in some factories, under some bad or careless masters; but that is not the side of things to which I wish to draw attention:—it is rather to the *inevitable* results of non-domestic labor for women and to the special duties it imposes on those of a higher class. In the first place, there are the obvious results of the absence of married women from their homes, an absence which I believe we may fairly state, should, in the majority of instances, be discouraged by every possible moral means, since the workman must be very wretched indeed before his wife's absence can be a source of real gain. Then there is the utter want of domestic teaching and training during the most important years of youth. How to help this is no easy matter, since, whatever we may do in regard to married women, we certainly cannot prevent girls from being employed in factories, nor, in the present state of civilization, provide other work for them if we could so prevent them; and lastly, there is what I believe to be the sure deterioration of health; we are as yet only in the second generation, but any one who has closely watched the effect of ten hours in England and twelve hours in France, of labor chiefly conducted in a standing posture amidst the noise and, in some cases, the necessary heat of factories, upon young growing girls, knows how the weakly ones are carried off by consumption, or any hereditary morbid tendency, and what the subtle nervous strain must be upon all.

Believe me, there is enough in the necessary, and what we have come to consider the natural, features of modern industry, to arouse the earnest conscientious attention of the wives and daughters of employers, and of all good women whom Providence has gifted with education and means. And the need is peculiar, and so must the help be. Except in some isolated cases we will hope and believe that it is not, strictly speaking, missionary work. It is not to teach the wholly uneducated, to reclaim the drunkard, to rouse the sinner; there is enough of that to be done in England and France, but it is not of that I am speaking. Help and teaching and friendliness are wanting for the respectable workwoman, such as have already been partly provided for the respectable workman. When Lord Brougham, Dr. Birkbeck, and others, started the Mechanics' Institution,[6] when clas-

---

6. George Birkbeck (1776–1841) is credited with founding the Mechanics' Institutes, educational institutions for working men. He was supported in this by Lord Brougham (1778–1868), the prominent reformist peer.

ses, and lectures, and savings' banks, and co-operative societies were created, it was to help those who were willing and able to help themselves, if put in the way. The Christian ministers of all churches and persuasions have generally of late years entered with warmth into these secular plans for the advantage of their flocks; and it is just such an intelligent effort, carried out by earnest and intellectual women, which is required wherever numbers of their own sex are gathered together to labor. I do not mean that the plans should be identical, but that the level of effort and of sympathy should be the same. I would see every large factory sustained in its moral advancement by female teachers capable of entering into the moral and physical life of the people; I would see evening classes, co-operative societies, and mothers' meetings of an upper sort, vigorously set on foot. I would have the amusements of the younger people guided, restrained, and elevated; and those women of the middle classes who crave for more activity, yet do not feel that they possess the peculiar characteristics needed to visit the very poor, to nurse the very sick, or to reform the very degraded, remember that there is an immense, an inspiriting field of exertion, one demanding intellect, study, and sympathetic apprehension of the social forces now at work in England and France, which calls for their religious endeavor and intelligent will.

HENRY BRISTOW WILSON

[The Clergyman and His Conscience]†

* * * As far as opinion privately entertained is concerned, the liberty of the English clergyman appears already to be complete. For no ecclesiastical person can be obliged to answer interrogations as to his opinions, nor be troubled for that which he has not actually expressed, nor be made responsible for inferences which other people may draw from his expressions.

Still, though there may be no power of inquisition into the private opinions either of ministers or people in the Church of England, there may be some interference with the expression of them; and a great restraint is supposed to be imposed upon the clergy by reason

† From "Séances Historiques de Genève: The National Church," in *Essays and Reviews* (1860). Wilson (1803–1888) was an Anglican clergyman who, as a result of his essay in which he argued for greater freedom for clergymen in matters of conscience, was tried by the ecclesiastical courts for heresy. He was convicted on three of the charges, but these convictions were quashed on appeal. *Essays and Reviews* is a volume of essays by liberal theologians and clergymen which attempts to introduce modern thinking on a number of theological issues. I have omitted Wilson's own footnotes [*Editor*].

of their subscription to the Thirty-nine Articles. Yet it is more difficult than might be expected, to define what is the extent of the legal
obligation of those who sign them; and in this case the strictly legal
obligation is the measure of the moral one. Subscription may be
thought even to be inoperative upon the conscience by reason of its
vagueness. For the act of subscription is enjoined, but its effect or
meaning nowhere plainly laid down; and it does not seem to amount
to more than an acceptance of the Articles of the Church as the
formal law to which the subscriber is in some sense subject. What
that subjection amounts to, must be gathered elsewhere, for it does
not appear on the face of the subscription itself.

The ecclesiastical authority on the subject is to be found in the
Canons of 1603,[1] the fifth and the thirty-sixth. The fifth, indeed,
may be applicable theoretically both to lay and to ecclesiastical persons; practically it can only concern those of whom subscription is
really required. It is entitled, *Impugners of the Articles of Religion
established in this Church of England censured.* 'Whosoever shall
hereafter affirm, that any of the nine and thirty articles, &c., are in
any part superstitious or erroneous, or such as he may not with a
good conscience subscribe unto, let him be excommunicated, &c.'
We need not stay to consider what the effects of excommunication
might be, but rather attend to the definition which the canon itself
supplies of 'impugning.' It is stated to be the affirming, that any of
the Thirty-nine Articles are in any part 'superstitious or erroneous.'
Yet an article may be very inexpedient, or become so; may be unin-
telligible, or not easily intelligible to ordinary people; it may be controversial, and such as to provoke controversy and keep it alive when
otherwise it would subside; it may revive unnecessarily the remembrance of dead controversies—all or any of these, without being
'erroneous;' and though not 'superstitious,' some expressions may
appear so, such as those which seem to impute an occult operation
to the Sacraments. The fifth canon does not touch the affirming any
of these things, and more especially, that the Articles present truths
disproportionately, and relatively to ideas not now current.

The other canon which concerns subscription is the thirty-sixth,
which contains two clauses explanatory to some extent, of the meaning of ministerial subscription, 'That he *alloweth* the Book of Articles, &c.' and 'that he *acknowledgeth* the same to be agreeable to the
Word of God.' We 'allow' many things which we do not think wise
or practically useful; as the less of two evils, or an evil which cannot
be remedied, or of which the remedy is not attainable, or is uncertain

---

1. The *Constitutions and Canons Ecclesiastical* were drawn up and debated at the convocation
of Canterbury in 1603. Although they lacked parliamentary authority, they became the
legal basis for the governance of the Church of England. The "Thirty-nine Articles" date
from 1562 and are effectively a list of requirements to which all Anglican clergymen must
subscribe when taking a new living.

in its operation, or is not in our power, or concerning which there is much difference of opinion, or where the initiation of any change does not belong to ourselves, nor the responsibility belong to ourselves, either of the things as they are, or searching for something better. Many acquiesce in, submit to, 'allow,' a law as it operates upon themselves which they would be horror-struck to have enacted; yet they would gladly and in conscience, 'allow' and submit to it, as part of a constitution under which they live, against which they would never think of rebelling, which they would on no account undermine, for the many blessings of which they are fully grateful— they would be silent and patient rather than join, even in appearance, the disturbers and breakers of its laws. Secondly, he 'acknowledgeth' the same to be agreeable to the Word of God. Some distinctions may be founded upon the word 'acknowledge.' He does not maintain, nor regard it as self-evident, nor originate it as his own feeling, spontaneous opinion, or conviction; but when it is suggested to him, put in a certain shape, when the intention of the framers is borne in mind, their probable purpose and design explained, together with the difficulties which surrounded them, he is not prepared to contradict, and he acknowledges. There is a great deal to be said, which had not at first occurred to him; many other better and wiser men than himself have acknowledged the same thing—why should he be obstinate? Besides, he is young, and has plenty of time to reconsider it; or he is old and continues to submit out of habit, and it would be too absurd, at his time of life, to be setting up as a Church reformer.

But after all, the important phrase is, that the Articles are 'agreeable to the Word of God.' This cannot mean that the Articles are precisely co-extensive with the Bible, much less of equal authority with it as a whole. Neither separately, nor altogether, do they embody all which is said in it, and inferences which they draw from it are only good relatively and *secundum quid* and *quatenus concordant*.[2] If their terms are Biblical terms, they must be presumed to have the same sense in the Articles which they have in the Scripture; and if they are not all Scriptural ones, they undertake in the pivot Article not to contradict the Scripture. The Articles do not make any assumption of being interpretations of Scripture or developments of it. The greater must include the less, and the Scripture is the greater.

On the other hand, there may be some things in the Articles which could not be contained, or have not been contained, in the Scripture—such as propositions or clauses concerning historical facts

---

2. Accordingly and in proportion to (Latin).

more recent than the Scripture itself; for instance, that there never has been any doubt in the Church concerning the books of the New Testament. * * * But as the canon grew, book after book emerging into existence and general reception, there were doubts as to some of them, for a longer or shorter period, either concerning their authorship or their authority. The framers of the Articles were not deficient in learning, and could not have been ignorant of the passages in Eusebius[3] where the different books current in Christendom in his time are classified as genuine or acknowledged, doubtful and spurious. If there be an erroneousness in such a statement, as that there never was any doubt in the Church concerning the book of the Revelation, the Epistle to the Hebrews, or the second of St. Peter, it cannot be an erroneousness in the sense of the fifth canon, nor can it be at variance with the Word of God according to the thirty-sixth. Such things in the Articles as are beside the Scripture are not in the contemplation of the canons. Much less can historical questions not even hinted at in the Articles be excluded from free discussion—such as concern the dates and composition of the several books, the compilation of the Pentateuch, the introduction of Daniel into the Jewish canon, and the like with some books of the New Testament—the date and authorship, for instance, of the fourth Gospel.

* * *

We have spoken hitherto of the signification of subscription which may be gathered from the canons; there is, also, a statute, a law of the land, which forbids, under penalties, the advisedly and directly contradicting any of them by ecclesiastics, and requires subscription with declaration of 'assent' from beneficed persons. This statute (13 Eliz. c. 12), three hundred years old, like many other old enactments, is not found to be very applicable to modern cases; although it is only about fifty years ago that it was said by Sir William Scott to be *in viridi observantiâ*.[4] Nevertheless, its provisions would not easily be brought to bear on questions likely to be raised in our own days.

* * *

If, however, the Articles of religion and the law of the Church of England be in effect liberal, flexible, or little stringent, is there any necessity for expressing dissatisfaction with them, any sufficient

---

3. Eusebius of Caeserea (c. 235–339), theologian and historian. His *History of the Church* in eight volumes was written between 308 and 311 and was a founding work of church history.
4. Broadly, "present to the minds of men"—i.e., in current observation (Latin).

provocation to change? There may be much more liberty in a Church like our own, the law of which is always interpreted, according to the English spirit, in the manner most favourable to those who are subject to its discipline, than in one which, whether free or not from Articles, might be empowered to develop doctrine and to denounce new heresies. * * *

* * * Obsolete tests are a blot upon a modern system, and there is always some danger lest an antiquated rule may be unexpectedly revived for the sake of an odious individual application; when it has outlived its general regulative power, it may still be a trap for the weaker consciences; or when it has become powerless as to penal consequences, it may serve to give a point to invidious imputations.

* * *

For, the act of subscription being abolished, there would disappear the invidious distinction between the clergy and laity of the same communion, as if there were separate standards for each of belief and morals. There would disappear also a semblance of a promissory oath on a subject which a promise is incapable of reaching. No promise can reach fluctuations of opinion and personal conviction. Open teaching can, it is true, if it be thought wise, be dealt with by the law and its penalties; but the law should content itself with saying, you shall not teach or proclaim in derogation of my formularies; it should not require any act which appears to signify 'I think.' Let the security be either the penal or the moral one, not a commingling of the two. It happens continually, that able and sincere persons are deterred from entering the ministry of the national Church by this consideration. * * *

It may be easy to urge invidiously, with respect to the impediments now existing to undertaking office in the national Church, that there are other sects, which persons dissatisfied with her formularies may join, and where they may find scope for their activity with little intellectual bondage. Nothing can be said here, whether or not there might be elsewhere bondage at least as galling, of a similar or another kind. But the service of the national Church may well be regarded in a different light from the service of a sect. It is as properly an organ of the national life as a magistracy, or a legislative estate. To set barriers before the entrance upon its functions, by limitations not absolutely required by public policy, is to infringe upon the birthright of the citizens. And to lay down as an alternative to striving for more liberty of thought and expression within the Church of the nation, that those who are dissatisfied may sever themselves and join a sect, would be paralleled by declaring to political reformers, that they are welcome to expatriate themselves, if they desire any change in the existing forms of the constitution. The suggestion of the alternative is an insult; if it could be enforced, it would be a grievous wrong.

*   *   *

CRITICISM

LOUIS CAZAMIAN

Mrs Gaskell and Christian Interventionism: *North and South*†

Six years separate the publication of *Mary Barton* and *North and South* (1854–55). In the interval the continental upheaval of 1848 had shaken the social order, and the resultant reaction had established it more firmly than ever. The tone of philanthropic literature after 1850 was different from what it had been before. A new timidity inhibited the most wholehearted supporters of intervention. The revolution in Paris had impressed itself on people's minds; they felt vaguely that moderation was necessary since excesses had been committed, and their reforming intentions were directed towards prudent solutions by a more or less conscious fear of starting something that might get out of hand. Mrs Gaskell too shared this general tendency. Or perhaps it should be said that the development of her thought led her to correct what over the years she came to see, as did other idealists, as the intransigence of her earlier beliefs. In the end she was hurt by the accusations of bias her critics threw at her. Moreover *North and South*, structurally, is to *Mary Barton* as *Coningsby* is to *Sybil*:[1] there is a similar change in the social basis: we are concerned with employers rather than workers, and from a vantage point among the middle classes, only see the proletariat from the outside. This changed point of view inevitably gave Mrs Gaskell a new perception of the problems. The tone of the book also led to a softening of *Mary Barton*'s impassioned eloquence. Nevertheless the new book, like the old one, demonstrates her familiarity with the workers. Some scenes take us into weavers' homes, and the general feeling is close to the interventionism recommended in *Mary Barton*.

In *North and South* the industrial question is no longer the whole of the novel. Manchester—renamed Milton in the book—stands for the industrialised, despoiled areas which, in turn, become one of the two poles on which England turns. The opposition is between the old and the new forms of civilisation, rather than merely capital and labour. The slow-moving agricultural South, pastorally idyllic, is contrasted with the feverish energy and tough austerity of the

---

† From *Le Roman Social en Angleterre* (1903), translated by Martin Fido as *The Social Novel in England* (London and Boston: Routledge and Kegan Paul, 1973), chap. 7, pp. 226–31. Reprinted by permission of Taylor & Francis Books, Ltd. Cazamian (1877–1965) was a French scholar and literary historian. His book is the first full-scale study of the industrial novel. Page references are to this Norton Critical Edition.

1. Novels on the industrial theme by Benjamin Disraeli, published in 1844 and 1845, respectively.

North. This profound contrast was, for the future, to be an essential part of English life and a fertile theme for moral, economic, and artistic consideration. It was quite an achievement on Mrs Gaskell's part to have grasped this clearly so soon, and to have characterised decisively some aspects, at least, of the question. Disraeli had gestured towards it in *Sybil*: the nation of the rich, by and large, live in the aristocratic South, and the reader is taken north to find the nation of the poor. But geography and economics did not tally precisely: the agricultural proletariat formed a 'Northern' enclave in Disraeli's South. He was, after all, primarily concerned with social opposition, to which he subordinated little picturesque effects. Mrs Gaskell, on the other hand, used her sensibilities to establish contrasts. Her imagination and senses could perceive the theoretical boundary dividing the green sunlit fields, where grey church towers rose behind aged oaks, and poets had idealised peasant poverty, from the noisy, smoky blackened cities, where the crowds moved gloomily between ugly little houses. Mrs Gaskell put a little of her own feeling into drawing the contrast. Her childhood and youth in Knutsford, and schooldays in Stratford, had given her a deep attachment to the splendid beauty of the English countryside. When she was abruptly uprooted she was only conscious of the full horror of Manchester, though as she became more accustomed to it she was won over by the affections and sympathy of the North. The personal note in *North and South* arises from this, as does the true feeling for modern England's economic dualism, which is so well conveyed.

Industrial civilisation had a certain grandeur and beauty. It shared the solid merits of the men who had built it: dogged energy and initiative. If its environment was joyless, its capacity for human passion ran strong and deep. If the social setting seemed drab and utilitarian, the class struggle was savage, and there was room for huge improvement through education. It was a harsh, unyielding soil, but it might bring forth fruits of peace and justice when tilled by gentle intelligence and religious or humanitarian missions. The proud and worldly London merchants and southern squires who dismissed Northern manufacturers as 'tradesmen' were making a grave mistake, as were the cultivated university-educated humanists, like Mr Bell the tutor, who detested the iron qualities of the steam age. Manchester's barbarism should be seen as the birth-pangs of a new civilisation in which Northern energy and Southern grace would be harmoniously united.

Here, as in Disraeli, a marriage symbolises the social reconciliation. Margaret Hale is the daughter of an Anglican parson in Hampshire. She is a gentle, sensitive beauty, with aristocratic good looks, but also a proud spirit and headstrong will. (Mrs Gaskell had no wish to give the North exclusive rights to character.) From her childhood she has loved the simple poetry of country life. Her heart goes out to ruined cottages as she draws them. She has not escaped the prejudices of her background: she condemns the spirit of commerce without knowing anything about it, and dismisses the work of the industrial bourgeoisie as all being selfishly motivated. And then her father gives up his parish, from religious scruples. He goes to live in Milton, in the heart of the industrial area. At first Margaret is made utterly miserable by the move. The city is ugly; the populace crude; and the upper classes blunt, opinionated, and narrow-minded. A manufacturer called Thornton comes to know the family better and better. At first he affronts Margaret's delicacy with his harsh manner, but she is compelled to respect his vehement independence. And after their hostile meeting, the two end in unity, by a slow progress whose minute stages are traced by Mrs Gaskell. Each yields a little intransigence. Thornton's association with the Hales makes him more gracious and cultivated. Margaret penetrates the dry, abrasive surface of the North, and finds the deep affections underneath. When she has been orphaned and enriched by a legacy, she sends for Thornton, who is threatened with bankruptcy as his business has been going badly. Will he accept a loan? And as the manufacturer, trembling with emotion, wishes to kneel before her, she rests her lovely head on his strong shoulder.

That is the main plot of *North and South*. It casts an interesting light on the differences between Northerners and Southerners, and is even finer as a psychological study in contrasting personalities. The moral drama, too, has a severe, powerful beauty. Mrs Gaskell evinces great skill in handling her characters' interior lives, in the scenes where old Mr Hale announces his cruel decision to his family, or where Margaret, in the midst of her daily tasks, reflects on her capacity for self-denial. But from our point of view, greater interest attaches to a sub-plot devoted to the problem of industry. The author found it easy to link the two narratives. The second, like the first, is built around the contrast between North and South, and Margaret Hale's influence converts Thornton to philanthropy. The manufacturer's faults, from the standpoint of that Christian kindness which ought to govern social relations, are similar to his cultural inadequacies, from the standpoint of superior cultivation. Once again the employer's failings are pride, severity, and want of feeling. His workpeople look upon him as

> what the Bible calls a 'hard man'—not so much unjust as unfeeling; clear in judgement, standing upon his 'rights' as no human being ought to stand, considering what we and all our petty rights are in the sight of the Almighty. (p. 152)

Like Carson,[2] Thornton is a self-made man. His father died bankrupt, leaving him debts which he paid off by determined work. His mother, whose nature is as indefatigable and indomitable as his own, helped him along the road to success with stern affection. He has worked on, absorbed in his daily tasks, his attention directed to the ambition which had become the focal point of his life: to win and maintain an honourable place among Britain's industrialists. Wealth is not an end in itself for him; only a means of gaining authority and social standing. He is proud of his factory, where the latest machinery is in use: 'There is not such another factory in Milton. One room alone is two hundred and twenty square yards' (p. 147). But his struggle has cut him off from any understanding of hardship. He is hard on the weak, and is too strong-willed to make any allowance for their weakness. He generalises from his own experience, and puts unbounded faith in the power of hard work and individual independence. 'It is one of the great beauties of our system, that a working-man may raise himself into the power and position of a master by his own exertions and behaviour' (p. 78). He is implacably opposed to restrictive legislation, and refuses to interfere in the lives of his workers: his ideas of justice come into conflict with charity itself. He is a bitter enemy of trade unions: 'Upon my word, mother, I wish the old combination laws were in force' (p. 132). He is the epitome of individualism's finest virtues, and worst excesses.

The industrial drama is similar to that in *Mary Barton*. Misunderstandings between the classes lead to a strike, and all the violence associated with it. Under pressure of competition from America the owners cut wages, although their own prosperity seems undiminished. Mrs Gaskell argues that the action was justified, but they should at least have explained it. Thornton refuses arrogantly: 'Do you give your servants reasons for your expenditure, or your economy in the use of your own money? We, the owners of capital, have a right to choose what we will do with it' (p. 108). As the strike goes on, he brings in starving men from Ireland, ready to undertake any work whatsoever. The workers immediately rise in protest. They have been worn down, and their morale is slipping as a result of their long patient strike. At home their wives and children are weeping with hunger, and now it seems that their last hope has been brutally overthrown, and the victory for which they have suffered so much will be taken from them. A maddened crowd storms the factory, breaks down the gates, and threatens to kill the Irish. Thornton defies them, standing on the steps of his house with folded arms while they hurl stones at him. His life is in danger, until Margaret throws herself before him to shield him with her body, and the rioters' hesitation

2. In *Mary Barton* [Editor].

is turned to flight when armed troops arrive. Soon the strike is over, and Thornton seems to have won outright. But he has been shaken by the challenge thrown at him by Margaret during the riot:

'Mr. Thornton,' said Margaret, shaking all over with her passion, 'go down this instant, if you are not a coward. Go down and face them like a man. Save these poor strangers whom you have decoyed here. Speak to your workmen as if they were human beings. Speak to them kindly. Don't let the soldiers come in and cut down poor creatures who are driven mad.' (p. 161).

For a long time, he is troubled by the implications of this reproach. And his heart has been softened by love, so that he can accept the value of charity which he has never thought about before. He learns that one of the ringleaders of the strike has been turned away from work everywhere, and has drowned himself. So when old Higgins, the trade unionist, comes to ask for work, and meets his reproof with a resolute defence of working-class solidarity, he 'forgets entirely the mere reasonings of justice, and overleaps them by a diviner instinct' (p. 296). A man-to-man sympathy grows up between master and worker, and gradually Thornton becomes involved with the lives of fellow-creatures whom he previously chose to ignore. We see him, rather hesitantly, help them in organising a co-operative dining-room. And we hear him expounding new ideas which echo Carlyle:[3]

'My only wish is to have the opportunity of cultivating some intercourse with the hands beyond the mere 'cash nexus'. . . .
'I have arrived at the conviction that no mere institutions, however wise, and however much thought may have been required to organize and arrange them, can attach class to class as they should be attached, unless the working out of such institutions bring the individuals of the different classes into actual personal contact. Such intercourse is the very breath of life.' (p. 391)

Margaret has come to know Nicholas Higgins. We follow her to the bedside of his daughter Bessy, who has contracted consumption as a result of long hours in the factory:

'I think I was well when mother died, but I have never been rightly strong sin' somewhere about that time. I began to work in a carding-room soon after, and the fluff got into my lungs and poisoned me.'
'Fluff?' said Margaret inquiringly.
'Fluff,' repeated Bessy. 'Little bits, as fly off fro' the cotton,

---

3. The reference is to Thomas Carlyle's comment that 'cash payment has become the sole nexus of man to man' in *Chartism*, chap. 2. There is a similar comment in Carlyle's *Past and Present*, bk. III, chap. 9.

when they're carding it, and fill the air till it looks all fine white
dust. They say it winds round the lungs, and tightens them up.
Anyhow, there's many a one as works in a carding-room, that
falls into a waste, coughing and spitting blood, because they're
just poisoned by the fluff.'

'But can't it be helped?' asked Margaret.

'I dunno. Some folk have a great wheel at one end o' their
carding-rooms to make a draught, and carry off th' dust; but
that wheel costs a deal of money—five or six hundred pound,
maybe, and brings in no profit: so it's but few of th' masters as
will put 'em up: and I've heard tell o' men who didn't like working in places where there was a wheel, because they said as how
it made 'em hungry, as after they'd been long used to swallowing
fluff, to go without it, and that their wage ought to be raised if
they were to work in such places. So between masters and men
th' wheels fall through. I know I wish there'd been a wheel in
our place, though.' (p. 94)

She has never seen the countryside:

'When I have gone for an out, I've always wanted to get high up
and see far away, and take a deep breath o' fullness in that air.
I get smothered enough in Milton, and I think the sound yo'
speak of among the trees, going on for ever and ever, would
send me dazed; it's that made my head ache so in the mill.'
(p. 93)

When Bessy dies, Margaret, on a kindly impulse, takes Higgins to
meet her father, and the old pastor finds himself confronted with a
working-class atheist. Higgins has the same blunt, sensible direct-
ness and simplicity as John Barton, with more good humour, and
less bitterness. He tells the decent, honest, middle-class folk around
him of his life and his feelings, and although Mrs Gaskell intends
that their religious faith should emerge comfortably superior to his
unbelief, she allows him some shrewd hits: 'If salvation, and life to
come, and what not, was true—not in men's words, but in men's
hearts' core—dun yo' think they'd din us wi' it as they do wi' political
'conomy?' (p. 208).

Mrs Gaskell appealed to her readers with sober, truthful realism.
Her characters were convincing, individual human beings. The
reader was made to feel that he was meeting people from another
class on an intimate footing. As he heard them he came to understand their joys and sorrows, and the justice of their inarticulate
complaints was made crystal clear. *North and South*, moreover, was
even more likely than *Mary Barton* to encourage every well-
intentioned individual without affronting anyone. Its more cautious
didacticism could only add to its effectiveness.

A. W. WARD

[*North and South* in Context]†

"North and South" has always seemed to me, and seems to me more than ever after a careful reperusal, one of the finest of modern English fictions. Like the great statue of the famous Florentine, it was cast, head and foot, in a single piece—all the metal flowing in from the same fire.[1] Human kindness, the sympathetic sense of contrasts in which resides the essence of true humour, and the burning passion of love—all these, with much else, contributed to the current. And yet, so it chanced, the novel was the first which its authoress wrote bit by bit; just as, by a curious coincidence, Dickens' "Hard Times," which preceded Mrs. Gaskell's story in the same periodical, and which presents other points of contact with its successor, was the first story ever brought out by him in weekly instalments.[2] It is well known that the inconveniences of the experiment, to which Mrs. Gaskell bears testimony in the Prefatory Note to the original edition, were, according to his wont, stated by Dickens in the most emphatic of terms. "The difficulty of the space," he wrote, after a few weeks' trial, "is CRUSHING. Nobody can have an idea of it who has not had an experience of patient fiction-writing with some elbow-room always, and open places in perspective. In this form, with every kind of regard to the current number, there is no such thing." "North and South" first came out in "Household Words," where it appeared in the numbers extending from September 2, 1854, to January 27, 1855. It was first published as a complete work (by Messrs. Chapman and Hall), in two volumes, in 1855, and went through many subsequent editions. A French translation of it, by Mmes. Lerau and H. de l'Espigne, was published in 1859, and, in a second edition, in 1865.

Although it was "Sylvia's Lovers"—a work of later date—which Mrs. Gaskell chose for dedication to her husband, he can hardly have taken a deeper interest in any of her books than that with which he watched, and furthered, the production, first of "Mary Barton," and then of "North and South." Mr. Gaskell's heart, like his wife's, was,

† From "Introduction to *North and South*," *The Works of Mrs. Gaskell*, 8 vols. (London: John Murray, 1906), "The Knutsford Edition," vol. 4, pp. xi–xxvii. Adolphus William Ward (1837–1924) was appointed as the first professor of History and English Literature at Owens College, later to become the University of Manchester, in 1866, the year after Gaskell's death. He knew William Gaskell, and remained in Manchester until 1897. His edition of Gaskell's works is the first comprehensive edition. Notes are the Editor's.
1. The bronze equestrian statue of Cosimo de' Medici that stands in the Piazza della Signoria in Florence.
2. This, in fact, is not so. Both *The Old Curiosity Shop* and *Barnaby Rudge* first appeared in weekly installments in *Master Humphrey's Clock* (1840–41).

as has been seen, with the people among whom they dwelt; and the best of his remarkable powers were given to his ministerial work in Lancashire—the sphere of his life's labours, though not, strictly speaking, his native county. As was written of him after his death by one who had long looked up to him as a teacher of literature, "much as he liked Nature and everything that was beautiful in scenery and in art, he was most at home in cities, where he could see and study, and love and guide, the men and women with whom he came into contact." He watched and noted the thoughts and feelings of the "Darkshire" folk as closely as he traced their ways and forms of speech. It was in 1854, the year in which the publication of "North and South" opened, that he brought out his two "Lectures on the Lancashire Dialect," which were in the same year appended to the fifth edition of "Mary Barton." He must at the same time have been pursuing his favourite study of German poetry—and hymnology in particular—among whose fruits were the translations contributed by him to Miss Catherine Winkworth's "Lyra Germanica,"[3] of which the first series appeared in 1858. Reminiscences of this study seem to have found their way into one or two of the mottoes prefixed to the chapters of "North and South," which are borrowed from Mr. Gaskell's favourites, Rückert, Uhland, and Kosegarten.

In "North and South" may easily be traced the effects of a perfect union of tastes as well as of affections, which made the companionship of her husband and daughters the greatest happiness of Mrs. Gaskell's life, and helped to mature in her the knowledge of men's and women's hearts—the supreme gift of the writer who undertakes to interpret to others the best, though they may not be the least common, experiences of human life. This book has much to tell of sorrow and suffering; and Miss Edgeworth, had she lived to criticise it, might have been excused for complaining of the number of its death-beds[4]—including those of Mrs. Hale and Mr. Hale, Mr. Bell, Margaret's generous guardian, and Bessy, her humble friend and admirer. Yet the work is, notwithstanding, the product of a happy mind in a happy mood—and at times this happiness finds expression in passages radiant with beauty, and glorious as testifying to the service of Love the Conqueror. Thus the force and charm of the personal sentiment with which the story is instinct correspond to what may be called its chief purpose (since a novel with a purpose it remains)—the endeavour to commend reconciliation through sym-

3. Catherine Winkworth (1827–1878), together with her sister Susanna (1820–1884), was a pupil of William Gaskell and a family friend. She remained unmarried and was active both as a translator of German theology and as a pioneer in the cause of women's education.

4. Maria Edgeworth (1767–1849), the novelist, had previously complained of the number of deaths in *Mary Barton*.

pathy; and this is the solution applied by it to the problems suggested by the nature of the plot and the course of the story.

Most prominent among these problems—though, as will be seen, most felicitously mingled and interfused with difficulties or contrasts of a wholly uncontroversial sort—is the national question as to the relations between masters and men, and the whole social condition of the manufacturing population, to which, in "North and South," the authoress of "Mary Barton" once more addressed herself. If she had in the mean time grown older, calmer—and why should we not say wiser?—without becoming untrue to herself and her noblest instincts, so too the conditions of the national life which affected this question had undergone an unmistakable modification. During the six years, or thereabouts, which passed between the writing of "Mary Barton" and that of "North and South," a change had come over the movement for advancing and improving the condition of the working population, more especially in the manufacturing districts of Lancashire and other parts of the North.

In the first place, few movements involving the interests and affecting the sentiments of large classes of the population are able to escape the common fate of being followed by periods of reaction. The triumph of the agitation against the Corn Laws, which went to the very root of the sufferings of the working-classes, had been complete; and the philanthropic activity of Lord Ashley, and of those who acted with him, had since his return to Parliament in 1847 been chiefly directed to matters of a less controversial character than the practices of the factories and the pits.[5] Moreover, about this time the condition of the Irish population, which went on rapidly from worse to worse, had begun to absorb a large share of attention and munificence. Finally, the revolutionary movements, which shook the Continent of Europe in the years 1848 and 1849, though they left England virtually unaffected, could not but leave behind them in a large part of English society a mingled sense of repugnance and relief. After the failure of the Chartist demonstration in London of April, 1848,[6] the cause which it had intended to advance seemed for many years dead in this country; the Chartist conference held in Manchester early in 1851 was attended by the representatives of not more than four localities; nor was it till 1855 that another attempt was made in the same town to revive the agitation. In general, although notwithstanding the gradual collapse of the Whig Govern-

5. The philanthropist Lord Ashley, later Earl of Shaftesbury, was heavily involved in the reform of working conditions through a sequence of factory acts in the 1830s and 1840s. He then turned his attention to matters of education and housing conditions.
6. In 1848 a huge petition in favor of universal suffrage was presented to parliament by a Chartist delegation. Its rejection marked a significant point in labor history. A fictionalized version of the event features in *Mary Barton*.

ment there was no question of any permanent acceptance by the nation of a Conservative policy, still less of any return to Protectionist principles, yet a period of compromise and tranquillity was at hand in home affairs and internal legislation, which covered both the building of the temple of peace in 1851 and the opening of the gates of war in 1854.[7] Finally, it must not be overlooked that in the manufacturing districts during these years the employed had become more accustomed to, and more expert in, the use of their readiest and most effective weapon of offence, as well as of defence, against their employers; and that strikes (though none seems to have been attempted on a large scale in Manchester between 1848 and 1854) were becoming more frequent in the manufacturing districts at large.

The reaction to which the above and other contemporary causes contributed could not but exercise an influence upon that group of English writers of prose-fiction who had shown so genuine and so special an interest in the condition of our working-classes; who had insisted so strongly on the justice as well as on the expediency of hearing both sides of the questions at issue; and who, whether from a national, a humanitarian, or a Christian point of view, had pleaded that justice should be done to the needs of the employed not less than to the claims of the employers, and that masters and men should meet each other as friends, not as foes.

It so happened that early in the year 1854 Dickens and Mrs. Gaskell, with whom his literary relations had of late been so intimate, each set out upon the composition of a story of which the scene was to be laid in the manufacturing districts, and which, under whatever conditions, could not fail to address itself to the perennial question of the relations between capital and labour—or, better perhaps, for much is involved in the choice of phrase, of the relations between masters and men. Dickens, though his wondrous activity of mind, his breadth of human sympathy, and his hatred of social injustice, could not but excite in him an interest in the manufacturing districts and their population—to which, as in "The Chimes" and "The Old Curiosity Shop," he had already given expression more passionate than convincing—possessed no intimate knowledge either of the North or of the manufacturing classes in general; indeed, neither his upbringing, nor his experience (except incidentally)—nor again, his reading and his tastes—had brought him into close contact with this particular class of our population. In this year, 1854, when he was revolving the story "Hard Times," which was (though somewhat late) to present the full deliverance of his mind on the condition of our manufacturing districts, he travelled to Preston, where at the time

7. The references are to the Great Exhibition at the Crystal Palace (1851) and the onset of the Crimean War (1854).

there was a strike, to catch what he could of the spirit of the conflict, and of its influence upon those concerned in it. But he was much disappointed with what he saw, or rather with what he did not see; and, having ascertained that the people "sit at home and mope," went off himself to witness an indifferent performance of "Hamlet" at the theatre. Even genius cannot satisfactorily report or reproduce what it only imperfectly understands. Dickens' intuitive perception of this truth will not be held to derogate from the characteristic candour and generosity of a passage in a letter which, four months later, he addressed to Mrs. Gaskell, with the general design of whose new story he must by this time have become acquainted:

> "I have no intention of striking. The monstrous claims at dim-inution made by a certain class of manufacturers, and the extent to which the way is made easy for working-men to slide down into discontent under such hands, are within my scheme; but I am not going to strike, so don't be afraid of me. But I wish you would look at the story yourself, and judge where and how near I seem to be approaching what you have in your mind. The first two months of it will show that."

While, from the nature of the case, the publication of the successive portions of "Hard Times," which appeared in "Household Words" from April 1 to August 12, 1854, could not have exercised any but a quite incidental influence upon the composition of Mrs. Gaskell's story, internal evidence shows the latter to have been written in absolute independence of Dickens' work. Thus, while it would be impertinent to offer here any general criticism of what can hardly be described as the earlier of the two works except by reason of their dates of publication, even a comparison between the pair seems superfluous. Yet the almost simultaneous treatment, by two eminent writers in close mutual touch, of themes which, though not identical, in many respects cover each other, is something more than a curiosity in literary history, and should not be lost sight of by critics desirous of applying a comparative treatment. Is it going too far to say that in "Hard Times" Dickens, whose creative power had then only just passed its zenith, sought to illustrate social conceptions fervently cherished by him by means of types drawn only in part from spheres within his own intimate knowledge; while Mrs. Gaskell sought to harmonise personal and social contrasts in conditions of life that came home to her with an intimate and familiar force? However this may have been—and we may be sure that no such conclusions were tried by her with her great friend—nothing could have been more delightful, and nothing more magnanimous, than the spirit in which Dickens applauded every stage in the progress of a story which he welcomed as an ornament, not only to his journal, but to the literature of English fiction.[8]

* * *

The scheme (to borrow Dickens' word) of Mrs. Gaskell's own story no doubt conformed itself to a wish, which may have been only half conscious though at the same time most genuine on her part, to find an opportunity for rectifying whatever misapprehensions might have arisen as to the real purpose—for purpose there had been—with which she had written "Mary Barton." Yet her object in sending forth "North and South" to take its place by the side of her early master-piece was by no means, as has been at times loosely suggested, to balance her previous advocacy of the claims of one class by showing what was to be said in favour of the other. Beyond a doubt, she desired to assert her sincere wish to be fair to both masters and men; and in "North and South" she succeeded better in the endeavour than she had in "Mary Barton." * * * Once more, she accorded the recognition which was its due to the heroic element perceptible in the conduct of the workmen, when persistently holding out together even to the disadvantage of their individual interests—"that's what folk call fine and honourable in a soldier, and why not in a poor weaver chap?" (p. 123). On the other hand, she cast no glamour round their unreasonableness in thought and in action, and exhib-ited them as clinging to their prejudices even where pernicious to themselves—like the men who "didn't like working in places where there was a wheel, because they said as how it made 'em hungry, at after they'd been used to swallowing fluff, to go without it, and that their wage ought to be raised if they were to work in such places" (p. 94). In Nicholas Higgins she drew to the life the best kind of Lancashire operative and the pitifulness of the likeness was attested by the great engineer, Sir William Fairbairn, who knew more than most men of Manchester workshops, and who wrote to Mrs. Gas-kell:

> "Poor old Higgins, with his weak consumptive daughter, is a true picture of a Manchester man. There are many like him in this town, and a better sample of independent industry you could not have hit upon. Higgins is an excellent representative of a Lancashire operative—strictly independent—and is one of the best characters in the piece."

But she depicted with no less force and fidelity the fanaticism of unreason in the personage of Higgins' *bête noire*, the unlucky Bou-

8. The correspondence between Gaskell and Dickens reprinted above (pp. 399–413) sug-gests otherwise.

cher—whose folly, dealing destruction to his nearest and dearest as well as to himself, his comrade was to requite by a self-sacrificing care for the suicide's widow and children.

But the companion picture to that of the working man typical of the best characteristics of his class—the picture of a master who, with the roots of his own strength in his native ground, aware of his power and jealous of all interference with its legitimate exercise, yet comes gradually to realise the whole of his duty towards his workmen—this was for the first time deliberately essayed by Mrs. Gaskell in "North and South." * * *

In "North and South" the whole course of the story, whose most dramatic scene has shown the master and his men face to face in all but internecine conflict, makes us understand how its hero, Mr. Thornton, a man of true Lancashire metal, possessed of a firm will, a clear head, and a true heart, gradually finds for himself the true solution of a problem of which he has come to understand the conditions in their entirety.

ELIZABETH HALDANE

[Elizabeth Gaskell and Florence Nightingale]†

Florence Nightingale, having the stronger character, broke from tradition more thoroughly than ever could have done her gentle contemporary. And yet such a hold did it have on the women of that time that in some respects she returned to the standards of Victorianism in later life; anyhow she resented John Stuart Mill's blandishments in regard to "coming out into the open." It is difficult to picture Miss Nightingale living quite the conventional life of a well-born Englishwoman of her period, and yet had she succumbed to the many efforts made to get her to give up her independent womanhood (which indeed one can hardly figure to oneself), married a clergyman and had four daughters, what would have resulted? The truth is that both—the one consciously, the other unconsciously— were breaking down the walls that Mrs. Grundy had built round women's lives in the nineteenth century. Miss Nightingale had no use for the sentimentality that was controlling the emotions and leading them into the beaten tracks of ordinary social life. Mrs. Gaskell had much of the romantic in her, but she was carried along by force with the life of her time and the manners of her time, and

† From Elizabeth Haldane, *Mrs. Gaskell and her Friends* (London: Hodder and Stoughton, 1930), pp. 108–12. Reprinted by permission of the publisher.

though she wrote of freedom from the shackles of the customs and conventions of her day it was perhaps only in her short romantic tales that she entirely escaped from their thraldom.

In her next novel, already referred to, which she wrote partly at Embley[1] and which was called "North and South" (Mr. Forster wished it called so rather than "Margaret Hale"), she deals with another moral question very different from that treated of in "Ruth," but one which was troubling many good men and a few good women of the day. The question was one of the conflict of moral ideas, and it was one that would have appealed strongly to Miss Nightingale, who was grappling with just such ideas. A clergyman, the husband of a good, ordinary, matter-of-fact clergyman's wife, and the father of a charming daughter, Margaret Hale, realises that he does not believe in the doctrines he is preaching, and must give up his living in an attractive country parish in the New Forest where he and his family are adored by the people. Mrs. Gaskell's father had done something of the kind in ceasing to be a minister and trying his fortunes in another line of life without too much success, so that she had an idea of what it would mean to leave a pleasant parsonage and go with an unsympathetic wife to "labour" in a smoky northern industrial town and to face obloquy on account of his beliefs.[2] The story is well told, though lacking in the unction of a later writer, Mrs. Humphry Ward, who dealt with a similar subject, and we can picture the feelings of the women of the family and their "superior" maid at finding themselves ensconced in dingy rooms costing thirty pounds a year, all they could afford, with overloaded cornices and a gaudy paper of pink and blue roses with yellow leaves, though indeed they were saved from the worst by a millowner whom Margaret to begin with held in disdain. The heroine herself is vividly described as she appeared to the same rough millowner, whom eventually she was to marry, however unlikely it seemed at first. "Her dress was very plain; a close straw bonnet of the best material and shape, trimmed with white ribbon; a dark silk gown, without any trimming or flounce; a large Indian shawl, which hung about her in heavy folds, and which she wore as an empress wears her drapery" (pp. 57–8). It sounds extraordinarily unlike the attire of a modern girl while house-hunting; but Mrs. Gaskell loved clothes, and, being famed for her good taste in them, liked to describe them. This was evidently the ideal wear of the time and no doubt it was becoming.

1. The Nightingale family home where Gaskell completed the writing of *North and South*, Haldane attributes the revised title to John Forster, rather than to Dickens.

2. Gaskell's father, William Stevenson, was in fact a Unitarian minister for a short period at Dob Lane Chapel near Manchester until he resigned on grounds of conscience. His situation was thus very different from that of Mr. Hale in the novel. See John Chapple, *Elizabeth Gaskell: The Early Years* (Manchester: Manchester University Press, 1997), ch 2. Gaskell would thus have had no personal experience of a "pleasant parsonage."

Mr. Hale had to act as tutor to such as he could get to instruct in order to make a livelihood. His whole action was no doubt guided by the highest dictates of conscience, but it strikes us at the same time as extremely selfish in its manner. The way in which not only the decision but the plans are made without once consulting the querulous but faithful wife, is typical of the attitude to the family so often adopted in those days by its head. The girl was marvellously loyal, but the maid who had always been in the "best families" had no compunction in setting forth her views. "And master thinking of turning Dissenter at his time of life, when, if it is not to be said he's done well in the Church, he's not done badly after all. I had a cousin, miss, who turned Methodist preacher after he was fifty years of age, and a tailor all his life; but then he had never been able to make a pair of trousers to fit, for as long as he had been in the trade, so it was no wonder" (p. 45).

The life at Milton (Manchester of course) is well described, the heavy smoky air and the rough outspoken factory workers whom gradually the girl came to understand and love after their independent ways ceased to astonish. Then comes the strike and the importation of Irish labour which drove the men into rioting, and Margaret's part in endeavouring to quell the riot and help Mr. Thornton, the millowner. The strike fails as did the general strike it is founded on, and then there is much talk of the Union, its benefits and faults. It is evident that the writer has had all the arguments of the "economists" pressed upon her since the days of "Mary Barton." Her deep sympathy with the "hands" and their suffering (we are not spared death-bed scenes in this tale, though they are not so frequent as before) are as real as ever, and her observation and description of their lives is as accurate. But the study is mainly from the point of view of the employer. Thornton is the typical employer of the straight, unbending kind who expects to be served well, and if he is not from his point of view, is adamant. Then there is the working man Higgins and his relations with his employer. Higgins is as independent as his master, and when they fall out and he loses his job, he is in a parlous state, especially as he takes over the care of the children of a fellow worker who drowned himself. The rights of the union and the action of the masters who will not take "union" men are dealt with very fairly. Mrs. Gaskell sees that the "South" has nothing to offer for these hard-headed workers, with its labour all the day long for nine shillings a week, the sameness of the toil deadening their imaginations as they were not deadened in a manufacturing town. At night these men were, as she says, brutishly tired and could think of nothing. She does indeed give a very true account of what the life of labourers was at that time in the Southern counties of which she knew from her country life before her marriage. They were no better and perhaps worse than those in the North.

Margaret's wooing, her father's death, and the account of the Oxford don, the friend of her father, who came into her life and made her his heiress is the best part of the book. Mrs. Gaskell excels in her description of the type that Thornton represents; she is at home in all her descriptions of his life and of the life of Milton; where she fails is when Margaret leaves her old surroundings and goes to live with the rich aunt and cousin in London. The life there is drawn conventionally and the rival lover does not interest us. * * *

RAYMOND WILLIAMS

[*North and South* and the "structure of feeling"]†

Our understanding of the response to industrialism would be incomplete without reference to an interesting group of novels, written at the middle of the century, which not only provide some of the most vivid descriptions of life in an unsettled industrial society, but also illustrate certain common assumptions within which the direct response was undertaken. There are the facts of the new society, and there is this structure of feeling, which I will try to illustrate from *Mary Barton, North and South, Hard Times, Sybil, Alton Locke,* and *Felix Holt.*

* * *

Mrs Gaskell's second industrial novel, *North and South*, is less interesting,[1] because the tension is less. She takes up here her actual position, as a sympathetic observer. Margaret Hale, with the feelings and upbringing of the daughter of a Southern clergyman, moves with her father to industrial Lancashire, and we follow her reactions, her observations and her attempts to do what good she can. Because this is largely Mrs Gaskell's own situation, the integration of the book is markedly superior. Margaret's arguments with the mill-owner Thornton are interesting and honest, within the political and economic conceptions of the period. But the emphasis of the novel, as the lengthy inclusion of such arguments suggests, is almost entirely now on attitudes *to* the working people, rather than on the attempt to reach, imaginatively, their feelings about their lives. It is interesting,

---

† From *Culture and Society* (London: Chatto and Windus, 1958), chap. 5, "The Industrial Novels." Reprinted by permission of The Random House Group Ltd. Williams's complete chapter lays the foundations for much modern criticism of the genre.
1. I.e., than *Mary Barton* [*Editor*].

again, to note the manner of the working-out. The relationship of Margaret and Thornton and their eventual marriage serve as a unification of the practical energy of the Northern manufacturer with the developed sensibility of the Southern girl: this is stated almost explicitly, and is seen as a solution. Thornton goes back to the North

> to have the opportunity of cultivating some intercourse with the hands beyond the mere 'cash nexus'.

Humanized by Margaret, he will work at what we now call 'the improvement of human relations in industry'. The conclusion deserves respect, but it is worth noticing that it is not only under Margaret's influence that Thornton will attempt this, but under her patronage. The other manufacturers, as Thornton says, 'will shake their heads and look grave' at it. This may be characteristic, but Thornton, though bankrupt, can be the exception, by availing himself of Margaret's unexpected legacy. Money from elsewhere, in fact—by that device of the legacy which solved so many otherwise insoluble problems in the world of the Victorian novel—will enable Thornton, already affected by the superior gentleness and humanity of the South, to make his humanitarian experiment. Once again Mrs Gaskell works out her reaction to the insupportable situation by going—in part adventitiously—outside it. * * *

* * *

AINA RUBENIUS

Factory Work for Women†

(i) * * * Work for women in the textile industries, the chief industry of Manchester, was nothing new. When work for the textile industry was carried out in the home, before the introduction of the power loom, weavers and spinners had taken the assistance of their wives and children for granted and counted on them thus to contribute to the family income—indeed, the loss of this income was one of the male weavers' most frequently repeated objections to work in the factories. The introduction of the steam loom broke up these working

† From "The Woman Question in Mrs Gaskell's Life and Works," *Essays and Studies in English Language and Literature*, V, The English Institute in the University of Upsala, (1950), (i) pp. 233–35; (ii) pp. 152–53. Reprinted by permission of the English Institute in the University of Upsala. Rubenius's study was the first full-scale feminist discussion of Gaskell. The first of these two extracts considers the situation of working women in the cotton industry in general terms, while the second focuses specifically on *North and South*. Notes have been edited and renumbered.

teams, and one man's wages did not suffice for a whole family. Most of the women workers in textile factories in the 'thirties and 'forties were therefore the wives and daughters of such weavers, simply carrying on the tradition from the time of the hand loom in the home. There were good opportunities of work for them, especially after the Factory Act of 1833 limited child labour, and consequently raised the demand for adult workers. Women were often preferred to men, because "The small amount of wages paid to women, acts as a strong inducement to employ them instead of men".[1] P. Gaskell gives the following information about textile workers in his *Manufacturing Population of England* (1833): "The individuals employed . . . are chiefly girls and young women from 16 to 22 or 23 years of age; indeed the weavers in many mills are exclusively females." Women seem to have been in a majority in worsted mills, and flax mills employed women workers only.[2]

The most frequently repeated objection to factory work for women in the Victorian age was its alleged tendency to break up the unity of the family, and unfit women for household work. "Woman's sphere is the home" was the favourite argument of the Victorians in discussions of this question, as well as of all others concerning a wider field for women's activities. The fact that most women workers in factories were single women who could not be supported at home carried no weight with those who constantly reiterated their phrase about woman's natural sphere.

Neither the women themselves nor the men workers seem to have regarded their factory work as worthy of comment until the late 'thirties and early 'forties, when a depression in the textile trade forced many mills to close down and many men found themselves without possibilities of work. From that time on, the effect of women's competition was taken into account when the distressed condition of factory workers was discussed. The argument was, however, generally concealed in phrases about women's natural place being the home. The *Manchester and Salford Advertiser* of January 8, 1842, for instance, printed an account of the reasons for which a "gradual withdrawal of all females from factories" had been demanded in 1841 by a Short Time Committee.[3] Factory work for women, said the article, was "an inversion of the order of nature and of Providence—a return to a state of barbarism, in which the woman

---

1. *Factory Inspectors' Report*, 1843, quoted by Ivy Pinchbeck, *Women Workers and the Industrial Revolution 1750–1850* (London: G. Routledge & Sons, 1930), p. 188.
2. 'In 1833 the cotton mills employed about 60,000 adult males, 65,000 adult females, and 84,000 young persons of whom half were boys and girls of under fourteen. By 1844, of 420,000 operatives . . . 242,000 were women and girls.' Arthur Bryant, *English Saga 1840–1940* (London: 1940), p. 59.
3. I.e., a Parliamentary Committee enquiring into the possibility of reducing working hours [*Editor*].

does the work, while the man looks idly on".[4] A deputation waited on Mr. Gladstone, requesting the limitation of the number of women workers in each factory in proportion to the number of men employed there. The deputation also demanded a law to prohibit married women working in factories during the lifetime of their husbands.

* * *

An objection to factory work for women that was frequently made about the middle of the nineteenth century was its disastrous effects on the health of the workers. Some kinds of work in which women were engaged were generally admitted to be extremely unhealthy. This applied especially to flax mills, where the method of so called wet spinning was in general use. In 1843 a factory superintendent by the name of Baker stated in a report that women worked all night in a temperature of 70° or 80°. In other cases, he had seen girls of seventeen who worked from six to ten o'clock, with only one-and-a-half hours a day for meals and rest. His report shows the necessity of the violently opposed Factory Act of 1844, which abolished the worst of these abuses. Critics of the factory system, however, often overlooked the fact that many of the disadvantages, such as the unsatisfactory sanitary conditions, were not confined to the factory, nor were at all new. Charles Kingsley showed in *Yeast* (1848) and *Alton Locke* (1850) that the poorer country population was no better off, and in a Report of Handloom Weavers of 1840 Hickson stated: "With regard to health, having seen the domestic weaver in his miserable apartment and the power loom weaver in the factory, I do not hesitate to say that the advantages are all on the side of the latter."[5] * * *

(ii) * * * That, in *Mary Barton*, Mrs. Gaskell considered only the effects that factory work for women had on the home is quite consistent with the attitude towards a wife's problems that she showed in her first stories, when she uncritically adopted the ideal from the "darkness where obedience was the only seen duty of women".[6] She then saw them only as appendages to men, without any intrinsic value in themselves. But her attitude gradually changed, and she came to think of women as independent beings, whose duty it is to have a will of their own and to accept moral responsibility. Thus, in 1853, the year when the story of a wife who rebels against her husband appeared in *Ruth*, Mrs. Gaskell began writing of the factory system in *North and South* from a somewhat different point of view than she had done in her first novel. In *North and South* there is no

4. Quoted by Pinchbeck, p. 200.
5. Pinchbeck, p. 197.
6. *Letters*, p. 109.

longer much insistence on the disastrous effects of factory work for
women on the home. It is mentioned, but only in passing.[7] Nor does
Mrs. Gaskell protest against or even comment on the fact that
women preferred, to domestic service, "the better wages and greater
independence of working in a mill",[8] a fact which had distressed her
in *Mary Barton*. Instead, she concentrates her attention on a point
which she had omitted in her earlier work, the disregard for their
workers' health which many mill-owners displayed.

Bessy Higgins, who dies as a result of the unhealthful conditions
under which she is obliged to work, is employed in a carding-room,
which implies that she performed the work which shared with "wet
spinning" a reputation for being the most dangerous in the textile
industry. This is what she tells Margaret about her work in the factory:

> " 'I think I was well when mother died, but I have never been
> rightly strong sin' somewhere about that time. I began to work
> in a carding-room soon after, and the fluff got into my lungs
> and poisoned me.'
>   " 'Fluff?' said Margaret inquiringly.
>   " 'Fluff', repeated Bessy. 'Little bits, as fly off fro' the cotton,
> when they're carding it, and fill the air till it looks all fine white
> dust. They say it winds round the lungs, and tightens them up.
> Anyhow, there's many a one as works in a carding-room, that
> falls into a waste, coughing and spitting blood, because they're
> just poisoned by the fluff.'
>   " 'But can't it be helped?' asked Margaret.
>   " 'I dunno. Some folk have a great wheel at one end o' their
> carding-rooms to make a draught, and carry off th' dust; but
> that wheel costs a deal of money—five or six hundred pound,
> maybe, and brings in no profit; so it's but a few of th' masters
> as will put 'em up; and I've heard tell o' men who didn't like
> working in places where there was a wheel, because they said
> as how it made 'em hungry, at after they'd been long used to
> swallowing fluff, to go without it, and that their wage ought to
> be raised if they were to work in such places. So between mas-
> ters and men th' wheels fall through. I know I wish there'd been
> a wheel in our place, though.' "[9]

It has been pointed out by most of Mrs. Gaskell's critics that she
showed more understanding for the mill-owner's point of view in
North and South than in *Mary Barton*, and some have even asserted
that she wrote the latter book chiefly to restore the balance in the

---

7. Bessy, the factory worker, says about her sister: 'who has she had to teach her what to do
   about a house? No mother, and me at the mill till I were good for nothing but scolding
   her for doing badly what I didn't know how to do a bit' (p. 95).
8. P. 65.
9. P. 94.

opinions concerning the factory system which she had expressed in *Mary Barton*. It might be argued that in the passage quoted above Mrs. Gaskell divides the blame between masters and men, but it should be noted that the reason given for the workers' opposition to the introduction of safeguards is ignorance, whereas that of the masters is a wish for gain. * * *

DOROTHY W. COLLIN

The Composition of Mrs. Gaskell's
North and South†

* * *

* * * There are two areas in which we may now place side by side two "versions" of the novel. In the first eleven numbers of the published serial it is possible to put side by side the divisions which Dickens recommended and those which were finally adopted;[1] and we may contrast the highly compressed final number published in *Household Words* with the more leisured conclusion of the novel as it was published in two volumes. Neither of these areas affords a simple comparison of editor's choice versus author's choice; the error in casting-off prevented simplicity of arrangements at any stage of serial publication, and it is clear that the final chapters were also rewritten under pressure of time.

Variations of part divisions in the early numbers show not so much differences in the technique of serialization between Dickens and Mrs. Gaskell, as emphasis upon one aspect of the novel rather than another. The first three serial parts were published as Dickens first divided them; his wish to shorten severely the second and third numbers so that they became one was overruled. Dickens made breaks following passages which would introduce an element of suspense (the announcement of Mr. Lennox at the end of part one) or point forward to a new prospect (the plan to stay at Heston at the end of part three). Mrs. Gaskell did not disdain the device of simple suspense; indeed, she exploited it fully at the end of part eleven, when,

---

† From "The Composition of Mrs. Gaskell's *North and South*," *Bulletin of the John Rylands Library*, vol. 54, no. 1, Autumn 1971, pp. 67–93. Published by permission of the John Rylands University Library, Manchester. Volume, chapter, and page references are given in this text and, unless they refer specifically to the *Household Words* text, which numbered its chapters in one continuous sequence, have been adjusted to those of this Norton Critical Edition. This selection should be read in conjunction with the correspondence between Gaskell and Dickens printed above, pp. 399–413. Notes are the Editor's.

1. For Dickens's proposed part divisions see his letter to Gaskell, [15] and 17 June 1854, pp. 406–07 above.

after Margaret is admitted to Thornton's millyard, she hears "far away, the ominous gathering roar" of the rioters (p. 157).

The fourth part was carried by Dickens beyond the Hales' arrival in the new house at Milton-Northern to the moment which turns the reader nostalgically back to the luxury of Margaret's London connections. The unreality of this part of Margaret's life is emphasized as she sits down to read Edith's letter from Corfu. At this point Dickens proposed to close the part. The division was actually made a few paragraphs earlier with the Hales' arrival at their new house. The significance of the change is that the final sentence now brings before the reader most effectively the power of Mr. Thornton: "There was no particular need to tell them, that what (the landlord) did not care to do for a Reverend Mr. Hale, unknown, in Milton, he was only too glad to do at the one short sharp remonstrance of Mr. Thornton, the wealthy manufacturer" (p. 60). It is an effective ending. Lingering with the reader, it suggests to him a set of northern values to which the Hales are strangers, directs his attention to the almost entirely unexplored territory of Milton, which is the novel's central setting, and opens the possibility of a developing connection between the Hales and Mr. Thornton.

The following part division again shows Mrs. Gaskell's preference for leaving the reader with his attention focused upon a new character. Dickens would have taken the number to Mr. Thornton's departure from the Hales after the tea-visit (vol. 1, chap. 10) when a conversation which lays emphasis on the north/south conflict is animated by a misunderstanding of manners upon leave-taking which leaves Mr. Thornton angry with Margaret's seeming haughtiness. The part thus closes without any promised incident in view. In publication this part concluded with a spirited disagreement between Mr. Thornton and his mother (vol. 1, ch. 9). The result is to lay emphasis again on the Thorntons, to invite the reader's attention to follow the development of Mrs. Thornton's aggressive character and to look forward with curiosity to the figure which this Northern manufacturer will cut in Mrs. Hale's drawing-room.

The proposed sixth part again closed with a leave-taking; again the published part held a visit in promise—that of Mrs. Thornton to the Hales (vol. 1, ch. 11), a mixing of characters as yet untried by the reader and promising a clash of temperaments. Dickens' division brought into prominence the working-class Higgins family, whereas Mrs. Gaskell continued for the third time to direct the reader's attention as the part closed to the Thorntons.

Comparison of the two plans of division for the second batch of manuscript is more difficult for the end of the published eighth part coincided with the end of Dickens' proposed seventh part and the discrepancy was increasing with each number. The overall difference seems to lie in the degree to which the divisions of the published parts emphasized these aspects of the novel which Dickens, for obvious reasons, could not foresee. The seventh part calls forth anxiety about Mrs. Hale's illness (vol. 1, ch. 13), the ninth part looks forward to the possibility of Margaret sinning (vol. 1, ch. 17). The tenth part closes quietly soon after Boucher's outburst has shown him to be emotional and unreliable, a necessary preparation for a later scene (vol 1, ch 19).

Dickens' skill in finding convenient dividing points in a manuscript is evident, but the variations made from his first scheme suggest that the advantage lay with the author who had already in her mind the outline and conclusion of the whole novel.

In preparing the first edition most of Mrs. Gaskell's attention was directed towards reshaping the material compressed into chapter 44 (vol. 2, ch. 19) which forms the latter part of the penultimate number in *Household Words*. This single chapter was expanded to make five. With the exception of breaking the original chapter 45 (vol 2, ch 20) into two, she made no substantial changes to the final number. One may assume therefore that it was the original chapter 44 which she felt to have suffered most severely from the "desperate compression" to which she "was compelled"[2] by the editors of *Household Words*. The appearance of the chapter itself, long unbroken passages of description relieved by only a few brief exchanges of dialogue, would certainly suggest this, and there is evidence that Dickens or Wills was partly responsible for its character.

It was thus that she carried out the intention expressed to Mrs. Jameson[3] of "(throwing herself) back a certain distance in the story and (re-writing) it from there". Although the first two pages of chapter 44 include in much the same order the material used in the first two paragraphs of the original chapter 44, there follows an extensive development of events only briefly mentioned in *Household Words* and considerable additional material. Chapter 45 is represented by a single sentence in the serial version, and there is no vestige of chapter 46 (vol. 2, ch. 21), the visit to Helstone. Chapters 47 and 48 (vol. 2, chs. 22 and 23), the last of the "new" chapters, return more closely to material found in the *Household Words* chapter 44 and sometimes present it in exactly the same order.

It has been indicated that the material in chapter 44 is most closely tied in with the writing of the additional chapters at their beginning and at their end. In some parts there are only slight variations of punctuation between the *Household Words* version and the first edition; other passages have been re-written. It is notable that the two sentences which are used twice in the first edition appear in pairs,

2. See Gaskell's letter to Anna Jameson [January 1855], p. 403 above.
3. Ibid.

as it were, on the first occasion just at the point where Mrs. Gaskell
moves away from material taken from the original chapter 44 and
on the second occasion just after she resumes close contact with the
Household Words version. This suggests that during her free excur-
sion into the new material she had forgotten which passages of chapter 44 had been "used up" already and that in writing new chapters
she was working without a systematic plan.[4]

The sentences which have been re-written show two main
changes: the sharpening of a word or phrase (e.g., "profound calculation" for "profound purpose") to produce a stylistic improvement, and some additions or omissions of material appropriate to the
new ending. Making allowance for the possibility that as a housewife
Mrs. Gaskell may have done a good deal of phrase-shaping in her
head without benefit of paper and pen to hand, the versions correspond so closely that it seems more probable that the variants are
deliberate alterations made while copying out a first text, rather than
that they arose because whole paragraphs were re-written from
memory.

In the new chapters it is possible to discern an attempt to restore
the balance of the novel by dwelling upon its southern aspects. There
are London scenes which counterbalance those at the beginning of
the novel and there is a delicious strawberries-and-cream visit to
Helstone. Yet in Harley Street there is acerbity, ambition and petu-
lance, and in Helstone there is the odour of roasted cat. Through
these scenes Mr. Bell travels; here he is developed with some of the
detail which he deserves as the agent of the Hales' removal to Milton,
the source of Margaret's wealth, and indeed the matchmaker in the
romance. Henry Lennox is given a second chance to prove himself
worthy of Margaret before he brilliantly and bad-temperedly fails.
The reader has no regrets that Margaret lost the opportunity of continuing the life of a London lady surrounded by "those Lennoxes".
The hopes first raised in Milton, that Frederick might be exonerated
and be free to return to England, are dispelled at sufficient length
to enable the reader to share Margaret's feeling that one more of her
supports is denied her. Indeed, these chapters might be seen as a
measured and relentless process of stripping from Margaret all her
attachments in preparation for her solitary encounter with Mr.
Thornton in which she recognizes and acknowledges to the reader's
satisfaction her only remaining support.

4. See p. 340, n. 5 above.

W. A. CRAIK

[The Topography of *North and South*]†

North and South, like *Ruth*,[1] uses geographical setting as an element
of its organization. It does so with even greater complexity and sub-
tlety, and with more daring. Here for the first time in a full-length
novel Elizabeth Gaskell moves out of her north-western England
native ground. The four places in which the action takes place are,
in the order in which we see them, London, Helstone in the New
Forest, Milton, and Oxford (which though only briefly visited, yet
has its own importance). In order of importance, Milton must take
first place, as most of the events take place there, but all the others
have their power and purposes, as do even remoter regions only
glanced at with reference to other characters—Spain, where Frederick lives, South America, and Scotland. Elizabeth Gaskell is using
a wider area than in any of her other novels, with increased assurance
and skill, yet without any need to develop a different attitude or
methods from those she has already tried and proved. Helstone and
Milton are both 'invented' in that they have neither the names nor
all the attributes of actual places, and are therefore more representative than an actual southern English village, or actual Manchester,
could be. They bear the same relationship to the actual that George
Eliot's Middlemarch, Trollope's Barchester, or Hardy's Casterbridge
do to their originals, giving the author the freedom to develop their
significance and symbolic qualities, alongside the sense of reality of
an actual place with which the reader can have some familiarity.
London does not require the same handling, because it has in itself
so many aspects that selection can be made without any sense of
distortion.

Whereas in *Ruth* the settings were used once only, as Ruth passed
through the phases of her life with which they were connected, in
North and South the pattern is more elaborate, with a design of
departures and returns, with the ending a balanced coming-together
of the aspects of life that each place presents and explores. Over-
simplifying severely, one could say that London revealed conventional upper-middle-class standards and behaviour; Helstone the
natural life of the country and the old rural standards; Oxford the
life of the mind—'sitting still, and learning from the past, or shaping
out the future by faithful work done in a prophetic spirit' (p. 301) as

† From *Elizabeth Gaskell and the English Provincial Novel* (London: Methuen, 1975), chap.
3, pp. 111–20. Reprinted by permission of Taylor & Francis Books Ltd. Page numbers are
to this Norton Critical Edition.
1. Gaskell's preceding novel (1853) [*Editor*].

Mr Bell puts it; and Milton a new world still in the process of creating itself, full of the troubles of adolescence, but with the power to develop and grow which the others lack.

Around these centres Elizabeth Gaskell suggests a much wider world than she has done before, of places which exist, and affect life in the most retired or self-absorbed provincial places. Edith's letters from Corfu, where her husband is stationed, Frederick's new and strange life in Spain, Thornton's business connections on the continent, even the consciousness of Glasgow and the Scottish universities, as the rare and only possible education for a Milton manufacturer's scion, all render the work and the reader aware of the whole contemporary world. * * *

We meet Margaret first in London, in the comfort and ease of her aunt's house, a dependent without cares or responsibilities, at the opening of her adult life, a looker-on at her cousin Edith's wedding. Elizabeth Gaskell firmly sets down here the main considerations of her novel; aesthetic and sensuous qualities, the emotions, and worldly success and honour. They are all present in an amorphous condition, with no sense of their relative importance, or of their implications. She does justice to them all, recognizing the genuine family affections of the Shaws and the Lennoxes; the genuine delights of a life containing Indian shawls with their 'spicy Eastern smell' and 'their soft feel and brilliant colours' (p. 11); and the pressures of personal ambition and the need for money, which make Henry Lennox, the rising lawyer, unwilling to yield to the attractions of the near-penniless Margaret. It takes its tone from the inhabitants we meet, their life and standards: they are all, though not unprincipled, partly enslaved to the comfortable and the worldly: Edith dislikes the idea of going to Corfu with her soldier husband:

> Yet had anyone come, with a fine house, and a fine estate, and a fine title to boot, Edith would still have clung to Captain Lennox while the temptation lasted; when it was over it is possible she might have had little qualms of ill-concealed regret that Captain Lennox could not have united in his person everything that was desirable. In this she was but her mother's child; who, after deliberately marrying General Shaw with no warmer feeling than respect for his character and establishment, was constantly, though quietly, bemoaning her hard lot in being united to one whom she could not love. (p. 9)

The handling is done with immense tact and economy, since Elizabeth Gaskell has to indicate that this opening chapter is merely a preface to what is to happen elsewhere. She avoids superbly any suggestion that London could provide a norm from which to judge the rest, since she carefully reveals that there are no standards in *this* London; and Margaret, plainly the main character, is an outsider, whose own world is elsewhere. * * *

Elizabeth Gaskell's delicately neutral attitude to London in Chapter 1 contrasts sharply with the impression she creates when Margaret returns, three years later, a woman, wise, independent, wealthy, and desolately alone in the world, for whom the round of daily comforts, family affairs, trivial occupations and dinner-givings falls into insignificance beside the sterner standards of life in Milton. She can judge 'a shade or two of coarseness' in Edith's finding her 'an attraction to the house' because 'ever so many men will be glad to visit here next year for your sake' (p. 371), and can find her own life in social work among the needy. It is a pity that Elizabeth Gaskell, cramped by the serial form in which *North and South* was originally written, was unable to develop the final London section as she obviously wished. Her intentions are clear, but she has not room enough for their execution, particularly that of its new aspect, which is as a neutral meeting-ground for the reconciling of the conflicts she has explored, and for the final coming-together of Margaret and Thornton in whom they are embodied.

The action proper opens at Helstone, the place Margaret thinks of as home. Her brief stay there, before she is ousted by Mr Hale's giving up his living and leaving the Church of England, renders its enchantment through the eyes of the enthusiastic and enchanted Margaret, and allows it both to exist in its own right, and to function as an extention of her nature. Because it does so, it can reveal and establish her connections and disunities with others. It is 'the place where Margaret grew to what she is', as Thornton says (p. 395); Lennox is clearly seen as no possible husband for her because he is out of tune with the place; Thornton becomes so when he has visited it: roses from Helstone have their part in his proposal and acceptance. Barely five chapters though there are of this first Helstone (its revisiting is a different world) Elizabeth Gaskell establishes it as a point of reference and contrast on a number of levels. All are seen through Margaret's eyes, and accepted by the reader as valid even though at a later stage Margaret's mature eyes, and the passage of time, create a different scene, and a different judgement. Helstone thus contrasts in impressions with London, where reservations were presented by the author herself. Helstone is both realistic and idyllic. Elizabeth Gaskell presents sensuously and faithfully the physical details of the country-side, 'the broad upland, sunstreaked, cloud-shadowed' commons, the forest trees which were 'one dark full dusky green; the fern below them caught all the slanting sunbeams; the weather sultry and broodingly still' (p. 18); and recreates equally faithfully the domestic minutiae of house and garden that she delights in. Her purely descriptive passages are brief and enchanting, and, while seeming to exist for their own sakes, always have a structured purpose. When Mr Lennox visits them, lunch ends in an *alfresco* dessert of pears gathered and eaten in the garden:

> Margaret made a plate for the pears out of a beetroot leaf, which threw up their brown-gold colour admirably. Mr Lennox looked more at her than the pears; but her father, inclined to cull fastidiously the very zest and perfection of the hour he had stolen from his anxiety, chose daintily the ripest fruit, and sat down to enjoy it at his leisure. (p. 27)

He continues to do so during the climax of the chapter, when Lennox proposes to Margaret and is refused. Both are disturbed and chagrined:

> It was well that having made the round of the garden, they came suddenly upon Mr Hale, whose whereabouts had been quite forgotten by them. He had not yet finished the pear, which he had delicately peeled in one long strip of silver-paper thinness, and which he was enjoying in a deliberate manner. (p. 29)

Such passages, which are many, act by transference to give the reader the sense of near-unconscious delight of the characters who share them. They render all the complexity of human experience: we register here Mr Hale's rest from his hidden trouble (whose nature has not yet been revealed) and feel also how, whatever startling changes have taken place in Margaret and Henry Lennox, the life of the rest of creation goes on at its own unregarding pace. The method is powerful in the very opposite way from the 'romantic' novel, where, to take an extreme like *Wuthering Heights*, all creation and nature participates in, or is seen as an aspect of, the characters themselves. Hardy can develop such techniques to his own ends, which drive home for him the bitter indifference of the universe to humanity. Elizabeth Gaskell may be less powerful, but she is wiser, in accepting such things as contingencies which, simply neutral, may be comfort as well as torment.

During Margaret's stay in Milton, Helstone is recalled in contrast, by allusion and recollection. Bessy Higgins sees it in imagination from Margaret's descriptions, and connects it in her mind with the Heavenly Jerusalem of the Apocalypse. Thus Helstone becomes more remote and idealized, even though Margaret occasionally acknowledges its drawbacks, such as that Higgins would be unable to stand the hardship of field labour there.

Three years later (vol. II, chap. 21) Margaret goes back to Helstone, for a single day, with Mr Bell. Elizabeth Gaskell treats it with the same honest and minute fidelity, through Margaret's now mature vision. Helstone has changed, both to reveal the changes in Margaret that make her see it now with a wiser perception, and in itself, so that it demonstrates its author's constant theme, the operation of time. The new clergyman and his wife have altered the vicarage—deliberately, by changing Mr Hale's study into a nursery, and unconsciously:

> The garden, the grass-plat, formerly so daintily trim that even a stray rose-leaf seemed like a fleck on its exquisite arrangement and propriety, was strewed with children's things: a bag of marbles here, a hoop there; a straw hat forced down upon a rose-tree as on a peg, to the destruction of a long, beautiful, tender branch laden with flowers, which in former days would have been trained up tenderly, as if beloved. (p. 357)

The change may pain Margaret, but there is nothing wrong about it: Elizabeth Gaskell's tone suggests that the signs of 'merry, rough healthy childhood' are an intrinsic improvement. On the other hand, Margaret interviews the old woman whose cat has been stolen by her neighbour (who has roasted it alive, in accordance with a local superstition that to do so would bring back clothes stolen by a gipsy); the comic-macabre account and the woman's conclusion leave no choice but to believe that change and education are all to the good:

> 'it were very cruel for sure, and she should not like to do it; but that there were nothing like it for giving a person what they wished for; she had heard it all her life; but it were very cruel for all that. (p. 355)

The nostalgia remains of rural enchantment in woodland walks, and the delights of washing in spring-water scented by 'fresh-gathered roses plunged head-downward in the water-jug' (p. 351), or lavender-scented towels, or a lunch of strawberries and cream, brown bread, and jug of milk, and Stilton cheese—but it is nostalgia firmly put in its place.

Milton, which occupies the main body of the novel, is equally a balancing of qualities valuable and reprehensible, or both at once, depending on the attitude and degree of understanding, and the social or aesthetic bias of the beholder. Milton is the symbol and embodiment of industry and of all the social issues between 'masters and men' that were at the heart of *Mary Barton*. It is also the catalyst for the working-out of the personal and spiritual progress of Margaret and Thornton, who change in relation to each other and to the place itself, and it is finally indicated, are beginning to change Milton. Elizabeth Gaskell has thus a more exciting as well as a more difficult area than George Eliot in *Middlemarch*. Middlemarch is inert or even destructive; it leads Lydgate into compromising his principles, trammels him, and ultimately, through its small-town politics and pressures and through Rosamund, its representative, destroys him; it offers no outlets for Dorothea's ideals, who can fulfil herself eventually only by escaping altogether with the aid of the outsider Ladislaw. No single reforming character changes *Middlemarch* which 'moveth all together if it move at all', to the great vague outside pressures (such as Garth's railways project) of time and the era. Those who succeed personally are those who, like Mary Garth, Fred Vincy and Celia Brooke, contrive to maintain their personal integrity within the confines of the society and its *mores*.

Elizabeth Gaskell, neither idealistic nor unrealistic, is not as unconsciously defeatist as George Eliot. Before the end of the novel, she not only suggests that improvement is possible, but how it may be brought about, and how it may be done by individuals, as well as by groups. Thornton is both a representative of the masters and a 'man' who has risen from those 'men' whose representative is Higgins, the mouthpiece of the unions, who as man to man can communicate and work with Thornton. Elizabeth Gaskell rests her faith on the position given in the crucial exchange between Thornton and Margaret:

> 'A man to me [he says] is a higher and completer being than a gentleman.'
> 'What do you mean?' asked Margaret. 'We must understand the words differently.'
> 'I take it that "gentleman" is a term that only describes a person in his relation to others; but when we speak of him as "a man", we consider him not merely with regard to his fellow-men, but in relation to himself—to life—to time—to eternity' (p. 150)

Higgins and Thornton are both men, in this sense; once they communicate, Thornton sees his way to providing for his workers' needs: the provisions are slight ones, not much more than allowing employees some self-organization within the factory—such as the canteen they run—and the more general hints of the penultimate chapter:

> 'I have arrived at the conviction that no mere institutions, however wise * * * can attach class to class as they should be attached, unless the working out of such institutions brings the individuals of the different classes into actual personal contact. Such intercourse is the very breath of life.' (p. 391)

Elizabeth Gaskell undoubtedly intended something more precise, but was, as we know, painfully short of space at her conclusion. However, it is clear that Milton, no less than Helstone, is not only a changing place, but one that can be changed by those within it.

She has thus set herself a hard and elaborate task, to show change in action and also to show changes of attitude in her observers towards Milton itself, in its essential being. She succeeds superbly in her task, of moving by way of observers and interpreters with several extreme positions, to a balance, partly of opposites, and partly of those who grow to see that qualities must have the defects of their virtues. Any method other than justice and fidelity in representing Milton is thus impossible for her. She avoids the unconvincing extreme delineations of Disraeli or Kingsley, while making many of the same points as they do about the enormous, fundamental, and horrifying problems in the new, fast-growing world based on the factory-city.

To do so she needs a variety of viewpoints: she uses Margaret and Thornton as those who are young, wise, and responsive enough to achieve the balance, and a variety of others, of whom the chief are Mrs Hale and Mrs Thornton, to state the unchanging extremes. It is Mrs Hale who is most troubled by the physical unpleasantnesses of Milton, who suffers from the cold and fog, who cannot come to terms with its new and alien class-structure, in which the prosperous and proud mother of a prosperous and proud manufacturer can boast of her son's having risen from penury by his own exertions. Mrs Thornton herself embodies the courage, the inaesthetic hardness, the strong sense of right, and proud self-respect of the Milton character. Through her, her house, and the way of life she embodies, Elizabeth Gaskell presents the private and domestic life of Milton. It is a hard but far from unfeeling life, governed by high and rigid standards whose satisfactions are not sensuous: her drawing-room is described with a faithful lightness of touch by the author:

> The walls were pink and gold; the pattern on the carpet represented bunches of flowers on a light ground, but it was carefully covered up in the centre by a linen drugget, glazed and colourless. The window-curtains were lace; each chair and sofa had its own particular veil of netting or knitting. Great alabaster groups occupied every flat surface, safe from dust under their glass shades. In the middle of the room, right under the bagged-up chandelier, was a large circular table, with smartly-bound books arranged at regular intervals round the circumference of its polished surface, like gaily coloured spokes of a wheel. Everything reflected light, nothing absorbed it. The whole room had a painfully spotted, spangled, speckled look about it, which impressed Margaret so unpleasantly that she was hardly conscious of the peculiar cleanliness required to keep everything so white and pure in such an atmosphere, or of the trouble that must be willingly expended to secure that effect of icy, snowy discomfort. (p. 103)

Thus Milton indoors. Outdoors is equally justly done. The Thorntons' house is next to the mill, across the mill-yard. The detail is
realistic, and, equally, signifies that, according to the values of Milton, work is the larger part of life. Elizabeth Gaskell avoids the usual
novelist's problem of rendering work as vivid and immediate as personal life by making the two inextricable. The noise and business of
the mill pervade the Thornton house, as much as the fluff from the
carding-room does Bessy Higgins's lungs.

Against these fixed views of Milton Elizabeth Gaskell charts the
gradually changing perspectives of Margaret and Thornton. For both
of them Milton is a place of testing, possibly uncongenial, undoubtedly hard, but able to call out and temper the virtue and strength of
the individual, and make him face and answer the questions about
his or her own nature, and about duties and links with fellow-men.
Margaret learns her own courage and power to fight, finds that her
simplistic ideas, based on human kindliness and the Bible, will not
answer with rugged natures like Higgins's and Thornton's, whose
arguments she cannot logically refute. Thornton, in his turn, sure of
his place in his society, and of belonging to it by birth, nurture, and
personal striving, learns to look upon it differently in the light of
Margaret's ideas.

The great strength of Elizabeth Gaskell's rendering of Milton is
that while sympathetically recognizing that Milton is socially and
economically viable as it stands, she reveals at the same time that it
is personally and morally inadequate and imperfect. The single man
can work his way up to become master providing he accepts that, if
defeated by the powers that gave him the chance to rise, he must
take that defeat—as Thornton does. Similarly the workers can break
the master's power, if they accept that by so doing they may also
break themselves. Each man has the opportunity of Samson to bring
down the temple over his own head, leaving others to rebuild in their
turn, and have the same choice. Milton is her final word on the city
of the industrial revolution. She never returns to it again, having
achieved in it a finer and deeper study than any other writer. When
the reader thinks back over this novel, he is likely to recall the
places—London, Helstone and Milton—and what happens in them
which partakes of their nature, quite as vividly as the industrial personalities. Milton is probably the greatest character in *North and
South*, more fully revealed and subtler than any single personality—
fine though they are—and more memorable. * * *

ROSEMARIE BODENHEIMER

North and South: A Permanent State of Change†

North and South was a title suggested by Dickens and accepted by Elizabeth Gaskell, who thought of her novel as "Margaret Hale" during the early stages of composition. The choice represents Dickens's imagination rather than Gaskell's; it sets up an absolute contrast, a sharpening of distinctions between pastoral and industrial worlds, that Dickens himself might have used to make his rhetorical points. His own "condition of England" novel, *Hard Times,* was running in *Household Words* as he received Gaskell's chapters, and it seems likely that he invented a title which would link the new novel with his own and with Disraeli's *Sybil, or The Two Nations* [1845], and advertise it as another account of the crisis of social division. But *North and South* is not really organized as a system of contrasts;[1] nor is it exactly a "social-problem novel," for it does not identify a clear version of industrial crisis and cry for a solution.[2] It is rather a novel about irrevocable change, and about the confused process of response and accommodation that attends it.

This essay is written from a desire to offer a reading of the strengths and the internal coherence of a book which strikes me as Gaskell's most radical and courageous work. *North and South* is so often treated as part of some other question—in comparison with *Mary Barton,* as one in a larger group of industrial novels, in relation to Charlotte Brontë, or as a book written under the stress of Gaskell's stormy relationship with Dickens—that it still deserves some attention to its own terms. It is by no means a formally perfect work; my argument is partly that it cannot be, because it is so good at posing knotted issues and feelings that cannot come formally to rest except in the depiction of ongoing process and readjustment. In its every situation, whether industrial politics or emotional life, traditional views and stances break down into confusing new ones, which are rendered in all the pain of mistakenness and conflict that real human change entails. To suggest how that principle works in all of the novel's parts, my discussion will move, roughly, from social to emo-

---

† From *Victorian Fiction* (now *Victorian Literature*) 34. 3 (Dec. 1979): 281–301. Reprinted by permission of the University of California Press and the author. Footnotes have been edited and renumbered by permission of the author.

1. The widely shared idea that the novel is organized by contrasts appears in Margaret Ganz, *Elizabeth Gaskell: The Artist in Conflict* (New York: Twayne, 1969), p. 81; Edgar Wright, *Mrs. Gaskell: The Basis for Re-assessment* (London: Oxford UP, 1965), pp. 132 ff.

2. This redefinition of Raymond Williams's term "industrial novel" (*Culture and Society, 1780–1950,* London: Chatto and Windus, 1958) may be found in John Lucas's article, "Mrs Gaskell and Brotherhood," in *Tradition and Tolerance in Nineteenth-Century Fiction,* ed. David Howard, John Lucas, and John Goode (London: Routledge & Kegan Paul, 1966). The article includes a strong and interesting assessment of *North and South.*

tional topics: from the social landscapes to the issues of class and industrial conflict, and finally to Margaret's character and interior life. Throughout, however, I want to emphasize how *North and South* depicts social change as personal change without dissolving either into an "industrial novel" or into a love story.

The novel's opening—the apparently multiple openings—have generated both confusion and criticism. First the fashionable London milieu, then the country parish of Helstone are depicted, only to be rather quickly left behind. Charlotte Brontë assumed that it would be a story about religious doubt and later readers with the whole novel in hand have criticized the treatment of Mr. Hale's defection from the Church of England as unmotivated, or without serious consequences, or as a mere pretext for the family's removal to Milton-Northern. But the consistency of the narrative emphasis on change itself makes these early chapters both emotionally coherent and socially significant.

Margaret Hale is introduced as she sits by her sleeping cousin's side silently brooding over "the change in her life" occasioned by Edith's marriage. The first extended attention to her consciousness comes as she remembers arriving at the London household nine years earlier, and crying "with such wild passion of grief" at the unfamiliar rituals and ceremonies of the place. Now she has come to love the London life and to regret leaving it; the Brontë-like childish passion has taken a normal human course of accommodation and learning. The theme would be unremarkable were it not to be expanded and explored in episodes of increasing intensity.

Helstone, the home to which Margaret returns, is quickly but carefully set up to represent a pastoral condition as apparently immune to change as any that could be imagined. Margaret thinks of it as "a village . . . in one of Tennyson's poems" (p. 13);[3] her impulse is to set it out of time altogether. A country village, a Church of England parson, a set of traditional charitable relationships with individual parishioners, a world more stable even than Jane Austen's—the danger would seem to lie only in domestic boredom. The point of Mr. Hale's decision is to overthrow all that, and to suggest how, by a murky and confused process of internal change, he has grown apart from his social role and come to a state of mind, indefinite and yet absolute, in which he cannot sign the Articles which signify his allegiance to a higher authority. Gaskell's refusal to investigate the substance of Mr. Hale's decision is not a weakness but a placement of emphasis: his irrevocable change, its statement of doubt in the face of a traditional order, his cowardice and ineptitude at facing its social consequences are the issues she attends to.

3. Chapter references are to the two-volume first edition, as reprinted in this Norton Critical Edition.

The function of the South is not to provide a contrast with the industrial North but to be itself the subject of changing perspectives. When Margaret and Mr. Bell return to visit Helstone near the end of the novel, the point about change there is quite obviously recorded—perhaps most delightfully in the detail that the school-children have modern terms for grammar that Margaret does not know, rendering her traditional social help obsolete. But by that time Margaret has experienced other pressures on her point of view. Trying to describe Helstone to Bessy Higgins, she finds her nature metaphors falling on uncomprehending ears, while Bessy, deafened by factory noise and dying of factory air, picks out the parts of the description which answer to her experience and desires (I, 13). Later Margaret thinks of the South as a workplace for Nicholas Higgins and recognizes the destitution and solitude of agricultural labor, as compared with the comradeship of factory life (II, 12). The New Forest is no longer a place for rustic sketching. Forced to think in class terms, Margaret sees the social reality beneath the picturesque view, and the necessity which drives the "romantic" poacher. The South, where social change is less visible, nonetheless requires a new vocabulary, and Margaret is a worthy heroine because she is able to learn it.

When the narrative moves on to describe Margaret's responses to the streets of Milton, the adjustment of vision is again an implicit organizing principle. The scenes are recorded in fluid terms which stress the mental activity of confronting and absorbing something new; the streets are not there to provide symbolic social geographies like those of Dickens or Engels. As Margaret and her father first approach Milton, they see a cloud which Margaret takes to foretell rain; later it proves to be factory smoke. Despite the mild irony in the mistake, there is little emphasis on the desecration of the natural landscape; the description of the "lead-coloured cloud" sounds like a precise report of weather conditions, told by a mind that wishes "sufficiently" to account for any phenomenon. Standing among the smaller houses, the factory looks "like a hen among her chickens" (p. 55); and the barnyard simile is also not so much ironic as oddly accurate, suggesting both Margaret's country sources of comparison and the economic structure of Manchester factory life. Much of this first description—of the width of the streets, the cargo of the lurries, the dress of the populace—is done through comparisons with London street life, and although monotonous Manchester loses by contrast, Margaret's careful distinctions emphasize her attempt to balance and come to terms with what she sees. It is the absence of controlling metaphor or generalizing vision which is powerful here: refusing the role of authoritative or didactic narrator, Gaskell renders the condition of intelligent openness without judgment.

The fluctuating mix of responses in class-sensitive Margaret is even more striking in the description of her encounters with factory crowds in the streets. The paragraph begins with a fearful, negative judgment:

> Until Margaret had learnt the times of their ingress and egress, she was very unfortunate in constantly falling in with them. They came rushing along, with bold, fearless faces, and loud laughs and jests, particularly aimed at all those who appeared to be above them in rank or station. (p. 66)

This vision quickly modulates into her acceptance of the women in terms which demonstrate the weakening of class vocabulary: "There was such a simple reliance on her womanly sympathy with her love of dress, and on her kindliness, that she gladly replied to these inquiries, as soon as she understood them." Her fear of the men is stronger, anticipating her prideful struggle with sexuality:

> She, who had hitherto felt that even the most refined remark on her personal appearance was an impertinence, had to endure undisguised admiration from these outspoken men. But the very out-spokenness marked their innocence of any intention to hurt her delicacy, as she would have perceived if she had been less frightened by the disorderly tumult. Out of her fright came a flash of indignation which made her face scarlet, and her dark eyes gather flame, as she heard some of their speeches. (p. 66)

There is a crucial movement in the whole passage, from class terms to psychological ones: Margaret's prideful and indignant responses are shown to be defenses against class fears and are quickly linked to fears about sex and violence, as they will later be with Thornton. In this way the problem of changes in class assumptions created by the massing of workers in towns is presented as a concrete case for personal adjustment, requiring not the practice of some general spirit of benevolence but real psychological stress and reorganization.

The case is further pointed at the end of the chapter, when Margaret meets the working-class hero, Nicholas Higgins. She makes the automatic class assumption that a charity visit will be in order, only to find it interpreted as a reciprocal "impertinence." Higgins reverses the roles, inviting Margaret to his house because she is lonely and kind; and Margaret's shock of pride is recorded: "She was not sure if she would go where permission was given so like a favour conferred" (p. 68). But Higgins has the last word: reading Margaret's face rather than her social status, he correctly predicts that she will overcome her pique. His insistence on a personal interpretation displaces the class reflex; and the scene serves not only as an introduction to Higgins—who will later insist on the same kind of reversal in relation to his employer—but also as a lively example of the novel's insistence on the difficult bending of conventional class assumptions into recognitions of individual character. The need for such delicate adjustments of status is always imaginatively dramatized: Margaret's complex relationship with the traditional servant Dixon and Thornton's with Higgins are prominent cases.

Gaskell's account of shock and revision in such personal encounters widens into a more theoretical concern for the correction of balances between asserted authority and accepted dependence. This issue is made explicit during the important "Masters and Men" dialogue among Margaret, Mr. Hale, and Mr. Thornton (I, 15); here the analogy between parents and children, masters and men, organizes the conversation about mutual duty and dependence. Thornton argues for the factory relationship which splits work from life, insisting on absolute authority during working hours and independence for his workers at other times. Mr. Hale, arguing by analogy with families, suggests that workers, like children, must be brought up to attain both independence and a measure of authority. Margaret, closest to the narrative stance, brings up the actual interdependence of workers and masters, stressing the need to share economic information and decisions with factory workers. But it would be a mistake to read these dialogues as abstract position papers which are meant to be "won" by one view or another. The social dialogues are dramatic—that is, truly novelistic—scenes in which the pressures of personal history can be heard, and the contradictions inherent in positions felt. The coalescence of personal and social vision is, in fact, closer to the point of the dialogues than is the content of the abstract statements. The way the talkers' views are shaped by domestic experience and personal history is emphasized when Thornton allows himself to tell his own story, but it is implicit throughout in the parental metaphor.

The views of Margaret and her father are consistent with their recent experiences. Margaret has suffered under Mr. Hale's inability to share his decision with his dependents, and her insistence on the need to share information with factory workers reflects her sense of that failure. Mr. Hale's withdrawal from authority in his very declaration of independence from the Church shows how fully he yearns not to wield power, and is reflected during the dialogue in his stress on developing independence in children or workers. His actual weakness makes a domestic parallel with Thornton's attitude toward his workers: "I can always decide better by myself, and not influenced by those whom I love . . . I cannot stand objections. They make me so undecided" (p. 37), he has earlier apologized; Thornton, of course, does not fear objections, claiming to relish honest opposition from an independent stand. But he too wants to decide by himself, and to deny the actual dependence of his employees. The parallel between the situations, though not the characters, of the two men defines Thornton's respect for independence in his workers as a similar withdrawal from responsibility.

Thornton's reliance on his righteousness as a master and on setting a good example for his men is also placed in relation to his own "thorny" relationship with larger authorities. If he had not altered his own factory chimneys before "parliament meddled with the affair," he tells Mr. Hale, he would have resisted the law and "given all the trouble in yielding that I legally could" (p. 76). The contradictions in his stance are apparent, yet they contain the potential for change on which the virtue of Thornton's character is built. He learns to respect the workers' right to give legal "trouble in yielding" and to recognize that he cannot be a law unto himself in the fortunes of the larger economic community. These changes, based on new personal experience, are also logically demanded by his earlier theoretical stance.

Such points are constantly made through parallels—between Thornton and Hale, Thornton and Higgins—and are rarely explicated by the narrator. But the technique meets us at every turn: Frederick's story reflects again the dangers of Thornton's authoritarian position, as well as the corresponding dangers for the striking workpeople. None of the painful paradoxes and consequences of Frederick's shipboard mutiny is avoided in the brief treatment of that subplot. Margaret's defense of her noble if impulsive brother echoes Higgins's vision of the strike: "Loyalty and obedience to wisdom and justice are fine; but it is still finer to defy arbitrary power, unjustly and cruelly used—not on behalf of ourselves, but on behalf of others more helpless" (p. 100). This idealistic rhetoric is quickly qualified, as it is in the strike plot. As their leader, Frederick is indirectly guilty for the hangings of his sailor-followers; his "right beyond the law" will never be recognized; he is condemned to fugitive exile. The story remains opaque and insoluble matter, resting, perhaps, only in the wry view of the law that is Frederick's legacy: a court-martial is, in his words, "a court where authority weighs nine-tenths in the balance, and evidence forms only the other tenth. In such cases, evidence itself can hardly escape being influenced by the prestige of authority" (p. 237). The fact that his sister is saved from judicial process by the prestige of Thornton's authority is yet another irony in the great accumulation of puzzlement and contradiction which the novel builds around this issue.

"I can not imagine a nobler scope for a thoughtful energetic man, desirous of doing good to his kind, than that presented to his powers as the master of a factory," Mrs. Gaskell wrote to Lady Kay-

Shuttleworth in 1850, musing about the manufacturing novel she wanted somebody else to write. "But I believe that there is much to be discovered yet as to the right position and mutual duties of employer, and employed."[4] Three years later she found that she was to be the author herself, and *North and South* reiterates the need for new relational concepts. Gaskell's pessimism about finding a good "system" for factory organization informs her letter, but her insistence that Thornton cannot be a good manufacturer on his own shows how clearly she came to see that the problem can no longer be conceived as one of making "better factories." Admitting the need for "discovery" is, then, Thornton's crucial shift in the novel: he switches tutors, leaving Mr. Hale's classical tradition aside in favor of the keen social intelligence of his workman Nicholas Higgins. Thornton comes to define the present as a time of "men groping in new circumstances" (p. 304); the phrase shows he has learned the lesson of the novel, that a deliberate exploration of assumptions about traditional roles must precede the leap to solutions.

Gaskell's commitment to the need for openness in industrial relations can be tested in her treatment of Nicholas Higgins. The genuine intelligence and autonomy with which his character is drawn would seem to be the best argument against the preference for *Mary Barton* that many critics share, for the portrait of John Barton—like the tragic poem Gaskell thought it was[5]—comes to rely on pathos, while Higgins is always represented with the respect warranted by his ability to think, learn, and change. Higgins's position as a political spokesman is equal and parallel to Thornton's, and it is accorded the same kind of critical hearing. But it is necessary to point out the conceptual limits within which that hearing is interpreted.

Gaskell's position can be distilled from the points in the dialogues that are not left open for further questioning. Most centrally, the novel takes a stand against the idea that labor and capital represent opposing interests which must be expressed in class struggle. In that sense, *North and South* falls squarely in the category of middle-class fictions which argue for the identity of interest between workers and owners. That view depends on an acceptance of the liberal principles of economy—the flux of the market according to natural economic laws—whose blows of fortune are seen as affecting workers and manufacturers with equally uncertain results. Higgins is given the strong argument that the liberal view is simply part of the masters' "line" to their workers. The weight of the novel's argument does not challenge the concept, but uses it rather as an economic basis for a

4. *The Letters of Mrs Gaskell*, ed. J. A. V. Chapple and Arthur Pollard (Manchester: Manchester UP, 1966), p. 119. (This edition, p. 399.)
5. Writing to her publisher, Edward Chapman, 1 Jan. 1849, Gaskell complained about the manufacturers' responses to *Mary Barton*, saying, "meanwhile no one seems to see my idea of a tragic poem; so I, in reality mourn over my failure" (*Letters*, p. 68).

stance which often moves into a religious appeal for the interdependence of human beings. When Thornton, near the end of the novel, comes to give Higgins work, the narrative reveals its bias: Higgins's patience and generosity have made Thornton "forget entirely the mere reasonings of justice, and overleap them by a diviner instinct" (p. 296).

Along with those tenets of the liberal position, the novel stands clearly against violent means of persuasion. But Gaskell does not identify striking with violence. She does a great deal of work to demonstrate the generous nobility in Higgins's conception of the union, his careful orchestration of the principles which are to determine the strikers' behavior, and his rage when those principles are violated by the rioters. Thornton himself is made to say finally, "this last strike, under which I am smarting, has been respectable" (p. 305). The serious criticism of union strikes is presented in a way that is not typically redolent of middle-class fears; it is the further issue of the problematical relationship between the union and the poverty-stricken workers who become victims of the union as well as of the masters. The fair-mindedness in Gaskell's account can easily be seen if it is compared with Dickens's version of unionization in *Hard Times*, which presents the organizer as a slick devil and the ostracism practiced against good hard-working Stephen Blackpool as forced collective torture. In *North and South*, the union as Higgins conceives it is admirable and intelligently directed, and the strike is justified by the despotism of the masters. What is wrong is simply that workers like Boucher cannot afford to strike; that the union has created a new class division with oppressive tendencies within the labor force itself. Boucher is made a weak but passionate character, and his suicide is treated unsentimentally; his case does not undermine Higgins's position so much as it demands further adjustment in its conception.

The criticism of Higgins's position, therefore, rests on two main points: that he conceives of industrial life as class struggle, and that his union can act to oppress poor people. Higgins's story, like Thornton's, is about the way personal experiences with individual cases teach one to modify strongly argued theoretical views. The outlines of the change are expressed in the difference between two statements assessing the relationship between labor and capital. "I'll tell yo'," he says to Margaret in early dialogue, "it's their part,—their cue, as some folks call it,—to beat us down, to swell their fortunes; and it's ours to stand up and fight hard,—not for ourselves alone, but for them round about us—for justice and fair play" (p. 124). The deliberate emphasis on "acted" social roles links Higgins with every other character in the novel who begins by seeing others in terms of their role or class. Later, after Higgins has seen some of the complications for "them round about us," he accepts Thornton's job offer with a line which represents what Thornton has to learn, as well as the modifications of Higgins's original antagonist position: "I shall need a deal o' brains to settle where my business ends and yo'rs begins" (p. 297). It is the touchstone of the novel's conclusion, a tentative openness to which Thornton also submits in the plan for the factory dining room.

That exploratory frame of mind is not charity, and the complexity of the concept marks another important advance from the position of *Mary Barton*. In the early meeting with Margaret, the job-offer scene with Thornton, and the dining-room scheme, Higgins consistently refuses the role of acceptor, turning charities around into invitations apparently initiated by him. His insistence on the equality of the participants in all these relationships is charmingly suggested in his ability to make analogies between his and others' situations. When he goes to visit Mr. Hale, for example, he identifies their positions, calling him "a parson out o' work" (p. 208). The similarities between his independent pride and Thornton's are, of course, clearly marked. Like Thornton, Higgins indulges in violent verbal anger, but his actions are generous. Despite his rage at Boucher's betrayal of the strike, he takes responsibility for its results by supporting Boucher's children; Thornton's second thoughts are also invariably generous. The equality which Gaskell extends in the portrait of Higgins is genuine and can be measured by the shock of her lapse into special pleading when Higgins's state of cleanliness and his class embarrassment suddenly come into focus during the visit to Mr. Hale.

What *North and South* finally has to say about its industrial theme is emblemized in the factory dining-room scheme, however summary the presentation of that plan may be. The dining room where Thornton eats by invitation is a symbol of his willingness to obliterate his earlier distinction between the men's lives as workers and as human beings. It is also a tentative forum for discussion, awaiting the growth of trust and the formation of personal respect between Thornton and his workers. No claims are made for its effectiveness, but the shifts in attitude to which the dining plan attests are consistent with the novel's theme of change through personal contact. Thornton refuses to present the plan as a model, but his way of talking about it stands for a change of heart. A fictional "solutions" go, this one has the virtue of tangible particularity and an appealing faithfulness to the rhythm of the workplace itself.

It has often been argued that Gaskell raises large social issues only to diminish them in merely personal solutions; that the love story is central, and that the marriage, a symbolic union of north and south, rural and industrial, traditional and modern, stands in for the author's position of compromise and accommodation. Yet in the textures of the novel that I have discussed so far, the equal weighting in the presentation of personal and social vision is especially remarkable. To make the point that political stance grows out of particular experience and that change is possible exactly for that reason is not to retreat so much as to focus on process. And, if Gaskell's call for dialogue between representatives of different views is, politically judged, a wobbly compromise position, it must also be seen as a deeply held sense of life. "I suppose we all *do* strengthen each other by clashing together, and earnestly talking our own thoughts and ideas. The very disturbance we thus are to each other rouses us up, and makes us more healthy,"[6] she wrote, not about politics but about the "good" that her correspondent had suggested she might do for Charlotte Brontë. The earnestness is Victorian, but the confrontation psychology is not; and such stress on the value of conflict makes *North and South* atypical among industrial fictions.

The story of Margaret and Thornton is strong for the same reasons that animate the social conflicts: because it is an account of deep confusion in a time of personal change and revision. Moreover, the issues in Margaret's emotional economy are closely related to those of the social plot. Margaret struggles with the implications of assumed authority and carries on a fierce internal battle between conventional female roles and feelings and the uncharted territory of personal impulse. These matters come to a head in two dramatic actions: Margaret's rush to protect Thornton from his strikers' threats, and her lie to the police inspector. The two acts of impulse— and Margaret's confused attempts to interpret them after the fact— are formally parallel and provide more evidence for the embedded coherence of the novel.

Amid critical demur at Gaskell's glamorizing of her heroine, her quite radical treatment of Margaret as a fully responsible human being has gone by with surprisingly little note. The predominant sense of Margaret's life—one which makes it an unusual account of a Victorian heroine—is that of a person forced continually into making decisions, alone and under pressure. In the early chapter "Decision" the shock of that change is recorded. In the London household, Margaret thinks, "everything went on with the regularity of clockwork. . . . Now, since that day when Mr. Lennox came, and startled her into a decision, every day brought some question, momentous to her, and to those whom she loved, to be settled" (p. 48). The quick confusion of refusing Lennox in the space of time it takes for Mr. Hale to peel and eat a pear is followed immediately by Mr. Hale's announcement and the removal to Milton; but the pace of events here is only a mild anticipation of the build-up of pressures that will accumulate to almost unbearable intensity at the novel's center. When Margaret goes to Thornton's to borrow a water bed for her mother and stays to protect Thornton from the strikers' violence, she has been up all night after her mother's attack of spasms, she is confused by her feelings about Thornton, involved in Bessy Higgins's dying, torn by Boucher's position in the strike, and sympathetic towards Higgins himself. All these situations, each demanding internal adjustment and outward moral action on her part, play into her responses to the strikers' convergence on Thornton's mill.

As in the "Decision" chapter, and often elsewhere in the text, Margaret tries in meditation to organize and separate these rapid changes of focus. Keeping watch beside her mother's sickbed, she thinks, "Not more than thirty-six hours ago, she cared for Bessy Higgins and her father, and her heart was wrung for Boucher; now, that was all like a dreaming memory of some former life;—everything that had passed out of doors seemed dissevered from her mother, and therefore unreal" (p. 155). That afternoon Margaret confronts the public mob in an action which mixes public and private motives inextricably. The next day, hurt and unrested, she refuses Thornton in an angry interchange, visits Bessy and hears about the pressures on the workers, hears her mother's dying plea to see her son, and writes the letter to Frederick that, she knows, may place him in mortal danger. This astonishing rapidity of event is experienced in the reading as it impinges upon Margaret's consciousness, with the effect that her actions and decisions about each event carry in them implicit pressures from all the others. The technique forces the reader into constant juxtapositions and comparisons that are not pointed out by the narrative. Feelings which rise out of one situation emerge in another one; thus, to give only one example, we hear Margaret speak of Frederick in terms which perfectly characterize the rejected parts of her action and feeling towards Thornton: "I will put my arm in the bolt sooner than he should come to the slightest harm. . . . I will watch over him like a lioness over her young" (p. 218). The result, so different from the sparse actions and spacious reflections of heroines like Austen's or Brontë's, is a sequence of strong feeling and quick action in a character whose natural bent is to control and meditate upon experience. At least in the central portion of the book, Margaret is not allowed a woman's leisure to learn, and the narrative emphasizes instead the sheer strength of character required to get through all those simultaneous crises, and the continual pressure of responsibility for actions that bear heavily on other lives.

Margaret's two actions push her into the public realm of men: she joins Thornton to confront the angry strikers ("A Blow and its Consequences") and lies to the police inspector, denying that she has been present at the railway station with her fugitive brother ("False and True"). In both cases her pleas have put a man in danger, and she moves instinctively to save him from the consequences of a situation for which she feels responsible. The unthinking gestures are, in both cases, indirectly successful in averting the danger, but once done, they seem riddled with moral ambiguity, and cause Margaret enormous shame and internal strife. In both cases, too, what she sees as a human action to save another is given a sexual interpretation by others; and in the strike scene, the action does in fact include passions which Margaret is yet unable to face. What Gaskell takes on here is remarkable for its demand that Margaret share the complexities of public and private motives with the male characters: she places her heroine in situations which force her to experience and to reconcile herself to the moral ambiguity of public actions and, while Margaret agonizedly attempts to separate her "personal" from her morally disinterested self, shows how inextricable her motives "as a woman" and as a moral being really are.

It is tempting to see the strike as an irritated response to the riot scene in Charlotte Brontë's *Shirley,* one manufacturing novel besides *Hard Times* that we know Gaskell read. In Brontë's story the theoretically feminist Shirley prevents her co-heroine Caroline Helstone from rushing to the aid of the besieged mill owner, Robert Moore. The assumptions about women's roles which underlie Shirley's reasons ought to destroy any pretenses about the nature of her feminism: she wants to keep Caroline from making "a spectacle of yourself" and argues, "And this is serious work: he must be unmolested."[7] What would happen if she *did* go, Gaskell might have asked, in defiance of that traditional stance. Having Margaret go, speak to the crowd, and suffer the blow meant for Thornton is a dare, and Gaskell does not avoid the consequences that Shirley foresees. Thornton is annoyed at the violation of his masculine world, Margaret suffers acutely from having become a "spectacle," and the impulsive action rebounds in unexpectedly sexual ways. The point is that Margaret is not allowed to hide and watch from the shadows, as Brontë's heroines do; she is made to share publicity and its attendant confusion with Thornton and to work out for herself the psychic consequences of her assertion.

I would emphasize the courage with which these situations are imagined, because it is so easy to criticize the scenes themselves. The writing in the chapters may well suggest a novelist pressed mistakenly into melodrama, for Margaret appears in them, too often, as the object of external regard, a suffering queen; and the strikers are turned for the purposes of the drama into a bestial force that betrays

7. *Shirley,* chap. 19.

the novel's otherwise clear-eyed individual attention to the work-people. The riot scene, with its focus on the sentimental force of Margaret's trickling blood, helps to justify the popular view that the social material is put in service of the love story. It is certainly true that the immediate consequence of "A Blow and its Consequences" is to turn our attention to the passional relationship of Thornton and Margaret and, for a time, away from the strike. But, together with the lie episode, the scene also does the more central work of impli-cating Margaret in the novel's questions about conventional—even legal—rules. Margaret violates a traditional idea about her place as a woman and commits perjury in a good cause. Like her father and brother, like Higgins and Thornton, she is placed in the position of asserting a personal stand in the face of a larger authority, and of enduring the complicated aftermath.

If the actions of Margaret's life stress her assumption of respon-sibility amid rapid changes of fortune, the story of her inner life renders the process of psychic change in terms that also move beyond our usual notions about Victorian analysis. At its best, the narrative describes the strong and contradictory feelings of the two lovers with an impartial, unmoralized recognition of their integrity that anticipates the method of D. H. Lawrence.[8] Gaskell's refusal to judge or categorize the feelings she names gives another kind of nar-rative validity to her view that honest feeling does not live by the rules of conventional role.

Margaret's transformation from child to acting adult occurs quickly, but the change from girl to woman is a far more muddled transition in which the appeal to Victorian "womanhood" is as much a mask for sexual fear as it is an assertion of adulthood. The early narrative is surprisingly honest about Margaret's sexual confusions. "If Margaret had not been very proud she might have almost felt jealous of the mushroom rival" (p. 11), we are told in relation to Edith's new sister-in-law; the narrator is clear about the force that prevents jealousy, and it is not a moral one. After Henry Lennox's proposal, "Margaret felt guilty and ashamed of having grown so much into a woman as to be thought of in marriage" (p. 32). This blunt and accurate piece of adolescent psychology establishes terms which anticipate Margaret's shamed response to her impulsive defense of Thornton.

The confusion of guilt and shame in the rejection of Lennox, pushed aside in waking life by Mr. Hale's decision, returns in a

---

8. Barbara Hardy recognizes and summarizes this as one of Gaskell's strengths, pointing out "how often the feelings are not specialized, not kept in separate compartments." "Mrs Gaskell and George Eliot," *The Victorians*, ed. Arthur Pollard (London: Barrie and Jenkins, 1970), p. 178.

remarkable dream that dramatizes the strength of Margaret's guilt and anger, suggesting at the same time her notion of "saving" as a primary impulse of love:

> He was climbing up some tree of fabulous height to reach the branch whereon was slung her bonnet: he was falling, and she was struggling to save him, but held back by some invisible powerful hand. He was dead. And yet, with a shifting of the scene, she was once more in the Harley Street drawing-room, talking to him as of old, and still with a consciousness all the time that she had seen him killed by that terrible fall. (p. 41)

What Gaskell herself would have made of the dream we do not know; that she invented it is one of the many signs of the powerful psychological intelligence that casually informs so much of her narrative. Similarly, Margaret's ambivalent stance toward free action is represented in waking scenes controlled by images of freedom and enclosure. Margaret's despair at her father's defection from the Church is expressed in images of lost boundaries: she sees him as an outcast, while the sky behind the church tower becomes "some farther distance, and yet no sign of God," and the earth seems "desolate" under "never-ending depths of space" (p. 40). When the cottage is nearly dismantled, Margaret goes out into the garden and experiences an analogous fear. The mystery of the forest life, the "wild adventurous freedom" of the poacher (p. 51), formerly sources of romantic pleasure, become threatening. Unaccountably afraid, Margaret rushes to the door of her house, " 'till she was safe in the drawing-room, with the windows fastened and bolted, and the familiar walls hemming her round, and shutting her in" (p. 51). The narrator does not tell us why Margaret is afraid, not choosing to interpret her character behind her back. We are left to observe the connection between her fear of boundless distance and the stress of change in her life without being put in a position of superior wisdom. At the same time we learn something of the tendencies in Margaret's unconscious life: bold imaginative romanticism on one hand, fearful retreat to the familiar or the orthodox on the other. The partial release of pent-up forces—both social and personal—in the riot scene is partly figured in a continuation of these patterns of imagery: the strikers break down the gates of Thornton's barricadelike establishment; Margaret sends Thornton out from the enclosed safety of his house, and then follows herself, going out of bounds into the "angry sea of men" on the tide of her passionate moral impulse (p. 162). The ambivalence in her earlier responses to such uncharted spaces makes no surprise of her reactions to this one.

Margaret's psychological task is to retreat from that chaotic territory by interpreting the incident in a way that will deny the feelings for Thornton which have been crudely observed by the vulgar eyes of Fanny Thornton and the servant Jane. She does so by making herself into a Victorian angel: "If I saved one blow, one cruel, angry action that might otherwise have been committed, I did a woman's work" (p. 173). This interpretation, which she uses again to defend herself against Thornton's declaration of love, is not Gaskell's retreat to Victorian convention but a canny conjunction of feeling and rationalization: Margaret clutches at the accessible stereotype in the face of her acute shame at having been "seen" in passionate action. In her fevered night thoughts,

> a cloud of faces looked up at her, giving her no idea of fierce vivid anger, or of personal danger, but a deep sense of shame that she should thus be the object of universal regard—a sense of shame so acute that it seemed as if she would fain have burrowed into the earth to hide herself, and yet she could not escape out of that unwinking glare of many eyes. (p. 174)

The shame is about having left the protected woman's place for one of unwomanly publicity, and Margaret's insistence that her act is a representative piece of woman's work takes on its full strength of defensive meaning in relation to the shame.

The scene in which Margaret and Thornton fight about that meaning, ironically titled "Mistakes Cleared Up," is a fine representation of confusions multiplied by the clash of the antagonists' different styles of anger. Under the circumstances, Margaret's stance of outraged modesty is almost comical: "We all feel the sanctity of our sex as a high privilege when we see danger," she says, and later accuses Thornton of being no "gentleman" if he could not perceive "that any woman, worthy of the name of woman, would come forward to shield, with her reverenced helplessness, a man in danger from the violence of numbers" (p. 177). The irony in such terminology is deepened by Thornton's insistence that he is a "man," and has therefore a right to express feeling, for Margaret's action as a particular woman has done precisely that. Her overly general and sentimental moral language gives away the shakiness of her emotional state, while Gaskell's clarity about its fraudulence shines through the extraordinary Lawrence-like account of Margaret's private condition of mind:

> As far as [her opinions] defied his rock-like power of character, his passion-strength, he seemed to throw them off from him with contempt, until she felt the weariness of the exertion of making useless protests; and now, he had come, in this strange wild passionate way, to make known his love! . . . And she shrank and shuddered as under the fascination of some great power, repugnant to her whole previous life. She crept away,

> and hid from his idea. But it was of no use. . . . She disliked him
> the more for having mastered her inner will. . . .
>
> And so she shuddered away from the threat of his enduring
> love. What did he mean? Had she not the power to daunt him?
> She would see. It was more daring than became a man to
> threaten her so. (p. 180)

The blunt linkage of sexuality and power-play is the kind of thing
that may suggest Brontë's influence; but Brontë would never have
come out with such stark formulations of pride, passion, and fear in
a controlling narrative voice. That inner/outer voice, with its almost
incantatory rhythms, is of Gaskell's invention. And this sequence of
feeling is not presented as a road to resolution; it remains a stubborn
set of contradictions. Margaret again returns to her Victorian solution, while the narrative simply shows the confused coexistence of
moral and emotional thoughts with the courage to leave them unin-
terpreted.

Thornton also gets his share of such internal life, for Gaskell—
again like Lawrence—makes no bones about her ability to enter his
mind with equal confidence. The description of Thornton's aimless
bus ride into the countryside ("Mother and Son") is perhaps the most
sustained example; in those paragraphs we get, for instance:

> He said to himself, that he hated Margaret, but a wild, sharp
> sensation of love cleft his dull, thunderous feeling like lightning,
> even as he shaped the words expressive of hatred. His greatest
> comfort was in hugging his torment; and in feeling, as he had
> indeed said to her, that though she might despise him, contemn
> him, treat him with her proud sovereign indifference, he did not
> change one whit. She could not make him change. He loved
> her, and would love her; and defy her, and this miserable bodily
> pain. (p. 191)

Among all the variations spun on the theme of change, "she could
not make him change" rings with special strength. Even more
impressive, though, are the cadences of prose. Like the treatment of
Margaret, this writing creates sympathy and admiration for a character on the basis of stubborn strength of feeling, presented without
the controlling terms of moral argument.

Elizabeth Gaskell's best writing—this originality of diction and
psychological honesty—is done with the unjudging openness to
experience that is also at issue in the story. But it is at odds with a
conventional Victorian novelist's conception of her duty, and with
the formal nature of the novel itself. The pervasive questioning of
conventional roles does not function on the level of explicit design
as clearly as it permeates pieces of narrative texture. Yet the novel is

strongest when it is most free to set down the rather chaotic matter of experience without an insistent directive bias.

North and South may well represent the furthest stretch of Gaskell's courageous sense of the clash between observation and form, for the novels that follow are, in some ways, retreats. *Sylvia's Lovers* and *Wives and Daughters* are formally better, but they lack the intense questioning which animates everything in *North and South*. Those stories work within the social order and its judgments, even if they are often acute about its stresses; and the demands of social change are no longer issues of character. Unlike *North and South*, both of those fictions seem "contained" in their forms.

In the final ten or eleven chapters, the narrative of *North and South* seems set on the task of bringing itself to some orderly conclusion, and the writing all too often summarizes with a lack of drama or conviction that suggests the dutiful completion of a project. Strained circumstances of composition need not suffice as an explanation; it may be that the difficulty of ending had something to do with the stubbornly open presentation of character and social change in the main part of the story. The constant questioning of the dynamics of authority and dependence, the insistence on the centrality of change in human experience, and the admiration for sheer strength of feeling in character—these attitudes are not easily shaped into the form of a Victorian story. If *North and South* ends with too much haste and inattention, it is perhaps because its author had dared to venture so much that did not lend itself to the demands of "resolution" in the conventions of serialized fiction.

JO PRYKE

The Treatment of Political Economy in *North and South*†

North and South has a good deal to say about political economy, and what it says is most characteristic of Elizabeth Gaskell. The subject, and the way Gaskell handles it, have special interest for us today, for the fundamental assumption of what we now call classical economics, that we are all subject to the laws of economic competition and must—paradoxically—be made free to obey them, has in this decade made a come-back as the dominant conventional wisdom, after a long period in the wilderness. Once again the arguments between

† From *The Gaskell Society Journal* 4 (1990): 28–39. Reprinted by permission of the Gaskell Society and the author.

Margaret Hale, Thornton and Higgins in *North and South* about economic individualism versus social responsibility, and free market forces versus justice and fair play, are to be heard on all sides. As before, what is at issue today is not merely an economic theory, but a mixture of moral and social values inextricably associated with an economic system whose virtues are once again being vigorously promoted. Moreover now, as in the mid-nineteenth century, these moral and social values are being used as material in contemporary culture. David Lodge's recent novel, *Nice Work*, is implicitly 'about' political economy, dramatising precisely, in the confrontations of its two central characters, the attitudes and practices which classical economics seeks to explain and justify, and the ways in which they can be challenged. The film *Wall Street*, the play *Serious Money*, the television serial *A Very British Coup* and even the comic TV character 'Loadsamoney' are further examples from contemporary culture of a renewed interest in the values of the profit motive.[1]

At the time when *North and South* was written, there were—broadly—two opposing conceptions of what was meant by 'political economy'; we find them dramatised in this text, and we recognise them as the terms of the debate today. On the one hand it was seen as a 'science', proving a set of propositions about economic life which everyone should know about, and which ought to regulate the behaviour of all, to their own and society's moral and material benefit. On the other hand, it was perceived as a set of self-interested theories developed to rationalise and justify the kind of economy that was developing; these theories were felt to be dangerous because they claimed—and exercised—a baneful influence over the discussion of economic, political, social and moral questions.

There were two essential elements in the simplified version of political economy used by both its supporters and its critics. The first was Adam Smith's 'general desire for wealth', assumed by his successors to have the status of a law of nature. Its corollary was freedom of economic action: no regulatory legislation, or well-meant but dependency-producing charity, must be allowed to stifle this universal motivation. Political economy's critics attacked this first and basic assumption as a perniciously limited definition of man, claiming that 'the dismal science' saw him *merely* as a creature of self-interest, connected to his fellow-man *only* by the 'cash nexus'.[2] From this point of view, political economy was often attacked as simply un-Christian.

The second essential element was the 'law' of supply and demand, determining the movements of capital, labour and commodities. A

1. Lodge's novel was published in 1988; the references to television material are to British television productions of the 1980s.
2. The term originates in the work of Thomas Carlyle. See p. 391, n.1 above.

popular image of this was of the working of the 'Invisible Hand', ordering all things harmoniously. Driven by the 'general desire for wealth', untrammelled by distorting constraints imposed by governments or workers, supply and demand (or market forces, in our current phrase) would ensure that the economy worked smoothly, to the enrichment of all. From the assumption of this law followed the belief in *laissez-faire* policies in trade, industry and social matters. The hostile view of the law of supply and demand saw it simply as the law of the economic jungle: political economy, in presenting it as inevitable and desirable, was merely expressing the heartless self-seeking and materialism of the age. In the 1980s these simplified ideas have once again become familiar currency.

Political economy appears both explicitly and implicitly in *North and South*. Rather than adopting a stance pro- or anti-, the book seeks to place and explain partisan attitudes on both sides. To do this, Gaskell sets them in the context of an economic system which is shown to be cruel and oppressive, but no more so than the one it is supplanting, and in which the text also sees the excitement and potential for good. In this setting, the events of the narrative itself enact the confrontation and modification of opposed ideas. Moreover, the structuring of the book by parallel as much as by contrast— of event, situation, character and attitude—equally enacts an exploratory and explanatory approach. In this article I have space only to examine the book's use of the 'conversation method' to explore the major questions.

Political economy is mentioned explicitly in three places in *North and South*; it occurs as one of the implicit terms in direct and reported conversations about economic issues and, more broadly, appears as part of the capitalist industrial system, being the theory used by its supporters to rationalise and justify it. Each explicit reference is in the context of discussion about the relationship between masters and men, and the attitudes on each side to the point at issue in the strike: who—or what—determines wages? The masters, as the instruments of impersonal economic laws, or the men, asserting their rights? The presentation of these questions within conversation means that there are no 'winners'. People are left in possession of their positions and only manifest the effects of the points put to them subsequently, gradually and partially.

Political economy first appears by name in Volume I, Chapter 15, when the coming strike is under discussion between Margaret, Mr Hale and Thornton. A strike conveniently dramatises the question at issue in any discussion of the capitalist industrial system which calls in aid its rationale, political economy, because a strike is, even if peacefully prosecuted, self-evidently a challenge to the *status quo* of a dramatic sort. The strike in *North and South* is in resistance to

a wage-cut, and for better pay: in other words, the workers are claiming some control over their industry. Thornton produces political
economy as the explanation and justification of the *status quo*, in
which the masters retain total control, as a matter of 'principle' not
revealing to the men their reasons for holding or reducing wages
(though this secrecy is not related to any theory of political economy). Their reasons are the poor state of trade, in other words the
functioning of political economy's law of supply and demand, which
is currently producing poor demand. This would, in fact, make it
beneficial to the masters if the men were to stop producing for a
while of their own accord, which is why they 'on principle' keep it to
themselves. Thornton refers to the state of trade as something to
which all must submit, masters and men alike, and to his autonomy
as a master as something he would not allow to be encroached upon
because his 'hands' are in a state of ignorant infancy as far as their
understanding of business is concerned, though he would never
'interfere' with their life outside work hours. His position has been
more crudely stated by his mother earlier in the chapter when she
tells Margaret that the workers are striking 'for the mastership and
ownership of other people's property' (p. 106), but Thornton displays
the same combative spirit: ' "Let them turn out! I shall suffer as well
as they: but at the end they will find I have not bated nor altered one
jot" ' (p. 111).

Margaret, however, challenges Thornton's all-embracing pro-
nouncement that ' "We, the owners of capital, have a right to choose
what we will do with it" ' (p. 108). She proposes the idea that the
proper relationship between masters and men should be based on a
Christian conception of stewardship but breaks off, saying ' "However, I know so little about strikes, and rate of wages, and capital and
labour, that I had better not talk to a political economist like you" '
(p. 108). In other words, political economy is something separate
and apart from Christian morality, and Margaret, in a move common
to its critics then as now, is shifting the argument onto a different
plane.

Indeed the issues on which a political economist would have something to say, the state of trade and the rate of wages, are lost as the
conversation returns to the central, obsessive question—who, out of
masters and men, controls whom? Thornton actually refers to the
conception of political economic theory, that the two are necessary
and equal components in a harmoniously operating society of free
individuals, but dismisses it as 'Utopian'. Thus he is no pure political
economist, but a practical businessman, dealing with facts as he sees
them, and praying in aid political economy's laws as they suit him.
Margaret, advancing her southern gentlewoman's conception of the
responsibility of the upper for the lower classes, and the Christian

minister, Mr Hale, suggesting that perhaps judicious 'bringing up', particularly through education, is what the hands need, are met simply with the practical businessman's reply: ' "I am sorry to say, I have an appointment at eight-o'clock, and must just take facts as I find them to-night, without trying to account for them; which, indeed, would make no difference in determining how to act as things stand—the facts must be granted" ' (p. 112).

Margaret, however, will not let him dismiss, in this way, the idea of society as an interdependent unity. Thornton questions whether the economic relationship—of labour to sell and capital to buy—gives him the right to assume any other relationship with the independent Darkshire men, but Margaret, in reply, offers an eloquent, Carlylean picture of industrial society:

> ' . . . not in the least because of your labour and capital positions, whatever they are, but because you are a man, dealing with a set of men over whom you have, whether you reject the use of it or not, immense power, just because your lives and your welfare are so constantly and intimately interwoven. God has made us so that we must be mutually dependent. We may ignore our own dependence, or refuse to acknowledge that others depend upon us in more respects than the payment of weekly wages; but the thing must be, nevertheless.' (p. 112)

Thornton counters this with the suggestion that the role dictated for him by this 'mutual dependence' may best take the form, not of interference, but simply of example, for what the master is, so the men will be. But Margaret (who certainly has the best of the argument in debating terms) once again brings a Christian text into her effective riposte. This is that, if the men are violent and obstinate in pursuit of their rights, it can, on Thornton's argument, be safely inferred that the master is too: ' "that he is a little ignorant of that spirit which suffereth long, and is kind and seeketh not her own" ' (p. 113). Here again there is an attempt to shift the argument away from the Gradgrindian 'facts' and towards the kind of values which yield to no computation, and again it provokes the response of the eminently practical man, who has in any case other things to concern him besides getting along pleasantly with his 'hands': ' "You are just like all strangers who do not understand the working of our system . . . you suppose that our men are puppets of dough . . . and you seem not to perceive that the duties of a manufacturer are far larger and wider than those merely of an employer of labour" ' (p. 113).

Far from being the cool representative of a rational science in this conversation, Thornton 'reddens' and speaks 'hastily', whilst Margaret remains cold; his arguments are heated, experience-based, hers clever, essentially theoretical, so that she can vex Thornton to speechlessness by pinpointing illogicalities: ' "I am trying to reconcile your admiration of despotism with your respect for other men's independence of character" ' (p. 114). His re-iterated position is essentially a statement of pure individualism, whilst Margaret opposes to it an idealistic communalism, the one position rationalising an atomistic, *laissez-faire* society, the other a hierarchical, deferential one. Yet while Thornton speaks from experience, the experience he articulates is one in which he does not yet, in practice, relate to individuals—his men are 'hands', Margaret a woman he is soon to 'worship'. At the same time the telling incident which so effectively closes the chapter shows how far Margaret has to go in genuinely acknowledging fellowship, for her failure to shake hands with Thornton, in the customary Northern fashion, interpreted by him as pride, in fact reflects the more hierarchical, less democratic society of the south (with regard here to relations between the sexes but the implication is wider) to which she still belongs—though, with her friendship with the Higginses under way, she is changing.

Political economy is thus seen as something used by the masters, as far as it suits them to use it, but co-existing with non-theoretical elements in their outlook. Its tenets are shown as arising from certain positions taken in the real world, and it is the method of the book to show those positions both as arising from other than abstract considerations, and as susceptible of modification. The idea that to think in terms of political economy is natural to some people in the economic system and not to others, because of their respective places within that same system, does not, of course, necessarily imply that political economic concepts are not valid absolutely, but the giving of equal weight to the view of the matter from each side, in the book's conversations, certainly contributes to the relativity of its treatment in many other ways. Later, in conversation with Mr Bell in Chapter 40, Thornton even attributes the qualities of enterprise and independence to the accident of Darkshiremen's Teutonic racial inheritance—the Greeks were different and wanted different things: an (unwitting) challenge, indeed, to the claim that political economy's 'universal desire for wealth', and the need to exercise it untrammelled, have the status of laws of nature.

The book's chief exponent of the relativity of the doctrines of political economy is, however, the redoubtable Higgins, with whom, in Chapter 17, Margaret discusses the strike after her first brush in the subject with Thornton. Higgins's way of thinking is as combative as Thornton's, focussed on teaching the masters the limits of their control, while Margaret's approach is, again, to look for recognition of common ground and common humanity: to strike merely damages everyone, the masters will surely give reasons for their action in cutting wages, such as the state of trade (the latter point nicely showing

the way in which characters incorporate arguments they have previously dismissed into their thinking). Higgins, like Thornton, sees
Margaret as an ignorant outsider, and expounds the view of the matter from his side of the battle lines, a view which, like hers, shifts the
basis of the argument: *justice* demands that the rate of wages, not the
state of trade, should be the issue, and he is prepared to die at his
post, in the way so admired in soldiers, sooner than yield: ' "I'll tell yo'
it's their part—[the masters'] . . . to beat us down, to swell their fortunes; and it's ours to stand up and fight hard,—not for ourselves
alone, but for them round about—for justice and fair play. We help
to make their profits and we ought to help spend 'em" ' (p. 124). In
parallel with Thornton, a relish for conflict characterises Higgins, as
well as an adherence to principle, which will combine to make him
an effective spokesman for scepticism and political economy:

> 'It's not that we want their brass so much this time . . . We'n
> getten money laid by; and we're resolved to stand and fall
> together; not a man on us will go in for less wages than the
> Union says is our due. So I say "Hooray for the strike, and let
> Thornton, and Slickson, and Hamper, and their set look to it!' "
> (p. 124)

Political economy does not come up again for directly dramatised
discussion until Volume II, Chapter 3, after the crises of the riot,
Thornton's proposal to Margaret, and the death of Bessy. In the
context of the Hales' care and concern for the bereaved Higgins, the
issues of the defeated strike are debated in their home, where Higgins is courteously received as a visitor, and where he correspond-
ingly behaves with dignity and restraint. The discussion has been
initiated by the Hales so that they can give Higgins the sympathetic
hearing he would have had from Bessy. His account of its failure is
reported in the explanatory, mediating tone which characterises the
approach of the book as a whole. The parallelism of over-confidence
in theory, on the part of masters and men alike, is made explicit in
this passage. The placing of it qualifies Higgins' ensuing attack on
the absolutism of political economy more effectively than would the
gentle remonstrances of Mr Hale alone: 'The workmen's calculations
were based (like too many of the masters') on false premises. They
reckoned on their fellow-men as if they possessed the calculable
powers of machines, no more, no less' (p. 210).

The political economic theory that is brought up for discussion is
the wage fund theory (popular at the time, though since discredited)
which lent intellectual conviction to a practical reluctance to
increase pay. If it is true, as Hale puts it to Higgins, that, when wages
are forced up by a strike, they will only sink again in greater proportion because of the effects of the strike, then clearly it is not legiti-

mate for workers to ask for a rise, as Higgins and his Union have been doing, because this is not only futile, and damaging to the employers, but actually self-destructive. The challenge mounted by Union action, and articulated by Higgins, to the control of wages arises, however, from the experience of the poor on the receiving end of the wage system, and it ignores the claim of the wealthy that such matters are not in fact under their control but determined by the laws articulated by political economy. It asserts a counterclaim for 'justice and fair play', calling in aid a universal morality:

> 'So I took th'book and tugged at it; but, Lord bless yo', it went on about capital and labour, and labour and capital, till it fair sent me off to sleep. I ne'er could rightly fix i' my mind which was which; and it spoke on 'em as if they were vartues or vices; and what I wanted for to know were the rights o' men, whether they were rich or poor—so be they only were men.' (p. 211)

Thus Higgins's reply to Hale's point about wages finding their own level once again shifts the perspective, and inserts the moral element into the debate. However, he makes practical points, too, about how men should be handled, given that matters continue as they are. He argues that political economy, whether or not it tells the truth on the limited subjects it does address—on which he reserves judgement—should be explained in terms that are intelligible. Then he asserts that even if it were so explained, it should not be assumed that everyone is necessarily going to agree with it, for there is not one absolute truth on the matter for everyone, and political economy may be truer for some than for others: ' "And I'm not one who thinks truth can be shaped out in words, all neat and clean, as th' men at the foundry cut out sheet-iron. Same bones won't go down wi' everyone. It'll stick here in this man's throat, and there in t'other's" ' (p. 212). Finally, even if the truth of political economy be granted, its prescriptions should not be forced on people regardless of their position and circumstances: its ministrations should be tempered to the recipient.

Hale, irredeemably the man of theory, can only respond, as we have seen, by wishing that masters ('some of the kindest and wisest') and men could meet for 'a good talk' in order to dispel the men's ignorance on ' "subjects which it is for the mutual interests of both should be well understood by both" '. His further idea, equally fanciful given the entire narrative so far, that ' "Mr Thornton might be induced to do such a thing" ' (p. 212), is effectively quashed by Margaret's brief reference to their own knowledge of Thornton's view of the men, as fit only for despotism.

Higgins's position on political economy is given considerable eloquence by the use of vivid pictorial and anecdotal language, and would dominate the chapter if it ended there, fitting as it does so well into the relative, experience-based value system of the book. The conversation method, however, prevents winners emerging in this way, for the mention of Thornton leads on to discussion of his treatment of Boucher and the other rioters, and thence to Higgins's attitude to Boucher. Margaret asks why Boucher was in the Union at all, if he was so feeble and undisciplined, and learns about 'sending to Coventry' to enforce Union membership. Her horror at this cruel coercion, and her comparison of this tyranny with the tyranny of the masters he complains of, draws from Higgins a defence based, like Thornton's in Volume I, Chapter 15, on experience, and the facts of the system. Here the facts are the history of tyranny by the masters, and the consequent necessity of unity among the workers for survival. Once again the voice of experience draws from Mr Hale a plaintive wish that divisions between classes did not exist, once again (in an echo of Thornton's less tactful response to father and daughter) met by the voice of practicality: ' "Oh!" said Mr Hale, sighing, "your Union would in itself be beautiful, glorious—it would be Christianity itself—if it were but for an end which affected the good of all, instead of that of merely one class as opposed to another." "I reckon it's time for me to be going, sir," said Higgins' (p. 214).

Again the incident that concludes the conversation is tellingly chosen. The chapter closes on a distinctly anti-dogmatic note, but with a heavy emphasis on common humanity and shared experience: 'Margaret the Churchwoman, her father the Dissenter, Higgins the Infidel, knelt down together. It did them no harm' (p. 215). Since political economy appears in this chapter, either as dogma from the point of view of a practical sceptic, or presented as fact by an inexperienced theorist, it continues to be seen as part of the shifting, apparently contradictory, puzzling phenomena of life portrayed in the text of *North and South* with an appropriately shifting, relative perspective.

Political economy is not again mentioned explicitly in the book. However the industrial system it has been presented as explaining and justifying continues as an important topic. It is important by virtue of the attitudes towards it of the major characters and the way these are modified and developed, and these attitudes imply views about the validity of political economy. Is the system to be seen as impressive and heroic, or as dirty and selfish? A Carlylean picture of industry as inspiring and invigorating is established and maintained throughout the book. It is a view not only given by the eloquence of the partisan Thornton, but one that Margaret and her father readily adopt. Thornton is given qualities of strength and sagacity that are suggestive of a Carlylean captain of industry. At the same time, the nature of the system as dirty, damaging for the workers, and (an equally Carlylean point) tainted with greed and selfishness, is regularly stressed. Above all, the inevitability of conflict in the system, the simple fact that it looks—indeed is—different from the respective points of view of worker and employer, is perhaps the most simple and obvious statement on the subject made by the text.

The modification of view of the industrial system is clearly carried in the development of Margaret, which is a dominant feature of the book, but in so far as the validity—or otherwise—of political economy is implicated, the development of Thornton is the more pertinent here because he is actively involved in the system and has to endure a crisis which ruins him; furthermore these things are presented in terms of the changes in outlook which they generate. Clearly, in narrative terms, Thornton needs to suffer a crisis, as Margaret has done, before they are both sufficiently chastened and mature to come together. In terms of the discursive structure of the book, he needs to modify his views considerably before he is suitably purged of dogma and theory about the industrial system to supply, with Margaret, its minimally progressive conclusion. Again the method of presentation, as well as the instrument of change, is discussion, either dramatised or reported.

The first of the two chapters concerning the final stage of his development, Volume II, Chapter 17, has Thornton describing to Mr Bell how he has set up a canteen for the workers in his factory. He presents it as a purely practical arrangement, pragmatic in origin, denying any theoretical base for his action, or any theoretical implications: ' "I have no theory. I hate theories" ' (p. 330). We have seen how he had earlier asserted, dogmatically, the separation between masters and men except for the transactions of work. He comes to the point of proposing the dining room through personal contact with Higgins (a contact which also leads to his paying for the Boucher children's schooling).

Volume II, Chapter 25, presents Thornton's ruin. The picture sketched here of the jungle world around Thornton at the time of his crash is particularly unattractive. The development of Thornton's thoughts and feelings in the period up to and including the crisis is presented through, and as a matter of, discussion. From the realisation that he and his workers led 'parallel lives, very close but never touching', his 'wonder' that he and Higgins, living by the same trade and working in different ways at the same objects, could look upon each other's positions and duties 'in so strangely different a way' (p. 381), had led Thornton into discussions with Higgins. Better feelings and improved knowledge had resulted on both sides, though no expectation that 'future clashes of opinion and action' would not occur. The prospect of his crash is thus poignant to Thornton because it will mean losing these human contacts. What he himself has presented earlier in the book as an entirely neutral event, morally or emotionally, is now experienced by him in human terms. The difference between such an event in theory and in practice turns out to be a difference in kind, and not merely in degree, of experience.

Furthermore the event is experienced in moral terms. Thornton's mother raises the same cry of protest at the system as Higgins, when he brought the question of 'rights' into economic discussion. For Mrs Thornton there is no 'justice' in the world if her son fails. Rather than correcting the misapprehension that it is inappropriate to expect morality in the workings of the economic system, Thornton comforts her in terms of Christian doctrine, telling her they must submit to what God sends, which is a different gloss on events from his earlier explanations to Hale. Moreover, Thornton, now seeking work in a 'subordinate situation', rejects the idea of being set up as partner for Hamper's son and having to fall in with the 'tyrannical humours' of a young man 'half-educated as regarded information, and wholly uneducated as regarded any other responsibility than that of getting money' (p. 386), a negation indeed of his earlier denials of wider responsibilities, or assertion of the benignly developing and self-righting nature of the system. Thornton can now see others as tyrants, from a point of view where he, with no money, has to submit to those who have it. What he wants now is rather to be 'only a manager, where he could have a certain degree of power beyond the mere money-getting part' (p. 386).

The kind of power he wants is explained in the final conversation 'about' political economy when, thus appropriately prepared, Thornton comes to London and to Margaret. In Volume I, Chapter 26, he appears at a dinner party, an object of interest to a bright young member of Parliament. His claims for the new-model manager are, however, minimal. Using the language of the critics of political economy, he expresses a wish to have a relationship with the workers that goes beyond the 'mere cash nexus', a phrase directly from *Past and Present*. Its use in itself suggests an acceptance of Carlyle's ferocious attack on life in a *laissez-faire* industrial society as not a fit life for humans and, again, an acceptance of obligations that Thornton, in that early argument with Margaret, so vigorously denied. The increased knowledge of each other that will result from personal contact will help to 'attach class to class as they should be attached' (p. 391). The vision suggested here of a purged, socially responsible industrialism, led by strong men like Thornton, does not, however, carry much weight. Despite his newly authoritative role in the book's discursive structure, the fact is that in its narrative Thornton is a ruined man. Moreover the very weakness, in structural terms, of the new Thornton (his last phase of development being so compressed, and of secondary emotional interest to Margaret's) detracts weight from his new theoretical views. Thus within the text as a whole his vision stands as a mere assertion of pious wish over against the resolutely experiential, relative approach of the book and the picture of industrial society it has painted in these terms.

Finally, Thornton's description of the kind of project he would like, in the interest of unity, to undertake, stresses the essential personal involvement of all concerned at every stage, an idea the exact reverse of the despotism he initially defended to Margaret. It is important to notice, however, that he explicitly denies that even such co-operative involvement in the running of industry would affect the basic structure of the system. The tone of his denial reasserts the voice of experience, and it stands as the book's final comment on a problem for which political economy, itself seen merely as one element in the intellectual and practical experience of industrial society, has offered no answer. Significantly, the catalytic questions raised by a strike are the final focus, as they have been in all the book's previous conversations about political economy:

> 'I would take an idea, the working out of which would necessitate personal intercourse; . . . . it might not go well at first, but . . . interest would be felt by an increasing number of men, and at last its success in working come to be desired by all . . . '
> 'And you think they may prevent the recurrence of strikes?'
> 'Not at all. My utmost expectation only goes as far as this—that they may render strikes not the bitter, venomous sources of hatred they have hitherto been. A more hopeful man might imagine that a closer and more genial intercourse between classes might do away with strikes. But I am not a hopeful man.'
> (p. 391–92)

In *North and South* political economy is lined up with the capitalist industrial system. Support for the one is support for the other. Willingness to disrupt the system goes with scepticism about the theory. The attitude arrived at by the text towards the one may therefore be taken to express a response to the other. The industrial system is seen, finally, in *North and South*, as something (presenting both admirable and evil qualities) which, for the present at least, has to be lived with. Since that is so, the view taken is that there is no point in hoping to do more than marginally improve the experience of working in it, exercising qualities of sympathy, self-discipline and honesty, whose value holds good whatever the social or economic system. At the same time, however, such a stance does not imply an endorsement of political economy—merely, again, a recognition of its existence, as a body of sincerely held ideas found in a particular social group and relating to its particular experience: a remarkably agnostic presentation, given the current attitudes on the subject.

HILARY M. SCHOR

["The Languages of Industrialization"]†

* * *

Margaret Hale's adventure in Milton-Northern is largely linguistic: the novel is almost a romance of the languages of industrialization, challenging characters and readers, enlisting a new vocabulary, offering itself as a dictionary, and using its heroine's consciousness to achieve all this. Repeatedly, the novel offers up a new term, runs through a series of definitions, explains what is at stake in each, and then allows Margaret to choose. As she is initiated into Milton (and into its new plot), she becomes increasingly fluent with the vocabulary she must learn there—and increasingly, as she serves as a translator for other characters and for readers, the novel serves as a glossary of industrialization. Take, for example, the question of the strike, which was of such importance to Gaskell that she wrote to Dickens to ask if he intended to have a strike in *Hard Times*, currently running in a serialized version in *Household Words*.[1] When Margaret asks, "What is a strike?" she is signaling her ignorance (with which a London reader might identify) and putting herself in the middle of social forces that shape her (smaller) individual plot; she is both a narrating intelligence (what Wayne Booth might call the reader's friend) and a narrative agent. The strike functions in that double-directional way we have been tracing (it is an agent in the romance plot, literally forcing Margaret into Thornton's arms, and the embrace in turn becomes a force in the "industrial action" of the novel, as the two plots blur), but it is also a linguistic puzzle, forcing new definitions and new "combinations" of words from a variety of characters.

Margaret's characteristic form, the question, with its necessary unsettling of prior meanings, is a question here of linguistic indecisiveness. Margaret must learn what the word *strike* means to a wide range of characters before she can mediate between them, and before they can learn to speak to each other. But the "question" of language is deeply vexed politically, a problem that resounds through *North and South* even more thoroughly than it did through *Mary Barton*. As with the politics of language, so the politics of the hero-

---

† From *Scheherezade in the Market-Place: Elizabeth Gaskell and the Victorian Novel* (New York and Oxford: Oxford UP, 1992), chap. 4, pp. 129–36. Used by permission of Oxford University Press, Inc. Notes have been re-numbered. Page numbers are to this Norton Critical Edition.

1. *Letters*, p. 281, 23 April 1854. Gaskell reports to John Forster that she had asked Dickens "& he says he is not going to have a strike,—altogether his answer sets me at ease."

ine's speech: where *Mary Barton* could frame its heroine's speaking
out as the heroic moment of connection and communication, no
such easy optimism obtains here, and the incoherencies of language
parallel some of the difficulties of plot we have been rehearsing.

What I mean to follow here is Gareth Stedman Jones's insight that
the language of political debates shapes their content: that "the form
in which [Chartist] discontents were addressed cannot be understood in terms of the consciousness of a particular social class, since
the form pre-existed any independent action by such a class."[2] The
language of any "class" (any social group; any "character") will in
turn "speak" that class or that character. Language does not refer
back "to some primal anterior reality, 'the social being' " (p. 20); on
the other hand, it cannot promise a transhistorical self, being shot
through with its own "social being." Class consciousness is "con-
structed and inscribed within a complex rhetoric of metaphorical
association, causal inference and imaginative construction" (p. 102).
If my earlier use of Stedman Jones, in discussing *Mary Barton*, was
to emphasize the language of representation at the heart of Chartist
politics, what I wish to emphasize here is the multivocal nature of
all discourses of class, and the political nature of all language, particularly the languages of fiction. What *North and South* will suggest
is Stedman Jones's warning that even his account of the languages
of Chartism cannot be complete, for it is taken from radical literature
and speeches reported in the radical press: "Quite apart from the
fact that such reported speech took no account of accent or dialect,
I am not arguing that this is the only language Chartism employed.
What is examined here is only the public political language of the
movement" (p. 95). Gaskell's account moves between "public" and
"private" languages as carefully as it does between the languages of
a range of characters, classes, "associations."

It is in this context that we must understand the novel's preoc-
cupation with language. At the time Gaskell was writing *North and
South*, her husband was offering a series of lectures on the English
language; they were published with the fifth edition of *Mary Barton*,
along with a glossary for the novel's dialect, which makes linguistic
the novel's social argument, that language itself is a social weapon,
and that the language of the workers (like the lives they lead)
demands both the respect and the special understanding of readers.
For the Reverend William Gaskell, language is the "close connection
between the present and the past," for language "ever runs backwards," but more appositely, the "slang" of Lancashire is not, "as
some ignorantly suppose, mere vulgar corruptions of modern

2. Gareth Stedman Jones, "Rethinking Chartism," in *Languages of Class* (Cambridge: Cambridge UP, 1983), p. 95.

English, but genuine relics of the old mother tongue."[3] In a building metaphor that will be resurrected in the factory vision of *North and South*, he adds, these "forms of speech and peculiarities of pronunciation . . . are bits of the old granite, which have perhaps been polished into another form, but lost in the process a good deal of their original strength."

The language that Margaret eventually learns in Manchester is one she praises for its strength, and for its absolute appropriateness to the new world in which she finds herself. Like all lessons of the novel, that of the new language is learned first by the heroine—and largely, at the risk of sounding too abstract, through her body; the strike literally "strikes" Margaret; the angry men throw stones at her; her body's signs are (mis)read sexually. Her acquisition of a new language is an initiation as central as the sexual initiation it signals; to use the word *knobstick* for a strikebreaker is like swallowing an olive; and to be ready to learn a language is as sure a sign of sexual readiness in this novel as is dancing in a novel by Jane Austen. The phrase "slack of work" that, to her mother, is a "provincialism . . . horrid Milton words . . . factory slang" is to Margaret only natural: "If I live in a factory town, I must speak factory language when I want it," and without "a great many words you never heard in your life," she would "have to use a whole explanatory sentence instead" (pp. 218). And the new language is not only economical but "expressive," sensual, usefully concrete, promising some kind of more direct representation. As she goes on to ask Thornton, to excuse herself for calling what she has "picked up" in Milton "vulgarity," "Though 'knob-stick' has not a very pretty sound, is it not expressive? Could I do without it, in speaking of the thing it represents?"

The slight confusion signaled here between new things and new words—what *knobstick* "represents" is the harshness of relations between workers and masters in industrial England, and the violence directed against the "knobsticks," or scab workers, themselves—is also a way of insisting on the novel's importance. To offer itself as a narrative dictionary of industrialization is both to constrict our point of view to what it can translate for us and to offer us the misspoken or misheard languages *around* Margaret, and the potential violence of these representations. Take again the range of answers Margaret receives to that central question, "What is a strike?" The novel so much expects readers to share Margaret's confusion that a whole chapter takes its title from the question; a reader might further echo Margaret's comment:

---

3. "Two Lectures on the Lancashire Dialect," by the Reverend W. Gaskell, M.A., in *Mary Barton*, 1854 (fifth) edition, pp. 9–10.

Why do you strike? . . . Striking is leaving off work till you get
your own rate of wages, is it not? You must not wonder at my
ignorance; where I come from I never heard of a strike. (p. 121)

"I wish I were there," is Bessy Higgins's response, coding our ignorance as truly social bliss; for Bessy, the strike is linguistic hell, "just
the clashing and clanging and clattering that has wearied me a' my
life long, about works and wages, and masters, and hands, and knobsticks," and she "could have wished to have had other talk about me
in my latter days than just [that]" (p. 124). For Bessy, the strike is
only more "talk," and even the by now infamous *knobstick* only one
more linguistic counter.

All the answers to Margaret's questions—all attempts to agree on
a definition for that one word, *strike*—end in a kind of linguistic
"strike" because none of the definers can agree on their terms. For
Mrs Thornton, the strike is "uncomfortable work . . . going on in the
town," and the men are only striking for "mastership and ownership
of other people's property" (p. 106). For Thornton himself, mastery
is capital, and the only language available that of captainship: the
strike is the workers' "next attack," and it is his "right" as an "owner
of capital" not to explain his action to his workers. Margaret, trying
to argue with him, invokes another discourse, of "a feeling which I
do not think you would share." There is, she says, a "human law" to
allow him to "do what you like with your own," but no religious right.
In an attempt at least to define his definitions, she declares, "I know
so little about strikes, and rate of wages, and capital, and labour, that
I had better not talk to a political economist like you" (p. 108). But
when she tries out these same phrases (those of political economy)
on Nicholas Higgins, asking if "the state of trade may be such as not
to enable them to give you the same remuneration," Nicholas replies,

State o' trade! That's just a piece o' masters' humbug. It's rate
o' wages I was talking of. Th' masters keep th' state o' trade in
their own hands; and just walk it forward like a black bug-a-
boo, to frighten naughty children with into being good.
(pp. 123–24)

Here, the masters' abstract language becomes a "bug-a-boo," "humbug," "walking . . . forward" to frighten the workers. But how could
such linguistic conflict lead anywhere but to a strike, to the failure
of language to do any of the work of reconciliation? The abstractions of trade and wages fade further in the face of Bessy Higgins's
account of the workers themselves during the strike:

Yo'd ha' been deaved out o' yo'r five wits, as well as me, if yo'd
had one body after another coming in to ask for father, and
staying to tell me each one their tale. Some spoke o' deadly

hatred, and made my blood run cold wi' the terrible things they said o' th' masters,—but more, being women, kept plaining, plaining (wi' the tears running down their cheeks, and never wiped away, nor heeded), of the price o' meat, and how their childer could na sleep at nights for th' hunger. (p. 138)

There seems *no* way to reconcile Bessy's account of starving children with the masters' discussion of the strike on "sound economical principles" in which Mr Thornton shows "that, as trade was conducted, there must always be a waxing and waning of commercial prosperity; and that in the waning a certain number of masters, as well as of men, must go down into ruin, and be no more seen among the ranks of the happy and prosperous" (p. 139). The gap between "be no more seen" and the "childer [who] could na sleep at nights for th' hunger" is no more—and no less—than the failure of any one language ever to represent the range of "waxing and waning" in Manchester. The narrator says Thornton spoke "as if this consequence were so entirely logical, that neither employers nor employed had any right to complain if it became their fate," but such suppressed "complaining" of employer and employed sounds far different than the "plaining, plaining" of the grieving mothers; they hardly seem in the same linguistic register—nor do the poetical emphasis of "waxing and waning" and the Wordsworthian echo in Thornton's speech do justice to the violence of class conflict.[4] If what Margaret pleads for at the moment of the strike is for Thornton to go out, like a man, and address his workers, to "speak to your workmen as if they were human beings," to "speak to them kindly," it is hard to see the novel's putting forward any language in which he could speak to them, as she implores, "man to man!"

What ends the strike and its potential violence is not, of course, any language, anything "man to man" at all; rather, it is the stone that strikes Margaret and her silent fall that silence the rioters. One might add, as well, that the inability of the strike to solve the workers' difficulties leaves us without any clearer answer to Margaret's initial question; a strike is leaving off work, but its ends remain as unclear in *North and South* as in more politically reactionary novels. No more than *Hard Times* can *North and South* recommend political action that will end the "plaining." More pointedly, what the novel leaves in question is the possible reformatory power of any language that remains "man to man": as in the gap between Bessy's and Thornton's accounts, the difference between the "strikes" of men and women informs the whole novel. If Margaret's conscious answer to the madness of the crowd is to send Thornton to "go out and speak to them," like *Mary Barton*, *North and South* is framed around a woman's trans-

4. I owe these suggestions to Donna Landry and Peter Manning.

gressive movement into the public sphere. Margaret's insistence that her stepping in front of the crowd is only using a woman's "high privilege," the "sanctity of our sex" to do a "woman's work" in preventing "one blow, one cruel, angry action that might otherwise have been committed," allows her to salvage her "maiden pride." But it also suggests again Gaskell's own much beleaguered sense of authorial modesty—one no longer quite in keeping with the authorial assertion of the preface to this novel, which carries into the public her quarrel with Dickens over the novel's serialization in *Household Words*, and one that is as strained as any in the novel over the status of the woman's "plaint."

Margaret's move into the public realm before the angry strikers and the connection between her actions and Gaskell's in speaking out before the crowd suggest again that the linguistic questions under discussion here have a gendered inflection, one that returns us to the question of the social economy of romance. To rephrase this slightly, we might ask, what happens to the tension between male speech and female silence, the masculine "political economy" and female "plaining" when we move beyond the "strike"? Is there a conflict between men and women that registers as deeply—that is, as linguistically—as that between masters and men?

There seems to be such a conflict in Manchester, for if the language Margaret learns is primarily one of labor ("slack of work," "knobstick") there is another language of commodification that is also new to her, and that she hears primarily in the conversations of women. The gendered languages surface at dinner parties as well as on the streets: when she dines at the Thorntons' in Milton, there is a "very animated conversation going on among the gentlemen; the ladies, for the most part, were silent, employing themselves in taking notes of the dinner and criticizing each other's dresses" (p. 148). When Margaret separates herself from the "ladies'" conversation, she catches "the clue to the general conversation," which she notes is "in desperate earnest,—not in the used-up style that wearied her so in the old London parties." Later, she is

> surprised to think how much she enjoyed this dinner. She knew enough now to understand many local interests—nay, even some of the technical words employed by the eager mill-owners. She silently took a very decided part in the question they were discussing. (p. 149)

But Margaret is "decidedly" silent at that moment. Her newfound vocabulary serves her well as a reader but not a speaker; she is no more vocal than she was in London, where the men sat downstairs after dinner, and the women's "fragments of conversation" that she overheard horrified her.

Her accounts of the women's conversations in Milton are hardly more encouraging. As she describes them to her father,

> the ladies were so dull, papa—oh, so dull! Yet I think it was clever too. It reminded me of our old game of having each so many nouns to introduce into a sentence. . . . They took nouns that were signs of things which gave evidence of wealth,—housekeepers, under-gardeners, extent of glass, valuable lace, diamonds, and all such things; and each one formed her speech so as to bring them all in, in the prettiest accidental manner possible. (p. 153)

The dinner-party conversation in some ways signals the old problem of "signs of things which gave evidence," recalling Margaret's earlier defense of her use of *knobstick*: "Could I do without it, in speaking of the thing it represents?" The dinner party is all "representations," all the "extent" of commodities, most especially in the formal fakery of the "prettiest accidental manner possible." It is as if the women were themselves dressed in language (in nouns, to be precise) that displayed their husbands' wealth even more conspicuously than the gentlemen's conversation "relative to the trade and manufactures of the place"; at the dinner table, the ladies are "employing" themselves in "taking notes of the dinner and criticizing each other's dresses." Similarly, when Margaret returns to London after the death of both her parents, and returns to the Harley Street wealth of her aunt, conversations reflect mere "cleverness" and "relentless ease"; "there might be toilers and moilers there in London, but she never saw them." The conversations, as much as the social whirl itself, exclude any life other than high society (the very servants, Margaret says, "lived in an underground world of their own, of which she knew neither the hopes nor the fears" [p. 339]), and it is only when she receives her inheritance and is free to begin the social work that occupies her until her marriage (and to which I will return) that she hears anything other than "the easy knowledge of the subjects of the day" or meets anyone other than people who "talked about art in a merely sensuous way," "lashed themselves up into an enthusiasm about high subjects in company, and never thought about them when they were alone," who "squandered their capabilities of appreciation into a mere flow of appropriate words" (p. 370). If female conversation is less economical than the men's ("squandered" as it is), it is also less useful; it offers no new words, no metaphors for social union, nothing except the "dress" Margaret is always rejecting. But Margaret cannot use the masculine language for her needs either; the novel seems to need some other language to describe what the heroine is now "silently" so decided about.

The isolation of male and female languages, which the novel in many ways refuses to "solve" artificially, is part of its larger dissatisfaction with old vocabularies, with the "flow of appropriate words," with a language that provides only lists of possessions, with the segregation of the male realm of business and the female world of party dresses; with the inability of conversation to incorporate new languages with which to describe "new things." What had seemed in Milton an anarchy of signification, with no agreement about the relations of words to things, gives way in the second half of the novel to the social stratification of language; men speak only to men, women only to women, and the toilers and moilers only to one another. With the recognition of this division, the novel also begins to express some doubts about its own role as mediator between one language and another, with its own models of reconciliation, with the mythic promise of a common language that will unite the two nations. It will register that ambivalence, as we have come to expect, first, with an attention to the difficulty of shared *written* languages, in which the novel must include itself, and then with its focus on the even more difficult role of the woman as mediatrix, poised between one discourse and another, one England and another, between masters and workers, men and women. It is to the mythology of the condition-of-England novel, the vision of a language that would unite all these Englands, that we must turn. What kind of dictionary is it that this novel tries to be or imagine, if its romance depends on the absence of any shared language at all?

TERENCE WRIGHT

Women, Death and Integrity: *North and South*†

The two elements in this title, it may be noted, are allowed to stand beside each other—North *and* South, not North *or* South. The point is important because, as we so often find in Mrs Gaskell's work, we are not invited to make a final and absolute choice, but are given the opportunity to weigh both experiences, both sets of values, and give each its due. When Margaret returns to Helstone at the end of the book, she sees much to awaken memories—things which have not changed and retain their charm, though they also hurt her with their continuing, indifferent beauty:

† From *Elizabeth Gaskell 'We are not angels': Realism, Gender, Values* (Basingstoke: Macmillan, New York: St. Martin's P, 1995), chap. 5, pp. 97–113. Reproduced with permission of Palgrave Macmillan. Notes are the Editor's. Page numbers are to this Norton Critical Edition.

It hurt her to see the Helstone road so flooded in the sunlight,
and every turn and every familiar tree so precisely the same in
its summer glory as it had been in former years. Nature felt no
change, and was ever young. (p. 350)

But much has changed too. The vicarage is now in the possession of
an ardent teetotaller, his bustling, organising, well-meaning but
insensitive wife, and their seven children. They are changing the
house, and the kind of education given to the village children. 'And
not before time, thinks Mr Bell, when he and Margaret are told of
a cat's being roasted alive as a charm by the villagers. He first was
opposed to the new educational plans, but later admits 'Anything
rather than have that child brought up in such practical paganism'
(p. 355). 'There was change everywhere; slight, yet pervading all'
(p. 358). Mr Bell has the resignation of age towards the subject:

> It is the first changes among familiar things that make such a
> mystery of time to the young, afterwards we lose the sense of
> the mysterious. I take changes in all I see as a matter of course.
> The instability of all human things is familiar to me, to you it is
> new and oppressive. (p. 353)

But he speaks from the point of view of an old bachelor, living in
scholarly obscurity with his manservant. For all his kindness he is
maimed, spiritually, thinking of his own comfort, security, and, most
grossly, his stomach. Change for Margaret is not something to be
dismissed so easily. In one of the most crucial passages for understanding this book, and indeed some others of Mrs Gaskell's, she
cries out to herself:

> 'I begin to understand now what heaven must be—and, oh! the
> grandeur and repose of the words—"The same yesterday, to-day,
> and for ever." Everlasting! "From everlasting to everlasting,
> Thou art God." That sky above me looks as though it could not
> change, and yet it will. I am so tired—so tired of being whirled
> on through all these phases of my life, in which nothing abides
> by me, no creature, no place; it is like the circle in which the
> victims of earthly passion eddy continually. I am in the mood in
> which women of another religion take the veil. I seek heavenly
> steadfastness in earthly monotony. If I were a Roman Catholic
> and could deaden my heart, stun it with some great blow, I
> might become a nun. But I should pine after my kind; no, not
> my kind, for love of my species could never fill my heart to the
> utter exclusion of love for individuals. Perhaps it ought to be so,
> perhaps not; I cannot decide to-night.' (p. 363)

But she will not follow her parents whither they have recently gone
(and where Mr Bell will shortly follow them). Absolute reconciliation

is not for this world, and the gloomy thoughts that evening induces are balanced by her morning mood:

> 'After all it is right,' said she, hearing the voices of children at play while she was dressing. 'If the world stood still, it would retrograde and become corrupt, if that is not Irish. Looking out of myself, and my own painful sense of change, the progress all around me is right and necessary.' (p. 364)

I say 'balanced', not 'dispelled', because the essential value which is lived out in this book—particularly by Margaret—is admission that different things may exist together in our lives without destroying us. There is an openness to instability, uncertainty, changeableness and ambiguity. Her final words before she leaves Helstone are an acceptance of perpetual change as a condition of life:

> 'And I too change perpetually—now this, now that—now disappointed and peevish because all is not exactly as I had pictured it, and now suddenly discovering that the reality is far more beautiful than I had imagined it. Oh, Helstone! I shall never love any place like you.' (p. 364)

When she has left the village she '[finds] her level' (p. 364). At the beginning of the novel she is less experienced, and therefore less able to be assured that uncertainty is an acceptable state. She despises the trivial fussing over Edith's wedding arrangements and the superficial, cynical wit of Henry Lennox, but when the possibility of marriage comes into her own life, via this same man, she finds herself far from being settled and confident in mood. First 'the brightness of the sun' comes over her face, in the glad pleasure of renewing a London acquaintance (p. 22) Her mother's complaints introduce a 'thin cold cloud' between her and the sun, but she and Henry set out 'in the merriest spirits in the world' (p. 24), a mood which lasts through dinner. As he works himself up to his proposal, however, she becomes disturbed, only to overcome her disturbance by standing on her dignity. Yet when he takes her hand the disturbance of her inward calm returns, and she finds she is 'despising herself for the fluttering at her heart' (p. 28). Once again she recovers her composure and refuses him, only to be reproaching herself a moment later for having given him pain. She puts him off by trying to close the subject entirely, but finds that this drives him into flippancy and her into a consequent return to annoyance and contempt. Finally she feels 'stunned' and 'unable to recover her self-possession enough to join in the trivial conversation that ensued between her father and Mr. Lennox' (p. 30). On his departure, she reflects:

> How different men were to women! Here was she disturbed and unhappy, because her instinct had made anything but a refusal

impossible; while he, not many minutes after he had met with a rejection of what ought to have been the deepest, holiest proposal of his life, could speak as if briefs, success, and all its superficial consequences of a good house, clever and agreeable society, were the sole avowed objects of his desires. . . . Then she took it into her head that, after all, his lightness might be but assumed, to cover a bitterness of disappointment which would have been stamped on her own heart if she had loved and been rejected. (p. 31)

We may notice that her first, absolute judgement is modified by the end of the paragraph. Perhaps, indeed, men and women are not so dissimilar, but it is her uncertainty, and openness to the possibility of alternatives, that allows her to perceive this. When she comes to make the judgement on Helstone established in the course of her final visit she can encompass the whole experience. It is beautiful, but it is past; it is unchanging in her heart, subjectively, but in common with all things it is constantly changing. And on the larger scale, Milton and Helstone both exist. They cannot be denied, nor can they be made more than they are. The return to Helstone is crucial to Margaret at this point in her life. It gives her the opportunity to come to terms with what her life has been and will be—an experience shared by some older companions as a prelude to death, but one reserved for her as a final step into freedom.

In the passage of night-time musing I quoted above, Margaret regrets the instability of all things mortal, and that mortal yearning after our own kind which makes us cling to unstable, restless, troubled life. For a moment she feels the attraction of having her heart stunned with some great blow. It is reminiscent of the moment when her father first mentioned his doubts to her, and the whole painful process of change began: 'it was better to be stunned into numbness by hearing of all these arrangements, which seemed to be nearly completed before she had been told' (p. 35). Such a lament is not surprising, in view of the changes that have come upon her (and are yet to come) in the course of a year or so. It is not simply a matter of change in itself, however. The texture of experience suggests uncertainty, indecision, dividedness and the instability of discontent from the beginning. In spite of the easygoing nature of the couple who are about to marry, a faint note of discord is struck by Edith's mother's bemoaning 'constantly, though quietly . . . her hard lot in being united to one whom she could not love' (p. 9). In this opening chapter Margaret herself is summing up an earlier phase of her life— her childhood—an experience which is a reconciliation to pain, involving self-repression. She hid her tears in childhood; is she to be condemned to the same experience again?

The character of the decision Mr Hale makes when he initiates

the enormous change in his family's life and fortunes is typical of
the man,but also characterises much of the 'feel' of experience
throughout[1] the book. His problem is, as Angus Easson observes in
his notes, historical rather than a matter of strict faith (*Easson 1973*,
p. 438). He feels he cannot subscribe to a Church which, it seems
to him, compels men's belief. He must therefore give up his living
and move the whole family to Milton-Northern. It is scarcely his
fault, since we cannot but believe that he is sincere in this rather
abstruse point of conscience, but his act of integrity is perforce a
rather negative one, involving doubt, uncertainty and withdrawal.
Moreover his whole manner of avowal, when at last it comes, is about
as far removed from a positive, clear declaration of some principle
by which he would stand, as it is possible to be. After days of inward
wrestling, and hours of sighing, he tells his daughter, being, as he
admits, too much of a coward to break it to his wife himself. He plays
with papers on the table in a 'nervous and confused manner', opens
his lips to speak several times without beginning. His face when he
has told her wears an expression of 'piteous distress . . . almost as
imploring a merciful and kind judgement from his child' (p. 32).

It is, of course, typical of this lover of 'speculative and metaphysical' problems that his one really active decision in the book, the
decision which in fact impels all the rest of the story, should arise
from abstruse doubt. Most of the practical consequences, in human
and material terms, fall on his daughter, since his whole life appears
to have been a retreat from the larger world into his parish, and from
his family into his study. There are three deaths which affect Margaret closely. Her mother has never quite reconciled herself to the
practical circumstances of her love and marriage. She cannot understand why her husband never sought preferment. She has not got
his interest in books. Mr Hale's whole life has been in a sense a
withdrawal from the world, and death completes that withdrawal.
Mr Bell has not even attempted wider engagement with the world
by marriage. His rooms in Oxford, closeted, lonely, self-centred, are
the type of his last 'narrow cell'. Parallel with these three examples
of lives which by their nature seem to anticipate the ultimate negative of death, Margaret encounters the pain of life as a means by
which she can encompass experience and advance in maturity.

The doubt and negativity of Mr Hale's initial decision to give up
his living is part of that general uncertainty which, as I have said,
informs the whole book, and is seen characteristically in human gestures and features. Margaret views her father asleep on the train, his
face in repose, but showing 'rest after weariness' rather than 'the
serene calm of the countenance of one who led a placid, contented

1. I.e., to the "World's Classics" edition of *North and South* (Oxford: Oxford UP, 1973).

life'. The lines on his face speak 'plainly of habitual distress and depression'. When he wakens, after the first smile his face returns 'into its lines of habitual anxiety. He had a trick of half-opening his mouth as if to speak, which constantly unsettled the form of the lips, and gave the face an undecided expression' (p. 17). But lest it should be imagined that uncertainty is confined to her father, we should note the many occasions on which Margaret herself feels changeable and undecided. To the world she appears 'superb', and assured even to the point of haughtiness, her habitual expression a direct contrast to her father's. This is how she first appears to Thornton:

> Margaret could not help her looks; but the short curled upper lip, the round, massive up-turned chin; the manner of carrying her head, her movements, full of a soft feminine defiance, always gave strangers the impression of haughtiness . . .

> She sat facing him and facing the light; her full beauty met his eye; her round white flexile throat rising out of the full, yet lithe figure; her lips, moving so slightly as she spoke, not breaking the cold serene look of her face with any variation from the one lovely haughty curve; her eyes, with their soft gloom, meeting his with quiet maiden freedom. (p. 58)

Something of the unique quality of this heroine is suggested in 'soft feminine defiance', and I shall return to this in a moment, but what strikes the reader most forcibly here is the carefully composite detail in the picture, and the physicality, indeed the fleshliness, of this detail. Mrs Gaskell is not afraid of suggestions of the statuesque in 'massive'. It is sensual to the point of eroticism. She has 'taken off her shawl' to reveal further charms in her 'round white flexile throat'. Our attention is frequently drawn to her 'taper fingers', perhaps as a balance to any suggestion of cumbrousness, but one cannot escape the sense of weight and solidity in the description, and an accompanying sensuality. In part, of course, this is because a man is viewing her. The combination of provocativeness and appeal in 'soft feminine defiance', or the excitement suggested in the 'lovely haughty curve' of her lip betray a sexual engagement, but she has also the largeness of figure associated with (potential) maternity. She is, as one might say, 'all woman', and this womanliness is conveyed in her centred, self-assured poise. It speaks in her eyes, 'with their soft gloom, meeting his with quiet maiden freedom'. There is no confusion here, no falsity and no attachment beyond the necessary social intercourse. The feeling of 'togetherness' is promoted particularly by her being presented as a portrait—it is as though the eye travels over the subject, noting each point and drawing them together for a total impression. It is the visual embodiment of a 'powerful and decided nature' (p. 46) but it suggests much more than simply strength of purpose.

The same sense of statuesque poise is apparent in Thornton's view of her at the dinner when their hands first touch:

> the curving lines of the red lips, just parted in the interest of listening to what her companion said—the head a little bent forwards, so as to make a long sweeping line from the summit, where the light caught on the glossy raven hair, to the smooth ivory tip of the shoulder; the round white arms, and taper hands, laid lightly across each other, but perfectly motionless in their pretty attitude. (p. 148)

The 'long sweeping line' suggests the line of the artist's pen, and again indicates unity and harmony. Thornton mentally compares her favourably with his restless sister, 'now glancing here, now there, but without any purpose in her observation' (p. 148).

We certainly cannot doubt the essential strength of Margaret. Dr Donaldson reflects on the literal strength of her handgrasp: 'Who would have thought that little hand could have given such a squeeze?' (p. 116). 'But the bones were well put together,' he reflects, 'and that gives immense power.' He speaks of her 'backbone', another metaphor suggestive of inward strength and well-composedness—a strength manifest in her handling of domestic problems, the reception of news of her mother's imminent death and the independence of her views on industrial relations. There is a special kind of integrity in Margaret which corresponds to the more obvious male integrity all around her. However negative his decision may be, Mr Hale's integrity in making it is undoubted, as is the personal integrity of his whole life. His son shows the same firmness in standing fast against injustice, even though it costs him his career, threatens his freedom and forces him to live abroad. Mr Thornton is self-made, clear-minded, determined, decisive; able (on the whole) to compartmentalise his life; sure of his own rightness in economic matters; incorruptible; the hard but just master. It is not open to Margaret to compete with men in integrity of their kind. All three of these men decide for themselves, and thereby define themselves. Their whole lifestyle is their self-definition, and as an inescapable result of the social order they carry their women along with them (if they have any). Mrs Hale must live in Milton; Fanny, and even the inflexible mother, are carried with the man's success or fall with him. The accounts I have quoted of Margaret's appearance and personality are by men. Thornton's admiration is frankly sexual, even if he does not at first recognise it himself, and Dr Donaldson, too, reflects 'Such a girl as that would win my heart, if I were thirty years younger' (p. 117). 'Integrity', involving wholeness, completion and untouchedness is perceived in

Margaret, but she possesses it as an object rather than a subject—it might be called an 'integrity of the flesh'—the wholeness of a portrait, immobile, to be contemplated. Her untouchedness is her virginity—nothing has detracted from her absolute purity—but it means that she is seen as something already formed rather than filled with the instability that means also potentiality.

For in fact there is a deep irony in all this. Despite all the apparent composure of Margaret, her 'togetherness' and surety, her success in keeping her parents' heads above water, her comforting and encouraging the Higgins family and arguing confidently with Thornton and his mother, she is as much a representative of the pervasive uncertainty as anyone else. Margaret's completeness, exclusivity, untouchedness is apparent rather than real, and apparent to men, who wish to see such integrity there. For Mr Thornton her immobility is essentially of the nature of her virtue, but in fact, as we shall see, movement, uncertainty and instability are far more fundamental values for both him and Margaret when they see aright.

North and South is a book full of pain—not the pangs of hunger, as in *Mary Barton*, but the pain of stress and disturbance, of pangs of conscience and sexual torment. It is also the pain of loss, particularly for the heroine, and indeed it seems surprising on reflection that a happy ending could be retrieved from such unpropitious material. Those who are not suffering are the exceptions, and they are generally not admitted to centre stage, but rather used as foils to the more anguished characters. The most notable is Edith, who is first seen 'rolled . . . up into a soft ball of muslin and ribbon, and silken curls . . . gone off into a peaceful little after-dinner nap' (p. 7). Her comfortable cocoon aptly suggests her sheltered existence, untroubled by any problems other than clothes and teething. Those whom we see in closer focus, of course, are always more likely to appear troubled than people we know distantly, but there seems little doubt that the sufferings of the Hales and John Thornton and his mother are real. The problems themselves are clearly enough stated, whether they be religious doubts, worry over illness or money, the consciousness of having lied, unrequited love, or bitter sorrow over the unhappiness of a beloved son. But the pain is embedded in the texture of the novel—in its kind of realism. Where *Mary Barton* is full of the stark shock of confrontation, *North and South*, with one notable exception, is diffusive. The weight of reality is borne much more by gesture and dialogue; two crucially repeated words are 'wince' and 'stun'. If the coin of experience in *Mary Barton* is moments, in *North and South* it is the rhythm of night and day.

Elizabeth Gaskell is very specific about times of day in this novel, and about what each of them means for her heroine. Mornings at the beginning of her story are a time of renewed hope for the future.

Her face, as she watches her father wakening, is 'bright as the morning', speaking of 'boundless hope in the future' (p. 18). After her father announces his planned change of life, sleep brings no refreshment. She drags herself up, 'thankful that the night was over,—unrefreshed, yet rested' (p. 174). For most of the novel, life for Margaret is a matter of anxious activity by day and restless worry or watching through the night. When she first returns to Helstone, before her father has mentioned his doubts, she finds evenings 'rather difficult to fill up agreeably' (p. 20). After Henry Lennox's proposal she finds herself wishing bedtime were come 'that she might go over the events of the day again' (p. 31). But it is not to bring her rest, since that very evening her father lays his doubts before her. At the end of the day she 'stole to bed after her father had left her, like a child ashamed of its fault'. 'Miserable, unresting night! Ill preparation for the coming day! She awoke with a start, unrefreshed, and conscious of some reality worse even than her feverish dreams' (p. 41). Next day, after the news has been broken to her mother, Margaret rushes upstairs 'to stifle the hysteric sobs that would force their way at last, after the rigid self-control of the whole day' (p. 45). She finds her daily life has changed immeasurably. In London there were few decisions left to her, but now 'every day brought some question, momentous to her, and to those whom she loved, to be settled' (p. 48). She reassures her father that 'it is only that I am tired to-night' (p. 52) but the evening of their first day away from Helstone 'without employment, passed in a room high up in an hotel, was long and heavy' (p. 53). On their first night in Milton, Margaret feels 'inclined to sit down in a stupor of despair'. (p. 61) She lies awake 'very long this night, planning how to lessen the influence of Milton life on their mother' (p. 82).

Few novels can have concentrated so much of their attention on the hours of darkness. Sometimes the nights are simply described as wakeful or restless, on other occasions the experience of wakefulness is described in some detail—'she was so tired, so stunned, that she thought she never slept at all; her feverish thoughts passed and repassed the boundary between sleeping and waking, and kept their own miserable identity' (p. 174). Sometimes, by a reverse process, the nightmare is brought into daytime experience as an image of terror or horror:

> The deep impression made by the interview, was like that of a horror in a dream; that will not leave the room although we waken up, and rub our eyes, and force a stiff rigid smile upon our lips. It is there—there, cowering and gibbering, with fixed ghastly eyes, in some corner of the chamber, listening to hear whether we dare to breathe of its presence to any one. (p. 180)

This hysterical waking vision is the result of Thornton's proposal, following upon the scene before the mob of strikers. On one occasion the subject of sleep and beds is actually discussed in a half-comic way, Mrs Hale suggesting that beds are not what they were in her youth, and that until she slept on a water-bed she 'did not know when she had had a good sound resting sleep' (p. 183).

The detailed accounts given of the passage of days and nights, and the constant marking of the beginning and end of the diurnal round gives a painful sense of the monotony of ordinary existence—a life not threatened with the absolute finality of starvation, but wearing in its demands on making-do, reconciling one's fellow-beings over trifles, feeling one's potential circumscribed while one makes unrecognised sacrifices. It is the realism of gentility. When they settle in Milton they must find rooms suitable to their size of family, their income, their taste and their social standing. Any place to rest their head will not do. Margaret must soothe her mother's fears about health risks, and conciliate her to a new life in a strange town, as well as placate or put down the maidservant who believes that her mother threw herself away on Mr Hale. All these things are unspectacular, but essential to bearable family life. At the end of the first year of her trials, Margaret looks back and wonders how she bore them:

> If she could have anticipated them, how she would have shrunk away and hid herself from the coming time! And yet day by day had, of itself, and by itself, been very endurable—small, keen, bright little spots of positive enjoyment having come sparkling into the very middle of sorrows. (p. 95)

'Where can we live but days?' asks the poet,[2] and it is a question clearly endorsed in this novel. But we also live in nights. Night should be the time of rest, and it is rest that Margaret covets throughout the book, from the 'indescribable weariness' she feels at the preparations for Edith's wedding (p. 12) to her lament at Helstone—'I am so tired—so tired of being whirled on through all these phases of my life, in which nothing abides by me, no creature, no place' (p. 363). She would seek 'heavenly steadfastness in earthly monotony'.

In its absolute form her desire for rest is the desire for death, an urge most clearly expressed here in Bessy Higgins' desire to view Paradise. The diurnal round which, for all its wearingness, is a source of strength to Margaret, is to Bessy simply a series of 'bits o' time'

---

2. The poet referred to is Philip Larkin; the words quoted are from his poem "Days." Philip Larkin, *Collected Poems* (London and Boston: The Marvell Press and Faber and Faber, 1988), p. 67.

which are a distraction from Heavenly rest. 'Do you think such life as this is worth caring for?' gasps Bessy (p. 83). Margaret urges her not to be impatient with her life 'whatever it is', but Bessy feels 'tossed about wi' wonder' (p. 84). Margaret cannot enter into her affinity with death, shrinking from it 'with all the clinging to life so natural in the young and healthy' (p. 82). Even revisiting Helstone, at her most exhausted, she desires calm and stability within, rather than beyond, life. Yet life seems to offer only insubstantiality and transience, as she reflects after a night's watching at her mother's bedside:

> The dull gray days of the preceding winter and spring, so uneventless and monotonous, seemed more associated with what she cared for now above all price. She would fain have caught at the skirts of that departing time, and prayed it to return, and give her back what she had too little valued while it was yet in her possession. What a vain show Life seemed! How unsubstantial, and flickering, and flitting! (p. 155)

In face of the possible loss of her mother she feels loss in everything—even the terrible night just past. Monotony is assurance, change means loss.

Margaret comes from a world that appears to represent stability and freedom. The stability is present in both her adopted London home, with its wealth and monotonous ease, and apparently in Helstone also. Having always disliked the decorum her aunt required of a woman walking the streets of towns, she becomes free to adopt her own rhythm of the 'bounding fearless step' in the woods about Helstone (p. 66). In Milton she finds this freedom curtailed in a new way. The townspeople violate her space by bustling close past her and even making remarks on her appearance. Yet it is out of this disturbance of her privacy that she meets Higgins and his family. She is 'shocked but not repelled' by his words on his daughter (p. 68), and 'half-amused, half-nettled' by his invitation to their home (p. 68). The feeling of disturbance and the mixed response are part of that uncertainty which is the quick of life and marks the beginning of Margaret's new openness to possibilities.

The two most important men in Margaret's life—her father and Thornton—seem respectively to represent, as sensitive speculator and man of action, the undecided she finds so painful and the decided and absolute she thinks she requires. Yet significantly she understands that 'the opposition of character . . . seemed to explain the attraction they felt towards each other' (p. 75). It is an observation that suggests how difference may be held in creative tension. For all that, she finds Thornton too absolute, and is glad when he 'looks anxious' (p. 152). He is 'as iron a chap as any in Milton'

(p. 149), and his ideas of the laws of economic life are rigidly hierarchical, Darwinian and determinist. They are the economic and
biological equivalent of Bessy Higgins' religious predeterminism
expressed just a few pages before. 'Margaret's whole soul rose up
against him while he reasoned in this way' (p. 140) but at almost the
same moment she is forced to acknowledge another side to the man,
and in doing so to feel again that anxiety, disturbance and uncertainty are of the essence of life:

> How reconcile those eyes, that voice, with the hard-reasoning,
> dry, merciless way in which he laid down axioms of trade, and
> serenely followed them out to their full consequences? The dis-
> cord jarred upon her inexpressibly. (p. 140)

They cannot be reconciled, in the sense of ironing out the differences
and saying they are the same thing. They both exist, and must both
be given their weight. Mrs Thornton, in her proud absoluteness,
speaks a great truth when she says that 'South country people are
often frightened by what our Darkshire men and women only call
living and struggling' (p. 107). Margaret is not afraid of seeing that
to live is to struggle, but life is also change, unease, instability, and
this is something Margaret could teach others as she experiences it
herself. To acknowledge our own uncertainty and dividedness in the
face of an uncertain, divided and mysteriously painful life requires
the greatest integrity.

We constantly witness the crumbling of absoluteness, the clear
becoming irresolute, the iron will a vulnerable flesh. The resolute
Mrs Thornton has an 'uneasy tenderness' over her feebly self-centred
daughter Fanny, but it is the only hint of a chink in her armour until,
following a conversation with her son in Volume I, Chapter XXIII,
'Her servants wondered at her directions, usually so sharply-cut and
decided, now confused and uncertain' (p. 170). The reason for this
unwonted behaviour is her son's possible attachment to Margaret,
and he himself, who has just been deciding on punishment for the
strikers 'clean and sharp as a sword' (p. 171) is a moment later
reduced to indecisiveness by the apparent forlornness of his hope.
He becomes exposed to feelings so disturbing and so mixed that he
cannot form his ideas into any settled response:

> And it doubles the gladness, it makes the pride glow, it sharpens
> the sense of existence till I hardly know if it is pain or pleasure,
> to think that I owe it to one . . . whom I love, as I do not believe
> man ever loved woman before. (p. 177)

Margaret finds her feelings changing the moment he has gone—from
'proud dislike into something different and kinder, if nearly as painful—self-reproach for having caused such mortification to any one'

(p. 178). The pain that both parties feel is part of the heightened emotional tension induced by passion, but pain, as I have said, is endemic in this work, particularly for the heroine. She is pained by leaving Helstone, by the death of her parents and Mr Bell, as well as that of Bessy Higgins, by false accusations and by her sense of wrongdoing when she lies to protect Frederick. Beyond all is that sense of daily pain involved in survival with an indecisive father, an ailing mother, a reduced income and an alien environment. The repeated references to 'flinching' and 'wincing' metaphorise the raw-ness of sensibilities open to acute pain. The complementary sensa-tion is 'stunning' or 'numbing'. Taken together the words suggest a sensibility heightened to the extremes of sensation, which can only be relieved by some shock that deadens the nerves for a while and gives insensitivity to pain by a violent blow.

Two crises clearly stand out as being of supreme significance in Margaret's story. The first is the episode in which she challenges Thornton to face the mob and then throws herself before him and takes the blow meant for him. Her intervention may well, as Thorn-ton says, have saved his life. In taking the blow, and indeed in her first facing the mob, she introduces that element of confusion and uncertainty which is a hallmark of this novel, into the 'man to man' confrontation. The presence of a woman turns the fierce determi-nation of the mob into something more 'irresolute' in a moment. The role of the woman is the traditional one of conciliation and martyr-dom as far as the public impression goes. She defuses the situation by taking the violence upon herself and becoming the injured body. But obviously, as both she and Thornton realise, the act has powerful sexual overtones. Her challenge to him to go downstairs is a sexual challenge, and her taking of the blow is a sexual reconciliation, marked by blood and wounding. Like so many encounters in this work it is notable for its self-contradictory nature. Having challenged him to go alone, she regrets the command and throws herself before him. In the light of this, how are we to take her avowal when she has recovered from the incident that she had been 'anxious that there should be fair play on each side' (p. 173)? It is surely a defensive rationalisation. Is it only a change in sensibilities between two ages that makes her traumatised reaction seem extreme? Whatever she felt for him before, it is clear that the incident is an advance in intimacy of a sexual nature, as her reference to her 'maiden pride' (p. 173) indicates. There is involved for her a real question of integ-rity. She will stand by her action, ambiguous though it may seem. But alone, she must test her *absolute* integrity, answerable only to God. There would seem to be two kinds of integrity—that we owe to our social and sexual beings, which is by definition not absolute, but a recognition of our own changeability, and a willingness to exist with it; and that we owe to ourselves alone, and which can only be measured in terms of that transcendent Absolute we call God.

Her second crisis is the lie she tells in order to allow her brother time to leave the country. At the moment she commits the sin there come together several elements we have already noted as crucially carrying meaning in the novel. First is Margaret's stillness; not here the stillness of repose, but the stillness and firmness of an indomitable will: 'She never blenched or trembled. She fixed him with her eye' (p. 249). As so often the key word 'now' makes an appearance. Of course her apparent calm masks an agonising struggle only to be overcome by that 'stunned' condition which here amounts to an almost trance-like state in which she wears a 'glassy, dream-like stare' (p. 251). The policeman 'thought to have seen her wince' (p. 251), but it is not until she is alone that she falls in a 'dead swoon'—a reaction to unbearable tension, but also the horror of being forced into a lie. The chapter is called 'False and True'; Margaret is false to fact and to herself in order to be true to her brother, but even the clearly mitigating circumstances cannot relieve her from the feeling of having violated her own integrity. She rejects the comfort of sharing her secret: 'Alone she would go before God, and cry for His absolution. Alone she would endure her disgraced position in the opinion of Mr Thornton' (p. 261). It would seem it is easier to admit one's fallibility to God than to man, but the seeds of that admission of dependency upon another which is the prerequisite of love have already been sown at the factory gates, although her heart cannot admit it.

When she finally comes to terms with the problem for herself, she has to go back to the nursery where:

> On some such night as this she remembered promising to herself to live as brave and noble a life as any heroine she ever read or heard of in romance, a life sans peur et sans reproche; it had seemed to her then that she had only to will, and such a life would be accomplished. And now she had learnt that not only to will, but also to pray, was a necessary condition in the truly heroic. Trusting to herself, she had fallen. (p. 373, n.2).

Putting away childish things, she realises her dependence upon a transcendent truth with which she must engage if she is to establish her integrity. True integrity is not defensive self-enclosure and self-dependence, but outgoing and creative, realising our own natures and giving ourselves to the necessary instability and imperfection of things. This she discovers socially, sexually and transcendentally.

* * *

Elizabeth Gaskell: A Chronology

1810	Elizabeth Gaskell born, 29 September, at Chelsea, London, the daughter of William Stevenson and Elizabeth Holland.
1811	After death of her mother she is taken to live with her maternal aunt (Hannah Lumb) at Knutsford, Cheshire.
1821–26	Attends boarding school at Barford, near Warwick, and Stratford-upon-Avon.
1826–29	Returns to Knutsford, then London. Stays variously with relatives in Liverpool and North Wales before visits to the family of Reverend William Turner in Newcastle and friends in Edinburgh. Her father dies, 1829.
1831	Stays at Woodside, near Liverpool; meets Reverend William Gaskell, junior minister of Cross Street Chapel, Manchester.
1832	Marries William Gaskell at Knutsford; comes to live permanently in Manchester.
1833	Delivered of stillborn child.
1834	Daughter, Marianne, born.
1837	Daughter, Margaret Emily ("Meta"), born. Aunt Lumb dies. "Sketches among the Poor, No. 1," a poem written jointly with her husband, published in *Blackwood's Magazine*, XLI, 1837.
1841	Visits the Rhineland with her husband.
1842	Daughter, Florence Elizabeth, born.
1844	Son, William, born. (Earlier, at an undetermined date, a son had been born who lived for only one week.)
1845	Son dies of scarlet fever.
1846	Daughter, Julia Bradford, born.
1847–48	First stories published in *Howitt's Journal*; *Mary Barton* published 1848.
1849	First meets Dickens, during visit to London.
1850	Publishes *Lizzie Leigh* in *Household Words*; will continue to write for *Household Words* until 1859, and then *All the Year Round*. Meets Charlotte Brontë.
1852	*Cranford* initiated *in Household Words*.

1853	*Cranford* completed and published in one volume; *Ruth* in three volumes.
1854	*North and South* initiated in *Household Words*. First of a sequence of visits to Paris during 1850s and 1860s.
1855	*North and South* published in two volumes.
1857	*The Life of Charlotte Brontë* published, exposing Gaskell to criticism. Visits Paris and Rome, where she establishes friendship with Charles Eliot Norton.
1859	Visits Germany and Paris.
1863	*Cousin Phillis* published in *Cornhill Magazine*; *Sylvia's Lovers* in three volumes. Again visits Paris and Rome.
1864	*Wives and Daughters* initiated in *Cornhill Magazine*.
1865	Dies, 12 November, with *Wives and Daughters* lacking final pages.
1866	*Wives and Daughters* published posthumously in two volumes.

Selected Bibliography

• indicates works included or excerpted in this Norton Critical Edition

BIBLIOGRAPHIES

Northup, Clarke Sutherland. In Gerald de Witt Sanders, *Elizabeth Gaskell*, New Haven: Yale UP for Cornell University; London: Oxford UP for Cornell University, 1929, pp. 163–262.

Selig, Robert L. *Elizabeth Gaskell: A Reference Guide*. Boston: G. K. Hall, 1977.

Welch, Jeffrey Egan. *Elizabeth Gaskell: An Annotated Bibliography 1929–1975*. New York: Garland, 1977.

Weyant, Nancy S., *Elizabeth Gaskell: An Annotated Bibliography of English-Language Sources, 1976–1991*. Metuchen, NJ: The Scarecrow Press, 1994.

———. *Elizabeth Gaskell: An Annotated Guide to English Language Sources, 1992–2001*. Metuchen, NJ: The Scarecrow Press, 2004.

JOURNAL

The Gaskell Society Journal, vols. 1–17, 1986–2003. (Articles published in this journal have not been listed individually below. Volume 16, 2002, contains author and subject indexes for volumes 1–16.)

BIOGRAPHY AND CORRESPONDENCE

•Chapple, J. A. V. and Arthur Pollard, eds. *The Letters of Mrs. Gaskell*. Manchester: Manchester UP, 1966.

Chapple, John. *Elizabeth Gaskell: The Early Years*. Manchester: Manchester UP, 1997.

Chapple, John, and Alan Shelston, eds. *Further Letters of Mrs. Gaskell*. Manchester: Manchester UP, 2000.

Foster, Shirley. *Elizabeth Gaskell: A Literary Life*. Basingstoke: Palgrave Macmillan, 2002.

Hopkins, Annette B. *Elizabeth Gaskell: Her Life and Her Work*. London: John Lehmann, 1952.

Uglow, Jenny. *Elizabeth Gaskell: A Habit of Stories*. London: Faber & Faber, 1993.

CRITICAL STUDIES

General studies with substantial commentary on *North and South*

Bodenheimer, Rosemarie. *The Politics of Story in Victorian Social Fiction*. Ithaca: Cornell UP, 1988. See pp. 53–69, "Elizabeth Gaskell and the Politics of Negotiation."

•Cazamian, Louis. *Le Roman Social en Angleterre, 1830–1850: Dickens, Disraeli, Mrs Gaskell, Kingsley* (1903). Trans. Martin Fido as *The Social Novel in England*. London and Boston: Routledge & Kegan Paul, 1973. See chap. 7, "Mrs Gaskell and Christian Interventionism."

David, Deidre. *Fictions of Resolution in Three Victorian Novels*. New York: Columbia UP, 1981. See Part 1, "*North and South*."

Gallagher, Catherine. *The Industrial Reformation of English Fiction: Social Discourse and Narrative Form 1832–1867*. Chicago: U of Chicago P, 1985. See chap. 7, "Relationship Remembered against Relationship Forgot."

Harman, Barbara. *The Feminine Political Novel in Victorian England.* Charlottesville: UP of Virginia, 1998. See chap. 2, "Women's work in *North and South.*"

Ingham, Patricia. *The Language of Gender and Class: Transformation in the Victorian Novel.* New York: Routledge, 1996. See chap. 4, "*North and South*".

Kestner, Joseph. *Protest and Reform: The British Social Narrative by Women.* Madison: U of Wisconsin P, 1985.

Nord, Deborah Epstein. *Walking the Victorian Streets: Women, Representation, and the City.* Ithaca: Cornell UP, 1995. See chap. 5, "Elbowed in the Streets: Exposure and Authority in Elizabeth Gaskell's Urban Fiction."

●Williams, Raymond. *Culture and Society.* London: Chatto and Windus, 1958. See chap. 5, "The Industrial Novels."

CRITICAL STUDIES OF ELIZABETH GASKELL

Bonaparte, Felicia. *The Gypsy-Bachelor of Manchester: The Life of Mrs. Gaskell's Demon.* Charlottesville: UP of Virginia, 1992.

Colby, Robin Bailey. *'Some Appointed Work to Do': Women and Vocation in the Fiction of Elizabeth Gaskell.* Westport, CT: Greenwood Press, 1995.

●Craik, W. A. *Elizabeth Gaskell and the Provincial Novel.* London: Methuen & Co Ltd, 1975.

Easson, Angus. *Elizabeth Gaskell.* London, Boston, and Henley: Routledge & Kegan Paul, 1979.

Easson, Angus, ed. *Elizabeth Gaskell: The Critical Heritage.* New York: Routledge, 1991.

Ganz, Margaret. *Elizabeth Gaskell: The Artist in Conflict.* New York: Twayne, 1969.

Hughes, Linda K, and Michael Lund. *Victorian Publishing and Mrs Gaskell's Work.* Charlottesville: UP of Virginia, 1999.

Lansbury, Coral. *Elizabeth Gaskell: The Novel of Social Crisis.* New York: Barnes and Noble, 1975.

Lucas, John. "Mrs. Gaskell and Brotherhood." In *Tradition and Tolerance in Nineteenth-Century Fiction*, ed. David Howard, John Lucas, and John Goode. London: Routledge and Kegan Paul, 1966.

●Rubenius, Aina. *The Woman Question in Mrs. Gaskell's Life and Works.* In *Essays and Studies on English Language and Literature*, V, ed. S. B. Liljegren. The English Institute in the University of Upsala, 1950.

●Schor, Hilary M. *Scheherezade in the Marketplace: Elizabeth Gaskell and the Victorian Novel.* Oxford: Oxford UP, 1992.

Sharps, John Geoffrey. *Mrs. Gaskell's Observation and Invention: A Study of her Non-biographic Works.* Fontwell, Sussex: Linden Press, 1970.

Stoneman, Patsy. *Elizabeth Gaskell.* Brighton, Sussex: The Harvester Press, 1987.

Webb, R. K. "The Gaskells as Unitarians." In *Dickens and other Victorians: Essays in Honor of Philip Collins*, ed. Joanne Shattock. New York: St. Martin's Press, 1988.

Wright, Edgar. *Mrs. Gaskell: The Basis for Re-Assessment.* London: Oxford UP, 1965.

●Wright, Terence. *Elizabeth Gaskell: "We are not angels."* Basingstoke, Hampshire and New York: Macmillan Press; St Martin's Press, 1995.

CRITICAL STUDIES OF *NORTH AND SOUTH*

●Bodenheimer, Rosemarie. "*North and South*: A Permanent State of Change." *Nineteenth-Century Fiction* 34.3 (Dec. 1979): 281–301.

Brown, Pearl L. "From Elizabeth Gaskell's *Mary Barton* to Her *North and South*: Progress or Decline for Women." *Victorian Literature and Culture* 28 (2000): 345–58.

Campbell, Ian. "Mrs. Gaskell's *North and South* and the Art of the Possible." *Dickens Studies Annual: Essays in Victorian Fiction* 8 (1980): 231–50.

Carnall, Geoffrey. "Dickens, Mrs. Gaskell and the Preston Strike." *Victorian Studies* 8 (Sept. 1964): 31–48.

Chapple, J. A. V. "*North and* South: A Reassessment." *Essays in Criticism* 17 (Oct. 1967): 461–72.

●Collin, Dorothy. "The Composition of Mrs Gaskell's *North and South.*" *Bulletin of the John Rylands Library* 54.1 (Autumn 1971): 67–93.

Easson, Angus. "Mr Hale's Doubts in *North and South.*" *Review of English Studies* 31 (1980): 64–78.

Gallagher, Catherine. "*Hard Times* and *North and South*: The Family and Society in Two Industrial Novels." *Arizona Quarterly* 36 (1980): 70–96.

Gill, Stephen. "Price's Patent Candles; New Light on *North and South.*" *Review of English Studies* 27 (1976): 311–21.

Harman, Barbara Leah. "In Promiscuous Company: Female Public Appearance in Elizabeth Gaskell's *North and South.*" *Victorian Studies* 31 (1988): 351–74.

ᴉson, Patricia E. "Elizabeth Gaskell's *North and* South: *A National Bildungsroman.*" *Victorian Newsletter* 85 (1994): 1–9.

Martin, Carol. "Gaskell, Darwin, and *North and South.*" *Studies in the Novel* 15 (1983): 91–107.

Parker, Pamela Corpron. "From 'Ladies' Business' to 'Real Business': Elizabeth Gaskell's Capitalist Fantasy in *North and South.*" *Victorian Newsletter* 90 (1997): 1–3.

•Pryke, Jo. "The Treatment of Political Economy in *North and South.*" *The Gaskell Society Journal* 4 (1990): 28–39.

Stevenson, Catherine Barnes. "Romance and the Self-Made Man: Gaskell Re-writes Brontë." *Victorian Newsletter* 91 (1997): 10–16.

•Ward, A. W. Introduction to *North and South. The Works of Mrs. Gaskell,* 8 vols. London: John Murray, 1906 4:xi–xvii.